W9-CKR-548

Warriors
of the
Steppes

The Complete Cossack Adventures
Volume Two

Harold Lamb

Edited by Howard Andrew Jones
Introduction by David Drake

UNIVERSITY OF NEBRASKA PRESS
LINCOLN AND LONDON

Library of Congress Cataloging-in-Publication Data
Lamb, Harold, 1892–1962.
Warriors of the steppes / Harold Lamb; edited by
Howard Andrew Jones; introduction by David Drake.
p. cm. – (The complete Cossack adventures; v. 2)
ISBN-13: 978-0-8032-8049-6 (pbk. : alk. paper)
ISBN-10: 0-8032-8049-1 (pbk. : alk. paper)
1. Cossacks—Fiction.   2. Steppes—Asia,
Central—Fiction.   3. Asia, Central
—History—16th century—Fiction.
I. Jones, Howard A.   II. Title.
PS3523.A4235W37 2006
813'.52–dc22
2005035140

Set in Trump by Kim Essman.
Designed by R. W. Boeche.

Contents

6/20

Foreword

When he began seeing print in magazines like *Argosy* and *All-Story*, Harold Lamb's fiction was competent but unremarkable. At first his work for *Adventure* was no better; Lamb wrote several forgettable South Sea tales and some stiff, contemporary pieces . . . and then suddenly he found his voice. In 1917 Harold Lamb created a wandering Cossack named Khlit and truly launched his career.

The tales of the wily Cossack helped transform Lamb into one of *Adventure* magazine's most popular writers. Khlit traveled through the plains of Mongolia, Tibet, China—places painted vividly by Lamb's prose, each exotic and deadly and teeming with adventure. In all, Khlit appeared in nineteen stories, and the historical accuracy of the series helped give *Adventure* its sterling reputation as a magazine of quality—*Newsweek* once proclaimed it the "dean" of pulp magazines.

In a little over two years Lamb had drafted ten Khlit stories, most of them novellas, but he took various short breaks from the saga to write other tales. There was such a demand for fiction at this time that the pulp magazines were printed frequently—*Adventure* was appearing on newsstands at least twice a month.

Prior to the first story in this collection, Lamb created Abdul Dost, who narrates four of the tales reprinted here and is a pivotal player in the short novel that follows them. Like Khlit, Abdul Dost is a talented swordsman and veteran warrior, though he is more straightforward than the Cossack. He is a devout Muslim and a loyal follower of his lord, Shirzad Mir. And therein lies the trouble, for Shirzad Mir is out of favor and unjustly imprisoned. The new Mogul emperor, Jahangir, turns a deaf ear to Shirzad Mir's defenders, and thus Abdul Dost must find a way to free his lord, avenge the wrongs done to him and his people, and clear Shirzad Mir's name. Fortunately for Abdul Dost, he soon meets a traveler from Frankistan well versed in all the stratagems Abdul Dost is not—and to say much more would spoil the tale.

Lamb had become fascinated with India, more precisely, India in the reign of Jahangir and his spectacular wife, Nur-Jahan, about whom Lamb would eventually write a novel. Both you, the reader, and Khlit were introduced to her in the final story of the first volume of this series.

While researching Khlit's time period Lamb probably was inspired to write tales set in India in which it would have been difficult for Khlit to play a part, and thus he developed Abdul Dost. Once through with Abdul Dost's story cycle Lamb wrote one more solo story of Khlit—the tale that opens this collection— and then seems to have decided to throw Khlit and Abdul Dost together to see what would happen. It *may* be that Lamb intended to unite the two characters the moment he created Abdul Dost—a note by *Adventure* editor Arthur Sullivan Hoffman indicates that Lamb was at least considering that idea from the start. I like to think Lamb realized the Khlit stories needed a new element, for the last two solo Khlit adventures, "The Rider of the Gray Horse" and "The Lion Cub," while enjoyable, lacked some of the fire and immediacy found in the high points of the series.

However Lamb came to combine the characters, the result worked; from the climactic story of their meeting in "Law of Fire" to their final scene together in "The Curved Sword," Lamb is once more on his best footing. Indeed, "The Curved Sword" is one of the best entries in the entire Khlit saga, and, strangely, like "Law of Fire" and "Masterpiece of Death," has not been reprinted since its appearance in *Adventure* magazine in 1920. It was likely intended to bring the series to a close; there is even a suggestion that Khlit's curved saber has been shattered in the battle that concludes the story, and there would be nothing more final than that, for the weapon was a touch point for many of the Cossack's adventures and his constant companion. Near the end of the story Lamb writes only that Khlit carried a shattered sword, but what other weapon might it have been?

Fortunately for himself, Lamb had not been explicit in the matter, for come 1925 he was to begin a final series of Khlit adventures in which the aging Cossack has handed over his famed saber to his grandson Kirdy and instructs him in the ways of adventure, Khlit style. But those tales, and the exploits of the Cossacks Ayub and Demid, will be found within the pages of volume 3.

For now, relax with ten swashbuckling tales abrim with action and adventure in perilous times and fantastic places, your guides none other than the daring Abdul Dost and Khlit of the Curved Saber.

Enjoy!

Acknowledgments

I would like to thank Bill Prather of Thacher School for his continued support, encouragement, enthusiasm, and friendship. I also would like to express my appreciation for the tireless efforts of Victor Dreger, who pored over acres of old maps to compile a map of the locations that appear in the final version printed within this book. Thank yous also are due to the tireless Bruce Nordstrom, Dr. Victor H. Jones, and Jan Van Heiningen for aid in manuscript acquisition, as well as S. C. Bryce, who kindly provided a timely and time-consuming last-minute check of some key issues of *Adventure*, and Dr. James Pfundstein and Doug Ellis for similar aid. A great deal of time was saved because of the manuscript preservation efforts of the late Dr. John Drury Clark. I'm grateful to the staff at the University of Nebraska Press, for their support of the project and for efficiently shepherding the manuscript through the publication process. I'm likewise appreciative and delighted by the hard work of cover artist and map artist Darrel Stevens. Thank you all for your hard work and dedication—you have helped bring Khlit the Cossack and his world to life.

Introduction

David Drake

The setting of Harold Lamb's Cossack stories is utterly different from the world of their readers, whether in this volume or in *Adventure* magazine in 1920, where the pieces first appeared. The difference isn't particularly a matter of geography; the hills of Afghanistan (where most of them take place) are mentioned, but rarely described in detail. Rather, it's culture. The stories are set in human society, and the mindset of the characters is nothing like that of the Western world.

A few of the stories include Sir Ralph Weyand, an envoy of the (British) East India Company attempting to gain trade concessions. They're not told from his viewpoint, however, and he's generally referred to by the deliberately un-English form "Sir Weyand." The reader either enters the world of the Weyand stories through the eyes of a local or is guided by an omniscient narrator who describes events, however horrific, with a complete absence of emotion.

And the events often *are* horrific; murder, torture, mutilation, and ruthless greed are the norm here. Faithlessness is almost universal among the nobility and common at all levels of society, so it's only among simple soldiers and crippled mendicants that fair dealing is to be expected. Courage and strength are as much the province of evil men as good ones, however, while intelligence is consistently the tool of amoral brutality rather than honor.

Khlit the Cossack, a major figure in most of the stories collected here, is shrewd but explicitly not as intelligent as the high-
ranking villains he ranges himself against. What carries Khlit
through to success—to the confusion of his enemies, at least—
is experience, a very different thing. Even experience wouldn't
be enough were not Khlit willing to accept the cost of victory
to himself, his friends, and his allies, because victory in these
stories never comes cheap.

Lamb makes his alien world real by making it concrete. The
clothing, equipment, and administration of Afghanistan in the
early seventeenth century are described precisely and in contemporary terminology. The author keeps the real historical background a shadowy presence enveloping his stories instead of trotting it out to prove his erudition, but the more a reader knows of
that background, the more certain he becomes that Lamb had all
the details at his fingertips.

And this brings me to a personal anecdote with which to
conclude these introductory remarks. My friend Manly Wade
Wellman was a pulp writer, but he was a successful journeyman
whereas Harold Lamb was "one of the lions," as Manly described
him in his journal.

They met once. Manly's brother Paul Wellman wrote best-
sellers in the '30s and '40s. When his publisher gave him a book-
launch party in New York City in the late '30s, Harold Lamb
was invited as an equal and Manly was invited as Paul's brother.
Manly vaguely alludes to the meeting in his journal, but the only
details are those which he told me in person after dinner one
night.

According to Manly, he and Lamb began talking about the rel-
ative merits of the Turkic composite bow and the English long-
bow. Lamb said, "But Manly, a Turkish bowman could send an
arrow two hundred yards." Manly retorted, "Two hundred yards
was a clout shot for an English longbowman!" Whereupon Lamb,
crushed, turned his back and walked away.

Do I believe that story? Yes, absolutely, but that's because I know what Manly did not know: he misheard what Lamb must have said.

Sir Joseph Banks's secretary in 1797 described a marble track in Constantinople where the best shots of the Turkish sultans were marked in gold. The longest shot had been over 800 yards. Lamb was certainly alluding to this record.

In the clamor of the party, Manly mistakenly heard "two hundred" for "eight hundred," and he didn't have sufficient background knowledge to realize that he *must* have misunderstood. Lamb walked away, presumably because he recognized the pointlessness of an argument in which one party relies on facts and the other on emotion.

That observation provides an insight into the strengths and weaknesses of both men's work. The reader of a Harold Lamb story may find himself without an emotional connection to its alien characters, but he can never doubt the reality of the factual background which Lamb paints in such bright, vivid colors.

Warriors of the Steppes

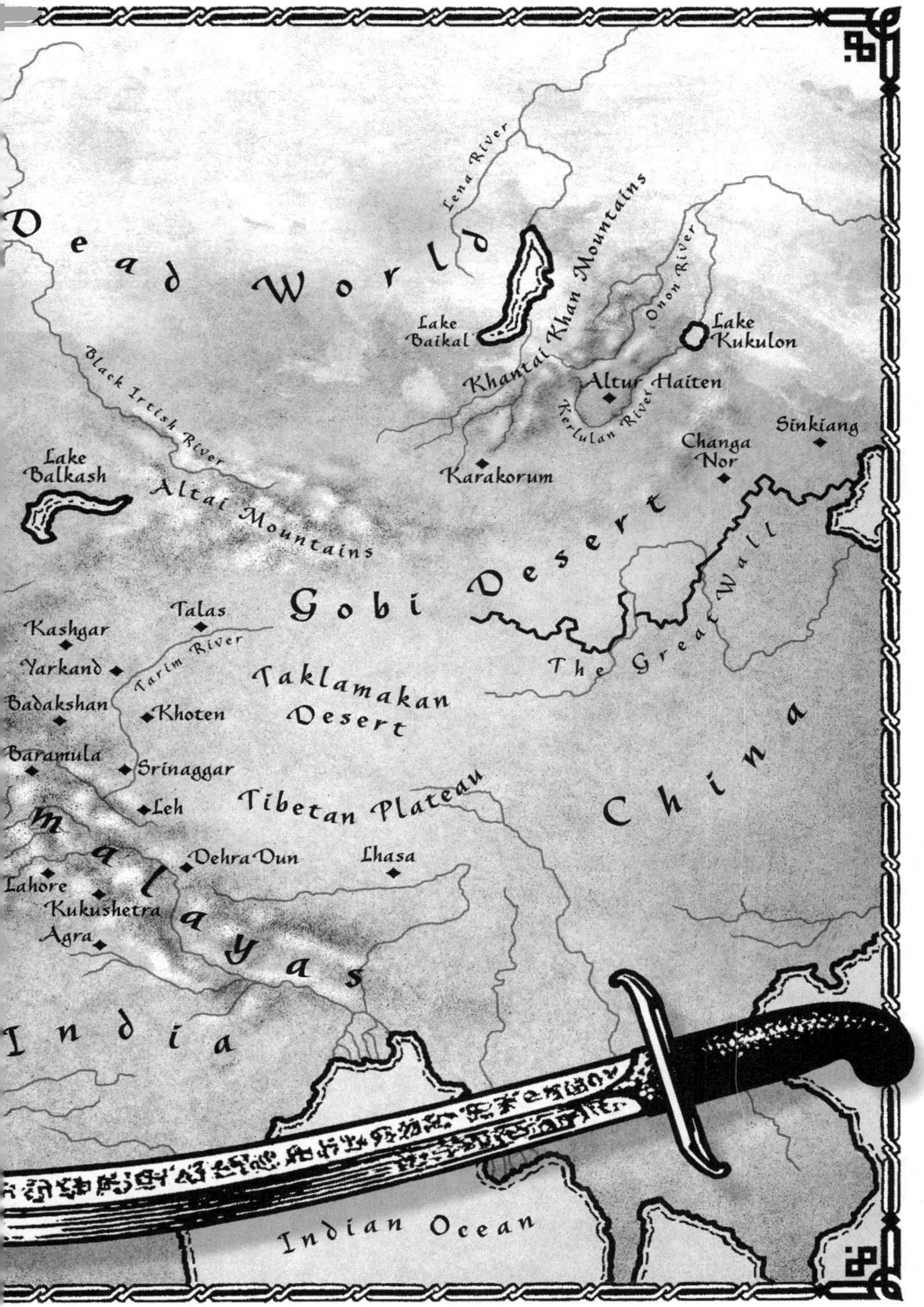
Dead World
Lena River
Khantai Khan Mountains
Onon River
Lake Baikal
Lake Kukulon
Black Irtish River
Altur Haiten
Kerlulan River
Sinkiang
Changa Nor
Lake Balkash
Karakorum
Altai Mountains
Gobi Desert
The Great Wall
Talas
Kashgar
Tarim River
Yarkand
Taklamakan Desert
Badakshan
Khoten
Baramula
Srinaggar
Tibetan Plateau
China
Leh
Himalayas
Dehra Dun
Lhasa
Lahore
Kukushetra
Agra
India
Indian Ocean

The Lion Cub

Who can lift the veil of the unseen! And who can read the hand-writing of Fate!

Jhilam the Mighty, the stronghold of the hills, had been fief of the sires of Sattar Singh since the time of Ram. Now Sattar Singh, Lord of Jhilam, was dead.

And Rani Begum, wearing the white robe of widowhood for Sattar Singh, brought the keys of Jhilam castle and laid them before Jahangir, the Mogul, as was the law. But her heart was heavy.

"Lord of the World," cried Rani Begum—and her fear was a great fear at sight of the mask of anger that overspread the face of the Mogul—"my Lord Sattar Singh swore that the keys of Jhilam of the Hills should be held by none but our son Rao Singh. Such is our right."

"Is the oath of a hill chief greater than the word of the Mogul?" said Jahangir. So it came to pass that Jahangir the Mogul, Lord of the Punjab, of the Dekkan, of Sind and all Hindustan, gave the fief of Jhilam to one Shaista Mirza, a Persian. But the allegiance of the men of Jhilam he could not give.

Allah in his mercy laid the hand of death upon Rani Begum. It was written that this should be.

Who can look beyond the veil of the future! Yet the thought came to me in a vision that the treasure of Jhilam should be found. And in the vision was the dark form of the Angel of Death.

From the tale of Ahmad Rumi

The hour of sunset prayer was past. Ahmad Rumi, teller of legends, folded his prayer-carpet neatly and placed it within his bundle and seated himself at the side of the caravan-track. This was the trail from the Wular lake to the southern border of Kashmir. And it was the year 1609 of the Christian era.

Carefully the legend-teller adjusted the folds of his white turban and ate sparingly of dates which he took from his girdle, leaning on his staff the while. The sun had gone down behind the willows at his back; the shadows lengthened, dwindled and formed again under the pale light of a new moon.

Except for the loom of the turban against the underbrush, touched by the faint fingers of moonlight, the form of Ahmad Rumi was invisible. He sat very quiet, sensing the change of hour by the night chill. For Ahmad Rumi was blind.

He lifted his head at a sound from above him on the caravantrack. Other sounds reached him, blended and confused, but clear to the blind man. Three horses were approaching.

Three Arabian horses, bearing heavy men perhaps in armor. So reasoned Ahmad Rumi and drew farther back into the willows. Years had taught him the different tread of a Turkoman's pony, a Kirghiz's quick-moving horse and the stolid gait of a Kabul stallion. He could distinguish between the bell-bearing mules of a Bokharan caravan and the laden beasts of Chinese merchants.

Slowly the three Arabs passed. They minced along after the manner of their kind, and their riders spoke Persian. The horsemen did not perceive Ahmad Rumi.

"Fresh horses, held in check," muttered the legend-teller to himself, "and going warily. Aye, verily, the tale of the Wular peasants was true. *Insh'allah!*"

He leaned slightly forward, facing up the trail expectantly and stroking the gray beard that fell to his girdle. His wide, brown eyes were closed, and the moonlight outlined shadows under his high cheekbones. Then he lifted his head again eagerly.

This time he scrambled to his feet, aided by his staff, and stepped into the highroad to confront the rider who trotted swiftly under the willows.

"Back, beggar," cried a high voice, not unkind nor harsh. "I have no silver—"

"I am blind," responded the teller of legends quickly.

He felt for the bridle of the horse that had been reined in sharply. His lean hand touched the bridle and the silk shoulder-straps, halting at the wrought silver ornaments.

"The Wular stallion," he muttered. "Allah is merciful."

A quick indrawing of breath escaped the rider.

"Back, Muslim. I must pass."

"Nay, Rao Singh. Not until you and I have spoken together."

For a space the rider was silent, peering at the fragile form in his path. He sat his mount easily, a slender figure nervously erect, in a plain white tunic with silk girdle bearing a light sword and a small, peaked turban.

"What seek you? How knew you my name?" he demanded suspiciously.

Ahmad Rumi felt for the hand of Rao Singh and pressed it to his forehead.

"Thrice blessed is this hour!" he exclaimed joyfully. "Aie—should I not know the name of the son of my lord? It is sweeter than the wind in the pine-tops in the hills and more fragrant than the scent of the lotus by the lake.

"Dismount, Rao Singh; dismount! At a distance of a bowshot wait those who would slay you and scatter your ashes on the wind of death. By the ford they watch—three, with arms and perhaps coats of mail."

Rao Singh lifted his dark head and glanced warily about into the thickets. In that age it was well to keep to horse on the caravan-routes, even within sight of the camp of the Mogul, as he then was.

But Ahmad Rumi was alone. Youth and aged man seated themselves on the bank by the willows.

"How know you this thing?"

Rao Singh spoke with the directness of a boy—which he was, barely attained to man's figure.

"You could not see them?"

Suspicion was in the last words and Ahmad Rumi smiled gently.

"They spoke Persian, which I know. They will wait at the ford for the one they seek. I heard the rattle of their weapons. Death is in the air tonight—for Rao Singh."

"Whence came the three?"

"From the Jhilam path."

"How knew you I should come?"

The teller of legends sighed, stroking his beard.

"Many are the mouths that will utter evil. The master of horse of the Lord of Jhilam spake to the slaves, the stable slaves, and they whispered to the cutters of wood, who bore the news to the forest men. Hence I, who wait at the Wular gate, heard that this night Rao Singh was to be slain at the ford near the outpost of the Mogul camp.

"So I came hither with a caravan from Khoten, bound for the camp. Even as I heard the thing has come to pass."

"Three common retainers from Jhilam," meditated Rao Singh.

"Nay; one was noble, for I caught the scent of musk as they passed."

"Nevertheless I must ride on."

The boy glanced up anxiously at the moon. "May the gods reward you for your tidings—"

"Aie, say not thus, my lord! For the space of four Winters since the death of Sattar Singh, who was master of Jhilam, I have lived but for one thing—to embrace the hand of the son of Sattar Singh, telling him the while that there are those at Jhilam who have not forgotten. It was our fate to suffer, and we have endured much, but we have not forgotten—"

"Peace!" whispered the boy.

Ahmad Rumi's keen ears had caught the sound—the swift clatter of horse's hoofs down the trail. But this time his memory was at fault. The gait was not that of Arab or Persian beast, nor yet that of a steppe pony.

Rao Singh had sprung to his feet, hand on sword. He saw a black horse sweep by bearing a tall form in sheepskin *khalat* and black hat. The rider glanced at him but did not pause.

"A hillman," he whispered to Ahmad Rumi, "perhaps a Kirghiz, yet I think not. Presently he will be at the ford."

"The trees are thick there, I have heard. It may be written that this one should be attacked and perish in your place—"

"Then must I mount and warn," cried the boy.

"You are too late, my lord."

The teller of legends raised his hand. From below came the sound of horses plunging in shallow water, a cry and the sharp clash of weapons.

"Siva! It is one against three."

Shaking off the protesting beggar, Rao Singh leaped to saddle and spurred down the track, drawing his sword as he went. Again the noise of steel striking steel, again a cry of pain, followed this time by the sound of a heavy body breaking through brush.

In the edge of the stream Rao Singh reined his mount and stared about him. A riderless horse, trembling with excitement, stood nearby, its reins tangled in a human body stretched on the grass.

Under the surface of the shallow water where a moonbeam pierced the curtain of trees he saw a second form that seemed to move as he watched. Then it was still. Silence held the ford, and he wondered at the swift change from tumult to quiet.

Not more than two minutes had passed since the first shout, and two men were dead and two had fled beyond sight and hearing. Into the silence, however, crept a *tap-tap*. It came nearer and Rao Singh's eyes widened as he gripped his weapon.

The *tap-tap* changed to a rustle, and as Rao Singh was about to voice a prayer to ward off the evil influence of a *rakzhas*—a malignant demon—he saw Ahmad Rumi's lean figure approach along the way he had come.

Reassured, the boy dismounted and guided the Muslim to the edge of the stream.

"Heard you the sword-blows, Ahmad Rumi?" he questioned uneasily. "All was over ere I reached the ford. 'Tis like to demonwork, for here be two slain as by magic. By Kali and Durga, protectress of the two worlds, 'twas magic!"

"Nay," returned the beggar calmly, "there is no enchantment save the will of Allah and the handwriting of fate, lord. I heard steel strike upon steel. Is the rider who passed us by slain?"

Rao leaned over the body by the horse. It was that of a commoner—a harsh face stared up at him above a blood-stained quilted tunic. Satisfied as to this, the boy inspected the form in the water. Caste prevented him from touching the dead. A strong smell of musk assailed him.

"The noble who rode with the three," Ahmad Rumi informed him promptly.

"Aye, he wears a gold chain, and the moonlight shows mother-of-pearl inlaid upon the scabbard at his girdle."

The blind man had run his delicate hand over the features of the bearded soldier. He drew in his breath sharply.

"Bairam, master of horse of Shaista Mirza, will breed no more foals," he muttered. "Just so was his beard ever trimmed and this is his Damascus steel cap. Little it availed him."

The two were silent a space, pondering what had passed at the ford. Plainly the rider of the black horse had been set upon by the three Persians ambushed at this spot. In all probability he had been mistaken in the deep shadows under the trees for Rao Singh. Yet he had fought off the three sharply, killing two, and had passed on his way.

"Truly a swordsman, he," sighed the boy. "Would I had seen him more closely and that he had joined his blade to mine, for I have need of such a one."

"You have many foes, lord," mused Ahmad Rumi, seating himself, for his aged limbs were not strong. "There be jackals aplenty who would pull down the lion cub of Jhilam. Aye, in the Mogul camp. After what has passed, is it safe to draw your reins thither?"

Rao Singh smiled, his white teeth flashing gaily from his dark face. His countenance was immature; the chin weak, the mouth delicate, the eyes somber. Like his slender figure, it bespoke nervous energy and willfulness rather than strength. There was pride in the lines of the thin nostrils, and the imprint of sorrow in the creased brow.

Rao Singh was eighteen years of age, yet he bore the cares of a man of thirty—not an uncommon thing in the Mogul era, when fortune or exile hung upon the fancy of an emperor and death was the reward of a slight offense.

"Nay," he laughed, "have not the gods favored me, Ahmad Rumi, this night? It is well, for I must accomplish a great thing before dawn—" He broke off to stare at the placid beggar suspiciously.

"Ho, Ahmad Rumi, how shall I trust you? You have come upon my path like a spy. You—a follower of the Prophet—claim allegiance to my father, who holds sacred the books of the Veda and the many-armed gods. That is not wonted."

The legend-teller leaned on his staff, his blind eyes seeking the boy with uncanny exactitude. Rao Singh fingered his sword nervously.

"Siva!" he muttered. "You have not the look of one who is blind."

Ahmad Rumi smiled patiently.

"Your temper, lord," he said slowly, "is like to that of noble Sattar Singh. He was ever swift to draw weapon, and heedless of danger. Wherefore his followers loved him and his name is still whispered among the forest men of Jhilam, who are of his faith."

He nodded slowly, pondering as the aged will on events that were past.

"I am not one of them, Rao Singh. That is true. But there was a day when I journeyed barefoot to Mecca, to the holiest of the holy. It was the sacred month of Ramadan.

"There came a Mogul noble with his followers—one who was hunting with falcons and had had poor sport. He mocked me and set his dogs upon me, who was in rags. With my staff I slew one of the dogs, wherefore the noble grew great in anger, and his servants pierced my eyes with the fire pencil."

Rao Singh leaned uneasily against his horse, glancing from the lean face of the beggar to the dead body in the shallow water, and up to where the round sphere of the moon showed through the trees.

"Came one who rode hastily and cried out in hot accusation against the noble," continued the teller of legends. "He cried that I had been wronged, and weapons clashed. I heard little, for the pain was great.

"Then the rider spake to me gently and had a skilled *hakim* make me a healing bandage. Eh—for that I blessed him and asked that I might be the servant at his doorpost."

There was a silence while Ahmad Rumi paused as if listening —a silence broken by the whimper of the stream and the rustle of the bushes in the night wind.

"I thought footsteps sounded," he observed. "Nay, what is written is written. It was written that I should be blind.

"Since that day I learned that the noble who hunted was Shaista Mirza of Rudbar, and the one who took up my quarrel was Sattar Singh; and men said that both had long been enemies at the court of Akbar, on whom be peace."

"Did you ask punishment for the wrong done?"

"Am I a paladin of Mogulistan or Hindustan to accuse those of high blood? Nay; Shaista Mirza is a Persian and the Mogul favors his race for their learning and their political power.

"But since then I have had a hut where the Jhilam road joins the Wular lake, and the fishers of the Wular have brought me food—until the evil day when Shaista Mirza became master of Jhilam. Since then there has been little food and my hunger has been great."

He stretched a trembling hand toward the boy.

"Come to the Wular lake, Rao Singh. I have heard evil spoken of you at Jhilam. Those who hold the fortress are powerful. The sword-arm of Shaista Mirza is long—enough to reach to the court of the Mogul. He and his astrologer, Nureddin, are very shrewd.

"In the Wular forest you will be safe, for there are those who will guard the path to your hut and watch while you sleep. The forest men and the fishers—who are Kashmiris—remember Sattar Singh. And they ask for Rao Singh, his son."

He salaamed before the youth.

"To those who asked I said that Rao Singh would come. The lion cub of Jhilam would come, and with their own eyes they would see he was like to his father. This thing I have sworn upon the *kaaba* and the holy names of Omar and Welid.

"I have told them the legends of Jhilam. Yet they have doubted. They have not seen the face of Rao Singh. Shaista Mirza they see and know his power. *Aie*, too well!"

"Has the Persian put hardships on the bent neck of the Jhilam people?"

"Aye, it was our fate that he should do so. The slaves he brought with him have been made overseers with whips in their hands. The eunuchs who guard his women have the power of life and death."

Words tumbled eagerly from the beggar's beard.

"The tithes of rice are doubled; men no longer work the soil, for the tithes are ruinous; instead they have turned wolf-like into robbers and as such are slain daily by the retainers of the Persian. The village oxen are taken without pay—"

"How could I alter this, Ahmad Rumi?" cried the boy. "Am I one to share the lot of peasants?"

"They ask but to see you. They would look upon the face of the son of Sattar Singh who was their lord."

And the boy laughed with bitterness.

"Truly a poor sight that, Ahmad Rumi—to see the blank eyes and woeful mouth of him who is a poverty-ridden hostage to Jahangir the Mogul."

The beggar touched the other's foot hopefully.

"Nay, lord. Is it not written that an omen may bring good? It would be an omen—for the forest men and the outcasts of Jhilam. They would know that you live, and their hearts would be lifted up as flowers at sight of the sun.

"This was the message I was to bring. And—our need is great."

He waited patiently while Rao bent his head in thought. Once he looked up hastily at the moon as if to mark the passage of time.

"Men starve in the forests of Jhilam, and the hills that are sacred to you and yours, Rao Singh, see nightly hunting of men like beasts along the lake. A pavilion of pleasure has been built by Shaista Mirza on the floating garden of the Wular and there Kashmiri women die slowly so their agony shall be longer and the pleasure of their lord the greater—"

In his earnestness Ahmad Rumi did not hear the slight crackle of brush that drew nearer the two.

"Verily, Rao Singh," he rose to his full height and extended an imploring hand," Jhilam cries for the son of Sattar Singh!"

The boy did not move, nor did his expression change. Meditating as he was, he did not hear the sounds in the thicket.

Rao Singh had the faults and the splendid virtues of his race. Proud, intolerant of personal wrong, and brave in battle to the point of folly, he was passionate, short-tempered and as yet indifferent to the misfortunes of those of baser birth.

His years of semi-captivity at the Mogul court had not made him a satellite of the throne, bred to flattery and intrigue, but they had branded suspicion into him, and boyish selfishness. And one other thing.

He was unwilling to take up the cause of his hereditary vassals as Ahmad Rumi had hoped; yet he saw in the suggestion of the blind man a possibility of obtaining new followers. The inbred restriction of caste kept him from association with outlaws and the poorer orders; yet his hopes were stirred of taking up arms against Shaista Mirza.

"Whither lies the place I should come—to the Wular?" he asked.

"At the end farthest from the palace and the pleasure island, lord," chanted Ahmad Rumi. "Up the course of a stream, an hour's fast ride, to where the pines give way to a cleared place. There is a place of many rocks called the Wular *davan*—where I have my hut."

Again the boy laughed softly.

"I have prayed to the many-armed gods, Ahmad Rumi. The time has come when I am no longer child but man. Tonight I ride to claim what is mine—"

"Allah is merciful—"

"Nay, it is a woman. There is one in the Mogul camp who has looked at me, and in her eyes burned the fire of love. I also feel love, and it is strange. I will take her from her guards, and I shall turn my horse from the court. If Jahangir's men would seek me they must come into the hills."

The teller of legends plucked at his beard, considering this. He shook his head doubtfully. Rao Singh had no friends in the court— such was the weight of Jahangir's displeasure—and women were ever the harbingers of strife.

Moreover the boy had not said that the woman was to be given him; he had declared that he would take her in spite of guards. Whoever stole the woman of another ran a great risk, for the Mogulis were even more jealous of their womenkind than the Hindus. "A slave, lord?" he questioned.

"Nay."

Rao Singh threw back his head proudly.

"A free-born maiden, fairer than the lotus."

"A concubine?" persisted the blind man.

"Not so. Kera of Kargan is hostage for her tribe. Her lot is like to mine."

"*Aie!*" Ahmad Rumi wrung his hands against his lean chest. "The maiden of Kargan Khan, hill chief of the Kirghiz, master of a thousand riders and lord of the northern hills beyond Jhilam. *Aie*! Verily Allah has thrown the dust of madness into the pool of your wisdom."

Rao Singh paid little attention. The rustle in the thicket had ceased save for a dull impact that might have been the stamp of a horse's foot.

"Kera of Kargan," he murmured. "Beautiful as the solitary moon at midnight. Fragrant as the jasmine—her lips like coral, teeth white as water-lilies.

"Her figure is slender as the young pine. And her eyes—dark as shadows in a forest pool at night."

"Hostage for the allegiance of Kargan Khan, who is ruthless as the storm-wind—"

"A pearl set in base silver. And Cheker Ghar, her buffoon, brought me word that she would mount my horse and go where I willed."

"Kargan Khan esteems the maiden as the jewel in the hilt of his sword. Only when Jahangir pledged her safety did he render her to the Mogul."

"Tonight I will seek her among the tents, and she will come."

Ahmad Rumi tore at his beard as he grasped the meaning of this.

"Eh—then she must be in the imperial seraglio. She is among those in the red imperial tents. Rao Singh, snatch from the jaws of a lion the calf which it is devouring, touch the fang of an angered cobra, but do not raise your eyes to a woman of the Mogul's tents!"

"Nay, she put on her ornaments that she should be fair in my eyes. Twice I saw her face, for she is not like the veiled mistresses of the Muslims."

"Kargan Khan will hunt you, and when he has found you cut you in many pieces which he will throw to the fish of a mountain lake."

"I have sworn to the conjurer that I would come this night to the imperial tents."

Ahmad Rumi sighed, hearing the willful pride that rang in the youth's words.

"It was the way of Sattar Singh to be rash," he mused, "yet this is madness—and death for the sake of a woman. Surely there be slave girls that can be bought—"

"I have spoken," said Rao Singh shortly. "It is late—"

He had turned to his horse when his figure tensed and his hand flew to his sword.

"Siva!" he cried softly.

Not ten paces away a man stood in the shadows, afoot, one hand holding the bridle of a horse, the other closed over the beast's muzzle. He was a tall man with high shoulders, wearing a long-sleeved sheepskin *khalat*, heavy horsehide boots and a black sheepskin hat.

"It is he of the black horse," the boy whispered to Ahmad Rumi, who had turned his head inquiringly.

The stranger had made no move. He stood with powerful legs wide apart, the set of the shoulders suggesting strength, although his figure was spare. The hat was perched on one side of his head. Rao Singh could make out that the stranger had long gray mustaches, and a beard.

Both men measured glances in silence. The boy was the first to speak.

"Whence came you?" he cried shrilly. "What seek you here?"

He had whipped out his sword and poised watchfully, one foot in stirrup.

"A jackal comes in silence," he repeated angrily, for he was startled.

"And jackals lie in wait," responded the other.

He spoke slowly in the deep voice of one well on in years, yet almost indifferently. He seemed careless of the threatening attitude of Rao Singh.

"What mean you? I wait for no one."

"This."

The man by the black horse spoke *Mogholi* somewhat brokenly. He moved forward and touched the dead Bairam with his foot.

Out in the moonlight his true height was revealed. He towered over the boy and the legend-teller. He glanced at the Hindu's mount appraisingly.

"A good horse, that," he grunted. "Yet the other three were ill-mounted and worse swordsmen."

Rao Singh hesitated. The swaggering, powerful figure was that of a warrior conscious of his power—resembling somewhat a Turkoman or Kirghiz. But the man's eyes did not slant, nor had he the furtive manner of a hill bandit.

His dress was rough, yet the curved sword in his leather girdle was richly chased and he had besides two costly Turkish pistols. His skin was lighter than that of an Afghan. Moreover his speech was strange.

"Dog of the devil," he observed meditatively, "this is a cursed spot. Here the three set upon me in the stream. When two were slain the third fled and won free in the thickets. I saw you and yonder beggar standing at the ford and returned to see whether you were kin to the three—"

"Nay, they waited here to set upon me."

The stranger looked at the boy keenly, but held his peace. Rao Singh wondered how much of their talk he had heard. The man had come from the brush with uncanny quietness, after the manner of one who was at home in such paths.

"Warrior," spoke Ahmad Rumi, "this youth mounted and rode to aid you when you were attacked."

"He came not overswiftly."

Rao Singh bit his lip.

"No fault of mine—you rode with speed."

He frowned.

"Are you a Muslim?"

"Nay." The stranger spat into the stream indifferently.

"Perchance a man of the Mogul."

"Nay."

Rao Singh sheathed his sword with sudden decision.

"Verily you are blunt of speech. Yet you did me a service. And," condescendingly, " ' tis plain you are not an ill swordsman. Will you enter my service? I have need of a keen sword this night."

At this the owner of the black horse tugged at his mustache thoughtfully. From far below the three came the shrill cry of the Mogul's sentries. The wind bore a faint echo of the imperial kettledrums and brass cymbals playing a festive measure.

"Harken, stripling," growled the stranger abruptly, "I like not many words. I eat the bread of Jahangir—"

Rao Singh stepped back instinctively, but the other waved a gnarled hand impatiently.

"I am no follower of the Mogul. In the Summer I came to his court from—another court. Because of a service Jahangir, who is lord of these lands, gave some horses and gold. Despite that his minions came near to slaying me."

He pointed down to the South, where lay the border of Kashmir.

"I saw some elephants bearing gilt castles, surrounded by fat horsemen, and watched, for I had not seen the elephants before. Then the horsemen and slaves with staffs began to strike me, crying that the Mogul's women rode upon the elephants.

"Blood of Satan! I cared not to see the women. The Mogul is tenderer of his women than a bear of a bruised paw. Bethink you and molest them not."

"Then you heard?"

Rao Singh gnawed his lip and sprang suddenly to saddle.

"Ho—wait here and you will see Kera of Kargan. Eunuchs are fat; they will make good slicing with a sharp sword!"

The stranger grunted, either in agreement or dislike.

"Wait here, Ahmad Rumi," cried the boy, fired with his purpose. "And at dawn you shall hear the music of the voice of the Flower of Kashmir. Aye, then we shall ride to the hills."

He spurred forward with a wave of the hand and vanished down the caravan path.

"Allah be kind to the youth!" cried the blind man.

"A pity," mused the stranger, "to hazard such a horse for a woman."

The stranger stared after Rao Singh, then glanced at the legend-teller's blind countenance. He tethered his horse carefully, then led Ahmad Rumi to a seat against a rock by the brook bed. He sat nearby, leaning upon the trunk of a fallen willow, his long, booted legs stretched idly before him. Here he could see both up and down the trail. Although his posture indicated idleness, even physical laziness, his eyes under tufted brows were keenly watchful.

Ahmad Rumi squatted passively on his heels, his gentle face turned upward, as was his wont, to the stars he could not see, and waited what was to come with the calm of a fatalist. He made a strange contrast to the scarred, moody face of the warrior.

"Ho, Ahmad Rumi," said the stranger at length, "you spoke of Jhilam and its lord. Something I have heard of it in the prattle of yonder courtiers. What is the true tale?"

Thus did Khlit, the wanderer and the seeker after battles, hear the story of Jhilam. While the two waited the return of Rao Singh they talked, and Khlit learned much of what went on in the hills by the Wular lake and how Shaista Mirza scourged the villages of Jhilam with the whip of fear.

II

It was the beginning of the third watch of the night and the revelers had retired from the imperial *kanates* when Cheker Ghar poked his head from his ragged shelter.

He scrambled nimbly to his feet, then drew a heavy pack wrapped in leopard-skin tenderly from the tent. Cheker Ghar was a wiry, bare-legged man of uncertain age with a crafty, fox face whitened with powder as a mark of his profession—conjuring.

With a sigh he shouldered his pack and began to trot through the tents, keeping well in the shadows and avoiding the slaves who guarded the barriers of each noble's camping-site.

The dense smoke rising from fires of dried dung and green wood had cleared away with the advent of early morning but a faint mist hung about the tents. Cheker Ghar sniffed the air as a dog does.

He marked the position of the Light of Heaven—the lantern on the lofty pole erected beside the imperial yak-tail standard at the gate of the Mogul's pavilions. Toward this he made his way, skipping over tent-ropes and avoiding snarling dogs with the skill of one familiar with encampments.

He avoided the avenue of torches by the imperial gate, and the tent of the *ameer* who was on guard that night. His way led to the *kanate*—the barrier of cotton cloth printed with flowers and supported by gilded poles—which surrounded the Mogul's enclosure. And to that portion of the cotton wall which veiled the tents of the seraglio.

Outside the *kanate* were no sentries, for the *ameer* on guard was supposed to make the rounds with a troop of horsemen from time to time. Within, however, were stationed wakeful eunuchs, armed. Cheker Ghar shivered. He knew the cruelty of the eunuchs.

But a stronger impulse than his own will drew him to the barrier. Here he listened attentively. Occasional voices reached him, showing that the guardians of the women were awake. Cheker Ghar glanced swiftly behind him to reassure himself as to his position.

About the *kanate* was a cleared space; on the farther side of this the horse artillery that always accompanied the Mogul was parked. Through the mist reared the summits of the tents of the *ameer*s and *mansabdar*s, illumined by the pallid moonlight. For several miles the camp extended, to the hills.

The only sounds were the measured cries of the outer sentries, the howl of a dog, the mutter of the hunting-beasts prisoned in the Mogul's menagerie, or the snort of a horse. The air was chill with a hint of coming dawn.

There was no time to be lost. Satisfied as to his position, Cheker Ghar bared his teeth and, taking his pack in his arms, slipped under the *kanate*.

He crept slowly into the moonlight on the farther side. A stout eunuch poised not twenty feet away saw him and squealed shrilly—then his warning cry changed to a laugh.

"El Ghias," the guard called softly to his companions. "The buffoon."

"Aye, gracious masters," bowed the conjurer; "aye, here is poor El Ghias. Eh—I starve for food. There is scanty picking among the dogs this night, and my belly yearns. I remember the gracious masters who gave me silver—"

"Begone," warned the eunuch carelessly. "Misgotten cur— mongrel of a jackal's begetting! We have no silver for you. Entrance here is forbidden—"

"O unutterable vileness, bred of dishonorable fathers and unknown mothers," said Cheker Ghar to himself. Aloud:

"By the gods, 'tis a dreary night, masters. See, I would beguile the hour with a clever trick. A rare sight, noble swordbearers of Jahangir!"

He shifted his pack from his shoulders to the ground, prostrating himself before the guardians. It was not the first time he had come, for he had prepared craftily for this night. The eunuchs had been amused at his arts.

"O thrice-defiled maggot of a dung-hill," he whispered under his breath, adding:

"Bara, grant me but a moment. I have an artful trick, taught me by my father's wisdom. The hour is fitting for such a feat. Watch in silence—"

He swiftly unstripped his pack, disclosing a pot of earth and a white silk cloth. Bara and the others drew near, fired with curiosity. They ran great risk in allowing the conjurer to stay, but his cleverness had whiled away weary hours before this, and now he promised a rare trick.

"In this pot," said Cheker Ghar solemnly, "aided by Hanuman, the monkey-face, and Ganesh, the elephant-head, I can make to grow—a tree. Name what tree you will, noble masters, and it will grow and bear fruit."

He squatted behind the pot, glancing up at them. From the corner of his eye he saw a shadow appear under the awning of the tent nearest on the right—the one that sheltered the women in attendance on the seraglio. Four eunuchs now stood about him, leaving a bare space of some two hundred yards along the tent-line.

"A lie," chattered Bara. "A tree! Nay, it cannot be, base-born."

"Even as I say," nodded Cheker Ghar, "it will appear. Name but the tree."

Incredulity, curiosity and uneasiness were in the black faces that bent over the conjurer.

"A plane-tree," hazarded one.

"Nay, a mulberry," broke in Bara, grinning. "Wretched one, sweeping of the offal-heap, noisome breeder of evil smells, grow me a mulberry tree with fruit! Six silver dinars if I taste of the fruit. The bastinado if you fail."

The others laughed and pressed closer.

Cheker Ghar did not laugh. Nor did he look up at Bara. Perhaps —for the conjurer had a way of hearing all the news of the imperial bazaars—Cheker Ghar had known Bara was fond of mulberries.

"Take heed, exalted ones," he muttered, "and speak not."

Whereupon he cast the white cloth over the pot. The trick was a favorite with Hindu conjurers but so difficult that it was not performed on ordinary occasions. The eunuchs had never witnessed it although they had heard of it.

Cheker Ghar raised his bare, brown arms and lifted the cloth. A tiny green shoot was disclosed.

"Nay," shrilled Bara, "that is no tree but a weed—"

"It is the seed-shoot of the mulberry," reproved the conjurer sternly.

Again he replaced the cloth with tense face. His half-closed eyes shot to the tent on the right. The slender shadow was still there. Without the enclosure sounded the trot of horses.

"The horsemen make their rounds," observed Bara.

He was unconcerned, for none of the outer guard would have dared look within the *kanate*.

"Behold!"

Cheker Ghar's bare arms writhed above his head and the cloth seemed to rise of itself into his hand. A young tree perhaps three feet in height stood in the pot.

"*Karamet, karamet!*" cried the onlookers. "A miracle!"

The conjurer's keen ears had noted that one horse lagged behind the others. A gleam of moonlight appeared against the *kanate* as if a weapon wielded from without had slit the cotton fabric. The eunuchs, absorbed in the tree, had sensed nothing untoward.

"Pluck the fruit, noble Bara," he wheedled. "See, within the leaves. The six dinars are mine."

Incredulously the chief eunuch, who bore the honorary title of Purified One of Paradise, felt among the branches of the tree. He plucked craftily at the stem, but it did not yield. The tree was in fact a mulberry.

He stared angrily at the ripe fruit he had found and fumbled in his girdle for coins which he flung down with an oath. Cheker Ghar clutched them eagerly.

Then the shadow flitted from the canopy toward the barrier. In the moonlight it was revealed as a veiled woman.

A eunuch saw her and cried out. At once with incredible swiftness Cheker Ghar clutched his pot, thrust it into the pack and gained his feet, holding the leopard-skin.

"Fools!" he chattered. "Offspring of swine!"

Bara's sword whirled at him but the conjurer leaped back, still reviling his enemies, and scurried under the barrier with crab-like agility.

The woman who had fled from the tent had passed through the opening in the cotton wall. Bara sprang after her, storming curses. As he plunged into the slit cloth a hand appeared in the aperture—a hand that grasped a dagger.

Bara staggered back with the haft of the dagger sticking from his broad girdle. He gripped the haft moaning and sank to his knees. His companions hesitated, making the night shrill with their screams. Others ran up.

On the outer side of the *kanate* the girl had been caught up in strong, young arms.

"Kera! Flower of my heart!"

She lay trembling in Rao Singh's grasp as the boy ran to his horse and swung into the saddle. He set spurs to his horse and wheeled away from the imperial enclosure as the beat of approaching hoofs neared them—but not before a diminutive figure had secured a firm hold on his stirrup and raced beside him, barelegged, a leopard-skin on its shoulders.

"Into the cannon, noble lord," warned Cheker Ghar. "The *ameer*'s guard is close behind."

Rao Singh swerved and traced his way among the picketed horses. Slaves started up to gaze, but hung back perceiving a nobleman with a woman on his saddle peak.

Behind them echoed the shouts of pursuers. Eunuchs and soldiers swept through the parked cannon, questing for the horseman they had glimpsed for a moment.

Out of the red imperial tents came women slaves who gathered together and stared at a fat figure prone on the earth, hands clasped about a dagger-hilt and wide eyes staring up into the moon with a kind of helpless surprise.

III

Khlit was making his morning meal at the ford in the Jhilam caravan-trail. The sky overhead had changed from gray to blue and the stars had paled before a rush of crimson into the eastern sky.

The wanderer had drawn rice-cakes and portions of dried mutton from his saddlebags and was eating hungrily, cutting the food with his dagger. He was alone at the ford. Fresh hoof prints showed on the farther bank. But here two trails crossed and the marks could not be traced beyond the stream edge.

Khlit eyed the stream meditatively. Often he frowned. He had much to think about.

From the Cossack steppe he had journeyed to the Tatar plains, where he had found men to his liking—indeed of his own blood. He had liked the life on the open steppe, where men lived on horseback and there were no cities.

Here matters were different. Wherever Jahangir the Mogul went, there was a city of tents. And myriad courtiers, ambassadors from outlying tribes, trade cities, and kingdoms.

Khlit had been interested at first in the splendor of the palaces and the temples of the Land of the Five Rivers (The Punjab). He had never seen such an array of soldiery assembled in one place. The very numbers oppressed him. Here was luxury, food in plenty. Here beat the pulse of the southern Asiatic world.

He had been favored with gifts at first—slaves, which he gambled away, and horses, which he liked and kept. But since the affray with the guards of the seraglio he had been ignored, although he might still claim the favor of Jahangir in memory of the deed that had brought the wanderer to Hindustan.

The heat of the plain had annoyed him and he was glad when the Mogul's court moved to the cool hills of Kashmir. And Khlit had been thinking. He saw unending caravans bear wealth to the Mogul, but he had noticed that Jahangir drained the nobles of their wealth to pay his enormous army.

He had seen a fortunate Rájput chief raised at a word to the rank of two thousand horse; yet another of the same clan had been beheaded as promptly for a whispered word against the Mohammedans. He had listened while emissaries from Khorassan called Jahangir monarch of the world to his face and debated among themselves whether they should shake off the Mogul's yoke and throw their fortunes with the Persians.

Curiously he had noted that Jahangir and his followers uttered their prayers even while drunk, yet massacred the garrison of a hill town with bland treachery when inviolability had been promised.

Khlit perceived the greatness of the empire of Hindustan, and marveled. Yet these hive-like human beings were not of his race. And he was weary of the silken luxury which enwrapped the camp.

The high civilization of the court held no interest for him. Khlit had seen too much of the evil ambition of the priests—for the most part—the astrologers and the physicians. With very few exceptions each man had his price.

These matters and others Khlit considered while the light grew in the East and he listened to the approach of a large body of horsemen. They came swiftly, but Khlit was not disturbed. He was not accustomed to yielding his place at the approach of strangers. Furthermore he had a purpose in staying where he was.

The leaders of the cavalcade swept up to the ford and reined in with a shout.

"Ho, graybeard!" one cried. "Saw you a horseman with a woman in his arms pass this way?"

Others appeared—cavalry of the imperial guard, eunuchs, archers, and one or two *ameers* of rank gorgeously clad and profane in their anger and haste.

"Speak, dullard!" exclaimed another. "A woman has been stolen from the exalted seraglio. Men will die for this. Saw you the traitorous rider?"

Khlit surveyed them in silence. He had watched while Rao Singh with Kera and Ahmad Rumi, mounted behind Cheker Ghar, had taken the upper turn to the hills. Both horses—they had availed themselves of the animal belonging to the slain Persian master of horse—had been carrying double and they had but a brief start.

If the pursuers were set on their tracks, at once they must be over-hauled. But Khlit was not minded that this should happen. His talk with Ahmad Rumi had not been in vain. Moreover, he had been pleased with the youthful Rao Singh.

"How should I know?" he growled. "I am no stealer of women."

The ranking *ameer* glanced anxiously at the divided trails and gnawed his lip. He had been commander of the guard when Kera escaped.

"Perchance this will quicken your memory, warrior," he cried, fingering a gold mohar.

Khlit's eyes gleamed shrewdly under their shaggy brows.

"Aye, that is well spoken," he responded. "A rider with a woman across his knees passed this way and took the lower turn."

He pointed to where the cross-trail led into the thickets, away from the path to the hills where Rao Singh had gone.

The *ameer* who was leader of the party was about to sign for an advance after tossing Khlit the coin when a small, dun Arab pushed in front of him and a high voice not unlike a woman's addressed him.

"Lord, I, all unworthy, have a word for your ear."

Khlit looked up swiftly, sensing a new development. He saw a withered, bent frame of a man with a singularly light complexion and sharp eyes. He wore a skull-cap, and his frail figure was enveloped in a white cloak, a garment of rich texture, with bracelets of pearls at the wrists.

"Speak, Bember Hakim—waste no words."

The *ameer* glanced at the newcomer half-scornfully.

"Lord, I spake with one who was sentry at the foot of this path. He said that when the moon was very bright there came two who stood on the hill above him and looked toward the camp. One wore the turban of an Afghan, the other was yonder graybeard.

"They watched, lord. For what? Perchance for the coming of one in haste from the camp."

The *ameer* glanced at Khlit, fingering his sword. The wanderer met his gaze squarely.

"This one remained at the ford," continued Bember Hakim shrewdly. "Wherefore if not to turn us aside from the fleeing rider? It is written that the evil-doers shall trip in their own snare. Why should the man we seek take the lower turn, which leads but to villages? Nay, we shall find him riding into the hills—"

"By the beard of the Prophet!"

The *ameer*'s dark face twisted in a snarl. He signed to his men. "Seize me this traitor and squeeze his gullet until blood or the truth come from his lips."

Khlit saw that others rode past him to the farther side of the ford to hem him in. His horse stood behind him, but he was surrounded save for the stream.

He did not move as two warriors approached, looking up instead at Bember Hakim.

"You be men of the Mogul's," he said slowly. "Know you Jahangir has promised me safeguard? Aye, his safeguard to Khlit. I have his oath."

The soldiers hesitated, but the *ameer* scanned Khlit sharply and bared his teeth in a grim smile.

"A favorite of Jahangir? In common garments? Nay, you be no Muslim."

"Nevertheless it is the truth. I give you warning."

"A woman has been taken from the imperial seraglio," broke in the Arab. "This man is a *caphar*, an unbeliever, by dress and speech. What matters a safeguard if he be a traitor?"

Khlit rose and faced the two.

"Take me then to Jahangir," he ventured. "He will remember the one who befriended Nur-Jahan."

"Spawn of an unbeliever!"

The *ameer* gripped his sword.

"Nay, I waste not words with such. Speak us the truth and you may save your life. Jahangir's memory is short."

"I have spoken."

Khlit noted that the ring of men pressed closer, and he saw a smile creep upon the thin face of the *hakim*. In a calmer mood perhaps the horsemen would not have dealt so harshly with him; yet it was a vital matter—since favor at court rested with the outcome—that they should find Kera and Rao Singh. Moreover the nobles of Jahangir were scarcely tolerant.

"We waste time!"

The *ameer* reined his horse forward.

"Bind me this wretch—"

"And the word of Jahangir?"

"Is a thing that is past. If you have aided the misdeed this night you will be given to the elephants to trample."

Khlit had been thinking while he talked. In fact he had played with words while he considered the situation. To his ability to weigh chances and to act swiftly in the face of danger he owed his long life.

If the *ameer*'s men had realized the character of the wanderer they would not have given him the chance to mount his horse. Khlit's enemies frequently underestimated his strength, and still more frequently his intelligence.

"Stay!"

Khlit grasped the reins of the leader's horse, forcing the beast back on its haunches.

"Behold what lies underfoot!"

Before this the newcomers had not observed the body in the deep pool where the current had washed it. The body of the Persian. They were startled, and their eyes were drawn to it for a brief second.

Time enough for Khlit to spring bodily into the saddle of his horse and plunge spurs into flank. Perfect rider as he was, trained in the Cossack school, it was no difficult feat to avoid the other horses and gallop up the bed of the stream.

A pistol echoed behind him. He bent low, avoiding the sweep of the branches overhead. The others were after him at once. But his course had surprised them, and the footing was of the poorest.

Khlit had chosen his present horse with care, and by keeping well in to the bank he drew ahead of his pursuers, who were on spent beasts. Their pistol-shots went wide.

Only one kept close to him. After an interval Khlit looked behind.

He saw the little Arab galloping through the brush by the stream, and he put spurs again to the black horse.

The stream turned into an open glade. Once this was passed, and the thicket on the farther side, Khlit reined in sharply. He drew a pistol from his belt and awaited the approach of the *hakim*, satisfied that the others had been left in the rear.

The Arab came into view and the rider slowed to a walk as he neared the Cossack. He seemed to be unarmed, wherefore Khlit did not fire his weapon but waited alertly.

The little man in the cloak surveyed him shrewdly and held up an open hand.

"Peace!" he cried.

He sighed, glancing back the way he had come.

"*Aie*—you can slay me if you will. By the holy names of Allah, I am a doomed man."

He faced Khlit with the calm of a fatalist and smiled. The Cossack lowered his weapon, frowning.

"By the delay," explained Bember Hakim, "the rider and the maiden will win free, and you also are safe—although you had best ride farther. But I am doomed."

"Wherefore?"

"Eh—you know not the Mogul. The girl is lost. And I was the physician, chosen last night to minister to the ills of the women. By the will of Allah I spoke blindfolded with Kera of Kargan. This will come to the ears of Jahangir, and I—"

He drew a lean finger across his throat and sighed.

"*Caphar*," he added reflectively, "I would have accomplished your death. That is a thing like to writing on the sand when the wind has passed. Will you grant me the hand of friendship? We be both branded men."

Khlit surveyed him with some surprise. Verily Bember Hakim
was a strange philosopher. Then he laughed. The offer appealed
to his fancy.

"Come then, if you will," he said gruffly and wheeled his horse
into the brush.

The physician trotted after moodily on his small horse.

Thus did Khlit leave the camp of the Mogul and lose the favor of Jahangir. But as he put the miles between himself and
the imperial pavilions his contentment grew, so that he laughed.
Whereupon Bember Hakim looked at him curiously, not knowing
Khlit was glad to be his own master again with a horse between
his knees and open spaces ahead.

IV

*In the lake waters glimmer the snow-crests of the mountain
peaks. In a mirror a woman looks upon her beauty and smiles.*
    *Within a mirage over the desert are caravans that leave no
trace, and wells that are barren of water.*
    But how shall we see the faces of the gods?
Hindu saying

The Wular lake was very old, older than the floating island and
older than the pillared halls of Jhilam. Older than the first myths
of the Hindus—than the ancient story of the *Ramayana*.

It was high in the mountains north of the pastureland of Kashmir. Yet it was below the Summer snow-line—low enough in
altitude to escape freezing in Winter. It was a sheet of turquoise-
blue water fed by cascades descending from the snow-line.

The southern end of the lake was occupied by the castle of
Jhilam with its gardens and the native village. At this point of
the lake was the floating island on which Shaista Mirza had
built his pleasure pavilion. Around Jhilam were the rice-fields,
the beehives—famous in Kashmir—and the fruit-groves that had
once belonged to the natives and now were the property of the
Persian lord.

At the northern tip of the Wular rose the mountains which
formed the foothills of the Himalayas—pine-clad and rocky, yet

richly verdant. Of late years many of the Hindus of the Jhilam village, as told by Ahmad Rumi, had forsaken their huts to flee from the ruinous taxes of their overlord and to take refuge in the pine forest, where game was moderately plentiful.

So it happened that the village of Jhilam came to be overrun by slaves of the Persian and in the castle proper were only adherents of Shaista Mirza—soldiers, Khorassanis, a few Pathans, Hazaras and the Persians. And as Jhilam was the fortress of northern Kashmir, all the province from the lowlands to the boundary of Kargan Khan's territory had come under the Persian's sway.

It was a clear morning in early Winter with a hint of snow in the air when a man in armor on an exhausted horse rode up the avenue of aspens through the gardens and dismounted hastily at the castle gate.

He was recognized by the guards and passed into the main hall by a gigantic Turk, Jaffar, sword-bearer of Shaista Mirza.

"The master!" cried the rider. "The master! I bear ill news."

Jaffar grunted as he parted the satin hangings over the portal of Shaista Mirza. The soldier, dust-stained and streaked with sweat, prostrated himself.

"Lord," he cried, "may your shadow ever be over us. Lord, I bring word from the Jhilam road."

Jaffar eyed him eagerly, but Shaista Mirza did not look up from his study of the chess-board. He sat on his heels on the tiled floor by the ivory chessmen—a lean man, wasted by illness, pockmarked and pallid with the expressionless gaze that is sometimes seen in animals.

Shaista Mirza was neither Muslim nor sun-worshiper. Some said that he was a survivor of the *Refik*, a follower of the Assassins, the secret order that had held power in northern Persia during the twelfth century. Shaista Mirza never admitted this, and those who knew him best—among them the astrologer Nureddin—said that the Mirza liked the title of Assassin yet did not belong to the order.

He was a man who chose to inspire fear among his followers and his enemies. He did this in a number of ways—availing himself sometimes of the arts of Nureddin, who was skilled in the magic of the time, and maintaining a network of spies among the Kashmir hills as well as in the Mogul court. He had chosen Jaffar with this end in view, and Jaffar's congenital cruelty fitted well with the needs of his master.

Such was Shaista Mirza's shrewdness that Jahangir saw fit to conciliate the Persian, fearing him more than a little and allowing him to accomplish his own ends in Kashmir. This was what the Mirza sought, and he sent the Mogul a small yearly tribute from the rich fief of Jhilam.

Beside the chessboard burned a brazier, tended by Nureddin, giving out the scent of sandal-paste and aloes. The Persian's gaze shifted from the mimic warriors of the board to the smoke of the brazier—a fixed, cold stare that resembled the unblinking scrutiny of a snake.

Beyond the brazier stood a small mirror, and in this mirror Shaista Mirza could watch the prostrate soldier.

"You have no weapon," he said slowly, and the man squirmed, for the *mirza*—so he thought—had not glanced at him.

How then was he to know that of which he spoke?

"*Akh!*" he cried. "Lord of Exalted Mercy and River of Forgiveness, my sword was taken from me by a demon on a black horse. Verily it was a demon, for it slew Bairam with one stroke and my comrade with another. In the time it takes to draw breath it slew the twain. Verily it was a demon."

Jaffar grunted at this, and Nureddin glanced up fleetingly. The astrologer was a handsome man, ruddy of cheeks, with black beard curled and scented—a man of manifest vitality. Some who stood in awe of Shaista Mirza whispered that the wasted master of Jhilam sucked blood and strength from the strong body of Nureddin.

Shaista Mirza did not look up, but toyed with the links of a gold chain about his lean throat.

"*Akh,*" protested the soldier volubly, "the demon warrior flung a black cloak of darkness about him—and how was I to see where to strike? By the ashes of death, I struck, and fire darted from the nostrils of the black horse and turned the blade, which fell into the stream."

Jaffar scowled, but the expression of the pale Persian did not change.

"Verily—" the soldier plucked courage from the silence, "a troop of accursed spirits were abroad in the night. At one stroke was Bairam slain—his head hanging to his shoulder by the wind-pipe. I rode without stopping for drink or meat until I should bear the news to my lord."

Shaista Mirza signed to the Turk.

"This man thirsts," he whispered. "See that he has drink. Wine he may not drink because of his faith, but water; ah, water, Jaffar. Bind a rope about his ankles and tie the rope to a branch of a tree overhanging the lake in the pear-garden. Thus may his head hang in the water, and he will drink—much."

A wail from the suppliant was interrupted by the sword-bearer, who jerked the soldier to his haunches. Jaffar had learned to obey Shaista Mirza swiftly—hence he was alive and in favor.

Fear lent the soldier brief courage.

"Lord," he cried, "Lord of Rudbar—I have further news. Grant me release from this punishment and you shall hear it."

Shaista Mirza lifted an ivory castle delicately from the board and set it down on another square.

"Wretched one," he said softly, "you and the twain were sent to slay me the stripling Rao Singh. Yet did you attack another man. The twain have atoned for their mistake. Shall you fare better?"

"Lord, I have rare news."

The Persian glanced at him fleetingly and the man shivered. "Speak!"

"Lord, will your exalted mercy pledge me life—"

"Speak!"

"Give tongue, dog."

Jaffar struck his prisoner with a heavy fist.

"My lord of Jhilam loves not to wait."

"This is the word, master," the man exclaimed, his eyes rolling from one to another of the group in feverish supplication. "In the third watch of last night Rao Singh did seize the woman Kera of Kargan from the imperial tents and bear her away."

Nureddin sucked in his breath with sudden interest and was silent, watching his master.

"He escaped?" demanded Shaista Mirza.

"Aye, lord."

"How heard you this?"

"From certain eunuchs who rode in pursuit."

"Whither went Rao Singh?"

"North into the hills, they knew not where."

"How large a following?"

"Lord, they knew not. A wild figure clung to his stirrup. Perhaps others went also. Allah alone knows the truth."

"Darkness doubles numbers—if they be enemies," smiled Nureddin, speaking his limpid mother-tongue. "Also—creates demons, my lord."

Shaista Mirza turned to Jaffar.

"Strip this scion of purgatory and bind him upon an ass with his face to the tail. Then summon the archers to feather him thick as a falcon is feathered with their shafts. Let the body be led through the village as a warning."

"*Akh!* My life was pledged—"

"Fool and nameless one," pointed out Nureddin coolly, "Shaista Mirza did but grant your prayer that the punishment be altered."

When Jaffar and his prisoner had gone—the man silent with the hopelessness of the fatalist—Nureddin lowered his voice.

"'Tis well, my lord. Wisdom teaches that a broken arrow should not be kept in the quiver. Rao Singh has scant friends, yet it were not well to have knowledge of your attempt on his life get abroad."

Shaista Mirza made no reply, whereupon Nureddin glanced at him appraisingly and bent over the chessboard.

Not until the last move had been made and the *mirza*'s king had been mated beyond all doubt—it was significant of the relations between the two men that the Persian would have flown into a rage had Nureddin not played his utmost, oblivious of the result—that Shaista Mirza leaned back on his cushions and allowed his mind to wander from the game.

"Aye," he mused, "the stripling lacks favor at Jahangir's court. Eh, at one stroke he has flown from his gilded cage and taken a mate. What think you of that?"

Nureddin smiled, stroking his beard.

"Never, my lord," he responded slowly, "will you occupy Jhilam in peace until the last of the brood of Sattar Singh has been laid in death. And now Kera of Kargan is one of the brood.

"The blood of youth is traitor to its own cause, lord. Rao Singh has stepped to the brink of a deadly cliff, whence by good fortune and some small arts of ours he shall doubtless tumble to his death."

Shaista Mirza was silent for a space. Then:

"Jahangir will give much for his punishment. Yet the Mogul departs with his following for the plains of Hindustan. It is my thought that Rao Singh will escape capture—by the Mogul's men."

Nureddin bowed assent, thrusting his hands—now that the game was ended—in his wide sleeves, as etiquette prescribed.

"The essence of truth, my lord. Yet perchance he will not escape us."

Shaista Mirza tapped his chain meditatively.

"Nor will Kera of Kargan. Verily the fool has dug a pit in which he shall be caught. Know you Kargan Khan?"

"Aye, being sharer of the wisdom of the Lord of Rudbar. A brainless hill chief blind in one eye because of a spear-thrust and likewise blind in his brain. Kin to his own clumsy yaks, my lord, he has room but for one thought at a time."

"And that thought?"

"To rend the man who has carried off his child. Kargan has love for his daughter."

Shaista Mirza made no response. Love was a feeling he had never possessed. Wasting sickness had stripped him of vitality, leaving a burning sense of injury—a craving to overmaster the happiness and the lives of others. Ambition and cruelty were the twin forces that gripped the Persian's keen brain.

Yet he was shrewd enough to make allowance for such feelings —in others. He had studied the human emotions, aided by Nureddin's knowledge of the sciences, of Avicenna's Law, and Galen's, and even Aristotle.

"Nureddin, you boast the foreknowledge of the stars. Can you answer me this: Where will a fox flee when pursued?"

"Nay," smiled the astrologer, "no divination is needed to speak you that. To his burrow."

"And when the goshawk mates, where will you find the female bird?"

"In the eyrie of her mate."

"Aye, Nureddin. Now while the heat of love, rising from the center of life in the human body, which is the stomach—"

"Nay; the kidneys." This was a debated point between the two.

"Nay; the Frankish philosophers claim the heart, yet the wisdom of Arabia, allied to the lore of Avicenna, proclaims it the stomach. The heat of love dulls the keenness of the brain. Yet Aristotle, who is the master of learning, proves by experiment that when animals mate the male is rendered doubly alert and jealous of danger. So with human beings, Nureddin—for we are naught but higher beasts—"

"The Buddhist priests claim we are animals reincarnate—"

"Then Kargan is a buffalo reborn. Yet what I would say is this: Rao Singh will be thrice as wary now as heretofore, on behalf of Kera, whom he has taken to himself. Therefore he will be crafty in selecting a retreat. Yet his instincts will lead him to flee near his homeland."

Nureddin raised his brows. "Jhilam?"

"Not near the castle. That were madness. Or supreme cleverness, such as—"

"Only Shaista Mirza possesses."

"Nay, but near to Jhilam are barren hills."

"Aye, lord; north of the lake."

"Yet he will not ride to the country of Kargan Khan. So perchance Rao Singh may be found north of the lake. Send riders out to over-cast the countryside."

Shaista Mirza stretched back on his cushions, his eyes closed. Frequently he was in bodily pain bred of his disease.

"Send a messenger to the Mogul saying that by his favor I, Shaista Mirza, will hunt down the lawless defiler of the seraglio."

"And Kargan Khan?"

The Persian opened his eyes, and their stare was baneful. "Nureddin, I have a thought that mighty omens are foreboding events in my favor. I ask for your wisdom, gleaned from the stars. Are the coming days favorable to me? Is my star ascendant?"

There was genuine anxiety in his voice. Like many men of genius Shaista Mirza trusted much in the potent element of destiny. Nureddin considered.

"The season of Taurus is past, lord," he responded. "Yet the days of Capricorn, of the Goat, are auspicious. Aye, your birth-star is high. Great events may be forthcoming."

"Then," cried Shaista Mirza, "we will deal with Kargan Khan —not now but later. First we will find Rao Singh."

V

It was cold among the deodars midway up the long slope that led to the Himalaya peaks. Animals here bore a thicker coat than those south of the Wular lake.

Yet in the Wular *davan*—valley—towered precipices, and in the base of these were caves. It was at the upper end of the *davan* where the gorge terminated in a rock-tangle that Ahmad Rumi had his hut, and the hut was but cedar slabs placed across the entrance of a cavern with skins of mountain sheep within to lie upon, and a cleft in the rock overhead to carry off the smoke from the fire.

Not that Ahmad Rumi could cut himself firewood. The Kashmiris of the forest saw to that—and likewise brought fish at intervals. But now in the first moon of the early Winter of the year 1609 they brought also smoke-cured mutton and goat's milk.

For instead of one there were now four in the Wular *davan*. And the Kashmiris ran from a great distance a few at a time to look upon the face of the son of Sattar Singh and his bride.

They were small squat men in ragged gray woolen tunics and round hats, and their women in shawls. They came a few at a time in spite of the cold. They came from their mountain nests, from the caverns by the lake and from the valleys as far distant as the border of Baramula, which was the land of Kargan Khan and his Kirghiz.

In fact many of them were Kirghiz—those that boasted ponies and felt *yurts*, and were of the breed of the northern steppe. And so it happened that Kera of Kargan, who was the mate of Rao Singh, felt no terror at sight of the ragged groups, for they were like to her own people, the Kirghiz, whom she remembered from her child-days.

They asked no gifts from Rao Singh, knowing the tale of his misfortune—how he had been kept as a prisoner at the Mogul's camp. In that Winter the verdant land of Jhilam was rife with poverty, arisen from the tithes of Shaista Mirza, and few but the *aksakal*s of the Kirghiz *yurts* possessed two horses.

It was a strange court that Rao Singh held. His bride, daughter of a Kha Khan and a beauty among the women of the Mogul, had no better quarters than the hut of Ahmad Rumi, which had been given up to her and her lord. She lacked the jewels and the perfumes bestowed upon their women by the southern *ameer*s.

Her lord owned but two horses, and only one of these better than the average—and his sword. He had no wealth, for he had been shown no favors by Jahangir—consequently none by the nobles of the empire, to whom Jahangir's disfavor was a potent ban.

Yet Kera of Kargan did not complain. She was happy in Rao Singh. Kera was barely at the verge of womanhood—a shy, dark-faced girl with splendid black hair that matched her eyes and a free spirit bred of her early life on the steppe. She was round of arms, with strength in her youthful limbs. This was well, since a woman of the hotter climate, accustomed to the luxuries of Hindustan, could not have survived the days in the hills.

She sang to herself and bound her silver ornaments in her long hair by aid of the mirror of the spring near the cavern. This she did to make herself fair in the sight of Rao Singh, who was her lord.

"Eh, my lord," she had said, "may it not be that we can ride to the encampment of Kargan? It would be well that we should do this, for evil tales will be whispered to him and he will hear naught that is good of you if I am not the messenger. Yet great is his love for me, and he will take heed when I speak."

"Nay; you are mine, no longer Kargan's," Rao Singh had replied fiercely.

He did not add that patrols of horsemen had been seen near the lake, or that the Kashmiris had reported search being made for the two. It would have been courting danger to venture from the valley.

Here the forest men kept guard vigilantly, and they were reasonably safe. Moreover the chance of discovery was lessened if they stayed in one spot.

"Who shall safeguard you, Light of my World," whispered Rao Singh, his dark eyes aflame with the beauty of the girl, "but me?"

Kera sighed. "We have many enemies, my lord. I have a woman's thought and wish that we could seek the Baramula and the might of Kargan. He has many horsemen—and his anger is quick. Who can pen the waters when the dam has burst? Let me speak with him and win his pride to our favor."

"Nay," said Rao Singh again, "will the Khan of Baramula look with favor on one who is an outcast? The time will come—so says the wise Ahmad Rumi—when I shall ride to meet Kargan with horsemen at my back as one chief to another."

So it happened that the pride of the youth kept Kera from sending a messenger to the Kirghiz. In this he blundered perhaps. If Kera had had her way it might have altered the events that came to pass in Jhilam during the space of that moon.

Kera was content to obey her lover. Cheker Ghar, who liked the cold little, still bestirred himself to amuse her—saying naught of his disappointment at the poor fortunes of Rao Singh.

"Ho, Flower of the Hills," he would cry, "when had a woman such rare followers? Here is Ahmad Rumi, who is councilor of owl-like wisdom and can repeat his Muslim proverbs and legends with the art of one who is schooled in chronicles and books. And I, my lady—behold the chosen buffoon of the imperial bazaar!"

He waved his lean hand toward his precious leopard-skin and salaamed.

"Aye, even unworthy I—unworthy in the fragrant splendor of your beauty—yet a paladin among conjurers, buffoon and mimic without a peer—"

Whereupon he gathered his cloak about his scant form and strode about in the semblance of an *ameer* until Kera clapped her hands in delight.

"Behold," he chattered, rejoiced to see her merriment, "a eunuch of the royal seraglio."

He puffed out his dark cheeks and bound his voluminous turban in the Turk fashion and clutched a stick, which he bore before him like a scimitar, scaling his voice to the shrill pitch of one of those unfortunate creatures. Rao Singh, even, smiled at his performance, and Ahmad Rumi turned his sightless eyes toward the mimic in gentle approval.

Secretly Cheker Ghar turned up his nose at association with the blind Muslim; yet he spoke not of this dislike, nor of the many things he did in defiance of the dictates of his caste for the sport of Kera of Kargan.

"If," ventured Rao Singh, "that was the likeness of him you named Bara, you need not fear he will call you to account. I left my knife in the chief eunuch's ribs."

"Ho, verily?"

Cheker Ghar smiled broadly.

"Then my heart is light, for the Purified One was such but in name, and he was like to a thriced-defiled swine that has eaten of filth."

The conjurer had an uncanny knack at mimicry. So great was his skill that he frequently confounded Ahmad Rumi, who thought that Rao Singh or another addressed him when Cheker Ghar spoke.

With others than the light-hearted Kera he took his profession with grave seriousness. He was at such times not so much the buffoon as the Hindu master of magic. Only for her would he powder his face white and make idle sport. Cheker Ghar loved her as a dog loves its mistress, and this love was to bear fruit in due course.

Often he would sit squatted opposite the fire from the legend-teller while Kera and Rao were together on the hillside and their Kashmiri followers were on watch.

"Harken, Son of the Owl," Cheker Ghar whispered to the Muslim, "and tell me what is this you hear—"

A plaintive cry floated through the cavern, coming apparently from the cleft overhead.

"It is *kulan*, the wild ass, calling."

The cry changed to a grunting, snapping torrent of sound, echoing from a corner of the cave.

"The wild pig of the jungle!" muttered the blind man. "*Bismillah*—does such an animal of filth approach?"

"Nay," said the mimic seriously, "have no fear; I will guard you from defilement."

He bellowed suddenly, hoarsely.

"The mountain buffalo, the yak, calling to its mates, Cheker Ghar."

A shrill, grunting moan issued from the Hindu in such a fashion as to appear as from a distance. Ahmad Rumi lifted his white head.

"A camel complains under its load as the pack is bound on by the camel man."

"Aye," assented Cheker Ghar, pleased. "Yet there is no yak, and no camel in the valley. Is it not magic then?"

"There is no magic but the will of Allah."

And so the days passed under the cloud of danger with scant food and comforts until Bember Hakim found his way to the hut; and with him came Khlit.

The wanderer entered quietly into the life of the valley, asking nothing from Rao Singh and providing his own meat, which he obtained in ways best known to himself.

He constructed a shelter of sheepskins not far from the cavern. Khlit disliked to live under a roof, and so pitched his *yurt* in a pine grove where his horse could be picketed.

Ahmad Rumi removed his prayer-carpet and skins to the *yurt*, where he fell to talking much with Khlit. The life suited the Cossack, and the *davan* provided good concealment from the riders who searched the hills.

The Kashmiris had reported that the Mogul cavalry were no longer questing for Rao Singh, but others kept up the pursuit. So well chosen was the hiding-place in the valley that it had not been noticed. The rock walls were sheer on one side, and on the other was dense forest. Nothing was to be seen from the lake side, and from the overhanging peaks the *davan* appeared nothing more than a break in the forest.

By now the searchers were striking farther afield to the North, and Rao Singh felt that they had escaped discovery. He himself began to make excursions to the haunts of the Kashmiris at the urging of Ahmad Rumi, who felt that the coming of Rao Singh would work a miracle of some kind and aid the suffering peasants of Jhilam.

"Verily," he assured Khlit, "is he not the son of Sattar Singh, who extended the hand of mercy to the wound of my suffering?"

"He is a man half-grown," grunted Khlit, "who loves a woman. What skill has he in warfare?"

"Eh, he may adorn the pearl of love with the diamond of mercy," said the legend-teller wistfully. "Allah grant I may see him Lord of Jhilam. I have prayed much, but the span of my life draws to an end."

He showed the Cossack a white garment wrapped beneath his clean tunic. It was a winding-sheet.

Except with Ahmad Rumi Khlit talked little. Rao Singh and Kera were wrapped up in each other, and Cheker Ghar in Kera. Khlit from long habit made no advances and kept to himself.

Rao Singh and his small colony entertained no distrust of the wanderer, for the reason that Khlit was an outcast such as they. They had heard from the Kashmiris that he was banned by the Mogul, and they knew that, having slain by chance two men of Shaista Mirza's, he could claim no alliance with the Persian.

As for Bember Hakim, he occupied himself in collecting herbs, a task which took him away from the valley for long intervals, and otherwise accepted his hard lot with characteristic philosophy.

"Now, my lady," quoth Cheker Ghar, squatting at the feet of Kera, "we have a physician of the court. What lack we now?"

He rose and began to move around, limping after the manner of Bember Hakim and uttering pseudo-learned remarks on the Arabic sciences until he saw her smile.

"Naught save the protection of Kargan Khan," she said, leaning her smooth chin on her arms. "Would I might send Khlit to him with word from me!"

"The rider of the black horse performs errands for no one, Flower of the Hills. His look fills me with a fear. It is like a wolf, looking into the distance."

He shook his turbaned head moodily. "A wolf—aye, for he is not one of us. And when did a wolf do a kindness to others?"

He sighed. "As for Kargan Khan, methinks the Kirghiz would welcome you to his *yurt*, my lady, but we others would have our blood let from our veins by his sharp sword."

Now it happened that it was night when Cheker Ghar said this, and they were seated by the fire in the cavern, Rao Singh being absent on one of his rides.

The hour grew late, and Kera, wearied with the tricks of the conjurer and becoming anxious for her lover, left the fire and sought the sheep path by which Rao Singh would ride back to the *davan*. She walked swiftly for the night was cold and she knew the way leading to a rock—a favorite resting-place of their guards—by the trail. But recently the Kashmiris had given over their vigil as the pursuing bands had not visited the vicinity.

Kera wrapped her sheepskin *khalat* about her slender shoulders and tripped along in her light leather boots. Unlike the women she had lived with in Hindustan, the solitudes of the forest held no fear for her. She passed between giant pine-trunks and slipped around trailing junipers. A scanty fall of snow had rendered it easy to follow the trail, outlining the bulk of tree and rock.

She seated herself on the stone she sought, drawing up her knees under her chin for warmth. Then she lifted her head alertly. She had heard a heavy tread along the sheep path. Her pulse quickened at the sound.

She had been moody that night, perhaps because of the absence of Rao Singh, perhaps because of the tales of Ahmad, who had been depressed in spirit. The legend-teller had said that he had a premonition of danger.

Kera stared at the dark form that paced toward her, coming from the valley. Opposite the rock it halted, and she heard Khlit's voice.

"Have you a fear, little girl?"

It was a deep voice without pretense of anything but gruffness. Kera sat up straight, her heart still beating swiftly.

"What seek you?"

Up to now she had felt more uncertainty than pleasure at Khlit's presence. The Cossack was not one to impress women favorably. Yet Kera was not afraid of him. She watched—seeing him dimly—while he scanned the trail, then leaned against the rock with folded arms, his head on a level with her own.

"I seek that which is a thorn in the side of Rao Singh," he said slowly.

Kera hissed angrily.

"I? A thorn? Dolt! One without understanding!"

She fumbled in her girdle for the dagger that she carried, but Khlit did not move, nor did he look at her. He was watching where the pine-branches took shape slowly against the sky and the gleam of the many stars paled as the moonlight flooded the vast spaces of the air from a hidden quarter somewhere behind the hills.

The snow summits were turning from dull gray to silver, and the shadows deepened. Shafts of silver shot through the branches, forming a tracery in the snow, outlining the sticks and rocks that had been invisible before.

"A thorn, Kera of Kargan. You are a woman and you love. See you not that Rao Singh is brooding?"

The girl considered this silently, peering at Khlit as if she tried to read his meaning in his face. She no longer felt disturbed at his presence.

"Aye, Khlit, my heart has told me that. Yet it is for me that Rao Singh has a foreboding."

"Ahmad Rumi has talked much. He is full of words. He has told me you left a silk couch in a velvet tent to be by the side of Rao Singh. Yonder hut is a poor shelter for a woman—they are like to birds who seek a soft nest. Is it not so?"

The Kirghiz girl laughed softly. "Who does not like the touch of silk? Yet with Rao Singh lies my path and my heart. My pride is his strength; he is a mighty lord."

"Without a follower save for yonder mummers. Kera, would you ride back to the tents of the Mogul? Then your body would again lie in ease."

Again Kera laughed, resting her face sidewise on her arms, which were clasped over her knees.

"Ho, the fool is a mighty fool," she whispered softly. "He is blinder than the poor Muslim. He has the wisdom of the dullard yak. Aye, though Ahmad Rumi said that he had once been Khan of the Horde. Nay, Ahmad Rumi lied, for you, Khlit, are the one that is—" again her laugh echoed softly—"blind. More blind than the teller of legends."

She glanced up the trail hopefully at the sound of a falling twig, and sighed.

"Aye, Ahmad Rumi is like to one that sits in the dark; still in his spirit there is a lamp by whose rays he sees an assemblage wherever he looks. So he said, and I wondered. Now I understand that he has within him a vision, while you—"

She broke off in contempt. Other women of her race perhaps would have cursed Khlit, being angry. Kera however was gentle.

"Where Rao Singh goes I guide my horse," she added as he did not speak. "His smile opens my heart like a flower. Why should it be otherwise?"

Khlit was satisfied. He had thought to test the girl's feeling for the Hindu. He had done so crudely. But it did not occur to him to explain this to her. He was indifferent to what she might think of him.

He returned to the thought that had impelled him to follow her along the sheep path.

"Kera, the thorn of unrest is in the side of the son of Sattar Singh. He has seen the evil that is wrought upon his people. And he is angry. He knows not the path he should follow."

The Cossack spoke gruffly.

"Likewise his thoughts are bound up in a woman."

The girl made no response, and Khlit went on.

"What has the stripling learned of war? He can think of naught but to find the path to your hut and to lie with your arms about him. Yet it is time he should mount and take up his sword. There be those who will follow."

"Nay."

Timidity—the shrinking of a woman who loves—gave Kera speech. "Here he is safe. If he rode far the men of Shaista Mirza would hear of it."

"The time must come, little sparrow," growled Khlit, "when your lord will try sword-strokes with this same *mirza*. It would be well were he to strike first."

"It may not be, *baba-ji*. *Aie*, how should that come to pass? The Persian is friend to Jahangir."

"Not so. The master of Jhilam—whatever name he bear—will be well treated by Jahangir. For Jhilam is a key to the hills. It lies too far to the north for the Mogul to muster his banners to attack it. So 'tis said, but I have a thought the Mogul fears to leave the Delhi court, and those who would plot against him, so far in his rear. So he must conciliate him who is lord of the fortress."

Out of his wisdom, hard-won in dealing with merciless foes, Khlit spoke. Out of her love for Rao Singh—blind love—the girl responded. "Does a hunting-dog walk into the den of a lion?"

"Aye, when death awaits him without."

"No danger lies about the *davan*. The riders have drawn their reins from these hills."

Khlit moved angrily.

"It is not I who am blind, Kera. Hide of Satan, see you not that Rao Singh must slay Shaista Mirza, or the Persian will sprinkle the cub's blood on the snow of his native hills?"

Kera drew back with a shiver.

"*Aie*—it is cold! Nay, *baba-ji*, it is said you are wise in battle. The gods may have so willed. Yet it is but the space of a short day I have Rao Singh at my side.

"The time for sword-strokes has not yet come; he lacks followers—perchance time will bring Kargan's riders to his aid, then proudly shall I gird the belt of war on the twain. Ahmad Rumi has said that this would come to pass."

Khlit would have turned away angrily, not knowing that the words of the woman were to come true. Yet in a manner such as he had not conceived. Ahmad Rumi possessed something of the gift of prescience which is found at times in men of frugal life and intensity of thought.

"Stay!" The girl touched his shoulder. "Shaista Mirza has five hundred horsemen under Jaffar his sword-bearer. I pray the gods that he will fall in the dust of defeat.

"I have heard it said that you are a father of battles. Will you ride with Rao Singh against Shaista Mirza when it is his fate that this should come to pass?"

The Cossack shook off the girl's hand impatiently.

"When Rao Singh is—a man," he growled.

"My lord will be a great *ghazi* conqueror," she cried proudly. "He is one among a thousand, and like to his father. So Ahmad Rumi swore."

Her mood changed swiftly and she looked up beyond the trees where the stupendous mountain peaks of the Himalayas were coming into view under the silver torch of the moon like sentinels taking their posts. A breath of the cold air from the heights above brushed her long hair across her face and she pushed it back, gazing up with eyes dark as fate.

"*Aie*—on the high places of the hills live the gods. Who knows what is in the heart of the gods? Who can pierce the cloud that covers the will of the many gods?

"I have prayed that they will be kind to Rao Singh! I have bent my head on the footstools of the gods, but they will not answer— save to send the wind and the cold."

She stretched up her slim arms.

"Why will the gods not answer? They hide their faces. Once I thought that they were near. *Aie*—they are cold, and I have naught to offer them. There is no mountain sheep to be slain for their pleasure. If they had an offering then they would turn the sun of their kindness on Rao Singh—"

She broke off in a moan that changed to a cry of delight as a rider came trotting down the trail on a spent horse, passing swiftly under the changing shadows of the moon.

Long after Rao Singh and Kera had gone, Khlit leaned against the rock, pondering many things. And in his thought Kera and her plaint had no place.

Khlit was not content with their position in the valley. The next day he went on a tour of inspection down to the lake. As usual, he went alone. The ride warmed his blood, and he sought for a fishing settlement that Ahmad Rumi had mentioned.

He was unable to locate it and wasted several hours, so it was late in the afternoon when he returned, hungry, for he had not eaten that noon. He was in high spirits, being naturally suited by a cold climate, and he had formed a plan which he intended to confide to Rao Singh.

The sun had set and Khlit had put his horse to a swift trot when he halted abruptly at sight of a body in the path. It was a peasant, an arrow projecting from his side. The man had been dead some time.

Khlit passed him by silently after observing that the trail of several horsemen led from the body away in the direction of the lake.

He was now in the *davan*, and scented smoke from the fire in the hut. He pushed his horse forward, rounded the turn by the spring, and then set spurs to flank.

Prone on his face in the snow lay Cheker Ghar, his small limbs twisted strangely. Beside the body of the conjurer were the tracks of many horses. Yet the valley was silent, strangely so. Khlit uttered a gruff exclamation. He was now before the cave entrance. Here the horse tracks ran, and among them the imprint of booted men. These footsteps led to the cavern.

The snow was gray with early twilight and trampled in spots as if men had struggled. And here and there were dark blotches of blood.

Just outside the door lay Ahmad Rumi, his white beard ominously stained. His turban was askew over one ear and the front of his tunic was slashed in a dozen places. From the pallor of his thin face Khlit knew that he was dead.

And beside the legend-teller was the form of Kera.

Khlit dismounted and stepped to the girl's side. Her dark hair flooded over the snow. She lay on her back, one hand clenched on her breast. And Khlit saw that her dark eyes were half-closed, the small, red mouth half-shut as if in a deep breath.

A scimitar stroke had slashed the base of her throat, severing the jugular vein. Her *khalat* was thrown back, revealing the grim message of death embodied in her torn and pierced chest:

> *Shaista Mirza has found those whom he sought.*

Bember Hakim hobbled from the nearby thicket fearfully and stared at the form of the girl and the blind man.

The story written in the snow was plain for Khlit to read. A group of horsemen had ridden swiftly up the valley, encountering Cheker Ghar on the way, and had surrounded the hut entrance. Some had dismounted and dragged Ahmad Rumi from the cavern.

Kera seemed to have attempted to flee but had been struck down beside the blind man. Her slender dagger lay near her clenched hand.

Then the riders had passed out by the way they came in, leaving the valley desolate with its dead. Of the Hindu youth there was no sign.

"Eh," cried the Arab, "I was at the cliff summit—Allah be praised—and I saw Jaffar and his men ride hither. It was an ill deed—"

"Rao Singh?" questioned Khlit sharply.

"He ran from the cavern at the cry of Cheker Ghar. Two horsemen rode him down and his weapon broke upon the sword-hilt of one. Then many seized him and he was bound. Allah the merciful laid the shadow of a swoon upon the youth—for he was struck heavily on the head with the flat of a blade—and he saw not the fate of Kera. Eh, it was a deed of shame—"

"They took Rao Singh?"

Bember Hakim's shrewd, dark eyes searched Khlit's face.

"Aye. Jaffar cried that Shaista Mirza would take pleasure in the sight of his foe."

Khlit said no more but walked heavily to the cavern, glancing within at the embers of the fire. Ahmad Rumi's prayer-carpet was in its place by the coals, and there also lay the sack of the conjurer. The Cossack stared at them meditatively. Then he flung up his head.

From down the valley came a mournful cry, rising and falling. It was like the cry of a madman. As it neared him Khlit could distinguish words:

"Wretched one, child of a thieving slave! O faithless and thrice accursed! O traitor to thy bread and salt! O snake that crawled from defiled flesh!"

It was a voice shrill, incoherent with rage. It panted as it cursed. And Khlit, striding from the cavern, swore in surprise.

Cheker Ghar was running up to the cavern, his puny fists clenched overhead. In the failing light his features showed distorted with anger. He was looking not at Khlit but at a form that climbed the opposite rock wall, where a cleft offered foothold.

Khlit peered doubtfully at the climber and recognized Bember Hakim, who passed from view behind boulders on the summit as he watched.

"O unutterable filth! O blood-guilty, and dog without a name!" Cheker Ghar shook his fists at the spot where the fugitive had vanished.

Abruptly he fell silent and sank on his knees by the body of Kera. He raised a twisted face to Khlit.

"Thus does one without honor reward the hand of mercy. I have seen what I have seen. The Turk and his men were led to this spot by Bember Hakim, accursed by the gods. Aye, for when the slaying was done he crept like a lizard from behind the warriors and smiled."

The conjurer moaned, touching the garment of his mistress.

"Bember Hakim set his foot upon the breast of the slain Flower of the Hills. For that I will follow the pursuit of blood. Aye, if the gods are kind I will tear open his breast and let his life run forth like water. Traitor to his salt—"

"Stay!" broke in Khlit gruffly. "Hide of the devil, how comes it that you live? With my eyes I saw you dead."

"A simple feat, lord, for one of my profession. When I saw the riders sweep up the valley I cried out. They would have seized me in their hands, but I slipped away. When they bore off Rao Singh I ran after, keeping to the forest, until my strength was spent.

"When I came hither again to bury my mistress I heard hoofs and lay like one dead. I saw not it was you until you had passed—"

"Then Bember Hakim was a man of Shaista Mirza?"

"Aye, yet we knew it not."

Khlit thought of the meeting at the ford when Bember Hakim had ridden after him. Seldom had Khlit been tricked by the art of another. But the physician was crafty and quick of wit and had told his lies readily.

Bember Hakim had guessed that the Cossack knew the hiding-place of Rao Singh. And his pretended search after herbs had afforded the opportunity to communicate with his master. Khlit had wondered when the other spoke the name how Bember Hakim had known it was Jaffar who led the riders.

Mechanically he seated himself by the fire and added fuel to the embers while Cheker Ghar labored at digging a grave with a Kashmiri tool.

Khlit had not eaten but he felt no desire for food. As was his habit when thinking deeply he drew his curved sword and laid it across his knees, stroking it absently. He felt no immediate fear that Jaffar and his party would return, for they must take Rao Singh to Jhilam. It was useless to follow Bember Hakim, who had gained a good start among the rocks, where there was little snow to reveal his course.

Several things puzzled Khlit. Why had Bember Hakim remained in the valley? Perhaps the Arab sought to trap him—believing all the others dead.

If so, why? Shaista Mirza would not want a living witness to the deed in the valley—one like Khlit who might bear the news to others.

Still Khlit was not satisfied with this reasoning. And it was not likely that Bember Hakim had remained to guard the bodies from the beasts.

Why had the Arab told Khlit the truth—in part—of what had happened? It seemed illogically cruel moreover that Kera should have been slain as she was. Why had she not been kept as a hostage? Surely by all accounts Kargan Khan was not lightly to be made an enemy of.

Khlit perceived that the Persian was a crafty foe. And his servants were like to him. In reasoning thus the Cossack came near to the truth. But he did not yet understand the masterly mind of Shaista Mirza.

He rose presently and aided Cheker Ghar in his toil. They worked in silence by the glow from the cavern mouth. Snow began to fall lightly. There was no moon.

When they had buried the two, they rolled rocks to the spot to protect it from the prying claws of jackals. This done, Khlit touched the shoulder of the conjurer, who squatted by the mound.

"We cannot stay," he pointed out. "By dawn Bember Hakim will bring others with him to search us out."

Cheker Ghar prostrated himself in the snow and clasped the boot of the Cossack.

"Lord," he whispered, "I heard it said in the Mogul's camp that you were crafty as the steppe fox and wise in war. Aid me to bear tidings of this thing to Kargan Khan over the Baramula trail. He will mount for vengeance, for Kera was his child."

"Nay," said Khlit.

Then, seeing the despair in the conjurer's dark face, he added: "Kargan Khan will not believe our tale. Shaista Mirza will send emissaries to the Kirghiz tribe. They would say that we lied." He withdrew his foot from the other's grasp.

"Come, Cheker Ghar. Gird on your pack."

"*Aie*, lord! Whither should I go, if not in the pursuit of blood? I have sworn an oath to the gods—"

"And I, too, swear an oath, Cheker Ghar, though to another God." Khlit's voice deepened with involuntary feeling.

"This thing I swear: I will not turn my horse's head from the Wular lake until Shaista Mirza be laid in death."

VI

In the end, a lion's cub becomes a lion, although brought up a slave.
                                                                      Hindu proverb

The floating island of the Wular lake had been built by human hands. The stalks of the rushes that lined its banks had been cut and fastened into bundles by withes. Rows of these bundles had been laid one upon the other, and over all earth. Under the reed bundles were the trunks of trees.

So it was that a grass carpet covered the floating island. And gardens bloomed with jasmine and wild rose in the Summer—gardens built upon the roofs of the arbors that surrounded the kiosk. This kiosk had been fashioned by artisans from Persia.

Slender pillars of marble—delicate, so that the foundation of the pleasure island should not be overbalanced—supported a cedar roof, the underside of which was enameled. Between the pillars were ranged gilded squares of wood upon which were blazoned certain words of the poets, and paintings from the Persian annals.

The porticoes were hung with brocaded silk. In the center chamber were placed brass braziers and incense pots that filled the air with a hot scent. Also they served to lessen the chill of the kiosk, for snow lay without on the bare rose-bushes; and

Shaista Mirza had chosen to visit the pleasure island alone with Nureddin.

"By slitting the tongue, O learned interpreter of the stars," he confided, "men may be made voiceless, and by piercing the inner ear, deaf. Yet it is well sometimes to go where there are none to hear or to speak."

Satisfied that the slaves had stocked the braziers well, Shaista Mirza lay back on his cushions, eyeing the vista of the lake through the open portal. The Persian was habitually watchful, for he did not fail to credit others with his own crafty nature. By virtue of this he was still alive.

Moreover he was well content this day. He scanned the kneeling astrologer through half-closed eyes, and Nureddin did not return his gaze. The astrologer had partaken of bhang to stimulate his brain.

Shaista Mirza however did not use opium, hashish or bhang. He was sparing of wine, for he would say that a man was witless to soften his brain with false pleasures.

"Verily, Nureddin," he mused, "my star is ascendant. Rao Singh lies in chains in the tower of Jhilam. Aye, the lion cub has dragged his limbs to the den of his sire. And his mate is where she will work us no harm."

"It was fated."

"Nay, I willed it. What is fate, Nureddin, but the whine of the low-born? When I placed my yoke on the neck of the Kashmiris, behold, they cried that it was fate. Believing this thing, they will not attempt to rise against me."

"Men do not rebel, my lord, without a leader. And you have the body of him they call master."

"A stripling, Nureddin; a broken pine that leans to the wind— aye, a weakling who found his happiness in the arms of a woman."

He stirred the coals of a brazier with his dagger and drew his cloak about his shoulders. He loved better the sun of Persia than the winds of Kashmir.

"Sattar Singh was a man, Nureddin," the high, soft voice went on, "a man of strength whose greatest foes were his own passions. Rao Singh is a child. I feared his mother more than the boy. So it happened that she partook of hashish from Rudbar in Persia—"

He broke off with a wave of the thin hand. The astrologer started. He had not thought until then that Shaista Mirza had conceived the death of the woman. He was not sure whether this was the case or not. The Persian, a master of intrigue, liked to be mentioned as the author of violence in which he had no hand, and likewise was silent about many deeds of which he was the author.

"Power, Nureddin, is built upon a multitude of swords. Sword-arms can be bought. Wealth we must have, and it comes from the labor of the low-born who are the peasants of Jhilam, and now—"

"The Kashmiris mutter and shirk, feeling the breath of the wind of rebellion, my lord."

"Aye, due to sight of Rao Singh, who is of the accursed brood of Sattar Singh. Verily they shall not see him long."

He leaned closer to the astrologer.

"The Mogul must have his tribute—silver coins, while gold mohars accumulate in the treasury of Jhilam."

He threw back his head with a silent laugh that changed to a grimace of hate.

"Nureddin, how shall we deal with the lion cub of Jhilam?"

The courtier meditated, seeking a clue in the face of his master.

"'Tis plain, my lord, the scoundrel came to Jhilam to stir the fires of strife. Is he not then a rebel against the Mogul? Should he not be impaled upon a spear and left to rot where the kites and the low-born may find him?"

Shaista Mirza smiled grimly.

"The stars have not taught you—policy, Nureddin. Nay, is it well to mention the Kashmiris to Jahangir? He is their overlord—though he keeps his army south of the hills.

"Harken—Rao Singh has outraged the seraglio of the Mogul. So shall we send a rider in haste with news of his capture and a prayer that Jahangir name the manner of his punishment. Thus

will we have the sanction of the Mogul for our action. And the
Kashmiris shall know this."

The astrologer bent his head and touched the floor with the
tips of his fingers as a sign of mute admiration.

"O wise reader of men! 'Tis an excellent plan. But if the punishment be not death?"

"A simple matter. The boy will sicken and—follow the shadow
of his mother. He mourns for Kera—the wanton. So shall he welcome the false contentment of hashish."

"And Kera of Kargan?" Nureddin looked up curiously. He had
not understood why Shaista Mirza had ordered Jaffar to slay the
girl brutally.

Moreover Nureddin was a trifle anxious concerning Kargan
Khan. If the truth were known the Kirghiz could muster a force
of warriors who were hardy men, bold riders and fearless.

"Jaffar mutilated the maiden as I bade him," responded the
Persian softly. "Already I have decided to send a messenger to
the Kirghiz tribe, relating how Kera was laid in the dust of death
by—a certain one. Bember Hakim, our worthy physician, saw the
deed."

The astrologer glanced admiringly at his lord. Truly Shaista
Mirza was a master of human fate.

"Then will come Kargan Khan to Jhilam like the breath of
the storm-wind to see vengeance done. And when he comes he
will look upon the body of the slayer of Kera. Because of this he
will yield me the hand of friendship which he has withheld until
now—"

Sudden suspicion flared in the cold eyes of the *mirza* and an
oath trembled on his lips as he stared through the portal. A fisher-
boat had drawn in to the landing-stage of the floating island.

Then he saw that the figure in the boat was Bember Hakim,
escorted by the mighty Jaffar.

The physician performed the triple salaam as he came into the
presence of his master. As a mark of favor Shaista Mirza bade
him be seated on the carpet. Bember Hakim's white cloak with

the pearls was stained with mud and his thin face was blue with
cold.

"Wherefore are you late?" demanded Nureddin sharply.

"Lord, and Monarch of Exalted Mercy," said the physician to
Shaista Mirza, "as you bade me, I awaited the gray rider of the
steppe. The words that you were divinely pleased to utter I repeated to him."

"What thinks the unbeliever?"

"Lord, one escaped death, a wretched Cheker Ghar, the buffoon. He upbraided me with treachery, and barely I escaped with
my life. Yet even in the cold—and the snow fell—I crept back to
the cavern from the rocks above and heard the Cossack vow—"

He hesitated in fear of the man who watched him silently.
"What, fool?"

"He vowed, lord, to seek vengeance for Kera, and to—slay the
master of Jhilam."

Nureddin laughed, but Shaista Mirza moved no muscle of his
face. "It is well, Bember Hakim," he said, and the Arab knew he
was pleased.

After a moment's thought he continued.

"Thus we have two alive who are our foes. Of Khlit of the
Curved Saber I have heard some talk. A wandering Christian who
was once khan of a northern clan. He dares not ride to the Mogul
with his news, for he is under the ban of outcast."

He played with the golden chain at his throat, frowning
slightly.

"'Tis unlikely that this aged unbeliever will seek Kargan
Khan, yet—shall we leave no hole through which the fox could
creep. Mount, Bember Hakim, this day, and ride by the Baramula
caravan-trail to the Kirghiz tribe.

"Seek Kargan and say to him that if he would look upon the
murderer of his daughter to come to the Wular *davan* with speed.
Your tongue is shrewd, Hakim—speak him well, but haste."

He sighed and fell to stirring the brazier.

"Nureddin, the dice fall as we wish—since we have doctored them. For who would play with life with unloaded dice? A fool! And who would invoke a god to aid him? A simpleton.

"Yet is this Khlit crafty after a fashion. Nureddin, talk with Rao Singh. The youth saw not the death of his wanton. Declare that Khlit sabered her. Thus will we plant a seed that may bear fruit."

"If he doubts, my lord—"

"Eh—remind him that Khlit owes his outlawry to Kera—" Bember Hakim had told his master all that had passed—"also that Khlit escaped hurt when Jaffar attacked Rao Singh."

"Yet the fight at the ford—"

"He saw it not."

Shaista Mirza turned to the waiting sword-bearer. "Jaffar, choose a following—nay, t'were best to ride alone. Fear you the Curved Saber?"

The broad Turk bared his teeth and touched his scimitar significantly.

"Then seek the man about the northern end of the lake. Take with you some trinket from Rao Singh. Say that the youth sends a message to the ear of Khlit, having promised you the jewel as reward. If he is puzzled in spirit by this and relaxes his guard—slay him. Do not fail this time."

Now as the four were ascending the bare gardens of Jhilam over the terraces to the palace proper, Jaffar espied in the distance on the crest of a hill something that might have been a rider on a dark horse.

Whereupon, after marking the position of the watcher at the forest edge, he mounted hastily without waiting to don his armor and spurred to the spot.

Here he found tracks in the snow made apparently by two animals. Doubtful now of what he had seen, he went forward into the pines, following the tracks leisurely. After a while they separated.

Jaffar turned his horse after one trail, taking the precaution of poising a primed pistol in his free hand. He was an experienced warrior, yet too vain of his strength, which was bred more of flesh than of spirit.

He hastened forward at a curious sound. It resembled the groan of a man. It proved to be but a mule.

A sick mule, wasted and trembling upon its legs. On its back was bound the blackened body of a man long, long dead, with arrows sticking from its chest. Jaffar's eyes widened and he cursed aloud until he remembered the soldier slain by order of Shaista Mirza a fortnight ago.

Then he thrust his pistol back into his girdle and had turned homeward something hastily, for the sight of his own handiwork was not pleasant, when he saw a strange form creeping from the thicket at his side.

It was a lean man in a green cloak, a knife between his teeth, which were set in a grin of hate. Seeing that he was observed, the man leaped forward, running with bent knees, silently intent.

Jaffar plucked the pistol from his belt and fired, only to see one corner of the cloak jerk. He had no time to draw a second weapon.

A black horse burst from the farther side of the thicket, snorting under the spur.

The Turk whirled to meet the rider of the black horse. Another second and his own mount had been knocked from its feet by the impact of the other's horse and Jaffar with a shrill cry of terror fell headlong.

For an instant before the creeping man with the knife reached him, Jaffar's eyes rolled in fear while he fumbled with his sword. Then Cheker Ghar with a low chuckle of joy sprang upon the powerful Turk, knife in hand.

That night Jaffar returned on his horse to his lord and to Jhilam. His horse wandered back to its stable by instinct. Yet slowly, for tied to the saddle-girth of Jaffar was the halter of the mule. Upon the back of the mule was the victim of Shaista Mirza.

And, as Nureddin observed sagely, the one was not more dead than the other.

Thus did Khlit throw down the gage of war to Shaista Mirza and did Cheker Ghar avenge her to whom he had given his allegiance and whom he still praised as the Flower of the Hills.

It was long before the conjurer was seen in the vicinity of the Wular.

VII

Jaffar's death did not disturb Shaista Mirza, after the first moment when the body of his sword-bearer was brought to him. His anger had blazed up at sight of the dead Turk and he spurned the body with a slippered foot.

"Fool," he whispered, "to be outwitted by a mummer and a graybeard. Waste not a dinar on burial, but cast this carrion into the lake."

Whereupon he fell silent and retired to his chamber, playing long games of chess with Nureddin while he awaited word from his messengers.

The first to arrive was the rider he had dispatched to the Mogul. Jahangir was rejoiced at the capture of Rao Singh. In the royal firman were many words of flattery and praise for Shaista Mirza.

Jahangir ordered that Rao Singh be confined in the prison cells of Jhilam. Death was the penalty for breaking into the imperial seraglio, but the cautious monarch suggested that the Kashmiris might resent the infliction of such a punishment on the son of Sattar Singh. Hence the decree of imprisonment.

Shaista Mirza spat upon the firman, then tossed it contemptuously to the astrologer.

"Behold the word of a monarch who is bound by the cords of his fear! Still it must suffice. When Bember Hakim returns, bid him prepare the drug that eats into the brain and creates a fever in the limbs—a wasting sickness. Did not the *hakim* prepare this physic for Rani Begum?"

Nureddin bowed in understanding. So the *mirza* had been the author of Rani Begum's death! After all, the astrologer reflected, it was wise, for so long as the brood of Sattar Singh lived, the Persian's seat upon the throne of Jhilam was not secure.

But Bember Hakim was slow in making his appearance. Knowing the uncertainty of travel over the northern passes where only the horns of mountain sheep and stags marked the caravan trails, Shaista Mirza was not disturbed. The man's patience where his schemes were involved was as great as his anger at the failure of a subordinate.

Yet he did not go again to the floating island, having in mind perhaps the death of Jaffar. He sat on the carpet of his sleeping chamber, hearing the reports of his vizier, the treasurer of the Jhilam fief, and playing at chess often—sometimes discussing with Nureddin the science of the stars.

Although a keen watch was kept around the outer gardens of Jhilam, Khlit was not to be seen. Shaista Mirza had issued a firman declaring death the penalty for any Kashmiri to give food or shelter to the outcast, also promising a mohar of rupees to whoever would bring tidings of Khlit.

No one came to claim the gold, and it is certain that the Cossack was given fodder for his horse at the Wular villages. The Cossack kept to the forest, pitching his *yurt* where he could watch Jhilam without danger of discovery.

This course of action suited Khlit well. He was accustomed to playing a lone hand, and the numerous followers of the Persian gave him no cause for concern. He hunted occasionally when he needed meat, and slept little, sitting in the door of his *yurt*, his sword across his knees and the brace of pistols on a sheepskin at his side. And he groomed and fed his horse painstakingly.

"Hey, black imp of hell," he observed caressingly, "eat well— yet not too much; for the day will come when you must gallop with the dogs of Satan at heel. Hey, that will be a ride of rides."

So Khlit waited in his *yurt* overlooking the fortress, and Shaista Mirza sat in an inner room and meditated.

Then came Nureddin to his master, smiling, with news on his bearded lips.

"O Lord of Exalted Wisdom," he announced, "there came Bember Hakim alone and pale with the cold of the hill passes. Verily the thin blood has dried in his veins and the fingers of one hand are scourged with frost. Barely he could whisper his message—"

"What said he, parrot-tongue?"

"This, my lord. He gave me a signet from Kargan Khan—" Nureddin handed the *mirza* a ring which his master scanned keenly and placed in his girdle, satisfied—"and reported that the wrath of the Kirghiz hill chief was like the blind rage of a wounded tiger—"

"Nay, a witless buffalo!"

"Aye, my lord. Kargan Khan musters his riders and girds on the sword of vengeance. In spite of the snow he will ride down the Baramula trail to the Wular *davan*, even as you advised."

The hard eyes of the Persian gleamed.

"Furthermore Kargan Khan would look upon the body of his child, so that the edge of his anger shall be sharp. Even now he tears his beard and cries upon his gods to speed the arrow-stitches of retribution."

Shaista Mirza stroked the wrinkled skin of his forehead reflectively.

"Why do men utter the name of a god when they feel pain? 'Tis like to the vain cry of a child newborn, Nureddin. Aye—not even the hand of a god may lift the shadow of destiny. Say on."

"On the fifth day will Kargan Khan be at the Wular *davan* by the grave of Kera. So said he at the border of his land. For three days Bember Hakim rode hither."

"Then," calculated the *mirza*, "on the second day from now will we meet with Kargan Khan. It is well. You have talked with Rao Singh?"

"Aye. Yet not as if there was a purpose in my mind. I spoke as if by chance, saying that Khlit had slain the woman. At first he believed not."

Shaista Mirza frowned, but Nureddin raised his hand deprecatingly.

"Not in vain have I knelt at the feet of the master of wisdom
of Rudbar, and disciple of the *Refik*. A thought came to me, and
I had slaves fetch the body of Jaffar—before it was thrown to the
Wular—as if by chance. And the slaves told the boy that Khlit
had slain Jaffar. They told how the unbeliever was an outcast in
the hills."

Shaista Mirza leaned forward expectantly.

"My lord," continued Nureddin smilingly, "the slaves were
simple folk and Rao Singh saw that they lied not. Wherefore a
doubt seized upon his spirit as the first sore of disease appears
upon the body."

"And then—"

"I sought out Bember Hakim's accursed store of herbs and powders. I bade the warders give him opium, a little at a time. And
Rao Singh began to brood. His doubt is heavy upon him. He re-
members little of the fight in the valley, for his brain is dulled
with the blow and with mourning for Kera of Kargan."

Nureddin stroked his beard tranquilly, aware that Shaista
Mirza was pleased.

"One thing further shall I do before the day of triumph. Bember
Hakim now lies abed, gripped by the demons of sickness, for his
body is frail and he has endured much.

"The malady has affected his tongue, but he is doctoring himself with rank smelling herbs and by the second day he will recover. Then shall I send him to the chamber of Rao Singh, and
his words will bear out my tale."

"Aye," assented Shaista Mirza; "Rao Singh knows that the
Arab saw the affray in the Wular *davan*."

"The boy is feverish with his grief. Truly it is strange that he
should grieve for one woman. Are there not round-faced maids
of Persia to be bought as slaves? Or pale and handsome maidens
from Georgia? And even the Kashmiris are not ill shaped, for I
have seized certain—"

Shaista Mirza waved his hand impatiently and the astrologer
was silent.

"Rao Singh is not like to Sattar Singh, Nureddin," he meditated.

"He is empty of mind and foolish as a young stag—eh, thereby we shall profit. For by your arts Rao Singh will believe Khlit slew the woman."

He glanced up at the water-clock that marked the passage of the hours.

"Soon, Nureddin, we shall take Rao Singh to the Wular *davan*, and with him Bember Hakim. Then shall they bear witness that Khlit is the slayer of Kera. And Kargan Khan shall hear."

"Most wise lord!" mouthed the astrologer.

"Take care that the Hindu is plied well with opium. Thus by the arts of Bember Hakim he shall say what we will that he should. And Kargan Khan with his steppe wolves will scour Kashmir until he hunts down Khlit."

"Aye, lord, and with Rao Singh gone to the portals of death you will be purged of the brood of Sattar Singh."

"And sole master of Jhilam, in favor both with the Mogul and Kargan Khan."

He looked up where the sky showed through an embrasure in the wall. Suspense crept into his crafty face. "The omens are good, Nureddin? My star will be ascendant in the constellation of the East?"

"Lord, the star of your birth will rise that night, foretelling a mighty event."

In a bed-chamber of the Jhilam palace a wizened man coughed and muttered on the cushions of the floor, wrapped in his cloak, while he prepared certain mixtures of powders, which smoked in a brass pot over the flames.

He ordered his trembling slaves to fetch a young goat, living, and to let some of its blood run into a dish. Whereupon he consulted the book of the two hundred and sixty medicinal substances, as written by the Arab scientists. He prepared a broth of the goat-blood and the contents of the vials at his girdle.

The slaves cringed and choked in the smoke from the foul mixture in the pot. Then he drank the broth and sighed, announcing that the elements of disease had been vitiated and that he would sleep until Shaista Mirza summoned him.

During that night and the next day fur-clad riders threaded through the lower passes of the Himalayas on ponies that stumbled ahead in blinding snow and a sharp wind that swept in their faces like a keen sword.

The riders bore spears at their shoulders, and under their furs wore shirts of Kallmark mail. They stopped only to make an offering of food before the shrine of the Altai-Nor god—a felt image fastened to a tree-trunk beneath a rough wooden roof—to insure their safe descent of the dangerous pass.

They dismounted only to run beside their horses and stir the heat of their bodies. They ate sparingly of dried horseflesh and frozen mare's milk.

Kargan Khan, who led the troop, had said that they would not rest until they reached the *davan* where his daughter was buried.

And during that interval Khlit sat by his horse in the snowstorm, having raised one side of the sheepskin shelter so that it partly covered the black stallion. His food was nearly exhausted but he did not venture abroad for more, having decided that the next day was the one in which he would seek out Shaista Mirza.

During the last week Khlit had formulated a plan. He had pondered it carefully and was content. It was a bold venture, depending for success upon the speed of his horse. Yet in his plan Khlit had been unaware of one thing—the consummate cleverness of the Persian, and the craft of his servants.

Khlit had faced many enemies and had lived while they had died by virtue of his shrewd brain. In Shaista Mirza, however, he had a foe who was no less shrewd, who planned as carefully, and who was master of many swords.

Yet Khlit did not intend to trust to his sword. Rather he put his trust in his horse, and in a thing that Shaista Mirza would have scorned—the faith of another man.

VIII

When the dead are placed in the earth or upon the burial-fire, they are not. Then is the burial-place a place of shadows. The caravan will pass by and see not the shadows. The singer will strike upon the guitar, and heed them not. The women will bear jars to the nearby well and know them not.

Yet there is one who will heed the shadows. Aye, the slayer of the dead!

Kirghiz proverb

The snow ceased not long after dawn, leaving its carpet over the breast of the Jhilam hills and its tracery upon the laden branches of the pines. With the clearing of the weather, Shaista Mirza ordered the kettledrums of the fortress to sound the muster of his forces.

The riders assembled in the snow-covered gardens—Persians in elaborate armor, Pathan mercenaries in cloak and hood, lean Hazaras in quilted corselets with quivers slung at the saddles.

The *mirza* inspected his men with care to see that they were well-armed and mounted. It was well, he thought, to make a good showing of force before Kargan Khan.

He was mounted on a beautiful Arab, his thin body wrapped in furs that covered all but his sharp face. Nureddin accompanied him, a handsome figure with jeweled saddle-peak and sword-belt.

Only a small force was left with the slaves in the fortress. Shaista Mirza completed his muster. He selected a group of heavily armed Persians—among them a few musket-men—as bodyguard for himself. Others he told off under Nureddin to escort Rao Singh and the master of physics, who was muffled in his soiled white cloak because of his recent malady.

The Pathan mercenaries Shaista Mirza placed in the vanguard, and he threw out two flanking parties of Hazara archers. In this manner they set out along the Jhilam road around the lake, leaving only slaves, servants, and a few soldiers under a Persian captain to guard the castle. On that day the *mirza's* riders numbered twenty-five score.

They rode through the village, flinging gibes at the few emaciated women who with children clinging to their shawls came to look impassively at the cavalcade. The men of the village were not to be seen.

Along the lakeshore the huts of the fishermen were empty; so noted the sharp-eyed vizier whose duty was to assess the taxes. Here the road wound into the pines.

The sun was high by now, giving out a cheering warmth. The riders, now that the early-morning chill had been shaken from their limbs, laughed and sang snatches of ballads, restraining their fresh horses with difficulty. Shaista Mirza smiled and plucked at his cheeks. He was treading the path of his destiny, and his plans were well laid.

Rao Singh, his arms bound behind him, rode with head downcast, saying nothing and only looking up at intervals to stare at the thickets that bordered the road. He paid no heed to the witticisms of Nureddin, who was in a high good humor.

Then Khlit rode into the path ahead of the vanguard.

A shout went up from the Hazaras, a shout which was repeated back until it reached Shaista Mirza.

"Let the archers pursue!" he cried shrilly. "Yet not more than a ten—all others keep to their files."

The black horse wheeled under spur as the nearest Hazaras urged their mounts forward. Khlit waved his arm as if making a sign to someone hidden from view. He bent low in the saddle, for the archers had sped a few haphazard shafts, and gave the black horse its head.

Rao Singh had raised his head dully at the shout, but seemed not to grasp its meaning.

"Eh, the wolf is seen by the pack, Bember Hakim," chuckled the astrologer. "The stars are kind to Shaista Mirza."

"Nay, 'tis a shrewd wolf," muttered the other, "and Jaffar sleeps with the fish for bedfellows."

Nureddin shrugged his plump shoulders, yawned, and glanced appraisingly at Rao Singh. "Gave you the youth opium?" he whispered.

"He is made ready for what is to come. See, where he reels in his saddle."

Khlit rode well ahead of the pursuers, keeping beyond bow-shot. His horse was fresh and had the legs of the others. Little by little he increased his lead, turning easily in the saddle to measure the distance.

He had lost sight of the main body of his enemies. He rose in his stirrups, plucking his curved sword from its scabbard and swinging it around his head, feeling the exhilaration of being again in the saddle and tasting the keen delight of peril.

Yet as he did so—obeying one of the instincts that were his heritage from his Cossack forebears—he sheathed his weapon and crouched forward watchfully. In the snow before him he had seen the tracks of many horses.

Into the broad trail left by these riders he urged his own mount, and a cry went back from the speeding archers to the men around Shaista Mirza.

"The outcast has turned into the Wular *davan*."

The Persian laughed, then scowled and snapped an order angrily. "Summon back the archers! Form in close files."

He was wary of riding haphazard into the valley where the men of Kargan Khan were waiting. And he knew that Khlit once in the *davan* was between his own men and the Kirghiz and could not escape without leaving his horse and climbing the slope—a course of action that would leave him afoot and consequently an easy prey.

Shaista Mirza was willing to believe that sheer good fortune had thrown the Cossack before his men. Yet his suspicions were sharp and he had heard how Khlit had once led two bands of soldiers into conflict with each other by just such a trick. He knew his own strength and the weapons he could employ to sway the mind of Kargan, and he could afford to be cautious.

"Perchance the outcast thought to bait a trap," he muttered to the leader of his musket-men. "If so he must be without hope, for he has ridden ahead of us into the *davan*."

It occurred to Shaista Mirza that Khlit might have hoped that Rao Singh could escape in the excitement that arose on his appearance. But the Hindu was in his place, leaning heavily on the peak of his saddle.

"If we find the Cossack in the *davan*," he called to Nureddin, "make no move to seize him until I command."

Whereupon he set his men in motion in orderly ranks, close-knit now that they ascended the slope that led from the lakeshore to the *davan*.

Meanwhile Khlit had not slackened the pace of his horse. The way was familiar, and those who had gone before him had trampled the snow crust into a compact footing.

He passed two sentinels—bearded men mounted on shaggy steppe ponies—without pause, only shouting the name of Kargan Khan. The two, seeing that he was alone, permitted him to ride on.

Now he saw slender blue spirals of smoke rising from the head of the valley and caught the stamp of horses' hoofs and the jangle of bits. Rounding the turn where he had once passed the form of Cheker Ghar, he came full upon the Kirghiz.

They filled the valley-head from cliff to cliff, squatting in circles around the fires, yet with their horses' bridles near at hand and their weapons across their knees—stalwart men roughly clad in furs and horsehide boots, their broad faces set with slant eyes that turned inquiringly upon Khlit.

The Kirghiz had come in peace to the Wular; still the tribesmen had no love for the mercenaries of Jhilam and they trusted no man's word—save only Kargan Khan's.

And Khlit reined in sharply, beholding one who sat upon a stone and watched him under shaggy brows. It was a man whose heavy head seemed sunk into massive shoulders, whose bent and mightily thewed frame was enclosed in a supple corselet of Turkish mail without the customary *khalat*.

A bronzed and hairy hand gripped each knee of the sitter, and Khlit saw that one eye was closed beneath a vivid scar that ran from chin to brow. By this Khlit knew that he faced Kargan, chief of the Baramula horde.

But already he had seen where the rocks over the grave had been rolled aside and the earth upturned. The *khalat* of the khan lay on the snow before him, and under the *khalat* the outline of a slender figure.

Thus did Khlit ride to meet Kargan Khan on the day that gave to the Wular valley the name of Kizil Yar, or Red Pass, in the tongue of the Kirghiz.

He lifted his right hand to show that he held no weapon and walked his horse forward slowly. The warriors on either side of the khan observed him intently but made no hostile move. "Dismount!" cried one gruffly.

Khlit made no move to do so.

"Shall a kha khan dismount before a khan, even the chief of a horde?" he asked, speaking directly to Kargan. "I am Khlit, called by some the Curved Saber, and once the yak-tail standard of the Jungar horde followed me."

A murmur went through the assembled warriors at this. The southern Kirghiz had never seen Khlit, but his name was known by hearsay. Many tales concerning the Cossack had been repeated throughout the nomad tribes.

Kargan Khan's harsh face showed no indication of his thoughts. "What seek you, Khlit?"

"I ride to Kargan Khan with a message. Behind me, in the space milk takes to boil, will come the slayer of Kera."

The muscles under the jaw of the Kirghiz tightened and the skin of his face darkened.

"It is well," he rumbled, the words rolling from his thick chest—the only sign of his emotion. "For I have come in the pursuit of blood. I have looked upon the dead body of Kera."

Shaista Mirza took in the scene at the valley-head with a swift glance. He sought out Khlit, noting his position a few yards from and slightly back of Kargan Khan.

He saw that the Kirghiz had mounted but were not formed in any order. They sat silently on their wearied ponies, staring at the gaudily attired Persians. Shaista Mirza reflected smilingly that they resembled a pack of wolves.

Whether Khlit was Kargan's prisoner or not Shaista Mirza could not guess. He considered it a stroke of rare good fortune that Khlit should have walked into the trap. Perhaps, he reasoned swiftly, the Cossack planned to denounce him—Shaista Mirza.

For this Shaista Mirza was prepared. Hidden among his followers, he reflected, were Rao Singh and Bember Hakim, whose testimony united to his own would overbear anything the solitary outcast might say.

So Shaista Mirza smiled and bent his head slightly in greeting to the khan.

"Hail, Kargan Khan," he began smoothly, "master of the Baramula and lord of the Kara Kirghiz. Auspicious is the day we can meet in friendship. Favorable are the omens for this day, and fain would Jahangir himself have been present to greet the chieftain he holds in honor."

He paused for a response, but Kargan Khan spoke not. The single eye of the Kirghiz roved over the Persian ranks as if seeking that which he found not.

"Happy am I, Kargan Khan, to bid you and your followers welcome to Jhilam, and to the castle."

Shaista Mirza's courteous words thinly veiled the scorn in which he held the clumsy figure on the rock. His glance wandered to the *khalat* and the form beneath it, and wavered. Then he summoned a ready smile.

"Think not, Kargan Khan, because I sent a single man to your encampment that I am unmindful of the honor due the Lord of the Baramula. Nay, Bember Hakim is the trusted servant of the Mogul himself, and a worthy messenger."

The Kirghiz lifted his shaggy head impatiently. "Aye," he responded, "the *hakim* swore that when I rode to this spot I would set hand on the slayer of my child. Name the man!"

The last words echoed forth as if torn from the muscles of the warrior's chest.

Shaista Mirza bent his head and glanced sidelong at Khlit. The Cossack sat his horse impassively, apparently indifferent to what was said. He also was scanning the Persian ranks.

In spite of himself the *mirza* wondered at the outcast's calm. He reflected that Khlit must be in truth dull of wit and not as the tales had painted him. Once Kargan Khan heard Shaista Mirza speak the name of Khlit, the Cossack would die as swiftly and mercilessly as a cornered roe deer is torn by dogs.

Wherefore Shaista Mirza smiled—a smile that ended in a sneer. He liked well to play with a victim, to tie slowly the knot of death upon the condemned.

Truly, he would have preferred to see a woman die rather than the gray-haired warrior. He regretted that he had not seen Jaffar deal with Kera. It would have been a dainty sight.

"My heart is heavy with your sorrow, O khan," he lisped. "And I have come prepared to see vengeance done. Aye, to see the end of the pursuit of blood. Yet you are a chief and a judge.

"Behold then, I would have the matter clear and purged of the cloud of doubt, so that none may whisper Kargan Khan slew wrongly."

He turned in his saddle.

"Nureddin!"

The astrologer pushed forward.

"Fetch Rao Singh and Bember Hakim."

Softly he added—"You have made certain the stripling is heavy with opium?"

"Aye, my lord. These past six hours has Bember Hakim been plying him with noxious physics and nostrums, so that he knows not his right hand from his left."

Satisfied, Shaista Mirza watched his two witnesses dismount and advance until they stood beside the *khalat*. Rao Singh, whose arms had been freed, stumbled, and was supported by the other. Khlit was watching not Rao Singh but the face of Kargan.

By now the sun was well down behind the mountain peaks and the shadows were gathering under the pines. Sometimes the shadows shifted as if wind had moved the pine-branches. But there was no wind.

From a cleft in the rock—the same as that by which Bember Hakim had made his escape—yellow rays of the sun shot across the ravine, falling athwart the figure of Rao Singh.

Kargan Khan had gripped his weapon spasmodically as the boy stood before him, wondering if the Hindu who had carried Kera from the seraglio was the one he sought.

Rao Singh looked up, and father and lover of Kera stared long into each other's eyes. Then the boy's drooping figure straightened and he flung back his head, crossing his arms on his chest.

Nureddin frowned, for he could see that a change had come over the face of Rao Singh. The lips had drawn firmly together. Suffering had wiped out the lines of youthful indolence. The eyes were level and purposeful.

Into the face of Rao Singh had come the stamp of grief and the strength that changes boy to man. Nureddin moved uneasily and would have spoken, but Rao Singh was before him.

"Kargan Khan," he said slowly, "the Flower of the Hills was my bride. Aye, she was the rose that made fragrant the garden of my heart. And she called me lord."

In the dark eyes of the Hindu shone a steadfast purpose. Kargan Khan stared at him with fierce intentness, his savage anger challenging the pride of the Hindu.

Shaista Mirza had not thought to find Rao Singh master of his senses and would have spoken, but the Kirghiz motioned him aside without taking his gaze from the Hindu.

"You feared to ride to me—Kargan—with Kera upon your saddle-peak."

"Nay," retorted the Hindu proudly, "that I could not do until Kera was mistress of Jhilam as was Rani Begum, my mother."

Long and steadily the Kirghiz measured Rao Singh, and a new gleam crept into his single eye.

"By the gods—name me the slayer of my child!" he roared, whipping out his sword.

Shaista Mirza put out his hands, then licked his dry lips softly, studying his prisoner craftily—as a man who scans the dice he is about to cast.

Rao Singh wheeled and pointed.

"Shaista Mirza," he said.

A rising mutter of anger from the ranks of the Kirghiz, a quick flash of weapons; ponies capered under the spur, an exclamation from the Persians, and Kargan Khan sprang to his feet. Then Shaista Mirza lifted his hand. Except for a quick spasm his face showed nothing of the rage he felt.

"Stay," he cried harshly, his high voice rising over the tumult. "Would you listen to one who speaks in the stupor of opium? Rao Singh has partaken of the drug. He knows not what he is saying."

The Persian would have urged his horse upon Rao Singh, but the Hindu leaped back and the Kirghiz interposed his bulk between them. The sword that the chief held was a heavy blade, but it trembled with the force of his anger and the strength that held the anger in check.

Khlit had not moved. Nor did he seem surprised by the speech of the boy.

"Nay, Kargan Khan," pursued Shaista Mirza swiftly, "is not Rao Singh my foe? Did he not seize your child? His false lips frame lies."

He clutched the khan's massive shoulder and whispered:

"Yonder sits the scoundrel. Aye, Khlit—he of the Curved Saber—is the man you seek!"

The Kirghiz shook his head angrily like the buffalo that Shaista Mirza was fond of calling him.

"Death of the gods!" he cried. "Would the slayer of Kera ride alone into my array?"

Then for the first time Shaista Mirza felt the chill of doubt, and paled. His voice broke as he called for Bember Hakim.

"Aye," said Khlit.

This was the only time he spoke during the judgment in the Wular *davan*.

"Let us hear Bember Hakim."

"Bember Hakim is the man of the Mogul," shrilled Shaista Mirza. "He is the faithful servant of Jahangir. His words are as the pearls of truth, for he saw the death in this valley—"

"He will say that Rao Singh is in a stupor," cried Nureddin.

"Let him speak!" growled the khan.

The wizened figure in the white cloak fell on its knees before the Kirghiz. "Rao Singh spoke not the truth," he cried.

Shaista Mirza smiled while the witness crawled closer to the khan and embraced his boots.

"*Aie*," chanted the figure at the feet of Kargan Khan, "I have seen what I have seen. I saw the fair head of the Flower of the Hills sink in death under the sword of the miserable Jaffar. I have heard Shaista Mirza boast that he ordered the death.

"*Aie*! My spirit is parched with the thirst of vengeance. Jaffar is slain. But Shaista Mirza lives—"

The pale face of Shaista Mirza flushed and his eyes widened. "Traitor! False to your bread—"

Shaista Mirza struck at the prostrate form with his dagger, realizing that the man had betrayed him and understanding now why Rao Singh, who had been placed in his care, was free from opium. The Persian's dark brow was rife with hatred and fear as he thought how Bember Hakim must have fallen in with Khlit at the Baramula trail on his quest to Kargan Khan. Kargan Khan read this swiftly.

The next instant Shaista Mirza reined back sharply among his bodyguard, who had pressed forward. For Kargan Khan had bounded upon him and struck down a shield that was interposed. His second blow felled the holder of the shield to earth and he sprang after the Persian, slashing at the spears of the riders who sought to ward him off and bellowing his war-cry.

And after Kargan came Rao Singh, who had snatched up the weapon of the felled rider. And upon his heels came the mass of the Kirghiz, fearful for their chief.

In an instant the valley resounded with the clash of steel, the frenzied snorts of horses and the cry of the injured.

The Kirghiz had attacked with fury, led by Kargan, who had mounted. In the confined space was no room for maneuvering or for the use of arrows. The compact bands of horsemen made one struggling mass, where knee pressed knee and shield clashed against shield.

Khlit had set spurs to his horse and forced his way into the center of the ranks. He found Rao Singh and drew the Hindu away from the Persian files, protesting.

"Have you forgotten?" the Cossack cried sternly. "There are those who await your coming."

At that Rao Singh had turned and sped to the cleft in the slope where he disappeared behind the rocks.

One other man had parted from the battle. Nureddin, after a glance around, had wheeled his horse and slipped back through the array of the Persians. Once clear of the valley he set out swiftly down the Jhilam road.

Kargan Khan had flung himself into battle with the sole thought of finding and striking down the *mirza*. His men had attacked readily, savagely, but without plan or formation.

The Persian's forces had given back at first, then closed in with the armored horsemen in front. Shaista Mirza, safe behind the cordon of his men, directed the fight craftily.

In the narrow quarters the Kirghiz could not employ their favorite tactics of enveloping their foe, and were forced to fight hand to hand. They had little armor, and their horses were wearied. The fury of their first onset waned, and they split up into knots of horsemen, wheeling and plunging at superior numbers.

All this Khlit noticed, and frowned.

Then that for which he watched came to pass. Down the cleft in the ravine, down the rock-slope, even down the cliff itself, swarmed dark figures chattering with eagerness and bearing knives, rusted spears, clubs or stones. And at their head was Rao Singh.

They raced behind the Hindu brandishing their makeshift weapons, and fell upon the flanks and rear of the Persians.

Thus did Rao Singh put himself at the head of the forest men of Jhilam even as his father Sattar Singh had done before him, though under different circumstances.

The Kashmiris were unskilled warriors but they had the agility of their kind, and their anger against the Persians was a great anger. With their coming the Kirghiz pressed in, raising their war-cry anew. Khlit could see the broad figure of Kargan Khan at their head, his weapon flashing.

"Hey," he meditated, "it is a good fight. Yet it is the fight of Rao Singh and Kargan Khan."

He fingered his sword, swearing anxiously. Never before had he been a spectator of a battle. Then he sheathed his sword and sighed.

The fight—the first phase of it—was over. The Persians, their ranks broken, were streaming back toward the valley entrance. By their flanks, clutching and stabbing, went the Kashmiris, and in their rear the Kirghiz struck down the fleeing riders. Half of Shaista Mirza's men lay in the *davan*.

Khlit, galloping among the Kirghiz, caught up with Kargan Khan at the edge of the lake. Twilight had fallen, and the cries of the stricken mercenaries were growing fainter down the Jhilam road.

Kargan Khan with a band of his men had halted to stare at a red glow on the lake. In the dusk it flickered from the surface of the water.

"'Tis witchcraft!" muttered Kargan Khan.

"Nay," laughed Khlit, " 'tis but the pleasure island of Shaista Mirza gone up in flames after the visit of the fisher-folk. The villagers have attacked the castle and overcome the scanty garrison."

"Praise be to the gods!"

Kargan Khan looked at Khlit curiously.

"Nay, did you plan this rising of the Kashmiris? It served us well."

"Rao Singh leads them," said Khlit, and was silent.

Then he laughed. "Nureddin—I saw the rascal flee—will be well greeted at the castle. And those of Shaista Mirza who reach there will fare little better."

While he trotted beside the Kirghiz after the fugitives Kargan Khan looked at Khlit long, wondering how much Khlit had fore-known of what came to pass at the Kizil Yar.

There were few of the Persians who escaped from Jhilam that night, and Shaista Mirza was not among them. And that night Rao Singh took the chair of his father in the council-hall of Jhilam.

Concerning Bember Hakim there is a strange tale. A forest man of Jhilam tells the tale. It was the day after the battle, at dawn, and he saw Khlit and Bember Hakim go into the forest along the Baramula trail.

Being curious, the man followed. He saw the two come to a heap of stones that seemed to mark a grave. There, so says the Kashmiri, Bember Hakim threw off his cloak, tunic, and sandals and washed some stains from his face with snow.

Then—such is the tale—Bember Hakim rewound his turban in a different fashion and took from the rocks a green cloak and other garments, which he put on, shouldering also a heavy leopard-skin pack.

Thus Bember Hakim the Arab physician became in the eyes of the Kashmiri Cheker Ghar, the conjurer and mimic—Cheker Ghar, who pressed Khlit's hand to his forehead and departed to the South, while Khlit rode alone to the North.

This tale of the Kashmiri was adjudged a lie by those who heard. For how could one man be like to two?

Doubtless, said those who heard, the Kashmiri had partaken of the good wine of Shiraz, for that night there had been great feasting in Jhilam, and much rejoicing among the men of Jhilam.

The Skull of Shirzad Mir

What is written in the book of Fate no man may read.

The grave of the rider of the desert will be dug in the blue hills of Badakshan; he will not know it until the dark angel of death is at hand.

The astrologer may sit on his strip of carpet in the cupola of the temple and seek the wisdom of the stars in the night. But he will not see the hand with the dagger that rises behind him.

Mogul proverb

The sun was high over the Shyr Pass when Gutchluk Khan reined his horse in my path. It was the year 1608 in the calendar of the Christian priests, and the year of the Ox by the reckoning of my people.

The Shyr Pass at this place is not wide, for one of the rivulets of the Amu Daria flows beside the caravan track. On either hand the willows and rocks press close. Likewise, Gutchluk Khan was a broad man, with a figure like a full sack of wine, and there were two with him. They carried bows and round shields, small and bossed with silver, after the manner of their race—the Uzbeks.

It is a saying of my master, Baber Shirzad Mir, who heard it said by the dead Mogul Akbar—on whom be peace—that, when in difficulty, put spurs to your horse and ride forward. It is well said. This thought came to my mind when I saw the turbaned bulk of Gutchluk Khan, and I pressed toward him, touching the hilt of my sword lightly with my free hand.

Gutchluk Khan was not the same man with a sword as with his speech. He watched, not pleased to stay where he was at the edge of the river but not wishing to rein back.

"Ho, Abdul Dost!" he cried loudly. "Whither go you?"

Speech is ever a trick of those who wish you ill. And I loved not the stout Uzbek, whose sword was too often for sale and who, in the year of the Ox, was numbered among the men of Jani Beg. Wherefore I pressed forward until the gold cloth at the peak of my saddle rubbed against the shoulder straps of his steppe pony.

Now I was at that time two-score years and lean. I have heard it said in the bazaars that I ride better than most and use my scimitar as well as any but a very few of the Mogul's picked *mansabdar*s. Doubtless Gutchluk Khan knew this, and stout men are tender of injury.

He reined his horse to one side and his followers likewise. Yet when I had passed them so much as a horse's length, I halted.

A thought had come to me. I was bound for Khanjut, where was my lord, Shirzad Mir. He was prisoner to Jani Beg. Gutchluk Khan had seen me and would follow if he suspected my horse's head was turned to Khanjut. He would doubtless be glad of an excuse to set his pig's face back toward the camp of Jani Beg, where were captive women and the musicians and wine of the Beg.

"I go," I said, "to Anderab to seek a new horse."

"Nay, Abdul Dost, your horse is good." His swine's eyes puckered at me. "It is one of the breed of Kabul. And you, truly, are a one-mount soldier."

It was true the horse was excellent. It was a gift of Shirzad Mir—may his soul have peace! Gutchluk lied when he swore I was a rider of one mount. Ten years ago, when Shirzad Mir was chieftain of Badakshan, the king of kings, whose court was a heaven and who was a warrior to warm the heart, the Shadow of God, Akbar, the emperor, had given me the rank of *mansabdar*, with the privilege of a double remount.

But Gutchluk Khan did not know this. Nor did I care if he knew. My heart was sore with thought of Shirzad Mir in chains and doomed to death.

"He is bred—" I patted the neck of Wind-of-the-Hills—"to take the road from mongrels."

"And from Moguls," chuckled Gutchluk Khan, who lacked not wit after a fashion. "He has learned that trick from his master. Aye, you and the other men of Shirzad Mir—those that still live— have earned the hatred of the all-powerful Jahangir, Mogul of India, whose whisper is a shout of command, even in these northern hills. Wherefore Shirzad Mir will die before sunrise tonight."

It was true that Jani Beg had so ordered. A boy shepherd had told me the news, down the pass.

"He will be slain," smiled Gutchluk Khan, "by a bowstring drawn taut around the neck. When he is dead, his head will be cut off. It will be emptied and the skull set in gold."

The two followers laughed, for they were three and I was one. Nevertheless they kept their bows in hand. I was very angry, and they had heard tales of my swordplay.

"The skull," mocked the Uzbek, "will be dried and will be a drinking-cup to fill with wine of Shiraz for the favorite of Jani Beg. The women will toy with it."

Gutchluk Khan was well pleased that he had angered me.

"Ho," he cried, waving his plump hand at me, "there will be rare sport when Jani Beg gives the order to hunt you down, Abdul Dost! He will fly his horsemen at you like falcons, and they will add your head to the minaret of skulls by the gate of Khanjut. But the skull of Baber Shirzad Mir, the Tiger Lord, he will keep for his women's delight."

Three years ago Akbar the Great, Mogul of India, had passed to the mercy of God. He had been the friend of Shirzad Mir. Jahangir, Akbar's son, had little liking for us hillmen.

Besides, Jani Beg, the Uzbek, had spent much gold among the courtiers of Jahangir and had whispered that Shirzad Mir was a rebel who sought Badakshan for himself. Shirzad Mir was a proud man; he did not give up the kingdom when Jani Beg came—with Jahangir's consent—at the head of an army to demand it.

It was false that he had rebelled against the Mogul. But we were far from the court—and Jani Beg had spent much gold. We had done no evil. Only, we had not gone to the court, as the Uzbek did. It is written in our annals—the annals of Badakshan—that the screech of an owl in the wilderness is more pleasant than the song of the nightingale in the grove; the caves of the mountain-tops are finer than the cities of the valley.

When it was too late, we understood. But the word had gone forth that we had taken up arms against the Mogul, and those who were of faint heart deserted us.

As a last resort I had mounted and gone through the Uzbek lines, through the pass, to Kabul to seek the governor of the Mogul. But at Kabul I found Said Afzel, the son of Jani Beg, who had given the governor much silk, camels, brocades and slaves. I could do naught, being a man of slow speech, without a present in my hand.

It was then, when I rode back through the pass, I learned that Shirzad Mir had, to save the lives of his followers, surrendered Khanjut and appealed to the mercy of Jahangir.

But the voice of the Tiger Lord carried no further than the foothills of the Hindu Kush. That night he was to be slain.

Knowing these things, what answer had I to the gibes of Gutch-luk Khan? It was an evil day.

Even at the last, Jani Beg and the courtiers who were with him had not kept faith with Shirzad Mir. They had promised him life, and they were making ready his death bed.

Verily, it came to my mind, when I heard the talk of the sheep-boy, that he who holds power under a prince should not be absent from the court. But it was too late.

If the Mogul had known the truth, it might have been other-wise. Aye, for his father was Akbar, who was a soldier. And a soldier understands justice.

It is written by the men of wisdom that he who sits down to the feast of life must end by drinking the cup of death. Yet the cup that was at the lips of Shirzad Mir was bitter as dregs of sour wine. For who wants to be branded a traitor?

Of this thought I said naught to Gutchluk Khan. Seeing that he was waiting for me to speak, I was silent. He watched me from owl-like, blinking eyes. He had the broad, hooked nose of the Uzbek men, but his face was heavy with flesh and his beard scrawny. Instead of the sheepskin saddle-cover that his tribe usually owned, his saddle glittered with jewels, and his *khalat* was silk. He had been at the sack of Khanjut after the surrender.

"When Shirzad Mir is dead," he said, changing his tone, "you will be a free man. Why not enter the service of Jani Beg? He has an eye for a veteran swordsman. And he has watched you among the defenders of Khanjut. Where else will you go?"

The thought came to me that Gutchluk Khan would like to wheedle me and so to carry my head to Jani Beg. I smiled and he said no more.

It was a fair sight, if I had been so minded—the valley of Shyr. The rivulet muttered nearly under our feet, down the steep bank. Overhead, through the thin arms of the willows, was the blue, blue sky of the hill country. On either hand rose the mighty peaks of the Hindu Kush with their pine garments and snow heads. *Hai*—it was well to feel the keen air of the higher levels after the hot dampness of the Kabul fields!

And then I saw that Gutchluk and his followers were not looking at me. Along the path in front of them had come two men.

No man—but only God—knows what lies before him. Here were two men on foot, and I had never seen their like before. None but peasants, shepherds and slaves walk afoot in my country. Yet these two had no horses.

Even the followers of Gutchluk Khan wore cloth of silver and had gems of sorts, such as turquoise, on the hilts of their scimitars. These strangers wore plain weapons of dull steel in leather scabbards and their swords were not curved but straight. The taller of the two had a cloak of dull brown with a plain metal clasp at the throat. Also boots of loose leather, such as the Tatars wear.

But he was no Tatar. His green eyes were level and his face was fair as a Circassian. His yellow beard and mustache were pointed. A plain ruffle of white cloth showed at his throat, which was bare. Instead of a turban he wore a small green cap with a long feather.

By these things I knew that the two were *Frank*s, or *Ferang*s, called by the black Portuguese priests of Agra Christian Europeans.

I stared, for I had not seen a *Ferang* before. Nor had Gutchluk Khan and his men. The taller of the two strangers lifted his hand for speech. And Gutchluk Khan rode toward him slowly, afire with curiosity.

It came about by chance. The arrogant bearing of Gutchluk Khan must have alarmed the shorter man, who had the rough garb of a servant, very dusty and tattered. This man stepped in front of the khan with upraised staff.

"Put down the staff!" cried the khan harshly.

He was quick to mistrust—especially those who were strangers.

The man either did not understand or would not obey. He planted his feet doggedly and waited. His eyes shone from a dusty face. Gutchluk Khan spoke a quick word to his followers and one of them fitted arrow to bow.

The shaft sped and I saw the feathers stick from the throat of the man with the staff, under the chin. He coughed and fell to his knees, spitting blood. Then he lay flat in the road, moving slowly.

The tall man gave an exclamation and stepped to the side of the servant. He bent over and touched the arrow; then he stood up, drawing his long sword.

In his face was distress for the man who had died. Yet it had been only a servant. The fellow had been a fool to threaten Gutchluk Khan with his staff.

"These men are foreigners and infidels," said the Uzbek loudly. I thought to myself that the religion of Gutchluk Khan was the faith of whatever lord he followed—Mohammedan, Uzbek or

Hindu. "They mean no good; we will take the sword of the tall one with the yellow mane and carry it to Jani Beg, who will be pleased."

He made a sign to his two followers to close in on the stranger. The man threw back his cloak, resting his sword-point in the earth in front of him. He was not ill to look on, with his legs planted strongly, his straight body bending forward from the hips slightly and his head high. His face seemed drawn. Later I knew that he had not eaten for a day and night.

The slaying of the servant had not mattered, but this man had not the bearing of a common person. Moreover, it was one without armor, afoot, against three mounted and with mail vests. I reined my horse forward.

"Only a wild boar hunts in a pack, Gutchluk Khan," I said. "Do you meet this man alone? He bears himself well. There will be more honor if you take his sword in fair play. Dismount! A coward seizes advantage when he can: a brave man will deal fairly with an adversary."

The pig eyes of the Uzbek glittered from me to the stranger. He liked my words little. I think it had occurred to him that if the three attacked the *Ferang* they would leave their backs open to me. And, as I have said, the Uzbeks know how well I use a sword.

He whispered to his men, who fell to eyeing me. I was within arm's reach and the way was narrow.

"If your servants slay the man and you take his weapon to Jani Beg, I shall tell the true story of what happened, Gutchluk Khan," I said again, "And the *bahadur*s of Jani Beg will make mock of you."

The words had their effect. The stupid Uzbek could not draw back now without disgrace. He scowled and whispered again to his men. Perhaps he urged them to put an arrow into me if chance offered. But it did not.

"So be it," he said with bad grace and sprang from his horse.

He was eager to gain honor by carrying the *Ferang*'s weapon to his chief.

He dressed his round shield and drew his scimitar. That which followed was swift in passing and I saw it well—although I watched the two followers from the corner of my eye.

Gutchluk Khan ran against the tall *Ferang*, seeking to catch the other's sword on his shield and cut him down with a scimitar stroke. Shields are a clumsy thing, useful for defense, but—is not a good thrust the best defense?

The tall *Ferang* poised his long sword straight before him and warded aside the scimitar. I saw that he watched not the weapon of Gutchluk Khan but the Uzbek's eyes. That is the mark of a good fencer.

Truly, it was strange swordplay. The scimitar of Gutchluk Khan could not beat down the guard of the *Ferang*. And almost at once the *Ferang*'s weapon thrust under the shield and bent sharply against the mail vest.

He gave an exclamation at that and turned his attention to Gutchluk Khan's neck. He was very cool and moved slowly; still, with good effect. Another moment and the straight sword had passed twice against Gutchluk Khan's fat throat, over the armor, and blood flowed freely.

The two followers shouted and Gutchluk Khan squealed like a hurt pig. He was afraid he was dying and the cuts had melted his courage, like snow before the sun of the desert of Khorassan.

With their shields the two covered Gutchluk Khan from the thrusts of the *Ferang* while the Uzbek ran to his horse and mounted. The khan spurred away up the path whence he had first come, followed by his two, without further heed to me. I laughed, for he had squealed just like a pig.

They passed me at a gallop, going toward Khanjut.

"Lend me your horse and I will go after them," cried the *Ferang* to me, coming to the bridle of Wind-of-the-Hills.

I laughed again. To none save Baber Shirzad Mir or the Mogul himself in battle would I render my horse.

He had spoken in broken *Mogholi*, a language which, in the spoken word, is my own. For writing, we use *Turki*.

"Nay," I answered in the same tongue. "You would be a fool. They would send an arrow through you, and—I have need of Wind-of-the-Hills. I ride to Khanjut tonight."

With that he glanced up the pass after the three angrily. Almost, I think, he would have run after them afoot. Yet he should have been thankful that he was still alive.

Then he turned to the servant, who was dead by now. He lifted the man in his arms and I saw that his grave face was marked with grief. He glanced once at the stream; then he walked up the hillside a few paces to a great poplar tree. It was a noble tree, with wide branches. Here, using his sword and the servant's staff, he fell to digging a grave between the roots of the poplar, where the soil was soft and there was no grass.

I could not help him, for it is forbidden. I dismounted, taking food—dried prunes and rice—from saddlebags. After washing in the stream, I sat and ate—after making the noonday prayer. It is well to pray and the hours of life that remained to me were uncertain. That night I was going to Khanjut—after that, who knows?

The *Ferang* did not cease his labors until he had hollowed out a hole sufficiently large to place the body in, when he doubled it up. Truly, that was an unwonted thing. The dead man had been a servant and the kites would have seen to the corpse. But the *Ferang* had unwonted thoughts.

When the grave was filled in with dirt, he brought several large stones, one after the other, and laid them on it so that the animals would not dig the body up. This done, he hacked a cross in the smooth bark of the poplar with his sword. He took off his hat and stood by the grave for the time that it took me to swallow four times.

It was a strange custom, even for a *caphar*—an unbeliever. The thought came to me that each race has its road to follow and at the end of the road, its shrine. I was meditating upon this and upon the skill with which the *Ferang* had used his straight sword when he came and stood by me.

Since then I have told many that the straight sword is a goodly weapon, but they would not believe—not having seen the *Ferang* use his.

"What was the name of the stout man who ordered my servant slain?" he asked.

I told him.

"He shall pay for what he did," he said.

He spoke directly, as he had thrust with his sword, in a clear voice that came from his chest as if he knew what it was to give commands to many men.

"Where has Gutchluk Khan gone?" he said again.

"To Khanjut."

He was silent, watching me eat. Then—"I have not had food for the space of a day and night," he said.

I made room for him beside me. He was a *caphar*, but a brave man. He ate very much. I gave him all the prunes and rice, because he was hungry and I did not know when I should eat again. When he had finished he sat back moodily.

Who was he? Where had he come from? What was his rank? I knew not. And there was the straight sword.

"Give me leave," I begged politely, "to hold your weapon in my hand. I have not seen the like."

He glanced at me quickly from his green eyes. Sitting shoulder to shoulder, he was my height, but broader through the chest and with more muscle on his forearms. His neck was round and firm and when he moved it was with the ease of one whose muscles are not slack. He had not put on his hat and the yellow hair curled around a broad, white brow. He was young—perhaps twenty-five.

"I heard what you said to Gutchluk Khan when the rascal was about to attack me with his two men," he said in his broken

Mogholi. "For that I give thanks. Yet how am I to trust another with my sword? I have no other weapon." His voice fell and I thought I heard him mutter, "Nor aught else."

"You have eaten my bread and salt," I reminded him. "And he who has done that is safe from harm at the hand of the giver of salt."

He looked at me again and handed me the sword without another word. It felt strangely in my hand. It would have been hard to deal a good cut with it. Still, the steel was very fine. I thanked him.

"What is your name?" I inquired, for my curiosity had grown.

"Weyand."

"Wey-and," I repeated. "Is that all the name?"

He told me that he was called Ralph Weyand; that he had the rank of Sir, or *Ser* in my tongue; that he had come from the country of Ferangistan, from a very large tribe, the English.

I had heard of them.

"Then you are a lord," I asked, not quite believing, for he had neither attendants, rich garments or horses, and the title of *Ser* is not less than the Persian *Shah.*

"Nay," he said. "My rank is not more than that of khan among your people."

That was little enough. Still, Sir Weyand carried himself like one accustomed to command.

He was a sailor—by which he meant khan of a ship—and a merchant. That is, he had not come to India to trade for himself but to make easy the way for others. After he had said that I would not have talked with him further—for a merchant is but a getter of coins, and a seaman is a man without wealth or honor—had it not been for two things.

He had used his straight sword well; and I was still curious.

Why was a man of the sea walking afoot in the hills of the Hindu Kush? Why was a merchant come to the highland of Badakshan, instead of the cities of Hindustan—Agra, Delhi and Lahore? Also, how had he learned *Mogholi?*

He told me all, sitting back against a willow and speaking sadly. I harkened, for I did not plan to reach Khanjut until nightfall. As for Sir Weyand, he must have cared little what he did. His was a great sadness.

Sir Weyand had been sent to India to the court of Jahangir by him who was the *ameer* of England. He had come, he said, in the service of his sovereign lord, the king. The English had a thought to make a company to trade with India. This they called the East India Company. They were merchants who knew something of fighting.

The *Ferang* had landed from his ship at Surat and had gone from thence to Agra. There, he had presented himself at the court of Jahangir. But he had few attendants and fewer presents. That was not well. As I, also, had learned at Kabul.

Likewise, the *Ferang* made enemies. In those years the Portuguese were in favor with Jahangir—the Portuguese, whose priests and traders had come from Goa and were at Agra.

The Portuguese, said Sir Weyand, knew that if the English received permission to trade in India for the East India Company, their own traffic would be hurt. I knew naught of merchants and their ways, but the *Ferang* said it and it may have been true.

The priests of the Portuguese had contrived to persuade Jahangir that the English were robbers. Sir Weyand was not granted a second audience. Some of his followers had died from illness; others returned to the ship.

Sir Weyand said the priests had tried to poison him. I know not. Priests, who are not warriors, may not be trusted. They had cut him off from his ship.

When Sir Weyand learned that Jahangir had been turned against him, he sent a message to the Mogul that he would return to the Presence. He swore this on an oath—that he would return to the court and gain the right to trade for the East India Company.

Then he went into northern Hindustan with one servant and studied *Mogholi* with certain *kwajahs*—learned men. He had come to distrust the interpreter of the court. And so he mastered *Mogholi*. But the priests had tracked him, and because they were afraid, they were dangerous. The *Ferang* had been attacked by paid men; he had left Kabul to seek refuge in the hills.

That was his tale. Much I believed, for he spoke frankly; some I could not believe.

"How is it," I asked, "that the Portuguese, who are Christians, wish your death, when you are also a Christian? It is not fitting."

"In your religion, Abdul Dost," he replied after a moment, "there are many sects. Are they always at peace?"

"Nay."

"Neither am I at peace with priests of Agra. We are two sects. Likewise Portugal is bitter to the English."

"Then," I said at once, for here was a plain puzzle, "why does not the *ameer* of the English make war upon the *ameer* of the Portuguese and try the issue by the sword?"

"We do not seek war, but peace." The *Ferang* looked long and thoughtfully at the distant snow peaks of the Hindu Kush. "War, perhaps, will come; if so we will have the victory."

"Meanwhile," I pointed out, "the Portuguese hold the favor of the Mogul and you are an outcast from Hindustan, like the lepers of Kashgar—not otherwise."

This being true, he said nothing.

"What do you plan to do?" I asked.

"In time," he said, "I shall return, as I have sworn, to the court of Jahangir, and the Mogul will hear my message."

Verily, this was strange. The *Ferang* had no thought of fate. It seemed that his fate was assured—as he was alone in the hills, his servant slain, without food or money. He had neither horse nor armor. Yet he spoke with conviction.

Some have said that it was not fitting that I, a *mansabdar* and warrior, should be named Abdul—the man of books. This, like many other riddles, may have been one of the unseen ways of

God. For I, by dint of fighting through many lands, had become a speaker of three languages; wherefore my account of the fighting in Badakshan in the year of the Ox has been written down by the Mogul's scribes in the annals of Mohulistan.

What is written is written. It was fate that brought Sir Weyand to me in the Pass of Shyr. And from this meeting was born the strange event at Khanjut that night.

Even as I had questioned the *Ferang*, he asked many things of me. And I told him what lay so heavy on my heart—the captivity of Baber Shirzad Mir, the Tiger Lord of Badakshan.

We were of an age, Shirzad Mir and I, although the *mir*'s curling beard was gray and his hawk eyes set in wrinkles. We had fought from Herat to Samarkand against the neighboring Uzbeks of Turkestan.

Before dawn on the coming night Shirzad Mir was to be bow-stringed. His wives had already been taken by Jani Beg, who was holding the women for the coming of his son, Said Afzel, from Kabul the next day or the day after. And Shirzad Mir had no sons.

"It was the will of God," I explained to the *Ferang*, who had listened closely, "that this heaviness should be laid upon us. No man may escape his fate."

"Then Shirzad Mir is a rebel—against Jahangir?"

I put my hand on my sword and scowled.

"Eh, *Ferang*," I said, being angry, "that is an ill word! You know not what you say. When a Mogul dies, the chieftains of the tribes send to pay fealty to the new Mogul—or they revolt. Shirzad Mir did not revolt. But Jani Beg had the first word to Jahangir at the court. He offered to take the hill country of Badakshan from Shirzad Mir—who had not yet sent homage, the distance to Agra being great."

And I told him how our fortunes—the fortune of Shirzad Mir—had fallen. Again he listened.

"If Shirzad Mir could live," he said, "he might make his peace with Jahangir. The Mogul would forgive him the war for the sake of the *mir*'s service to Akbar."

I was silent. The *Ferang* knew not the ways of the court. Jani Beg had been clever. And he held Badakshan in the palm of his hand. Likewise, the memory of a Mogul is short.

"So you are going to Khanjut," went on Sir Weyand, "to make an effort to save your lord?"

"Nay," I said. "No man may escape his fate. Shirzad Mir will go to the mercy of God tonight and perhaps I shall keep him company. I shall ride in front of the gate of Khanjut and shout an insult to the men within. Riders will come forth, and of these I may slay several before I am slain. This will be an honor to Shirzad Mir. For there will be one man to strike a blow for him, even when his hour has come."

"Then you are a greater fool than I, Abdul Dost," he replied.

"How?"

"Because Jani Beg has the upper hand, you say it is your fate to die."

"It may be written that I shall slay the men at the gate of Khanjut and live," I pointed out.

"Your fate, Abdul Dost, lies with Shirzad Mir; if you are a true follower of his, you will try to save his life."

"It may not be."

I lay back and watched the white flecks of clouds moving across the blue, blue veil of the sky above the pine-tips of the hills. They were like foam flung from the muzzle of a horse. The *Ferang* was silent for a long time, perhaps the time that it takes milk to boil.

"What manner of place is Khanjut, Abdul Dost?"

Now Khanjut is the citadel of Badakshan, for the great city of Balkh has dirt walls and is not easily defended; the Pass of Shyr ends at Khanjut. Wherefore the citadel is called in the language of my people the Iron Gate—*Khalga Timur*. Caravans bound from Kabul to Kashgar and Balkh pass by it. It was built in the time of the first Mogul, of stone from the quarries, and it has walls to four times the height of a man. Also four towers built inside, to

command the walls. It is a small fortress, made to be held by a
picked army. And it had never been taken by storm.

"Jani Beg has made his camp within the walls," I said, "with
fifteen hundred horsemen and as many more bazaar followers.
An outpost is kept at the cliff gate. Sentries are on the walls at
night."

"And where is Shirzad Mir kept?"

"In the tower by the hill."

So the sheep-boy had told me.

"Can the cliff be climbed?"

I laughed. Many had tried it during the siege. But the cliff is
the height of many spears, facing the plain. Below it runs the
caravan track. On the top—as those who climbed it learned—is
dug a moat against the castle wall.

In the rainy season and in Summer, when the snows on the
peaks melt, the water from the river beside which we sat is at the
flood. God has given this fine water to Khanjut and Badakshan.
It flows from its gorge into a covered way, built cleverly of brick,
which leads into the citadel from the hillside of Khanjut. Thus,
we have water for drinking and to fill the moat.

So much I told the *Ferang*.

"Is the stream at flood now?" he asked.

"Nay; it is the season of harvest, when the snows above have
melted and the rain is not yet."

He sat near me, nursing his sword. I was fain to sleep, for I
would need my strength that night, but still he talked.

"Are any followers of Shirzad Mir within call, Abdul Dost?"

"Nay—save for old Iskander Khan, the Kirghiz, who with his
two striplings of sons tends sheep on the mountain near Khanjut."

"He is a friend?"

"Aye. He fought in the siege of the citadel until the time of
surrender; then he slipped away to the hills, with others. But he
is old."

"Could you reach him by nightfall?"

"If it suited me."

"Has he cattle with his sheep?"

"Doubtless."

"And he loved Shirzad Mir?"

"All did," I answered, sitting up and thinking of the Tiger Lord, "who followed him and heard his voice ring out in battle."

"Where does Iskander Khan keep the cattle?"

"Out of eyeshot of the walls of Khanjut, or Jani Beg would have taken them. In the hills, an hour's fast ride from the citadel."

"Where goes the caravan track from Khanjut?"

"It passes under the cliff, fords the stream which flows down over the cliffs, and passes straight out into the plain."

"Does Iskander Khan keep his sheep and cattle at the right hand or the left of this pass?"

I was becoming angry with long questioning; yet there was a purpose in the words of the *Ferang*.

"As we leave the pass," I said, "Khanjut is close on the right hand, with the Amu Daria—the stream—on that side. Iskander Khan's *aul* is away to the left."

For a long space Sir Weyand stroked his sword in silence. Then he stooped and gathered up a little dust in his hand.

"See you this dust, Abdul Dost?" he said, looking at me strangely. "By it, and the will of God, we may save Shirzad Mir this night."

I stared. The *Ferang* was a merchant and an unbeliever. How could he hope to do what the army of Jani Beg had not done—break into Khanjut?

"It may not be," I said.

We were two men with one horse, without firearms or food. The *Ferang* had spoken of Iskander Khan; but the Kirghiz was an old man, lacking strength to swing a sword. The two striplings of the khan were apt at herding, or perhaps a bowshot; still, they could not be reckoned on in a fight.

And it would take fighting and good sword-strokes to gain inside the walls of Khanjut. Once there, we would yet have to

assault the tower wherein was Shirzad Mir. Also we could not
know how many men guarded him. Even could we gain my lord,
we three, horseless, would be pent within the walls. The dark of
the coming night would not aid us overmuch, for there would be
a clear moon.

"Nay," I said, thinking of these things, "it may not be."

"How far can you see in the moonlight, Abdul Dost?"

"As much as a bowshot," I responded—for moonlight obscures
outlines, as if you were looking through very fine silk.

"Then it may be done."

Surely, I thought, the *Ferang* could have no real plan—for what
have moonlight and dust to do with the way into Khanjut? Still,
he was not content.

"What will cattle do if they see danger approaching from a certain quarter and are not sure what the danger is?" he questioned.

"They will face toward it and prick up their ears. Then, if it is
real danger, they will push together and lower their horns."

"Are humans so different from cattle?" he said, more to himself than to me. "And it has not rained for two weeks in this
country."

I looked him full in the eyes.

"Have you a plan?"

"Aye," he said, "a plan."

And he told me what it was. I listened carefully. Truly, it was
a strange thought that had come to him, sitting with me in the
Shyr Pass.

When he had finished I remained silent for a long time. Then
I asked why he was willing to do this thing.

"I am now without friends, Abdul Dost," he replied. "If we
save Shirzad Mir, I will at least have one friend—nay, two." He
smiled at me.

Later I came to understand that he looked further ahead than
this, into the veiled future that only astrologers can pierce.

"Gutchluk Khan will warn Jani Beg that he has seen me, and
they will guess that I come to Khanjut tonight," I told the *Ferang*.
"They will watch—"

"So much the better," he said and laughed, stretching his powerful arms. This was a good omen—that a man should laugh before battle.

"I will do as you say," I agreed. "It may be our fate—"

"Our fate, Abdul Dost, is in our own hands."

Whereupon we rose up and went to Wind-of-the-Hills, who was cropping grass near the grave. Sir Weyand mounted behind me and Wind-of-the-Hills carried double down the pass as far as the first villages, which are around Khanjut.

Here we turned aside to the left, along paths known to me, and passed through the ravines that led to the *aul* of Iskander Khan. We went quickly, for time was short.

The sun had left the ravines and the shadows were long out in the plain of Badakshan that we could see through the willow groves when we came out on the encampment of the Kirghiz. He and his sons and daughter were at sunset prayers.

Iskander Khan took the bridle of my horse and greeted me warmly. His encampment was shrewdly placed to escape the eye of Jani Beg's foragers; the sheep lay about it among the trees and the ground was black with their dried droppings. Further out, at the edge of the plains, the two boys had left the cattle. Their ponies were standing at the door of Iskander Khan's tent.

When we had dismounted we ate food with Iskander Khan, who glanced curiously at the *Ferang* but asked no questions, knowing that I would explain in due time.

When the meal was done I talked to Iskander Khan alone, as had been agreed upon between me and Sir Weyand. I told him what we wanted done.

"It is to save the life of Shirzad Mir," I ended, "if God so wills."

Iskander Khan was silent for a very long time, because I had asked a great thing of him.

"*L'a iloha ill Allah*," he said at length. "For what Shirzad Mir has done for me, and what his father did for my father, I will do this thing."

"At the beginning of the third watch of the night," I repeated, "when the shadows of Khanjut's four towers fall across the caravan track—then is the time."

Again he promised. And the *Ferang* left the encampment with me. Darkness was falling, but who should know the paths of the Badakshan foothills better than I?

We pressed forward quickly, running at times, holding our swords so they would not strike against our legs. Wind-of-the-Hills I left with Iskander Khan, for where we were going the horse could not take us. We went due east, crossing, in the second hour of the night, the caravan track of Shyr down which we had come, and entered the ravines on the further side. Here we began to climb, going up, up, until our breath came in pants.

Many to whom I have told these things have doubted at this point that what I said was true. This was because there were three weak links in the chain by which we hoped to pull Shirzad Mir free of Khanjut.

One of the weak links was Iskander Khan. We had put our trust in the old Kirghiz and risked our lives on his spoken word. If he should fail us, we should die. The other links were my knowledge of Khanjut and the wit of the *Ferang*. If either did not serve us, the plan of Sir Weyand would fail, Shirzad Mir would be slain at dawn, after the banquet that Jani Beg was holding that night—and we would be dealt with likewise.

Another thing: we were not going to enter a citadel held by foolish Hindus or drunken Sarts, but by warlike Uzbeks—and there are few better soldiers—and my countrymen of Badakshan who had joined the standard of Jani Beg.

So many who have heard this doubted. I also doubted at the time when we were climbing among the heights behind Khanjut. But Sir Weyand was full of cheerful words and I was ashamed to speak my doubts. Besides, we had agreed with Iskander Khan.

A horseman is at loss when afoot and I was leg-weary by the time we gained the precipice over the stream of the Amu Daria.

Perhaps because of this, or because he was accustomed to command men, the *Ferang* assumed the leadership in spite of my better knowledge of the place.

Hai—it was a good sight when we stood on the cliff over the stream. In the East, in our faces, the full moon—that of harvest—rose among the tall cedars and poplars. The silver mistress of the earth rose into the sky and pointed her finger down into the ravine through which muttered the hidden little river.

Looking down the gorge, we could see in the distance below us the black walls of Khanjut and beyond, in the green haze, the plain of Badakshan. The four towers stood out against the haze and I thought of Shirzad Mir, who was making his final ablutions in one of them, the one nearest us.

We could not see the sentries on the walls. Still, they were there. Jani Beg was a careful leader, as I had learned to my cost. Afterward, I heard that because of the warning of Gutchluk Khan the guards had been doubled, and also the outpost in front of the one gate of Khanjut that looked out over the plain. Truly I have something of a name as a warrior in Badakshan, for all this they did on my account.

Higher rose the moon, until it topped the cedars across the gorge. We had gained our breath by now.

"It is the beginning of the second watch of the night—even later," meditated Sir Weyand. "Know you a path down the cliff?"

There was no path. But at a point near where we stood I had seen goats descend the precipice in my youth. We went down, helping each other as best we could. It was an evil half hour.

Once Sir Weyand's heavy shoes slipped and he clung to a ledge with his fingers until I could reach him. Another time I fell the length of two spears, being checked by a stunted tree. It bruised me badly and strained the muscles of one armpit.

Had it not been for the moon we could not have done what we did. Perhaps in daylight we would not have tried it. The green haze of the silver light concealed the perils of the way. *B'illah*! A man is not a goat!

When we sat at the bottom of the cliff, with our feet in the water of the stream, the sweat was running from my chin. Sir Weyand, having suffered no hurt, left me and returned bearing the trunk of a dead cedar.

"The second watch is two-thirds passed," I said, looking up at the stars.

I had had command of sentries in the night too often to be mistaken.

"Soon you will be cool," laughed the *Ferang*, who threw himself down by me to rest.

I doubt, however, if he was tired. The man had good muscles and carried his weight easily, whereas I was not used to climbing or walking.

He stripped the branches from the cedar with his sword. As he did so he sang to himself a deep song of his tribe which I did not understand. He was a strange merchant. No man of our bazaars would have climbed down the cliff of the Amu Daria or sung to himself when about to enter Khanjut in the face of the men of Jani Beg. I wondered how he would bear himself in what was to come, in Khanjut. I doubted then if he would see another sun— for in a skirmish a man must look out for himself and I must see to Shirzad Mir.

"Come," he said; "it is time to go forward."

So I rose, being stiff with my bruise, and stepped into the river, carrying one end of the cedar and he the other. It was not deeper than our waists, since this was the dry season.

The moon was almost directly over our heads when we came near the end of the gorge. Here we could see the walls of the castle plainly, some five bowshots in front of us. We could hear the sentries crying one to the other. And the shouting in the bazaars around the walls, where the camp-followers were feasting at Jani Beg's bidding.

Then we stepped forward and, stooping over, entered the covered way through which the stream ran into the moat of

Khanjut—into the moat and under the wall to the great reservoir which stores water for Khanjut in time of siege.

The cedar floated in front of us and we gripped it. At times the water was over our heads, and these times we swam, holding the tree. Often we struck our heads against the brick above, for the tunnel was not large.

The current gripped us and thrust us forward into the dark. We went quickly down, down. Aye, we were little better than the big water-rats that swam away from us, as our wet clothing pulled at us and our swords tugged at their girdles.

The worst was when we came to the arch that marks the wall of Khanjut. Here the tunnel closes down on the water and we were thrust under the surface. It was an ill moment. The cedar caught and we left it, swimming forward. Sir Weyand caught me and jerked me with him, for he swam well.

The evil passed. As I had known we must, we rose up through the water presently to the surface of the reservoir and caught our breath—with great gasps. The *Ferang* drew me with him until our hands touched stone and we sat on the side of the cistern where the women come with their water jugs.

The tank was built after the Hindu fashion, roofed over, with stairs and balconies leading down to the water. Thus it provided a cool spot in the hot season. We waited not to rest but climbed the steps and passed through the galleries until we stood at the door, where were some women looking out into the street. They were wringing their hands and clutching at their hair.

"What has come upon us?" I asked them, for I heard horses galloping about the courtyards.

I was glad of the dark, for my face is known in Khanjut.

"It is the enemy," they cried. "The sentries have sounded the call. Some men of Shirzad Mir, led most like by the accursed outlaw Abdul Dost, are at hand."

These words told me we were late. I signed to Sir Weyand and ran forth into the streets, keeping in the shadows and avoiding the torches some horsemen carried. Following back alleys, I came to the tower where I had heard Shirzad Mir was.

Before the door of the tower a hulking Kurd leaned on his spear. He stared at the form of the *Ferang*, who was close on my heels.

"Gutchluk Khan has sent for us," I cried quickly, lest he become suspicious, "to come here. Where is Jani Beg?"

"With the horsemen at the gate," answered the Kurd, still looking at the *Ferang*. "Gutchluk Khan is within, watching from the tower."

"Doubtless he is guarding Shirzad Mir," I said calmly, for this thing I needed to know.

"Two men guard the *mir* before the door on the third landing."

I think the man—although he could not see our faces—was ill at ease. Yet we were going into the tower and not out, and Gutchluk Khan was within. So we pushed past him and began to climb the stair, for there was no time to be lost. Already we were late.

We climbed up in silence. I was listening to the clatter outside the tower. Men were crying and running about. There was much noise. Plainly the Uzbeks had been alarmed. And our period of grace was nearly over.

Embrasures in the walls lighted our path up. But at the second landing Sir Weyand checked me and pointed from the embrasure.

We were now higher than the walls of Khanjut. Beyond the walls and the roofs of the buildings we saw the plain. Over it lay the haze of moonlight.

And far out on the plain we saw a great cloud of dust. It was moving nearer to the gate of Khanjut, coming from the West and circling. In the dust we caught a flicker of light here and there, reflected on something hard—also streamers that might have been attached to spears. In front of the cloud of dust a horseman was wheeling.

In the plain below us Jani Beg's men were gathering in ranks as they emerged from the pathway that led down at one side of the cliff. They formed swiftly. Jani Beg was a good leader. Our time was short. Already one or two horsemen were riding out toward the dust.

Sir Weyand noted all this and turned to me.

"Iskander Khan has kept his word," he said.

I thought to myself that Iskander Khan would never see his cattle or his sheep again. It was the reflection of moonlight on their horns we had seen and the streamers in the dust were rags tied to the horns of bullocks. The rider in front of the herd was one of the boys of Iskander Khan.

Truly, the stripling made a brave show—although we could barely see him at that. He must have shot arrows at the horsemen who were coming out, for they hesitated, waiting for the main body of Uzbeks to come up.

It is written that the faith of a true man is firm as steel. Sorrow came upon Iskander Khan for that night's work. Did he not render the service, however, to Shirzad Mir?

So far the plan of Sir Weyand had borne fruit. While the eyes of the Uzbeks were all turned to the plain, we were in the tower. And on the landing above, thanks to the confusion which had followed sounding the alarm, there were only two men.

They were sitting on their haunches, two mail-clad Uzbeks. But they sprang to their feet at sight of the *Ferang* running up the steps. Here was no time for talk.

I drew my scimitar and struck at the first man, leaping to the landing at his side. He warded clumsily and my second stroke bit deep into his neck through the shoulder muscles. He sank to his knees.

The *Ferang*, I saw, was engaged with the second man, his long sword thrusting silently at the fellow's neck. The shouts below drowned the dull mutter of steel against steel. I had seen the *Ferang* use his weapon and I wasted no time in turning from him to the door.

Two strong bars were in place. These I pulled down and threw open the door.

Within, a broad figure rose to its feet from kneeling over a wash basin. My heart rose in me as sap rushes up a tree in Spring. For here was Shirzad Mir, clad in the clean garments in which he was to go to his death.

I caught his hand, while he stared, and touched it to my forehead. God gave me great happiness in that moment!

"Come with us, Lord of Badakshan," I cried. "We have little time."

Behind me I heard the second man fall to the floor. Shirzad Mir lacked not wit. In a second we had passed out of the door.

I looked for the *Ferang* but he was not to be seen. Shirzad Mir and I could not wait. We were obliged to be free of the walls of Khanjut before Jani Beg's horsemen should discover the trick we had played on them and rein back toward the castle. And there was but one gate.

Verily, I was rejoiced to see the curling beard and stout figure of my lord. The Kurd spearman at the tower entrance gave no trouble. Before he could turn I had struck him once with the flat of my sword under the ear and he fell to earth like a stricken ox.

Nevertheless, we waited at the tower gate while a man could drink a beaker of wine slowly.

"There was one with me, lord," I explained to Shirzad Mir.

"Then we must wait," he said, being an upright man.

The skin prickled up and down my back while we lingered, for it was foolhardy of the *Ferang* to delay.

Then he came and I nearly struck him, for he had put on an Uzbek turban. It was well, though, for when we ran from the tower and sought out two horses which I had marked in the courtyard nearby, none of the Uzbeks noticed him. One horse Shirzad Mir mounted. The other I gave the *Ferang*, running by his stirrup from the courtyard to the outer gate.

I had feared that Gutchluk Khan would have seen us from the tower. No one challenged us, however, as we fled through the gate among the scattered horsemen. In a night alarm there is much confusion and no man knows his neighbor.

At the bottom of the cliff path we left the horsemen and struck through the camp bazaar, where there was great outcry and running about of women and slaves. I was watching for a horse to seize. None was to be had; yet on the edge of a village I spied a *kulan*—a wild ass. This, being desperate, I seized and mounted.

Then I rode after Shirzad Mir, who was leading the way into the ravines.

Truly, many have laughed at me when they heard I had ridden a wild ass to safety. Nevertheless, few have ridden such. It was no easy matter to stick to the beast's back.

Shirzad Mir was laughing at my riding. Perhaps I did cling to the *kulan's* neck. Who would not? It was I who led the way into the forest of the hills back of Khanjut. We rode until the night was spent.

Then, in the dawn, which is the blessing of light, we dismounted in a grove and stretched on the ground. Shirzad Mir was still laughing at my riding. To take his mind from that and to satisfy my curiosity, I asked Sir Weyand why he had risked our lives by delaying at the tower.

The *Ferang*, who was lying beside me, stretched his arms over his head.

"I went to find Gutchluk Khan," he said.

"Did you find him?" asked Shirzad Mir, watching him, for, despite the turban, he had noted the strange dress of the *Ferang*.

"Aye," said Sir Weyand and threw the turban from him. "That was his."

Said Afzel's Elephant

Put cloth of gold upon a fool and a multitude will do reverence to him; clothe a wise man in beggar's garments, and few will honor him. Yet those few will have their reward.

Turkestan proverb

We were three men with two horses and two swords. We were outcasts in the thickets of the foothills of the Badakshan, under the peaks of the Roof of the World. We had earned the wrath of the Mogul of India and there were two thousand riders searching for us.

It was the year of the Ox—the year 1608 by the Christian calendar—and Jani Beg, the Uzbek, had taken Badakshan from my lord, Baber Shirzad Mir, sometimes called the Tiger Lord.

Nevertheless, we three were happy. We had taken Shirzad Mir from the hands of Jani Beg, who had marked him for death.

Aye, Shirzad Mir sat in the clean white robes in which he had prepared to die by a twisted bowstring around the neck, and laughed for joy of seeing the sun cast its level darts of light over the peaks and through the trees that gave us shelter. Our hearts—the *Ferang*'s and mine—were lifted up for a moment by the warmth that comes with early morning. We had an ache in our bellies for lack of food; we had not slept for a day and a night. Also, I was stiff with many bruises.

"Tell me," said Shirzad Mir, fingering his full beard, which was half gray, half black, "how you got me out of the prison of Khanjut."

While I watched, lying at the edge of the thicket on my side, the *Ferang*—the Englishman, Sir Ralph Weyand—explained how we had climbed through the water tunnel of Khanjut into the

walls, and how we two alone had freed the *mir* while Jani Beg
and his men were tricked into looking the other way by a herd of
cattle that we had sent to the gate of Khanjut.

He spoke in his broken *Mogholi*, but Shirzad Mir, who was
quick of wit, understood.

"And whence came you?" he asked.

Sir Weyand told how he had been sent to India as a merchant,
and had been driven from the court of the Mogul by the wiles of
the Portuguese priests. When he had done, Shirzad Mir rose up
and touched his hand to earth, then pressed the back of it to his
brow. This is something he has seldom done, being a chieftain by
birth, and a proud man. Sir Weyand rose also and made salutation
after the manner of his country.

I watched from the corner of my eye, for my curiosity was still
great concerning the *Ferang*: also, for all he had borne himself like
a brave man that night, he was but a merchant and I knew not
how far we could trust him. While I lay on the earth and scanned
the groups of horsemen that scurried the plain below us, seeking
for our tracks, the thought came to me that our fortunes were
desperate.

We were alone. The followers of Shirzad Mir were scattered
through Badakshan, or slain. The family of my lord was in the
hands of Jani Beg—upon whom may the curse of God fall. North
of Badakshan we would find none but Uzbeks, enemies. To the
East was the nest of bleak mountains called by some the Hindu
Kush, by others the Roof of the World. To the West, the desert.

True, to the South, the Shyr Pass led to the fertile plain of
Kabul, but up this pass was coming Said Afzel, the son of Jani
Beg, with a large caravan. I had heard that Said Afzel was a poor
warrior, being a youth more fond of sporting with the women
of his harem and with poets than of handling a sword. Still, he
had followers with him, for he was bearing the gifts of the Mogul
Jahangir from Agra to Jani Beg.

Something of this must also have been in the mind of Shirzad
Mir, who had been lord of Badakshan for twice ten years, during
the reign in India of the Mogul Akbar, peace be on his name!

"I am ruler," he smiled sadly, "of naught save two paces of forest land; my dress of honor is a robe of death. For a court I have but two friends."

Shirzad Mir was a broad man with kindly eyes and a full beard. He had strength in his hands to break the ribs of a man, and he could shoot an arrow with wonderful skill. He was hasty of temper, but generous and lacking suspicion. Because of this last, he had lost Badakshan to Jani Beg, the Uzbek.

He knew only a little of writing and music; still, he was a born leader of men, perhaps because there was nothing he ordered them to do that he would not do himself. Wherefore, he had two saber cuts on his head and a spear gash across the ribs.

Thinking to comfort him, I rose up from the place where I was watching and squatted down by them.

"There are many in Badakshan," I said—long ago he had granted me leave to be familiar with him—"who will come to you when they know you are alive."

"Who will tell them, Abdul Dost?" he asked mildly. "We will be hunted through the hills. The most part of the nobles of Badakshan have joined the standard of Jani Beg."

"The men of the hills and the desert's edge are faithful, Shirzad Mir," I said.

They were herdsmen and outlaws for the most part. Our trained soldiers had been slain, all but a few hiding out in the hills.

"Aye," he exclaimed, and his brown eyes brightened. "Still, they are but men. To take up arms against the Uzbeks we need arms—also good horses, supplies and treasure. Have we these?"

So we talked together in low tones, thinking that the *Ferang* slept or did not hear. Presently I learned that he understood, for, with many pains, he had taught himself our tongue.

We spoke of the position of Jani Beg. Truly, it was a strong one. He himself held Khanjut, which was the citadel at the end of the Shyr ravine leading into India. Paluwan Chan, leader of his Uzbeks, was at the great town of Balkh with a garrison. Re-

inforcements were coming through the passes to the North from
Turkestan. Outposts were scattered through the plains. Jani Beg
was a shrewd commander. Only once did I know him to err badly
in his plans. Of that I will tell in due time.

Shirzad Mir, who was brave to the point of folly, said he would
go somehow to Agra and appeal for mercy from Jahangir himself.
I had been to Kabul and I knew that the intrigues of Jani Beg
had made his quarrel seem that of the Mogul and—such is the
witchery of evil words—Shirzad Mir seem to be a rebel.

"That may not be," I answered.

Then the *Ferang* lifted his yellow head and spoke in his deep
voice.

"I heard at Agra, Shirzad Mir," he said, weighing his words,
"that you were a follower of the Mogul Akbar."

"Of Akbar," nodded my lord, "the shadow of God and prince
of princes. He was a soldier among many."

"So it has been told me." Sir Weyand rested his chin on his fists
and stared up where the blue sky of Badakshan showed through
the trees. "When Akbar was in difficulty, what plan did he follow?"

"He was a brave man. God put a plan into his head when it
was needed. He had the wisdom of books and many advisors."

"And with this wisdom, I have heard he always did one thing
when he was pressed by great numbers of enemies."

Shirzad Mir looked thoughtfully at the *Ferang*. It was a strange
thing that this merchant, who carried a straight sword and came
over the sea in a boat, should know of the great Akbar. Verily,
wisdom travels hidden ways.

"Aye," he said, "the Mogul Akbar would say to his men that
they should attack—always attack."

"Then," repeated Sir Weyand promptly, "we will attack. It is
the best plan."

I threw back my head and laughed. How should the three of
us, with but two horses, ride against the army of Jani Beg? How
should we draw our reins against Khanjut? We should be slain as

a lamp is blown out in the wind. A glance from Shirzad Mir, who frowned, silenced me when I was about to put this thought into speech.

"How?" he asked, still frowning.

Then I remembered that I also had asked this question of the *Ferang* and that his answer had freed Shirzad Mir. I drew closer to listen.

"In my country," said Sir Weyand, "there is a saying that he who attacks is twice armed."

He then told how an *ameer* of Spain whose empire extended over Ferangistan and the lands across the western ocean had sent a fleet of a thousand ships against England in Sir Weyand's youth, and how the Queen of England had fitted out a much smaller fleet, dispatching it to sail against the invader.

"Had we waited for the Spaniards to land, the issue might have been different," he said. "As it was, few of the Don escaped with a whole skin. The advantages of those attacking are these: they can choose the ground best suited to them; they can strike when they are ready; also, their numbers appear greater in a charge or onset."

The thought came to me that perhaps the *Ferang*, being a bold man, would not hesitate to turn against us if the chance offered. After all, he had been sent by his king to get money and trade concessions from India, and the small province of Badakshan could mean little to him. What did we know of the king of England except that he had ships and very fine artillery?

Still, at this time Sir Weyand needed the friendship of Shirzad Mir. And, although he was a merchant—which is a getter of money—he never in the weeks to come, and I watched closely, shunned the dangers we faced. Instead he welcomed a battle, and laughed, when he swung his long sword, as if he were about to go to a feast. It is written that a fight is like a cup of strong wine to some. Sir Weyand was such a man.

"True," nodded Shirzad Mir, who had listened with care, "the great Mogul Akbar, once, when his men were wavering, went forward on his elephant to a knoll where all could see him; then he ordered his attendants to shackle the legs of the elephant with an iron chain so that he could not retreat. Whereupon his men rode forward, and the battle was won. Yet we are only three against as many thousands. In what quarter should we attack?"

"Aye," I put in, "where? We are not yet mad."

"We are like to be so from hunger or thirst," replied the *Ferang*, "if we do not better our fortunes. I heard you say we had no place to flee, and so we must attack."

"Khanjut?" smiled Shirzad Mir almost mockingly.

But the *Ferang* was not in jest.

"If we had a few score followers, it would not be a bad plan. But that is for you to decide, Shirzad Mir. You know the country. If I think of a plan, I will tell you."

That was all he had in his mind. I was disappointed. Perhaps I had expected too much of him.

"Meanwhile we must eat," I pointed out, feeling the urge in my stomach. "Iskander Khan will surely give us food, also weapons, if he has any."

I did not add that my horse was at the *aul* of Iskander Khan. Last night I had ridden a wild ass from Khanjut. But I did not want to do so again—until my bruises healed.

"It is well," said Shirzad Mir.

So he mounted one horse and the *Ferang* the other. I trotted before them, to spy out if the way was safe. Iskander Khan was the friend who had aided us with his herd of cattle and his two sons the night before. His *aul* was hidden in the hills not far away. But, as we traveled, we did not think to find what was awaiting us there.

II

About the time of noonday prayers we came to the Kirghiz's *aul*—three dome-shaped tents of willow laths covered with greased felt and hides. Over the opening of the biggest tent were yaks' tails, also an antelope's head. Under this sat Iskander Khan, cross-legged on the ground.

He was a very old man, bent in the back, with the broad forehead and keen eyes of his race and a white beard that fell below his chest. His eyes were very bright and his skin had shriveled overnight. His turban was disarranged as if he had torn it in grief.

He rose unsteadily to his feet when he saw Shirzad Mir. But my lord—because Iskander Khan had rendered him a great service, and because the Kirghiz was the older man—sprang down from his horse and went to meet him. Iskander Khan touched his hand to the earth and to his forehead three times; then Shirzad Mir embraced him.

"We have come for food," I said, looking for Wind-of-the-Hills but seeing him not.

Iskander Khan lifted his hands in despair and pointed to the empty huts.

"It is my sorrow," he said, "that Shirzad Mir of Badakshan should come to my aid and ask meat when I have none to give. There is *kumiss* in the cask, and this I will bring you."

He did so, filling a bowl with the mare's milk, which is the distilled drink of the Kirghiz. Neither Shirzad Mir nor I liked *kumiss*. When we saw how disappointed Iskander Khan was at our refusal, we forced ourselves to drink some. As it happened, this was well, because the strong fluid eased the pang in our insides.

Shirzad Mir glanced curiously about the vacant *aul*. In the days when he had known Iskander Khan, the Kirghiz had many sheep and cattle.

Then Iskander Khan told us what had happened. The herd and flock which his sons had driven to the gate of Khanjut had been taken by Jani Beg, who was greatly angered at the trick we had played on him. Also, the two boys and the daughter of Iskander Khan had been taken by the Uzbek horsemen.

One of the youths Jani Beg had impaled on a spear which was then fastened to the gate of Khanjut. The other Kirghiz had been shot in the stomach with a matchlock ball and thrown from the walls of the citadel.

The girl Jani Beg had had flayed alive. Iskander Khan had been too feeble to ride with his sons. News of what happened had been brought him by a Kirghiz sheep-boy who saw. Truly, a heavy sorrow had been laid on the khan for what he had done for Shirzad Mir.

My lord put his hand on the arm of Iskander Khan and spoke softly.

"It is written that what evil-doers store up for themselves they shall taste. You shall have revenge for the death of your sons. By the beard of the prophet, I swear it."

He felt at the peak of his turban for the jewel he had been accustomed to wear there, intending to give it to Iskander Khan as a token. He smiled ruefully when his hand met naught but the cloth. The small turban of white cotton he wore was part of his grave clothes.

"Truly, Iskander Khan," he meditated aloud, "I am a beggared monarch. I have not even a token to give you for this service."

"I am content, Shirzad Mir."

I thought of the riches that the poet son of Jani Beg was carrying to Khanjut from the Mogul Jahangir, while Shirzad Mir had not so much as a spare horse, and I voiced this thought, being embittered by hunger and much soreness. At this the *Ferang* sprang to his feet so swiftly that I thought he had seen some Uzbeks approaching, so I did likewise. He clapped me on the back, rudely.

"Ha, Abdul Dost!" he cried, "that is the word I have been waiting for. So the caravan of Said Afzel is now in the Shyr Pass? Here is our chance. We will attack Said Afzel!"

"Ride against two score, when we are but three?" I laughed at the man. If he was mad, I must see to it that Shirzad Mir did not suffer from his folly. "I was in Kabul three days ago, and Said Afzel was just setting out. Besides his slaves and personal servants he has a bodyguard of some Pathans. They are well armed; the pass is narrow. Also they have many camels. You know not what you say!"

"Peace, Abdul Dost!" called my lord, whose eyes had taken on a strange sparkle. "You have not wit to see farther than your horse's ears. Let the *Ferang* speak!"

"It is better to be mad than calm at this time when caution will gain us nothing, excellency," said Sir Weyand respectfully. "Here is a noble chance. Said Afzel does not yet know you have escaped. He will not be watchful of danger. His caravan may be numerous but it is made up for the most part of women and eunuchs. Moreover, in the narrow ravine they must extend their line of march. We can choose our place of attack—"

"And they will dig our graves there," I said.

Shirzad Mir frowned at me.

"And we will have the advantage of surprise," continued the *Ferang*. "Jani Beg will hardly think to send reinforcements to his son because he knows that Said Afzel is well attended. We will have time to gain the narrow point of the pass just before dark—the best time to strike."

"How can three horsemen ride against camels and an elephant in a ravine?" I asked, for I was not to be silenced.

Shirzad Mir was foolhardy of his life and it was plain to me he liked well the words of Sir Weyand.

"We will not ride against them, Abdul Dost. If you had thought, you would remember that we could stand on the ledge above the caravan trail, where our arrows will command Said Afzel's men."

It was true I had not thought of that, in my concern for Shirzad Mir. It angered me—a *mansabdar* of the army—to be corrected by a foreign merchant, and I was silent for a space. Not so the Tiger Lord.

"*Hai*—that was well said!" he cried. "Such a plan warms my heart. Now if we had the strong sons of Iskander Khan—" he broke off with a glance at the mourning Kirghiz. "What men and slaves are with the caravan?"

"I heard at Kabul," replied the *Ferang*, settling his tall body against the tent, "that Said Afzel was a courtier and a gallant— fond of music, toys, verses and the Indian dancing girls. He is bringing a throng of such with him, also several camel loads of treasure as gift from the Mogul. What do we care for eunuchs and Ethiopian slaves?"

"Said Afzel has at least seven Pathans with him," I reminded him. "They are good fighters."

"Are you an old nurse, Abdul Dost?" cried my master in great anger. "Speak again, and I will set you to tend swine!" He turned to the *Ferang*. "Said Afzel is truly called 'the dreamer,' Sir Weyand. He is the most elegant in dress and can recite verses as well as his boon companion Kasim Kirlas, the professional courtier. It is true that he travels with cumbrous baggage—unlike his father—and is usually stupefied with bhang and opium. I would risk much to set hand on his jewels."

"We would risk much," nodded the *Ferang* bluntly, as was his custom, "especially as there is one of the big Indian elephants in the caravan."

"An elephant!" Shirzad Mir clapped his stout hands and laughed. "*Hai*—an elephant. That would be Most Alast from the stables of Jahangir. I heard it said at Khanjut when I was prisoner. Verily, the star of our good fortune is in the ascendant."

I thought the madness that had come upon Sir Weyand had bitten my lord, for he laughed again and fell to talking in low tones to the other. I strained my ears but could not hear. Being angry and perhaps a little jealous, I withdrew slightly to show them I did not care what they said.

Once Shirzad Mir called to Iskander Khan.

"Have you a great cauldron?" he asked.

The Kirghiz pointed to the ashes of the fire, where a pot stood, large enough to boil a sheep whole.

"Will you give it me?"

Iskander Khan made a sign to show that all he had was Shirzad Mir's for the asking. Once more the two talked together, and I saw them glance at me and laugh. Then Iskander Khan lifted up his white head.

"You will need a good horse, Shirzad Mir," he said slowly. "The one you have is a sorry pony. In a thicket yonder I have Abdul Dost's horse, also an Arab stallion that has carried me for five years. I will fetch it for you so that you may mount as is fitting for a king."

The eyes of the Tiger Lord softened.

"Thrice happy is the man who has a faithful friend," he said, and with his own hand helped the aged Kirghiz to rise.

Before the two left the tent to go for the horses, he spoke quickly to Sir Weyand.

The *Ferang* rose and stretched his big frame. I did not move, for they had not confided in me. He disappeared into the tent and presently came forth, lugging a basket filled with something heavy. I wanted to see what was in it, but I would not show him that I was curious.

He was singing to himself after his strange fashion. He moved with his hands that which was in the basket and put it in the cauldron. I watched him.

When he had nearly finished there came a dog that was hungry and whined. Seeing the dog, Sir Weyand threw him a piece of the stuff he was handling. The dog wagged his tail and carried off the stuff. I saw him eat it.

This was very strange, so I rose up without seeming to be interested and walked toward Sir Weyand, until I could see into the pot.

"*B'illah!*" I cried, for the stuff was rotting swine's flesh, which it is defilement for a follower of the prophet to touch. It had been used by Iskander Khan to grease the tents. The *Ferang*, who knew this, laughed.

"Tell me, Abdul Dost," he smiled, rising from his labor when the pot was nearly full, "is that dog better than you, or are you better than that dog?"

He was a *caphar*, one without faith. Those words might well have cost him his life.

"I have faith," I answered him sternly, "I am better than that dog; if I have not faith, he is better than I." I laid a hand on my sword. "If you wish a quarrel—"

"Peace!" cried the voice of Shirzad Mir behind us. "It is time we mounted."

He was leading a fine gray stallion, and Iskander Khan had Wind-of-the-Hills. Likewise, the Kirghiz gave to us two good bows and quivers full of arrows—also he brought his own sword from the tent and girded it on Shirzad Mir. What man could do more than Iskander Khan did for us?

"The blessing of God go with you, Shirzad Mir," he said in parting. "I shall stay at this tent, and perhaps—"

"I will come back," said my lord swiftly. "I will not forget."

We watched the bent form of the old man go into the empty tent, then we set spurs to our mounts. The cauldron Sir Weyand had slung on a long pole, one end of which he carried and I the other. Shirzad Mir rode bridle to bridle with him—I following behind. Still they talked together eagerly, like boys with a new sport. Once Sir Weyand looked back at me and grinned.

"If you are afraid to come, Abdul Dost," he said, "you are free to drop the pole and go."

Before I could think of a fitting answer, he was speaking again with Shirzad Mir. Verily, I was angered. The pole leaped and jumped, and I was forced to watch lest the vile fat should fly out on me. There was no doubt in my mind that lack of food had unsettled my lord's brain.

Why else should we ride at a fast trot through the hot ravines of the hills to the Shyr Pass, where at any moment we might meet a wandering patrol on the watch for us? And why did we carry that accursed pig's flesh?

As for Sir Weyand, my brain was black with anger. I wanted to swing my scimitar against his long sword. Had it not been for the events of that evening, I should have done so.

Our horses were steaming when we came out of a poplar thicket on a hill near the caravan track and saw a boy shepherd watching us from his flock. When he recognized Shirzad Mir, the lad put down his bow and dropped to his knees.

"*Hazaret salamet!*" he cried joyfully, in the dialect of his tribe.

He had thought Shirzad Mir was dead. My lord questioned him swiftly. The boy told him that the caravan of Said Afzel had not yet passed this point. Our good fortune still held, yet I was doubtful of what was to come. Shirzad Mir bent over the boy.

"Speak, little soldier," he laughed, "how would you like to shoot an arrow in the service of your lord?"

The boy's eyes brightened and he fingered his bow, being both pleased and shy with the attention paid him. He was a slight, dark-skinned Kirghiz—the same that had visited Iskander Khan's *aul*—and the words delighted him. Shirzad Mir honored him by taking him up behind on his horse. My belly yearned for the mutton that we might have cooked and eaten, but my master would not linger.

It was mid-afternoon, and the sun was very hot. We were in the pass now, and once we met a runner coming up the ravine. It was a man of Said Afzel, and when he saw us he bounded up into the rocks. But Shirzad Mir fired an arrow swiftly. My lord was an excellent shot. From the body we took the message.

It said that Said Afzel would camp that night at a certain level spot in the pass, for the caravan track was too narrow, besides being on the bank of the turbulent stream Amu Daria, to travel at night. Probably Said Afzel liked better to sit on the cushions of a silk tent than to ride.

"God is good to us," exclaimed Shirzad Mir and pressed forward.

Although I still said nothing, I had a great foreboding. No man has ever called me a coward, but our strength was sapped by hunger—we had no armor or firearms. We were acting on the mad whim of the *Ferang*, and for the first time in his life my master had put aside my advice for another's—that of the merchant who made me carry the pot of swine-flesh.

We passed the open place where Said Afzel had planned to camp. We knew now that the caravan could not be far away, and Shirzad Mir sent the boy ahead to spy. He ran swiftly, like a young mountain goat.

We came to the very place where I had first met the *Ferang*, and I bent my ears back like a horse, listening for hoofs on the trail behind us, for here we were in a trap. On one side the cliff rose sheer for perhaps four spear lengths. On the left hand the slope, steep and strewn with rocks and thorns, dropped abruptly to the rushing stream which was deep enough to drown a man.

Truly, I thought, the madness of Sir Weyand had brought us to an evil place. If a patrol of Uzbek horsemen should come behind us we would be caught between them and the caravan.

Even a brave man feels a prickling of the flesh when he knows not what is before and behind him. The mad fantasy of the other two had veiled their minds from danger. Shirzad Mir, to make matters worse, set Sir Weyand and me to rolling some stones into the path from the slope. While we were doing this, he dismounted and led our three horses by a roundabout path up to the top of the cliff.

Not until we had the stone-heap nearly the height of a man and were panting from the toil—my bruises had not yet healed— did he call for us to cease. Then Sir Weyand made me take the pole with him and carry it up the slope to the top of the cliff. If the foul fat had fallen back on me, I should have struck him, but it was my fate that it did not.

Back into a cedar grove we carried the accursed thing. Here Shirzad Mir had kindled a fire from dried cedar branches.

"The trees may hide the smoke," he said. "Quick—our time is little!"

As if possessed of a demon, Sir Weyand worked at the fire, placing the cauldron over the logs so that the fat began to heat. Meanwhile, Shirzad Mir stood at the edge of the cliff to watch for the coming of the boy.

The sun had dropped behind the peaks at our backs. There was no wind. The scent of the cedars was sweet in my nostrils, but Sir Weyand made me labor over the evil-smelling pot. I had none of his wild hope. For, without doubt, Said Afzel, whom we sought, would ride the elephant, and I had once tried to attack one of the beasts in a battle.

The ravine in which the stream muttered was clothed in shadows and it must have been the time of sunset prayers when the boy came running back up the path, looking for us.

Shirzad Mir called to him, and the youth came nimbly up the cliff, clinging somehow to the sheer rock, until my lord reached him a hand. Then he bowed his head to Shirzad Mir's feet.

"The caravan comes, Lord of Badakshan!" he cried eloquently.

"How many and in what order?" asked Shirzad Mir swiftly.

"Some horsemen, riding slowly, are in front. Then a group of slaves with burdens on foot. Following them some armed riders. Then a black elephant with a glittering *howdah.*"

"God is with us!" cried Shirzad Mir. He turned to me merrily. "Ho—Abdul Dost of the dark brow! What think you of an elephant in the ravine of the Shyr?"

We had seen none of the beasts in Badakshan before, but something of Shirzad Mir's purpose flashed on me, and I felt the heart-leap of the hunter when he sees game approach his hiding-place. Sir Weyand stirred the fat, which was now boiling and bubbling odorously.

Above the place where we had piled the stones so they would look as if they had fallen down the slope, my lord sent the boy with his arrows. He, himself, took his bow and crawled forward to where he could see him down the pass.

At a sign from Sir Weyand, I helped him lift the cauldron from the fire by its stick. We carried it to the edge of the ravine.

"Go with your master," said Sir Weyand to me under his breath, "and take your bow. I will manage the rest of my task alone."

Nothing loath, I obeyed. Crouching beside Shirzad Mir, I could see the caravan coming up the pass, in the quiet of the evening.

The bearers and camelmen were pushing ahead with loud cries, for the camping-place was just around a turn.

It was a brave sight. The Pathans, as the boy had said, were in the lead—lean men, riding easily and fully armed. Next came the Ethiopians, with their heavy burdens. They, of course, were unarmed. I counted seven Pathans.

Then appeared Most Alast, the elephant of the Mogul. He had two red stripes down his forehead, and silver bells at his neck. I could see the white heron's plume of Said Afzel in the *howdah* behind the *mahout*. Slowly, slowly, they came forward.

"It could not be better, Abdul Dost," cried my master joyfully.

I took heart from this. For, though his eyes were shining, he was laughing to himself, which was a good sign. He was not mad. I had begun to see his plan.

Last came the long-haired camels, bearing the women, the baskets which probably contained the treasure, and the eunuch guards of the harem. A few slaves in gorgeous tunics walked with the dirty camelmen.

A lone Pathan brought up the rear. I felt Shirzad Mir's hand on my arm.

"Shoot your arrows among the camelmen, Abdul Dost," he said. "I will take care of the leading riders—I and the boy. When I shout, raise our battle-cry and shout as if you were many men."

I nodded to show that I understood. I strung my bow and waited, lying on my belly. It was just as if Shirzad Mir and I were stalking antelope. Yet never had we stalked such game as this.

The sun had left the pass, but there was still light when the Pathans passed under us and arrived at the heap of stones. After talking together, three of them dismounted and began to clear away the stones, dropping them down the slope into the stream to free the path for the elephant.

We four were silent on the cliff, though I could hear Sir Weyand working at the fire. The swaying *howdah* of Most Alast came nearer—so near I could see the jewels set in the turban of Said

Afzel, who was laughing with a fat man on the cushion by him—
Kasim Kirlas, I thought. I could have almost reached down and
touched their heads.

Then Shirzad Mir bellowed his battle-cry.

"Hai—Shirzad el kadr—hai!"

He leaped to his feet and began to speed arrows down at the
riders.

"Hai—Shirzad el kadr—hai!" I echoed, twanging a shaft
among the camels.

It must have reached its mark, for one of the beasts yelled with
pain. I heard the shrill shout of the boy and startled cries of the
slaves below us.

Then Sir Weyand came to my side.

"Saint George for England!" he cried. I asked him later what
it was, and he told me.

As he shouted, he pushed the cauldron over on its side. The
boiling fat fell on the broad rump of Most Alast.

An elephant has a thick hide, but he is sensitive and nervous as
a woman—and the boiling grease was very hot. Most Alast lifted
up his trunk and bellowed his pain. Then he charged forward.
The howdah, with Said Afzel and Kasim Kirlas, slipped its girths
as Most Alast shook himself—the fat had missed the howdah, to
my sorrow—and the two went to earth.

Then Most Alast dashed among the riders. Several horses
leaped over the slope in their fright. Finding himself against the
stones, the elephant turned in the narrow path and charged back
against the camels, which gave way before him. Some stumbled
into the brush of the slope. Others pressed against the cliff wall.
B'illah, there was much confusion!

The camels, being frightened and hurt, began to yell also, and
the horses too. The black slaves had leaped to shelter and stood
watching, their eyeballs showing white. The camelmen sought
safety where they could.

Shirzad Mir had reckoned well what havoc an angered elephant
would make along that narrow path.

I was a middling shot with a bow, but my lord was a marksman among many. His shafts sought out the Pathans, who had no time to use their matchlocks before they had to leap out of the way of Most Alast. Yet he killed none. Before long, I knew why.

"*Hai—Shirzad el kadr—hai*!" cried my lord for the last time, and ordered me to seek the horses.

While the boy plied his arrows from the cliff, we two, with the *Ferang*, rode rapidly down until our horses stood at the slope above the pile of stones. Here Shirzad Mir called upon the Pathans to throw down their arms.

A Pathan is a good fighter when and if it suits him. These men were less afraid of us than of Most Alast, who was trumpeting back and forth along the path, heedless of the efforts of his *mahout*. They saw that we were armed and ready. They did not know how many more of us there were.

Three of the Pathans were hurt by the arrows of Shirzad Mir. Two others had fallen among the rocks and thorns of the slope below. The other two were afoot and watching the elephant.

All who could do so put down their muskets and swords and said that they had had enough of the affair. Shirzad Mir would not move until he had seen the two who were in the thorn thicket climb out, cursing, but little the worse for their fall, and join the others. Then we left Sir Weyand, who had picked up a brace of their discarded pistols, to watch the group, and Shirzad Mir went forward with me at his side.

"Find Said Afzel," he ordered me.

I saw the Uzbek prince leaning turbanless against a rock, feeling of himself tenderly. It is no light thing to fall from the *howdah* of an elephant. Kasim Kirlas, the professional courtier, was stretched on the ground at his feet—but this was no salaam; the man was stunned.

Shirzad Mir caught the dazed prince by the shoulder and bade him sternly walk before his horse. My lord had drawn his sword, and this he kept near the bare neck of Said Afzel.

"Where is the elephant?" he asked me.

I pointed to the stream below and Shirzad Mir laughed aloud. He ever appreciated a good jest. Most Alast had smelled water, and had somehow got himself down the slope to the stream unhurt.

He was drawing water up in his trunk and squirting it over his sore back—*mahout* and all. Later Most Alast lay down in the mud. It was many hours before we could get him to leave it.

Shirzad Mir pushed through the bewildered bearers swiftly. Half of the camelmen had fled. One or two of the eunuchs drew their scimitars when my lord came near the camels on which were the women, but when they saw the plight of Said Afzel, with my lord's sword at his ear, they threw down their weapons.

It was a sorry gathering that we grouped against the cliff wall. Eunuchs and slaves are masters of brave words, but I have yet to see the ones who will face danger to their bodies without shrinking. I cast about and discovered that the Pathan who had formed the rear guard had fled.

Shirzad Mir was now master of the field. He called to the boy on the cliff—our foes thought that many more were there—to shoot down the first man of the caravan who moved from his place.

Then he ordered me to ride my horse slowly back and forth among the remaining women and their attendants, and see that none escaped.

It was now growing dark, so of my own will I set four of the camelmen to building a great fire at the lower end of the caravan and another by the heap of stones. So it happened that when it grew dark we had our prisoners securely between the two fires and could see all that passed.

Shirzad Mir had gone straight to the Pathans and talked with them a long time. Presently he came to me and said:

"They will join my party, being men who sell their swords. For this reason I did not slay them. They were near enough for good shooting. I have cared for those who were hurt. The others are

cooking food. In the morning we will give them a sword apiece—
perhaps."

With the other attendants we did not speak. They were men
of low breeding and jumped to obey our orders. Shirzad Mir kept
Said Afzel ever at his side, in case of treachery.

One at a time we ate of the food for which we yearned. The
boy joined us proudly, and Shirzad Mir set him to collecting the
few weapons of the eunuchs. Of these he made a pile and sat on
it, feeling greatly the honor we did him.

Shirzad Mir talked with Said Afzel through the night. There
was no chance for me to sleep, but I think Sir Weyand slept a little
during his watch over the Pathans. Before dawn I had spoken with
the *mahout* of Most Alast and given him a handful of gold from
the treasure bags. He—one master being as good as another—
consented to serve us.

At dawn I had finished my task. The loads were all recovered
and placed on the camels and the slaves' backs. All had eaten. The
women were put back on their camels, and the eunuchs herded
in front.

At first break of light in the sky we set out, my lord and Said
Afzel mounted on the elephant, who was now quiet, the injured
in litters borne by the slaves, the Pathans on their own horses,
and the sheep-boy on another.

We struck away from the Shyr Pass into hills. Then, for the
first time in two days and nights, I slept a little in the saddle,
being weary, but only a little.

III

Said I not our star was in the ascendant, so that for a space we
were given strength to trick our enemies? Later, evil fortune came
upon us again, but not then.

Three courses were open to my lord. He could slay Said Afzel,
to strike terror into the Uzbeks; he could exchange the prince
and the women for his own family, and perhaps a strip of Badakshan; or he could ransom our prisoners for gold with which to

pay an army. I urged the first plan, Sir Weyand the second, and
the Pathans, who had now cast their fortunes with us, the third.

Our danger was great, for when news of what had happened
in the pass reached Khanjut by way of some escaped bearers, the
whole army of Jani Beg was sent to hunt us down. As yet we had
no followers other than the four injured Pathans and the sheep-
boy, whom Shirzad Mir appointed head of the camelmen and gave
a sword, to his great satisfaction. The bearers, the slaves and the
camel-drivers were useless to us and would have been glad to
fall again into the hands of Jani Beg, who would not drive them
through the bypaths of the hills, as we did.

It is written in the annals of India, the curious thing that my
master did in this difficulty.

"We will keep the prisoners and the treasure," he said, "and
we will regain the foothills of Badakshan from Jani Beg; also we
will gather together a small army."

And this thing we did, by the will of God. How was it done?
We held a *durbar*—that is, a crowning ceremony. The people of
Badakshan had been told my lord was dead. The *durbar* showed
them he was not.

Verily, not before or since has such a *durbar* been held in Hindustan or Badakshan or Turkestan. We traveled with the caravan through the villages of the hills. At each village Shirzad Mir
would dismount from Most Alast and spend money—from the
bags of Said Afzel—for a feast.

Wine he bought freely, and food, and scattered silver among
the people. So that all might see, he held his *durbar*. Said Afzel,
the opium-eating prince, he forced to do homage in public to
him; fat Kasim Kirlas, the professional courtier, Shirzad Mir made
pay him extravagant compliments; El Ghias, the buffoon of the
caravan, performed his tricks; the musicians of Said Afzel sang—
at the sword points of the Pathans—and the dancing girls danced.
It was a great feast. Shirzad Mir, looking the proud king he was by
birth, sat on cushions under a cloth-of-gold tent which we found
in the baggage, and watched idly, saying nothing.

Sir Weyand cleaned his soiled garments and sat at the right hand of Shirzad Mir, as the ambassador from England. Only I did not attend, for at every feast I was out in the lookout places with certain men of the hills who rallied to our standard, keeping watch. The men of Jani Beg pressed us close. We moved each day, marching in the night to a new village. I kept a good watch and at each new place more of our men came in to see and hear, for rumors of what had happened spread through the hills. Shirzad Mir gave to them gold and weapons from the store we had taken.

In the plain of Badakshan we could not have avoided being overtaken by the cavalry of the Uzbeks. But in the hills they were at a loss—and the people aided us. It was a mad scheme, yet its very madness protected us.

Shirzad Mir himself put on the jewels he took from Said Afzel, and—sitting placidly on Most Alast, the black elephant, with the two crimson stripes of the Mogul on his nose—he looked the king he was. The hearts of his old soldiers, who thronged to us from the hills, were uplifted at the sight.

Always Shirzad Mir directed me to travel in a circle, through Anderab, Ghori, and Bamian, back to where we had started, at the Shyr Pass. In spite of danger he did this, and we all wondered, until one day, we came to the desolate *aul* of Iskander Khan, as Shirzad Mir had planned.

When the old Kirghiz chieftain came forth and lifted up his hands at the sight, Shirzad Mir in his gorgeous robes dismounted from Most Alast and embraced Iskander Khan, while we all watched.

Then my lord pointed to the caravans, the camels, the treasure and the women.

"Choose," said he to Iskander, "it is all yours for the asking."

But Iskander Khan would not, saying that he was unworthy of such honor. Whereupon Shirzad Mir called for us all to see. He loaded the horse Iskander Khan had given him in his need—the fine Arab stallion—with pots of gold and gems, and put the bridle in the Kirghiz's hand himself.

He put a robe of ceremony on Iskander Khan and girded on him the sword from his own waist.

"This man," he said loudly "shall be always at my left hand until he dies. Those who do homage to me shall bow to him also."

In this manner did Shirzad Mir pay debt to Iskander Khan. He was a good man. A man among ten thousand. Aye, among ten times ten thousand.

Prophecy of the Blind

A fool covers himself with cloth of gold and laughs; while a wise man sharpens his sword.

Ask a fool what is hidden within the temple wall, and he will answer, "Stone." But a blind man may see what is hidden. Aye, he will read what is not written by the hand of men.

Muslim proverb

It was on the road to Balkh that the boy was playing in the dirt. And down the road was trampling a herd of frightened buffaloes.

With my eyes, I, Abdul Dost, hereditary follower of Shirzad Mir, saw what came to pass. This was in the year 1608 of the Christian calendar.

The boy was very young and could not walk except when guided by a stronger hand. He was intent upon his play, facing us. His companion was the *kwajah** Muhammad Asad, who sat upon a rock beside the road.

Muhammad Asad was blind.

The buffaloes, frightened by something down the road, were coming swiftly. And still the boy kept at his play, moving tiny sticks about in the dust. Muhammad Asad heard the beat of the animals' hoofs, but he could not see the danger to the child. I saw it, so likewise did Sir Weyand.

Sir Weyand, as I have said, was the *Ferang*, the Englishman, who had joined me in the hill country of India. He was a man who acted quickly. Some men are readier at making words fly than at drawing a sword, but the *Ferang* was not such.

---

* Holy man, or man of wisdom.

In a second he was down from his horse and running toward the child. His stout legs flew through the dust, and as he ran he loosened his brown cloak. The buffaloes were very close.

Sir Weyand did not slacken his pace. It seemed to me as if he sprang among the running animals and snatched up the boy under one arm; with the other be waved the cloak.

It was a goodly sight—the broad *Ferang* with both feet planted wide, his green cap with the feather on one side of his yellow curls and the cloak waving about his head.

The beasts could not stop, yet they parted in the middle and swept by the Englishman on both sides, bellowing and tossing their horns. The waving cloak had frightened them. In the dust that rose around him I could see the straight figure of the man. Yet why should Sir Weyand have put his life in risk for the sake of a *mullah*'s child?

The buffaloes forced my horse aside, up the bank of the road. When they had passed I caught Sir Weyand's mount and reined down to him. The child was frightened and cried. At this, the holy man came toward us, feeling the way with his staff. The feelings of the blind are quickened by the affliction that God has laid upon them, and Muhammad Asad knew that the child had been in peril. He reached forward with his thin hand until he had touched the boy and made certain that no harm had come to him.

"Peace be unto you, Muhammad Asad," I greeted him, knowing the holy man.

"And unto you be peace."

He asked what had passed, and when I told him he lifted blind eyes to heaven while Sir Weyand stared curiously at his lean face and venerable beard. "It is a blessing from the Prophet. Yet I have no gift to reward this deed."

Now I know not if the blessing of the *kwajah* aided the *Ferang*, who was an unbeliever. Still, he was a brave man and because of this and the strange events that followed, I think the *kwajah*'s thanks bore fruit.

That was well, for it was the whim of Sir Weyand that had brought us here, on the way to Balkh, in grave peril. He had become wearied of the inactivity at the camp of Shirzad Mir, my master, where the hill tribes were gathered. Sir Weyand had made common cause with us after he was driven from the Mogul's court by intrigues of Portuguese priests who were foes of the English.

"Idleness will breed defeat for us, Abdul Dost," he had said to me.

When I asked what else we might do, he laughed and said, "We ride to Balkh." This was a mad whim, for we were outlaws with the hand of the Mogul against us. The plain of Badakshan was filled with the Uzbeks, our foes, and Balkh itself was a great city of trade with high walls. But his whim would not be denied.

"We saved our lives and that of Shirzad Mir by attacking when we were starved and lost and defeated. Now we will attack again. Shirzad Mir cannot leave his men, but you, Abdul Dost, do you fear to come with me?"

When he said this, I mounted my horse. Who can speak of fear to Abdul Dost, *mansabdar* of the dead Mogul Akbar— commanding officer of the Mogul army below Amira, and best master of scimitar in northern Ind?

Now Sir Weyand had been thinking as he watched the *kwajah*, and thought with him led to deeds.

"It has been told me, Muhammad Asad," he spoke gravely, "that your priesthood have sight into the future. Is it so? Can you read me the future?"

"It is so with one who has fasted until the thread of life between soul and body is thin. What would you know?"

Thus came the prophecy of Muhammad Asad, written in the annals of Badakshan, from which befell the strange event at Balkh.

"A *Ferang* is within the borders of Badakshan," answered Sir Weyand, speaking respectfully—for the *kwajah* was loved of God—and motioning to me to be silent. "What is to be his fate in this moon?"

Muhammad Asad turned sightless eyes to him and to me. Then he took the hand of the boy and walked up the hillside, signing for us to follow. We dismounted and did so. A short distance away was a stream known to travelers along the caravan route to Balkh. By this Muhammad Asad halted. He released the child and felt his way to the water, where he knelt and performed his ablutions, as prescribed in the law.

I did likewise, for it was the hour of noonday prayer. Sir Weyand took the child on his knee and watched.

"By your tread—" Muhammad Asad turned to me when he was finished—"and by your voice it is clear that you are a warrior. Have you arrows?"

At his command I handed him a shaft from my quiver. This the *kwajah* broke into two parts. He felt on the ground and took up a stick. This also he broke. Then he was silent in prayer with the sticks in his hand.

He chanted softly the sacred invocation:

> *Allah ho Akbar, Allah ho Akbar.*
> *Arsh haddu unlah Illah ha Illahah,*
> *Arsh haddu unnah Mahomeda Razul Allah.*
> *Hyah Allah S'allah,*
> *Allah ho Akbar, Allah ho Akbar.*

This was the blessing upon the name of the prophet. Verily, Muhammad Asad was holy and he had fasted long. It is given to few to dwell so near the thoughts of the other world.

He took the four sticks and tossed them into the air. Then he felt them as they lay on the ground.

"I heard it said in the bazaars of Balkh," he uttered, "that the *Ferang* is the foe of Jani Beg, the Uzbek."

Again he laid his hands on the sticks. This time he turned to the *Ferang*. Sir Weyand waited gravely. He had not meant to make sport of the holy man. If so, I should have drawn sword against him.

"A thought has come to me," spoke Muhammad Asad. "It is this. Within the moon the *Ferang* shall be master of Jani Beg's stronghold."

That was the prophecy. It seemed to please Sir Weyand. Truly, I took it for a good omen. But he conceived of another thing. Verily, his whim was strong upon him.

"Will you render me a service, Muhammad Asad?" he inquired.

The *kwajah* bent his head.

"Ask, and I will do what I may. But I have nothing which I may give you for the act which saved the life of this boy that I found playing naked in the bazaar of Balkh."

Sir Weyand's cheeks reddened at this.

"It is not a gift," he said quickly. "You are going east where Jani Beg's forces lie?"

"Aye."

"Then go to the camp of the Uzbeks. Tell them of your prophecy. Will you do this?"

"If God wills," assented the holy man, "it shall be done."

"But do not say that you met with us."

Again Muhammad Asad agreed. It is the way of such men to be of service. I knew that he would do as he said. So, I think, did Sir Weyand. Yet I could not see how the tale would serve us.

Many things were not given to me to see. I saw not how two men—and outlaws—could make themselves masters of a walled city filled with foes. Never before or since in the annals of the Moguls had this been done.

Sir Weyand was full of his new thought.

"Ho, Adbul Dost!" he cried, setting himself sidewise in his peaked saddle to look at me. "Abdul Dost of the somber countenance and the wary glance! Ho, *mansabdar* that was, leader of a thousand horsemen in battle, champion of the scimitar, man of the Moguls, sword-bearer of Badakshan—"

"Nay," I growled, though not ill-pleased, for Sir Weyand was a merry man.

"—Entitled to the rank of triple remount, veteran of fifty onsets—what think you, Abdul Dost, we will do now?"

"God alone knows," I made reply, for there was no telling what his whim might be. "Perhaps you seek to cut Jani Beg from his men. If so, your grave will soon be dug, for the Uzbeks are skilled soldiers."

"Nay; if that were so we are riding in the wrong direction. I have seen you play at chess, Abdul Dost, on a carpet by the evening campfire. In the mimic battle of the chessboard, what is it you seek to do?"

"To capture the strong pieces of the enemy."

"Even so. Now what is the stronghold of Jani Beg?"

"Khanjut," I said bitterly, thinking of the fortress on the rock at the pass of Shyr that the Uzbeks had wrested from us.

Sir Weyand was thoughtful at this, but he shook his yellow curls.

"Nay, Abdul Dost. You, who are a soldier, think of a fortress. I, who am a merchant, a servant of my sovereign lady the queen, think otherwise."

Long after the events which were about to come had passed back into the abyss of time, I heard it said that when the Englishman spoke these words, his queen was dead and a new monarch sat the throne of the *khanate* of England. I know not. But Sir Weyand had been several years in reaching the hills of India and he had not heard from his own country for a long time.

"Think, Abdul Dost," he said; "what is the precious jewel in the turban of Jani Beg? What is the reservoir from which he draws strength? And do you remember where the caravans pass from Kashgar to Persia, from Samarkand to India?"

"Balkh," I responded unwillingly, for Khanjut was the real citadel of Badakshan, holding as it did the stores of Jani Beg and controlling the pass into India.

"Balkh!" he cried. "What else? Balkh, the ancient mother of cities. Balkh, the walled town toward which we have turned our horses' heads. Truly, I have coveted Balkh for the space of a moon.

And now we have met with Muhammad Asad, which is a brave omen."

"An omen will not give us men or weapons."

"Nay, but it will uplift our spirits." He threw back his sturdy head and laughed aloud, as a man will do who is proud of his strength. There was a twinkle in his gray eyes and his firm lips curled with delight. "You and I, Abdul Dost—the *mansabdar* and the merchant—we will capture Balkh."

Verily then I looked upon him as one who is light of wit. This was worse than I had thought.

"Nay," I said clearly, "that may not be."

Sir Weyand was but a merchant—although master of that long sword of his—while I was a leader of horsemen. How could two men seize a city, walled, and within the walls ten times a thousand men, all of whom carried swords? True, they were of every party and race—Sarts, Pathans, Persian merchants, hillmen, desertmen, and Ghils, but we were only two.

"What did Muhammad Asad prophesy?" he asked swiftly.

I had no answer to that, as the *kwajah* was a holy man. Nevertheless, I had been thinking. Wise men in the mosques have said that a holy man who fasts can perceive the thoughts of others. Perhaps Muhammad Asad did but echo the thought he had caught from Sir Weyand.

"Be there many Uzbeks in Balkh?" he asked meditatively.

"Nay; they are in the field with Jani Beg. The people of Balkh are of every race.

"Then we will seize the city."

"God writes the future in the book of fate. But it is madness to seek to write therein ourselves."

Then I told him how Balkh was like a hub, a hub in the wheel of Badakshan. Its people were traders and were very wealthy. They cared little what master they served so long as the caravans came and went. And, like ants, the riders of Jani Beg scurried over the spokes of the wheel of Badakshan. He kept in touch with the wealthy city, although his forces were pinning Shirzad Mir to the hills in the East.

We were even then in danger of discovery and death, but Sir Weyand would not listen.

"We have had an omen, Abdul Dost. And, as for fate, did not Muhammad Asad make a prophecy?"

II

Thus did the mad whim of Sir Weyand lead us to Badakshan's great city of Balkh. It was useless to argue with him. He had the stubbornness of a wild ass and the quick wit of a falcon. When I said that Shirzad Mir had ordered me to keep him from danger, he asked if I was growing old, that I feared sharp sword strokes. He cried that with the jewels and *lakh*s of rupees he had in his saddlebags he would buy me a silk carpet from Isphahan and a soft wife from Persia to comfort my old age.

When I asked how we, who were but two, and marked men, could take a walled city, he made answer in curious fashion.

"In Cathay—" by which he meant the Han Empire of China— "it is said there are dwarfs with two heads, one looking forward and one back. Thus their face will speak one tongue, and their back another. We will make ourselves two-headed and speak with two tongues. In this way we shall be masters of Balkh."

This was madness, and I made no answer except to say that there would then be four heads instead of two to place on spears at the gates of the city when Jani Beg should hear of our folly. And I paid little heed to his questions about the two great gates of Balkh which are the only entrance through the walls, and the evil bazaars wherein the hillmen find their bhang and opium and women of Persia—also the distance from Balkh to the camp of Jani Beg. It was but a day's fast ride.

I liked the venture little, although I would have risked much to attack Khanjut, because Balkh was a city of trade; and what would the bazaars and the marble palace avail us, who even then were fugitives from the power of the Mogul?

So I brooded as we rode to Balkh, keeping to the by-paths and riding at night. Sir Weyand still had a grain of sense, for he brought a dirty shepherd's *khalat* to put over his strange clothes, and a greasy turban which he bound over his cap with a grimace.

Thus it was at night that we entered the east gate of Balkh. There were no guards, for traders are slack in such matters. Nevertheless, the walls loomed over us like grim things of evil omen. No horse could jump them, and the gates could be closed.

We were like antelope walking into the nets of hunters. On each side of the gate I saw some dried heads hung in cages. Jani Beg was a hard master and he inspired submission by blood. A night-bird flew away at our approach.

At Sir Weyand's bidding, I led him to the bazaar quarter where are the caravansaries under the eastern wall. Here, there were much light and noise. The curtains over the fronts of the shops were closed, but candlelight shone through them.

The caravansaries were aglow with torches, for many hillmen had brought in sheep and skins to trade—and to steal what they might. The mud-and-thatch taverns were tumultuous with merrymaking and the laughter of light women.

Odors of musk, civet, stale wine and dirt crept into my nostrils. It was like a den of animals. And we had come into the pen.

It did not displease Sir Weyand. I had thought that he would turn back when he saw the numbers that were in Balkh. But he gazed keenly at the figures that slipped past us in the shadows. And he dismounted at a tavern somewhat back from the others—a mere roof of cane, over some carpets on which many men lay drunk with wine of Shiraz cooled by snow brought from the mountains.

I loosened my scimitar and tethered the horses well in back of the place, as I knew it was a den of the hillmen, where a man's life hangs lightly.

Still, I would not draw back, for his taunts had angered me and I had ceased to point out his folly.

Madder than ever he appeared that night. He stepped over the squatting Afghans and Ghils, heedless of the sharp looks they cast at us. The light from a few candles was bad, so they did not at first mark him for a *Ferang*. Nevertheless, they were astir with curiosity and watched while he drank in the corner he had chosen and laughed as he pointed at the harlot that had brought him his wine. Beside her toddled a Khotanese dwarf—one of the wretches that dance in the bazaars to earn the leavings of wine and meat that are tossed to them.

"A second omen, Abdul Dost," he whispered.

"Nay; it is a misshapen thing. These men have marked us. Tomorrow the word of our coming will be through the bazaars."

"Know they your face?" he asked sharply. "Are there Uzbeks here? I do not think so."

"They are not Uzbeks—" I glanced covertly around the place— "but they are masterless men who would cut your throat for a single jewel of those you carry." As I spoke, I noticed a hillman watching us. "There is one who knows me. Kur Asaf, a low-born Ghil whose name is thievery, who is an evil snake, a toad, who can not frame a word but it is a lie—"

"Good," he broke in. "Summon him hither."

If I had needed further proof of his folly, here it was. Given a glimpse of the coins and jewels the *Ferang* carried, and we should not live to be staked on Jani Beg's spears. Kur Asaf would slit our throats and bury us in the mud behind the bazaars. "Eh," he grinned as he squatted in front of us, with two yellow teeth showing through his thin mustache.

"Peace be upon the worthy Abdul Dost," he muttered unctuously—he had never taken off his shoes within a temple. "What brings the *mansabdar* to Balkh, which is the city of Jani Beg?"

I would have answered sharply, but Sir Weyand pressed my knee with his arm.

"Spoil, Kur Asaf," he smiled back.

The Ghil—may his ancestors have sorrow from his knavery— drank a bowl of rank wine to hide his surprise at sight of the *Ferang*. I think he had never seen such a man before.

"There is spoil to be had in Balkh, Kur Asaf," repeated Sir Weyand.

The hillman was at a loss. He could not guess what lay behind
Sir Weyand's words, nor why I should be with him. His curiosity
grew, and the mention of loot was like added brush to a fire.

Then Sir Weyand, before I could prevent, plucked out a double
handful of silver coins, with several good diamonds, and showed
them to Kur Asaf.

"Here is some," he said softly, "and we will gain more. I am
a merchant and I will not waste my time without profit. Abdul
Dost says that you are a shrewd man. Doubtless you have followers in the bazaars."

Kur Asaf drew a long breath at sight of the money. He peered
at Sir Weyand keenly. Truly, he knew not what to think. Nor did
I—save that my friend must be mad.

"Ten score," he said, and lied. Perhaps he had two score. He
was a power among the thieves.

"Good." Sir Weyand leaned close to him, in spite of the smell.
"I find you to my liking. Come here after sunset tomorrow night,
and we will talk together, you and I. There will be spoil for you."

The Ghil looked knowing, but he was as much at a loss as I. He
could not believe the good fortune that had brought Sir Weyand
to his hand for the plucking. I think he suspected we were spies
for Shirzad Mir. Yet the thought was strong upon him that we
might have betrayed Shirzad Mir and joined Jani Beg.

"Say nothing of our coming to other than your own men," I
cautioned him, thus arousing his curiosity further.

"We are not strangers to Jani Beg," added Sir Weyand calmly.

Was there ever such a man? It was all I could do to keep from
a grunt of surprise. I looked wise, yearning for a chance to speak
alone with Sir Weyand.

This mystified the Ghil the more.

"It shall be done," he said at length.

"Good," echoed the *Ferang*, and handed him a large diamond.
He put it in a fold of his turban, looking around to be sure he was
not observed.

As he left the tavern, Kur Asaf spoke briefly with some of the
hillmen. I guessed that he told them to watch us, and not to

harm us until he should order it. Verily, we must have aroused his curiosity.

"Kur Asaf," Weyand said thoughtfully, "will not lift weapon against us until he knows for certain what master we serve. Likewise, Abdul Dost, is it not true that he will keep the other thieves from us until then?"

He was a shrewd man, my comrade, but he had the *Ferang*'s intolerance of robber folk which I did not share, being wise in those matters.

Whereupon he said that he would sleep. Later, he added, I might do so, for I would need my strength presently. He fell into slumber while I meditated upon what had passed. I could not tell head from tail of the matter. Nevertheless, it was clear that Sir Weyand was acting upon a plan. And from this I took some comfort, not knowing at that time the gigantic folly of what was in his mind.

As he had ordered, I slept for some hours after he had wakened at dawn. Being a little wearied by the ride and more by the heat of the place, I did not arouse until after the midday prayers.

We were alone in the tavern, although men came from time to time to look in on us, and I guessed they were friends of Kur Asaf who wished to satisfy their curiosity. Our plight was that of a bullock bound.

"We will take Balkh, you and I," he said idly.

"How?" I asked.

He had no answer save a jest.

"Have you forgotten your own words? You said, Abdul Dost, that if we had two heads and they were set on the gate-posts, we would face two ways."

B'illah—he angered me! He would say no more, only cautioning me to help him make Kur Asaf believe we had much wealth to reward the Ghils with. Truly, this mattered little, for the Ghils would cut our throats as readily for a single silver coin as for many.

"Is it your thought," I asked, "that with the score of thieves we may take Balkh? That may not be. The townsmen, although merchants, are like dogs that lick the sandals of Jani Beg. And they are ten thousand with swords."

"We will not strike a sword-stroke," he made reply. Then I knew he must be touched with madness. He threw off his *khalat* and the greasy turban and washed himself. I did likewise, wishing to perform my lawful ablutions before the angel of death summoned me. Then he slumbered, and I watched until after the evening meal and sunset prayers. I heard the *mullah*s call the holy words, and the sound was as welcome as a mountain breeze in the filth of the bazaars. With darkness came various painted women and the dwarf. Guitars and tambours struck up around us. Still our tavern was empty of men, which I took for a bad sign.

Then came Kur Asaf, swaggering, and squatted down on the carpets in front of the *Ferang*. With him entered a score of men—I counted thirty, and well-armed—who stared at my comrade.

Kur Asaf waited for Sir Weyand to speak the first word. I, likewise, waited, being angry. When he spoke it was not what I thought.

"Have you kettledrums?" he asked sharply. The words had the ring of an order. Kur Asaf growled that the drums might be bought in the bazaars. Sir Weyand tossed one of the Ghils money and the man went out.

The men pressed closer at this, but Sir Weyand did not look up, nor did he move. This impressed them and they fell to talking among themselves. Their curiosity was great. Also, they were afire to learn how they could gain the more spoil—by robbing us here, or robbing others for us and keeping the reward for themselves. God has sown naught but evil thoughts in the hearts of Ghils, although they are bold men after a fashion.

They stirred and scratched uneasily as the silence grew. They were slender, dark-faced folk, dirty of dress, yet with excellent weapons. Jani Beg had many in his army, as he paid well.

"I have come as I promised," uttered Kur Asaf when the drums were brought. "And here be my men. What have you to offer us?"

"Are you afraid to take a risk?"

"Nay," replied the Ghil complacently, "we have no fear."

"Then I will divide among you a *lakh* of rupees and diamonds —one to each man. Also a handful of pearls to the one that bears my message to Shirzad Mir. You will be paid when our task is finished."

I pricked up my ears at this. As for the Ghil, he was more mystified than before. First Sir Weyand had spoken the name of Jani Beg. Now he named Shirzad Mir. The men of Balkh—even the hillmen—were little better than driven dogs that fawn upon a master. Aye, that is the curse of India—save for the Rájputs and mayhap the Pathans—that they are born to feel the yoke of a master. Kur Asaf dared not offend an envoy of Jani Beg, lord of ten thousand Uzbek swords, nor did he desire the enmity of Shirzad Mir, who loosened the arrows of vengeance swiftly, and might again be in power as he once had been.

"This is the message," continued the *Ferang* before the other could meditate fully upon the matter, "to be delivered by word of mouth. It is that Shirzad Mir should pick twenty-five score good riders and come by night to the ravine just north of the great well of Ghori."

Now, the three places of Balkh, Khanjut and the camp of Shirzad Mir make a triangle—such as is used by the astrologers— a triangle with the sides equal. And the camp of my master lay to the east of the triangle. Khanjut was to the South, and Balkh to the West.

The ravine north of the well of Ghori was just in the center of the three points. So much I knew.

"Say to Shirzad Mir," added the *Ferang*, "that I, Sir Weyand, send the message. He is to be at this place of meeting by the third watch of tomorrow night. He must not fail. By this sign he will know the message is true."

The Englishman took from his hand a ring Shirzad Mir had given him. It was a fine sapphire. Also, he dropped into the claw of the Ghil three small pearls.

"The rider who carries the word," he explained, "will have twice this number of pearls when I rejoin him at the well of Ghori."

The thought came to me that the rider would not take the message to Shirzad Mir, but to the Uzbeks, and claim a greater reward. Sir Weyand's next words showed that he had reasoned upon this also.

"The rider must go swiftly, for this matter affects Jani Beg." He lowered his voice, but not so the others could not hear. "Jani Beg's men will be in Balkh by nightfall on the morrow. There will be a tumult in Balkh, Kur Asaf, and those who are nimble of wit will not lose thereby. Aye, blood will be shed at the gates and spoil taken in the bazaars. Much hangs upon this—even the power of the Mogul."

By now Kur Asaf was groping for the meaning of this in darkness. How was he to know what we were? The *Ferang*'s words had hinted we were traitors to Shirzad Mir. Our presence in Balkh seemed to confirm this, yet the message was to Shirzad Mir.

I, also, was puzzled. Perhaps Sir Weyand meant but to deceive the Ghils. Yet why had he appointed a meeting-place with my master?

Kur Asaf whispered to one of his men and gave him two pearls. The other he kept for himself. I have keen ears and I overheard him say to deliver the message as he had heard it if he would keep his hide whole.

The Ghil scented mighty deeds, and his greed was inflamed. Whatever happened, he could slay Sir Weyand and me and take our wealth. At the same time he was sure he was aiding either Shirzad Mir or Jani Beg—he thought the Uzbeks.

Sir Weyand allowed him no time to meditate further.

"Ho, Kur Asaf," he cried, rising and stretching himself, "are you a man for a daring deed? Do you fear to take plunder from

these fat swine of merchants? Will you join forces with me and
Abdul Dost?"

Will a jackal go to the smell of meat? The Ghil's small eyes
gleamed. He would come with us, he said. Verily, he did not want
to let us escape from his sight with the *lakh* of rupees.

"Good!" cried the *Ferang* with his broad smile. "Then choose
a dozen of your men. They must ride a circuit around Balkh with
break of day. They must make a chain in the plain without the
walls and keep back any that seek to leave the town from dawn
until dark."

This promised well and the Ghil did as he was directed, counting off and dismissing twelve of his rascals. This left sixteen in
the tavern.

These Sir Weyand divided into two equal groups.

"What is it you seek to do?" asked Kur Asaf shrewdly.

"Soon you will see. Remember I do this for one who is greater
than I. You and I, Kur Asaf, will take the kettledrums and go to
the eastern gate. The other party, under Abdul Dost, will seek the
western gate. There are but two. Then we will seize the gates."

I stared, and the Ghils grunted their surprise. But I was more
surprised than they. Seize the gates of Balkh! When we were no
better than outlaws! When a day would bring an armed party
from the Uzbeks to cut us down—

But Sir Weyand had me by the arm.

"You will act as follows, Abdul Dost," he said loudly. "When
you are at the west gate, close it so only one man can slip through.
Station men outside and within. Remain without, yourself. To
those who approach Balkh from the plain, say that Shirzad Mir
has captured the city. To the townspeople within, say that Jani
Beg has closed the gates for two nights and a day."

His stern face became harder as he spoke.

"Slay any who try to force the gate!" he ordered. Then, sinking
his voice as he strode to the door of the tavern: "Take your horse.
Keep him near. Send messages by the outer riders to me as long
as all is well. By nightfall on the morrow you will hear shots.

Mount at once and ride through the town to me. Cut down any who get in your way."

His grip on my arm tightened.

"Ho," he whispered, "we are playing with death this night, you and I, Abdul Dost. But we shall be masters of Balkh."

"Nay," I whispered, thinking swiftly of many dangers.

"These be orders, Adbul Dost!" he cried roughly. "Go to your post!"

The Ghils looked at me mockingly, and I went.

III

Is any plight so uneasy as that of a man on outpost who knows not what goes on in his rear? Verily, he is like a blind, led horse which hears the noise of battle but cannot see.

And I, at the west gate of Balkh, heard battle drawing close and smelled blood in the dusty air. Aye, for at dawn people began to approach the gate. The cry of the *muezzin* had scarce silenced when women appeared in the hamlets without the walls, bearing jars to the wells; burdened donkeys passed here and there; a barking of dogs resounded, and now and then the song of a witless girl.

Aye, I smelled danger and my heart closed upon itself heavily.

We had no trouble in holding the gate. Some travelers came first on camels from the plain. These turned back in alarm when I cried that Shirzad Mir had taken Balkh. They gave the news to the hamlets, so that the women and children and donkeys began to flee away from us.

But within the walls there was more confusion and outcry. Throngs gathered in the roadway when the Ghil, standing just inside the wooden gate where I could hear what passed, said that Jani Beg had ordered the walls of the city closed.

So the high walls of Balkh were closed. The townspeople dared not force an outlet through us, fearing the name of the Uzbeks who held the reins of power in Badakshan. After a while came sundry *kwajah*s and high merchants who questioned the Ghils.

They responded as I ordered that Jani Beg had done this thing, and they must wait until after nightfall, when a party would come from the Uzbek camp to learn the why of it.

Said I not it was the fate of my people to bend the neck to a master—even to the invading Uzbeks? The Ghils swaggered, and the townspeople did not doubt—at first. In time they did so, but in time many strange things came to pass.

Then came a caravan from Herat. To them we told the same tale. Our outriders must have told Sir Weyand, at the other gate, of the caravan, for the kettledrums—which are a sign of authority—struck up loudly, and there was a great outcry.

The merchants withdrew. I saw several horsemen leave their party and strike off, around the city. I judged that they went to seek Jani Beg. Yet others must have gone before them with the news. Jani Beg would pay well for tidings that Shirzad Mir was in Balkh.

One of the Ghil outriders galloped up and told me that men had left to inform the nearest Uzbeks of what had happened before dawn. He asked if this was what we wished.

"How should it be otherwise?" I responded, putting on a bold face. "A wise man reads the writing of fate."

The man trotted off to think this over.

Thus it was that we two held the gates of Balkh. It was clear now what Sir Weyand had said about our faces being turned two ways. To the people of Balkh we seemed men of Jani Beg. To those outside we were sentries of Shirzad Mir. To the Ghils we were a mystery.

Aye, the sun climbed high and the herders brought their flocks but did not try to enter the city to the market. And we held the gates of Balkh.

At intervals the kettledrums echoed. It was a feast-day, and the noise within did much to convince those who watched from the plain that a party of Shirzad Mir was in truth in Balkh. Sir Weyand's orders—so said the Ghils who were watching the streets—had encouraged the celebration of the feast.

Presently one of the Ghils approached me where I sat by my horse and salaamed.

"The *Ferang*," he said covertly, "has sent a message to you. He asks what Jani Beg will do when he hears the news."

This speech smelled strongly of a lie. It was the Ghils, not Sir Weyand, who were waxing curious. I pondered the matter for the space milk takes to boil.

"Tell the *Ferang*," I made answer, "that Jani Beg will turn his horse's head to Balkh with the pick of his followers. Others he will leave to watch the rebel, Shirzad Mir. Still others he will send with his important stores to the citadel of Khanjut. There they will be safe while his army is removed, for Khanjut is impregnable. It is written that while water flows in the rivers of Badakshan, Khanjut will not be taken by siege."

Thus I put in his ear a small grain of truth that left him none the wiser. Yet as it proved, my judgment was true. I spoke bitterly, for the man's words had made clear that the Ghils were becoming doubtful of us. And by now the Uzbeks must be on the march toward Balkh. The Uzbeks are good fighters and ride swiftly. They would not be long in coming. And what was to become of us when they arrived?

I knew not. I sat by my horse and waited while the hours passed. Smoke appeared in the sky overhead. Looking through the opening in the gate, I saw the Khotan dwarf running about among the legs of the watching townspeople and heard him cry that the Ghils had set fire to the bazaar.

By now the outriders on the west of the town had assembled and drawn in to the gate. They talked with those of my party and looked at me.

"The Uzbeks—many hundreds of armored riders—have been sighted nearing Balkh," they said to me, and waited.

"Said I not they would come?"

But the Ghils were not content. They had had time to think. By now they had satisfied themselves that we—Sir Weyand, and I—

were not of the Uzbek party. And they were growing frightened lest Jani Beg should cut their heads from their shoulders.

I read their thoughts as clearly as a black stone shows through shallow water. They had assembled outside the gate to prevent me from escaping. They planned doubtless to slay us and take the *Ferang*'s money. Or perhaps to bind us prisoners and deliver us to Jani Beg for torture. I think if Kur Asaf had been at the west gate, swords would have been drawn by now. Yet Sir Weyand's wisdom had kept the leader of the Ghils with him, and without a leader they were slow to act against such a swordsman as I.

Still was my heart sick as the long shadows began to fall across the brown plain of Balkh.

My back was itching to be up and join Sir Weyand. It would not be long before both of us would stand before the dark angel of death, for Sir Weyand still did not give the signal, and each moment was closing the toils of the hunters about him, taking him between the oncoming Uzbeks and the Ghils. As for me, I had my orders, and never have I broken my word in order to turn my back upon peril.

I bade the Ghils fetch me clean water, and I made my ablutions. They gathered around me like vultures sitting beside a dying horse. They dared to laugh at me, sitting beside my mount. Some of the townspeople stared from the walls.

The men of Balkh had recognized the *Ferang* by now, from the walls, and I think if it had not been for the conflagration in the bazaar they would have slain us.

No man likes to look full into the pathway of death, as it opens before him. Few would have sat still as I did and waited while the shadows came closer to the walls, and twilight drew a veil over the plain.

"The Uzbeks have been sighted from the east wall, Abdul Dost," said one of the Ghils mockingly.

"Jani Beg will be well pleased to see you," added another, fingering his sword.

"There will be new heads in the cages," spoke up a third.

They edged closer, looking one at the other like curs ready to spring—if one would make the first move.

I said nothing, watching them while the glow from the fire began to light the sky overhead. My ears were pricked for sound of the shot Sir Weyand had promised, but it did not come.

"The Mogul loves not traitors," gibed one. "Is he the master you named?"

I heard a stir on the wall above the gate. The Ghils looked up uneasily, and then a shot sounded.

It is no easy feat to spring from a seat on the ground to the back of a horse; yet this is what I did that same instant.

The Ghils snatched at their swords and spread around me so that I could not ride through to the plain. This was a mistake. I wheeled my mount on two legs round to the gate and spurred through it.

Two there were who struck at me as I passed. They did not strike twice. I am not an ill master of the scimitar.

The gate was wide enough to win through. Surprise at my sudden move had kept the Ghils back, but now they were after me with loud cries.

Nevertheless, I had a start of half a bowshot, and my horse was a good one. The people in the streets drew back hastily, and I kept well ahead of the Ghils, past the palace of Balkh, past the registan and the marketplace, to the farther side of the town.

It was good to be in saddle again with a sword in my hand. I rose in my stirrups and cried loudly, and the men of Balkh gave way to stare and curse. In the dusk they could not see my face.

The glow from the fire grew stronger, showing me dark packs of thieves who were looting the bazaar where the flames had not yet come. The painted women were running about in fright. More than one body was in the alleys.

By this light I saw Sir Weyand as I neared the gate.

He was standing with his back to it, his long sword bare in his hand. He was fronting the Ghils who ringed him about.

One lay on the earth—one that I judged to be Kur Asaf. But the Ghils had Sir Weyand's horse. The sweat was shining on his face, and he was smiling as he fenced with two of the rascals, who were not overanxious to try the taste of his long sword.

Yet he had an eye for what went on around him.

"Ho, Abdul Dost," he cried angrily, as his blade made play, "you are late—almost—" the Ghils drew back at the sound of horses' hoofs—"too late."

Uncertainty in a battle is a two-edged sword. The Ghils did not know who was on the horses they heard. When they saw me and others behind me they sprang back warily. Men of that breed are ever mindful of their own skins.

"To me, Abdul Dost!" cried the *Ferang* impatiently.

I spurred forward, while he pulled at the gate to open it. An angry shout came from the pursuers behind me, and the Ghils plucked up heart. A pistol echoed from near at hand—then another.

My horse quivered under me and stumbled. He had been hit and sorely hurt. I sprang from the saddle, lest he fall upon me, and he ran to one side, neighing and plunging blindly as he went. It was a stroke of bad luck.

The Ghils were running toward us now, mounted and afoot, taking courage from the fact that we were but two and unhorsed. I could hear Sir Weyand's heavy breathing. The scene was bright with the flames at one side of the gate, but on the outer side of the wall darkness reigned.

"The Uzbeks are within bowshot of the gate," the *Ferang* called to me, and I thought that our fate had come upon us.

But he wasted no time in thought. Plucking the pistol from my girdle, he discharged it at the nearest Ghil, who coughed and dropped to his knees.

"*Shirzad el kadr!*" Sir Weyand cried our battle-shout, and I echoed it, turning with bared weapon to face the Ghils. A third shout came from the Uzbeks at some distance on the farther side of the wall.

Verily, it was a tight place. The Ghils were coming forward slowly, being wary lest we have another pistol. I felt a tug at my arm. Without turning, I stepped back one pace and then another.

I felt my shoulders scrape through what seemed to be beams of wood. Then the light and the Ghils were blotted out in darkness.

Sir Weyand had opened the wooden gate enough to slip through and had pulled me after him. Then he had closed the gate. He was a strong man.

Said I not it was dark without the wall? We were in its shadow. But the glow from the flaming bazaar lit up the countryside faintly.

I saw a body of horsemen coming along the road at a walk. And behind them the light glittered on hundreds of spears and swords. Among the leaders I thought I saw the broad figure of Jani Beg.

They could not see us, for we were in the blackness of the wall. All they had seen was that two men on foot had appeared for an instant in the crack of the door, and they had other things to think about. They thought that Shirzad Mir and his men were in Balkh.

Aye, they came forward slowly. They were no cowards, but within the wall where a tumult echoed might be the army of Shirzad Mir. Meanwhile Sir Weyand and I were running to one side, keeping in the gloom of the wall.

My lungs were near to bursting with the effort, when Sir Weyand checked me. The gate of Balkh was opening slowly. We could not see it pulled back, but we saw the light grow as it opened.

Slowly, slowly the square of the gate became light. I had no great fear that the Ghils would rush out. They could not wish to face the angry Jani Beg.

But the leading Uzbeks halted their horses, and I heard a mutter spread through their ranks. And the skin grew cold along my spine.

In the red light of the fire a figure appeared in the gate of Balkh. It strutted and cried and gibbered. It laughed wildly and fell to dancing.

There in the roadway was the dwarf of Khotan, inspired by the madness of what was happening. The red flames flickered on his grotesque figure as he flung his arms about in the dance.

We did not linger to watch. When we had gained the bushes where the conflagration no longer lighted us we ran toward one of the hamlets near the wall.

I knew the place, by the will of God. And before an hour had passed I had found two good horses which we paid for with jewels.

By now there was a cry raised after us from within Balkh, and the Uzbek riders were out seeking us.

But it was not our fate that we should die that night. The stars were bright overhead and we left Balkh behind us, feeling the fresh night air in our faces.

"Ride to the well of Ghori!" said Sir Weyand harshly. "We are late. Shirzad Mir is waiting for us. As I thought, the prophecy of Muhammad Asad and the news from Balkh has brought Jani Beg and his army hither, but ride! Eh, Abdul Dost, we must be in Ghori by midnight!"

By sheep-paths and cuts through the plain I took him to Ghori and past that village to the well. Was this not my own country? At places we were seen. Yet the villagers had love for Shirzad Mir in their hearts, and they speeded us on.

It did not seem fitting that we should kill two horses in needless haste, yet when I said this to Sir Weyand—now that our skins were safe—he stormed at me. Aye, so I fell silent, and rode in the dark without regard to beast or man.

Once we gained a remount at a friendly village. By this, and the hand of God, we passed the well of Ghori at midnight. We passed the well and drew up at a sharp challenge beyond.

The challenge had come in our own tongue, and I answered gladly. A rider came out of the shadows and led us on our quivering horses to where Shirzad Mir and his *ameer*s and *mansabdar*s sat their horses at a crossroad. Along the road the men of Shirzad Mir, to the number of more than a thousand, sat by their mounts, ready and waiting.

My master had kept the time and place of the meeting. Likewise he held prisoner the Ghil we had sent.

And then I saw that I had been blind. Aye, for Sir Weyand and Shirzad Mir talked together the space of a moment and the whole of our men were set in motion. With Sir Weyand at our head we went forward at a fast trot, which is the most swiftly a body of men can move in the night.

What we did that night is written in the annals of Badakshan. We rode until the morning mists were turning gray with dawn and we could see one another's eyes. We rode away from Balkh while the army of Jani Beg held that city. We rode to Khanjut.

Aye, we entered the citadel of Badakshan, the stronghold of our country, at dawn. The gates were open for the scattered parties of Uzbeks who were bringing in the stores, the bulkier treasure and the women of Jani Beg. At Khanjut none suspected we were anywhere save at Balkh.

In the mists we entered Khanjut, the citadel on the rock that has never been taken by storm. This was what Sir Weyand had planned.

And then a thought came to me. I spoke of the thought to Shirzad Mir, who gave praise to the mercy of God; and I spoke likewise to Sir Weyand, who laughed after his fashion, and said nothing.

My thought was that the prophecy of Muhammad Asad had come true.

Rose Face

Where is the man who knows what is hidden in the heart of a woman?

Muslim proverb

My master and Jani Beg, the Uzbek, had been at drawn swords. Jani Beg had built a tower of the skulls of my master's retainers that he had slain. On the other hand, Shirzad Mir, who was my master, had taken prisoner the son of Jani Beg, who was called Said Afzel, the dreamer and eater of opium and bhang.

Verily, it is written that the clashing of bright swords delights the soul of a brave man. Yet in this year—early in the seventeenth century of the Christian calendar—Jani Beg put aside the sword. He took up another weapon. He called upon Krishna Taya, a girl of the Rájputs.

This was because we, the hillmen of Badakshan, led by Shirzad Mir and the English merchant, Sir Weyand, had taken the citadel of Badakshan. It was by a trick, but nevertheless we sat securely behind the high stone walls of Khanjut and ate of the stores Jani Beg had gathered there for himself, and we were content. He could not take Khanjut by storm. No man has done that since the citadel was built under the white peaks of Kohi-Baba at the mouth of the pass that leads to Hindustan.

So Jani Beg, who was a man of guile, thought that he, also, would play a trick. And for this he chose Krishna Taya. He whispered an evil thing in the tiny ear of the girl, and she listened. Since the memory of our fathers, woman has played the part of treachery and her beauty has made blind the eyes of warriors.

Aye, it is so. I, Abdul Dost, the *mansabdar*, have seen it. And I watched the coming of Krishna Taya and harkened to her soft words, which were as artless as those of a child. Too late I saw what was in her heart.

She was the one Sir Weyand named "Rose Face." She was no taller than the armpit of my mail shirt and no bigger around than two small shields joined together. She was not a common courtesan, for she was of the Rájputs, who hold honor higher than life. Nevertheless, what is written is true—the face of a fair woman holds a spell.

I saw it all. It could not have happened had we and our men not been idle in Khanjut after many labors. We had starved and grown lean in the hills. Now we ate and slept. At such a time a warrior grows sluggish and his wits become dull and the sight of a shapely woman is not unwelcome.

This is the tale. There be few to tell it, for many in Khanjut died quickly and went to paradise or to the devil, after the coming of Krishna Taya.

The days had become still and the warmth of the sun tranquil, as Autumn spread its arms over the hills of Badakshan. The sheep from the hills were pasturing in the valley as Jani Beg, in his camp at Balkh, sought out the tent of Krishna Taya. I was not there to see, but much I heard from one of the eunuchs of Said Afzel, and more came to my ears from a woman of the Uzbek harem.

Krishna Taya was no better than a slave. Said Afzel had seen her when he was with the Mogul, and Jahangir, the Mogul, had her carried off to please the prince, since Said Afzel's father was Jani Beg, who commanded twelve thousand swords and twice that number of horses.

She was playing with pigeons in a pear garden when they took her. She had come from the Rájputs. There she had been a free woman and high-born, yet Jahangir was Mogul of India, lord of the Deccan, Kashmir and Sind. She was given as slave to Said Afzel, who was well pleased, for she was fair of face and body. Many thought—so said the eunuch—that Krishna Taya would slay herself, being of the Rájputs, where no women may be slaves.

Whether it was because she was a child, or for another reason, I know not, but Krishna Taya did not thrust a dagger into her throat. She became the property of Said Afzel and said little, waxing thinner of face as dark circles came under her calf-like eyes.

Said Afzel tired of her swiftly. Those who eat much opium are not firm of purpose. He left her in the tents of the Uzbek harem, where she was dressed in the white silk trousers and cap of cloth-of-silver that the Uzbek women wear. Said Afzel's eunuchs kept her from meeting with the Rájputs who sometimes came from the camp of Jahangir, fearing that they might do her harm. By the law of the Marwar, no high-born woman may be a slave to an enemy.

Krishna Taya had broken this law. She had not done as her ancestors, who dressed in their bridal clothes and followed the queen of the Rájputs into the funeral flames when Chitore fell to the enemy.

Yet—so the eunuch whispered—she was but a child and might well fear the cold touch of death. Likewise, she ate opium, which kept her quiet and wrought upon her fancies. She had been partaking of it when Jani Beg visited her.

He sat on the carpet by her and talked. He was a shrewd man and her brain was aflame with the drug.

"The *Ferang* is the shield on the arm of Shirzad Mir," he said. "He is like to a devil loosed from the Christian purgatory. Without him, Shirzad Mir would fare ill at our hands. He it was who took my son prisoner."

She lifted up her soft eyes at this and plucked at the cap which she wore instead of the veil of her people.

"Yet he is his own man," continued Jani Beg. "He serves himself. None other. What reward he seeks I know not, save that he has sworn to obtain certain trade concessions from the great Mogul. Jahangir will not see him so long as he fights with the rebels of Shirzad Mir."

Aye, Jani Beg, who was an Uzbek of low birth, dared to name Shirzad Mir, whose father and father's father ruled in Badakshan, a rebel.

"Mayhap," whispered Jani Beg, "Sir Weyand does not know that I am allied to the Mogul. If he knew this—" Jani Beg smiled—"I might forget certain wrongs he has done me. Aye, and Jahangir might also forget, for the Mogul has counted the swords I lead. Say this to the *Ferang*—"

"How?" asked Krishna Taya softly.

The woman of the harem was listening behind the hangings of the tent and heard what passed.

"It is in my mind," said Jani Beg, stroking his long beard, "to send a present to this *Ferang* dog. He is a merchant, and when did a merchant mis-like the sight of gold? I will send a Persian sword with gold hilt, certain rubies, and woven cloth-of-gold. I will send—" he touched the long hair of the girl, and Krishna Taya's cheeks grew red—"you."

The girl was silent, being afraid to speak.

"The *Ferang*," went on Jani Beg, "has a heart for fighting. But now there is a truce. I have willed it so. The men of Shirzad Mir think I am weak." He laughed and closed his hand on the girl's arm so her fingers became numb. "As for you, be not so blind. I am master of Badakshan, a frontier of the Mogul. I can ask and receive much, and I seek much." He broke off to finger his beard again. "Win me the *Ferang*; aye, win me Sir Weyand. I reward those who serve me."

He unwound a long string of small pearls from his turban, where he had placed it in imitation of the Mogul fashion. This he laid about her throat and peered at her curiously.

"Can my words aid you, my lord?" she said, feeling the pearls with a trembling hand.

"Aye," smiled Jani Beg. "Put this thought in his head and you will serve me well."

"How?"

His brows knit together in a swift frown. He plucked forth his dagger and, so quickly that she had no time to draw back, passed the blade before both her eyelids, which fluttered in alarm. So near came the blade that it touched the skin. So said the woman who saw.

"Are you a *begum*—a wife of a noble—to question my words? So! Tell me in one word. Will you do this thing faithfully? If not—" His glance strayed to the dagger.

Perhaps he would have liked to slay her, for the blood lust was strong in him. I have seen Said Afzel, who was his son, wring the neck of a white pigeon in order to feel the life quiver out through his fingers. Nevertheless, Jani Beg was an excellent soldier and full of guile.

He had stirred the girl.

"Aye," she cried, looking wide-eyed at the dagger, "I will sever the prop from him who seeks the throne of Badakshan!"

"It is well," he said indifferently and rose. "Say what I have told you."

He lowered his voice, so the woman behind the curtain did not hear. Presently he laughed in his beard.

"So, Krishna Taya! Soon six men will stand alone together but, before they part, they shall be four and two."

This is what they said in the tent of Krishna Taya that night. I did not hear of it until long after—until what Jani Beg had promised had come to pass and ten thousand Uzbeks were storming the walls of Khanjut.

II

It was a late watch in the afternoon and I was drowsy, for the sun was warm on the stones of Khanjut and no wind stirred in the dried leaves of the poplar trees that fringed the garden of the castle.

Past the corner where I sat on my heels one of the hillmen bore a jar. He had come from the cellars of the castle and I suspected there was wine in the jar, so I rose and followed silently.

Truly, I was a follower of the prophet, but my thirst was great. Where there was wine, I knew there would be drinking. I dogged the hillman past the battlements to the center garden. He went down some steps and I did likewise.

I came full upon my lord, Shirzad Mir, and the Englishman, lying on some pleasant carpets under the trees. The bearer was just setting down the jar between them. Said Afzel was nearby, lying at full length.

"Ho, Abdul Dost!" cried Shirzad Mir, who had a quick eye. "You have come like a dog at the smell of meat in the pot. Nay, do not leave us. Come, here is another bowl. Said Afzel will not need his. He is rightly named the dreamer; he has taken opium until he is like a full-fed snake."

I looked at the Uzbek. His head was slack on the carpet, crushing the white heron plume on the turban. His olive face was red and he breathed heavily, while his slant eyes were glazed. They looked at me but seemed to see not. Truly they were like those of a snake. A snake that smelled of musk and attar of rose.

"Peace be unto you, my lord!" I greeted Shirzad Mir, and sat. "I do not seek the wine."

"A lie!" cried Sir Weyand jovially, shaking his yellow head. "Come, let me fill your bowl, Abdul Dost."

But I would not, as it would put me in the wrong. Then there came a soldier from the gate.

"A message comes for the lord *Ferang*," he said, after his salaam. We saw coming toward us under the trees a fat eunuch leading a slim girl by the wrist, and after them a white horse of excellent breed. The saddle cloths were silk and there were jewels in the peak of the saddle. A scimitar with gold hilt and some rich stuffs were on the saddle. I stared and Sir Weyand sat up and looked at this curiously.

The eunuch dropped to his knees and made the triple salaam, beating his head against the ground. The girl, who was veiled, fell also to her knees.

"What means this?" asked Shirzad Mir in surprise.

"It is a small, a very small gift from the treasury of Jani Beg, O lord of Badakshan and descendant of illustrious ancestors, O most munificent Shirzad Mohammed el Baber Hazret Mir," whined the eunuch.

"Ho!" muttered my master, who was not slow of wit. "Jani Beg sends me a horse and sword that I may mount and fight him. Then I will send back a silk rug of Persia and a spindle, for he seems more inclined to sit in a corner than to fight—"

"Thrice blessed, pardon!" the eunuch chattered. "The gift is for the *Ferang*. It is for the illustrious stranger in our country. Jani Beg does not wish to be thought an ungenerous foe."

"For me!" Sir Weyand looked from the eunuch to the girl and then to the horse.

"Aye, may it be pleasant in the sight of your nobleness! Truly, the woman is of the Rájputs and surpassingly fair. I have guarded her with zeal. There is not a blemish on her—"

"Please!"

Sir Weyand's cheeks became red. Shirzad Mir began to laugh.

"Jani Beg honors you with a wife," he chuckled. "Now that you have taken Khanjut, he sends you a slave."

I did not laugh, considering what this might mean. The eunuch plucked the veil from the woman's face, enough to show her beauty.

"It is a slave," he boasted. "And such a slave. I will take good care of her for my lord the *Ferang*. I like not the service of Jani Beg."

He caught sight of Said Afzel and gasped. The poet's heavy eyes had turned slowly to the girl and he was twisting his thick black beard. The miserable guardian of the harem quivered in fright like a fish caught between two nets.

But Sir Weyand looked long into the dark eyes that sought his and fell silent.

"She is not ill to look upon," commented Shirzad Mir gravely. "Jani Beg is unusually thoughtful. I would have said this woman was chosen by Said Afzel, if we had him not prisoner for the last moon."

"A royal gift to one who deserves it, lord," whined the eunuch, who thought this, at least, was safe to say.

"And are you also a royal present?" demanded my master quickly.

"Nay," the fat one salaamed. "I am but dirt from a dunghill."

"Do we deserve dirt?"

"Nay," the unhappy man wriggled, fearing that his death was near, but voluble after his kind. "I meant that I was but a servant who had come to a garden of paradise from a swine-pen."

"From the Uzbeks?" The merry eyes of Shirzad Mir twinkled.

The eunuch lifted his head long enough to see that Said Afzel was listening.

"Have mercy, lord! What was in my mind was that your presence has made me blessed, like one who comes from darkness to light. Now that I know the gift of the illustrious Jani Beg has been well received—"

"Enough!"

Shirzad Mir frowned. He whispered to Sir Weyand that a eunuch was a breeder of trouble.

"Get to your feet, O dunghill-that-came-to-the-garden-of-paradise! Abdul Dost, go to the battlements and take up the first bow that comes to hand. This dog may now begin to run out of the gate. Bring him down with an arrow, if you can, from the wall. If not, he goes free."

He waved his hand and the fat man galloped off like a frightened elephant. I, also, made speed to the wall. I would have been well content to plant a shaft in his haunches.

But when I gained the battlement he was far below me. He had rolled from the winding road down the slope of the cliff. His bones must have been well shaken; still, he saved his life.

So it happened that when I reached the spot under the trees again, all were gone but the soldier, who was taking a drink from the jar. I upbraided him well, for I had remembered the jar and was still thirsty.

He said the girl had fallen to weeping and Sir Weyand had softened to her tears when she cried that it would be her death to send her back to Jani Beg.

The *Ferang* had offered her a room in his residence. The horse and sword he had presented to Shirzad Mir, who had taken them readily, saying that he would ride the one and cut off Jani Beg's head with the other.

But I was not content, knowing it was not wonted that a woman of the Rájputs should consent to be a slave.

I dismissed the man. There was still some wine in the jar and no one was looking.

So the girl of the Rájputs came to Khanjut.

But I knew that any gift from Jani Beg was not meant for our happiness. I sent the soldier who had drunk from my jar of wine— Bihor Jan, a long-legged Afghan with nimble wits and a quick ear—to Sir Weyand to serve as a guard for the woman. Thus Bihor Jan would tell me what she did.

A day passed and then another. Then I sought out Bihor Jan, who was squatting on the stone of the entrance hall of the castle. I asked him what had passed between the woman and Sir Weyand.

"Eh!" The Afghan spat and looked about him. "The *Ferang* has seen her but once. It was when she carried his curry and wine from the kitchen to his room."

"What did Sir Weyand?"

"The *Ferang*? What you or I would have done, Abdul Dost. He ate of the food."

"And the woman?"

"She said in a soft voice, so I could scarce hear, although the door was open, that she was his slave. She asked why he turned his face from her service."

"What said he?"

"He became red and said that in his country they had no slaves. He did not wish her to wait upon him."

That was well, so far. But before long the Afghan came to my room—an alcove opening from that of Shirzad Mir—and greeted me. I saw from his dark face that he had news on his stomach and invited him to kneel and eat, as I was doing.

This he did readily, scooping up in his dirty fingers some choice sugared fruit that I had selected for myself.

"This day," he grunted between mouthfuls, "Krishna Taya seated herself by the embrasure of the *Ferang*'s room and waited for his arrival. When he came she salaamed and cried that her heart was troubled with loneliness."

He took up the bowl of jelly for which I had been about to reach. Now that it was too late, I pretended that I did not want the jelly.

"She was lonely with desire for her own country. She asked the *Ferang* if he would help her to get back to Rájputana. Then he questioned her concerning the Rájputs and their alliance with the Mogul. I could not hear what they said after that, though I sat with my back to the door. But the name of Jani Beg was spoken."

From this time forth I sometimes saw Sir Weyand walking about the garden with the woman. They talked much, for she was trying to teach him the language of the Rájputs and he was anxious to learn.

How is a man to scent danger in the perfume of a woman's robes or the quick glance of dark eyes?

Once, when they had been sitting under the bare pomegranates, I watched her walk back to the castle. She carried herself proudly, for all she was a slave.

"Eh, Sir Weyand," I said curiously, "she is fair. Jani Beg sent you a princely gift."

"Nay, I know not what to do with her, Abdul Dost," he said quickly. "Jani Beg will not take her back, nor will her own people, now that she is under the cloud of dishonor. "

"Why not sell her? It would not be hard to find a buyer."

"That I will not do—unless it should be her will."

Truly, the *Ferang* had a strange nature The woman embarrassed him; he would not let her serve him and wait on him; yet he would not take a round sum for her or even sell the fine necklace she wore.

Then I saw he was frowning, looking out under the trees. I also looked and noted that the Uzbek prince had stopped her. Said Afzel was leaning close and whispering, fingering the pearls at her throat, for he knew not we watched.

She listened to what the Uzbek said, but when the poet laid hand on her arm, she freed herself and ran off into the building.

"Once," I whispered, wishing to test the *Ferang*, "Said Afzel owned Krishna Taya. He it was who took her for a slave against the law of her people. Perhaps she loves Said Afzel."

He looked at me keenly.

"Think you so, Abdul Dost?"

"Aye," I lied; "why else did she not slay herself, as is the custom of her people after an injury that they cannot avenge?"

He fell silent, but the look he cast after the languid figure of the Uzbek was not friendly. I thought of the verses in the Koran which say that fire, once kindled, is put out with difficulty. Why had the *Ferang* named the girl Rose Face if his heart had not warmed to her?

For the moment all thought of the girl was driven from my mind. Bihor Jan approached and said that Shirzad Mir demanded my presence.

A rider had been sighted in the plain before the citadel. He had made signs to our outposts that he was on a mission of peace and would speak with those in Khanjut.

It was Shirzad Mir's order that I should mount and ride to meet this man. I donned a clean tunic over my mail and wrapped a white turban about my head. I chose a good sword and a sightly horse.

While the others watched from the wall, I passed down the cliff road, over the drawbridge and neared the rider. Then I saw that it was Raja Man Singh, one of the highest *ameer*s of the Mogul court and general to Jahangir himself, also leader of the Rájputs.

He was very elegantly dressed, with a jeweled sword stuck through his girdle and a single large diamond on the front of his turban. He rode excellently well and seemed quite fearless. He had a neatly combed black beard divided on each side of his chin, and his glance was that of a man of many followers.

Raja Man Singh greeted me in soft Persian, somewhat contemptuously. I did not dismount, despite his high rank, for I considered myself the emissary of Shirzad Mir. Besides, I was the older man.

I lifted my hand to my forehead and bent my head very slightly. I waited for him to speak my own tongue, as I knew not Persian. This he presently did.

"Have you learned manners among the dogs, soldier," he cried harshly, "that you know not the courtesy due an *ameer* of the Mogul?"

"Nay, Raja Man Singh," I made response, "I was bred in the camp of the great Mogul Akbar, on whom be peace. There I also was given rank—on the battlefield."

His horse was moving restlessly, but he did not sit the less straight for this. He was a splendid horseman and a soldier among many. It surprised me that he had come alone to Khanjut. Later, however, the thought came to me that he was but just arrived from Jahangir's army and sought to look upon the strength of the fortress.

"The greater shame to be a rebel now!" He cried with all the intolerance of his race.

"Nay," I said again, "Shirzad Mir has been faithful to the Moguls before the barbarian Uzbeks set foot in Badakshan."

He merely grunted, fingering his beard disdainfully.

"Take me then to Shirzad Mir," he ordered, "since I come on a mission of truce."

"Shirzad Mir bade me bring the message to him, not the messenger."

"Dog!" he gritted his white teeth. "Am I one to exchange words with such as you? Tell your master that Jani Beg would speak with him. The Uzbek *ameer* will ride to this spot when the sun is at noon. He and I will be alone. Let Shirzad Mir come hither with one man—no more. We seek a parley, not war—at present. Let him come or not, as suits him. I care not."

Wheeling his mount, the Rájput spurred away, raising a cloud of dust. He was a fearless man, although merciless.

III

It is the wisdom of God that no man can know the fate in store for him. It was our fate that we should not see the black cloud of peril rising over Khanjut, or the toils of the snare that closed about Shirzad Mir.

My men gambled and ate and were happy thinking of insulting things to say to the Uzbek patrols that sometimes neared our walls, and I, also, would have been happy, but for Krishna Taya.

I could not linger, yet I whispered a word of caution to Bihor Jan as I rode off with Shirzad Mir to meet with our foes.

If the Rájput had not been with Jani Beg, we would not have gone. But the Rájput was a man of his word, as was Shirzad Mir.

I was proud of my lord as he cantered to meet the other two. Jani Beg, who was there first, thought to impose a hardship on my lord by dismounting and sitting upon his cloak. Thus he hoped to make Shirzad Mir approach him on foot as an inferior in rank. Raja Man Singh, impatient of such pettishness, kept to his horse.

But my master saw through the artifice. He cantered straight up to the sitting Uzbek and he did not dismount. He reined in his horse only when its hoofs were fair upon the silk cloak of Jani Beg. In spite of himself the Uzbek drew back and scowled.

I turned my head to hide a smile and I saw the Rájput's beard twitch. He and Shirzad Mir greeted each other briefly. Jani Beg was made to look ridiculous, squatting beneath our horses' legs, so he rose and mounted, and I saw the pulse in his forehead beating. I, being inferior in rank, made the salaam from the saddle, which is not customary, yet I followed the example of Shirzad Mir and he cast me an approving glance.

"We have come, Shirzad Mir," said Raja Man Singh, "to arrange certain terms between the Uzbeks and the rebels. Jani Beg desires to treat for the ransom of his son."

The Uzbek chieftain looked darkly at the general of the Mogul. He would have liked better to play with words, but the Rájput was impatient.

"We—" Jani Beg waved his lean hand toward the Rájput— "will offer you a continuation of the truce you desire if you will release Said Afzel and his personal followers."

Again Shirzad Mir smiled.

"Is the truce of our seeking, Jani Beg? Nay, you have chosen it. For my part, I shall not rest from fighting until Badakshan is free from invaders."

"Then you will continue to rebel against the Mogul?"

"Nay. Badakshan is part of the Mogul Empire. I fight only with Uzbeks."

"Yet I and my men are serving the Mogul. And you see Raja Man Singh."

Shirzad Mir did not smile this time.

"Let the Rájput give heed to this," he said slowly. "Lies have been spoken against me in court, and I have taken up the sword of vengeance against the author of those lies. My quarrel is not with the Mogul. When the fighting is ended, he shall receive my allegiance."

They were bold words, spoken by an outlawed chieftain with only a handful of hillmen opposed to the Uzbek Army, which possessed powder and artillery and was strengthened by a force of the invincible Rájput cavalry. I held my head high with pride and listened keenly. Jani Beg began to speak words of another color.

"You have an ally, Shirzad Mir," he observed shrewdly, "a *Ferang*. You owe him much. Tell him, as ransom for my son, I will procure his pardon from Jahangir, who is at Kabul, and also an audience with Jahangir. Thus he may obtain the trade rights he seeks, for England."

Truly, the guile of the Uzbek was great. If Shirzad Mir should refuse this offer, it must offend Sir Weyand. Should my master keep the offer secret from the *Ferang*, Jani Beg would find means of getting the news to the Englishman's ears. Yet both Shirzad Mir and I knew that it would not do to give up Said Afzel for a promise of Jani Beg.

Shirzad Mir fingered his beard thoughtfully. Then he turned to the elegant figure of the Rájput.

"Do you also pledge your word, Raja Man Singh," he asked courteously, "that this privilege will be granted the *Ferang* and that he will not be harmed?"

Jani Beg had spoken cleverly. He knew that we could ill afford to lose the services of Sir Weyand, but the Rájput cherished the righteousness of his spoken pledge as a woman guards her honor.

"Nay," he cried, "this is not my affair. I have no authority to give a promise for Jahangir. Settle the matter between yourselves."

I pricked up ears at that, for it sounded as if the Rájput were not overfond of the Uzbek. Jani Beg had hinted that the two were as brothers. The Uzbek frowned slightly; then his brow cleared. He smiled with thick lips.

"I will give up Balkh as ransom for my son."

When he said that, I saw the Rájput's brows twitch in involuntary surprise. The thought came to me that Jani Beg was offering more than he intended to pay. Shirzad Mir was not one to be caught by such a trap.

"Nay," he said pleasantly. "Does a falcon give up its perch to strut on the ground where are many wolves? Keep Balkh—if you can."

By now Raja Man Singh was waxing restless. His handsome face was petulant.

"Shiva—and Shiva!" he cried. "Name the rebel a price, Jani Beg. I am thirsty. Give him a camel-load of gold!"

He lifted some grains of brown powder from a jeweled box that hung at his throat and placed them on his tongue. Jani Beg thought swiftly. He had no wish to exasperate the Rájput.

"Two *lakh*s of rupees and twenty horses of Arabia—" he began, when Shirzad Mir broke in.

"We have no need of such." He turned to the Rájput. "Give me twelve donkeys heavily loaded with powder and two others bearing camel-swivels, also twenty-four good matchlocks and as many braces of Turkish pistols, and you shall have Said Afzel."

The Rájput seemed to be about to refuse. Powder and cannon—even such small pieces of brass—were beyond price in Badakshan, and I judge that the swivels belonged to Raja Man Singh himself. Sir Weyand had said that there were many in the Mogul's army, although the Uzbeks had them not.

But Jani Beg cast him a glance.

"It is well," the Uzbek said swiftly. "Two days we must have to make ready the things. We will then bring them to this place when the sun is at the same hour."

"The beasts of burden must be driven by a half-dozen unarmed men on foot," bargained Shirzad Mir.

"Aye. And Said Afzel must be unharmed."

"Not a scratch will be on his skin. He shall be whole, although probably drunk, as is his custom."

So it was agreed. Jani Beg's party, including the beasts with the ransom, would ride to this spot in the plain. We would come forth to meet them. Then, while we still held Said Afzel and any who came to attend him, the men who drove the beasts would retire to the Uzbek lines. Then we would join Jani Beg's party and deliver the prisoner and they would ride away, leaving us the animals with their valuable burden.

"I will come alone with Raja Man Singh," added Jani Beg. "And you will bring only Sir Weyand."

Shirzad Mir was surprised and hesitated. I was angered that I should not accompany my lord, as was my hereditary right,

but Jani Beg said smoothly that both he and the Rájput desired
to look upon the *Ferang*, and Shirzad Mir assented, saying only
that in case Said Afzel was drunk I should be allowed to escort
his litter down to the meeting place and should remain ten spear
lengths distant. He asked this because it was my right by custom.

"Likewise—" and he looked at the Rájput, not at Jani Beg—
"this thing shall be done in peace and the curse of God be on the
man who sets hand to sword. I pledge this for myself and those
with me."

Then I noted that Jani Beg spoke swiftly before the Rájput.

"Aye, we trust you, Shirzad Mir."

Whereupon both wheeled their horses and made off. Not however, before I saw a gleam of satisfaction on the Uzbek's hawk-like
face. For some secret reason he was well pleased with the bargain.
The thought came to me that he was using the Rájput's honor as
a shield and that Shirzad Mir had got too readily what he asked.

Jani Beg glanced back shrewdly over his shoulder as he rode,
but the Rájput, who was a fearless man, looked neither to right
nor left. In spite of my foreboding, my heart swelled at the
thought of possessing the powder and the brass cannon.

"Eh, Abdul Dost," cried my lord, "we have strengthened
mighty Khanjut at the price of an opium-guzzling animal."

And think as I would, the bargain seemed safe to me, notwithstanding my distrust of Jani Beg. Sir Weyand and my lord would be
alone with Jani Beg and the Rájput. If swords should, by chance,
be drawn, the odds would be even and I should not be far distant.
Men have said I am an excellent hand with the scimitar. Likewise, there was the honor of Raja Man Singh, who would not
draw the first sword, although in a quarrel he would be forced to
side with Jani Beg. As for Said Afzel, he could not lift a weapon.

A change had come upon Sir Weyand. He fell moody and he
seemed to avoid Shirzad Mir and me. Bihor Jan reported that he
talked long and quietly with Krishna Taya and at other times
walked by himself on the ramparts.

This was not wonted, for, when himself, the *Ferang* was a merry man, although not fond of words. Once I asked him if the devil of illness had gripped him.

"I know not what devil it is, Abdul Dost," he made reply. "There is a matter lies heavily on my mind. It is not always easy to settle what is right and what is wrong."

He spoke with seeming frankness, yet the words had a strange ring. He turned on me suddenly.

"Is it true, Abdul Dost, that Jani Beg offered to give me a safe conduct to Jahangir?"

I started, for how could the news have come to him?

"The words of Jani Beg are false as a wolf's whine," I replied after thinking upon the matter. "If he made an offer, he did not mean to keep it. When Shirzad Mir gives his pledge of friendship, he will abide by it."

"I doubt it not!" he muttered. "It is long since I came to India, yet I am no nearer the ear of Jahangir than at first. I cannot forget my mission—"

He broke off and walked away.

There came Bihor Jan, on the *Ferang*'s footsteps, and whispered to me in passing.

"Rose Face is beloved."

"Ho!" I was surprised "The *Ferang*?"

"I know not. I have watched Said Afzel. The poet's eyes follow the girl when she walks by and there is a gleam in them. He plays to her on a guitar, lying at her side, and strokes the pearls of the necklace she wears. Sir Weyand likes it not. Why should he waste thought on the woman?"

Perhaps Bihor Jan would have liked the necklace of pearls for himself. For many hours I considered the matter. The *Ferang* had known of the offer of Jani Beg, yet neither Shirzad Mir nor I had spoken of it.

God has strengthened the walls of Khanjut. I did not think any spy of the Uzbeks had climbed within them, so the thought came to me that someone had known the offer was to be made. Perhaps Said Afzel, perhaps Krishna Taya and perhaps Sir Weyand.

Here was a horse that would require grooming. I went to Sir Weyand and spoke what was on my mind. How was I to know that I blundered?

"The girl distresses you, Sir Weyand," I said bluntly. "Why not give her to Said Afzel? Then she will have a master. It is true that you do not desire a slave."

"Death's life, Abdul Dost!" he swore. "It is true." He fell silent. "That might be best. Krishna Taya must be cared for. I think Said Afzel is fond of her. She is no more than a child."

I did not smile.

So it came to pass that Krishna Taya consented to serve Said Afzel. She gathered up her belongings in a bundle and went to the dwelling of the Uzbek prince.

Yet that night I found Sir Weyand walking moodily the length of her room, which was now empty as a year-old nightingale's nest. I think it was the first time he had been there. The room smelled of attar of rose, after the manner of a woman's apartment. I did not speak to him, for his face was not pleasant.

Nevertheless, I considered it was well. Now that Krishna Taya was with the Uzbek, she would not bother Sir Weyand—nor would it be so easy for her to talk with him.

I kept thinking of the meeting with Jani Beg which was to take place the next day. There seemed to be no danger. The plain before the castle was bare and no followers of the Uzbeks could approach the spot without being seen from the battlements. Since I was old enough to shoot an arrow at a stag, it was my task to safeguard the person of Shirzad Mir. I wearied my brains upon the matter of the meeting—without result. God had willed that I should not foresee what was to come to pass.

Still, one thing I did see.

The demon of unrest kept me awake that night and I walked the edge of the garden, past the stables and the door of Shirzad

Mir. It was a still night and the splendor of the stars beat down on Khanjut. I harkened to the challenges of the sentries and the stamp of a hoof among the horses.

Then I heard voices among the bare trees of the garden. For the space milk takes to boil I waited, holding my breath. Then I stepped softly nearer the voices.

The *Ferang* and Krishna Taya were talking together. By staring for a long time I made out their forms against the gray stretch of a wall. They stood close and whispered.

I heard Krishna Taya laugh and it sounded like the low murmur of a rivulet. Sir Weyand's voice came to me, harsh and urgent.

"You must not do this thing, Rose Face," he said.

Again I held my breath, but her whispered words were not clear. His reply was spoken in the swift, broken phrases of a man who is troubled by a great trouble. I caught the name of Shirzad Mir and bristled. Then—

"You will come and be at my side when the time is near," she whispered wistfully after the fashion of a woman who has bound a man by the silken cord of love.

"Aye, Rose Face."

Sir Weyand had made a decision and it had cost him much. For a space the two forms by the gray wall merged together, and the thought came to me that he had kissed her before she sped away through the garden. Thereupon he turned and went to his own quarters.

B'illah! If I had had her slim throat between my hands, I should have strangled her by the rope of pearls, for there had been pain and unwillingness in the voice of Sir Weyand, and this betokened ill to my lord.

This thing I told to Shirzad Mir after the dawn prayer, and he laughed in his beard.

"Of the servant who brings me food and of my foster brother, I might believe evil, Abdul Dost," he responded, "but not of Sir Weyand."

Yet I marked a flush in the cheeks of the Rájput maiden that morning and heard her sing in the apartment of Said Afzel for the first time since she had come to Khanjut.

What was I to do?

Noon came, the hour we were to ride to meet Jani Beg. Bihor Jan told me with a grin that Said Afzel was wrapped in opium dreams and lay like a stricken pig.

So, as this was my task, I had a litter brought, and the Afghan and I placed Said Afzel upon it. Then Krishna Taya, who watched, came and said that she also was to ride on the litter, as she would go with the Uzbek.

I would not consent. I smelled evil in this, as a hound smells the trace of a hare. Striding to Shirzad Mir, I demanded angrily that Krishna Taya should not go. Sir Weyand, who was listening, spoke curtly.

"It shall be as she wishes, Abdul Dost. Did not your master promise that any attendant of the prince might accompany him?"

Shirzad Mir made me a careless sign to be about my business. He was not one to suspect treachery, yet the *Ferang*'s eye had not met mine as he spoke.

As I had been ordered, I did. I placed a Kashmir shawl over the frame of the litter where Krishna Taya sat by Said Afzel's head. This was to guard the two from the sun and from curious eyes.

When it was time, I summoned Bihor Jan with seven others and accompanied them as they bore the litter from the castle across the courtyard and down the winding road to the plain.

Out over the drawbridge the litter passed. When we reached the spot of the meeting, I bade the eight set down their burden. When Shirzad Mir and Sir Weyand rode from the castle gate, I ordered the bearers to retire to Khanjut.

I sat moodily on the horse, watching the languid movement of Said Afzel's slippered feet—all that I could see of the poet—and thought blackly upon the danger to Shirzad Mir.

When he and the *Ferang* gained my side, Shirzad Mir bade me
withdraw ten spear-lengths toward Khanjut. This I did and when
I turned at my new station, the Uzbek party came in view.

Raja Man Singh, in all his finery, was leading with Jani Beg,
who sat his horse in grim silence. Behind them came the cavalcade of donkeys ushered by four or five miserable slaves. The
little beasts carried weighty packs. I caught the glitter of brass
upon one.

A cloud of dust rose about them and hung in the air, for there
was no wind. The jewels gleamed in the turban of the Rájput and
he laughed more than once, but Jani Beg did not laugh.

Nearer they came and nearer. I could see the sweat on the
donkeys' shoulders and marked the outline of the powder boxes
under the packs.

God has given me keen sight, and all that followed I saw
clearly. I saw the Rájput halt the donkey-men and order them off
with a contemptuous gesture and Jani Beg and Sir Weyand peer
at the packs as if to make sure of what they held. I saw the beasts
begin to nuzzle for grass to crop, and Raja Man Singh ride up to
the waiting two. By now the donkey-men were a good bow-shot
distant.

Then all four of the riders dismounted, watching one another.
I leaned upon the peak of my saddle and swallowed hard, for
my throat was dry. The dust settled down. I marked a pigeon
wheeling overhead.

There was a great stillness on the plain of Badakshan. Khanjut
was far, far distant and Shirzad Mir stood with three men at his
side, all being armed.

The Rájput's white teeth showed in a laugh. This time Jani Beg
smiled. He was in a cordial mood, for he advanced to Shirzad Mir
and made a low salaam.

Afar off, I heard a holy man cry to prayers.

Then suddenly I saw the lean arms of Jani Beg spring forth and
grip Shirzad Mir. Like a swift snake he twined about my master,
holding Shirzad Mir's arms to his sides.

"Strike him!" cried Jani Beg. "In the throat above the armor!"

It was to the *Ferang* that he had said this. The eyes of Raja Man Singh widened in astonishment.

Sir Weyand's muscles quivered, but he did not move to aid the treacherous Uzbek. Instead he stepped toward the litter.

The thing was clear to me. Jani Beg had thought that the *Ferang* would slay Shirzad Mir, as he had cried for him to do. Something had gone amiss with Jani Beg's plan, for neither Sir Weyand nor the Rájput moved. Aye, the Rájput was a man of high honor.

Shirzad Mir strained at the Uzbek's grip. Jani Beg's face grew dark with rage. I dug my spurs deep into the side of my horse. He sprang forward—a leap that would have unsettled another rider—and I bore down on Jani Beg.

Hot was my heart with anger at the sight of Shirzad Mir helpless among the three. I had lifted my scimitar to strike down Jani Beg. I had galloped within arm's reach and there reined in my mount on its haunches.

Aye, I drew rein at sight of the three, for the Rájput and Sir Weyand and Shirzad Mir were staring not at Jani Beg but at the litter, and on the three faces was the mark of amazement and horror.

I also looked down at the litter. Krishna Taya had pushed back the shawl. She sat upon her knees with the head of Said Afzel on her lap. The sleek face of Said Afzel was red and his eyes glazed, as in the opium trance. He lay still, very still.

From his gaping mouth hung the end of a string of pearls. The pearls looked like the tip of a necklace. I had seen them before. I looked from the mottled face that glared up at me to the neck of the maiden. The necklace had gone from the throat of Krishna Taya.

She sat very straight on the litter and there was a smile on her childlike face.

"Here is Said Afzel, Jani Beg," she said softly, "whole and without a scratch upon his skin."

The Uzbek looked from her to the head of the dead man on her
knee, and his mouth opened slowly. His arms that were about
Shirzad Mir dropped to his side and he tried vainly to swallow,
like one who has the palsy. I heard my lord mutter in his beard—
"By the ninety holy names of God, I knew naught of this."

Yet I heeded not. The pigeon overhead fluttered away.

Then hate leaped into the evil face of Jani Beg as flame sears
paper.

"Wench! Child of sin—traitress—" he gasped, and then choked
to silence.

"Nay," she spoke calmly, "What I promised you has been done.
I have cut the prop from him who would usurp the throne of
Badakshan."

So great was the rage of Jani Beg that his hand trembled so he
could scarce grip the dagger in his girdle. He raised the dagger
with one hand; the other he twisted in the hair of the maiden,
who looked up at him and smiled.

"It is well," I heard her whisper. "I have made clean the honor
of the Rájput."

Neither I nor Shirzad Mir would have checked Jani Beg in the
slaying of Krishna Taya, but the dagger did not reach her slender
throat. Sir Weyand had gripped the hand that held the weapon.
For the space of a long breath the eyes of the *Ferang* and the
Uzbek met and held. The arms of the two quivered and strained.
The lips of the *Ferang* were closed in a tight line.

Then Jani Beg spoke in level words.

"Every soul in Khanjut shall die if this woman is not slain."

Sir Weyand did not relax his grip.

"She avenged the wrong that was done her." His voice was
curiously strained. He turned his face to the Rájput.

"Krishna Taya needs the protection of the Rájputs."

Raja Man Singh sighed and twisted a strand of his curly beard.
His glance went from the end of the pearl necklace that had strangled Said Afzel to the woman.

"Come," he said at length, curtly. He took the girl and lifted
her to the back of his horse behind the saddle. We knew and Jani

Beg knew that Krishna Taya was now safe under the sword of the Rájput.

Many things were in my mind as I drove the donkeys up to Khanjut, following after Shirzad Mir and Sir Weyand. I thought of the reckless honor of Shirzad Mir that had let Jani Beg depart unharmed, because of his pledge. I wondered whether one of us would live to tell of the Uzbek storm that would be launched upon us because Sir Weyand had guarded the life of Krishna Taya when Jani Beg lusted for vengeance. But among these thoughts one was uppermost. It was a verse from the Koran:

Who knows what is in the heart of a woman?

Ameer of the Sea

In a hundred ages of the gods there is no glory like the glory of the hills.

Before Ganesh, the elephant-head, and Hanuman, the monkey-god, walked the night together, the snow-peaks of the Himalayas rose to the stars.

In the hills may a man find peace. Men die but the hills do not alter. They bless the eyes that look upon them. Where else is there such a place as this?

Hindu saying

Dawn was striking against the snow peaks of the Koh-i-Baba Range, among the foothills of the Himalayas. It was the year of our Lord 1608, and of the Ox, by the Muslim calendar.

The sky behind the peaks was streaking red, but in the valleys the cold morning mist still held. Through the mist rose the black towers of Khanjut. There was just light enough to make out the upper surface of stones and the glint of running water, when a man bobbed to the center of a pool in the stream.

He had not stepped into the stream. He broke through the surface panting as if he had long held his breath, and swam soundlessly to the rocks at one side. He glanced back once over his shoulder at the loom of the towers in the midst and began to run forward up the rocky *nullah*.

The light was strong enough for him to choose his way, and he threaded the boulders in the manner of one who knew his course. On either side, thick-set pines pressed upon him. The summits of the cliffs over the pines were still invisible.

The man ran steadily upward, any noise that he made being lost in the rush of the stream. The spreading dawn overhead showed him naked to the waist—a lean, dark body, its white muslin loincloth and trousers plastered tight by the water. A hillman—by his gait and his tireless progress—of the northern Afghan mountains.

At sight of light glinting on steel in a thicket ahead, the man swerved nimbly up into the pines. He caught the scent of the watchfire kindled by the sentries, whose helmets he had glimpsed, and passed the half-dozen figures lying about the embers without pausing.

Once safely by the outpost, he dropped into the trail that ran by the stream. Then he halted in his tracks, crouching instinctively as a cat does at sight of danger.

Ahead of him the figure of a sentry leaning on a spear was visible. The watcher was alarmed, had heard something, and was glancing into the pines with the indifferent caution of one who has been long on post and expects relief.

The hillman advanced swiftly, still crouching. Within two paces he leaped, metal gleaming in his hand as he did so. His free hand struck on the brow of the sentinel, two fingers catching in the nostrils, bending the other's head back.

The hand with the dagger smote softly into the throat, above the coat of mail. Three times the hillman plunged his weapon in. Coolly he caught the spear that was about to fall to the stones. For a moment he held the sentry, then lowered the body to the ground.

Dexterously the slayer unlaced the throat fastenings of the Turkish mail and drew it over the head of the dead man. He donned the mail, tucking its loose ends into his loincloth. He put on the pointed Kallmark helmet, thrusting his long, black hair up under it as he did so.

Then he resumed his run up the *nullah*.

The sky was blue overhead—the clear, tranquil blue of Afghanistan—and the pines had turned from black to gray to green when the runner reached the summit of the pass and turned aside from the stream into a sheep-track.

He went forward more confidently now, as if he had left his enemies at his back. He had passed under the siege works of the enemy, slipped around the outpost in the *nullah* and was free from all except wandering cavalry patrols.

He avoided the caravan track that ran beside him, leading from Khanjut over the Shyr Pass to the Kabul Valley and to the city of that name, the farthest walled town of the Mogul, his Majesty, the King of Kings, whose court is a heaven, the shadow of God, Jahangir, emperor of India.

Then, crossing a cleared space, he came upon several horsemen. Their shaggy ponies and the bows slung at their shoulders indicated to him that they were Uzbeks, even if the distance was too great to distinguish their drooping mustaches and high cheekbones.

The hillman hesitated only a brief second and went on as if unconcerned. The Uzbeks glanced at his mail and were passing on when one reined in sharply and shouted a challenge, pointing at him.

The runner did not answer. Altering his course, he ran for the nearest pine grove. He had not noticed, or had forgotten, the crimson stain on his mail that had come from the throat of the man he had slain.

This was what had aroused the suspicion of the riders. They spurred after him with growling curses. An arrow flicked into the sod ahead of him.

His legs were moving more slowly now; yet he was near the protecting pines. He glanced back, calmly measuring the distance to his pursuers—and fell with an arrow in his thigh.

He was up at once, limping forward. He heard the beat of horses' hoofs and wheeled, drawing his dagger with a grin of hate. The foremost horse ran him down. He struck vainly at the rider, who turned in the saddle.

The second Uzbek bent in his stirrups and slashed down with his scimitar. The curved blade bit deep through the mail; the hillman's limbs twisted, then fell limp.

Dismounting, the Uzbeks inspected their victim. At a sign from the leader one tore open the dead man's flimsy garments and ran his hand through the muslin. His effort was rewarded, for he stood up with a small square of parchment in his hand.

After a brief conference the leader of the patrol took the paper and the head of the runner and galloped off to the caravan track.

It was just after sunrise prayers that he threaded his way through the tents of the Uzbek camp, to the red felt *yurt* of Jani Beg, chieftain of the Uzbeks.

Jani Beg looked up as the guard at the door passed in the patrol leader. His broad, seamed face rested close to a pair of massive bent shoulders. A thin mustache drooped over a broad, hard mouth.

The eyes that scanned the newcomer sharply were peculiar. Jani Beg had tawny eyes, almost yellow, with the iridescent quality sometimes seen in those of an animal. The visitor put hand to forehead and bent in an uneasy salaam as he extended the paper, explaining how he had chanced upon it.

"The head is that of a thrice-cursed hillman," he added. "But none of the *ameer*s of the guard can read the missive. Thus it was that they ordered it brought before you."

The eyes of Jani Beg focused on the man without expression.

"Leave it and go!" he ordered in a high voice strange in a man of his bulk.

Idly he turned over the paper on the silk rug. He scanned the writing at first indifferently, then with as much curiosity as he ever permitted himself to show. Not for some time did he speak to the man at his side.

"May I rot on camel's droppings, Shah Abbas! By the beard of my grandsire—may he rest in peace—but I know not this unblessed script.

"You are a learned man even among the astrologers and fools of Isphahan. You can recite the Koran and read the portents of the stars. Read me this!"

The Persian who sat on his heels at the farther side of the rug scanned the Uzbek coolly. Deciding that no affront was meant, he bent his bearded head over the missive.

Shah Abbas, chief of the Persian generals in the first decade of the early seventeenth century, was a bulky and handsome man. He formed a striking contrast to his gaunt companion. His mellow eyes were those of a voluptuous liver, his high, smooth brow under the heavy turban that of a philosopher and scholar.

He was a poet of no mean ability, a master of the chessboard, well versed in Greek medical lore and in the mingled culture of Damascus and Bokhara. A follower of no single religion, he was a diplomat of the highest intelligence, a plausible talker and a man without faith except when it suited him to keep his word.

His person, from the sky-blue cloak to the carefully trimmed beard and the silk vest that exuded musk, was that of a dandy—setting off the rough, fur-trimmed tunic of Jani Beg, and the latter's dingy morocco shoes.

"Who am I," he responded in limpid Persian, "to interpret this thing, which the wisdom of Jani Beg has failed to read?"

"Dog of Satan!" fretted Jani Beg. "Did I ask for riddles from your smooth cat's tongue? Read me this writing!"

The Persian stroked his beard delicately and surveyed the rubies on his plump fingers with the utmost calm.

"It is written, Jani Beg, in the books of wisdom, that by his words the speaker may be known. Doubtless you are familiar with the breeds of dogs, even mongrels. Were not your grandsires mongrels?"

Jani Beg's hazy eyes glowed with a sullen fire. Few men dared to match words with him.

"Aye, you know that I am descended from Timurlane the Great. Where is the equal of the lame Conqueror?"

"Doubtless," purred Shah Abbas. "Yet it is a strange thing, for while the Conqueror was lame, he was a man of honor and he lacked not wits."

The Uzbek glowered. "Ho—you prate like a woman. We Mongols care not for the dusty Persian plain."

"Aye, the dust of Persia is not to be compared with the glories of the Mongol steppe."

"You are ripe with words. You are not the same figure with a sword as with speech."

"Nay, I waste not good steel upon a boaster."

Jani Beg's hand jerked toward the hilt of his scimitar. Shah Abbas surveyed him mildly and he dropped his hand. He could not afford to quarrel with the powerful Persian and the latter knew it. At mutual recrimination Shah Abbas was much the better.

Both were serving the same cause. Jani Beg had volunteered to serve the Mogul himself in the northern hills, and for a space Isphahan was at peace with Delhi. The Uzbek chieftain had sent Shah Abbas treasure to the amount of a dozen camel-loads of gold to come to aid him in Afghanistan.

The Persian had come with several thousand picked and excellently mounted horsemen, for two reasons. He knew that Jani Beg was at war with Shirzad Mir, known in Persia as Shah Beg, who was his own enemy, and he knew that Jani Beg had reasons for sending for him other than the crushing of a few hundred hillmen under Shirzad Mir, beleaguered in Khanjut.

But for the moment both ostensibly were acting in the interest of the Mogul and must remain friends.

"Nay," muttered Jani Beg with ill grace, "I meant not to offend you. But surely your wisdom can decipher this accursed missive. It may be a matter of moment, and I am not learned in script."

Shah Abbas shrugged his plump shoulders "The writing is not *Turki* and certainly not Persian. Nor is it the tongue of Hind. Nor Greek, with which I am familiar."

Both stared at the letter in silence, and in both minds was the same thought. The bearer should not have been slain. Torture—molten silver poured into ears or the fire-pencil applied to the man's eyes—would have elicited the truth of the matter. Now all they knew was that the missive had been sent from the citadel of Khanjut down the pass toward India. Jani Beg, in spite of his professed ignorance, was scholar enough to be aware that his companion spoke the truth concerning it.

As a matter of fact, the intercepted message—which never reached its destination—read as follows:

To the Notorious and Honourable Captain Hawkins,
Servant in like Manner as the Writer to
Our Sovereign Lord, James I, king of England—
Greetings from ye Fortress of Khanjoot
in N.W. Ind, N. of Kabool.

It has been told by divers Personne that ye be laden for Surat, with certain Goodes. Wherefore, sink the Fleete of the Portugals to Hell in Surat, and make shift to accompanie me to the Moghooul with a Companie of Musket Men and Falcon Gunnes.

I have beene kept from the Personne of ye Moghool by divers evil Stratagies of ye Portugals; still, I have taken Oath to gain the Trade for Our Lord, and this I shall yet do with the Grace of God; despite the Portugals, who are like to mad Dogges, labouring to work my Passauge out of the World.

I shall contrive to haste to meet you, as beseemeth fittinge, despite the black Peril frome ye Idolators and Portugals alike.

The name signed to the scrawled and misspelled missive was that of Ralph Weyand.

"It may work us evil; we had best be rid of it."

Jani Beg took up the letter in his huge claw of a hand and tore it into shreds. These he tossed indifferently into the brazier that warmed the interior of the *yurt.*

"And now, Lion of Persia," he whispered shrilly, "I would tell you a thought that is in my mind."

Shah Abbas yawned and felt for the gold box of hashish that hung from his girdle.

"Truly," he responded, "I find you and your thoughts wearisome. I came not to the hills to sit on my haunches before Khanjut."

"A wise man chooses a goodly weapon of the best temper to deal a death blow. Perhaps you are the weapon to fit my hand."

"Is this your wisdom?"

Shah Abbas smiled enigmatically, as if at the reflection that he should be a tool of Jani Beg.

"It is a fitting time to strike—for ourselves."

"At yonder miserable hillmen?"

"Nay, elsewhere. Perhaps—" Jani Beg's yellow eyes grew lustrous—"perhaps at one who is at Kabul."

The Persian, in spite of his habitual indifference, drew in his breath sharply.

"Have care!"

He glanced swiftly at the *yurt* entrance.

"Have you grown mad by the moon to say this aloud! The Mogul is in Kabul."

"Aye, Jahangir is visiting the gardens of Kabul."

For a long second the two measured glances. Then the Persian rose.

"Verily madness has come upon you," he sighed. "But this tent is no place for speech."

He led the way without. The red tent of Jani Beg stood on a hillock which overlooked the plain before Khanjut, the camp of the Uzbek and Persian besiegers, and the trenches built up the slope of the citadel.

It was a fair scene for a soldier's eyes, and Shah Abbas was a veteran of many wars. Banners fluttered in the breeze beside the tents of his Persians. High piles of stores were ringed about by tethered camels.

On the Uzbek side of the encampment there was less display; the men were quartered in haphazard fashion, but their shaggy horses were well cared for and their foragers dotted the distant fertile plain.

Captured Afghans were laboring in the trenches and saps that were slowly eating their way up the slope of Khanjut. A high mound of earth had been built; from its summit brass cannon belonging to the Persians pointed their carved and ornamented muzzles toward the walls.

At intervals, these cannon spoke and a swirl of smoke drifted over the camp. The wall opposite the earth mound was crumbling.

Occasionally the sunlight glinted on arrows that sped upward from the Uzbek trench, from behind the shelter of giant trees laid with their tops toward the walls. Behind this trench loomed the bare timbers of a battering machine, as they called it—a survival of the Middle Ages that served to cast rocks against the walls.

Boulders thrown down from the Khanjut ramparts had disabled the battering machine. But the Persian cannon were safe from harm.

In the course of time, as water eats through a dike, they would breach the stone wall that surmounted the rocky mass of Khanjut. Barrels of powder assembled at the head of saps at other points would be fired and Persian and Uzbek would surge to the attack.

The scene of bee-like activity, revealed by the clear sunlight, pleased Shah Abbas—even as the sight of the green hills and the snow peaks in the distance appealed to his poetic sense, stirred by the hashish, which had begun to have effect. He smiled at the gangs of sweating prisoners that were herded past the hillock—women as well as men—gleaned from the peasantry of the plain by his horsemen.

A goodly scene, he reflected, but one of little moment. The crushing of a rebel hill chief was scarcely game worth the hunting. It was pleasanter and less troublesome to fly falcons at the game-birds of the Koh-i-Baba or to linger in the rose-gardens of Isphahan . . .

This brought him sharply back to Jani Beg's remark. The two stood apart on the hillock and the Uzbek was smiling at him intently.

"Persia is at peace with Jahangir—for a space," he purred, stroking the gems on his fingers. "It has been said by those who are loose of tongue that the Mogul lacks the generalship and fire of Akbar, his father."

"They spoke truth. Jahangir is hot-headed and impulsive. His head falls easy victim to wine-fumes—or flattery."

"There are rare wines at Kabul."

Smilingly Shah Abbas repeated a verse to the effect that a man who feasts well must prepare to drink the cup of death. Jani Beg was still watching him narrowly. The Persian was a past master at saying what he did not think.

"There is better sport than looking at the bottom of the wine cup, Shah Abbas."

"Aye, God has given us slender women—"

"A nobler sport, even for Jahangir, the shadow of God on earth, is—warfare. I have sent him two *lakh*s of rupees with the humble request that he deign to visit this camp and see the fall of Khanjut."

Shah Abbas was silent for the space of a breath.

"It will be a pleasant sight. The hillmen have a proverb that Khanjut will never be taken by storm. It will please the eyes of the Mogul," Shah Abbas responded indifferently. "How came it that Shirzad Mir, chieftain of these Afghan hillmen, rebelled against Jahangir?"

"Shirzad Mir was my enemy," said Jani Beg. "I picked a quarrel with him and dispatched shrewd men with presents to the Mogul offering my fealty. Shirzad Mir, having been regent of the Mogul Akbar in the hills, was late with his offer of service to Jahangir. It was not hard to convince those at the Delhi court that Shirzad Mir was a rebel—especially as I had already gained the ascendency over him in the field."

Jani Beg lowered his voice.

"Your wisdom has read aright that I have other things in view than the crushing of Shirzad Mir and the barbarous Englishman with him. I seek power. You also thirst for conquest. The sword of Persia is sharp, so keen that it might cut even the pearl tiara from the turban of a Mogul."

Apparently Shah Abbas was tranquil, but the pulse in his throat throbbed strongly. Jani Beg did not miss this.

"What is the Mogul but the Muslim master of many peoples? A figurehead over armies of a dozen faiths?" he whispered. "Wherein lies the control of India, save in the person of the Mogul?"

"That person is well guarded. And the witless Rájputs serve him because his mother was of their race. Who could stand against the horsemen of Marwar?"

"No one—in the plains of Hindustan. Here in the hills—" Jani Beg glanced at the towering slopes at their backs—"it is another matter. Likewise the main army of the Rájputs is but returning to Delhi, after subduing a revolt in the Dekkan. Jahangir has with him many followers, but not an army."

"Think you he will turn his horse toward Khanjut?"

"Aye—he loves to be amused. He will come to see the hunting-down of Shirzad Mir, whom he believes to be a traitor. Harken, Shah Abbas, may not other snares be set? Greater game hunted? Who would trap a wolf when a stag may be pulled down?"

This time there was no mistaking Jani Beg's meaning. A flush dyed the yellow cheeks of the Persian.

"What snare can be set for a stag?"

The Uzbek laughed and pointed to the camp. He was more certain of his companion now, knowing the hereditary enmity between Persian and Mogul. But it would not do to commit himself fully as yet.

"When a stag walks into the hunters' toils, who is to blame?" he whispered. "Jahangir is not overcautious. We have twelve thousand retainers.

"If the Mogul should fall ill we might be forced to guard his sacred person. Aye, even to advance upon the rich city of Kabul, and then Lahore. We would gain allies among the Mohammedans north of the Indus. I—" a fleeting smile crossed his hard mouth— "have become a follower of the Prophet. Why not? If the Mogul should fall ill—"

A warning glance from Shah Abbas silenced him.

"Peace! This is the speech of madness."

He leaned closer to the Uzbek.

"Nay, sometimes it is folly to be sane. We will talk again. Yonder is the Rájput of Jahangir, his beloved watchdog."

Approaching the knoll was the slim figure of Raja Man Singh in a close-fitting white silk tunic. He rode a splendid Arabian, and the sun struck upon jewels in his saddle peak, on his sword hilt and turban.

He dismounted gracefully and came toward the two—a tall, long-striding warrior with delicate, boyish features and a frame that appeared too fragile to be that of one of the most noted swordsmen of Hindustan. He greeted the two carelessly.

"Ho, Jani Beg, the sun is at the hour you appointed for our conference. What have you to say?"

He spoke proudly. This pride—characteristic of the Rájput princes, who held themselves superior to nobles of other races, who boasted that they were descended from the sun-born kings of Ayodhya, from the mighty Ram himself—grated on his two allies. Raja Man Singh cared little what they thought, being of the blood of the Ranas of Chitore and Oudh, and the chosen companion of Jahangir.

Jani Beg peered up at him inscrutably.

"How like you the service of the Mogul?" he asked slowly. "Is it to your taste to wait upon the word of another man? I have marked your courage and ability, Raja. You are one who should lead and not follow."

"Siva! Am I not a leader? Have we of the Rájputs not a hundred thousand swords at our command? Did we not subdue the Dekkan for Jahangir?"

"For Jahangir, not yourself."

"Even so. He is of our blood, by his mother, and our faith—those who know him well know this. Jahangir is more Hindu than Muslim. Our fathers gave their fealty to Akbar; we are true to their word."

He stared disdainfully at the two. Shah Abbas made a warning sign to the Uzbek. It would not do to say too much to the Rájput. Nevertheless, he could not refrain from a barbed shaft of witticism.

"We have marked a stag nearby," he purred. "A noble animal, by my faith! Jani Beg says the hunters have set the toils."

He smiled contentedly at the baneful glare of the Uzbek.

"A stag!"

The Rájput's sleepy, opium-darkened eyes opened in interest.

"And a noble head! By the sword of Ram, let us ride him down. Snares are for the low-born. Come!"

"To ride him down would be—dangerous."

The Rájput's lip curled scornfully.

"Nay," put in Jani Beg hastily, "Shah Abbas jests. I asked you hither, Raja, to learn your opinion of the siege. Think you it progresses favorably? Will our plans meet with the approval of your master?"

He emphasized the last word slightly, but the Rájput took no heed.

"Aye, well enough," he grumbled. "Yet this digging and bombarding is the work of peasants. Give the word to storm the walls. The hillmen are few."

"Yet Shirzad Mir is their leader."

"Ho!"

Raja Man Singh laughed. "You have crossed swords with him before, Shah Abbas, at the siege of Kandahar. It has made you cautious. Siva Koh—"

"Not so," put in Jani Beg smoothly, noting the quick flush that overspread the Persian's olive throat. "We delay the assault for another reason. This is the news I promised you. Jahangir himself and his court may come hither from Kabul. When he arrives we will launch the storm and raise the standard of the Mogul for his pleasure—"

"By the gods!"

The Rájput's white teeth flashed in a delighted smile.

"That is news as sweet as the snow-cooled wine of Kashmir."

"Under the eye of Jahangir, you and the Rájputs of the court will doubtless desire to lead the assault."

"What else? Since the birth of Ram the warriors of the raj have taken the front of the battle. Truly we have but few of our race with the Mogul at present; yet we will show your northern dullards how to wield sword."

"Since you ask it, we will grant the favor," assented Jani Beg.

Shah Abbas smiled, stroking his beard gently. His respect for the Uzbek was growing. If the Rájputs led the assault many would be slain, and while they were engaged at the wall—

"The hillmen grow weaker daily from hunger," he added tranquilly.

"Not so," corrected Raja Man Singh. "Look yonder. It struck my gaze as I rode hither."

He pointed toward an open space on the walls. The cold Autumn air which caused the heat-accustomed Rájput to shiver revealed the distant scene in clear detail.

On the roof of a Khanjut building several men sat at meat. The watchers on the knoll could see attendants bringing bowls and vessels of food and wine.

"I went near the spot, for I was curious," he explained. "They shot arrows at me; nevertheless, I saw they were partaking of rich food. Is this a sign of starvation? Rather, it is a feast of plenty."

"That must be Shirzad Mir and his accursed companions," ventured Jani Beg. "Aye, it is a sign."

"Of abundance. They feast openly to let us know they lack not."

Shah Abbas frowned meditatively.

"I have reason to suspect the cunning of Shirzad Mir," he murmured. "It is more like that this scene is planned to deceive us."

Jani Beg grunted disdainfully.

"What else? Opium has eaten up your wit, Raja. Shirzad Mir feasts to conceal from us that they have little food. The garrison is near starvation."

"But I saw meat and fruit," insisted the Rájput, who did not love to be contradicted.

"Send an envoy into Khanjut to parley on some pretext or other and spy out the truth of this," grumbled Jani Beg. "I can spare no time for such child play. I have said our enemies lack food. It is the truth."

II

On a sunny spot overlooking the wall of Khanjut a carpet had been spread and a white cloth upon this. At either end of the cloth two men were seated. Before each was an array of bowls containing curried rice, spiced mutton, sugared fruits, jellies and beakers of good Shiraz wine.

"Drink, my excellent *Ferang*," quoth the stout man in the flowing *khalat*.

"Aye, drink, Shirzad Mir," cried the powerful Englishman in the leather surcoat and green cap. "This feast must serve our bellies for two days."

"May God grant it serves our foes with the thought we have food a-plenty."

"Amen."

Sir Ralph Weyand lifted his glass, shaking back the tawny curls that ringed his sun-burnt forehead. His gray eyes were alight with grim humor. The hand that held the beaker was veined and corded—an indication of the muscular strength concealed in his stocky frame.

"To my sovereign, the king of England," he added soberly in his own tongue.

"May the mercy of Allah give us aid," responded Shirzad Mir, not understanding.

"And speed the runner with my message."

"If it is the will of Allah."

Sir Ralph eyed his portly companion with affectionate interest.

"Truly, our lot is wretched, Shirzad Mir. A rebel baron, you— trapped by pride, Jani Beg's gold, allegiance to your fathers, devil knows what. It matters not."

"All things are written in the book of fate by the hand of the angels."

"Perhaps. They wrote my poor destiny in ill fashion. Spurned from Jahangir's court by the evil-tongued Portuguese, half-poisoned and starved in these friendless hills—"

"Nay, I am your friend."

"Granted," said the Englishman warmly. "I ask for none better. 'Tis well! We are yet alive, and here is—wine."

"The sweeper-away of care."

Shirzad Mir lay back comfortably on his pillows and sipped at his cup.

"May we confound our enemies," he added.

"Perchance we may, if the Afghan with my billet escaped through the underground watercourse to the hills."

Sir Ralph drained his beaker at one throw and sighed. He glanced appraisingly over the siege-works below them, and noted the flight of an arrow overhead. Standing by the battlement a few yards away were several Afghans, who watched them eat enviously. The men were gaunt with hunger.

The Englishman signed to one of the attendants.

"I have finished," he said gruffly. "Take these bowls to the sentries yonder."

While the hungry soldiers ate and Shirzad Mir, who with all his good qualities lacked solicitude for his men, stared quizzically, a slave salaamed and announced the coming of the *mansabdar*, Abdul Dost.

Adbul Dost was commander of the garrison, a long-striding Muslim with one cheek mutilated by a scimitar stroke. He raised his hand with dignity at sighting the two.

"Peace be unto you, Shirzad Mir," he greeted his master.

"And unto you be peace."

"The Rájput general, Raja Man Singh, has sent an envoy to the road that winds up to the gate. I spoke with him when he made a sign of peace. He would parley terms with you."

Shirzad Mir adjusted himself comfortably and sipped at his wine. His broad brow puckered in thought.

"Our trick has born fruit," laughed Sir Ralph. "Yonder chieftains think we have food in plenty."

Shirzad Mir glanced up at the *mansabdar*.

"What think you, Abdul Dost?"

"Does a tiger play with a trapped goat?"

"When it suits his whim," meditated the *mir*. "Say you the man came from the Rájput?"

"Aye."

"Then this is something evil. For Jani Beg would parley with hell itself, but the Rájput prefers to let his sword do the talking. Nay—!" he clapped his hands delightedly—"I have it. Our foes seek to learn whether we truly have food in the granary!"

"Then we should not admit the envoy," suggested Sir Ralph; but Shirzad Mir grew thoughtful.

"Not so. Verily it is written that a wise man profits by his enemy's mistake. Come, we will prepare a spectacle for the Rájput's man. Ho, Abdul Dost!"

He scrambled to his feet nimbly, for all his bulk. His broad face gleamed with childlike pleasure at a new thought.

Shirzad Mir, once regent of Akbar, lord of Badakshan and the Koh-i-Baba, was little more than an overgrown child. Impulsive and unsuspicious, he lacked the craft of his enemies—which was why he fought ever against odds. Petulant as a woman, indifferent to good or ill fortune, he had a generosity and sheer courage that kept friends steadfast until the end.

"Muster half the garrison, Abdul Dost. Count off gangs of a dozen, and send them into the cellar granary. Fetch forth every sack of grain and stack them along the alleys leading from the gate to the center of the garden. Haste!"

The *mansabdar* hesitated.

"Pour the grain on the ground along the way the envoy is led."

Shirzad Mir stamped his foot impatiently.

"Fetch every sack. Order no one to touch the grain, under pain of being beaten by bamboos. Keep the envoy waiting without the gate until this thing is done. Eh, he will then see what he came to see."

"But our men, lord—"

"See that they obey. Go!"

So it happened that when the emissary entered the gate of Khanjut, across the drawbridge that spanned the moat, some hours later, he saw a strange sight.

Grain, gray and golden, lay strewn in every quarter. Men passed indifferently over the piles and horses nibbled hungrily at it. Even oxen bearing carts along the alleys paused to snatch up a mouthful.

As he had been instructed by the raja, the man kept his eyes open. He was suspicious, but he saw nothing amiss. He left Khanjut after some empty words concerning a truce which neither side believed possible. And he was convinced that Shirzad Mir and his men did not lack grain.

He did not see, after his departure, that a hundred men fell upon the grain piles and stowed them into sacks which were carried back under armed guard to the granary. Or that half-famished horses came to nuzzle scattered particles along the alleys, and boys fought each other for a fistful of the golden treasure plucked from the passing sacks. Or that the men of the garrison muttered angrily as they boiled their half rations of rice over the fire that evening.

"Grain they have in plenty," he informed Raja Man Singh and the two leaders. "It is stored haphazard in the filth of the alleys and the animals eat of it when they will."

"This must be true," announced the Rájput triumphantly. "That is well, for who would fight a starved foe?"

Jani Beg and Shah Abbas glanced at each other significantly.

"If Shirzad Mir," continued the chivalrous raja, "had lacked food, I would have sent it in to him. It is the law of the raj that one of our blood may not strike a weakened foe."

At sundown a week later there was unwonted activity in the courtyard that led to the main gate of the castle. For the first time in a week a dense mist overspread the plain below Khanjut—the forerunner of the Winter mists.

Abdul Dost, mounted on a fine Kabul stallion, was grimly seeing to the mustering of a group of picked horsemen. As the last rim of the sun vanished over the blue summits, the horsemen, led by the *mansabdar*, heard a long, quavering cry from one of the towers. To a man they dismounted and kneeled on the stones of the court, facing the *Kaaba*.

It was the hour of sunset prayer.

"*Lailat el kadr*," cried the mollah. "*Allah il, Akbar!*"

"*Allah il Akbar!*," repeated the deep-throated chorus.

Shirzad Mir and Sir Ralph, stepping from a tower door, halted at sight of the tableau.

The genial face of the *mir* was more sober than usual.

"I have a foreboding, Sir Ralph," he said gravely. "Perhaps the hand of fate has written in the page of destiny that our plan is not to prosper. I know not."

"Your offer was generous," responded the Englishman bluntly. "Still, I like not to risk the lives of many when I might go alone through the secret watercourse under the walls and swim out into the mountain stream."

"By the face of the Prophet!" protested his companion. "Am I a jackal to send you unescorted into peril? Nay, it is written that peril shared among friends is a feast. Yet I like not to part with you."

"We have decided. I am useless here. By now my messenger will be well into Hindustan, on the way to Surat. It is time I followed."

"Think you the other *Ferang* will truly be at the seaport? I have heard it is fortified by the Portuguese."

"The more reason that Hawkins will come to Surat," said Sir Ralph grimly. "When I was last at Agra I heard it rumored that the English fleet lay at Mozambique. It was agreed before I left England that Hawkins would visit Surat this year. He will arrive before the Winter season sets in."

"I know not of such matters."

Shirzad Mir glanced at his sturdy companion regretfully.

"By the beard of my grandsire, I have a heavy foreboding. I fear that I will not set eyes on you again."

"Nay, I shall return to Khanjut. Think you I would leave as a coward flees, glad to set his back to danger?"

"Not I. Yet how will you do this thing? Granted that you meet with the other *Ferang* noble and that many ships are with him, you cannot sail ships to Khanjut."

The Englishman tightened the saddlebags and the girths of his horse. Lighted candles appeared among the men who were now— having finished their prayers—quietly mounting.

"We will go to the Mogul, Captain Hawkins and I. He will bring letters and presents from the English court. Likewise he will have musketmen and cannon. Jahangir will listen to the message from my king."

An eager light shone in the Englishman's honest face.

"Those at court have seen me but once. They will not mark my presence among the new embassy until the message is delivered. Then I shall ask pardon for you and those at Khanjut.

"I will explain how Jani Beg has deceived the Mogul and made you appear a traitor. Jahangir will listen, for I speak his tongue, and—he will respect the power of England that has sent a score of ships half around the world."

He struck his fist forcibly on the saddle.

"A great company has been formed in my country to bring the benefits of trade to India. Your people and mine are destined to be friends. The English deal fairly with those to whom they offer the hand of friendship—"

"But the Portuguese—"

"We will deal with them shrewdly if they hinder us. This time we will have an ample force of armed men."

Shirzad Mir puckered his brow. To him Jahangir was monarch of the world and the court at Delhi the center of the universe. He did not credit the intriguing nobles at court with respect for an unknown ruler whose servants appeared as if by magic out of the southern sea.

"What will be, will be. We cannot escape our fate, Sir Ralph. Ho—" the bored look vanished from his bland countenance at a fresh thought—"by the beard of the Prophet, I shall ride with Abdul Dost when his men cut a path for you through the tents of our foes. Ho, Abdul Dost! My horse!"

The Englishman protested against the risk Shirzad Mir was taking, but the impulsive chieftain would not wait even for his armor.

Abdul Dost, also, found his objections overruled.

"Dog of the devil, Abdul Dost!" cried his master. "Said I not I had a foreboding concerning this sally party? I will lead it myself, and if it is the will of God I will tumble Jani Beg's red tent over his ears.

"I will trim Shah Abbas's beard," he muttered delightedly. "Have the houris of paradise grown ill-favored, Abdul Dost, that you shirk sword blows riding bridle to bridle with Shirzad Mir? Nay, lead on, or you stay behind the walls of Khanjut."

Sir Ralph had adjusted the trappings of his horse to his satisfaction. He was more at home on the poop of a ship than in a saddle, but in the sally they planned it was necessary for him to be mounted.

The venture, although daring, promised success, thanks to the mist. The camp in the plain was spread over a wide area. Once past the entrenchments of the foe it would be possible to strike swiftly through the tents and escort the Englishman out to the open plain.

Free of the Persian lines—they had chosen the Persian camp as the most vulnerable—Sir Ralph was to circle to the Koh-i-Baba hills and strike through the Shyr Pass to the South.

The enemy would not be prepared for a sally, and once the group of horsemen had won back to the Khanjut wall, they would not think to look for a lone rider on the plain. And the mist would serve as a veil for what passed.

In fact, the danger would be greater for the horsemen riding back after the sally than for Sir Ralph. It was this that had made him reluctant to try the sortie. But Shirzad Mir would not be denied.

They walked their horses through the open gate and felt the cold mist strike their faces. It seemed to Adbul Dost, who was a veteran at night warfare, that the mist was thinning more than they had thought, looking down on it from the battlements.

Nevertheless, they pressed ahead as silently as possible, listening to the calls that passed from sentry to sentry along the entrenchments. There was no sound except a muffled jingle as a horse tossed its head, or an unavoidable click of hoof on stone.

Abdul Dost had effectively discouraged the presence of enemy outposts nearer than the first of the siege works. He had marked out in his mind the course that he would follow, down the ramp, out along the road, down the gentler slope to the plain. Then sharply to the left, past the earth mound that served as foundation for the Persian guns.

Here there were no trenches dug and the way was clear to the tents.

He led Shirzad Mir and the Englishman to the bottom of the winding road. They paused for several moments to note if they had been observed and to permit the horsemen in the rear to come up with them. The lights of the watch fires seemed peculiarlv clear to Sir Ralph, and he touched Abdul Dost on the arm.

"The mist is thinning," he whispered.

"*B'illah!*" grunted the *mansabdar,* casting a swift glance upward.

The stars were clear to view.

"No matter," urged Shirzad Mir impatiently. "We have come this far and we will not turn back without a few good sword strokes. Come!"

He spurred his horse forward, and Abdul Dost set his into a trot. They could see the earth mounds of the entrenchments on either hand and the occasional blurred form of a sentry. Sounds of revelry and quarreling came from the camp ahead, partially drowning the growing beat of the horses' hoofs.

A hasty challenge rang out in front of them. Abdul Dost reined his horse forward and struck down the sentinel, who had scrambled sleepily to his feet.

"Haste!" cried Shirzad Mir.

The trained horsemen behind them closed in and the troop thundered around the base of the artillery mound. Torches flashed along the lines in front. Startled cries resounded.

They swung past the mound and galloped into the torchlight. Foot outposts fled away from their course.

"*Shirzad el kadr*!" they cried.

"—and Satan's beldame!" swore Abdul Dost, pulling in his mount and snatching at the bridle of Shirzad Mir.

Across their course, hidden until now by the earth mound, was a line of felled trees formed into a *chevaux-de-frise*. A network of tangled branches stretched between them and the tents.

The Persians had not lacked the forethought to guard their camp against just such a sally.

Likewise a dozen alarm flares were kindling into glow, lighting the scene clearly. Abdul Dost saw at once that they were in grave danger if they should press on. But his attempt to check his master had been fruitless.

The lord of Badakshan spurred on along the line of branches, seeking a path through the obstacle. Perforce his men followed. Each moment the glow was revealing more clearly the secret of their scanty numbers.

The few foot soldiers in front of the barrier were cut down. But the commotion in the camp beyond showed that the Persian horse were assembling.

"*Ho níla—ki aswár!*" came an answering shout from the tents.

"The Rájputs," muttered Abdul Dost grimly. "This is an ill place. We must go back—"

A splendid Arab cleared the *chevaux-de-frise* in front of Shirzad Mir. The figure in its saddle was familiar to them all. Raja Man Singh had not waited for his men before riding to repel the sortie. He faced them with drawn scimitar, a slender warrior sitting his horse magnificently.

"Eh—that was well done!" laughed Shirzad Mir, spurring forward. "You shall not lack for sword strokes, Rájput!"

He pressed forward, swinging his curved blade. The raja waited his coming tranquilly. The two swords flew together, flashed and struck again.

The Rájput drew his mount nearer his enemy. While the horsemen watched, their swords thrust and parried at close quarters. The force of his onset lost, Shirzad Mir paid for his boldness in engaging the finest swordsman of Hindustan.

He guarded his head with difficulty, panting as he turned his stout body in the saddle. Raja Man Singh smiled, drawing closer until they were knee to knee. A swift stroke, and his scimitar bit deep into the side of Shirzad Mir under the armpit.

The lord of Badakshan swayed in his saddle, but did not loosen his grip on his weapon. Abdul Dost, frantic with fear for his master, reined his horse between the two and engaged the triumphant Rájput.

"Back to Khanjut, dogs!" he cried over his shoulder. "See to Shirzad Mir! Bowmen, form a rear guard."

Raja Man Singh was now fronted with a swordsman of equal skill, and neither of the two veterans were able to break through the other's guard until Abdul Dost, seeing that his men were drawing back with their wounded lord, wheeled and galloped back under cover of a flight of arrows.

The archers kept to the rear while Shirzad Mir was led up the castle road. Sir Ralph and Abdul Dost were the last to ride up to the gates, where a hundred archers on the walls kept their pursuers under the leadership of the impetuous Rájput at a distance.

The gates of Khanjut closed behind them, shutting out the tumult of the camp.

They had paid heavily for the sally. A dozen men were left stretched along the road behind them. On his cloak in the courtyard Shirzad Mir lay quiet, perspiration dotting his brow. Sir Ralph walked over to him gloomily.

"I foretold . . . the ill omen," muttered the *mir*, looking up at him. "But for the cursed Rájput we might—have won through."

Later came Abdul Dost to the Englishman with a long face.

"The *hakim*s have bound the wound, and the *mullah*s are chanting prayers. Shirzad Mir is sore hurt. He bade me give over the leadership of the garrison to you."

"Nay, Abdul Dost. Be you the leader."

Sir Ralph walked beside him thoughtfully.

"God grant our friend recovers," he added. "Bid him be of good cheer. I must go hence, as we planned."

In answer to the other's startled grunt Sir Ralph pointed to the mountain summits.

"The Uzbeks," he explained, "will not look for a second attempt to leave the citadel this night. I shall strike out for the Mogul court. That is our remaining chance. Do you hold Khanjut—"

"Khanjut will not fall to the besiegers."

The confidence of the *mansabdar* did not surprise Sir Ralph, who knew the belief of the hillmen. He clasped the other's hand.

"See to it, Abdul Dost. I go by way of the watercourse and the hills."

An hour later Sir Ralph descended into the well of Khanjut by torchlight. Diving under the rock arch of the cistern, he swam out into the water tunnel which led to the valley behind the citadel. He went alone.

Some time before sunup he climbed from the stream in the gorge whither his messenger had passed. In this way he began his journey to the South, half across India, to the rendezvous with his countryman, Captain William Hawkins.

III

In England in the year 1600 sundry knights, aldermen and merchants under leadership of the Earl of Cumberland had been enrolled and granted a royal charter in the East India Company.

This venture was planned to dispute Portuguese monopoly of trade from Aleppo east along the Malabar coast to the Moluccas. It was intended to win for England a share of the riches gleaned from the spice, silk and jewel trade with the Indies. It was hazardous, for the Portuguese had a dozen caravels at sea to one English sail; neither side scrupled to employ force.

When Sir Ralph left London it was agreed that a strong fleet under Captain Hawkins was to set out in 1607 for the west coast of India. This fleet was to despoil whatever Portuguese carracks fortune put in its way—thus repaying similar depredations of the doms—and enter the port of Surat before the Winter season.

Sir Ralph's mission was to obtain from the Mogul the right to trade. Without this, Hawkins' expedition could accomplish nothing.

It is easy to say, in retelling history, that the boldness of a project ensures its success. But both Weyand and Hawkins had been launched on their task ill prepared, in almost total ignorance of what they were to meet. The very boldness of the English reacted against them with the first Moguls.

Akbar and Jahangir were actually potentates of all the surrounding lands they cared to bring under their yoke; they drained into their treasuries the wealth of a golden continent. Outside nations, such as Ethiopia, Tibet and Khorassan, voluntarily sent envoys to tender their submission. Emissaries from Portugal were well received and granted *firmans*—trade concessions—because it flattered the vanity of the Moguls.

Under the circumstances it did not occur to the Moguls to respect the growing power of European nations outside their

known world—especially as the medieval Indian Empire neither
desired nor understood sea power. Portuguese and English were
curiosities at court; the former were tolerated because of their
astute diplomacy and generous bribes among the satellites of the
throne; the latter—of whom Weyand was the first to seek trade
concessions—were regarded with indifference because of their
apparent poverty and sturdy independence.

Bitter experience had taught Sir Ralph the difficulties con-
fronting himself and Hawkins. It was all-important that he
should meet the sea captain at Surat. The whole future of English
trade with India depended upon this.

And Sir Ralph was but ill-equipped for his venture south. He
had been marked as an accomplice of the outlaws of Afghanistan;
his life would hang by a slim thread if he fell into the hands of
the Portuguese, whose caravans passed from Surat up the Indus
to Agra.

And he was setting out alone, with his only resource his sword
and some gold and jewels that he had brought with him from
Khanjut, floating the bag that contained them, with his long
sword, tied to a log through the watercourse.

He had at that time no friends in the Mogul's land except
wounded Shirzad Mir in the beleaguered fortress of Khanjut—
save perhaps Krishna Taya, the Rájput girl whose life he had
saved. But she had returned to her own clan of Marwar in Rájputana, near the mouth of the Indus.

A man lacking Sir Ralph's dogged determination would not
have attempted the journey south—eight hundred miles from the
northern mountains to the dry, heat-ridden plain of Hindustan.
He had set his heart, however, on meeting with the English fleet
and returning with Hawkins's papers and presents to the Mogul's
court, then at Kabul.

He knew the way up the valley to the trail that led to the Shyr
Pass. He pushed ahead steadily, the exertion warming his limbs,
which had been chilled by the swim. He tied the bag of gold to
his girdle and wiped his blade dry on a tuft of grass.

As his messenger had done, Sir Ralph caught sight of the Uzbek outpost in the ravine and circled it, cursing the watchfulness of Jani Beg. He made more noise than the slain hillman, but—as he had guessed—the sentries had heard of the unsuccessful sortie and were lax in their watch. Nor were the mounted patrols alert in the Shyr Pass.

Crossing a cleared space, Sir Ralph sighted a form prone in the lush grass. Dawn was revealing his surroundings, and he identified the figure by sight and smell as that of a dead man. The head, he saw, had been cut off.

Thus it was that the Englishman came unwittingly on the body of the Afghan who had failed to get his message through the Uzbek lines.

Noting the rusted helmet that lay beside the body, he paused thoughtfully, then stooped and undid the throat-lacings of the mail. He forced himself to the disagreeable task.

Doffing his own surcoat and boots, he drew the mail over his shirt with a shiver of disgust. The cotton wrappings from the legs of the dead man he twisted about his own limbs. Putting on the helmet, he found that it effectively hid under its loose curtain of steel links his own yellow curls.

The peak of the helmet came far down over his eyes. He bound his own girdle about the mail, attaching to it the bags and his sword.

At first glance he would now pass for an Uzbek in Kallmark armor. The skin of his face had been deeply tanned; his brown mustache was little lighter than those of the Uzbek Mongols.

His knowledge of *Turki* would serve him well, although he could not hope to deceive an Uzbek or a Turk. Only the light hue of his hands, his gray eyes and his European weapon would be likely to stir the curiosity of the casual passerby.

He rolled his well-worn clothes into a bundle which he thrust into a thicket. This done, he struck off through the pines on a course parallel to the Shyr Pass, knowing that he would meet before long with shepherds or wandering hill tribes.

As a matter of fact it was a settlement of nomad Hazaras that he first came upon. These Muslim tribesmen were encamped in a clearing overlooking the southern slope of the Koh-i-Baba. They were a ragged crew, preying on stragglers from caravans and the camp followers of the army before Khanjut.

The young warriors of the tribe were absent on a raid, so there were few but women and old men to guard the ponies grazing by the tents and the camels kneeling in the sun.

They looked up curiously as Sir Ralph approached—their curiosity tinged with well-founded fear that the newcomer might be bearer of punishment from the Uzbeks.

He knew better than to accept their volubly proffered hospitality, contenting himself with purchase of some uninviting-looking rice, dates and dried horseflesh. Then he announced that he would barter a mount.

A graybeard, torn between evil curiosity as to the strange appearance and speech of the newcomer and fear of the Uzbeks, answered.

"We be men of the desert, valiant Mongol," he muttered righteously. "Our horses are our dearest possession; their flesh our food. Would you rob a long-suffering tribe on which Allah has laid the heavy hand of sorrow—"

"Nay, I will buy for gold—a camel."

Sir Ralph was no horseman; he had decided that he would fare better between the humps of a long-haired camel, besides journeying more swiftly. The graybeard whined and bargained for a heavy price.

"Yield me the camel, fool," growled Sir Ralph, "or I will summon the nearest Uzbek outpost—"

"*Aie!*" muttered the other. "That would bring a blight upon our women, and we should be all borne off as slaves to work at carrying earth for the siege. Nay—" a shrewd gleam came into his bleared eyes—"you be a strange Uzbek. And they do not ride south—"

"Perhaps I have taken gold from the *ameer*s and ride to save my skin." Sir Ralph tapped his sword hilt meaningfully. "Peace! And be content that you have gold and not a broken skull."

Nevertheless, when he left the camp he felt that the suspicions of the Hazaras had been aroused. When he mounted his protesting beast and struck south through the rock ravine of the Koh-i-Baba, he was not sure that boys from the tribe did not follow him for the space of a day's journey.

He found the camel uncomfortable but swift. Once they had descended the hills and gained the comparatively level valleys that ran past Kabul, the clumsy animal stretched into a long stride that ate up the miles.

This was to the liking of Sir Ralph, who was anxious to make all speed to the Indus. He allowed the camel to choose its path, so long as they kept to the South. He had only a hazy idea of that region, but knew that if he stuck to his present course he must come out on the river.

He avoided the larger villages, stopping only at shepherd hamlets for food and resting for the night in thickets beside the caravan trails. Once or twice he sighted strings of camels and horses forming merchants' caravans. These he skirted carefully, being content to meet only unwarlike people to whom the double argument of money and a weapon was sufficient to gain him food readily.

The cold of the hills diminished under the strong sun of the plains, and Sir Ralph knew that he must be near the Indus. Questions put to passersby assured him that this was the fact.

So far fortune smiled upon him. He was skirting the Mogul kingdom where few soldiers were to be met with. And his course was across rather than along the main caravan routes from Herat or Kandahar.

At the Indus he was equally fortunate. He came out upon a village whence native fishermen journeyed south in their small craft. Here he sold his camel and bargained with the natives for a place in one of their boats.

A week after his departure from Khanjut he was seated in the
stern of a barge headed down the broad current of the Indus. To
the best of his knowledge his course to the river had not been
observed by his enemies. But he had not reckoned with the speed
with which rumors spread in the congested plains of Hindustan,
nor with the curiosity which his advent had aroused.

All seemed well. There were only two men in the boat, miserable and half-naked fishermen who barely understood his *Turki*.
He had made them build him a shelter of bamboo in the stern,
for the double purpose of shielding him from observation and
protecting him from the unpleasant intrusion of the sun.

But he had not stilled the tongues that were wagging behind
him; nor had he guessed that his person was sought by others
than the Uzbeks.

It was a relief to change from the camel to the boat. The dirty mat
sail propelled them downstream at fair speed. The mud villages
along the banks became more frequent, as did the sight of boys
watering buffalo.

Sir Ralph's character was shaped for action. The idleness irked
him. Time was passing, and he knew that the citadel of Khanjut
could not hold out much longer.

Many things worried him. The time was drawing near when
he would have to leave the boat and strike south, where the Indus
swept to the West. Here travel would be more difficult.

He reasoned that he would then need to traverse the Rájput
province of Marwar not far from Chitore. It would be hard to
avoid questions; likewise, few Hindus would understand *Turki*.

He wondered if his messenger had reached Hawkins. How had
the English fleet fared at the hands of the Portuguese? He longed
for sight of an English face and the grip of a countryman's hand.

He became restive and uncomfortable in the heat. Long since
he had been forced to discard the helmet with its shielding curtain, and the sight of his yellow hair had clearly startled the worthy boatmen. They talked together frequently.

Sir Ralph, ill-tempered from gnawing anxiety and confinement, kept careful watch on them. He prevented them from talking with those on shore. Plainly they had come to fear his presence on the boat.

"This will be a thing of evil omen for us, master," muttered one. "The gods will not smile on us if we serve one of strange oaths who does not bend his head at the waterside shrines."

"Evil omens will bear fruit if you complain or turn back, dolt!" snarled the Englishman. "Pray to the gods if you like, but keep to your oars."

The two fell silent. But that day a party of horsemen watered their mounts at the bank while the fishing craft was passing. Sir Ralph recognized them as Rájputs of the warrior caste.

A rider challenged the men in the boat sharply. One of the fishermen replied. Whereupon the Rájputs wheeled their mounts up the bank and disappeared into the jungle.

"What said the horseman?" demanded Sir Ralph.

"He bade us beware of polluting the water where the horses of nobles drank, master," evasively responded the man who had spoken.

The Englishman guessed that he lied.

"Where be we now?" he asked shortly.

"I know not."

"O one of small wit, answer not thus when I speak. What kingdom lies along this bank?"

His tone was ominous, and the man cringed.

"Jesselmir, lord. The great city of Chitore lies not a week's ride beyond."

"See to it that I am not molested. If harm comes to me both your carcasses will descend into the maw of Father Indus to be food for the fish you catch."

The men bent over their oars in sullen silence. That night a crescent moon tinged the riverbank with an eerie light.

The Englishman, suspecting treachery, kept awake. He resolved to leave the boat after the next night. Any course of action was better than lying helpless in the boat at the mercy of the fishermen.

The next night the moon was fuller. He could see the cypress jungle that lined the river and listen to the cries that floated over the water from the villages. The odor of dried mud, decaying fish and human dirt was overpowering.

Under influence of the heat Sir Ralph slumbered. He woke abruptly, feeling that something unfamiliar had changed the motion of the boat.

His two rogues told him that they were stuck upon a mud bank. Overhead was the tangle of trees, through which glimmered the moon.

Then came the swift splash of feet in the water. Sir Ralph struggled to his knees, cramped by his sleep, and felt for his sword. It was gone.

With a crash the bamboo shelter tumbled in on him under the weight of a heavy body. Dark figures sprang into the boat. He struck out, cursing and pushing erect through the wreckage. Wiry arms seized him, dragged him down. He was pinned to the bottom of the craft, among the odorous fish.

He felt his arms drawn behind his back and bound. Then the arms released their grasp. He was pulled to his feet and pushed from the boat to the shore.

Horses were tethered under the cypresses. These his captors mounted, assisting him to do likewise. Bound as he was and unskilled in horsemanship, it was no easy matter to clamber into the high-peaked saddle.

A glance back at the river, illumined by the faint moonlight, showed him that the boat had pushed off and was heading away from shore with all speed. He reflected grimly that the two rogues had probably known of the ambush.

"My sword?" he demanded in *Turki.*

One of the warriors exhibited the weapon. Sir Ralph reasoned that one of the fishermen had removed the blade while he slept and given it to his captors.

Further speech was checked by the man who held his sword. This individual signed for the riders to move into the jungle.

They struck into a trail through the brush at a brisk trot that jarred the Englishman to the teeth. The trees closed in upon them. Hot scent of the jungle mesh struck his nostrils.

From either side came the subdued cries of bush life. Somewhere far off the deep diapason of a lion rumbled. The heat brought sweat to his forehead. In the half light he could not make out the features of his escort, but they presently came to a clearing where a half dozen torch-bearers were waiting.

The horsemen did not slacken their pace. The native linkmen trotted beside them, their torches serving the double purpose of lighting the way and guarding against possible assault from beasts of the bush.

The light showed Sir Ralph what he had suspected—that his captors were Rájputs of the military caste. He turned awkwardly in the saddle and addressed the one who understood *Turki,* the rider that held his sword and seemed to be the leader of the group.

"What master do you serve?"

The man's lip curled scornfully.

"Since when have the men of the raj owned a master? Nay, for three times ten times a life my fathers have been free warriors."

"By whose order do you seize me?"

"By the word of one whose speech is law in Marwar."

Sir Ralph reflected that they were probably in the Marwar land, near Oudh. He knew nothing of the rajas. Krishna Taya had said that the Rana of Oudh was with the Mogul's army newly returned from the Dekkan. He wondered fleetingly if the Rájput girl had known of his capture.

"The order is that of Raja Man Singh," said his informant complacently.

More than this the man would not say. The Englishman fell into moody silence.

Weariness settled upon him heavily. His long journey had taken toll of his strength.

Little comfort was to be extracted from his present situation as prisoner of the Marwar general. With a shrug he let the matter slip from his mind, accepting his bad fortune with what philosophy he could muster.

The trail widened again into a glade, and water glinted ahead. The link men turned aside to go around a pool. This Sir Ralph noted vaguely. It seemed built in a rough garden. The scent of jasmine hung in the hot air. Torches ahead revealed a pavilion facing the tank.

Here the horsemen halted and dismounted. They lifted him down and led him stumbling forward. He was very weak from lack of food and from the nauseous sickness bred of the days on the boat. Through the opening in the latticework of the pavilion he went and looked up wearily.

Candles lighted the interior of the tent, which was hung with flimsy silks, redolent of sandalwood. On the carpet in front of him a woman was seated. She sat very straight, a slim figure with white robe thrown back over one shapely shoulder, and black hair bare of ornament. Lustrous eyes looked up at him from a grave, childlike face.

"Krishna Taya!" he exclaimed.

She did not answer. Her glance held his steadily, while his dulled wits groped for the meaning of her presence here. The men left the tent to attend to their horses, with the exception of the leader, who stood at his side impassively.

"Krishna Taya!"

Relief crept into his voice, mingled with bewilderment.

"So I am your prisoner?"

"Nay."

The girl spoke quietly.

"You are prisoner to Raja Man Singh, whom I serve."

"Wherefore?"

"You drew sword against the Mogul."

Her eyes wavered and sought her hands, which played with silk bracelets.

"Did you think you could march through half the Mogul's land unseen, Sir Ralph?" She laughed softly, even sadly. "That might not be. A tribe of Hazaras reported your escape, and a search was ordered by the raja. They found the body you had despoiled of its mail and also your garments. Villagers at the Indus had seen you bartering with the fisherman.

"The boat was recognized several day ago," she added in explanation. "The raja's order had been brought hither by riders. My men are his followers. They have brought you to me as I bade them."

Sir Ralph smiled grimly, thinking of the false security he had felt on the journey down the Indus. Krishna Taya had changed. She was no longer the hand maiden of the Uzbek chief. She had slain the man who had taken her from the Marwar clan of the Rájputs, and the act had restored her to the protection of Raja Man Singh.

It was not strange that the Rájput had availed himself of the services of the girl after she had been restored to caste in her own land. Krishna Taya knew much of the secrets of the Uzbek camp and of the citadel of Khanjut.

The Englishman had once guarded her life at risk of his own. And Krishna Taya had looked long on the *Ferang* and kissed him farewell.

Yet he knew the implacable pride of the Rájputs and their devotion to the Mogul. Now that Krishna Taya served another master he would ask no leniency from her.

He confronted the girl calmly, standing erect with difficulty against the weakness that gripped him.

"What does the raja plan to do with me?" he asked bluntly.

"When the time comes you shall know."

"Am I to be held a prisoner here?"

"Nay. Those who command in the raj have planned otherwise."

He shrugged his shoulders.

"Whither were you going?" Krishna Taya glanced up with quick curiosity.

"Why should I tell?"

A flash of annoyance passed over the girl's delicate face. "It were best to answer, Sir Ralph. Here you are not among friends. I must know."

"Know then that I journeyed to Surat."

"To the Portuguese?"

"Where else?"

He smiled at the unbelief mirrored in her dark eyes.

"Then you fled from Khanjut to seek safety on the Portuguese ships?"

"Aye, I fled."

"Fool!" An angry flush mounted in her smooth cheeks. "Do you seek to deceive the servants of the raj? Your life hangs on the word of Raja Man Singh. Oh, you are a dullard of the sea, mingling in matters which concern you not. You fashion a lie clumsily—"

She broke off, eyeing his gaunt face with sudden understanding. The man at his side spoke to her in their native Urdu. Her glance softened.

"Udai Singh says that you lacked food and are beset by a fever. He will take you to his tent, where you must rest this night and the next day. Come then to my pavilion.

"But you must say what is true. I cannot send an answer of lies to Raja Man Singh, and there are certain things he must know."

Sir Ralph suffered himself to be led away. Udai Singh loosened his bonds and drew off the tormenting mail shirt. At his bidding the Englishman went to the far corner of the tank.

Here he was stripped and bathed by the attendants. This done, they gave him clean muslin garments and conducted him to the Rájput's tent, where he fell at once into a broken sleep.

Udai Singh had spoken the truth when he asserted that Sir Ralph was ill. Bad food and the change from the pure air of the hills had inflicted upon him a mild dysentery coupled with fever.

Throughout the next day he lay in the tent. Udai Singh brought him certain doctored drinks which smelled of herbs and the bel-leaf.

Once he thought that Krishna Taya came and looked in on him. A slave was sent who stirred the air over him with a peacock fan. From the fan came the faint scent of attar of rose—a favorite perfume of Krishna Taya.

This care and the Englishman's willpower staved off a more serious illness. By the evening of the second day he was able to go to the pavilion.

It was twilight. He reflected that at this time Abdul Dost would be performing his evening ablutions before the sunset prayer and Shirzad Mir would be calling loudly for scented wine.

How had Shirzad Mir fared? What was the situation in Khan-jut? What did Raja Man Singh seek to learn from him?

He did not know. Nor did he hope greatly that he could win free to Surat.

He groaned at the thought of Hawkins waiting for his arrival. His delay might work hardship for the sturdy English captain at the hands of the Portuguese.

He stifled his impatience as best he could, determined to gain his freedom, if it were possible, by his wits. In this frame of mind he joined Krishna Taya at the edge of the tank, where she was seated on some cushions, attended only by slaves. The Rájputs, however, were not far away.

"Vishnu and Siva have harkened to my prayers," the girl greeted him, "for Udai Singh says you are nearly free of the fever, al-though weak."

"Udai Singh has been kind."

Her glance swept over him inquiringly. She rested her chin on her small hands and gazed out over the water under dark lashes.

"It is the way of the Rájputs to care for a stricken enemy," she said softly. "That is the law of those who dwell ever in the shadow of Yama."

"So you are my enemy?" he responded bluntly. "There was a time when you sought to serve me—"

"And you freed me. The ways of the gods are hidden. Who am I but a servant of my clan and its leader, Raja Man Singh? From birth to death we women of Marwar must be ready to take the hand of Yama and pass to the fellowship of the *bhanuloka*, who are the spirits of the dead."

She sighed, and sighing fell to stroking the silk bracelets. When she looked up she was smiling.

"Ho, Sir Ralph, do you remember the thick-skulled Muslim Abdul Dost and his foolhardy master? They feared that I might do them a mischief. Nay, I am but a poor girl.

"How fare the men of Khanjut? Are they ready to place the sword of submission on a cord about their necks and yield to the Mogul?"

The Englishman looked away obstinately.

"Abdul Dost and Shirzad Mir once allowed you to leave the walls of this same Khanjut," he remarked grimly, "and by so doing earned the hatred of Jani Beg. Have you forgotten that?"

"Perhaps. There is a rumor Shirzad Mir is dying. The siege works of the great Persian, Shah Abbas, have reached close to the walls. His cannon have near completed a breach. Prisoners say that food is short in the garrison, although Raja Man Singh doubts."

"That I know not."

"Doubtless Abdul Dost, who is a warrior of sense, advises surrender?"

"Doubtless."

Sir Ralph was little inclined to tell her what she sought to know.

"Or you would not have left Khanjut."

He remained silent, and she sighed. Her hand touched his arm.

"Will you not trust me, Sir Ralph?" she whispered softly. "Those who are traitors to the Mogul may not live. You are like one who is walking blindly among snares.

"I have not forgotten that you saved my life. And I would do you a service. You seek a *firman* from Jahangir for your countrymen. That you have often told me. See—"

She loosened one of the fragile silk bands from her arm and placed it in his hand. It was a childlike ornament, fringed with red tassels. He looked down at the smiling girl inquiringly. She clapped her hands and called to the Rájputs.

"Raja Man Singh ordered that you should be brought to the Mogul court," she whispered swiftly, while Udai Singh and the others approached. "Pledge me that you will come to the court."

He reflected that this was what he planned to do.

"Quickly," she warned. "I know you seek Surat, to gain word of your countrymen. You shall yet do this, but—promise. You are a man of your word."

"I shall go to the court of Jahangir," he assented.

Udai Singh was near enough to hear.

"Now, speak freely," she cautioned under her breath.

"Witness this, Udai Singh—" she turned to the leader of her men-at-arms—"witness and tell others what you have seen. I have given the silk bracelet to Sir Ralph the Englishman, and he has taken it."

The eyes of the Rájput widened in genuine surprise. Sir Ralph looked at the silk-and-tinsel ornament curiously. It seemed a slight thing to have such an effect on Krishna Taya's warriors.

"Witness, Udai Singh, that he is now my *ram rukhi*—bracelet brother. He is bound to my service, for he has taken the token in his hand. In whatever I do, he will aid me. That is the custom of our clan and people, from the time the first queen of Chitore sent the *ram rukhi* to Privthi Raj—"

Sir Ralph had heard Shirzad Mir speak of this ceremonial of chivalry by which women of the raj obtained the aid of powerful chieftains when in need. The token he knew was never refused. It was considered more binding than a pledge, by the giver as well as the one to whom it was sent.

Udai Singh, however, was far from pleased. His dark face was harsh, and he gnawed at his mustache.

"This is not fitting, Krishna Taya," he said boldly, and the others murmured assent. "Who should aid you except us? This *Ferang* was to be bound and brought prisoner to Raja Man Singh—"

"Fool!" cried the girl musically. "Because you wield a sword well do you question in wisdom? Am I not vested in the authority of the raja himself? Does not the law of our people permit the *ram rukhi* to be sent to any one, slave or king?"

Udai Singh was silent but plainly ill pleased.

"And now, Sir Ralph," went on Krishna Taya, "what do you seek in Surat? It is not the Portuguese."

Quickly he pondered what he should answer and decided it was best to be frank. For some reason best known to her the woman seemed anxious to be his friend. Likewise, he was by nature a blunt man who had no love for lies.

He explained the visit of Captain Hawkins, the plan of the English to occupy Surat in spite of the Portuguese and to win the friendship of the Mogul by bold measures.

"The sea captain is an *ameer* in my land," he said. "He brings gifts and friendship to Jahangir. But his success depends upon me. It was agreed that I should meet him."

"Are you also an *ameer* of the sea, whence you came?"

Sir Ralph nodded assent.

Krishna Taya was silent for a long space, whether pleased or not he could not tell. Idly she tossed tiny crumbs of cake from her lap into the pool, where a flurry of silvery fish fought for the dainties.

"You shall go to Surat," she decided, "with Udai Singh and his following of six. Nay, you were witless to venture alone. Does a man hunt tigers afoot and without nets?

"Guide the English emissaries direct from Surat to Kabul," she commanded Udai Singh. "To the court of Jahangir himself This you may do, but not otherwise," she added, turning to Sir Ralph. "Udai Singh will see to it.

She glanced up meaningfully at the sulking Rájput.

"I give you this as a duty, Udai Singh."

She smiled mockingly at Sir Ralph, whose heart had leaped in pleasure.

"Do not think to escape from my men, *Ferang*, or to turn back from Kabul. You are a prisoner, under pledge. If the pledge is broken you will suffer. Nay, if you are wise you will trust us—for the Uzbeks and Persians will not be so gentle with you. Do not hurry; time is not lacking—"

"Not so, Krishna Taya," he said, disarmed by her artlessness. "I must be at Kabul before the citadel falls. The embassy will intercede with Jahangir for the lives of those at Khanjut—"

He broke off, cursing his plain-speaking tongue.

"O wise *Ferang*," she laughed. "Is not the citadel stocked with food to last for months? Surely you do not fear it will be taken?"

Caught off his guard by her nimble tongue, Sir Ralph could think of no plausible answer.

"Harken, Udai Singh," she chattered gaily, "how the dull *Ferang* tells me what I wish. Now I know that the granaries of Khanjut are near empty. I know that he has left Khanjut seeking aid for those within, who must be hard pressed. Nay, more he hopes to intercede with Jahangir through the English embassy for his friends.

"I must hasten to Raja Man Singh with these tidings. There is much to be done at Kabul—"

She rose lightly to her feet and fled into her pavilion, still laughing gaily. Once within the hangings, however, a change came over her. The mirth faded from her dark eyes and her slight lips trembled.

She flung herself on the cushions, staring through the sandalwood lattice at the group of men. The pulse in her smooth throat beat swiftly. Long she watched without moving.

When the men had made their preparations and mounted for the journey, her eyes followed them out of sight among the cypresses. Then she lay back upon the pillows, sighing.

Her attendants came to light the tapers, but she sent them away impatiently. Twilight merged into darkness. A faint glitter of moonlight showed on the surface of the pool. Still Krishna Taya did not stir.

The moon was high over the jungle mesh before she slept.

On the trail to the South Sir Ralph rode silently, angry with himself and the girl. Only once did he speak to Udai Singh.

"So the pretty play of the *ram rukhi* was a mockery," he observed scornfully, "and Krishna Taya played upon me as upon the strings of her guitar?"

The Rájput reined in his horse sharply.

"Those words were ill spoken, *Ferang*," he stormed. "By Siva and Kali the many-armed, you shall answer for them. Never is the *ram rukhi* given in false faith. My scimitar will cross with your long sword the day I have brought you safely to the court at Kabul."

"I have no sword."

Impatiently the other loosened Sir Ralph's blade from his own girdle and thrust it into the hand of the Englishman.

"Take this, then, and be content. Remember, you fight with Udai Singh the day we reach Kabul. One of us shall slay the other for the words that passed this night."

"So be it," said Sir Ralph shortly.

He had seriously offended the sensitive pride of the Rájput, but he was not the man to soften his own words, nor—in his present mood—did he greatly care whom he fought.

Yet the thing puzzled him. Apparently Krishna Taya had cleverly deceived him, while Udai Singh hotly maintained this was not the case.

There had been a wistful note in the girl's voice when she asked him to trust her. Yet she seemed heart and soul with his enemies.

However, she had paved the way for bringing the English embassy to Kabul. This meant much to Sir Ralph. He cared not how many quarrels he took upon his shoulders, if he could present Hawkins to the Mogul. As for Krishna Taya—

He was mystified by the girl. But he was not the only one in India who was curious as to the true character of the Rájput woman.

Like the breath of wind in the trees, Krishna Taya came and went from camp to camp, laughing at the men who sought to call her to account, and following her own whim. If she played a part, it was well played. If she served a master, no one could name him.

It was with relief and high expectation that Sir Ralph climbed the hills back of Surat after a short hard ride from the Indus bank. To add to the discomfort that horseback entailed for him, rains had been constant. The companionship of the Rájputs, who resented their errand and were afire to ride back to Kabul, was hardly cheering.

At Surat, he consoled himself, he would find the adventurous Hawkins and clap eyes again upon good English faces, bearded and weather-stained. He would feel the deck of an aftercastle under his feet and hear the pennon of the king snap in the shrouds overhead; he would have news of London and the court for the first time in close to four years; perhaps even receive a budget of letters.

So it was with a light heart that he urged his horse to the summit of the rise overlooking the city. The rain had ceased for a space and the sun beat fairly upon them. They had left the green wilderness of bush behind and were out upon the high road again.

At the top of the rise Sir Ralph drew in his horse, drinking in the sight before him. There were the flat roofs and the temples of Surat. At one side of the city were the storehouse and other structures of the Portuguese trading station. Out in the harbor four ships were anchored.

Sir Ralph's gaze riveted upon these. He scanned the high, loopholed fore- and aftercastles, the muzzles of cannon that peered forth amidships and the long pennant stirred by a faint breeze.

He had keen eyes and was familiar with the lines and rigging of ships of several nations. He even distinguished the coat of arms painted on the stern of one caravel.

He could not tear his gaze from the ships. These were what he had come across half the Mogul Empire to see. He remained sunk in a muse so long that the Rájput stared at him curiously.

The four ships were Portuguese.

IV

So long as the hills endure, a Rájput will keep his word.

Illness leaves its mark on a man's spirits, as it saps his strength. Sir Ralph had passed through an attack of dysentery coming on the heels of his long journey. His vitality had been drained more than he was aware while he was buoyed up by the prospect of meeting with Hawkins.

Now he knew that the English fleet had not appeared at Surat. Udai Singh made inquiries in the town and reported that the Portuguese had no knowledge of Hawkins, or of any vessels except their own along the west coast of India.

Sir Ralph had calculated that Hawkins would have arrived a month or two before. It was not likely that he would come during the Winter season.

Instead—so Udai Singh learned—a Portuguese fleet bearing envoys with letters and gifts to Jahangir had put into Surat some two weeks ago. There had been rejoicing at the trade station at this, and the newcomers were being dined nightly pending their departure into the interior.

It was the irony of fate, thought the Englishman, that an enemy squadron had put in an appearance on a mission like that of Hawkins. The arrival of the Portuguese—the first envoys from Europe to greet the new Mogul, Jahangir—would strengthen the hold of the Lisbon adventurers on India and would nullify Hawkins's mission when the latter arrived.

"We will wait," he told Udai Singh. "My companion may be delayed by storms."

"It was the word of Krishna Taya to return straightaway to Kabul," retorted the plain-spoken Rájput, who entertained no expectation of seeing an English fleet appear out of the sea.

They occupied a deserted caravansary on the slope overlooking the seaport. Sir Ralph deemed it best to keep out of sight of the Portuguese, and sent the Rájputs to the city bazaars for food. As he still wore a Rájput turban and the native garments he had donned perforce at Krishna Taya's pavilion, the peasants who sometimes came in sight of the caravansary did not suspect the presence there of a *Ferang*.

His companions, out of humor from their fruitless trip, returned from the bazaars with tales of the Portuguese, their supernatural power of sailing the seas to India, their lavish promises, the influence of their *padres* at Agra, and the glories of great Goa.

In all India, they reminded Sir Ralph skeptically, there was not another Englishman. The promised *ameer* of the sea had not appeared. They believed their own eyes, which told them that the Portuguese ships, not the English, were bringing gifts to the Mogul.

"Moreover," they said, "the low-born Portuguese at the trade mart have a tale that the king is not fit to wipe the dirt from their own boot soles. Verily, they are a race without caste. Are not all *Ferangs* merchants? If so, there are none of the warrior caste in all Ferangistan."

"Wait for a space," counseled Sir Ralph, keeping his temper, "and if the *ameer* of the sea comes you will behold a warrior among many."

"But you have said that you also are an *ameer* of the sea. Yet you have neither the garments nor following of a noble. How may we then believe?"

"What your eyes behold, you may believe."

"We see no *ameer* of the sea. Naught but a prisoner, poor as a Gulf Arab, and friendless save for—"

He broke off moodily.

In this manner they grumbled. Idleness was irksome to the hard-fighting, opium-eating Rájputs, who scented activity at Kabul and were loath to remain. Sir Ralph spent most of his time on the hill overlooking the town, where he could watch the coming and going of the men from the ships.

The sailors were conveying the cargoes ashore—bales of broadcloth, as nearly as he could judge. Each night a banquet was held at the trading-station. The Portuguese factor was in no hurry to see his distinguished guests depart. Tales were circulated from the storehouse of the splendid gifts brought for the Mogul.

It was not a pleasant watch that Sir Ralph kept. He searched the horizon against his better judgment for sight of an English sail, and thereby fretted himself the more.

"God's love!" he cried to himself. "Shall I go here hence empty-handed, to become a pawn on the Mogul's chessboard?"

He brooded on this thought, oppressed by the heat and his own ill health. The sight of the hybrid sailors who held revelry in the town of nights wore on his frayed temper, as did the prospect of the stout pursers and trade clerks who were carried about in pomp in native sedan chairs.

He heard no more from Krishna Taya; Khanjut was as if it never had been; he could hope for no word from England.

Then one day he returned to the caravansary from his lookout with a new light in his eyes.

Udai Singh was polishing his weapons; two others slept under their thatched shelter; no one looked up.

"Tomorrow," he said to Udai Singh, "we will turn our horses' heads to Kabul."

"It is time," yawned the Rájput.

"After nightfall I will pay a visit to the town."

Udai Singh scowled.

"Nay, the Portuguese will lay hands on you."

"Not so."

A new alertness in his gruff voice made the Rájput look up from the sword on his lap.

"Think not, *Ferang*," he responded grimly, "I would risk losing you. There are many of the fat merchants in Surat who would be glad to have you in their grasp. And I have whetted my temper for our meeting at swords' points in Kabul."

"I will not fail you. But, look you, Rájput, I will be in Surat this night and furthermore upon the deck of yonder ship."

The others stared.

"The heat has bewitched your brain," muttered Udai Singh.

"Krishna Taya," smiled the Englishman "bade you go wherever I went. You also will come to the ship."

"I will have you bound and set upon your horse's back."

"Nay; was it not the order of Krishna Taya that I should be free of bonds? If you seek to do such thing, Udai Singh, we shall have our bout here and now and one or the other of us will remain at Surat."

The Rájput hesitated, plainly at a loss. Seeing this, Sir Ralph drew Krishna Taya's bracelet from his girdle.

"Have you forgotten this, Udai Singh?" he demanded. "Will you keep the pledge made by a woman of your clan?"

"By Siva and Vishnu—aye!"

"Then you will do this one thing that I ask. You will go to the bazaars before sundown and buy extra horses. I will give you gold. And bring back with you two of the Portuguese traders."

"Nay; how may that be done?"

Sir Ralph pointed significantly to the other's sword. By now the remaining Rájputs had become interested and clustered around the two.

"I have no quarrel with the traders of Goa," observed Udai Singh after some thought, "although I love them not. The Mogul might be angered."

"Have you a fear? Nay, I shall take the blame. Ho, men of the Marwar clan, do you draw back when swords are pulled from

sheath and there is a fight afoot? Then you are not like to Raja
Man Singh's men."

"Nay, we be also from Marwar!"

"Then you will come with me this night."

Sir Ralph laughed at the mingled feelings expressed in Udai
Singh's dark countenance. The Rájput was doubtful of the new
venture, yet secretly pleased with the prospect of action and unwilling to be thought lacking in courage.

For a long time Sir Ralph talked with them, outlining what
had come into his mind when he was watching on the hill. His
bearded face was aglow with eagerness. The force of his conviction won a grudging assent from the Rájputs.

"The heat has eaten under his skull," they said one to the
other, "but we must go with him or he will never return. Likewise, it will be excellent sport."

When the Mohammedan traders of Surat were at evening prayers
and the bazaars were closing for the day, two things came to pass.

One was the seizure of a Portuguese chirurgeon on his way
to the house of his Excellency, the Portuguese governor of Surat.
The chirurgeon was a stout man who loved his comfort and enjoyed the rest after the long voyage from Europe. For this reason
he was traveling from the waterside to the governor's residence
in a palanquin borne by native coolies.

This worthy individual was passing through the bazaar quarter
meditating upon the rival merits of stuffed fowl and seasoned fish
washed down with spiced wine when he received a startling jolt.
The bearers let the palanquin fall to earth.

Several mounted men had spurred up. A cloak was promptly
dropped over the head of the worthy doctor. He heard harsh commands issued to the coolies, who took up the staffs of the palanquin again and set off at a frightened trot in a new direction.

Suspecting something decidedly amiss, the chirurgeon emit-
ted a series of bellows, reinforced by the jolting of his vehicle.
Whereupon the front of the cloak was lifted and the naked blade

of a sword caressed his beard. At this pantomime the Portuguese fell silent save for a string of muttered blasphemies.

When he tried to lift the cloak to peep out from under it, he received a blow on the head which made his ears sing. By its nature he judged it to be delivered by the flat of a sword.

"Santa Maria!" he muttered, and changed from oaths to prayers, occasionally mingling the two.

In time the jarring ceased. The cloak was snatched off, and he beheld his four bearers panting like dogs upon the ground. The horsemen conducted him by methods not soothing to his dignity to a walled space in which a tawny-bearded, gaunt white man in native garments confronted him.

"Santa Maria!" he said again.

Whereupon the man fell to questioning him fiercely in very broken Portuguese and the worthy chirurgeon received another shock. The man was English.

The questions were about the town of Surat, the habits of the Portuguese, the goods left on the vessels, the envoys and the guard that remained on the ships at night. The captive was allowed no time to adjust either his rumpled finery—he was a lover of good dress—or his wits.

When he had answered to the satisfaction of the Englishman, he was again seized, bound, gagged and laid none too gently under a thatch shelter. Whereupon the men left him.

The second event of importance—and this excited more alarm in Surat—was the fire that started shortly after nightfall in the bazaar quarter near the storehouse of the Portuguese.

Building materials were scarce in Surat, so the structures were of cane, straw and dried mud, all of which burned readily on a night like the present, when there was a brisk wind and no rain.

So aroused was his Excellency and his servants and guests that the dinner was abandoned at its midway point—to the irretrievable damage of certain well-cooked dishes. The small force of soldiery were mustered out to move the trade goods from the menaced storehouses. Even the sailors in the town were summoned, with the two left as a guard for the great boat that had brought the envoys ashore.

These last two could not be found and were deemed probably drunk. The fire raged strongly in the thatch huts and required the attention of all able hands until near midnight, when other matters engaged their attention.

The Portuguese wronged the two sailors, who had been only slumbering by the boat at the waterfront. Their dreams were disturbed by certain white-robed assailants who stunned them without compunction and had them conveyed to a nearby fisherman's hut. When they were discovered the next day they united in saying that devils had descended from the heavens and darted brimstone upon their heads.

Sir Ralph and his Rájputs were not devils, but they worked fiercely and without regard to the feelings of those they encountered. Once the venture was afoot the men of Udai Singh carried it on with a will. Hereditary dislike of the merchant class rendered their task agreeable.

Sir Ralph took the short oars of the great-boat, for his companions were no sailors. The harbor was dark, except for the lanterns high on the sterns of the moored vessels. From the deck of the craft that the chirurgeon had pointed out as the flagship came the sound of a chantey that bore evidence of a wine-butt opened in the absence of the officials.

The five Rájputs—two had been left ashore for pertinent reasons—eyed the looming vessel with curiosity. They had never seen a ship of the *Ferang*s before.

When the great-boat rocked on the slight swell, they gripped its sides uncomfortably. They had little liking for their present position, but as Sir Ralph was smilingly confident they were unwilling to show anxiety.

On the poop of the vessel a petty officer—the purser—leaned on the carved railing and cursed the ill luck that had left him in charge of the ship and its valuable cargo for the night. In the waist, a half-dozen of the hybrid crew discussed the merits of their wine by lantern light.

Below decks a swabber slept heavily beside a huddled group of African slaves destined as a present for the Mogul.

The purser ceased his maledictions to stare at a suspicious glow that had appeared in the town near the storehouse. A muffled tumult came to his ears. So it happened that he did not see a skiff drift toward the ship in the darkness under gentle impulse of a pair of oars skillfully wielded.

The tumult in the bazaar quarter grew to a clamor and he could see native figures outlined against the red glow of flames. A slight scraping overside on the quarter away from shore did not stir his interest.

Some of the men had risen to look at the fire. Then a man by the wine-butt looked up and swore aloud.

"Por Dios!"

Several white figures had climbed over the rail by the shrouds and dropped to the deck.

Those who sat at wine started up with oaths in mingled tongues. They felt for their cutlasses. No natives were allowed aboard the vessels, and these had appeared with an eerie quiet.

The purser turned at the clash of steel in the waist. He was in time to see two men tumbled to deck with bleeding scalps and others run to the tiny door of the forecastle.

It had taken the bewildered and befuddled crew a scant moment to find that the newcomers were not thieving river pirates but expert swordsmen who thoroughly relished a clash of weapons.

The worthy purser snatched a pistol from his belt, only to have it struck up by a long sword in the hand of a tall man who sprang up the after ladder with the skill of long practice.

"Let fall the weapons," hissed a voice in hearty English. "Kneel upon the deck. Kneel, dog!"

Menaced by a steady sword point, the purser had no choice but to obey. The newcomer took up the pistol and deftly wound a turn of rope about the prisoner's wrists, pinioning his arms behind his back. His legs received like treatment, secured by knots caught sailor fashion.

Then the temporary master of the Portuguese flagship was laid on his fat belly on the deck.

"Struggle or shout, my friend," advised the Englishman, "and yonder murderous natives will grant ye short shrift."

Whereupon the purser heard his assailant run to the waist. He lay where he had been placed, listening with distended ears to occasional groans from the crew.

Once the men were safely secured by his own hand, Sir Ralph went to the ladder leading down to the gun deck. Here he could make out a black mass, which he identified as the slaves, and their sleeping guardian. Stationing one of the Rájputs at this point, he inspected the door of the aftercastle.

It was locked, but an ax commandeered from the forecastle, whence the fugitives had been routed, soon splintered the oak panels. Sir Ralph led his party within. He glanced curiously at the carved beams overhead and the Flemish tapestries.

These he tore down and adjusted over the square ports as a precaution against discovery from the shore.

In the cabin of the Portuguese officials stood several stout chests. It took some time to force the lids with the ax. Once this was accomplished a variety of articles was disclosed—good broadcloth garments, velvets, elegant ruffles, plumed hats.

Here also were the gifts destined for the Mogul—firearms, clocks from Brandenburg, inlaid comfit-boxes of gold, silver statues of the saints, a volume of illuminations, among other things.

Sir Ralph sought and found the papers of the embassy. He knew enough Portuguese to make certain they were what he wanted. There was no mistaking the ornate seal of Portugal.

The Rájputs would fain have examined the treasure at leisure, being curious, but the Englishman set them to work carrying the spoil to the waist of the ship.

Cautioning Udai Singh to watch the prisoners, he descended to the great-boat and stowed away the objects his companions passed down. Then he took up the oars and with a single Rájput in the skiff struck out for the dark shore.

He landed at a spot outside the limits of the town and left the warrior to guard his plunder. By the time he regained the ship the tumult on shore was at its height and small boats were passing to Surat from the other vessels of the fleet anchored some distance away.

Sir Ralph worked swiftly, for he knew there was danger of a boat from the other ships coming to his prize. Once he heard a hail in the darkness and rested on his oars. But the cry was not repeated, and he safely rejoined Udai Singh.

The Rájputs had assembled the remainder of the spoil on deck. Not content with this, however, Sir Ralph stripped the cabin of an oil painting of Philip the Second, of sundry brass candlesticks and gilt pikes.

"These we will need Udai Singh," he observed thoughtfully. "Nay, we must have more."

His glance ran along the deck, which was dark except for a solitary lantern.

"Eh—we will take a cannon; nay, a brace of cannon."

Udai Singh grunted.

"What if we are seen by the *Ferang*s in the other sea-castles?"

"The rail protects us from observation," Sir Ralph made answer readily. "Come, I will need your help."

He collected various loose ropes and attached them to two brass demi-culverins—light pieces with the coat of arms of Portugal carved on their breeches. Under his directions the Rájputs lowered the two cannon overside into the boat.

The skiff was now dangerously loaded. But Sir Ralph had seen a cock-boat perched on the poop. This he lowered into the water by the ropes detached from the cannon.

"Death's blood!" he cried. "Almost I had forgotten our hostage."

They hauled the stout purser from his abiding-place.

"The cock-boat will hold you and your men," Sir Ralph informed Udai Singh, "and this stout rascal must needs be towed. Well, a wetting will do him no great harm and it will still his tongue."

It was a strange procession that wended its way from the flagship to the dark shore shortly before midnight that eventful evening. In the van the Englishman rowed the heavily laden skiff. A rope attached to the stern guided the Rájputs in the cock-boat, who splashed clumsily with their oars and breathed dark curses upon seacraft, large and small.

Another rope led from the cock-boat to the struggling purser, who had been informed that if he made outcry he would be beheaded.

"Surely we must strike off the heads of the others," Udai Singh had objected.

It was peculiar to the Rájput chivalry that their splendid fairness to foes did not extend to commoners.

"Nay; they will be safe, trussed in the forecastle," laughed his leader. "They saw little of what passed, and we do not wish to slay men needlessly."

So it happened that when the admiral and his companions returned to the flagship later in the night they found the crew bound and clamorous in the foredeck, the slaves excited and fearful, and the purser nowhere at all.

The seamen when released protested that demoniacal river pirates had stormed the ship. Both the chirurgeon and the purser were missing. Natives of Surat said the next morning that they had seen the palanquin of the former conveyed to a caravansary up the hillside.

But no chirurgeon was to be found at the caravansary. Numerous horse tracks led into the interior from here, and under threat of torture natives disclosed that certain Rájputs had been seen in the vicinity.

This however did not aid the Portuguese to recover their missing papers and treasure. A hastily formed search party returned in two days without news of the daring invaders.

The Rájputs and their spoil had vanished into the jungle.

Sir Ralph and Udai Singh were for the moment in accord. Both wished to make speed to Kabul. The horses were pressed to their limit, and camels were procured when they reached the province of Marwar, and their friends.

Here a rider joined them with word from Krishna Taya:

"Haste to the court. Raja Man Singh has need of you and those you bring."

This was the message, and it accorded with the wishes of Udai Singh, who was secretly pleased at the new importance of his cavalcade.

Sir Ralph found food for thought in wondering if Krishna Taya had learned of their looting of the Portuguese fleet. The woman had an uncanny knowledge of all that passed in the Mogul's land.

But he was now able to face the issue with confidence. He had a game of his own to play, daring and difficult, yet one that was to his liking.

He had abandoned his horse for a camel, and his native garments for the finest velvet suit in the purloined wardrobe of the envoys. A plumed hat sat his yellow curls jauntily; a silver chain supported a jeweled cross at his throat; his beard had been trimmed and scented by the involuntary aid of the sulky chirurgeon; his cloak was of finest purple plush.

"Ho, Udai Singh!"

He waved his gloved hand at the laden caravan and his two captive Portuguese.

"Behold the Portuguese embassy, bound for Kabul!"

"And at Kabul—"

Udai Singh touched the hilt of his scimitar meaningly.

"'Tis well." Sir Ralph offered his recently acquired snuff box to the Rájput, who took a pinch with the courtesy that custom prescribed for his rank and caste.

"Tomorrow we be enemies, and today we be—friends."

Udai Singh glanced at him curiously. The new splendor of his companion was not lost on him.

"You have put your hand on the knees of the many-armed gods, *Ferang*," he said.

V

In his red tent Jani Beg sat at chess with Shah Abbas. The Uzbek bent his massive shoulders over the ivory board and scowled. The Persian, his dark eyes mellow with hashish, moved the tiny gold warriors with consummate skill.

"I take your *rukh*, my friend," he smiled, removing a miniature castle from its square.

Jani Beg muttered an oath and reached for his wine cup. It was empty, and Shah Abbas motioned for one of his girl slaves to refill it.

"You must taste my wine of Shiraz," he urged politely.

Then, as the other hesitated, he signed to the girl to fill his own bowl first. He glanced as he did so with lazy admiration at the smooth form of the half-nude slave.

"Nay, I also will drink," he laughed, "lest you think there be poison in the cup. How runs the verse?

> *Life drags its steps from day to day*
> *To Death's dark caravansary.*

"If I quaffed poison from your cup," quoth Jani Beg grimly, "my dagger would let out the life of one poet whose spirit would anger the stars with verses as bad as the scent of a decayed flower."

"Eh, your eloquence astounds me!" Shah Abbas exclaimed in mock delight. "Nay, I know a verse to cap your speech—

> *Nowhere blows the rose so red*
> *As where some Persian sultan bled.*

"I think Omar himself could not have said it better," he added complacently. "I must have my scribe write it down with the couplet I uttered to the Mogul's messenger. It was my wit, I doubt not, that made Jahangir decide to journey hither."

"Ho, I thought I had arranged that matter."

Jani Beg glared at his companion like a dog seeking a bone of contention. The veiled mockery of the Persian always angered him, and tonight the nerves of the two men were on edge.

"You take a mimic castle with brave skill, but you have not yet forced the Khanjut wall with your cannon."

"Fool! It is not yet time for the assault. Jahangir does not leave Kabul for several days, and we planned to delay the storming till his arrival."

"True," admitted Jani Beg morosely.

He studied the chessboard and moved a piece. Shah Abbas smiled.

"You have entered the trap I set, Jani Beg. See—I advance this pawn, so, and—*shah m'at!*"

"*Shah m'at** the king is dead."

Jani Beg glanced up curiously.

"A good omen, that," he added.

"Yes, a castle is taken and a monarch dies. That likes you well."

"And you."

The Uzbek looked about the tent cautiously. Only two slave girls were present.

"Our plans go well. Khanjut is beset on every side. The breach is wide enough now for the attack. The garrison is thinned by arrows and hunger."

"It is rumored Shirzad Mir lies on his death bed. Only that stout scoundrel Abdul Dost remains to be reckoned with. The *Ferang* has vanished somewhere—to purgatory, I hope."

"Doubtless he has forsaken a falling house. He is but a merchant, when all is said—though the witless raja names him an *ameer* of the sea."

------

* Checkmate.

"Raja Man Singh hunts in the hills of Koh-i-Baba, complaining that we do naught here but sit on a carpet."

"The Rájput will awake to his error when his hundred horsemen face my three thousand Persians."

"And—" Jani Beg lowered his voice cautiously—"I have summoned new levies of Uzbeks from Ferahana and the Kara Kirghiz. Between us we will muster a full eleven thousand men-at-arms."

"Jahangir has no thought of our numbers," assented the Persian, "or even that foolhardy prince would not venture to Khanjut with his four thousand-odd followers."

"Bazaar hangers-on, eunuchs and slaves for the most part. I doubt if Jahangir could mount two thousand able-bodied soldiers in all his camp."

The Uzbek's tawny eyes gleamed.

"My spies have reported the main army of Rájputs still in northern Hindustan."

"A good place for them," approved Shah Abbas smilingly. "I like not these horsemen of the raj. They are furies from hell in battle, as they reck not of their own lives."

"They are distant. They could not ride here in half a moon, and Jahangir has pledged his coming within a week."

Jani Beg could not refrain from speaking the exultation that heated his brain, warmed by the strong wine the slave girls had given him.

"Great stakes are on the gaming board, Shah Abbas. Once we have seized the Mogul—"

"Or he dies—"

"—Better our captive—the artificial empire of India will be rent. Your home levies from Isphahan and Khorassan will move across the border to the Indus. My Uzbeks will unite with the Hazaras, and I shall be joined by the Mongols from the northern steppe. Kabul and Lahore will fall like rotting fruit—"

"Kandahar is ours for the plucking—"

"We will sweep down to the plain of Hindustan once the northern Mohammedan tribes have joined my standard—as they will if the cry of a holy war is raised. The chieftains of Kashmir are in half-revolt at this moment. The Dekkan is but half subdued. Only the Rájputs will remain."

His high voice had risen in spite of his caution.

"The rajas will be content to hold their own lands again. Nay; with Raja Man Singh in our hands we can treat with them to our advantage. Once the figurehead of the Mogul is severed from the empire, it will be open to conquest by the sword—"

"By the beard of my fathers!"

Suspicion gleamed in the Persian's glance.

"Your plan leaves little comfort for me. Eh—how do I know you mean to play fair? No one may trust your word—"

"*You* must abide by it."

Jani Beg caught the other's plump wrist in his iron grasp. The slave girls stared at the stark passion mirrored in his broad face.

"By the blood of the Prophet and the ninety-nine holy names of Allah, can you afford to question me? Whose horsemen hold this plain? Who has the soldiery powerful enough to take Kabul this moment? Who has the means and the will—if he choose—to slay you in this tent?"

Shah Abbas was no coward. But the ferocity of the Uzbek held his gaze in fascination. Slowly the light faded from Jani Beg's slant eyes.

"Nay, Shah Abbas," he growled, "you and I have one hate and one foe. We will keep faith in this."

"I doubt it not."

The Persian was once more master of himself.

"As surety," continued Jani Beg, "I will take on myself the more hazardous task of the two. When Jahangir lifts the royal standard for the assault of Khanjut, I will lead my Uzbeks in the rear of the Rájput horsemen. The men of Hindustan will claim the van of assault by hereditary right. This will rid us of some troublesome swords, for the garrison of Khanjut is not yet powerless."

"The stars betoken good omens."

Jani Beg snorted.

"Believe ye the message of the stars?"

"Believe ye the word of Allah, Jani Beg?"

"When it serves my need."

The Uzbek reached for a wine cup and, finding it empty, dashed it on the ground.

"But the Rájputs will not return from the assault. My men will outnumber them nine to one, and those that escape the arrows of Abdul Dost will fare worse at my hands. That will account for the elegant Raja Man Singh."

"And I?"

"You will remain near the person of Jahangir with your Persians. You have friends among the court

"Aye; they will be warned of what is to be."

"See to it. Jahangir will keep about him a strong personal following. When you see my sword drawn against the Rájputs, turn on the Mogul's guards. He will have elephants. So much the better."

"Aye; it will then be hard to escape."

"True. Once we have the Mogul among our men it should not take long to scatter any following that might muster from his camp."

The Persian stroked his beard tranquilly.

"Before the assault I will station outposts in the Shyr Pass," he observed. "So may we keep news of what has happened from spreading too swiftly, and gain time to mobilize our reinforcements."

"'Tis well thought on, Shah Abbas."

Jani Beg stretched his powerful arms and yawned.

"You warm my heart, Shah Abbas. Truly they have named you the Lion of Persia—"

The effect of the hashish had worn off when Shah Abbas summoned in the two slave girls and called loudly for his palanquin. He was consequently irritable. When he flung himself across the knees of one of the women on the cushions of the palanquin, he felt for the other and found her missing.

"Ha, wanton!" he snarled. "Where is your mate? Two of you I brought with me—the other being a newcomer in my tent."

"I know not, my lord."

But a clearer head brought sudden suspicion. Shah Abbas jerked around his bulk and seized the slave's slim throat.

"Speak, misborn *katchani*!" he cried. "Open that lying mouth!"

He twisted the girl's neck unmercifully.

"Whence fled the other? Nay, I remember now that she asked to come to attend me—"

The unhappy woman gasped and clutched at the arms that pressed her into the cushions.

"I know her not, lord!" she whimpered. "She offered a small string of pearls if she could come with me—"

"Death of the saints!"

Shah Abbas was genuinely alarmed, reflecting how freely he and his companion had spoken.

"Know you where she went?"

The slave shivered and felt of her throat.

"She asked me the way to the Rájput tents—"

At the Persian's bellowed command his bearers halted. Shah Abbas leaped from the palanquin and swept the nearest rider of his escort from saddle, mounting in his place.

"Ho, follow me!" he shouted to his cavalcade of riders.

Cursing his drug-heated brain, he sought the nearest path to the tents of Raja Man Singh. He had wondered, in the tent, why the girl pleased him so. Now he knew it was because he had not seen her before. A strange woman had heard what passed between him and Jani Beg, and, being an unknown, might have understood *Turki*.

He spurred his horse on furiously and gave a cry of delight at glimpse of a slender figure wrapped in a shawl that ran toward the nearby pavilion of the Rájput chieftain.

"A shirt of cloth of gold," he cried, "to the man that brings her down with an arrow. Speed, fools! She must not gain the pavilion—"

Several of his escort plucked arrows from quivers.

"Haste!" he stormed. "A purse of rubies goes to the one—Ha!"

He reined in his horse on its haunches. He had seen the woman stumble and fall with a piteous cry. The feathered shaft of an arrow showed between her shoulder blades.

Attired in lounging robes, Raja Man Singh and attendants appeared at the entrance of the tent, attracted by the outcry. The Rájput stared from the girl to the mounted Persians.

Shah Abbas leaned over to look into the tortured, upturned face of the slave girl.

"Know you this wanton, Raja Man Singh?" he asked sharply.

The chieftain scrutinized the dying woman.

"Not I," he responded frankly, "although her dress might be that of the Rájput slaves. By the fire of *bhairobi*, it is ill to slay thus."

Shah Abbas turned away indifferently.

"She stole—a small string of pearls," he said. "Almost she escaped."

Into the rocky pass leading to Kabul the caravan from the Portuguese fleet wended its stately way. The cooler air of the hill country made its passage easier, and it was within a few day's march of the Afghan city when Sir Ralph urged his camel beside that of the stout Portuguese chirurgeon.

He swept off his hat in an elaborate bow.

"I have not yet asked your name, *seignior*."

The other greeted him with an angry stare. Sir Ralph, however, had ascertained at Surat—at the caravansary—that his captive understood English.

"So the *seignior* is pleased to be haughty? Ah, well, it matters not. There was a distinguished sailor of your country whose name was da Gama. Perchance you have heard? I will call you da

Gama. Know that here hence you are Seignior Emanuel da Gama, minister of the Portuguese court, chirurgeon and confidant of— myself."

Curiosity loosened the man's tongue.

"And who, in the name of purgatory and hellfire, are you?"

Sir Ralph shook his yellow curls reprovingly.

"Nay, you must not pry into such a weighty matter, da Gama. Udai Singh might tell you, but sometimes questions are ill-advised, *seignior*."

"The Rájput admits you are his prisoner."

Sir Ralph frowned.

"Fie, *seignior*! You have long ears. Must I crop them? Udai Singh means but that he is bound to convey me safely to the Mogul's court.

"Which brings me to the point of my discourse. I shall present you and the worthy purser to Jahangir himself."

The chirurgeon's black eyes glinted shrewdly.

"The purser," continued Sir Ralph, "is none other than his Excellency the Vice-Admiral of Portugal, as related in certain papers which I have been perusing at sore labor—for I know little of Portuguese script."

Da Gama—as he had been christened—bristled.

"That dog of a scurvy seaman—"

"Nay; his Excellency."

"Whelp of Satan!"

"Mayhap, yet for the nonce Dom Pedro Raymundo is he anointed. For the space of seven days I have been reading him his lesson, and he has it well by heart. Don Raymundo is a noble of acute perception, *seignior*, and he knows on which side of the gangplank he had best plant his foot."

"You cannot force me to betray my honor by threats."

Sir Ralph twirled the nose-cord of his camel reflectively.

"Did I say aught of threats, Seignior Chirurgeon? Nay; I have appointed you to a higher rank and granted you a crest. Are you not fain to be content? My faith, I would be in your boots."

The Portuguese shrugged his bulky shoulders and subsided into irate silence. He was a man of temperament, not without courage, and he had tried several times to escape the caravan, hoping to reach the priests of Agra.

But the watchful Rájputs had restrained him. Udai Singh was not altogether content with the new whim of the Englishman; yet he was keen enough to see that it was best to keep the two Portuguese under close watch lest they work harm.

For the rest, Udai Singh had reasoned that by bringing Sir Ralph to Jahangir he was but fulfilling his duty. If Sir Ralph chose to carry along the spoil and the two prisoners, it was no concern of Udai Singh.

True, the Portuguese were somewhat in favor at court and there might be complaints; but Udai Singh knew that the Mogul would not be angered at receiving the gifts, and the responsibility for the whole matter lay upon the shoulders of the Englishman. Moreover, although he would not admit it, Udai Singh was led to follow out Sir Ralph's wishes by the fact that the latter was the *ram rukhi* of Krishna Taya. So the worthy chirurgeon had met with little comfort in his attempt to escape and was consequently worried. He was the more troubled because he did not know what Sir Ralph was planning to do when they met the Mogul. But this last the Englishman was now ready and willing to explain.

"Riders have been sent ahead, *seignior*," he observed thoughtfully, "to inform Jahangir of the coming of the Portuguese embassy. Nay, do not scowl. Are you not the embassy? Have I not the papers from Lisbon?

"Do not forget, *seignior*," he added coldly, "that I am in command of your person and that of the purser. I want you to play the part I have described. That is—be silent when you appear at court. That is all I ask.

"I will do the talking. Obey me and you will be well treated. You will be able to return in safety to Agra or the ships."

"Santa Maria! I will not do this—"

"It is the fortune of war, *seignior*. You will!"

Sir Ralph's steady eyes hardened.

"Your worthy countrymen once put poison in my food at Delhi. Their intrigues drove me penniless and afoot into the hills. They befouled my name and would have got rid of me if they could."

The chirurgeon shrugged his shoulders. Such measures were by no means strange to him.

"I shall deal with you fairly, *seignior*. All I ask is—silence. For a brief space."

"Scoundrel! Low-born—"

"*Seignior!*"

Sir Ralph's voice was dangerously mild. "Perhaps I have not told you that I was once knighted by my sovereign lady the queen on the deck of my ship after that slight affair of the Armada. It was my neglect not to tell you before. But do not forget that you have been told."

The Portuguese looked full on his enemy.

"What seek you to do?" he demanded skeptically. "I have heard that you once failed in your request of a firman from the Mogul. You are a discredited man, an adventuring seaman. What do you hope to gain from your stolen finery and the papers you have stolen—"

"My faith!" Sir Ralph glanced at him whimsically. "All this is true, and it has tried me sorely. Yet now do I see a chance to achieve what I had near despaired of. Aye, with your merciful assistance, *seignior*, I shall gain the *firman* for my king. Remember, I ask silence. Nay, there is another small matter."

He cast a meditative eye along the dusty cavalcade ahead of them.

"'Tis true I have small skill in reading. Still, certain phrases of your credentials please me not, Seignior da Gama. They vilify my king and my countrymen. They were ill thought on. Now the letters patent of the Portuguese embassy to Jahangir should not be marred by slanderous utterances."

"What would you have me do?"

"Cross out the blasphemous sentences, *seignior*. It would not be fitting for my hand to touch your papers, but you—being one of the envoys—may do so."

"Nay, I shall not."

"I think you will. It would like me well to make a fair and proper copy of the letters in *Turki* to present to the Mogul, but—I love not such remarks concerning England. Tonight I will give you a pen—"

"You waste words."

"My faith—no."

Sir Ralph turned and called to Udai Singh, who brought up in the rear.

"This nobleman," he informed the Rájput, "is weary of his camel. He would fain walk, or rather run."

Udai Singh looked doubtfully at the chirurgeon's bulk.

"Walking, *seignior*," remarked the Englishman politely, "is excellent for the understanding. It clarifies the clouded intellect. Dismount, therefore, and think upon your stubbornness."

Confronted by his enemies on either side, the Portuguese at first tried to cling to the neck of his beast. Propelled earthward by Sir Ralph's heavy hand, he subsided into the dust with scant dignity.

Once afoot, Udai Singh was in no mind to allow the captive to fall behind. So the chirurgeon was forced to keep up with the caravan at a round pace, half walk, half run, that tried him sorely.

Clouds of dust choked him. When he lagged he heard the impact of Udai Singh's steed at his heels. The sweat poured from his face and chest, and his legs, which had rarely been obliged to bear his weight for long, shook under the strain.

The attention of others in the cavalcade was attracted to this unusual spectacle, and da Gama's dignity suffered accordingly. When he beheld the mirthful gaze of the purser, smugly seated on a horse, he gave in.

"The foul fiend take your papers!" he gasped. "I will swear by all the saints that I was tortured."

"Nay—" Sir Ralph pulled his camel away—"that sounds ungracious. Of your own will and accord you will do it."

The stout Portuguese glared, rocking with unaccustomed fatigue. The mirthful scrutiny of the Rájputs, who had small sympathy for a pampered body, decided him.

"Have done," he groaned. "I shall do it."

"From very love of me?"

"Sant . . . From love of you."

"Mark, Udai Singh," observed Sir Ralph, "what a man's legs will bring him to. The fat captive cries that he loves me."

That night they pitched their tents within sight of the towers of Kabul. And after the evening meal Sir Ralph sought out the Rájput leader, first making sure that the Portuguese were safely guarded.

"We are at Kabul, Udai Singh," he said, sitting on the carpet beside the other, "and it is time you and I settled our quarrel."

The Rájput glanced at him inquiringly.

"It is not permitted to draw sword at Jahangir's court, Udai Singh. This is our last night, and the ground is fair for sword play. I will keep my promise."

Udai Singh did not speak for a long moment.

"It is well, *Ferang*," he responded mildly. "The gods are angered by a broken pledge. Yet I am bound to others."

"The quarrel was not of my seeking. I knew not the meaning of the *ram rukhi*."

Udai Singh seemed to be wrestling with a serious problem.

"Once, *Ferang*," he said, "the Queen of Chitore sent the *ram rukhi* to Humayon the Mogul and he took it. He mustered twice a hundred thousand spears to ride to the aid of Chitore, which was besieged. Eh, he rode slowly, slowly. He dallied, full of the idea of chivalry. But while he dallied the siege was pressed."

Sir Ralph waited, knowing by experience that Udai Singh never talked without a purpose.

"Chitore was the gem of the Rájputs, *Ferang*. It was the jewel in the diadem of Marwar. It is like music in the mouths of our children.

"My grandmother was in Chitore at that time. To hearten her husband she mounted, with other women, and took up a spear. She rode down the cliff and found death on the lances of the enemy. It was well done."

He glanced reflectively over the huddle of small tents and the kneeling camels to the evening sky, which was fast changing from purple to a full, blood red.

"Humayon and his men rode slowly. When was a Mogul swift to aid others? Chitore fell."

"And Humayon?"

"He kept the *ram rukhi*, for he loved to tell of his chivalry. Eh—could he name back his fathers for thirty-six generations, as we of the Marwar clan of Chitore? Yet he was fond of a good tale."

Udai Singh traced patterns idly in the sand with the point of his scimitar.

"The sin of the sack of Chitore," he added, "has become an oath of the Rájputs. It was taken by the army of Khorassan.

"The queen who sent the *ram rukhi* put on her bridal garments and ran into the *johar* fire kindled by the women in the vaults of Chitore. Since then the doors of the vaults have been closed. Twelve thousand women followed their queen."

Sir Ralph fumbled for words and failed to find them.

"The men," concluded Udai Singh tranquilly, "donned the saffron garments of death and painted their faces with turmeric. They ran forth with jewels upon their turbans, and there were none who cared to survive the death of their women. Such is our custom."

The picture Udai Singh had painted with a few words was vivid even to the unimaginative Englishman.

"Why should a man shrink from the halls of Yama, or the hot embrace of the *bhanuloka*? His name will live in the annals of his clan. Few know the heart of the Rájputs. If they knew that, they would read the secret of India."

He turned suddenly on his companion.

"Such is the *ram rukhi*, *Ferang*. You did not know its meaning, and you do not now. But before you leave India, if it is the will of the many-armed gods that this should come to pass, you will perhaps understand more.

"You will understand the strength of the bond that unites you with Krishna Taya. Not in the warmth of love, but in the colder tie of honor."

"But what need had Krishna Taya of me?" demanded the Englishman awkwardly.

"Nay, am I the one to say? But she has willed this thing, and it will suffice. What is in her mind you may learn. The shadow of a great happening is in the land. The rumor of war passes over the Mogul land."

Sir Ralph stared at his inscrutable companion.

"Has Krishna Taya said so?"

As Udai Singh was silent, he pressed his inquiry.

"Whom does the woman serve?"

"She serves the Rájputs."

"And Raja Man Singh?"

"He also serves the Rájputs." Udai Singh glanced around cautiously. "We shall not fight, you and I, *Ferang*. The gods have willed otherwise. I have thought upon it long; and I will not draw weapon against the *ram rukhi* of Krishna Taya. The Mogul has left Kabul and is on his way to Khanjut."

"And we—"

"Shall follow. Word has reached me from Krishna Taya. We must make all speed to the pass of Shyr though which Jahangir and his court are now proceeding."

Many things raced through Sir Ralph's mind—the difficulty of meeting the Mogul as he had planned, the urgent necessity to reach the court before it gained the Khanjut camp, where he would at once be recognized. Udai Singh, however, was a man of one idea.

"We will not cross swords, *Ferang*," he declared, "because Krishna Taya has need of you. It is my task to bring her to you."

The Englishman looked up frankly.

"You and I have fought side by side, Udai Singh, and eaten of the same bread and meat. Why can we not be friends?"

"That also may come. But only when you have served Krishna Taya."

He bent his handsome head nearer.

"Do not dally with your own thoughts as Humayon did."

With that he rose and stalked away through the tents. Sir Ralph gazed after him uncertainly.

VI

When the Mogul mounts for war the standard of yaks' tails is lifted; the elephants sound their challenge and lift a knee in the loyal taslim. *A million men will follow the standard.*

But in the sight of Allah is the Mogul more than one of the million!

Muslim proverb

The narrow pass of Shyr had been transformed by the advent of the camp of Jahangir. The Mogul traveled slowly, taking his ease and attended by the court, men of all ranks and provinces. Midway in the pass Jahangir had received news from Rájput messengers of the coming of the Portuguese embassy.

He decided, against the advice of his Persian followers, to receive the foreign emissaries in the pass. Being a lover of amusement, he was more inclined to this from the reports of valuable gifts brought by the strangers, and by his intention to hold a festival of the harem at their arrival.

These festivals were a part of the court life, and one was now due. On such occasions the royal tents were given over to the harem and the *katchani*s, who received sundry presents from the *ameer*s and *mansabdar*s.

It was also prescribed by custom that the Mogul should not see the ambassadors until they made their formal entry. In this instance Jahangir arranged a reception of the usual splendor.

The royal pavilions had been pitched along the clear stretch by the bank of the Amu Daria. A double line of cavalry extended down the pass. Cannon were sounded as the embassy reached the first of the cavalry.

A group of *ameer*s rode out to meet the cavalcade that came up the pass. They turned and rode back at the head of the procession. A lane had been cleared through the throngs of onlookers to the royal pavilion, where the elephants were drawn up.

The beasts were robed for ceremony in their cloth of gold and breast- and head-pieces of gold and silver. The sides of the pavilion were drawn up, disclosing a gallery of carved sandalwood inlaid with mother-of-pearl, wherein sat Jahangir.

Two railings extended beneath the gallery, the inner one containing the higher *ameer*s of the court—the Persian councilors, northern emissaries, the leading Rájputs and a group of black-robed Portuguese priests who were given this position by special favor.

Such was the scene that opened before Sir Ralph when he rode up at the head of his men. A setting of splendor in the barren, stony valley, ringed with its sunlit pine slopes.

Sir Ralph reflected grimly that the setting was different from that of his first visit to the Mogul. Then he had got no nearer the peacock throne than an audience with certain high *ameer*s of the Persian party and an unpleasant encounter with Portuguese priests.

He could not be sure that some of the men who had seen him at Delhi were not now in the pavilion of the Mogul. If so, they would be likely to recognize him in spite of his change of costume.

But they would scarcely identify him until he stood before Jahangir. He had studied the etiquette of the court, and he knew that once he had been presented in person to the monarch no one would presume to interrupt the ceremony.

By now they had reached the twin lines of waiting elephants. Behind the beasts the imperial kettledrums sounded a roll, beaten by musicians who squatted in the dust. Sir Ralph cast an appraising glance over his cortege.

The two Portuguese rode close behind his horse. They were scowling, but appeared in no mind to make trouble for him, especially as Udai Singh in all the finery that he could muster was within arm's reach, mounted on a splendid Arab that danced playfully under touch of spur.

Udai Singh seemed impassive, but the Englishman knew that the Rájput was keenly nervous at the importance of the coming ceremony and the part he had to play therein. However, Udai Singh had his orders from some one—perhaps Krishna Taya—and was prepared to aid Sir Ralph at all cost.

Behind the remaining Rájputs shepherded the led animals with the presents, attended by a company of slaves mustered by Udai Singh from somewhere.

So it was that Sir Ralph came to the audience with Jahangir that he had sworn he would obtain—came with an escort of two captive Portuguese and gifts plundered from his enemies. And the court that he approached was beset with his foes. Not easy circumstances for any envoy, but doubly difficult for the Englishman, who was known to have sided with the rebels of Khanjut.

In his favor were three things. He was reasonably sure that his caravan under Udai Singh's guidance had outstripped any couriers sent from the Portuguese fleet. He had laboriously acquired a knowledge of *Turki* and so was able to speak direct with the Mogul. And he alone of the assembly knew what course of action he was going to follow.

This last was a vital point. Neither the Portuguese priests nor the Persian councilors could prevent his speaking to the Mogul now. This opportunity was what he had craved.

For the moment the priests believed him to be the envoy from the fleet, arrived with unexpected speed. The chirurgeon and the purser behind him knew better, but—Udai Singh had his orders.

For the moment the cards were in his hand. He asked nothing better. Afterward would come recrimination, opposition, a storm of protest. Yet he had the opportunity to play his trump and win the favor of Jahangir.

He dismounted a dozen paces from the pavilion entrance. Within the shadow of the awnings he could see the watching throng and the gallery of the Mogul.

Over the head of Jahangir was a canopy of velvet and silk. From the feet of the sitting monarch a carpet stretched from gallery to floor and led between the lines of courtiers out to where he was standing.

A glance showed him that the two Portuguese and Udai Singh were afoot. He strode forward and paused at the pavilion entrance. A buzz of expectancy went through the crowd, who were waiting to see whether he would perform the prescribed low salaam or risk the displeasure of Jahangir by a European salutation.

Sir Ralph did neither. He spoke in a low aside to a watching *mansabdar* who was acting as captain of the guard. The officer took his message to a councilor of the outer railing, who in turn repeated it to a vizier directly beneath the balcony. This official spoke the message to Jahangir.

"The envoy, sire," he whispered, "begs that you will grant him leave to make the salutation of his country."

At Jahangir's assent Sir Ralph swept off his plumed hat and made a courteous bow. He advanced to the first railing and repeated it. Here he waited until Jahangir signed for him to advance to a spot directly in front of and below the gallery.

With another bow the Englishman complied. He had learned his lesson in court etiquette. The Portuguese imitated him clumsily. Udai Singh salaamed in the customary manner, but with a splendid swagger which was pardoned in the Rájputs.

Jahangir glanced down with pleased expectancy. He was a broad man with slender wrists and ankles, richly robed, wearing the small turban with plume and tiara of the Moguls—a full-bearded, calm-eyed man, somewhat bored, vain, yet instinct with courtesy and a genuine desire to play the part of a benevolent monarch despite his self-indulgence in powerful stimulants and the vices of the age.

Sir Ralph glanced up at him confidently, eagerly, holding his excitement under iron restraint.

He extended his documents to a waiting eunuch, who conveyed them abjectly to the hand of Jahangir. The Mogul took them, opened the scrolls and glanced at them impassively.

They were in Portuguese, but Jahangir recognized the crest. He beckoned to a second attendant.

"Clothe the envoy in a *serapah*," he commanded.

Sir Ralph allowed himself to be robed in a brocade vest, a silken sash ornamented with gold, and a turban. While this was being done he glanced back at his companions.

The Portuguese had caught the eye of the watching priests. A nudge from Udai Singh had restrained any impulse on their part to speak, but the priests within the railing had scented something amiss.

Perhaps they had failed to recognize the officials; perhaps Sir Ralph's un-Portuguese appearance had stirred their suspicions. They were frowning and whispering among themselves.

Clad in the robe of honor, Sir Ralph turned and nodded to Udai Singh. The Rájput signed to the waiting slaves, who advanced bearing the gifts.

The Portuguese had chosen their presents well, with a knowledge of the fancy of Jahangir. Gold or jewels would hardly have appealed to the man who owned in person the treasure of a hundred kingdoms.

But the quaintly wrought clocks, the engraved comfit-boxes and the illuminated volumes aroused his keen pleasure. He fingered the silver images of the saints and the silver-chased pistols with satisfaction.

He received the painted portrait of a Portuguese monarch with critical complaisance. The art of portraiture was well known in India, where the artists were almost as skilled as in Europe. The Flemish tapestries and the brass cannon likewise met with his approval.

Sir Ralph then took from his throat the crucifix, which was handed to Jahangir as the personal gift of the envoy. This completed the ceremony of the presents.

"Will the Conqueror of the World* receive my letter and read what is written therein?"

A murmur went through the assembly. Few had thought that the envoy would speak fluent *Turki*.

"It will be a pleasure greater than words can paint to read what is brought from without the World Empire."

Silently the Englishman extended a missive which he took from his girdle. A eunuch broke the seals and held it for the Mogul to read. There was an involuntary craning of necks behind Jahangir, who studied the letter intently.

Once his brows went up and he stroked his beard. Surprise and bewilderment were slowly mirrored in the faces that read over the monarch's shoulder. The missive, which had been written in *Turki* by Sir Ralph himself, was readily understood.

Jahangir glanced from the letter to the waiting envoy, from Sir Ralph to the letter.

"By all the gods," he exclaimed involuntarily, "this is a riddle. This letter is from one who calls himself the king of England. It asks for a trade alliance between my empire and the distant kingdom of England."

Sheer bewilderment held the throng of courtiers silent. The priests, who had caught what was said, pressed nearer the gallery,

---

* Interpretation of the name Jahan-Gir.

scowling. The two Portuguese behind Sir Ralph looked on blankly. They knew no word of *Turki*.

"Nay, sire," Sir Ralph said instantly, "I am the envoy of my sovereign the king."

"Of England or Portugal?"

"Of England."

A Persian councilor who had been listening closely attempted to whisper to the Mogul, but Jahangir motioned him impatiently aside.

"This is verily a riddle," he frowned. "I was told that the embassy from the Portuguese, who are my friends, waited speech with me. Did my *ameer*s seek to deceive me?"

"Nay, sire. I am come from the Portuguese fleet. I have placed in your hand the credentials of the Portuguese. But my message is from one who would be your friend, who desires your good will and amity. From my lord of England."

At this point one of the black-robed priests raised his hand and endeavored to gain the attention of Jahangir. The Mogul, however, was waxing curious. Sir Ralph had carefully planned the effect of his words.

"I know naught of the English," he exclaimed irritably. "They live beyond all the seas. They have sent no embassy to my court. The Portuguese have said that they are evil-souled pirates—"

"Sire," Sir Ralph broke in audaciously, "will you grant me leave to explain my presence? Two years have I waited to address the World Conqueror. I bear tidings that have been kept from you—that should reach your ears."

Curiosity is a potent force. Fronted with a riddle, Jahangir was in no mind to let it pass without explanation. He signed angrily to those who were trying to distract his attention.

"Speak!" he ordered, and to his followers:

"Peace! The man has been presented to me in audience. I would hear what he has to say."

"Intrigue and bribery, sire," began Sir Ralph promptly, "have kept me from your presence. If I had not escaped poison I should not be here."

He spoke forcibly, directly. Sir Ralph was at best no courtier, and he had the blunt speech of an English seaman. In the court where he now stood, plain speaking and honesty were an unknown quantity. Yet his only chance lay in arousing the interest of Jahangir.

"The Portuguese drove me from Delhi when I first came. They won over my interpreter and the *ameer*s to whom I spoke. They whispered to those near you that the English were pirates."

He had the attention of the Mogul now. Jahangir was nervously alive to hints of bribery about his person.

"A hundred years ago the Portuguese first came to India. Two years later a fleet under da Gama captured and slew a shipload of Muslim pilgrims bound for Mecca; later this same envoy of Portugal hanged fifty fishermen seized in the harbor of Calicut.

"This policy of aggression was followed by Dom Francis Almeida, who broke up and harassed a Muslim fleet off the Gulf of Cambay. In the lifetime of Akbar, your father, the Portuguese operating from Goa, which they had taken, defeated the combined princes of Bijapur, Ahmadnagar and Calicut."

Just as the first of the speech had been greeted with a murmur of approbation from the Mohammedans of the court, so now this reference to Goa drew forth a stir from the Rájputs.

Sir Ralph, now sure of undivided attention, outlined briefly the evils of the Portuguese regime in the empire, the religious bigotry of a people that preached holiness and oppressed captured natives.

"Only the Mogul should hold power in India," he said boldly. "Yet these poisoners and intriguers of Goa keep whom they choose from your presence. They have promised riches to the Moguls from their trade. Have you seen those riches?"

He could guess nothing from Jahangir's face, but the priests were obviously disturbed.

"The power of the Portuguese on the seas is waning. The flag of England is entering the Indian Sea. Half a lifetime ago there was a great sea-battle between the ships of England and the empire of Philip, of which Portugal is only a part. Our enemies were crushed and lost many thousands. "

"How may I know the truth of this?" broke in Jahangir.

Sir Ralph smiled.

"Nay, I was there. And another who fought the Armada will come to your court. His word will bear out my tale, and he is Captain Hawkins, an *ameer* of the sea."

He swept his hand at the pile of gifts.

"Here is witness. Nay, I alone with Udai Singh and some Rájputs have stripped the wealth of the Portuguese embassy. Because of my wrongs I have done this. Yet he who is coming after me will do greater things."

He faced the scowling Portuguese.

"Is it an evil thing to avenge a wrong? What says the law of the Prophet? I and those of my country and my king desire to despoil no one. We seek the rights of trade. But an injury we never forget."

"How came the Rájputs to aid you?"

"In the bonds of friendship. I alone take the blame. They obeyed orders. I brought the message of my sovereign to the Mogul. If I have done ill it is for the Mogul to say. None other."

Something like admiration showed in the handsome face of Jahangir, but also misgivings. A vizier whispered to him. Sir Ralph awaited his reply quietly. When he would have spoken, one of the Portuguese stepped forward with a low salaam.

"Harken, sire," the man exclaimed forcibly, "to the word of your servant. Like the warmth of the sun your righteous judgment nourishes the land and its people. Whithersoever the wind blows the uprightness of Jahangir, Conqueror of the World and Ruler of the Earth, is known.

"An offense has been committed against our countrymen. I ask that you pass judgment upon the offender."

He glanced at Sir Ralph scornfully. The early Portuguese in India were not lacking in boldness. But they were political tools, sent to win favor from the broad-minded Akbar and Jahangir. Their accomplishment in India was purely in the way of temporal power.

"What is this man but a sea-robber?" he cried, his hatred gaining the upper hand. "He is an adventurer, without caste or rank. Before your wisdom answers him I plead that you will hear our speech upon the matter.

"Let time and wise counsel influence your decision. Do not grant him what he asks now, but later when you may inquire fully into the rights of the matter."

Sir Ralph threw up his head.

"Soft words are the tools of the evil, Conqueror of the World," he said calmly. "Is it not the law of the Moguls that a visiting ambassador may not be threatened with such a charge? I claim the privilege of an envoy."

Jahangir stroked his beard meditatively. He was by no means a weak-minded man. But his position as ruler of a half-dozen nations and as many religions made caution a necessity.

"I pledge the safety of your person, Sir Ralph," he responded mildly.

"Sire," put in the Portuguese shrewdly, "you are beset by many cares. Tonight is the festival of the harem, which has long been prepared for your delight. Nay, it would be a sin if your honored enjoyment were impaired by this upstart. Postpone the matter until you can weigh both sides."

"Time," objected Sir Ralph, "will not make right a wrong. England asks the open hand of friendship. Will you refuse?"

But Jahangir was thoughtful. The power of England was still unknown in India, and—he had honored the Portuguese with his favor.

"I must think upon this," he decided. "Verily, I will speak with you again. Tonight you will make merry with us. For you are a bold man, and I am fain to like you."

With that he rose. The interview was at an end, the papers handed to his courtiers. Sir Ralph bowed.

He had played his trump card. And it had failed.

That night the bank of the Amu Daria was transformed into a torch-lit garden. It was the evening of the harem festival, when women could be seen by courtiers half veiled or unveiled, the hour when the charms of the *katchanis*—the dancing-girls—were bared for all who would to see.

The shrill music of Hindustan crept from concealed coverts along the bank of the river. The plaint of hidden musicians swept the silk-booths, wherein clustered the women of the harem.

Among the booths wandered Persian, Rájput, and Muslim nobles. High *ameers*, arm in arm with sturdy *mansabdars*, sought out the booths where ornaments, perfumes and trifles of various kinds were bartered with the utmost good nature.

A bearded Kashmir lord attracted attention to himself by loudly declaring that a jade bracelet offered by the wife of a Khorassan chieftain was worth scarce an ounce of silver, while the woman, nervous yet pleased at the publicity of the occasion, demanded at least two pieces of gold.

Such was the spirit of the festival—jest and a play of wit.

The dark-faced Kashmiri raised his price to two ounces of silver, while the *begum* with great display of dark eyes and flashing teeth insisted that he was verily a thief of thieves, a true Kurd. She cried for gold. The onlookers smiled.

The noble shrugged his robed shoulders.

"I will give three pieces," he laughed. "By the beard of my father, you are a shrewd mistress, *begum*!"

And he tossed down three pieces of gold. The watchers applauded, save for a few Mohammedans, who disliked the appearance of women unveiled in public.

Through the crowd wended slim *katchani*s, reveling in the music and high spirit which were twin partners of their profession. For the space of the festival they were on an equal plane with the wives and families of the nobles. And Jahangir himself talked and jested with them.

Such was the evening of the harem—when the Mogul's court forgot intrigue and ambition in child play. But there were many who did not forget.

Among the court were certain northern nobles who talked briefly with elegantly dressed Persians. And certain eunuchs who bore messages from those who did not like to be seen conferring with the Persians. Under the mask of light-hearted abandon there ran an undercurrent of suspense and expectation unperceived by Jahangir and his immediate friends.

The Mogul himself was well content.

He was playing the part of a gracious host to his court, laughing at the wit of the women and loudly exclaiming upon the by-play of a certain *katchani* who had made a Muslim merchant pay many times its value for a pair of pearl earrings.

"Ho," he chuckled, "here is one who is by breed a getter of profits; yet this sightly maiden has taken him by the ears!"

The courtiers echoed the good humor of their lord, save for Sir Ralph. The Englishman had been forced to join Jahangir's party by the hospitality of the Mogul. But the scene of that afternoon would not be dismissed from his mind.

He had made a bold stroke. He had claimed the firman for England from the Mogul. Interference by his enemies the Portuguese had checkmated him. He had no delusions concerning what was in store for him.

It mattered little that Jahangir had sworn that his person would be inviolate. The Portuguese of the court entourage had delayed Jahangir's answer. They were even now probably comparing notes with the two Portuguese he had taken prisoner. For neither Udai Singh nor his charges were to be found.

Time would serve his foes. Pressure would be brought to bear upon *ameer*s and eunuchs close to Jahangir. He would be painted as little better than a pirate. Other presents would be hurried from Surat to the court. Bribes would not be spared.

His attempt to win Jahangir's favor had been foolhardy. If it should fail, as seemed likely, he would endanger the success of Hawkins's embassy when that should arrive.

Sir Ralph was moody. He suspected rightly that many of the *ameer*s who were most attentive to him were leagued with the Portuguese.

Outwardly he was smilingly observant of all that went on. But he missed Udai Singh. In fact he saw few Rájputs in the throng.

Jahangir, who seemed to have lightly dismissed the affair of the afternoon, drew him toward the *katchani*'s booth.

"Verily, Sir Ralph," he whispered heartily, "here is a beauty whose face is like a rose, who is a stranger to my harem. She wears the dress of a Rájput, although the women of Marwar and Oudh are not of the *katchani* caste."

He pointed out the woman who had just sold the pearl earrings. Sir Ralph followed him perforce to the booth, while other courtiers pressed around.

"Ho, Pearl of the Harem!" exclaimed Jahangir in high spirits. "Have you a bracelet that I may buy? Nay, I am but a poor man, and I can pay no more than some few copper coins."

"Then you can do no business with me, O Poverty-Stricken Dweller of the Exalted Throne," she chattered, and the courtiers, scenting the interest of their lord, applauded. "My bracelets are those of Oudh, and their worth is beyond price."

Sir Ralph started. Until then in the faint light he had not looked fully upon the face of the woman. But he knew well the voice of Krishna Taya.

"Take pity upon me, Nightingale of the Twilight," smiled the monarch. "I must have a bracelet. Perchance there is some poor ornament of silk—"

"Nay, would you have what cannot be bought?"

Krishna Taya's white teeth flashed. Sir Ralph thought she cast him a warning glance.

"Surely you would not buy for gold a *ram rukhi*!"

Again the flicker of the dark eyes seemed to caution him not to recognize her.

"Such as the *Ferang* at your side has in his girdle?"

"By the splendor of Lakshmi!" swore the surprised Mogul. "Has the *Ferang* envoy bought a *ram rukhi*?"

Curious glances turned toward the straight figure of Sir Ralph. He was silent, pretending he had not understood, and wishing for the presence of Udai Singh.

That Krishna Taya was acting a part he knew. But what part? And what was her purpose in calling Jahangir's attention to the pledge he carried?

"Nay, Lord of the World," she responded swiftly. "The bracelet was given. The *Ferang* is the bracelet brother of the Rájputs. There is a service he must perform for the woman that gave it."

Even the keen wit of Jahangir could not quite fathom whether the woman jested. He looked curiously at Sir Ralph.

"What grain of truth is in this?" he asked. "Have you truly the silk bracelet?"

Krishna Taya nodded imperceptibly.

"Aye, sire," said the Englishman.

He showed the silk ornament, and Jahangir fingered it with a frown. The pretty ceremony of the *ram rukhi* was not lightly bestowed, especially upon a foreigner.

"Where got you this?

"At Marwar."

"From whom?"

Sir Ralph thought swiftly. "From a woman of Raja Man Singh. I know not her rank."

Again Krishna Taya signaled almost imperceptible approval.

"'Tis a riddle!" The frown had not left Jahangir's broad brow. "Eh, you also are a riddle, *Ferang*—an English pirate who dares to confront me with stolen gifts and demand the royal firman—who makes grave charges against those high in my trust—"

"Who is a consort of rebels, sure," put in the Kashmiri as if in jest.

"And a *ram rukhi* of a noble Rájput woman, sire," smiled Krishna Taya, twisting an errant lock of dark hair into place behind the silver band across her forehead.

"And envoy of the King of England, sire," amended Sir Ralph quietly.

Jahangir threw up his hand in mock bewilderment. Nevertheless, there was acute uncertainty in the long look he cast at the Englishman.

In the brief interval since that afternoon, Portuguese money had begun its work among his followers. The favorable impression made by Sir Ralph's bold words at the reception was being rapidly effaced.

Sir Ralph could not fathom why Krishna Taya had called attention to the *ram rukhi*, unless it was to show Jahangir that he was allied after a fashion with the Rájputs.

The girl was as much a mystery to him as ever. He felt that he was a pawn, a piece moved hither and thither on the chessboard of intrigue.

More and more he began to sense the byplay of great political forces in the trifling events of the evening. And the feeling grew on him that Krishna Taya was disposed to be his friend.

"Can a man serve two mistresses?" demanded Jahangir, looking from him to the woman.

"Aye, when both have one heart," responded Krishna Taya promptly. "Have you forgotten, O Lord of the World, that your mother was of the Rájputs?"

Seeing Jahangir's frown deepen, her tone changed swiftly. She clapped her hands as if at a delightful thought, and became again the light-minded *katchani*. She was a woman who could play many parts.

"Is this a riddle, sire?" she chattered. "Nay, will you know the answer? In a pavilion behind this booth is a wise prophet of

Hindustan, one who can trace the shadow of the future on the scroll of fate.

"He will answer your questions. Your heart will be gladdened by sight of him.

"Come, then. Take my hand, and all mysteries shall be unveiled for the sight of the World Lord!"

Boldly she caught Jahangir's arm and drew him laughingly into the booth. Some of the attendants started forward, but Krishna Taya waved them back.

"Nay, the Lord of the World will come with me alone."

She seemed animated by the spirit of the festival, even perhaps by an overdose of bhang. Yet it was a serious matter for the Mogul to go unattended anywhere.

Jahangir followed her half-curiously, half-distrustfully. He motioned to the bearded Kashmiri.

"Attend me," he said curtly.

Krishna Taya cast a mocking glance over her shoulder.

"Then shall the *Ferang* come," she smiled. "Is he not the man of mystery?"

Jahangir nodded. The three followed the swaying form of the girl. It was a jest to Jahangir, who was more than interested in the wilfulness of Krishna Taya. The Kashmiri stalked after his lord with a dark glance at Sir Ralph, who kept pace with him.

They passed through the scented darkness behind the booth to the riverbank where a small tent loomed in the shadow under a giant willow. Into the tent Krishna Taya disappeared.

"Come, Monarch of Asia," she called from within. "Come; for here is one who will delight your heart—a prophet of prophets, a master of the secrets of evil. Come, do you fear?"

Jahangir motioned the Kashmiri into the tent ahead of him. The warrior strode forward alertly, hand on sword. The Mogul and Sir Ralph followed curiously.

The interior of the pavilion was scantily lighted by a single brazier, from which came scent of ambergris and sandal-paste. A cloaked form stood behind the brazier, its face concealed as it made the low salaam.

Then the figure cast aside the cloak. It was Raja Man Singh. Krishna Taya's laughter echoed musically.

The Rájput stood at ease before Jahangir, his elegant attire bearing no sign of the hard ride that had carried him from Khanjut. He greeted Sir Ralph with calm courtesy, seeming not a bit surprised to see the Englishman. He lifted his dark head jauntily, looked full into Jahangir's eyes, and smiled.

"No soothsayer or magician am I, Lord of Asia," he said directly, "but a bearer of grave tidings. It was best that we should speak alone"—he glanced once significantly at the Kashmiri—"hence the pretty trick of the *katchani*, who is a servant of the Rájputs and may be trusted."

"Greetings, Raja Man Singh."

Jahangir overcame his surprise.

"This man is a councilor of the Persians. You may speak before him."

Raja Man Singh hesitated briefly, then bowed.

"Let the Kashmiri look to his ears then," he said plainly. "Here be only friends and we seek no wolf's friendship. Harken, Jahangir. I rode down the pass from Khanjut in the space of a single watch. Others who were on the way, I passed."

"I knew not of your coming."

"Nor did others, sire. Save for Krishna Taya. At Khanjut I scented evil in the air. Treachery lurks at the end of the pass—"

"The rebel, Shirzad Mir—"

"Nay, the hill chief is sore wounded in his fortress. By Siva, he was a brave man. The thought has come to me that we wronged him. Was he not the chosen man of Akbar?"

"He took up arms against the Lord of the World," put in the Kashmiri smoothly.

"Nay, against Jani Beg." The Rájput turned from the other scornfully. "At Khanjut, Jahangir, I hunted stags in the hills. The Persians and Uzbeks thought that I idled. Eh—I let them think so. And I counted the levies that came down the northern passes from Ferghana and the Kara Kirghiz. Lord, many thousands of horsemen are mustered before Khanjut."

"To storm the citadel of Shirzad Mir," growled the councilor.

"Five thousand would have sufficed for that. Three times five thousand are waiting in the foothills of the Koh-i-Baba. For what? Nay, it has an evil look."

Jahangir stroked his beard in silence. Sir Ralph thought that the girl crept nearer to his side.

"Where falcons wheel and point," continued Raja Man Singh boldly, "there is game marked for the slaying. Lord, I have followed your standard since I was a boy. I am of the blood of your mother.

"And I smell evil in the air of Khanjut. Jani Beg and Shah Abbas speak smooth words, but they whisper together. Many messengers have been sent back into Persia. Why has the storm of Khanjut been delayed?"

"For my coming," Jahangir admitted tranquilly.

"In battle many things may happen. How many trustworthy horsemen are with you, lord? Perhaps two thousand, and of these scarce the same number of hundreds are Rájputs."

"Nay, come not to Khanjut. Mount your followers and ride down the pass to Kabul. There you may meet the main Rájput army which hastens north. That is my message."

Jahangir bit his lip.

Sir Ralph glanced curiously at the keen, delicate face of the Rájput and the stout countenance of the Kashmiri. He understood little of what passed. But he felt the tension in the air.

"Sire—" the councilor bowed servilely—"surely Raja Man Singh has partaken too freely of opium, which is his failing. Jani Beg and Shah Abbas have invited you to their camp. Would they dare molest the Mogul? Is their friendship to be spurned on a breath of suspicion? That would be a serious offense.

"They are loyal now, and they number their followers by the thousands. Trust them, and they will be like a good scimitar in your right hand."

"Perchance a dagger in your back, Jahangir." The Rájput folded his arms defiantly. "I have seen what I have seen, and my eyes do not lie."

All the merriment had fled from the Mogul's handsome, indolent face. Graven lines of care appeared about his brow.

"Nay, Raja," he temporized, "should I rein my horse from Khanjut now it would be taken for a sign of weakness."

"Better that than death at the hand of a traitor."

"The Rájput seeks to place your person in the hands of his army," sneered the Kashmiri, emboldened by the hesitation of the Mogul.

Raja Man Singh's lean hand shot out and closed about the hilt of the other's scimitar. He whipped out the curved blade and thrust it into the Kashmiri's hand, drawing his own at the same instant. So swiftly had he moved that the other could do naught but stare.

"Another word, O wise councilor," he whispered, "and your sword will cross with mine. If that happens, look to your life."

The man's eyes gleamed in the faint light from the brazier and sweat showed on his forehead. He edged back toward the entrance of the pavilion.

Another moment and he had turned, to run swiftly into the darkness. The Rájput sheathed his weapon with a laugh.

"A scimitar tests a warrior's words," he said shortly. "Come, lord, give the order to mount and ride down the pass while yet there is time. Eh—I passed sentries by the Amu Daria who were newly posted. The nets of the hunters are closing about us. Trust your safety to the sword of Rájputana."

"If you had proof—"

Jahangir was disturbed. It is possible that he might have followed the advice of his general if he had been allowed to decide the matter for himself. But while he hesitated and Krishna Taya added her voice to that of the raja, there was a commotion without the tent.

The flare of torches showed through the silk. Voices and footsteps came rapidly nearer. Another moment and the pavilion opening was filled with courtiers, eunuchs and *ameers*. In the front of the group was the stout form of Shah Abbas.

"Greeting, Lord of India, and a myriad blessings."

The Persian salaamed and stood erect, his mellow eyes taking note of the three others in the tent. Sir Ralph guessed that the Kashmiri had not been slow in bearing news of what was passing to his friends. Likewise, he wondered whether Shah Abbas had been with the party the raja had seen in the pass.

"No longer," cried Shah Abbas eloquently, "could I restrain my desire to look upon the Presence, unworthy though I am. So I rode hither with a small escort to announce that those before Khanjut await your coming anxiously."

"I am honored, Shah Abbas."

Jahangir bent his head gravely. The coming of his courtiers seemed to have reassured him. He was a man of infirm purpose.

"Tomorrow," continued Shah Abbas, pressing his advantage swiftly, "Jani Beg hopes to welcome your standard. The day after we have prepared a goodly spectacle for your pleasure. Nay, it will be finer than a score of elephant contests or the hunting of a hundred tigers. The rebel stronghold will be laid low and the Mogul will ride his elephant into Khanjut."

For the first time he seemed to take notice of Sir Ralph.

"By the ninety-nine holy names of God!" he swore. "How is this? The *Ferang* dog at the side of the Mogul! Why, this scoundrel is escaped from Khanjut! He is a man with blood upon his head—the one that slew a score of Jani Beg's men."

Jahangir glanced at Sir Ralph uneasily. The Englishman realized the seriousness of his position. Shah Abbas had known of his presence in Khanjut—a fact which Raja Man Singh, for reasons of his own, had seen fit to overlook.

The Persian's nimble wit let slip none of his advantage. His visit to Jahangir had been decided upon when he and Jani Beg learned through their spies that Sir Ralph had appeared in the Mogul camp.

The Persian had seen a chance to deal a shrewd blow for himself. His craftiness was the one thing needed to swing Jahangir's decision.

If Shah Abbas had not visited the camp in the Shyr Pass that night the trap at Khanjut could not have been sprung; and the bloody scene before the Iron Gate, as Khanjut has been styled in Indian history, could not have been enacted.

"I have been told, sire," cried Shah Abbas, "that this rebel is masquerading as the *ram rukhi* of a Rájput woman. Nay, I have myself seen him on the walls of khanjut."

A clever stroke this, for it coupled in Jahangir's mind Sir Ralph with the Rájputs, and by implication cast suspicion on the latter.

"It seems to be true," the Mogul admitted.

He wheeled impatiently on Raja Man Singh.

"Proof! Give proof of what you have whispered, and then I may believe. Not otherwise. Shah Abbas is our ally."

The Rájput's hand went to his sword. But Krishna Taya stepped forward.

"A woman of mine, sire," she cried, "joined the slaves of yonder Persian. She overheard the talk between Jani Beg and Shah Abbas. Straightway—so important did she deem it—she fled to the tent of Raja Man Singh. But Shah Abbas struck her down when she was about to breathe her message. Ask him why that was done."

But Shah Abbas was not to be taken by surprise.

"Eh," he muttered, "so this is Krishna Taya, who was once the slave of Sir Ralph. Jani Beg has said it. Perchance she is also his *ram rukhi*?"

He glanced coolly at the startled girl.

"A woman without caste, a wanton—" he continued blandly.

"Nay," growled Raja Man Singh furiously, "she has honor in the Marwar clan—"

"And sees fit to consort with rebels?"

The Persian waved a jeweled hand amiably.

"I question not the honor of the Rájputs. Yet why is this woman dressed as a *katchani*? Surely her tale is wild. Doubtless she has drunk much bhang during this festival. The slave girl she mentions I slew for—a theft."

He smiled triumphantly at Raja Man Singh.

"As for this *Ferang*," he added swiftly, "the Lord of the World will surely not permit him to go free. I have heard it said he should be tried as a pirate for an offense against your good friends the Portuguese."

"Jahangir," said Sir Ralph, "has pledged my safety. I came to his court as envoy."

Shah Abbas's brows went up, and he fingered his scented beard daintily.

"As envoy from Shirzad Mir?"

"From England."

"I have not heard of that *khanate*." Shah Abbas turned deferentially to Jahangir. "I have a thought, sire, that this man is dangerous. We know naught of the tribe of England. But we have seen his sword drawn against you from behind the walls of Khanjut. Nay, your word is sacred. But surely he may be confined as prisoner until his story can be examined?"

Jahangir glanced at his courtiers dubiously. A murmur of assent greeted the words of Shah Abbas, who seemed to have many friends present. At a sign from the Mogul two soldiers stepped to Sir Ralph's side and bound his arms tightly behind his back.

"When we have dealt with the traitors of Khanjut," added the Persian smoothly, "this man may be tried. Jani Beg waits to welcome you. Surely you need not doubt the Uzbek who has taken up your quarrel with Shirzad Mir. Have I not shown good faith by coming hither alone?"

"Nay, I doubt you not, Shah Abbas."

Jahangir lifted his broad head with sudden decision.

"There is peace between Persia and Delhi. Tomorrow I ride bridle to bridle with you to Khanjut that all may know you are dear to me as my own blood."

"Your words, sire, are like drops of water upon a parched garden."

Shah Abbas turned aside to hide the exultation he could not keep from his eyes. But Raja Man Singh stepped forward.

"Then let me guard this man, sire," he suggested bluntly. "It is the privilege of the Rájputs to watch over the person of the Mogul. The *Ferang* will be safe with me—safer perhaps than elsewhere."

To this Jahangir assented, glad to have the troublesome matter settled. The Mogul departed to entertain his new ally, Shah Abbas, and Raja Man Singh accompanied Krishna Taya out into the darkness, motioning the Englishman to come with them.

Back in the camp the music had struck up again and they heard the murmur of voices that greeted the appearance of the Mogul. The three were walking by the riverbank, the raja talking earnestly to the girl.

"There should be three horses here," he said, glancing into the shadows. "Udai Singh was ordered to await our coming with the beasts. I had planned for Jahangir to leave swiftly."

He cast about among the bushes, then called Udai Singh. There was no answer.

"Here is the spot," said the girl anxiously. "And Udai Singh does not fail—"

She uttered a soft cry of alarm. Sir Ralph saw her stoop down. A glow from the distant torches struck through the foliage.

Bending close with the raja, he saw that Krishna Taya had raised something from the ground to her lap. He could make out the head and shoulders of a man.

"Udai Singh!" swore the Rajput.

"His tunic is damp with blood," sighed the girl. "And the skin of his face is cold. *Aie*—he was a faithful man!"

The raja rose, his voice calm.

"Shah Abbas works swiftly. I will fetch you a horse. Remain here with the *Ferang*."

He strode away into the shadows, and Krishna Taya replaced the body of her servant on the ground. Her light hand drew Sir Ralph back into the shelter of a thicket where the glow from the bazaar did not penetrate.

"Where the wolves have passed," she said bitterly, "they may not come again. But we must have a care. Shah Abbas would fain lay your body and mine by poor Udai Singh. *Aie*—the curs!"

She was very quiet for a space, her hand still touching his arm. He could feel her silk veil against his cheek, and the faint scent of attar of roses crept into his senses. He was conscious of the throb of a beating pulse against his arm.

"The Mogul is blind!" she cried softly. "He does not see the pitfall set for him at Khanjut. There is a doom preparing for him— and for us of the Rájputs. A heavy doom. The river of Khanjut will run red. You will see it—"

She broke off, a catch in her limpid voice. The grasp on his arm tightened involuntarily. Sir Ralph, conscious that she was looking at him, was taciturn, as was his wont.

"I will not be there," she whispered. "But I pray that the *ram rukhi* may safeguard you."

"Tell me, Krishna Taya," he asked seriously, "the meaning of the bracelet. Is there a service I can do you?"

"O foolish *Ferang*," she laughed, "must you have a plain an- swer to all your thoughts? Seek you to learn truth from Krishna Taya? Know then the time will come when Raja Man Singh will stand with his back to a wall ringed around by many foes. Strike then to aid him.

"I have told him that in you we have a swift sword and a keen brain. When that time comes the *ram rukhi* will be fulfilled."

The words of the dead Udai Singh came back to Sir Ralph's mind.

"My friends are in Khanjut—if they still live. Shirzad Mir and Adbul Dost are my comrades, Krishna Taya."

"Nevertheless, the Rájputs will fight beside you. I have a feeling that this will be."

He laughed without merriment. "Death's love, Krishna Taya. I am a prisoner, and already I have failed in my mission. A poor tool you have chosen. It is but a step from this bondage to the cells of Gwalior, and—my foes have the ear of the Mogul."

"Trust Raja Man Singh. He is minded to aid you for my sake. And he is a man among many."

Sir Ralph sought to look into her face.

Barely he could discern the dark mesh of her hair and the changing glimmer of her eyes. Her breath touched his cheek gently.

He pondered curiously upon the mystery of the girl. She had risked the anger of her clan to help him to Surat. His venture there had failed.

Still, she had spoken in his behalf boldly to Jahangir. He guessed that the *ram rukhi* had safeguarded him more than he was aware.

It had saved him from crossing swords with Udai Singh, and now it had—so Krishna Taya assured him—earned the goodwill of Raja Man Singh.

Owing to this he had been left unguarded with the girl. Yet he had no desire to attempt escape from the camp. Whither was he to go? Moreover, the raja had as good as given his parole.

"Why have you done this, Krishna Taya?" he asked bluntly.

She drew a quick breath, half sigh, half gasp.

"From the time I was given you as slave, Sir Weyand," she whispered, "and you freed me, I have formed an image of you and placed it in my heart. I have prayed many times to the gods and bathed in the sacred river, yet the image has remained. So it cannot be an evil thing, but good."

The words came swiftly in a torrent that would not be stayed.

"My heart became a garden that felt the warm sun of Spring. I watched you fighting on the walls of Khanjut when the men beside me sped arrows at you.

"I saw the sunlight strike on your hair that is like the brown mane of a lion. Truly, you walked among your men like a lion. It was my men who traced you down the Indus."

He felt her hand pass over his forehead and touch his cheek.

"I interceded for you with Raja Man Singh. *Aie,* my lord, you were wildly foolish in what you did. Thought you to overmaster such foes by sheer bravery?

"Nay, you are like a child among my people and those of Shah Abbas. Yet I loved you for it.

"Are you not one fit to walk with the sun-born kings of Ayodhya? Or to bear the gold-rayed orb on your breast?"

Sir Ralph lifted his head uneasily at sound of a horse's tread in the darkness. Krishna Taya also had heard it.

"My pride is great in my lord," she said simply. "And—Krishna Taya glories in the *ram rukhi.* You are bound to me in the swami dharma—the brotherhood of my people in common danger—"

"Nay, I am a blunderer, Krishna Taya—"

"Nay, a warrior worthy to wear the ostrich feather, of the parentage of Ram. So I have told the raja, my lord. *Aie*—the image of my lord weighs heavily in my heart; now I must leave him—"

She dropped to her knees and for an instant pressed her slender body against him, clasping his bound hands with hers. Krishna Taya was but a child in years, and her love was that of a girl who has found a hero.

Sir Ralph would have loosened her grasp, but could not.

"Think not ill of Krishna Taya, my lord," she whispered. "My time is now come, and the need of my clan has laid a task upon me. But as the falcon comes back to its master, I shall come to Khanjut and my lord."

She sprang to her feet as twin shadows appeared beside the thicket. Raja Man Singh's voice summoned her.

Sir Ralph, confused and embarrassed by the girl's eager words, saw her form blend with the other shadows. Then the horse moved away at a walk and the Rájput came toward him alone.

"Whence went Krishna Taya?" asked the Englishman.

"To the army of the Dekkan, *Ferang*. She bears word for the Rájput cavalry to ride to Khanjut with all speed."

"A girl—on such a mission?"

"Udai Singh is dead. Whom else may I trust—for the Rájputs of the army to believe?"

Raja Man Singh spoke moodily. Sir Ralph had never seen him so out of spirits.

"She can win through the network of Persian spies if any can, *Ferang*. Twenty thousand good horsemen ride from the Dekkan toward Kabul. But six days must pass before they can gain Khanjut, even though they ruin a horse apiece and sleep not on the way."

He stooped and gathered up the body of Udai Singh.

"Eh—who knows what is the will of the gods? Come, *Ferang*, we will bury our dead; then I shall partake of opium and talk much, for I am eaten with a sore trouble."

VII

The toil of the hunters is not to be seen in the jungle, but when the hunted beast leaps, the snare is disclosed.

Jani Beg and Shah Abbas had planned well.

Throughout the three days after the visit of the Persian to Jahangir, their plans came silently to a head. Outposts in the passes prevented *dak* runners from the Mogul from passing to the South. Khanjut and its thousands, besiegers and besieged, was isolated from the rest of India.

But not before a girl on a very good horse had slipped through the ravines of the Koh-i-Baba and circled Kabul, riding fast to the South.

At the polite request of Jani Beg, Jahangir pitched his great camp between the Persians and the Uzbeks. And the Mogul was given little chance to inspect the formation of the besiegers. Banquet followed banquet, drinking-bout drinking-bout. Khans of the northern tribes paid their respects to the Mogul with a great array of presents.

What was more natural than that these same khans should be attended by a numerous following of horsemen? So squadrons of Khorassanis, Hazaras, Afridis, and Kara Kirghiz assembled unnoticed—save by the alert Raja Man Singh—about the camp of the Mogul.

The reception to the Mogul took on the character of a triumphant *durbar*, under cover of which Shah Abbas moved his men with the same skill with which he manipulated the ivory and gold myrmidons of the chessboard.

The battalions of northern riders that had swelled down the passes from Ferghana were concealed in convenient *nullah*s. The human network was drawn about the Mogul and his followers, and closed.

Standing on the mound by the red imperial tent in front of which the yak-tail standard was planted, Raja Man Singh and Sir Ralph watched mail-clad, mounted archers of the Uzbeks form in position, ostensibly for assault. They saw hooded riders from the Irak plain wheel by in swallow-flight and halt their mounts beside the motley array of Jahangir's followers. They sometimes caught glimpses of helmeted and quilted Black Kirghiz—fierce fighters and lawless—mustering to the banners of their leaders.

Meanwhile the few Rájputs and Muslims of Jahangir drank and slept. Raja Man Singh, however, slept little.

"What force has Jahangir—that he can trust?" he demanded bitterly of the Englishman. "A score of armored elephants— eunuchs—slaves—priests—water-carriers. None fit to wield a sword save my Rájputs and a few hundred Muslims."

Sir Ralph had eagerly scanned the battered walls of Khanjut.

The Persian cannon had effected a wide breach. Inside this the defenders had stacked bales of cloth and cotton, and fagots smeared with oil.

But under another section of the walls reached the saps from the Uzbek camp. At daybreak on the morrow these saps would be exploded, tearing a new and wider breach.

On the heels of the explosion it was planned to launch the Rájput storm. Sir Ralph had little doubt of the success of the attack. Months of hardship and harrying by arrow and catapults had left their mark on the garrison.

Few hillmen were to be seen on the walls—or rather the stone heaps that had been walls. These few were ragged, their armor dulled. Sir Ralph saw men stagger from weariness as they labored to build up the crumbling ramparts.

The Khanjut River, flowing past the slope of the citadel, had been sturdily bridged by the Persian engineers. All the green verdure of the slope had disappeared, leaving a gray-brown stretch of torn earth and sliding rock.

He looked long and thought that once he saw the tall figure of Abdul Dost. The *mansabdar* had taken his stand on the wall over the mined section, where he could look down into the nearest trenches, protected by rawhide targets. Adbul Dost paid no heed to arrows that glinted by him.

"A brave man, that," grunted Raja Man Singh, who had also noticed the defender of Khanjut. "It is an evil fate that bends our sword against him and Shirzad Mir. Jani Beg called them traitors, but Jani Beg—"

He waved his lean hand about the encircling camp of the Uzbeks and laughed shortly. Sir Ralph looked up quickly.

"If you respect them, why not send them food, raja?" he asked in a curious tone. "Is it the custom of the Rájputs first to starve a foe—"

"Shiva—no! The law reads, 'When an enemy is weakened, tend him; take no advantage from his misfortune.'"

"Then," said Sir Ralph gravely, "obey your law. Send grain to the men of Khanjut."

The Rájput stared at him almost suspiciously. He had not forgotten that the Englishman was the friend of Shirzad Mir.

"Nay, do it not if you have a fear, raja. But your chivalry would be recorded in the chronicles of your clan if you do this thing."

The doubt vanished from Raja Man Singh's boyish countenance.

"What matters it, *Ferang*?" he laughed. "Jani Beg will scowl, yet I have small cause to love him. Nay, I recall that I once proposed it and he growled. Tomorrow we will all pass under the gateway of Yama, to be born anew—hillman, Abdul Dost, Rájput and I—perchance yourself as well. Let their bellies be filled, so they may feel themselves men when they meet us—"

He turned away indifferently and gave an order to his captain of the imperial guard. The man disappeared with Raja Man Singh.

Presently the Rájput returned in somewhat better humor.

"The Persian spat in horror," he informed his companion. "After all, it matters little to them. Rájputs will be in the van of the storm. It will be done. See—"

He pointed out where certain mules were being laden with sacks of grain, rice, and dates. This done, the beasts were led up over the trenches under a flag of truce.

Sir Ralph saw the provisions disappear into Khanjut.

The reckless chivalry of the Rájput had supplied the garrison with food. Pique, bred of Sir Ralph's words and desire to annoy the Persians and Uzbeks, had been responsible for his act. As Raja Man Singh had said, it mattered little whether the hillmen in the citadel were fed before they were cut down.

Yet, as it proved, this move was of vital import. Sir Ralph had seen this, and he was pondering it while the two watched and the sun lowered its red ball over the smoke-veiled plain of Khanjut.

"It was well done," admitted Raja Man Singh moodily. "I thank you for your word, *Ferang*. But how came you to think of such a matter of chivalry?"

Receiving no answer, he fell to watching the clearing away of the *chevaux-de-frise* preparatory to the assault of the next day. Festive murmurs reached the two from the red tent of Jahangir, where Shah Abbas was being feasted.

"How thought you of sending the food into Khanjut?" persisted the raja.

Sir Ralph sighed. He had been thinking deeply. "They are my friends," he said.

The Rájput glanced at the silk bracelet on the Englishman's wrist. His thin lips curled as he responded—

"And the *ram rukhi, Ferang*?"

"Krishna Taya trusted me."

"Aye, she said you were a leader of men."

Sir Ralph smiled grimly, feeling the cords which Raja Man Singh had thought best to keep upon him. The last mule had been lost to sight within the walls, which seemed bare of defenders. From the citadel he heard the long-drawn cry of a *mullah*, calling to evening prayers as shadows gathered to the East.

"Could you trust me, raja?"

"Wherefore? Yet you are a bold man, and frank. For Krishna Taya's sake I have kept you with me. Still, the shield of your honor gleams bright compared to that of the false Persian. May he be born again as a female gully jackal—"

The Rájput spat, voicing his bitter resentment.

"Because," Sir Ralph weighed his words with quickening pulse, "if you would trust me I could save you—and Jahangir."

He had been pondering this for the last hour, silently, with the perseverance of an alert, steady-going mind. And now he was ready to put the matter to an issue.

The Rájput general sat close beside the Englishman, a single cloak forming a carpet for both. His teeth gleamed through his well-kept beard in a mocking laugh.

"Ho—that is a goodly jest! Bold words from a bound captive! So, you have a thought to wrest Jahangir and his Rájputs from the trap of Jani Beg? Perchance you would arm the many-handed gods, and call them from the sacred abode of Himachal!"

Sir Ralph faced him patiently, knowing that the raja was worn with anxiety and that his opium no longer sufficed to keep his temper even.

"Tell me one thing," he suggested quietly. "Has Jahangir begun to suspect his danger?"

"He grows uneasy. But the wily Persian surrounds him with talkative women and buffoons. Even me, his general, they keep from his side."

"And the Dekkan army will arrive—"

"In time to bury our corpses that the kites have plucked bare."

Raja Man Singh's feverish eyes glowed with sudden fire.

"Death of the gods, *Ferang*, think you I feel nothing of what is to come to pass? I, the highest *ameer* of the court—head of the Marwar clan? Nay, just now one of my patrols came upon a *dak*-bearer of mine, slain in a by-path of the Koh-i-Baba. Some of my horsemen have vanished. The hand of Shah Abbas closes upon us."

Veins stood out on his forehead, and his lips twisted in an access of rage. Sir Ralph had not known until then the strain under which the Rájput labored.

"By Hanuman and Ganesh! By Kali, mistress of blood! What can I do? It avails naught to attempt to cut through the Persian camp. By placing Jahangir on his elephant among my horsemen we could win through the camp. But—each pass to the South is fortified by our foes, and guarded. We would be cut to pieces in the Koh-i-Baba, even if 'twere possible to form in battle array unmolested by the Uzbeks and Persians—which I doubt."

His voice had risen in snarling rage.

"We are trapped, *Ferang*. India will blame me—"

"You are not guilty of carelessness."

"Who will believe? In the network of lies whispered after the death of the Mogul the name of Raja Man Singh will be linked with treachery.

"Eh—this place is foul with evil. Yet I am helpless. If Jani Beg suspected what I knew, the cup-bearer who hands Jahangir wine would plunge a poniard into the Mogul's back! The creatures of the harem would drag him down, to be strangled—"

He waved his clenched hands before his closed eyes.

"The fate of India hangs upon the life of Jahangir, *Ferang*. It is the curse of India that she shall destroy herself, one clan fighting the other, if there be no leader."

He broke off into curses that Sir Ralph barely understood.

"It was our fate that this should come upon us. Jahangir, half-drunk, perceives his peril, but falters, and drinks more to forget. *Aie*—it will not be long before he drains the cup of death. For if a Rájput comes within earshot, a dozen hands fly to the courtiers' daggers; if Jahangir steps without his tent, twenty pairs of evil eyes follow him and Shah Abbas bows himself up with new presents."

Sir Ralph waited until the man's outburst had ceased. It was now early evening, and the men of the camp below them were passing about to their meat. Khanjut was a wall of shadows. Lights twinkled out here and there among the tents.

"Have you any plan?" he asked thoughtfully.

"Who may outvie fate? Nay, I and my Rájputs shall spread a carpet of slain for the Lord of the Exalted Throne—if he must die."

Rajah Man Singh was quieter now, cynical of the fortune in store for him.

"There is a way to save him—"

"It may not be."

"—if the army of the Dekkan can win to Khanjut in three days. I do not think Jani Beg will look for reinforcements for Jahangir so early."

He glanced about to make sure they were alone.

"Could the Rájputs from the Dekkan force the Persian guards in the Koh-i-Baba passes?"

"Can a mountain stream eat through a mud wall?" Raja Man Singh was contemptuous.

"Then Jahangir may be saved, and—the name of Raja Man Singh will be on the lips of every tribe in the empire."

"Nay, how can the Mogul escape?"

"He will not escape. Tomorrow he will watch the assault form against Khanjut."

The Rájput was silent for a long space.

"Speak, *Ferang*," he said moodily. "Krishna Taya said that you had a rare wisdom, of other gods than ours."

While the evening activities of the camp went on and the watchfires gleamed forth in a circuit around the invested fortress, Sir Ralph told Raja Man Singh what was in his mind.

He talked with the earnestness of a man that has much at stake. He told his companion what he had reasoned out. And he told his plan.

Raja Man Singh listened, at first irritably and skeptically, then intently. He was a man of limitations, but the general of the Rájputs was far from stupid. He had been tricked, after a fashion, by Shah Abbas; yet his loyalty to Jahangir had helped to accomplish this.

He sucked his breath in through his teeth when Sir Ralph finished. He was silent for a long time.

"Verily," he said softly, "that is a plan."

In the darkness Sir Ralph had no means of reading the Rájput's face.

"How may we get word of this to Jahangir, *Ferang*? He will doubt greatly, for he knows not all we know."

"Tell him naught. He is half-dazed with opium. You alone must lead in this, raja."

Again the Rájput was quiet, faced by the necessity of a vital decision.

"The *mahouts* of the imperial elephants are men of Marwar and Oudh," he meditated aloud. "They will listen to my words—

aye, they will obey me. Am I not leader of their clan? They are but servants."

"You must be leader."

"Shall I take the reins of India into my hand?"

The Rájput clapped his hands softly and laughed.

"Verily it is a plan of plans. If we should succeed—"

He broke off swiftly.

"How am I to trust you, *Ferang*? I have not forgotten there is a part you must play—"

"You cannot be sure of me," said Sir Ralph steadily. "But if the word of an adventurer . . . Krishna Taya is the only one who believes in me," he concluded grimly.

"A slender staff to lean on, *Ferang*. Yet Udai Singh spoke well of you. You have taken the *ram rukhi* of my clan—"

He sprang to his feet abruptly, laughing. "Ho, *Ferang*, I shall do this thing. As you have told it to me, I shall do it."

He loved action ever better than thought.

"If it comes to pass as you have thought, *Ferang*, it will be verily a jest for the gods and a thing like to none other in the annals of the Rájputs."

It was then dark. Before the second watch of that night was ended, Sir Ralph had passed with a small party of Rájputs to a certain valley near the Amu Daria—a gorge whence the river of Khanjut flowed down.

He was unbound, and when he stepped into the stream and swam out into the current toward Khanjut the Rájputs made no attempt to stay him. Sir Ralph had prevailed upon Raja Man Singh. He had secured his freedom from the custody of the Rájputs.

And now, he, reflected, as he sought for the watercourse that led under the Khanjut wall, he might obtain that for which he came to India.

There was no flaw in the scheme of Jani Beg and Shah Abbas—no break in the net that had been thrown around Jahangir.

Dawn showed the squadrons of Uzbek cavalry drawn up on one side of the Mogul's camp, with the Persians on the other. Behind the camp the plain seemed to have filled suddenly as the waiting battalions from the North emerged from their *nullah*s and closed in toward Khanjut. If Jahangir had doubted before, he was more than anxious now.

But he was allowed no opportunity to consult with Raja Man Singh. Jani Beg did not wish to strike until the Rájputs had been thrown against Khanjut, and the sharp edge of their attack dulled. So he escorted Jahangir in person to the waiting elephants, where they feasted briefly and drank under a temporary pavilion erected for that purpose.

Wine had little effect upon the Uzbek leader. But it dulled the faculties of the anxious monarch.

"Lord of the Exalted Throne—" Jani Beg bowed to hide his exultation and the suspense he could not altogether keep from his scarred face—"the storm is prepared, and the mines await but your auspicious word before they hurl the ramparts of Khanjut into the air."

"Where is Raja Man Singh?" demanded Jahangir uneasily.

"With his Rájputs yonder."

Jani Beg pointed to where the Mogul's horsemen had formed directly in front of and beside the royal elephants.

"All goes well," he cried exultingly. "Mount, sire, and view from the back of your elephant the spectacle we have prepared for you."

"Mount, sire," echoed Shah Abbas suavely, "and give the word that shall crush the rebel of Khanjut as a snake's head is crushed."

Both the traitors wished the Mogul to be upon his beast, so that he could not by any chance escape in the throng. Once installed in the gilded *howdah*, behind the armored head of the royal elephant, every move of Jahangir would be clear to view and descent from his elevation would be difficult.

Jani Beg whirled his horse away and Jahangir sat alone with a *mahout* in his accustomed station.

Around him formed a half-dozen of the royal beasts, bearing Rájput *ameer*s and Muslims of his personal following. But Raja Man Singh, the general who might—so Jahangir in his anxiety reasoned—take command and offset the treachery he had begun to dread, was not to be seen.

And Raja Man Singh was the one man who could enforce an order among the Mogul's followers. Jahangir himself was no warrior—he scarce knew how to phrase an order in the heat of battle.

From his elevation he could see that the Hazaras and Afridis who should have held the other side of the fortress had formed behind his own camp. In fact, the whole of the Uzbek and Persian troops were now in a semicircle about Jahangir and Khanjut.

The Rájputs, aroused as always by the prospect of action, were intent on their own counsels, *ameer* whispering to *mansabdar* and *mansabdar* to troopers.

It was a glorious sight, gray Khanjut ringed about by its foes under the clear sunlight of Afghanistan. In the distance, the snow peaks of the Himalayas frowned down on the mass of fighting men, ready to be launched into conflict. On the walls few of the garrison showed.

Shah Abbas signed for his men to draw closer to the Rájputs around the elephants. True, the Mogul's followers were but one in ten, yet—Shah Abbas was wary.

He reined his Arab near the royal elephant. "Give the word, sire," he cried, gnawing hard at a lip that quivered in spite of his self-mastery.

"Give the word, sire," repeated blue-robed Persian councilors, their eyes hard with greed and cruelty, bred of what was to come. Jahangir cast a look around, seeking for Raja Man Singh, who was not to be seen. Then he raised his hand. This was the signal. The Mogul's jeweled hand trembled, for a great fear had touched his placid heart.

The royal *nacars*—kettledrums—sounded a long roll. From the midst of a group of Rájputs the imperial yak-tail standard was raised high for all to see. A roar burst from a battery of brass camel-guns beside the red tent.

From the entrance to the saps the figures of miners scrambled. They joined the ranks of the Persians and waited. Throughout the watching host the warriors shifted their swords and pikes in their hands, tightened their girdles, and breathed prayers in many tongues and faiths. The leaders, on horseback, watched the walls of Khanjut.

A dull, gigantic thud, a quiver of earth underfoot, and a black cloud rose and swelled about the walls. A second roar, and both mines had exploded. Stones, earth, and beams tossed skyward in the murk. Dust rose in a dense cloud.

The engineers of Shah Abbas had done their work well. The celebrated Persian smiled and recited a verse in poetic gratulation. He missed the sight of bodies of the garrison hurled into the air, but—the storm was launched.

As a man the Rájputs sprang forward afoot.

"Ho—níla ghora ki aswár!"

Their battle-cry answered the tumult of trumpet and cymbals that echoed in the Persian camp. Shah Abbas saw the lines of saffron-robed warriors climb up the debris-strewn slope to where, under the dust cloud, a wide breach had been blown in the wall.

They scrambled upward at a swift trot, scimitars swinging free. The first ranks vanished in the dust cloud.

"To their fate they go like driven dogs, exalted Majesty," fawned a Persian master of horse at his side.

"'Tis well to have them out of the way," he responded softly.

The excitement had affected the elephants. The black beasts, brilliant in their paint and armor, stirred under the spears of their mahouts. They moved forward at first slowly, then with gathering momentum.

On either side of the royal elephants, the squadrons of Muslim archers and Rájputs moved upward with drawn weapons. On their flank the waiting ranks of Uzbeks stared and mocked.

The gold *howdah* of Jahangir glittered in the sun as it went forward.

"He goes to gain better sight of the storm," meditated Shah Abbas aloud, paying little heed to the elephants, so intent was he in watching the walls.

But the elephants did not stop. Nor did the *mahouts* cease to urge them onward. The beasts, trained to war, trumpeted, feeling the nearness of strife. Shah Abbas dispatched his master of horse to bring up his waiting ranks.

"Close in after the Mogul," he whispered shrilly. "But slowly, slowly. Jahangir was unwise to venture into the battle. Under the walls we will swarm against him and his thin following, and he will be beset from two sides—"

So he watched complacently while the royal *howdah* bobbed upward along the slope leading to the breach. In the midst of his followers the Mogul neared the Khanjut wall.

A rider came from Jani Beg.

"Sire," he cried to Shah Abbas, "the Mogul must seek to force the breach with his elephants."

"The gods favor us," muttered the Persian. "Jahangir will die in the breach by an Uzbek sword."

There was something strange in the silence of the assault. While Persian and Uzbek watched, the Rájputs leaped within the walls. Still no defenders were to be seen. Silence reigned along the Khanjut wall.

"Death of the gods!" swore Shah Abbas.

He reasoned that the garrison must have erected a barrier farther within the citadel. Assuredly, he thought, they had known the position of the mines, or someone had given them this knowledge. For none of the hillmen were caught in the explosion.

The Uzbek banners stirred uneasily. Shah Abbas could see the breach plainly, now that the dust had subsided.

And what he saw amazed him. The ranks of the Rájputs were filing through the gap unopposed. No arrows were shot from the walls at the oncoming elephants.

He had thought to see stones and fire hurled upon the van of the attack, and bales of lighted pitch rolled against the dangerous elephants. But not one of the garrison was to be seen. Not an arrow glinted in the sunlight.

Now, as had been planned, the ranks of Uzbeks moved forward, on the heels of the Mogul's following.

"Something's amiss," snarled Shah Abbas to those near him.

He could not take his gaze from the royal elephant. That great beast was urging forward, diagonally up the slope, as fast as the *mahout* could force him to go. The gold *howdah* rocked perilously. But it was now in the breach.

And still not a shot had been fired or a spear lifted against the Rájputs.

"Forward," cried Shah Abbas. "Gain the Mogul! May the gods destroy—"

The Persians closed in behind the Uzbeks.

Then the mellow eyes of Shah Abbas widened, and he and his men halted in astonishment. The *howdah* of Jahangir bearing its precious load had passed within the breach, like a ship entering the sheltering wings of a harbor. It turned to one side, and was lost to view.

Simultaneously the aroused ranks of Uzbeks plunged after it. At once the rear ranks of the Mogul's men turned in their tracks. Rájput horsemen spurred down upon the Uzbeks, casting them back. Jani Beg spurred forward furiously.

A line of Mogul spearmen formed athwart the breach. Through their dressed spears the horsemen of the rear guard trotted safely after their sally. The Uzbeks, who had sought to fall upon an unguarded rear, were faced by a ring of steel."

And now the hillmen appeared on the walls. Arrow flights sped into the confused ranks of Uzbeks. Muskets barked, and fireballs were flung from the half-demolished battlements.

Then Shah Abbas and Jani Beg saw the yak-tail standard of Jahangir raised on the walls.

They heard the battle shout of triumphant Rájputs. And they knew that, while they had watched passively, Jahangir had passed safely into Khanjut and now held the citadel against them.

Those who were first of the Rájputs into Khanjut saw a strange sight. Passing warily through the smoke, scimitar in hand, and climbing over the debris upheaved by the mine, they beheld safely removed from the area of the explosion groups of tattered men. These hillmen were like to remnants of warriors, for their armor was broken and oddly pieced out, with helmets and targets taken from the dead. They were hollow-eyed and scarred. They leaned wearily upon spear and pike, with bows dangling in their hands.

Beside these silent watchers were ranged piles of brush and sacks of earth, ready to form a barrier within the breach. Yet the barrier had not been put in place.

The Rájputs had their orders not to lift weapon against the defenders of Khanjut. Even so, with the care of veterans they advanced distrustfully. Perhaps they would have been loath to enter the silent breach save for the presence of Raja Man Singh in the first ranks.

Intrigue and rumors in the camp they had left had bewildered them. But the word and the face of the Rájput general was a beacon to their loyalty, and they followed him steadily, peering at the battle-worn groups that loomed out of the murk.

In the foremost group three men waited. There was bent Iskander Khan, leader of the hill Kirghiz, and tall, battle-stained Abdul Dost, worn to a lean semblance of a warrior; and there was a steady-eyed man with tawny hair who rested on a long, bare blade and smiled at the raja.

Seeing this, the Rájputs advanced more readily.

"Sir Ralph," they whispered among themselves. "The *Ferang* has come before us as the raja said. Even as he promised, the way has been cleared. And he has said there will be good sword strokes presently. He told us that we who were of the besiegers should be besieged. And his lips give forth the truth."

Whereupon, obeying a sign from their leader, they spread to either side along the ramparts, making way for those who pressed after them.

"The royal standard follows," they whispered, eyeing the assembled rocks and bundles of arrows with the keen appraisal of veterans. "This is a strange thing—and the fortress is but a ruin— yet Jahangir will join us."

With the acute curiosity of alert soldiers they watched Raja Man Singh advance alone to Abdul Dost, who stopped to meet him. For that instant Rájput and hillman fingered weapons distrustfully, uncertain of the outcome of the meeting. But they saw the raja and *mansabdar* salute each other and join Sir Ralph.

"It is said the *Ferang* swam down the river, through the water-main into the well of Khanjut," they informed one another. "Raja Man Singh trusted to his good faith that we should not be molested. Even so has it come to pass."

Satisfied that all was well, they fell to repairing the defenses. Trumpeting announced the coming of the elephants through the breach. Abdul Dost watched, grim eyed.

"Welcome to Khanjut, raja," he growled

"Jahangir was long in seeing the truth—that we of Khanjut are faithful to the Mogul, while Jani Beg is the traitor."

The Rájput scowled; then his brow cleared.

"The Mogul makes amends for his mistake, Abdul Dost."

"Too late."

"Nay, my men are fresh. We have food for two days, and in two days the van of the Dekkan army will strike through the passes."

"Too late, I said. And it is the truth. God has laid a heavy hand upon Khanjut. When you seek my master, Shirzad Mir, you will know whereof I speak."

With that he turned away, giving orders to his men, who staggered as they trundled the trees of the barrier into place.

Through the breach passed the elephants with the Mogul and his *ameer*s. Tumult and trampling of horses echoed without as the Rájputs turned against the oncoming Uzbeks. Raja Man Singh seized the royal standard and hurried to the wall.

Sir Ralph accompanied him as the last of the elephants passed the fresh-forming barrier.

Without, they saw the Rájput pike-wall, and beyond this the climbing masses of their enemies. The horse of Jani Beg was close to the spear-wall.

"Yield Jahangir, raja," cried the Uzbek angrily. "What means this treachery? Ho—the Mogul is betrayed!"

"No lie, that, Jani Beg," retorted the Rájput scornfully. "You are the traitor, not I, nor Shirzad Mir. The Mogul holds Khanjut. If you seek peace, even now, go hence to your northern steppe."

The Uzbek flushed darkly, then took heart from sight of his numerous followers. "Yield Jahangir and tie the sword of surrender about your neck, raja. This is my last word."

"When has a Rájput yielded? We guard Jahangir."

"Then it is war—and the fate of war for those in Khanjut."

"Nay—" the Rájput laughed grimly—"would you harm the Mogul?"

Jani Beg hesitated. But behind him were many thousand disciplined Uzbeks, Persians and plainsmen. His was still the upper hand, and he was not the man to let bloodshed stand in the way of his ambition.

"Let Jahangir look to himself, for his name will soon be as dust on gravel!" he cried, drawing his scimitar. "The star of Jani Beg rises over Hindustan. War!"

He shouted at his men. A score of arrows flew past the raja and Sir Ralph. With a cry the Uzbeks pressed forward. Muskets flashed from wall and trenches. The ominous thunder of battle rolled around Khanjut.

Almost Jani Beg held the prize he sought in his grasp. His mail-clad ranks clashed against the Rájput spear-wall. Raja Man Singh sprang down among his men, leaving the defense of the battlements to Abdul Dost and Sir Ralph.

The breach was filled in a moment with a mass of struggling men. Rájput faced Uzbek; scimitar grated against pike. The few horsemen who attempted to stem the wave of attackers were pulled down and slain.

But now arrows and rocks made gaps in the Uzbeks. Abdul Dost posted his men where the scaling ladders rose against the damaged ramparts.

For a space the storm swept against Khanjut, mingling assailant and defender in a swaying mass. Meanwhile the old men and boys of Khanjut labored at the barrier within the breach.

Raja Man Singh glanced behind him and waved his hard-pressed men to either side of the opening in the wall. He had seen the elephants of the Mogul form in a monstrous line and advance to the breach.

Not alone was Jahangir now in the *howdah*. A group of dark-faced Muslim archers knelt beside him and plied their small bows swiftly. In the other *howdah*s the *ameer*s were likewise reinforced.

"The Mogul!" cried the hard-breathing Rájputs. "Jahangir comes. Way for the imperial elephants."

No coward was Jahangir when it came to an issue. Sight of the battered garrison that fought for him had stirred his placid heart. And his father Jalal-Ud-Din Akbar had sat upon the back of a chained elephant in the pitched battle that had won him mastery of India.

"The Mogul!" cried his men as the gold-plated head of a swaying elephant with armored shoulders and sword-tipped tusks forged into view.

The trained beasts lined the breach, trumpeting with the fury of battle, and the Uzbeks gave ground down the slope. Persian horsemen pressed up to aid them. But from the backs of the elephants flooded a steady stream of arrows from chosen archers. And from the walls above them came the missiles of the heartened garrison.

"God's love!" swore Sir Ralph. "Here is a worthy onset!"

With that he leaped down among the Rájputs and called together a group that followed his long sword into the battle around
the elephants.

The foot soldiers under the Englishman arrived in good time,
for they diverted the attention of the Persian horsemen from the
elephants after one or two of the giant beasts had become infu-
riated with wounds and dashed down the slope, trampling their
assailants underfoot and plunging the men on their backs headlong to death.

On difficult footing, and harassed by the arrows from above,
the Persians were forced to give ground. They drew back to allow
Jani Beg to form a fresh assault, driving his savage Uzbeks into
the breach.

Raja Man Singh, who had watched coolly all that passed, urged
back the *mahouts* of the royal elephants and the remaining men
under Sir Ralph.

"Form behind the barrier," he cried. "It is near completed and
will be closed when you are through!"

So when Jani Beg's second storm swept into the breach it was
met by a flaming wall of cotton bales coated with pitch, behind
which stood an orderly array of the Mogul's men, fresh because
they had not yet been in the fight.

It was near evening when Jani Beg, twice unhorsed by arrows
from the walls, called off his baffled men and left the breach still
in the hands of its defenders. Not until then did Jahangir cause
his *mahout* to make his elephant kneel.

The Mogul dismounted stiffly and advanced to where Abdul
Dost and Sir Ralph waited. The *mansabdar* bent his head, and
the Englishman swept off his helmet in a bow.

"Take me, Abdul Dost," said Jahangir quietly, "to your master,
Shirzad Mir. I would tell him with my own lips that he has been
a faithful servant of the Mogul."

"You wronged my master," said the *mansabdar* fiercely.

"How was I to know?" Jahangir's handsome face was troubled, for his vanity had suffered in the past hours. "Treasure and honors will atone for my mistake. I pardon freely the pride that gave him the semblance of a—of one who defied me."

"Come, then, and pardon if you will."

So saying, Abdul Dost turned and led the two into the tower that formed the abode of Shirzad Mir.

It was empty of attendants, and dark save for a candle that winked in the wind from open embrasures. The couch that had formed the bed of Shirzad Mir had been removed. His scimitar and armor lay on a long table.

Jahangir paused and looked around expectantly.

"Summon the *mir*," he said impatiently.

Abdul Dost smiled.

"That I cannot do," he responded. "I buried my master under the floor of this chamber two moons ago."

Jahangir stared down at the stone flags under the table, and at the guttering candle. He looked at Abdul Dost, and at Sir Ralph.

"So Shirzad Mir was slain?" he asked curiously.

"Aye—by a sword stroke of Raja Man Singh, who warred against him, by your order."

This time Jahangir did not speak. He stirred uneasily, for the level gaze of the wearied soldier oppressed him and he liked not to be uneasy.

"Shirzad Mir—" Sir Ralph broke the silence—"was faithful to you, as to your father, Akbar the Great."

At length Jahangir threw off the spell of discomfort that had gripped him. He spoke impulsively, with his customary generosity.

"You have been a faithful man, Abdul Dost," he said kindly, "and you shall have due reward as such. I shall grant you rank of a lesser *ameer*, with a *jagir* in Guzurat, and two hundred good horses. Come, this is a sad place. You shall dine at my side this night."

"Nay," said the *mansabdar*. "My place is here."

So that night while Sir Ralph and Raja Man Singh in turn took command of the guard, and Jahangir feasted late in a pavilion that had been erected for him and listened to a Muslim poet extol his bravery of that afternoon, Abdul Dost squatted on the stone floor of the tower repeating prayers at the appointed hour, and facing toward Mecca.

For the next day and night and part of the following day, the storm swept against Khanjut.

The powder of the defenders was exhausted and the greater number of the elephants rendered useless. But Raja Man Singh was skilled in fortress warfare, and his Rájputs, aided by the survivors of Abdul Dost's force, fought desperately.

The Persian cannon had resumed their play against the battered ramparts. Fresh levies were formed for each assault. Trenches and ramparts were half-obliterated in the mass fighting that cast Uzbek against Afghan, Persian against Muslim, and Hazara against Rájput.

When Abdul Dost was wounded, he had himself conveyed to the summit of the remaining tower, and Sir Ralph took over the command of his men. Iskander Khan, the graybeard of the Koh-i-Baba, had died of an arrow the second day. The royal *ameers* presented little better appearance than the tattered soldiery.

It was then that Jani Beg, believing that the citadel was doomed, ordered the last assault. It is written in the annals of Afghanistan that he led this himself.

The wave of Uzbeks broke through the new breach made by the Persian cannon and swept around the tower whence Abdul Dost watched silently.

Then from the base of the tower issued a strange throng— graybeards and boys bearing arms that they had picked up from the slain.

"*Shirzad el kadr!*"

They shrilled the war-cry of their dead lord and plunged into the ranks of the northern swordsmen. They were singled out and slain, one by one, for the name of mercy had been forgotten in the struggle around Khanjut.

Sir Ralph, who had drawn aside to gather his strength, saw Jani Beg pushing toward the tower, and went to meet him with grim intentness.

The attackers had been driven back to the breach by the Khanjut townspeople. And it was here that the Englishman took his stand between two piles of stones.

"Come, Jani Beg," he called. "This is the way into Khanjut!"

He was weary and reckless with the ceaseless strife. The Uzbek hesitated. But his men had heard, and turned toward him. Seeing this, Jani Beg knew that he could not afford to draw back.

"Eh, *Ferang*," he growled, "your body will not stay me!"

He leaped forward, scimitar swinging overhead. His curved blade met the Englishman's long sword. Sir Ralph thrust strongly, using his point against the other's edge. And as he thrust he forced back Jani Beg.

Both men were tired, and their weapons, which had clashed sharply at first, moved more slowly. Once Sir Ralph's point struck and bent against the mail armor of the Uzbek's broad chest. His gaze held the other's furious stare steadily.

It seemed to him that the noise of battle about them dwindled as they fought. He was very tired.

The Uzbek fenced cunningly, guarding his vulnerable throat above the mail. His scimitar bit into the leather vest of the Englishman and drew blood. He drew back farther, smiling as Sir Ralph came on steadily.

Sir Ralph's long sword weighed heavily in his hand, and a blur passed across his sight. The cut in his shoulder troubled him. And still Jani Beg stepped back until he was close to his own followers.

A thrust of the long sword, a parry of the scimitar—and Jani Beg leaped clear of the Englishman's reach. Sir Ralph swayed, his knees quivering with fatigue. Jani Beg laughed, brushing the foam from his mouth.

"Slay him!" he panted to his men, who had watched irresolutely. "The *Ferang* is wearied and there are none to defend his back. Strike and slay—"

The Uzbeks stepped forward while Sir Ralph lifted his blade weakly. Jani Beg watched sneeringly. Then his great frame stiffened and his arms thrust out with a stifled screech.

The feathered end of an arrow projected under his chin. The Uzbek clawed at it wildly. He sank to his knees, gripping the shaft, blood running from his mouth.

"'Twas a goodly shot," said a voice calmly.

Glancing up at the sound, Sir Ralph saw Abdul Dost leaning against the battlement of the tower directly overhead. A bow was in his hand.

"Harken!"

The *mansabdar* raised his hand. Then Sir Ralph knew that a silence had indeed fallen over Khanjut and the men that stood within it.

In the distance below the citadel he heard a shout.

"*Ho—níla ghora ki aswár!*"

The Uzbeks heard and straightaway turned to run from the breach. Sir Ralph leaned on his weapon, wondering, for his senses were dulled with the conflict.

"The Rájput war-cry," he said.

"Aye," nodded Abdul Dost. "The Rájputs. In the plain their cavalry has deployed from the passes of the Koh-i-Baba. Their standards are those of the army of the Dekkan."

Sir Ralph was slow to comprehend this.

"I have been watching them for the space milk takes to boil— while you were engaged with the carrion that was Jani Beg."

The Englishman straightened with a laugh.

"What of the Persians?" he asked.

Abdul Dost cast an indifferent scrutiny over the plain.

"The Persians draw rein for Persia," he said grimly. "I think Shah Abbas leads them. He has the best horse."

It was not long after this that Sir Ralph said farewell to Krishna Taya in the hill gardens of Kabul, at the festival attending Jahangir's departure for the court at Delhi. His tent was near to that of Raja Man Singh, and here he found Krishna Taya waiting when he returned from his leave-taking at the Mogul's pavilion.

It was in the afternoon when few people were stirring, and the garden was quiet. This was the first time that the Englishman had seen the Rájput girl alone since the night of her ride to the Dekkan army.

"It is a fair day," she said softly, "when I see a smile upon the face of my lord. Jahangir is liberal with those who have won his favor. It is said that you have earned his good will—"

"For a time, Krishna Taya," he nodded, "my enemies are silenced. But I cannot afford to overstay my time."

"The slaves said today," the girl resumed wistfully, "that you received rich presents. They talked of high rank bestowed upon you, and treasure, and a *jagir* on the Guzurat coast, not far from Marwar—"

"Nay, I took it not. Instead I asked Jahangir for this."

Sir Ralph drew a folded paper from his tunic.

"It is the *firman*, Krishna Taya," he explained as she looked to him for an answer. "The trade concession for my country from the Mogul."

She turned her dark head aside.

"Then—you will not take the title and land of Guzurat, my lord?"

"Nay."

"It was said also that you might leave Hindustan."

"Aye. My work takes me to England, and those who sent me."

She sighed, resting her slender chin on clasped hands. She looked at him curiously.

"You still wear the *ram rukhi*, Sir Ralph. Has it served you— brought you happiness? The gods have smiled upon you since you took it."

He removed the silk bangle from his wrist cheerfully and handed it to the girl.

"My thanks, Krishna Taya. It has been a boon to me. Without it, I might not have gained the *firman*."

With that Sir Ralph stooped and raised her hand to his lips. The girl quivered under his touch, and her eyes closed. Her lips framed a word she did not speak.

"You are content, my lord?"

"Aye, Krishna Taya."

He stared at her in some surprise. Surely the girl was changed from the willful mistress of the Rájputs who had made him prisoner some months ago. She was very lovely, after her fashion, and he owed her much. She bent her dark head so that he could not look into her eyes.

"Your country and mine, Krishna Taya," he said, seeking to break the silence, "will no longer be apart."

"But you will not come back, Sir Ralph?"

"Another *ameer* of the sea will come."

He looked around at the rose-garden, now bare of flowers, and even to his blunt senses the place held a witchery that caused him some vague regret.

"I have seen much of India, and I have learned much of her people, Krishna Taya. I have known the loyalty of the Rájputs."

Krishna Taya smiled ever so slightly and stroked the silk bracelet on her wrist.

"So much, my lord? I—I also have known—much."

At loss for further words Sir Ralph bent again and kissed her hand. Then he strode away past the tent, while she looked after him wistfully.

Seeing that he would not come back, she rose and went into the garden. There against a stone gate of a well she sat, chin on hand, while the sunlight dwindled to the twilight.

Came long-striding Raja Man Singh, swaggering after his wont, in elegant attire, his beard new-trimmed and redolent of musk.

"Ho, Krishna Taya," he cried carelessly, "I have seen your bracelet brother leave with the caravan that goes overland to the northern sea. He was a brave man and I have thought that the *ram rukhi* was not ill bestowed upon him."

"Aye, my lord," she said.

"And you, little Krishna Taya," he added, for he was in high good humor with the events of recent days, "what think you?"

"The *ram rukhi* was well given."

Whereupon the raja departed about his business, leaving Krishna Taya staring wistfully out over the darkened garden, and holding close to her breast the hand that wore the bracelet.

Law of Fire

In the city of the silent lie those who are dead. Their blood is like to dried dust; over their faces the rose bush blows.

Even thus do they lie.

Between the hills of the Mustagh Ata the camels pass—one by one like shadows passing into the night. The riders of the camels lift not their veils; they look not upon the right hand or the left.

They stoop not to the rose bush; nor do they eat when it is time. For they are the dead who have not died . . .

Even thus do they ride.

It was a fair day in the early Spring of the year of 1609 of the Christian era. And it was in the hills of northern Kashmir, on the outskirts of the empire of the Mogul, a day's fast ride from Srinaggar, the City of the Sun.

Khlit had gone from his *yurt* to water his horse at the spring that lay in the valley through which ran the caravan track from Leh.

The site of his *yurt* had been carefully selected, being halfway up the mountain slope within the forest line. It enabled him to see down the caravan route and to observe who came and went from Srinaggar to Leh.

And not to be seen himself—a matter of some moment for one who was outlawed by Jahangir, the Lord of Lords, and King of Kings, the Shadow of God on Earth, his Majesty, the emperor of Hindustan.

The edict of Jahangir did not greatly trouble Khlit, who was accustomed to choose his own path in life and to ride alone. In this manner he had passed from the Cossack steppe to the Tatar steppe; from there to the mountains of Kashmir.

Yet a recent exchange of sword strokes with sundry Persians and Pathans had made the name of Khlit notorious about Srinaggar. Some called him the Wanderer, others the Curved Saber—in reference to the Cossack blade that was his favorite weapon.

Khlit's hair was gray and his tall figure spare with age. Of recent years he had trusted more to shrewdness than to the sword—which he still wielded, however, with a master hand—to preserve his life from the enemies who beset the hills and caravan paths of Central Asia during the era of the Mogul.

In his felt *yurt* Khlit had had a companion other than his horse. It was the spirit of loneliness, bred of days of watching by the fire and nights of scanning the majestic slopes that thrust their splintered ice crests into the moonlight.

Even as the spirit of the sword had risen beside Khlit when a boy and driven him to saddle and to the open steppe, the pang of loneliness irked him.

Not that Khlit was eager for the companionship of the Kashmiris of Srinaggar. He had visited the court of Hindustan, and the ways of the Hindus were not his ways. He longed for sight of the men of the northern hills, who rode where they willed and slept under the stars.

It was a great hunger, this hunger that had come upon Khlit. It came of years of riding knee to knee and bridle to bridle with men of his own kind, who had no master, paid no tribute and owned no slaves. And it would not be denied.

Perhaps the season had something to do with it. The snow by Khlit's *yurt* was melting and the freshets were breaking from the ice barrier. The sun shone warmly into the entrance of the felt shelter and the mountain ash and poplar were breaking into leaf. It was the season when the Cossacks were wont to be afoot with their comrades.

Khlit had been meditating and had walked slowly down through the pines, drawing his horse after him. As he came out upon the spring he halted abruptly.

A group of men were squatted on carpets by the spring, watering a score of horses. Khlit stared at them thoughtfully. He had taken pains to observe—as was his custom—that no caravan was in view when he started down to the spring.

These men must have come down the valley swiftly if they had reached the watering place before him. Moreover, it was not a caravan.

Khlit wondered if they were horse thieves. But if the horses had been stolen they were going in the wrong direction for safety—being headed for Srinaggar.

Only a half-dozen of the animals were laden, and these with light packs. He noticed that the horses were Arabs and Turkoman beasts, of excellent breed. Then his own horse neighed before he could prevent, and the group at the spring glanced up hastily, leaping to their feet and laying hand to weapon.

Whereupon Khlit walked forward, having no mind to turn his back on the watchers. They eyed him in silence as he reached the spring, which was already muddied by the hoofs of the other beasts. Seeing this, Khlit hauled at a bridle of one, making room for his own thirsty horse to drink.

"*Bismillah*! Dog and gully jackal! Would you take what belongs to others?"

The words were *Turki*, and sharply spoken. The speaker was a wiry Arab enveloped in a voluminous brown cloak, girded by a shawl in which were stuck an array of weapons, ranging from silver-chased Turkish pistols to a pair of Damascus scimitars—upon the jeweled hilt of one the Arab's lean hand trembled.

Khlit gnawed at his mustache calmly, making no move to withdraw his horse.

"Back, dog of a *caphar*. Wretched son of many fathers, and eater of filth—back!"

The man stepped closer, his dark face flushed with anger.

"Your horse had finished," remarked Khlit, speaking broken *Turki*. "And the clear spring was becoming muddied, even as this soil is defiled by your presence, O maker-of-lies."

With a grunt the Arab snatched at a pistol—only to have it struck from his grip by a swift slash of Khlit's sword. The mas-

ter of the curved saber had learned by experience never to draw
without striking, and always to be the first to strike. Moreover he
had acquired a trick of thrusting with the same movement that
drew his blade from scabbard.

The pistol had fallen into the pool, and the angered Muslim
snatched at a sword. Khlit's blade flashed before his face and
touched his turban, severing the folds over his forehead. The ends,
dangling down, blinded the Arab, who stepped back.

"Peace!" said a harsh voice. "Peace, swallower of flames, and
seeker after blood. Stay, Nasir Beg! The graybeard is your master."

Nasir Beg fumbled at his weapon uncertainly, his thin lips
drawn back in a snarl. Khlit glanced at the speaker and saw a
little man huddled in fur robes, over which two alert black eyes
peered at him.

"Am I one, Pir Kasim, to suffer a blow like a dog?" muttered
Nasir Beg.

"Peace!" cried the little man again impatiently, and Khlit
sheathed his weapon, seeing that Pir Kasim was master of the
Arab.

Nevertheless, he did not cease to watch Nasir Beg, who was
assuaging his injured feelings by muttered curses.

By his dirty turban, on which were strung valuable pearls,
Khlit guessed Pir Kasim to be an Uzbek—probably a merchant
and a man of some importance. The third of the group was a
stout eunuch, richly garbed in silk. The two others who sat apart
and watched were servants.

Khlit considered them without apparent interest yet with
some curiosity. They were the first men he had spoken with
in several moons. Moreover, Pir Kasim, who was undoubtedly a
merchant, was traveling without goods, while the fat Ethiopian,
who was a eunuch, had no women to guard.

In his days at the Mogul court Khlit had seen many strange
assemblages, yet never before an Uzbek allied with an Arab and
an Ethiopian.

Pir Kasim seemed to be owner of the horses, but these were not the kind ordinarily bought and sold in Kashmir, nor did the Uzbek appear to be a seller of horses.

Who were they? Whither were they bound? And what manner of goods did Pir Kasim have for sale?

Khlit's horse had quenched its thirst by now, and he swung himself into the saddle Cossack fashion without touching stirrup. Whereupon Pir Kasim combed at his thin beard and frowned.

Backing his horse slowly from the pool, Khlit eyed the merchant, and presently, as he had anticipated, the Uzbek lifted a crooked forefinger and spoke.

"A fair horse that, noble sir. You have him well to hand."

"Aye," grunted Khlit, "I have trained him. Ho, merchant, I would have a fellow to him. Sell me one of yonder beasts—I have gold mohars."

"Nay—" Pir Kasim did not shift his scrutiny—"I now have need of them. We be desert men, by the face of the Prophet, and when did such sell their horses for gold?"

He traced patterns in the dust beside the carpet as if meditating. "Nay. What name bear you, and whence come you?"

"I have drawn my reins from the Mogul court," responded Khlit grimly. "As for a name—is there not writing on my sword? Aye, for him who can read."

Pir Kasim's shrewd eyes blinked. Wrapped in his robes, from which his yellow face and claw-like hand protruded, he resembled a hawk meditating upon its nest.

"Your sword, noble sir? You use it well, as Nasir Beg can bear witness. Whither ride you?"

"Where goes the wind from the hill gorge?"

"Out upon the plain. Harken, warrior—" Pir Kasim, being somewhat at a loss as to Khlit's race and rank, was cautious— "the thought has come to me, nay, it is but an idle thought, you may desire to draw your reins to the border. Away, perchance—

Allah is my witness that 'tis but an idle thought—from the tents and riders of the Mogul. Will you join us?"

Khlit considered, leaning on the peak of his saddle.

"Devil take it!" He growled. "Plain speech is best! You ride to Srinaggar, not to the border land."

Pir Kasim rubbed his lean hands together and stretched them out to the sun as if to a fire. He smiled craftily.

"Nay, we will turn back from the City of the Sun—in the space of fifteen days. Aye, when we have that for which we come we ride to the hills of the Mustagh Ata, past Ladak to Yarkand, which is in the northern plain. You will have a double handful of gold at Yarkand."

"A horse is more to my liking."

"Aye, a horse if you wish—the pick of the herd," assented Pir Kasim, adding hastily, "in place of the gold, noble sir."

"Does a fox run blindly with the wolfpack?"

Khlit made as if to turn away, but the merchant scrambled to his feet and was at the wanderer's knee.

"Before Allah, good sir, my words are the very gems of truth. Nay—" he sighed— "I will grant you a copious handful of gold and a silver-chased saddle with the horse."

"When did a merchant of Samarkand give much for little? What seek you of me?"

Pir Kasim glanced at Khlit reflectively and hazarded well.

"Sword strokes, noble sir. Verily, the path we tread from Sri-naggar to Yarkand will be one of peril. It may be our fate to be pursued—for we have a rich burden. I have need of one who can wield well his sword."

He could not have framed a speech that fell in better with the wishes of Khlit. The wanderer sought the northern steppe and wished companions. Here both were offered him.

"A good horse," whispered Pir Kasim—"an Arab. And your share of the gold."

"Hey, I have a mind to ride with you. Yet it is not wise for me to go to Srinaggar—"

"Excellent, noble sir," purred the Uzbek. "Have we not all some petty place where we ride not? 'Tis easily contrived; meet me at the caravansary of the river Sindh, an hour's ride west of Srinaggar at dusk on the fifteenth day. On the following dawn we shall mount for Yarkand."

He smiled up at Khlit, caressing the silver ornaments of his bridle.

"Aye, noble warrior, that day we shall ride hard—and scatter the dust of our going upon these accursed hill villages of the unbelievers, and upon our pack animals we shall bear—spoil! Will you be one with us? The peril will be great—"

"It is well."

Khlit spurred away, up the pine slope.

"Fail not!" cried Pir Kasim anxiously. "The Sindh caravansary —on the fifteenth evening—"

The rider of the black horse did not look back, and Pir Kasim returned to the group by the spring, rubbing his hands with the air of one who has made a good bargain

Nasir Beg swaggered in front of the merchant, scowling.

"Eh, one without wisdom!" the Arab sneered. "Will you number among us an unbeliever, a *caphar*—"

"Even so, windbag, and witless mouther of words! This unbeliever is Khlit, he of the curved saber."

Nasir Beg glanced after the Cossack, trying not to show his surprise.

"The Curved Saber knows the paths through the Mustagh Ata. Aye, the tribesmen know him. His name will be a shield over the dust of our going, Nasir Beg."

"Had I known it was he I would have struck more swiftly—"

Pir Kasim laughed at the moody Arab.

"Eh, you are a brave figure with your tongue, Nasir Beg. But with a sword it is otherwise."

With a grunt of anger Nasir Beg whipped out a dagger and clutched the shoulder of the merchant. Pir Kasim shivered.

"Nay, good Nasir Beg—it was but a test. Let not the cloud of vexation arise between us, good Nasir Beg. Verily, I would not mar with my breath the mirror of your bravery."

He pushed back the threatening dagger and freed himself from the other's hand.

"Likewise, Nasir Beg," he pointed out, "those who know our purpose will not join with us because of the shadow of peril. Khlit will serve us well—"

"Think you he will come to the caravansary?"

"I doubt it not."

Pir Kasim meditated swiftly, watching his comrade. "If you would cast the cloak of blood upon the fire of your quarrel with Khlit, let the matter rest until we reach Yarkand. Then, if you choose, deal with him shrewdly, and—his horse; nay, his own horse and that which I shall give him—will be yours, with half of his portion of gold."

The Arab smiled grimly.

"So be it, Pir Kasim. Yet I will not share bread and salt with the unbeliever."

II

Like the kites that fly over a battlefield and the ravens that follow a caravan are the hallal khors. *Yet the* hallal khors *are not birds but men.*

In the round window overlooking the fountain of the seraglio knelt Yasmi Khanim. She lay curled upon the cushions on the tiled floor—a slim girl whose form bespoke youthfulness. Her attar-scented black hair fell about her slight shoulders. Her *kohl*-darkened eyebrows matched her eyes, which gleamed in the twilight like soft pansies.

"Eyes like a gazelle—hair blacker than the storm wind—a mouth like the seal of Suleiman—teeth finer than matched pearls—her form like a willow, a slender willow."

So had said the Persian merchant who sold Yasmi Khanim to Raja Ram-Dar adding, "Aye, lord of exalted mercy, Yasmi

Khanim, the Persian singing girl, is a rose from the gardens of Isphahan, a diamond-sheen of the gems of Kuhistan!"

Well-content was the raja with his new purchase, for the girl's face was fair as a Hindu woman of the higher caste, and her voice sweet. Yet only once did he hear her sing.

A great sickness had come upon the raja, such a sickness as the fresh water and cold of Kashmir served to heal not. Nor did the sacred water of the Ganges—the river that flows from the feet of the gods—cure him, although brought by the Brahmans themselves.

On the night before, Raja Ram-Dar drank plentifully of the Ganges water and thereupon died.

Upon this matter and other things Yasmi meditated. From without the silent seraglio came the moaning cry of women's voices. This, Yasmi knew, was the cry of the mourners, of Darayshi Krisna and the other wives, of the slaves and the women who had been hired to wail.

For the funeral of the raja was to be that night. And fitting honor was to be paid the dead.

> Our lord has gone before us to the halls of the Bhanuloka! Ai! He has set the seal of Yama on his brow. Ai! Our lord has bent his royal head at the footstools of the gods!

The chant echoed ceaselessly. Yasmi wondered if the women were tearing their garments and letting their hair fall about their faces. So did the Muslim women of Persia.

But the Hindu women were strange. Yasmi wondered at the fierce exultation of the chant, which was led by the shrill voice of Darayshi Krisna, the favorite wife of the raja.

Yasmi herself was a Muslim, being from the hills of Kuhistan in northern Persia. She was a child of fifteen Summers, raised in a hill village on the Afghan border—an onlooker at the mysteries of life, such as the splendor of a Hindu funeral.

From the burial place came the high plaint of music. Fiddles and guitars were sounding the *ragim bhairabi*, the music of the fire spirits.

Yasmi stirred uneasily and snuggled down on her cushions. She had chanted the death song at the grave of her father's father, who had been laid in the earth in a clean winding sheet with his face toward Mecca, as was the law. But her song had not been like this.

Yasmi closed her eyes uncomfortably, then opened them alertly to watch a band of white-robed, shaven Brahmans pass through the courtyard toward the burial place. The Persian girl was oppressed by a vague foreboding, bred of the silence in the woman's court and the shrill music without. She had heard of the burial of the sun worshipers, who were infidels, such as the Hindus. The sun worshipers had burned the bodies; perhaps these people did likewise.

Snuggling her feet into their slippers and drawing her velvet bodice closer about her waist—for the evening grew chill—Yasmi waited, looking very much like a brown fawn peering from its nest.

Hurried footsteps sounded in the corridors behind her, and she wriggled farther into the cushion, not wishing to be seen.

"Ho, base-born and shameless!"

The harsh voice of Sasethra, mistress of the slaves, assailed her.

"Wench without honor! Wouldst thou hide when the all-potent lord, thy master, is placed upon the *ghat*? Come!"

Sasethra clutched the girl's arm and jerked her to her feet, staring at her.

"How is this? Thine ornaments—necklaces—pearls! Where are they?"

The mistress of the slaves hurried Yasmi to her chamber and hastily arrayed her in bangles upon wrist and ankle, in silver-broidered cap that fitted over her splendid hair. She thrust jade earrings rudely into her ears, inspected her slim hands to see if they were henna-stained, and coiled a pearl necklace over her throat and breast.

"Ignorant sparrow!" she scolded. "So thou wouldst hide? *Ai*—is this not the night of nights?"

"Verily," protested the girl, "I had a fear—"

"A fear?"

The woman screamed with sudden laughter.

"Nay, the Persian songstress trills of fear? Knowest not, wanton, there are those who will see that thou treadest the path of honor—"

She broke off at a new note in the chant without.

"Come! Already we are late."

Despite her words she fingered the bracelets covetously.

"Ho, these be rare stones—"

"My father's gift—"

"Speak not, shameless one, of thy father on this night when thy lord ascends to a thrice-purified life. Aye, the jade earrings will fetch a good price. And the pearls—"

Her eyes glinted evilly in the dim light, and she urged the child abruptly into a corridor leading to the garden. From there Sasethra sought a small gate which conducted them through the wall of the woman's courtyard out to the glen by the Sindh bank. Seeing many people, men among them, standing about, Yasmi would have drawn her veil over her face but the woman jerked it rudely back.

The river bank and the glen were lined with watchers who faced a large pit. This pit had been nearly filled by a pile of brush and logs, neatly arranged.

By the light of the numerous torches Yasmi could see the body of the raja on the pile, resting on a couch covered with costly satins. At the head of the body a small hut had been built of brush.

And within the hut at the end of the couch sat Darayshi Krisna. The favorite wife of the dead man sat erect and silent, holding her lord's head on her knees.

Beside the *ghat* squatted musicians. And Brahmans came and went through the assembly, instructing the slaves how to pour oils and *ghee* upon the brush. Not far from the pit the women rocked, wailing.

Yasmi thought that it was to be a burial like that of the sun-worshipers. And even more ceremonious. Darayshi Krisna, she meditated, must have loved the dead raja with a great love since she waited until the last minute before tearing herself from her lord.

Beyond the pit and the watchers the broad current of the Sindh swept under the willows. A sharp wind from the mountain summits that Yasmi could vaguely see against the stars caused the torches to flicker.

She caught the scent of musk and ambergris. Truly this was to be a lordly burial!

But why Sasethra had dragged her there she did not know. For she could not sing the music that the fiddlers played.

"Honor to the son of Ayodyha and Ram! May he live again as a prince of princes, a king of kings. *Ai*! May he be purified by the sacred water and the thrice-sacred fire."

So chanted the women, their voices rising over the sound of the instruments. Then the music changed. Tambourines and cymbals clashed harshly, drowning all other noises.

"The hour of thy lord is at hand, Persian," whispered Sasethra. "Behold, the high Brahmans have come from Srinaggar, that all due honor shall be paid him by those who were the dust under his exalted feet."

Yasmi did not reply, for Darayshi Krisna had taken the torch that one of the priests handed her. The wife of Raja Ram-Dar thrust the torch into the brush of the wall of the hut at her side. At once the Brahmans scurried about the pyre, lighting the wood in a dozen places.

"*Aie!*" cried Yasmi, "she does not move. She will be harmed!"

An angry hiss from the mistress of the slaves silenced her. Then she saw in the light from the growing blaze Darayshi Krisna clad in all her ornaments, with unbound hair, remain tranquilly at the head of her lord.

"Twice, and the blessed five!"* cried a priest, raising his arms.

Others echoed the speech. But Darayshi Krisna did not see them. She was smiling, although the walls of the hut were crackling and blazing. She did not move when the perspiration poured from her set face and the fire caught her loose hair.

"Blessed is Darayshi Krisna!" cried the priest again in a loud voice.

Yasmi shivered and clasped her hands to her throat. She could no longer see the form of the woman who was burning herself on the pyre. The body of the raja was still visible, his sword on his hands.

By now the fire had filled the whole pit, soaring upward in swirling flames that illumined every person in the glen. The women had ceased their mourning and joined hands. They were running about the pit, crying out something that Yasmi did not hear.

Darayshi Krisna, she thought, wondering, had uttered no sound.

Several Brahmans stood as close to the flames as the heat would permit, leaning on long poles. Yasmi had begun to realize the significance of the poles, and she shuddered, whereupon Sasethra tightened her grip.

Just behind the priests were several men in armor, cloaked. Yasmi noted them only fleetingly, for Sasethra suddenly began to run toward the pit, drawing the girl after her.

Then Yasmi saw that the fire had caught the garment of one of the women—a slave, who straightaway cast herself into the fire. A faint cry echoed above the roar of the flames—a cry that was drowned at once in the blast of noise from tambourines and cymbals.

"High honor shall be paid thy lord!" whispered Sasethra, harshly. "The low-born slave felt the fierce kiss of the fire,

---

*Reincarnation. If she should die twice again in this manner—so the Hindu doctrine maintained—it would complete the five deaths which would win blessed immortality.

and her spirit was weak—but the music overbore her plaint.
Come!"

"*Aie!*" cried the girl in sudden terror "Nay, Sasethra—I am
one—"

"Thy lord is dead. Join thy spirit to his!"

Saying this, the mistress of the slaves stripped a costly bracelet
from the arm of the trembling singer and thrust the bangle into
her own girdle.

Terror-stricken, Yasmi saw one of the armed watchers seize
and speak to a woman who danced about the fire. The slave tore
herself from the man's grip and plunged into the pyre.

"Pity, Sasethra!" Yasmi implored. "Think, Sasethra—I am not
a follower of the Hindu gods."

"Thy place is with thy lord, shameless one."

The stout woman tugged at the girl, who recoiled weeping
from the heat of the fire.

"Ho, servants of Ram-Dar," shrilled Sasethra, "cast me this
faithless one after the others! Shall a slave outlive her lord?"

Several of the onlookers caught the girl, tearing the pearls from
her throat and the jade from her ears. Yasmi whimpered, helpless
in their grasp.

"The seal of death is set in her forehead!" screamed Sasethra,
who had taken the pick of the girl's jewels. At the words a priest
poured scented oil from a jar over her abundant hair.

"See, she feels the kiss of Yama!"

Then a hand gripped Yasmi, and a voice whispered to her in
Turki.

"Life! Would you have life, little slave? Speak!"

The last of the dancing-women had vanished and already the
fire had taken on a ruddier tinge, as the flames died. But Yasmi
quivered with the heat that struck through her thin garments.

"Life—by Allah—grant me life!" she cried.

She felt the pole of the priest thrust at her back and heard the
complaisant tones of Sasethra: "'Tis done. The holy Brahman has
anointed her for death."

Then the pole was thrust aside and Yasmi was picked up bodily. The arms that gripped her were mail-clad. Two cloaked figures joined the man who held her as he turned back from the flames.

In sheer surprise the priests and the watchers gave back before the group of men who had seized the girl. Availing themselves of this, they moved hastily toward the edge of the glen.

"*Ai!*" shrilled the voice of Sasethra. "The *hallal khors!* Oh, the robbers of the *ghat!* Oh, the wretched scavengers of the dead!"

A command from one of the priests silenced the strident woman. Yasmi saw an emaciated form appear before them, a figure turbanless, with unkempt beard and hair, who lifted lean arms.

"Back!" commanded the form with calm authority. "No man may take her on whom is the seal of death and live."

One of the warriors with an oath struck down the *yogi* and a wail went up from the priests and the unarmed watchers. Some ran toward the group, but drew back at the flash of ready weapons.

Swiftly Yasmi was borne to where horses waited in the shadow of a grove, and the man who held her mounted and wheeled his horse away along a path through the trees, throwing her carelessly over the peak of his saddle.

"A rare jewel we have plucked this night, Pir Kasim," he said.

For some time the horsemen rode at a rapid pace, and Yasmi Khanim believed that they went in the direction of Srinaggar. They slowed down among some huts, and at the bank of a canal she could see that the others of the party rode off, leaving her with the man who had first addressed her.

He sought for a space among the rushes of the canal and drew in a small skiff, which he bade her enter. He rowed out into the canal, and then more cautiously down the shadow of the bank under a bridge until he paused at what seemed a small gate in the steep slope of the bank.

Yasmi could make out the roofs and towers of the Srinaggar streets rising against the stars. She lay quiet in the boat, watching the man.

He stepped ashore and bent over the wooden door. This was opened presently from within and a gleam of light showed.

"Haste!" grunted the warrior. "And step softly."

She passed through the narrow door, which smelled strongly of mud and foul weeds. A hand gripped her shoulder and pushed her, stumbling, up a flight of steps. The passageway led toward the light, and Yasmi passed through a poorly walled cellar into a room where the air was stale in spite of the heavy scent of sandal-paste.

Here the hand on her shoulder wheeled her around, and she faced a stout eunuch who eyed her with a grin.

"Here is a pretty pearl, Nasir Beg. Her mouth too wide, perhaps. Ho, a shapely parrot, taken from the grip of the hawks."

"A necklace-string stripped of jewels," grunted the Arab. "The accursed women took even her earrings."

Yasmi glanced at him gratefully and fell on her knees.

"May Allah reward you," she cried in *Turki*, as they had spoken. "May you find honor and live forever in the sun of prosperity. Happy am I to be among true believers."

She had spoken impulsively, but there was pride in her voice—and the tone of one more accustomed to command than to obey. The eunuch grinned the more while Nasir Beg scanned her in surprise.

"A Muslim wench, Mustafa," he observed. "Verily, she is not the less handsome for that. And I heard those who said at the fire that she is a singer with a voice like to the Persian nightingale. Your name?"

"Yasmi Khanim, warrior."

The girl flung back her dark hair, resentful at the Arab's tone.

"My father is Sheikh Ibrahim of Kuhistan, master of a hundred swords."

"The sheikh has a fair daughter," responded Mustafa.

"He has gold, and his hand is generous," said Yasmi in sudden misgiving. "He will reward well one who brings his daughter to the hills of Kuhistan."

The Arab yawned, and Mustafa shook his head.

"Kuhistan is many days' ride, little sparrow. Tune your voice to a sweeter note and Mustafa will find you a silken nest."

"Nay, I must ride to Kuhistan. A Persian merchant—may he be forever without honor—seized me at the border of my father's land."

"*Bismillah*!" The eunuch spread out his plump hands. "He had an eye to a comely face, Yasmi. Aye, it is fate. And who can outrun the shadow of fate?" His expression hardened. "Do not weary Nasir Beg with your whine but join the others."

He pointed to an alcove in the cellar. There Yasmi saw for the first time some four women seated on a ragged carpet. By their dress she knew them to be Hindus. All were young possibly, but haggard as if from sickness. They did not look at her.

"Nay—" Nasir Beg ceased yawning and stared at the girl speculatively—"I would hear her sing. If it is true that she is skilled it will increase her value. The wretched Faizuli Anim owns—besides his wine jars—a lute. She can come to the tavern safely."

"Have a care, Nasir Beg," warned the eunuch. "Pir Kasim would not thank you if you take the wench before the eyes of men. If our abiding-place be found—"

"There will be slit throats and molten silver poured into the eyes of the *hallal khors*, Mustafa!" amended Nasir Beg grimly. "Nay, cease your whine. Fain would I hear the voice of the song-bird. In the tavern of Faizuli Anim none come but Muslims. Eh— is she not also a follower of the Prophet? Who will suspect?"

Yasmi's pale cheeks burned. She made as if to protest, then, on second thought, followed the Arab passively. Nasir Beg motioned her to a flight of steps leading upward from the cellar.

The steps terminated in what seemed a small and odorous chamber. It was, actually, a huge empty wine vat. Nasir Beg kicked impatiently at the wooden side of the cask, and it opened.

Mustafa accompanied the twain, muttering angrily.

III

Singing gently to himself, beating time complacently with a plump, bejeweled hand, Shir Mujir ibn Khojas of Baghdad, the *hafiz*—reciter of poems—wended his way importantly through the back alleys of Srinaggar.

His gait resembled that of a crab, inasmuch as when a belated group of Kashmir nobles passed down the streets intersecting the alleys, accompanied by armed guards and link-bearers, the *hafiz* scuttled sidewise into the shadows, but when he encountered a cortege of slaves he lifted the skirts of his tunic and placed a scarf, musk-scented, before his broad nostrils, crying loudly:

"Passage-way for the deputy of the Lion of Persia! Back, scourings of the offal-pot! Scrapings of the mud! Infinitely foul! Ditchborn, gully jackals!"

Luckily for the fat Khojas, *Turki* was not readily understood by the Kashmir slaves. In this manner did Mujir ibn Khojas, who was slightly the better—or the worse—for numerous potations, thread his way from the bazaar quarter to the riverfront at an hour so late that even the bazaar stalls of the Muslims, who were celebrating the feast of Bairam, were closed.

But the *hafiz* was in no mind for sleep since he had repeated lengthy versions of the *Shah Namah* at the board of wealthy merchants and was consequently the richer for silver and gold coins, both dinars and shekels.

"Nay, the night air is soft—soft as maidens' tresses and fragrant—fragrant as the essence of roses on the brow of a sultan's favorite," he muttered uncertainly, lurching over a heap of refuse which was far from sweet, "and I, the golden-tongued Mujir, peer of reciters, bedfellow, nay, boon-fellow, of princes; I, the diamond in the tiara of Allah, the flower i' the mantle of the Shah—may he bellow, or is't mellow, i' his grave? I, the *hafiz* of the chosen of Allah, the Commander of the Faithful, the Caliph who is the very substance of blessedness, the essence of divine light, and the spotless robe of honor—I am also a gleam of radiance and a pearl of precious substance. Where lies that accursed hovel of Faizuli Anim?"

Pursuing the uneven tenor of his way, the *hafiz* halted to beat at a closed door only to be confronted by the emaciated figure of a Kashmiri child.

"Verily," he cried, "by the beard of the Prophet! Faizuli Anim has shrunken most strangely in form, for he was once handsomely fat, even as I—although not quite so handsome or so fat. Ho—oho, Faizuli Anim! Nay, what is't?"

The boy had been snatched back and a hag, on whose wrists clinked the chains of bondage, faced him. In a trembling hand she held a knife and cursed fearfully from a mouth that was toothless and sore-ridden from disease,

"Nay," meditated the worthy *hafiz*, "now is Faizuli Anim in the shape of a vixen, a toothless vixen. Here is the work of evil magic and no place for the high-born Mujir. Farewell, shade of Faizuli. Farewell, hag, whose tooth hangs from her hand like the fang of a wolf—"

He aimed an unsteady kick at the twain and passed on until he reached the carpet-hung entrance of the Muslim tavern which overhung the riverbank.

The light from a solitary candle showed him Faizuli Anim seated on a carpet within. Mujir jerked off his leather shoes and replaced them, not without difficulty, with a pair of slippers.

"By the mole on the face of Mohammed," chanted the *hafiz*, "I have found you at last, worthy Faizuli Anim—after a struggle with an evil angel who was all but toothless, and that one tooth a thing of ill omen! Ho, good keeper of the blessed wines—a goblet of snow-chilled Shiraz!

"Verily I have a thirst that is a mighty thirst, wherein all the sands of Khorassan do itch in my throat. Aye, how runs the verse—

> *Leave't to others to cant and to repine*
> *When You and I embrace our life—the vine.*

"Nay, methinks the verse is mine. 'Tis excellently attuned. Ho—I will sit in the inner chamber—"

Despite the tavern keeper's remonstrance Mujir stepped gracefully over the prone forms of slumbering camelmen in the outer stall and pushed through the curtains that veiled a separate compartment of the inn.

Here he salaamed before a seated figure and slumped down heavily on the carpet. The other glanced at him once sharply, then looked away indifferently. Not so Mujir.

"Come, brother in wine and watcher of the night, let us tickle our throats with that which Mohammed scorns but I do not."

The seated figure made no response. Struck by a new fancy, the *hafiz* unrolled his prayer-carpet from his waist and hung it with drunken seriousness over the opening in the curtain—after Faizuli Anim had brought him his jar of wine and left.

"Thus," he explained, stroking his dyed beard, "do I veil the aspect of our delightful sin as a radiant damsel shrouds the beauty of her face. Come, brother! My eyes tell me you are a soldier, and your rich armor and jeweled ornaments bespeak rank and prowess.

"When did the wild ass keep his muzzle from the fresh grass, or a warrior his lips from wine—or the wine of a woman's mouth for that matter?"

The stranger made no response. He was a straight-backed man, wearing travel-stained mail, nearly concealed by a cloak of rich texture. His cotton trousers were clean and his red morocco shoes costly. The hilt of his scimitar was a mass of jewels, and a blue diamond shone from his turban crest.

These things the *hafiz* had noticed. But he had not observed the dark face under the turban with the scar on one cheek from chin to brow, the thin, hooked nose, and the hard eyes which moved slowly from object to object with a purposeful stare.

By face and form the stranger was an Afghan of a northern tribe, by dress a follower of the Mogul, and one of rank, who had prospered in war.

But the *hafiz* was in a mellow mood.

"Nay, have I not earned a kiss from the grape, O warrior?" he appealed. "'Twas a rare feat to thread the streets of the City of the Sun this night.

"Patrols of cursed unbelievers, godless Hindus and their like, search the bazaars and alleys for certain evil-doers. 'Tis said in the bazaars that a woman of the dead raja was snatched from the *ghat*, and the evil Brahmans are astir like a nest of angered bees."

This time the soldier looked up.

"Eh—why do they search in Srinaggar?"

"Because—so 'tis said—the woman was carried hither. Nay, I would she had been burned to a crisp on the *ghat* for the trouble she has made me. When the shaven priests have anointed a woman for death what else is she fitted for? Ho—the wine is cool!"

Whereupon he quaffed deep and lay back upon the carpet with a watery sigh, his plump limbs lax, and the Afghan regarded him with disfavor.

"Would they had burned—shriven—her, for by Allah she was a dainty morsel; verily the fire would wrap her limbs, licking them with ardent tongues, and she would have cried out."

So mumbled the *hafiz*, and the warrior's eyes narrowed while he bit at his beard.

"Methinks, aye, verily I think—sweet thought, choice as a pearl in a goblet of wine, red as blood—she would be reshriven, nay reshaped, into a houri fair as a blown rose, for she was Muslim. *Aigh*—"

Mujir groaned from the capacious depths of his stomach and would have sat up, but his palsied muscles refused their office. The flat of the warrior's scabbard had descended with no little force on the highest point of the wine-bibber's outstretched form—which was also his tenderest point.

"Toad, evil mouther, and worm!"

The Afghan spoke with slow decision.

"Stand!"

"Nay—akh, by Allah! I am death-smitten—"

"Verily, such will be your fate if you obey not. Stand!"

There was the sharp ring of anger in the soldier's abrupt command, and Mujir, who had scanned him with a rolling eye, clambered to his feet wide-eyed, holding his round belly tenderly in both hands.

"Now what mean you, warrior?" he panted. "Nay, are we not both servants of the pr—"

"My rank is *mansabdar* of Jahangir the Mogul. My title from the lips of such as you is lord."

"Nay, you are graceless—"

Mujir's words ended in a squeal, for the Afghan's sword flashed in his face. Twice the weapon struck as the soldier gained his feet and the right and left edges of the *hafiz's* cherished red-dyed beard fell to the floor. He stared at the wisps of hair blindly, then abruptly his stout knees began to shake.

"Harken, reader of poems and guzzler of forbidden wine." The Afghan scowled at him and spat in disgust. "Shall one without honor claim mercy? Shall swine taken in sin be treated as men? Put down your prayer rug on the floor."

In silence Mujir did so. In a moment he had become half-sober.

"It is near the hour of dawn, Mujir. Can your evil lips frame a prayer?"

"Aye—lord. O excellent guardian of the faith—"

"Speak not of faith. Is there faith in a body such as yours? I think not. Pray!"

The *hafiz* choked, but could not take his blinking eyes from the harsh face of the *mansabdar*.

"Lord, and fountain of all the virtues, shield of the faithful, favored of Mohammed. Harken to your slave. 'Tis in truth the feast of Bairam. And I—"

"Perform your ablutions."

With that the soldier snatched up the heavy wine-goblet and placed it gently at his feet.

"By your favor, Abdul Dost," came the servile voice of Faizuli Anim from the door. "Here is one Nasir Beg with the slave Yasmi who would hear the music of her golden throat. Knowing that Mujir ibn Khojas was skilled in such things, I ventured to bring the twain here that the *hafiz* might render judgment on the voice of the maiden.

"The *hafiz*," growled Abdul Dost, "is at his ablutions."

Behind the stout form of the tavern keeper he caught sight of a slender woman, held firmly by a lean Arab. Mujir also had seen the newcomers and his jaw dropped.

Abdul Dost considered, then seated himself on his heels, nodding to Faizuli Anim.

"Let the girl enter," he commanded. "And the *hafiz* render judgment."

Yasmi stepped within the curtain wearily, a lute in her hand. Nasir Beg squatted down at her side, eyeing the kneeling teller of poems with some curiosity. At Abdul Dost also the Arab glanced twice, then turned moodily upon the girl.

The tavern keeper had left them. But a moment later the curtains parted slightly, and a black, round face peered through the aperture.

Mustafa was keeping watch over his charge.

"Sing!" growled Nasir Beg. "Must I lose sleep because of such as you? Yet it was the command of him who owns you that trial be made of your voice. Haste, for I am weary."

By the faint light of the bronze lantern overhead Yasmi scanned the two beside her. She looked indifferently at Mujir over her veil, and long at Abdul Dost. She was worn with the hardships of the night, and tears trembled in her dark eyes. But Nasir Beg was impatient.

She bent her head over the lute, striking the strings feebly. Her slender shoulders shook with a brief sob.

"Haste, wanton," growled the Arab. "Must I summon Mustafa with his lash?"

He clutched at her shoulder, but the girl drew away swiftly. She lifted her head in sudden decision and to Nasir Beg's surprise let fall her veil.

Mujir sucked in his breath with admiration at sight of the delicate face framed in dark hair and glanced apprehensively at Abdul Dost, who was watching the girl closely.

A quick flush came into the cheeks of Yasmi, and she looked up at the lamp, a half-smile at the edge of her lips.

Then she sang, striking the lute softly, the song of the hill-tribes of Khorassan, the song that begins:

Where is the falcon's nest?
And the nest of his mate . . . Where,
save in the wind! And the wind is the breath of the hill.

Mujir hardly listened. He marked the trembling of the girl's lips, the rise and fall of her breast under the veil, and her slight hands upon the cords of the instrument. And he sighed noisily.

Nasir Beg lent an attentive ear, for he had the Arab's natural love of melody. Yet the song was not to his liking, and—seeing the goblet—he drank.

Behind the curtain Faizuli Anim crept to Mustafa's side to hear the better. Only Abdul Dost seemed not to listen.

But the Afghan was strongly moved by the song. He had heard it formerly in the tents of the hillmen of Khorassan, in the camps of the riders of Badakshan. It brought before his memory the time, long past, when he had tended horses for the lords of Afghanistan, now dead or servants of the Mogul.

Yet, being what he was, Abdul Dost allowed nothing of this to show in his scarred face. Indeed he resolutely put from him the impulse of memory that had been born of the girl's song.

Yasmi did not reach the end of the song. Her voice quivered and she dropped the lute, throwing herself on the carpet before Abdul Dost.

"Pity, lord; have pity!" she cried quickly. "By your dress you are of the Afghan hills. Verily the heavy hand of wrongdoing has taken me from the tent—"

"Peace, wench!" Nasir Beg struck her savagely across the shoulders. "Would you turn from those to whom you owe life?"

"Aye." The girl faced him resolutely. "For I am free born."

"No longer such," responded the Arab grimly, his hand on her arm. "Have you not sold your body to us?"

Yasmi cast the lute from her.

"I knew not what I did," she pleaded. "I thought you were— friends."

She touched the foot of Abdul Dost. "Lord, will you believe? By Allah and the face of the Prophet, this is naught but the truth. I am no slave, yet would this man and his kind hold me—"

"Faithless, and teller of lies!" snarled the Arab. "Come, *hafiz*, the song is ended. Speak—is her voice worth silver, gold, much?"

Mujir glanced apprehensively at Abdul Dost, who seemed lost in thought. Then he waved his plump hand doubtfully.

"'Tis true I am a rare judge of such matters, excellent sir. The sound of the woman's song is like the nightingale.

"Yet it would be well to teach her what best pleases her masters. Now if it is your will to sell her in the Baghdad market she should trill naught save the soft and amorous Persian airs—"

"Nay," grunted Nasir Beg, "she is to be sold to the wealthy mandarins of China, the men of Han, at the Yarkand mart. They pay well—"

"*Ai!*" moaned Yasmi. "Shall a Muslim be sent to the worshipers of the lotus-eyed god?"

She had appealed to Abdul Dost. The Afghan bent forward, searching her face earnestly, then looked long at Nasir Beg.

"She is yours?" he questioned sharply.

"My master's. We have risked our throats that she should live. She has given her body to us. *Bismillah!* We will not yield her up."

Nasir Beg spoke decisively. Abdul Dost frowned. If the girl was truly the property of the Arab it would be a delicate if not hazardous matter to interfere on her behalf. Moreover, Abdul Dost had no use for a slave, even such a one as Yasmi.

He had marked the movement of the curtains and suspected that Nasir Beg was not alone in his guardianship of the singer. Still—the song had touched his memory.

"Did she yield herself as a slave, Arab?"

"As a slave."

"A lie!" exclaimed Yasmi defiantly.

Abdul Dost considered, then spoke coldly to Nasir Beg.

"What price will she bring in the Yarkand slave-bazaar?"

Nasir Beg calculated shrewdly. "Eh, she has a face like a rose, and her form is rounded. Eh, you who have heard know that she graces the necklace of beauty with the pearl of song. Mujir ibn Khojas, who is a judge, has said that her voice is like to a nightingale. At Yarkand she will fetch twelve—nay fourteen—gold mohars."

Yasmi sighed and drew her veil about her face. Her glance was still fixed hungrily on Abdul Dost.

"That is her price?" inquired that warrior.

"Aye."

Abdul Dost put his hand to his girdle. "I have a whim, Arab." He opened his band over the carpet. Gold coins tumbled to the floor and rolled about.

"There be mohars—gold. Count seventeen, and take them. The girl's song pleased me, and—she is a free-born Muslim. Shall a falcon of the hills die in a foul cage?"

Wild hope leaped into the eyes of the singer. Mujir stared, licking his lips. Verily, he thought, this was a great lord who could shower gold like copper coins and let another count the tally.

But Nasir Beg drew back with a smile. He bowed and stroked his beard craftily.

"Seventeen? Nay, the generosity of the lord is like to the light of the sun. Yet—" he smiled again—"at Yarkand gold is worth more than here. At the market of the Han slave-merchants Yasmi would fetch twenty such coins."

"Count then the twenty, and be gone," Abdul Dost snarled, and the mask of indifference fell from his face.

Nasir Beg still smiled. Without consulting Pir Kasim he did not dare sell the girl. Besides, if she were sold to Abdul Dost it would be known. She would be recognized as the singer who had been stolen from the raja's *ghat*, and search would be made for those who had taken her from the priests.

The Arab was no coward, yet he knew how closely the Hindus had ransacked the byways of Srinaggar for his party, and he suspected that the *yogi* he had struck down in their flight had been badly injured.

The fate of the *hallal khors*, if discovered, was a thing not to be lightly contemplated. And if in addition they had slain a priest death by torture would be the least thing in store for them.

"Nay," he announced. "My master will not sell Yasmi."

Abdul Dost rose to his feet, hand idly at his belt. Yasmi followed his every movement with anxious eyes, scarcely breathing while she harkened to the argument between the two.

"Arab," said the Afghan slowly, "here is the price you named—and more. Take it or be false to your word."

"Nay." Nasir Beg still smiled. "The thought came to me that you jested, so I also made a jest."

"I do not jest. Twenty-two gold mohars lie on the carpet. Take them!"

The Arab rose lithely, drawing slightly back and glancing at the curtain. But then the voluble *hafiz* gave tongue.

"O lord and ocean of the nectar of kindness, and mountain of holy righteousness, I, the teller of poems, the faithful Mujir, will tear the veil of blindness from your exalted eyes. O leader of the faithful—" the *hafiz* saw in a flash, or thought that he did, a chance to redeem himself with Abdul Dost—"talk not of paying such a sum for this worthless one. O noble warrior, she is worth not one silver dinar."

He paused, pleased at the attention he was receiving—though Abdul Dost was watching the Arab more closely than the speaker. Yasmi tried to take the soldier's hand.

"With my eyes I saw it, lord," resumed Mujir. "This very night. By chance, it was verily by mere chance, I came upon the *ghat*. Nay, I knew naught of what was to come to pass, but some worthless beggar had whispered that women were to be burned—not that I believed, lord.

"Nay, by chance I watched—that is, I could not help but see— this very woman led to the *ghat* and anointed by the priest for death. And then snatched by force—"

For the first time Abdul Dost glanced down at the *hafiz* angrily. As he did so, Nasir Beg smote the lamp with the flat of his sword. The chamber was in darkness.

A cry from Yasmi—hurried footsteps. An oath from Abdul Dost, who had groped for the girl and finding her not, had sprung for the curtains, drawing sword as he went. His foot struck against something that quivered, jelly-like, and he rolled to the floor over the prostrate form of Mujir.

He was up immediately. But the curtains were cast loosely over his head. He felt the impact of a dagger against his mail shirt and jerked free of the entangling cloth. Then he halted perforce to listen for footsteps, as the tavern was in darkness.

No sound rewarded his seeking. Only the pale light of the new day outlined a window faintly.

"Lord," muttered a suppliant voice, "have I not saved your—"

Abdul Dost was lean, but there was great strength in his arms—the deceptive strength that had made him one of the finest swordsmen of northern Hindustan.

He caught the *hafiz* by girdle and collar and dragged him to the tavern door. Outside the dawn marked the riverbank, high above the water at this point.

"Harken, *hafiz*," said Abdul Dost. "I swear an oath on the faith of my fathers that I shall seek the girl Yasmi until she is free or Nasir Beg is dead.

"It is time," added Abdul Dost grimly, "that you performed your ablutions."

Whereupon he raised the struggling man to his shoulder and flung him outward, watching with satisfaction the resulting splash. He was content when the fat bulk of the *hafiz* failed to climb from the current.

Running footsteps sounded and two armed men hastened up.

"Sluggards!" snarled the *mansabdar*. "Ahmed—Rasoumi! Heard you not the struggle?"

"Lord," panted one, "we slept, being weary. Has hurt come to the favored of Allah?"

"Nay. Search me the tavern. Come."

But their efforts ended in the cellar filled with giant wine-casks. None were visible save the snoring and drunken camel-men.

Abdul Dost passed through the empty rooms, noting grimly by light of the torches his men had kindled that the gold coins were gone from the carpet. Either Mujir or Faizuli Anim had made good use of his time.

But he did unearth the cowering tavern keeper in the rear of a wine vat.

"Speak the truth, or follow Mujir into the river," he informed the man. "Who is that Arab Nasir Beg? Who was his master? Whither went they?"

By degrees Faizuli revealed the secret of the passage behind the wine cask. But when the Afghan entered it cautiously the lower cellars were bare and the door to the riverbank open. No boat was to be seen.

"Lord, and mountain of mercy," wailed the tavern keeper, "I know naught of them save that they planned to depart eastward and north along the Sindh caravan route, and they are many. They ride to the Darband Pass in the Ladak border."

"Thither we also will ride," said Abdul Dost.

So it happened that the *mansabdar* and his two men without waiting for further preparation set out along the Sindh trail in the early morning of the day after the feast of Bairam.

And when they had departed a woeful figure, mud-coated and gasping, dragged itself from the reeds by the river and lay cursing the day that Abdul Dost was born of his mother, the day that he had come to Srinaggar, and his father and his father's father, even to all his forebears.

<h2 style="text-align:center">IV</h2>

The lightning strikes down a tall tree, but it does not linger to be seen. Not otherwise strikes the sword of a skilled warrior.

Kashmiri proverb

Khlit was glad to be in the saddle again. He was well content to turn his back upon the City of the Sun and journey into the mountain passes. And the rapid pace that the caravan struck satisfied him.

In truth he saw no need for haste. Yet Pir Kasim, who led the cavalcade, pressed the horses to their limit.

No stop was made during the day. Only after dusk did the caravan halt, in a valley near the highway where water was to be had. And Khlit, who was well versed in such matters, noted that the merchant posted sentries. Also that the fires were put out after the dinner had been cooked.

He saw too that they avoided the villages. Once, when they passed through the outskirts of a collection of huts, ragged Kashmiris ran forth and stoned them. A sally by Nasir Beg and two of his men drove back the villagers, but not before blood had been shed.

Another thing struck Khlit. It was when they met a group of three Hindu riders going in the opposite direction. The men drew back from the trail, scanning the caravan and scowling. Weapons were drawn and Nasir Beg summoned Khlit to his side to wait with their attendants until the horses of Pir Kasim had all passed the spot.

Then they rode after the caravan. But Khlit, looking back, saw the three sitting in their saddles and watching. As long as the caravan was in view the riders watched.

Directly afterward Pir Kasim turned aside from the main highway and led his troop through an unfrequented pass, where the cold—even in early Summer—was great, and the women suffered.

Khlit had noticed with some surprise that the merchandise of Pir Kasim was women. He had met the caravan on his way to the rendezvous at the Sindh road. And the women had been with it then. They rode heavily veiled and closely watched by Mustafa.

For some time Khlit paid no heed to the women. He supposed —since neither Pir Kasim nor Nasir Beg spoke of the matter—that they were slaves.

He did not at first connect the anger displayed against the caravan in the villages with the women. For Khlit cared little for the female sex, slaves or otherwise. He was only annoyed that they were with the caravan, since he knew the cold of the higher passes in the Himalayas would cause them to complain.

Khlit did not even try to understand what was to be done with the women at Yarkand. Presuming them slaves, he thought vaguely that they would be sold and dismissed the matter from his mind.

Not so an event of the first night after they left the main caravan track. This was two days' fast ride up from Srinaggar, due east along the bank of the Sindh, at the Zodjila Pass.

Pir Kasim's change of course had brought them into waste rock ravines through which the tired beasts wound slowly. Twilight found them without food other than some oaten cakes.

Khlit had his own stock of provisions in his saddlebag—dried horseflesh and milk curds—for he disliked to eat with Mustafa, who shared the merchant's board.

They had come upon two donkeymen who had pitched their *yurt* in a hollow and were stretched beside the fire on their sheepskin cloaks. Besides the donkeys the men had several sheep of the thick-haired Kashmir species.

Pir Kasim halted the cavalcade and descended with Nasir Beg to bargain with the peasants for mutton. Khlit had dismounted to look to the leather shoes of his black pony—he had become attached to the strong horse during their Winter companionship, and the rocky going had caused the beast to limp.

So he did not see the merchants barter. He looked down, however, at sound of raised voices. Nasir Beg had flown into a rage, while the Kashmiris were protesting.

"Eh, will you not give food to women who hunger?" snarled the Arab.

"Aye, lord," remonstrated a ragged *bhikra*—beggar. "Yet that our women should have meat, and so yield milk to their babies, we must have a price for the two sheep you ask—"

"Wretch!"

Nasir Beg spurred upon the two donkeymen. Khlit saw that the Kashmiris had made no move to draw weapons, yet the Arab struck one down with his scimitar. It was a shrewd blow at the base of the throat, and the man lay dying where he had fallen.

The other turned and ran up the gorge. Pir Kasim dismounted and drew a Turkish pistol from his girdle. This he leveled across the saddle of his pony. Khlit heard the roar of the report and saw the Kashmiri stagger and fall to his knees.

Then Nasir Beg trotted up to the wounded man and returned presently, to wipe his blooded blade upon the garments of the first Kashmiri.

"Eh," he called to Khlit, "we shall eat well tonight, and the donkeys will serve us well in the hill paths where the horses are apt to fall."

Khlit turned back to his own horse in silence. He had been surprised at the uncalled-for slaying. Perhaps—although he had heard it not—the Kashmiris had given cause.

Still, why should Pir Kasim have shot down the wretched beggar who was fleeing? He could not have harmed them overnight.

Pir Kasim, however, set two men to cover the bodies with stones. "By the tracks of blood is the path of the wolf known," he grinned at Khlit. "And we must leave no trace."

The Cossack did not share the mutton.

That night they felt the full force of the wind down the gorge. As usual there was no fire. Khlit did not mind it, for he was accustomed to cold and his *khalat* was well lined.

The three caravaneers managed to sleep among the packs of stores. Pir Kasim had his *yurt* of hides, which he shared with Mustafa.

But Nasir Beg roused Khlit from a light sleep, and his dark face was blue with chilled blood, in the light of a small torch he had kindled on returning from his watch.

"Be not angered, Khlit," the Arab said, civilly for him. "My eyes are heavy with sleep, for it is the third watch, and the blood in my limbs is turned to ice. The caravan rascals are too wearied to be trusted. Will you keep watch until dawn?"

Khlit yawned and cursed forcibly.

"Are we hunted antelope, Nasir Beg, that we should stand guard in the darkness? What fear you?"

Nasir Beg was urgent, and took pains to be plausible.

"There be robber folk in the passes, Khlit. Lawless Kirghiz, and without doubt outcast Kashmiris. Pir Kasim, who is wary as a steppe fox, believes they have scented the caravan. 'Tis but three hours to dawn."

Khlit rose silently, taking his *khalat* with him and stamping warmth into his feet. He drew on his boots, tightened his belt and strode off to the point where Nasir Beg had stood.

"By Allah, Pir Kasim will thank you," the Arab called after him softly. "Beyond the rock on the farther side is a nook where you can see up and down the pass and be sheltered from this accursed wind."

Khlit grunted and wrapped his sheepskin robe over his high shoulders. He did not intend that Nasir Beg should occupy the warm nest where he had been sleeping. Beyond the line of tethered horses he halted to see where the Arab would seek refuge.

He had not long to wait. As soon as his tall frame had passed beyond the torchlight Nasir Beg threw the burning brand to the ground. By its failing light the Cossack saw Nasir Beg slip off his outer cloak and the long white robe that he wore and pass swiftly into one of the *yurts* occupied by the women.

There were six women, and they slept—or tried to—two in each shelter. The one the Arab had chosen had been pitched by Mustafa for the youngest of the women—one wearing Persian dress as Khlit had noted—and a slender Hindustani whose ankles and wrists were heavy with bracelets.

As Khlit turned away to his lookout he fancied he heard a cry from the *yurt*. He reflected grimly that the post Nasir Beg had mentioned was behind the rocks and out of sight of the camp.

Here he sat and watched the sky change in the East from crimson to saffron and gold. He saw the giant peaks overhead take shape against the dawn, first black, then silver, and finally white.

High overhead an eagle rose from a nest of pines and circled against the blue of the sky. He heard the horses stumble to their feet. Even before the sun's rays struck down the pass he heard the caravaneers grumble as they kindled the fire, and caught the pungent scent of green wood.

From the camp his glance wandered to the rock piles that marked the graves of the Kashmiris, and to the donkeys, standing passively in their tethers awaiting their morning meal of dried grass, indifferent as to who their master might be. And he scowled moodily.

He was no longer content with his surroundings. Well as he liked to be in the highlands of the Himalayas, he had begun to meditate upon the character of his companions and the nature of the caravan.

When Pir Kasim called him to the simmering pot of mutton, Khlit replied gruffly and ate where he sat of his own dried meat.

That day the march was harder than before. Pir Kasim had ordered the packs to be placed on the donkeys; this gave them extra mounts, but they made slow progress along the winding trail that threaded the surface of the cliff, over the gorge a thousand feet below.

The merchant posted Khlit in the rear of the caravan and bade him keep a keen watch over the path behind them. So it happened that the Cossack knew they were followed.

He could see black dots moving along the face of the cliff a mile in the rear. What their pursuers were he could not tell. He counted three dots and so reported to Pir Kasim, who alternately cursed and called upon Allah to hasten their progress.

It was unwise to hurry over the evil footing, where a sheer drop fell to the rocks below, beside a freshet that roared down the cleft of the gorge, sending up a steam of spray in which the sun formed the splendid arch of a rainbow. Once a led horse stumbled and vanished over the brink with a shrill neigh of terror. But Pir Kasim did not slow their gait.

Khlit was riding in the rear of the women. He saw how they shivered at sight of the unfortunate horse. The altitude was affecting them, and they sat miserably in their saddles, hunched under their robes.

Once the rearmost of the group threw back her cloak. Khlit saw her lift her veil and recognized her as the Hindustani of the bracelets. For a moment she stared back at him, her beautiful face wan, and circles under the dark eyes.

Then she jerked the rein of her horse. Khlit saw the beast stumble, rear, and plunge headlong from the path.

A wail from the women and an oath from Pir Kasim. Khlit himself stiffened in his saddle with surprise. The woman had done the thing deliberately.

"*Akh*, the cloud of madness gripped her spirit," mourned the merchant. "Yet why was it written that she should be the one to fall? Allah knows she wore the costliest bracelets.

"*Akh*—I let her keep the ornaments, for she had been the wife of the Maharaja of Guzerat. And this is the reward of my mercy. Verily, it is an evil fate!"

Complaining querulously, Pir Kasim halted the caravan and ordered one of the caravaneers to climb down a cleft in the cliff—a perilous path—and recover the gems the woman wore.

Nasir Beg protested, but the merchant did not cease to wail about his loss.

"Oh, evil hour!" he cried, twisting his beard. "Oh, verily the dust of ill fortune strews my path! A horse! One of the fairest of the women!

"And then, by the beard of the Prophet—the gems. Such gems! Gifts from the dead monarch himself. A fool of fools was I to let her keep them when she begged that they should rest on her limbs—"

"Verily," swore Nasir Beg loudly, "you are witless to linger here when riders follow along the path. If it be the Muslim—"

"Peace!" Pir Kasim glanced sharply from the Arab to Khlit. Then more calmly: "The lawless ones will not attack where the path admits of but one man."

He left Nasir Beg to watch the trail with Khlit while he peered eagerly down the cleft, marking the difficult progress of the man he had sent after the jewels.

It was long before the caravaneer returned to the ledge. Pir Kasim seized the jewels avidly and examined them, mourning when he saw a dent or break in the gold made by the fall.

"Wretch! Scorpion!" he cried. "All are not here. There was a diamond—a blue diamond set in jade that she wore about her throat. Faithless dog—"

"Nay, master," said the man stoutly. "Even as I took them from the body they are here."

The merchant counted over the bloodied trinkets and insisted that the diamond brooch was missing. But the caravaneer obstinately denied having it. Khlit, who was watching keenly, saw Nasir Beg's hand go to his throat and fumble at the opening of his cloak, then steal to his girdle. The Arab had taken something from his neck and placed it in a pouch at his waist.

And Khlit knew that the caravaneer had not found the brooch upon the body of the woman.

The dispute delayed them, and it was late afternoon before they reached a plateau where the trail widened to a ledge, upon which certain caverns faced, spacious enough to shelter the party.

So great was the cold that night that Nasir Beg was obliged to keep the fire going in spite of the scarcity of fuel, which they had been forced to bring on the donkeys.

Khlit had taken the first watch, and sat slightly down the cliff path between two rocks where he was in shadow.

He had seen no more of the three who followed in the path of the caravan. Perhaps they had turned aside. Yet, he thought, there was no other trail.

Unless they had turned back, the horsemen were still close in their rear. Khlit did not doubt that they sought the caravan. Otherwise they would hardly have taken the hazardous way around the Zodjila Pass, which Nasir Beg had contemptuously dubbed a "goat path."

Moreover, if their purpose had been friendly the three would have ridden up to the caravan when it halted. Khlit wondered briefly whether they had paused to go down the cleft to examine the body of the woman.

He wondered who the three were. Surely they were bold, for they were but three and there were six armed men—not counting Mustafa—in the caravan.

He sat up alertly at a slight sound—a light footstep. It came slowly over the rocks, from what quarter he could not decide. He half-drew his sword, then slipped it back into its scabbard with a grunt. He saw the slim figure of the Mohammedan girl—she who had been tentmate with the Hindu—standing before him in the glow from the firelight.

Her veil was back and she seemed to peer eagerly into the darkness down the trail. She looked back over her shoulder at the fire, and Khlit saw that horror was mirrored in her tense face—the face of an anxious girl, fearful and yet wistful.

She crouched as if afraid of being seen and began to move slowly past him. Khlit could hear her quick breathing.

She did not see him, as he was in deep shadow. But she seemed to be looking anxiously to mark his position. Evidently she was aware that a guard was posted near her but did not know the spot.

Then at the sound of heavy, hurried footsteps she sank to the ground. Mustafa appeared, framed against the firelight, staring out along the trail.

It was some time before he saw the girl; then he gave a shrill exclamation of pleasure.

"Evil wench! Wanton!" cried Mustafa. "So you would steal off as if on indoor slippers like a slave sneaking away to henna-nights! So you would leave me—Mustafa."

The sound of a blow accompanied the name. The girl did not cry out.

"Eh—ungrateful one! You had a thought to follow your mate. *Darisi bashine*—may her millet fall on thy head. Have a care lest her fate is yours—*Bismillah!*"

He cringed and stared as Khlit's tall form loomed over him. Then, seeing who it was, he made as if to strike the girl again. But this time under his nose was the glint of steel, and he felt a keen blade touch his throat.

"Enough, Mustafa!" growled the Cossack.

The eunuch peered at him angrily. "Will you come between me and my duty? Am I a slave to be commanded by such as you—a hired swordsman—"

"Yet a swordsman, Mustafa, and not a beater of women. Is it enough, or will you prove my words?"

At this the eunuch retreated backward and sought the fire. Yasmi did not follow. She took Khlit's hand in both hers.

"*Aie, baba-ji*—father-lord! I have a fear. It is a great fear. Nasir Beg has looked upon me with an evil light in his eyes.

"Last night he came to our tent, and this day Rani Kayastha is dead. Now his glance follows me.

"*Aie*—he took a jewel from Rani Kayastha, who was the wife of a king. But I have no jewels—"

Silently Khlit returned to his nook and sat upon his stone. Yasmi crept after and curled at his feet, much like a dog who fears to be spurned. Khlit rather expected that Mustafa would return with Pir Kasim to claim the girl. But though he glimpsed a shadow moving near him and suspected that someone kept watch upon them, he was not molested.

"Yasmi," he said slowly, "what manner of women are the wives of nobles, yet the property of such as Pir Kasim?"

"*Baba-ji*," she responded softly, "they are the dead."

For an instant Khlit was disturbed, thinking of the wan face and the dark eyes that had looked into his for an instant before Rani Kayastha died. Then he laughed. "Nay, you know not what you say, little sparrow. For you are one of them, and you are—living."

But Yasmi did not laugh.

"It is true," she whispered, "that my lot is not quite so evil as theirs. For I am not of their faith and I have not—as they have—broken the law that they must not break.

"But they are truly the dead; and I am like to them. We cannot look into the face of the people of Hindustan; where we go we are stoned. The village dogs are higher caste than we. The souls of those—" she pointed back to the camp—"are shriveled. They cannot live. They are the dead."

Khlit recollected the stones that had been cast at them when passing through the Kashmiri village, and the strange conduct of the two riders, and grunted.

"Yasmi," he observed presently, "I have a thought that you know those who follow. You are a Muslim, and Nasir Beg named them Muslims. Likewise you crept down the path tonight seeking someone. Is not this the truth?"

The girl would not answer. And after a time Khlit saw that she was shivering with cold. Whereupon he threw his *khalat* over her as she sat by his feet.

Yasmi slept, but Khlit did not close his eyes. The girl's words had stirred his curiosity, and after his fashion he pondered them.

The next day, and the next, Yasmi kept close to Khlit. His rough touch of kindness—giving her his *khalat*—had been the first she had received for many months and Yasmi was grateful. She kept her pony at the side of the black horse where the narrow track permitted, and at other times in front of Khlit.

On the second day at the noon halt Mustafa approached the two and with him Pir Kasim. Khlit, according to his custom, was preparing his own food, which Yasmi chose to share. Poor as the Cossack's fare was, the caravan fare was worse, now that the mutton was about gone.

Khlit did not look up when the shadows of the two men fell across his feet. He felt the girl draw closer to him.

"Ho, Khlit," began the merchant in a friendly tone, "we make good progress, and by the will of Allah tomorrow will see us through the Darband Pass, and out on the open ground leading to Yarkand. It is well, therefore, that the women be kept together lest one escape."

Khlit continued to toast the strips of meat in the flames without response.

"Mustafa waxes anxious for the girl Yasmi," continued Pir Kasim. "He fears she may fall from the trail."

"Nay," protested the girl, "my pony does not stumble."

Pir Kasim scowled at her.

"Nevertheless, you shall stay under the eye of Mustafa."

"I will not!"

The merchant, angered, caught her arm. She struggled, striking at his face, until Mustafa came to his aid. Then she ceased her efforts, glancing imploringly at Khlit.

The Cossack regarded a portion of meat with a favorable eye and proceeded to eat. Seeing this, Mustafa ventured a furtive blow upon the girl's back.

The eunuch had been reared to safeguard women for his master. It was his one duty, and after his kind he was faithful to it. But he also had the cruelty that was part of his office.

"Pir Kasim," observed Khlit thoughtfully, "would you lay hand on the blue diamond that Rani Kayastha wore?"

The merchant stiffened as a hunting dog at scent of game. His black eyes snapped, and he stepped closer to the sitting man, fairly quivering with eagerness.

"The blue diamond? Aye, the one that was set in rare jade. 'Tis said the maharaja paid for it the price of twenty fine horses." He stared at Khlit uncertainly, yet covetously. "Then it was not lost with the woman—may her soul never see paradise? Aye, it was a fine stone. You have seen it, Khlit?"

The Cossack chewed slowly on his meat, wiping his beard with his sleeve.

"Perchance you hold it, Khlit?" Pir Kasim affected a friendly laugh. "Nay, 'tis well. You thought to keep the stone safe for me. By the beard of the Prophet, I bear no ill will. Eh—but it would be safer in my hands."

Khlit nodded. Pir Kasim stretched out a claw that trembled with eagerness. He had completely forgotten the girl.

"Ask Nasir Beg for it," said Khlit.

Pir Kasim blinked. Then with an angry cry he hurried off to seek the Arab. Khlit looked up at Mustafa under shaggy brows, and the eunuch made as if to haul Yasmi away.

"Mustafa!" said Khlit. "Look behind you."

The eunuch glanced over his shoulder hastily.

"What see you?" asked Khlit, reaching for more meat.

"Naught. Save the precipice."

"Nay. Your eyes are dull. I have seen two things in the gorge below."

Mustafa glanced at the Cossack dubiously. Then, still holding Yasmi, he stepped nearer the edge to peer down. The invisible pursuers who had been barely noticed during the last two days had got upon the nerves of the men of the caravan.

"Nay, there is naught," he snarled. "I see only rocks."

"And the kites," amended Khlit. "The rocks and kites—there are the two things of which I thought. It is dark down in the *yar*; perhaps the bones of dead horses lie among the rocks, and the place is a feasting-place for the kites."

Mustafa drew back from the cliffside with some alacrity.

"Look, Mustafa, upon your hand!"

The eunuch did so uncertainly. He had a plump hand, generously adorned with rings. After considering this member of his person, he glared at Khlit.

"Your tongue jests," he cried shrilly.

"Nay, Mustafa, when did you know me to jest?" Whereupon Khlit took his sword from scabbard and laid it across his knees, stroking the blade meditatively against one leather boot.

"Harken, O Purified One," continued Khlit, addressing the eunuch by his actual name. "Consider those three things—and a fourth. Consider the rocks a bow-shot beneath, the kites and the tenderness of your skin. Mark it well."

Mustafa still glared but was silent. Yasmi laughed softly.

"And then the fourth thing, Mustafa. You said that I jest. It is a lie."

The eunuch loosed his hold upon Yasmi abruptly. Whereupon she slipped to Khlit's side, her dark eyes dancing at the discomfiture of her guardian. Mustafa would have left them to go after Pir Kasim, but a glance from Khlit staved him.

"*Kukuria*—little dog," the Cossack growled, "you would like to run whining to your master—"

"Pir Kasim will see that you suffer—"

"Nay, Mustafa. Consider yet another thing. Tomorrow Pir Kasim plans to attack those who follow us. I am—as you once said—a swordsman, and valuable to him. You are a servant."

The eunuch bit his thumb and scowled.

"Then, Mustafa, meditate upon these four—these five—things. But chiefly upon the rocks and the kites and your—hide, Mustafa."

Khlit rose, towering over the stout Ethiopian.

"A fitting place to meditate, O Purified One, is the precipice edge. Seek it!"

Not until Mustafa was enthroned upon the brink of the cliff, his legs hanging over the edge—to the wonder of the caravaneers—did Khlit leave him and return to his interrupted repast.

Yasmi's merriment at the plight of her master vanished swiftly, and she gazed moodily into the flames, chin upon her hand. Khlit also was silent.

He had felt when he first saw the women in the caravan that they would breed trouble. Now it was coming to pass even as he had foreseen. But the hardships inflicted on Yasmi stirred his anger.

Khlit glanced around. The others were resting on their robes, wearied by the hard marches and the poor food. Pir Kasim and Nasir Beg were not to be seen, although their angry voices echoed somewhere behind the rocks where the Arab was on watch. Mustafa, although eyeing them, was beyond hearing.

"My heart is heavy, *baba-ji*," mused Yasmi. "I have a foreboding. Last night the jackals howled in the gorge, and the kites screamed at dawn, and the sky was red as blood.

"Smoke came from the arrow Nasir Beg shot fruitlessly at a mountain goat. I dreamed that headless men walked toward us from the hill passes."

She sighed, twisting her fingers in the mass of her black hair. And she glanced involuntarily back along the cliff—a look which Khlit did not fail to notice. He put his gnarled hand on her slim one.

"Yasmi," he growled, "you are a sparrow; nay, a singing bird. Aye, the talons of the hawks are near to you. Speak, then, before it is too late.

"There is one thing I would know. Who are they that follow us?"

The girl searched Khlit's lined face with a woman's intentness. What she saw must have satisfied her, for she told him what had passed at the tavern in Srinaggar.

Khlit listened closely.

"Say you this Afghan warrior paid Nasir Beg the price he asked?"

"Nasir Beg made an excuse and did not take the gold."

"What did the Afghan?"

"The mask of anger fell upon his face, *baba-ji*, but then Nasir Beg thrust the lamp to the floor, and Mustafa, reaching from behind the curtains, seized me. I kicked and bit his arm.

"Yet he stifled me with a cloth, and bore me down into the cellar. Whereupon Nasir Beg kicked the women and bade them prepare to leave the cellar. He rowed us away in the boat. I looked back and saw the Afghan running from the door, and his sword was drawn."

She sighed, looking up at Khlit. "I think it is he who follows. He was very angry, and—he liked my song. He was a tall man—as tall as you—and his armor was very costly."

"Aye. He was a Muslim?"

"Even so, my lord. Methinks he was faithful to the law of Mohammed, as was father."

"These women—" Khlit nodded toward the group—"what is their faith?"

"They are unbelievers, who bow down before Vishnu and Shiva. Yet they are not godless. Their sorrow is great. The heat of the flames affrighted them, *baba-ji*, and they drew back from death—and so fell into the hand of the *hallal khors*."

"They do not wish to be sold at Yarkand?"

"Nay, my lord. They are of high caste, and their grief is like a cloud over the sun. But how could they escape Pir Kasim? Even like to theirs will my fate be."

Khlit did not answer. Presently, seeing the bustle of the caravan men, he arose and went to the eunuch, telling him that he had meditated sufficiently for the nonce.

Mustafa made off promptly, muttering.

Khlit smiled grimly when Pir Kasim directed the order of march and placed him with Yasmi in the center of the line, giving the rear to Nasir Beg. He noticed also that the servants kept watch on him.

Pir Kasim, however, made a great show of cordiality toward the Cossack. He rode at the warrior's side, explaining that he had recovered the gem from Nasir Beg—at a price.

"Tomorrow, Khlit," he vouchsafed, "will the path widen into the plateau of the Darband. 'Tis a wide, level expanse of stone, open to the eye. At the farther end, however, a swift stream rushes. Beyond the stream are many great rocks of sandstone."

He smiled, combing his beard.

"In those rocks we will lie in wait—you and I and Nasir Beg with the caravaneers. Only at one point—where the trail crosses—can the stream be forded. When the three unbelievers appear, we will see, and when they urge their horses into the current we will let fly arrows and pistol balls, aimed at the horses.

"Then—may Allah will it so—we shall ride forth and smite down those who live. Thus we shall be free of the robbers. It is a good plan."

The project was well-conceived, as Khlit saw. But his voice was gruff as he answered the merchant, "Have you seen those who follow us—near at hand?"

"Nay. You know they have kept shrewdly beyond view."

"How know you then they are—robbers?"

Pir Kasim stared, then laughed. "What else should they be, Cossack? Were they honest folk they would not lurk behind the rocks."

Khlit did not laugh. He pointed to the women who followed them, hunched miserably in their saddles.

"What manner of women be these?"

"Slaves."

"Then, Pir Kasim, have you paid the full value of their slavery?"

The merchant was too surprised to respond quickly. He had not thought that Khlit was interested in the caravan. Before he could answer Khlit turned on him, his teeth gleaming through his gray mustache and his eyes hard.

"Can you say, Pir Kasim, that you are less a thief than those who follow—"

He scowled moodily and struck his fist on the saddlepeak so that the black pony jumped. "Yasmi has a foreboding, Pir Kasim. Nay, I know naught of omens. But take care lest the evil fortune she has foretold comes to pass."

With that he spurred on to the head of the caravan, leaving the merchant sunk in thought. Pir Kasim dropped back until he was abreast of Nasir Beg.

"The wretched Yasmi has been using her tongue upon Khlit," he whispered. "The Cossack waxes insolent, Nasir Beg."

"What think you? If he rides to Yarkand he may breed evil for us. Yet we need him to deal with the Muslims."

"When the hour comes I shall strike the Cossack. Then the name of Khlit will be no more than the writing on sand when the wind has passed over."

Pir Kasim nodded shrewdly.

"Bethink you, Nasir Beg. There will be much confusion when we ride upon the Muslims. Perhaps it is written that Khlit should die by the hand of the unbelievers.

"If not—" he measured his words slowly "it may even then come to pass. A blow in the back—Khlit wears no armor—or an arrow at the base of the brain. The Cossack is a foolhardy dog—he will be in the front of the fight, eh, Nasir Beg?"

The Arab's eyes gleamed.

"*Bismillah*! I have a mind to his black horse and the curved sword. Yet—I have heard tales of Khlit. A price should be paid for such a deed—a good price. The blue diamond of the rani."

Pir Kasim squealed angrily.

"Nay, by the beard of the Prophet!"

He considered a moment, glancing sidewise at his companion.

"Yet I am generous, Nasir Beg. Methinks there is a thing other than jewels you have a mind to. If Khlit dies at the Darband you shall have—Yasmi."

"So be it," agreed the Arab.

There was a good reason why Pir Kasim had not seen Abdul Dost near at hand for some time. The Afghan was not there to be seen.

From the night at the Srinaggar tavern Abdul Dost had pressed the pursuit closely. He had soon ascertained that Pir Kasim had taken the Sindh caravan route. He had traced the merchant through the village where the caravan had been stoned, and was close upon them when Pir Kasim turned aside by the Zodjila Pass.

This move had checked the Afghans. They soon discovered that Pir Kasim had not continued along the Sindh, but it was the better part of a day before Abdul Dost, chafing under the delay, learned from a shepherd that the caravan had been seen ascending the Zodjila.

When they came into view of those they sought, the caravan was threading the path along the cliff. Abdul Dost, despite his impatience, was too experienced a soldier to venture to attack in such a location. He ordered his men to fall back and keep Pir Kasim in view.

Until the day when Khlit had sat Mustafa on the cliff ledge. Then Abdul Dost went back a space along the trail to a ravine which led to the gorge below and to the broken body of a woman. Down the ravine they had led their horses, and throughout that night they rode quietly along the valley bed until they had passed the caravan, which was encamped on the mountainside above.

At dawn Abdul Dost halted only long enough to water his horses. Then, munching their graincakes and dates as they rode, they struck through the pine forest that would lead—as one of the soldiers informed him—to the trail Pir Kasim was taking, ahead of the Darband Pass.

"Then will we ride back," explained Abdul Dost grimly, "and come upon them at the ford in the Darband."

But to do this he was forced to cross the stream below the pass, and at that season it was swollen with the melted snows from the heights above. The two men halted, staring at the rush of water and marking the rocks underneath.

"Those who pass here say it cannot be crossed, save at the Darband ford," they told the *mansabdar*.

Abdul Dost glanced up at the sun which was slanting through the pines and smiled.

"Then," he laughed, "it will be told how the Darband stream has been crossed."

He did not laugh as he forced his horse into the stream and saw how the beast drifted down with the current. The two men hesitated, then plunged in after him. The bad footing and the strength of the current soon forced the horses to swim.

Three men and two horses crossed the stream. The third beast floundered in the current with a broken leg until its rider drew his knife and ended its pain; then this man swam ashore, holding to the tail of another horse. Abdul Dost waited, for the two remaining mounts were badly winded.

Before noon he was again in his saddle. The dismounted warrior girded his tunic about his loins and ran, clinging to the stirrup of his comrade. For Abdul Dost had said they must hasten if they would reach the Darband in time.

"Eh, my children," smiled Abdul Dost, "I have sworn an oath. Shall I not keep my word?"

"We are your men, Lord of Badakshan," spoke up one, "and our swords are yours that your word may be kept. We will pray that our strength be increased."

So they spurred forward. But the sun was high when they neared the caravan track beyond the Darband Pass.

V

*Only for the space of a moment can a warrior say, "I am the slayer
and he the slain."*

*He hears the joy cries of the women at his wedding feast, and
his dull ears harken to the lamentations at his deathbed. Always
the voices of the women cry out. Nay, are they not the handmaidens of Life and Death!*

Kashmiri proverb

The sun filled the Darband Pass with a red light—red because it
was reflected from an expanse of sandstone that made the bed of
the pass level as the court of a palace.

High in the Himalayas was the Darband Pass, walled by slopes
of brown sand that were in turn surmounted by crumbling brown
cliffs, beyond which glittered the blue expanse of the glaciers that
filled the ravines descending from the rock peaks.

No grass grew in the Darband Pass; nor did pine trees fringe
the sand slopes. The only life was that of the kites and rooks
who circled overhead, following the course of the caravan. In and
about the Darband was the great silence of the heights, broken
only at the farther end where the stream rushed down through
the rocks.

The ford at this point was shallow; the opposite side, strewn
with sandstone ledges and gullies, was steep. Pir Kasim marked
this with a satisfied eye. He urged the women and the laden beasts
hastily over the stream.

Mustafa, sensing the need of haste so that they should be in
their hiding places before the pursuers appeared, cried angrily at
the women, striking one with his hand when her horse delayed
in the stream to snatch a mouthful of water.

"Get you hence, wanton," he commanded, and did not see the
glint of hatred intensified by terror in the Hindu's eyes.

Yasmi he did not strike, contenting himself with a mocking
whisper.

"Tale-bearer and infidel, soon you will have a new lord and
then you will feel the hand of Mustafa."

She passed by in silence—unusual for her—and glanced back at Khlit. Her eyes met the glance of the Cossack and he nodded as if approvingly. Whereupon she urged her horse up the steep slope.

Here were the sandstone gullies, a honeycomb of fissures and grotesque summits of the weather-worn stone. Yasmi fancied that each ledge bore upon it the semblance of a face—some leering evilly, some grinning. Some resembled animals.

It was as if the gigantic creatures of a long dead race had here been frozen into immobility. They stood watching the passing of the beasts and men of the caravans—so Yasmi fancied.

But Pir Kasim was well content. In the sandstone gullies were hiding places aplenty. The merchant disposed of the caravan swiftly and with much shrewdness.

On the top of the rise he placed the horses and donkeys in a ravine, the steep sides of which afforded exit at only one point. He commanded the women to remain here and at the entrance to the gully posted a caravaneer armed with a bow as guard.

Pir Kasim cared to take no chances with Khlit, so he had selected the place with care—a depression into which the sun shone fully, where the guard could watch both women and horses without moving.

"Because, Nasir Beg," he whispered to the Arab, "it is said the Cossack is like an evil magician with the black horse between his legs. Aye, like to a conjurer who can summon the powers of darkness, and the horse his *djinnee*. But here he will be afoot among the rocks."

Not less craftily did the merchant arrange his men. He chose the rocks just where the trail rose to the summit of the slope by the riverbank. Here they were a scant fifty paces from the horses—which were of course out of sight—and even less from the edge of the stream. They could see down the length of the Darband and watch their enemies as the latter rode up to the ford—as Pir Kasim believed they must do.

"Then, Khlit," he smiled, rubbing his hands together, "a volley of arrows—a shot from Nasir Beg's Turkish pistol—and all is done. Save the slaying of the wounded. It is a good plan."

"Aye," admitted Khlit.

"And you—" Pir Kasim's keen eyes were fastened on the Cossack's girdle—"where are your pistols? Eh—there were two fine weapons that you are wont to wear—"

"I have them not today," explained Khlit indifferently. "The sword, the curved sword, is the better weapon."

"Good!"

Pir Kasim had reason to be satisfied. Without his pistols Khlit would be an easy victim, he reasoned. The Cossack wore no armor, not even a quilted surcoat. Even if he should suspect treachery and try to defend himself he would be one against six—and Nasir Beg and the caravaneers had shirts of Damascus mail.

Pir Kasim was shrewd enough to perceive that Khlit was distrustful of him. The Cossack's words of the day before had served to put the merchant on his guard. He counted on the fact that Khlit would be stirred by the attack on their pursuers and would be taken unawares.

"If not," he confided to Nasir Beg, "he will be afoot, and crafty though he be at swordplay, my two men have orders to strike him down with their arrows. What avails a sword against arrows? Nay, he was a fool to put aside the Turkish pistols!"

"Even thus," suggested Nasir Beg, "it would be well to find those two weapons and take them in your hand."

Pir Kasim scurried off to ransack the saddlebags of Khlit's horse, leaving the Cossack surrounded by his men. His hasty search was unsuccessful, yet it gave him opportunity to see that all was well by the horses.

The women sat muffled in their robes at the feet of the guard—Yasmi among them, as Pir Kasim was careful to note. The horses were tethered securely. The caravaneer stood at the break in the sandstone ridge, which was the only entrance to the gully.

Fearful lest his enemies appear while he was absent, Pir Kasim ran back to the ambush over the riverbank. Khlit had not moved.

The Cossack sat idly on a rock where he was concealed from view from the ford, Nasir Beg within arm's reach on one side, the Arab's hand near the pistol in his belt. Mustafa leaned nearby, holding a sharp knife.

Within five paces of the three the caravaneers kept watch over the ford, their bows strung and their quivers ready to hand. Pir Kasim, like the eunuch, was armed with a knife. The merchant chuckled silently.

"*Akh*," he muttered in his beard, "the dolt! The tall fool of the steppe! The fox that is blind! The wolf that has seen many fights, who is heedless of peril thereby! Akh, another hour, and the three who follow will lie dead in the ford and Khlit will be overmastered. Then—I shall repeat the *namaz gar*—the evening prayer. For Allah favors me this day."

He surveyed the scene again before joining Nasir Beg. So well had he planned that a thrill of self-satisfaction chased up his bent spine. After all, Pir Kasim was an artist in his way—a master of treachery.

"Another hour, my lord," he smiled at Khlit, "and the way to Yarkand will be clear. Their rich gold will be ours from the women."

"Aye," said Khlit.

Pir Kasim nodded, thinking that Yasmi had foretold truly when she said that she had beheld evil omens. He watched Khlit contentedly.

The Cossack was stroking his bare blade back and forth over his boot top, and polishing the shining steel with his neckcloth. He was fingering the chasing in the blade with evident pride, his long legs sprawled before him, his sheepskin hat well to the back of his gray head.

And at this hour the sun was near its highest point.

Then Yasmi began her song.

It came clearly down to the waiting men. It echoed melodiously among the rocks of the Darband. And it was echoed back from the farther side of the ford—each word distinct:

Oh, where is the falcon's nest. . . .
Save in the wind . . .

The song swelled forth with the full power of the girl's throat. And it seemed to mock the men, as if Yasmi sang with the lilt of laughter. At the same time there was a murmur as if the women were stirring.

"*Bismillah!*" swore Pir Kasim. "Has the caravaneer taken leave of his wits that he lets Yasmi sing? Mustafa, go you and choke the song in the vixen's throat! Fail not, for there must be silence at the ford."

The eunuch needed no second bidding. Clutching his dagger, he stole off up to the gully where the women were.

Pir Kasim scowled at Khlit, wondering if the Cossack had had a hand in the girl's singing. Yasmi, he reflected suspiciously, might have intended to warn their pursuers of the ambush.

But Khlit sat passively gazing at his feet and stroking his weapon. Perhaps a trace of a smile twitched at his gray mustache.

Presently Yasmi's voice faltered in the midst of a word. Silence followed, broken by a faint murmur of voices in their rear. Pir Kasim peered across the ford and noted with satisfaction that the three riders were not yet in view.

"Mustafa has stilled the songbird," he whispered to Nasir Beg, "and doubtless bound and gagged her as she deserved—"

He broke off in sheer surprise. Yasmi had resumed her song at the point where she had ceased. Even louder than before, the girl's voice floated down from the rocks above them.

"By the ninety-nine holy names of Allah!" swore the Arab. "Will you let the wanton betray our abiding place?"

Khlit alone of the men at the ford seemed not surprised at the song of Yasmi. He pulled his sheepskin hat over one ear and glanced up solemnly at the sun.

Pir Kasim fidgeted in an agony of impatience. Their enemies, he knew, might even then be within hearing.

Yasmi must be silenced. He looked once more across the ford, and at Khlit basking his tall frame in the sun; then he stole off to the rear toward the women.

Nasir Beg looked after him, scowling. What had become of Mustafa and the guard, that they let Yasmi sing? He did not understand.

There was something uncanny in the note of the song. And Yasmi—"The Muslim girl is an evil enchantress," he growled to Khlit. "*Bismillah*! She has laid a spell with her song on the caravaneer and Mustafa."

Khlit responded quietly, leaning closer to the Arab.

"Aye, a spell, Nasir Beg. A spell of steel and powder. Yasmi has one of my brace of Turkish pistols. The mate to the weapon is in the hand of a Hindu woman—the same Mustafa struck in the ford."

"Ha!"

Nasir Beg looked up keenly and rose to his feet.

"A potent spell, Nasir Beg. Doubtless it has rendered the caravaneer and the dog of a eunuch powerless, each in turn, while the women bound them. And—doubtless—Pir Kasim has come under the spell. Did not Yasmi sing that he might hear?"

The two caravaneers gaped. Nasir Beg fingered his weapon. Khlit had neither moved nor looked at him.

"Pistols have their use, Nasir Beg," he mused calmly. "Aye, Yasmi uses them boldly. But for my hand, Nasir Beg—the curved sword."

He drew the cloth along the shining blade carefully. The three men watched him as if fascinated.

"The sword, Nasir Beg," said Khlit, "that you covet—with the black pony—after you had slain the Cossack who is called the Curved Saber. Aye, so Yasmi told me, and her ears are keen to hear—"

Nasir Beg caught at the pistol in his belt. Then, just in time, he snatched out his sword instead.

Khlit had struck without rising from his seat. Leaning toward the Arab, his long arm flew out. Though Nasir Beg partly parried the blow a crimson cut showed above the man's brow where Khlit's sword had touched—no more than touched—the skin.

And even as the wound in the Arab's forehead was the weakness that seized upon his heart. A crafty and experienced swordsman, Nasir Beg fought best when the odds were in his favor. Now, in the eyes that burned into his from under gray brows, he read—death.

So he gave back swiftly, parrying desperately. And as he gave back Khlit was upon him, the curved saber slashing at his throat above the armor.

"So, Nasir Beg," Khlit growled softly, "you coveted the sword? Nay, have it then. So the girl Yasmi was to be your slave? Nay, the steel is your reward, for treachery, Nasir Beg."

And Khlit's weapon flashed before his eyes. Nasir Beg cursed, giving ground again. Then, feeling the blood stream down into his eyes, the fear that had clutched at his heart overmastered him.

"Let fly, dolts!" he screamed to the staring caravaneers. "An arrow in his back—"

The cry ended in a grunt which changed to a gasp that shrilled and broke midway. Khlit had smitten down the Arab's guard and poised his sword for the death stroke. An arrow whizzed and tore through the Cossack's boot below the knee.

Khlit shifted his weight silently to the other foot, placing himself so that the Arab was between him and the archers, feinted at Nasir Beg's head and struck him savagely across the knees. The Arab staggered, cursing. The next instant he threw his arms wide, his skull split between the eyes nearly to the chin.

Khlit wheeled alertly, hearing stealthy steps behind him. A caravaneer had crept within arm's reach, dagger uplifted.

The Cossack, who was fighting with the cool intentness that was peculiar to him, had expected such a move, and the man fell back. His neck had been half-severed by a short stroke of the curved saber. Khlit reached behind him and pulled the sinking body of Nasir Beg between him and the second caravaneer. And the arrow the man aimed embedded itself in the form of the Arab.

Holding Nasir Beg in one arm—his sword arm—Khlit felt for and found the pistol in the Arab's girdle. Before the archer could fit another arrow to bow, the pistol bellowed in his face, sending its heavy ball through his brain.

Khlit cast down the smoking weapon, watching the man reel to the earth. A shrill cry from Yasmi came to his ears. He caught the arrow that had pierced his lower leg, broke it and limped upward through the rocks.

He heard a shout, the beat of hoofs. A horse plunged forward into view, sweating and sobbing with weariness—plunged and fell. A mailed form sprang clear, casting aside a flying cloak that glittered with jewels.

The newcomer alighted on his feet, gained his balance deftly and sprang at Khlit with uplifted scimitar.

Khlit caught a fleeting glimpse of a small, jeweled turban, a silvery coat of mail, and a dark, scarred face, dust-stained and alight with the joy of battle. He saw white teeth bared in a smile, and black eyes that bored into his.

"*Hai—hai*—look to yourself, graybeard! Stealer of women and seller of the death anointed! Ho—graybeard—Pir Kasim! The thread of your life is thin. Look upon the angel of death, Pir Kasim—"

The whirlwind attack of the warrior left Khlit no time to consider or to speak. The next instant he was fighting for his life, his saber crossing a blade that had an arm of steel behind it.

Many times and often had Khlit fought with the swordsmen of Tartary and Hindustan, but now he was faced by a master of the scimitar and one who fought as recklessly as Khlit himself.

The two retainers who had scrambled down over the rocks, panting, looked upon the combat and paused, observing the play of the blades with eagerness, and staring one upon the other in wonder.

1

36LAW OF FIRE

"*Hai—hai—*" Khlit's hat had been struck from his head and his fur *khalat* slashed by a glancing blow—"I have trimmed your scalp, graybeard; look to your beard."

A blow of the scimitar nearly found Khlit's throat.

"Does Abdul Dost keep his pledge!"

For several moments the two swords held in never-ceasing play.

And ever Khlit grew weaker, his knees trembling with fatigue. No chance was afforded him for a trick of the sword, nor any respite.

The lean muscles of the Cossack's long arm were quivering, and his vision blurred. Still the scimitar flashed almost in his eyes.

He did not give ground. Nor did he speak. He smiled upon Abdul Dost.

Then the two watchers saw a strange thing. They saw Khlit exhausted and at the point of death. They noted that Abdul Dost was panting, fighting with savage intentness. And they saw the man whose strength had ebbed gather himself together, limping, his weight upon one leg.

And Khlit sprang at Abdul Dost with the curved saber gripped in both hands, hacking and hewing, beating down the other's weapon, slashing at his mail so that the sparks flew from the steel. Then Abdul Dost sprang back.

The two watchers saw Khlit sink upon his knees and the saber fall from his hand and his head fall upon his chest. The last effort of the Cossack had exhausted the remnant of his strength and had blinded him.

Abdul Dost surveyed his foe, panting and half-stunned by the unexpected attack.

Then a small figure rushed upon the Muslim, and Yasmi cast her arms around him.

"*Ai*, lord—stay your hand!" she cried. "This is not Pir Kasim. The dog of a merchant has fled afoot up the mountain. Nay, this is he who took my quarrel upon him, my *baba-ji*—father-lord."

Abdul Dost was quick of wit. He sheathed his weapon. Then he stared around, marking the bodies of Nasir Beg and the caravaneers. He wiped the sweat from his brow and seated himself wearily upon a stone.

One of his men approached.

"The eunuch will watch no more women, Lord of Badakshan," he informed Abdul Dost grimly. "He was in the hands of the women and—the hatred of the high-born is not akin to mercy."

Abdul Dost stirred the form of the Arab with his foot and glanced up at Yasmi, who was watching him fearfully.

"Rightly have they named this the caravan of the dead, little Yasmi. My eyes tell me the truth of this and what I have seen I have seen."

Abdul dost rose, not oversteadily, and stared at Khlit, who still rested on his knees, drawing gulping breaths.

"Did the hand of this warrior slay these three?" he asked.

Yasmi looked around with a shiver.

"Aye, my lord."

"What name bears he?"

"He is Khlit, who has come from very far. It is said he was once Kha Khan of the Jungar, and leader of the Tatar horde. He it was who brought Nur-Jahan, wife of the Mogul, from China. He is my *baba-ji*."

Abdul Dost leaned over Khlit and lifted him to his feet. He noted the arrow in the Cossack's leg and swore under his breath.

Then he helped Khlit to a seat on the stone where he had been resting. Yasmi noticed the Cossack's sword lying on the earth and would have picked it up, but a sharp command from the Muslim stayed her.

Motioning the girl aside, Abdul Dost picked up Khlit's weapon, wiped it clean, weighed it curiously in his hand and laid it across the other's knees. Khlit glanced up at this, for the stupor of weariness had passed from his sight.

"Hey—it was a good fight, warrior," the Cossack said.

His head sank once more between his shoulders. He lifted a lean hand and gazed wonderingly upon its trembling.

"I have met many swordsmen in Hindustan and in Badakshan," responded Abdul Dost gruffly, "but none equal to you. Aye, it was rare swordplay. Yet was the fault mine, for I—in armor—set upon you unknowing—"

Khlit shook his head indifferently. The lines of his harsh face had deepened within the hour. Then he sought to take his sword but could not, for his strength was gone.

His head sank again, near to his knee. He lifted it with an effort.

"I shall not wield sword again, warrior," he said, breathing heavily. "The strength that was once mine is gone. My arm is weak. Something that was here—is sped."

He touched his chest.

"You—overmastered me. It is my last fight."

Abdul Dost would have spoken but checked himself. He turned aside, musing.

"The blame is mine," he said to Yasmi. "I would that I had known."

He ascended the rocks, for there was much to be done. In an hour he had arranged for Yasmi and the other women to be conducted back to the territory of her father, the Sheikh of Kuhistan, by way of the northern passes, and had mounted them under escort of his two followers, for food was lacking in the caravan and their departure was pressing.

"None will molest my men, who will go by the route through Badakshan," he told Yasmi. "And in the camp of your people these women may have peace."

"Aye, my lord," assented Yasmi.

When she would have knelt and poured forth her thanks, the *mansabdar* stayed her gruffly.

"Go—and sing among your hills, little Yasmi," he bade her. "Here is but an evil spot for such as you. In Kuhistan young warriors will give you their love, doubtless."

Khlit raised his head as the caravan moved off. He saw that his horse was not among those that went. Then he fell again into meditation, for he was very weary and his wound pained him.

He wondered why Abdul Dost had not gone with the caravan. Then he saw the *mansabdar* approach with his cloak again on his shoulders.

Khlit lifted his hand. He was not troubled at being left alone, but he was very tired and he wondered—without being concerned—whether Abdul Dost had thought to leave him food.

"Farewell, warrior," he said gruffly. "Ho—it was indeed a good fight."

Abdul Dost did not reply. He was carrying an armful of wood. This he laid on the ground and presently kindled into flames by use of his flint and tinder. Then he approached the Cossack and drew off his boot.

He cleansed and washed Khlit's wound with water from the ford after drawing the arrowhead, which Khlit suffered him to do silently. This accomplished, he bound the leg with some strips of cloth tightly.

By now the fire was blazing. Abdul Dost returned and presently came back carrying many things.

He laid Khlit's sheepskin robe on the ground near the fire, and his own beside it. He drew some meat from his saddlebags and began to toast it on a stick in the flames.

By now it was twilight, and the Darband was in deep shadow. Abdul Dost helped Khlit to lie on his sheepskin.

"Eh, Khlit," he said, "the horses are fed, and it is now our turn."

Not until then did the Cossack understand that Abdul Dost would not leave him. He looked at the Muslim in surprise. Never before had another tended him in this manner, or given him such comfort.

Neither man spoke. But Khlit was strangely content.

He had found a friend, and he who had been named the wanderer was no longer alone.

The Bride of Jagannath

Down past the stone shrine of Kedarnath, down and over the tall grass of the Dehra-Dun, marched the host of the older gods. The Pandas marched with feet that touched not the tall grass. Past the deva-prayag—*the meeting-place of the waters—came the older gods bearing weapons in their hands.*

In the deva-prayag *they washed themselves clean. The gods were very angry. The wind came and went at their bidding.*

Thus they came. And the snow-summits of Himal, the grass of the valley, and the meeting-place of the waters—all were as one to the gods.

The Vedas

The heavy morning dew lay on the grass of the land of the Five Rivers, the Punjab. The hot, dry monsoon was blowing up from the southern plain and cooling itself among the foothills of the Siwalik in the year of our Lord 1609 when two riders turned their horses from a hill path into the main highway of the district of Kukushetra.

It was a fair day, and the thicket through which the trail ran was alive with the flutter of pigeons and heavy with the scent of wild thyme and jasmine and the mild odor of the fern trees. The sun beat on them warmly, for the Spring season was barely past and they were riding south in the eastern Punjab, by the edge of Rajasthan, toward the headwaters of the Ganges, in the empire of Jahangir, Ruler of the World and Mogul of India.

"A fair land," said one. "A land ripe with sun, with sweet fruits and much grain. Our horses will feed well. Here you may rest from your wounds—"

He pointed with a slender, muscular hand to where a gilt dome reared itself over the cypress tops on a distant hill summit.

"Eh, my Brother of Battles," he said, "yonder shines the dome of Kukushetra. Aye, the temple of Kukushetra wherein dwells an image of Jagannath—"

"*Jagannath!*"

It was a shrill cry that came from the roadside. A small figure leaped from the bushes at the word and seized the bridles of both horses. They reared back and he who had pointed to the temple muttered a round oath.

"Jagannath!" cried the newcomer solemnly.

He was a very slender man, half-naked, with a gray cloth twisted about his loins. The string hanging down his left chest indicated—as well as the caste-mark on his forehead—that he was a Brahman, of the lesser temple order.

"The holy name!" he chanted. "Lord of the World! Brother to Balabhadra and to Subhadra! Incarnation of the mighty Vishnu, and master of the *Kali-damana*! Even as ye have named Jagannath, so must ye come to the reception hall of the god—"

"What is this madness?" asked the elder of the two riders gruffly. The Brahman glanced at him piercingly and resumed his arrogant harangue.

"The festival of Jagannath is near at hand, warrior," he warned. "This is the land of the mighty god. Come, then, to the temple and bring your gift to lay at the shrine of Jagannath of Kukushetra, which is only less holy than the shrine of Puri itself, at blessed Orissa. Come—"

"By Allah!" laughed the first rider. "By the ninety-nine holy names of God!"

He shook in his saddle with merriment. The Brahman dropped the reins as if they had been red hot and surveyed the two with angry disappointment.

"By the beard of the Prophet, and the ashes of my grandsire— this is a goodly jest," roared the tall warrior. "Behold, a pilgrim hunter come to solicit Abdul Dost and Khlit of the Curved Saber."

He spoke *Mogholi*, whereas the misguided Brahman had used his native Hindustani. Khlit understood Abdul Dost. Yet he did not laugh. He was looking curiously at the marked brow of the priest, which had darkened in anger at the gibe of the Muslim.

"Eh—this is verily a thing to warm the heart," went on Abdul Dost. "A Brahman, a follower of Jagannath, bids us twain come to the festival of his god. He knew not that I am a follower of the true Prophet, and you, Khlit, wear a Christian cross of gold under the shirt at your throat."

He turned to the unfortunate pilgrim hunter.

"Nay, speaker-of-the-loud-tongue, here is an ill quarter to cry your wares. Would the wooden face of armless Jagannath smile upon a Muslim and a Christian, think you?"

"Nay," quoth the priest scornfully, "not so much as upon a toad, or a pariah who is an eater of filth."

In his zeal, he had not taken careful note of the persons of the two travelers.

He scanned the warriors keenly, looking longest at Khlit. The elegantly dressed Afghan, with his jeweled scimitar and his silver-mounted harness and small, tufted turban, was a familiar figure.

But the gaunt form of the Cossack was strange to the Brahman. Khlit's bearded cheeks were haggard with hardship and illness in the mountains during the long Winter of Kashmir, and his wide, deep-set eyes were gray. His heavy sheepskin coat was thrown back, disclosing a sinewy throat and high, rugged shoulders.

In Khlit's scarred face was written the boldness of a fighting race, hardened, not softened by the wrinkles of age. It was an open face, lean and weather-stained. The deep eyes returned the stare of the priest with a steady, meditative scrutiny.

Abdul Dost was still smiling. His handsome countenance was that of a man in the prime of life, proud of his strength. He sat erect in a jeweled saddle, a born horseman and the finest swordsman of northern Hindustan. He rode a mettled Arab. Khlit's horse was a shaggy Kirghiz pony.

"It is time," broke in Khlit bluntly—he was a man of few words—"that we found food for ourselves and grain for our horses. Where lies this peasant we seek?"

Abdul Dost turned to the watching priest, glancing at the sun.

"Ho, hunter of pilgrims," he commanded, "since we are not birds for your snaring—and the enriching of your idol—tell us how many bowshot distant is the hut of Bhimal, the catcher of birds. We have ridden since sunup, and our bellies yearn."

The Brahman folded his arms. He seemed inclined to return a sharp answer, then checked himself. His black eyes glinted shrewdly. He pointed down the dusty highway.

"If the blind lead the blind, both will fall into the well," he chanted. "Nay, would you behold the power of the name of Jagannath whom you foolishly deride? Then come with me to the abode of this same Bhimal. I will guide you, for I am bound thither myself on a quest from the temple."

"So be it," nodded Abdul Dost carelessly and urged his horse forward, offering the pilgrim hunter a stirrup which the Brahman indignantly refused.

Abdul Dost was not the man to repent his own words, spoken freely. But he understood better than Khlit the absolute power of the Hindu priests in the Land of the Five Rivers.

The fertile province of Kukushetra was a favorite resort for the Hindu pilgrims of the highlands. Here were the ruins of an ancient temple, near which the new-gilded edifice—a replica of that at Puri at the Ganges' mouth—had been built. Here also were gathered the priests from the hill monasteries, to tend the shrine of the Kukushetra Jagannath.

Religious faith had not made a breach between Khlit and Abdul Dost. The Cossack was accustomed to keep his thoughts to himself, and to the *mansabdar* friendship was a weightier matter than the question of faith. He had eaten bread and salt with Khlit.

He had nearly slain the Cossack in their first meeting, and this had made the two boon companions. Khlit had treated his wounds with gunpowder and earth mixed with spittle—until Abdul Dost substituted clean bandages and ointment.

The two ate of the same food and slept often under the same robe. They were both veteran fighters in an age when a man's life was safeguarded only by a good sword-arm. Abdul Dost was pleased to lead his comrade through the splendid hill country of northern India, perhaps influenced—for he was a man of simple ideas—by the interest which the tall figure of Khlit always aroused among the natives.

Khlit was well content to have the companionship of a man who liked to wander and who had much to say of India and the wars of the Mogul. Khlit himself was a wanderer who followed the path of battles. From this he had earned the surname of the "Curved Saber."

It was the first time that Khlit had set foot in Hindustan, which was the heart of the Mogul Empire.

The priest, who had maintained a sullen silence, halted at a wheat field bordering the road. Here a bare-legged, turbaned man was laboring, cutting the wheat with a heavy sickle and singing as he worked.

The Brahman called, and the man straightened, casting an anxious eye at the three in the road. Khlit saw his eyes widen as he recognized the priest.

"Greeting, Kurral," spoke the man in the field; "may the blessing of divine Vishnu rest upon you."

"Come, Bhimal," commanded the Brahman sharply; "here be barbarian wayfarers who seek your hut. Lay aside your sickle. Your harvesting is done."

With a puzzled glance over his shoulders at the half-gathered grain, Bhimal the *chiria mars*—Hindu of the bird-slaying caste—led the way to his cottage beside the field. It was a clay-walled hut with a roof of thatched roots, under the pleasant shade of a huge banyan.

On either side of the door within the shade grapevines were trained upon a lattice; in the rear an open shed housed two buffalo—the prized possession of Bhimal and his brother.

At the threshold, however, the slayer-of-birds hesitated strangely and faced his companions as if unwilling for them to enter. Khlit and Abdul Dost dismounted, well-content with the

spot, where they had heard a good breakfast for a man and beast
might be had from the hospitable Bhimal. They had unsaddled
and were about to request a jar of water from the cottage tank
under the banyan when a word from Kurral arrested them.

"Stay," muttered the Brahman.

Turning to Bhimal, he smiled, while the simple face of the old
peasant grew anxious.

"Is it not true, Bhimal, that this cottage belongs to you and
your brother, who departed long ago on a pilgrimage to Puri?"

"It is true, Kurral," assented Bhimal.

"That you own two fields and a half of good wheat ready for
the harvest? And two buffalo? This cottage?"

At each question the peasant nodded.

"And a few rare birds which you caught in snares?"

Kurral drew a folded parchment from the robe at his waist and
consulted it. Then he tossed it to Bhimal.

"You cannot read, O slayer-of-birds," he smiled. "But this is a
bond signed by your brother. You can make out his scrawl, over
the endorsement of the holy priest of Puri, the unworthy slave of
Jagannath. The bond is for the cottage and all the goods, animals
and tools of your brother and yourself. It was sent from the mighty
temple of Puri to the lesser shrine at Kukushetra. And I am come
to take payment."

Khlit, not understanding Hindustani, yet read sudden misery
in the lined face of Bhimal.

"How fares my brother?" cried the peasant.

"He brought fitting gifts of fruit, grain and oatmeal to the
shrine of Jagannath, Bhimal. His zeal was great. All the coins
that he had, he gave. But mighty Jagannath was ill-rewarded by
your brother, for you came not with him on the pilgrimage."

"Nay, I am sorely lame."

Bhimal pointed sadly to a partially withered leg.

"No matter," declared Kurral sternly. "Is Jagannath a pariah, to
be cheated of his due—by miserable slayers of carrion birds? Your
brother wrote the bond for this cottage and the fields. He offered

it to the priest and it was taken. Thus he gained the blessing of
all-powerful Jagannath."

"Then—he is ill?"

"Nay, I heard that he died upon the return journey, in the heat.
By his death he is blessed—as are all those who perish on behalf
of the All-Destroyer, whether under the wheels of the sacred car
or upon the path of pilgrimage."

Bhimal hung his head in resignation. Abdul Dost, with a shrug
of his slender shoulders, was about to take the jar of water from
the tank when Kurral wheeled on him vindictively.

"Stay, barbarian!" he warned. "This tank and the cottage and
the food within is now the property of the temple of Kukushetra.
No unclean hand may be laid upon it."

Abdul Dost stared at him grimly and glanced questioningly at
Bhimal.

"It is true," admitted the peasant sadly. "A bond given to the
god by my brother is binding upon my unworthy self. Yet—"he
faced Kurral beseechingly—"the wheat and the rare birds are all
that I have to live through the season of rains.

"Suffer me to stay in the cottage and work on behalf of the
god. I shall render you a just tribute of all, keeping just enough
for my own life. I would strew the ashes of grief upon my head
in solitude—"

"Nay," retorted Kurral; "would you mourn a life that has
passed to the keeping of the gods? I have marked you as one of
little faith. So you may not tend this property. Another will see
to it."

A rebellious flicker appeared in the dim eyes of the peasant.

"Has not Jagannath taken the things that are dearest to me,
Kurral?" he cried shrilly. "My brother's life and these good buffaloes? Nay, then let me keep but one thing!"

"What?" demanded the priest, still enjoying his triumph over
the two warriors.

"A peacock with a tail of many-colored beauty. I have tended
it as a gift to my lord, the Rawul Matap Rao, upon his marriage.
I have promised the gift."

Kurral considered.

"Not so," he decided. "For the Rawul—so it is said—has not bent his head before the shrine of Kukushetra in many moons. It is rumored that he inclines to an unblessed sect, the worshipers of the sun-image of Vishnu—the followers of the *gosain* Chaitanya. He is unworthy the name of Hindu. Better the peacock should adorn the temple garden than strut for the pleasure of the bride of Rawul Matap Rao."

Then Khlit saw a strange form appear from within the entrance of the hut. In the dim light under the great tree it appeared as a glittering child with a plumed headdress. Kurral, too, saw it and started.

"Who names the Rawul with false breath?" cried the figure in a deep melodious voice. "Ho—it is Kurral, the pilgrim hunter. Me-thought I knew his barbed tongue."

By now Khlit saw that the figure was that of a warrior, standing scarce shoulder high to the Cossack and the tall Afghan. A slim, erect body was brightly clad, the legs bound by snowy white muslin, a shawl girdle of green silk falling over the loins, a shirt of finely wrought silvered mail covering the small body, the brown arms bare, a helmet of thin bronze on the dark head.

The man's face was that of a Hindu of the warrior caste, the eyes dark and large, the nostrils thin. A pair of huge black mustaches were twisted up either cheek. A quiver full of arrows hung at the waist-girdle.

In one hand the archer held a bow; under the other arm he clasped a beautiful peacock, whose tail had stirred Khlit's interest.

"Sawal Das!" muttered Kurral.

"Aye, Sawal Das," repeated the archer sharply, "servant and warrior of the excellent Rawul Matap Rao. I came to Bhimal's hut at sunup to claim the peacock, for my lord returns to his castle of Thaneswar tomorrow night. And now, O beguiler-of-men, have you wasted your breath; for I have already claimed the peacock on behalf of my lord."

"Too much of the evil juice of the grape has trickled down your gullet, Sawal Das," scowled the priest. "For that you came to the hut—under pretense of taking the bird. You are a dishonor to your caste—"

"Windbag! Framer-of-lies!"

The archer laughed.

"*Ohé*—are you one to question a warrior? When the very clients that come to your cell will not take food or water from the hand of a *Barna** Brahman. *Oho*—well you know that my master would hold himself contaminated were your shadow to fall across his feet."

He paused to stare at Khlit and Abdul Dost, whom he had not observed before.

"So you would steal from Jagannath!" fumed the priest.

"Nay."

The white teeth of the archer showed through his mustache.

"Am I one of the godless Kukushetra brethren who gorge themselves with the food that is offered to Jagannath? I plunder none save my lawful foes—behold this Turkish mail and helmet as witness!"

"Skulker!"

The hard face of the Brahman flushed darkly.

"Eavesdropper!"

"At least," retorted the warrior, "I take not the roof from over the head of the man whose guest I am."

He turned to the mournful Bhimal.

"Come, comrade, will you let this evil lizard crawl into your hut? A good kick will send him flying."

"Nay—" the peasant shook his head—"it may not be. My brother gave a bond."

"But your brother is dead."

"He pledged his word. I would be dishonored were I not to fulfill it."

---

*One of the lowest orders of the priesthood.

Sawal Das grimaced.

"By Siva!" he cried. "A shame to give good grain and cattle to these scavengers. Half the farms of the countryside they have taken to themselves. Even the might of my lord the Rawul can not safeguard the lands of his peasants. If this thing must be, then come to Thaneswar where you will be safe from the greed of such as Kurral."

"I thank you, Sawal Das."

Bhimal looked up gratefully.

"But I would be alone for a space to mourn my brother who is dead."

"So be it," rejoined the archer, "but forget not Thaneswar. Rawul Matap Rao has need of faithful house-servants."

"Aye," observed the priest; "the time will come when he who sits in Thaneswar will have need of—hirelings."

Khlit, indifferent to the discussion which he did not understand, had watered his horse and searched out a basket of fruit and cakes of jellied rice within the hut. Coming forth with his prize, he tossed a piece of silver money to Bhimal.

The peasant caught it and would have secreted it in his garments, but Kurral's sharp eye had seen the act.

"Take not the silver that is Jagannath's!"

He held out his hand.

"Or you will be accursed."

Reluctantly the peasant was about to yield the money to the priest when Sawal Das intervened.

"The bond said naught of money, Kurral," he pointed out. "Is your hunger for wealth like to a hyena's yearning for carrion? Is there no end of your greed? Touch not the dinar."

The priest turned upon the archer furiously.

"Take care!" he cried. "Kukushetra has had its fill of the idolatry of the Rawul and the insolence of his servants. Take care lest you lose your life by lifting hand against mighty Jagannath!"

"I fear not the god," smiled Sawal Das. "Lo, I will send him a gift, even Jagannath himself, by the low-born Kurral."

So swiftly that the watching Abdul Dost barely caught his movements, the archer dropped the peacock and plucked an arrow from its quiver. In one motion he strung the short bow and fitted arrow to string.

Kurral backed away, his eyes widening in sudden fear. Evidently he had reason to respect the archer. A tree-trunk arrested his progress abruptly.

Sawal Das seemed not to take aim, yet the arrow flew and the bowstring twanged. The shaft buried itself deep into the tree-trunk. And the sacred cord which hung to Kurral's left shoulder was parted in twain.

Kurral gazed blankly at the severed string and the arrow embedded not two inches from his ear. Then he turned and fled into the thicket, glancing over his shoulder as he went.

"A good shot, that, archer," laughed Abdul Dost.

"It was nought," grinned Sawal Das. "On a clear day I have severed the head from a carrion bird in full flight. Nay, a good shaft was wasted where it will do little good."

He strutted from the hut, gathering up the peacock.

"If you are strangers in Kukushetra," he advised, "you would do well to seek the door of my master, Rawul Matap Rao. He asks not what shrine you bow before, and he has ever an ear for a goodly song or tale, or—" Sawal Das noted the Afghan's lean figure appraisingly—"employment for a strong sword-arm. He is a just man, and within his gates you will be safe."

"So there is to be a marriage feast at Thaneswar?"

"Aye," nodded the archer, "and rare food and showers of silver for all who attend. This road leads to Thaneswar castle by the first turn uphill. Watch well the path you take, for there are evil bandits—servants of the death-loving Kali—afoot in the deeper jungle."

With that he raised a hand in farewell and struck off into a path through the brush, singing to himself, leaving Bhimal sitting grief-stricken on the threshold of the hut and Khlit and Abdul Dost quietly breakfasting.

II

On that day the young chieftain of Thaneswar had broken the *torun* over the gate of Rinthambur.

The *torun* was a triangular emblem of wood hung over the portal of a woman who was to become a bride. Matap Rao, a clever horseman, rode under the stone arch, and while the women servants and the ladies of Rinthambur laughingly pelted him with flowers and plaited leaves he struck the *torun* with his lance until it fell to earth in fragments.

This done, as was customary, the mock defense of Rinthambur castle ceased; the fair garrison ended their pretty play and Rawul Matap Rao was welcomed by the men within the gate.

He was a man fit to be allied by blood even with the celebrated chiefs of the Rinthambur clan—a man barely beyond the limits of youth, who had many cares and who administered a wide province—Thaneswar—with the skill of an elder.

Perhaps the Rawul was not the fighting type beloved by the minstrels of the Rinthambur house. He was not prone to make wars upon his neighbors, choosing rather to study how the taxes of his peasants might be lightened and the heavy hand of the Kukushetra temple be kept from spoliation of the ignorant farmers.

The young Rawul, last of his line, was a breeder of fine horses, a student and a philosopher of high intelligence. He was the equal in birth to Retha of Rinthambur—the daughter of a warlike clan of the sun-born caste. She had smiled upon his wooing and the chieftains who were head of her house were not ill content to join the clans of Rinthambur and Thaneswar by blood.

War on behalf of the Mogul, and their own reckless extravagance with money and the blood of their followers, had weakened the clan. The remaining members had gathered at Rinthambur castle to pay fitting welcome to the Rawul.

"We yield to your care," they said, "her who is the gem in the diadem of Rajasthan—Retha of Rinthambur—who is called

'Lotus Face' in the Punjab. Guard her well. If need arise command our swords, for our clans are one."

So Matap Rao joined his hand to that of Retha, and the knot in their garments was tied in the hall of Rinthambur before the fire altar. Both Matap Rao and the Rinthambur chieftains were descendants of the fire family of the Hindus—devotees of the higher and milder form of Vishnu worship.

"Thaneswar," he said, "shall be another gate to Rinthambur and none shall be so welcome as the riders of Rinthambur."

But the chieftains after bidding adieu to him and his bride announced that they would remain and hold revelry in their own hall for two days, leaving the twain to seek Thaneswar, as was the custom.

Thus it happened that Matap Rao, flushed with exultation and deep in love, rode beside his bride to the boundary of Rinthambur, where the last of the bride's clan turned back. His followers, clad and mounted to the utmost finery of their resources, fell behind the two.

The way seemed long to Matap Rao, even though a full moon peered through the soft glimmer of twilight and the minstrel of Thaneswar—the aged *Vina*, Perwan Singh—chanted as he rode behind them, and the scent of jasmine hung about their path. In the Thaneswar jungle, at the boundary of the two provinces, a watch tower stood by the road, rearing its bulk against the moon.

Here were lights and soft draperies and a banquet of sugared fruits, sweetened rice, jellies, cakes and curries, prepared by the skilled hands of the women slaves who waited here to welcome their new mistress. And here the party dismounted, the armed followers occupying tents about the tower.

While they feasted and Matap Rao described the banquet that was awaiting them on the following night at Thaneswar hall, Perwan Singh sang to them and the hours passed lightly, until the moon became clouded over and a sudden wind swept through the forest.

A drenching downpour came upon the heels of the wind; the lights in the tower were extinguished, and Retha laid a slim hand fearfully upon the arm of her lord. "It is an ill omen," she cried.

"Nay," he laughed, "no omen shall bring a cloud upon the heart of the queen of Thaneswar. Vishnu smiles upon us."

But Retha, although she laughed with her husband, was not altogether comforted. And, the next morning, when a band of horsemen and camels met them on the highway, she drew closer to Matap Rao.

A jangle of cymbals and kettledrums proclaimed that this was the escort of a higher priest of Kukushetra. Numerous servants, gorgeously dressed, led a fine Kabul stallion forward to meet the Rawul, and its rider smiled upon him.

This was Nagir Jan, *gosain* of Kukushetra and abbot of the temple.

He was a man past middle life, his thin face bearing the imprint of a dominant will, the chin strongly marked, the eyes piercing. He bowed to Retha, whose face was half-veiled.

"A boon," he cried, "to the lowly servant of Jagannath. Let him see but once the famed beauty of the Flower of Rinthambur."

Matap Rao hesitated. He had had reason more than once to feel the power of the master of the temple. Nagir Jan was reputed to be high in the mysteries of the nationwide worship of Jagannath.

Owing to the wealth of the priests of the god, and the authority centered in his temples, the followers of Jagannath were the only Hindus permitted by the Mogul to continue the worship of their divinity as they wished. The might of Jagannath was not lightly to be challenged.

But Nagir Jan was also a learned priest familiar with the Vedas and the secrets of the shrine of Puri itself. As such he could command the respect of Matap Rao, who was an ardent Vishnu worshiper. For Jagannath, by the doctrine of incarnation, embodied the worship of Vishnu.

"If Retha consents," he responded, "it is my wish."

The girl realized that the priest had come far to greet her. She desired to please the man who was more powerful than the Rawul in Thaneswar.

So she drew back the veil. But her delicate face wore no smile. The splendid, dark eyes looked once, steadily into the cold eyes of the priest.

"Truly," said Nagir Jan softly, "is she named the Lotus Face. The lord of Retha is favored of the gods."

While the twain rode past he continued to look after the girl. Glancing over his shoulder presently, the Rawul saw that Nagir Jan was still seated on his horse, looking at them. He put spurs to his horse, forcing a laugh.

But after the festival at Thaneswar Matap Rao would have given much, even half his lands, if he had not granted the wish of Nagir Jan.

The same thunderstorm that so disturbed the young bride of the Rawul caught Khlit and Abdul Dost on the open road.

The warriors had lingered long at the hospitable hut of Bhimal to escape the midday heat. So the sun was slanting over the wheat fields when they trotted toward the castle of Thaneswar. It was twilight when they came upon the crossroads described by the archer, Sawal Das.

Here was a grimy figure squatted upon a ragged carpet, the center of interest of a group of naked children who scampered into the bushes at sight of the riders.

The man was a half-caste Portuguese, hatless and bootless. On the carpet before him were a mariner's compass, much the worse for wear, and one or two tattered books, evidently—as Khlit surmised—European prayer-books. He glanced up covertly at the warriors.

"What manner of man is this?" wondered Abdul Dost aloud in Hindustani.

"An unworthy astrologer, so please you, great sirs," bowed the half-caste.

He closed both eyes and smiled.

"My mystic instrument of divination—" he pointed to the compass—"and my signs of the Zodiac."

He showed illuminated parchment pictures of the saints in the prayer-book.

"It is a goodly trade, and the witless ones of this country pay well. My name is Merghu. What can I do for the great sirs?"

"*Jaisa des waisahi bhes*!"—for such a country, such a masquerade—responded the Afghan contemptuously. "Will not the priest of Kukushetra beat your back with bamboos if they find you here at the crossroads?"

Again the man's eyes closed slyly and his sullen face leered. He lifted a corner of his cloak, disclosing a huge, ulcerous sore.

"Nay, noble travelers. They may not touch what is unclean. Besides the festival of *Janam* approaches, and the priests are busied within the temple—"

"Enough!" growled the Afghan at a sign from Khlit, who had marked a cloud-bank creeping over the moon that was beginning to show between the treetops. "We are belated. We were told to take the upper hill trail to Thaneswar castle, but here be two trails. Which is the one we seek?"

"Yonder," muttered the astrologer, pointing. "The other leads to the temple."

Khlit and Abdul Dost spurred up the way he had indicated. Glancing back at the first turn in the trail, the Cossack noticed that the sham astrologer had vanished, with all his stock in trade.

But now wind whipped the treetops that met over the trail. Rain poured down in one of the heavy deluges that precede the wet season in this country.

Khlit rode unheeding, but Abdul Dost swore vehemently as his finery became soaked. He spurred his horse faster into the darkness without noticing where they went save that it was upward, trusting to the instinct of his mount to lead him safely.

So the two came at a round pace to a clearing in the trees. A high, blank wall emerged before them. This they circled until a gate opened and they trotted past a pool of water to a square structure with a high-peaked roof whence came sounds of voices and the clang of cymbals.

"The wedding merriment has begun!" cried Abdul Dost.

He swung down from his horse and beat at a bronze door with fist and sword-hilt. Khlit, from the caution of habit, kept to his saddle. The door swung inward. A glare of light struck into their faces.

"Who comes to the hall of offerings of Jagannath?" cried a voice.

Khlit saw a group of Brahmans at the door. Behind them candles and torches lighted a large room filled with an assemblage of peasants and soldiers who were watching a dance through a wide doorway that seemed to lead into a building beyond.

In this farther space a cluster of young girls moved in time to the music of drums and cymbals, tossing their bare arms and whirling upon their toes so that thin draperies swirled about their half-nude forms.

Abdul Dost, who was a man of single thought, stared at the spectacle in astonishment, his garments dripping and rain beating upon his back.

"Who comes armed to the outer hall of the Lord of the World?" cried a young priest zealously. "Know ye not this is the time of the *Janam*?"

"I seek Thaneswar castle," explained the Afghan. "Is it not here? Nay, I am a traveler, not a slave of your god—"

"Be gone then from here," commanded the young priest. "This is no place for those of—Thaneswar. Be gone, one-without-breeding, low-born—"

"By Allah!" shouted Abdul Dost angrily. "Is this your courtesy to wayfarers in a storm?"

He swung back into his saddle, drawing his sword swiftly. Khlit, lest he should ride his horse into the throng, laid firm hand on the arm of the irate Muslim. They caught a passing glimpse of the dancing women staring at them, and the crowd. Then the door swung to in their faces with a clang.

" 'Low-born,' they said, in my teeth!" stormed the Afghan. "Base mouthers of indecency! Mockers of true men! Saw you the temple harlots offering their bodies to feast the eyes of the throng? Saw you the faithless priest offering food to the sculptured images of their armless gods—"

"Peace," whispered Khlit. "Here is an ill place for such words."

"Why laid you hand on my rein?" fumed Abdul Dost. "If you had fear in your heart for such as these—offscourings of thrice-defiled dirt—why did you not flee? I would have barbered the head of yon shaven villain with my sword. Eh—I am not an old woman who shivers at hard words and sword-strokes—"

Khlit's grasp on his arm tightened.

"The rain is ceasing," growled the Cossack. "I can see the lights of Kukushetra village through the farther gate in the temple wall. Many men are afoot. Come. Thaneswar is a better place than this."

While the Cossack eyed the surroundings of the temple enclosure curiously, Abdul Dost shrugged his shoulders.

"Age has sapped your courage, Khlit," muttered the *mansabdar*. "Verily, I heard tales of your daring from the Chinese merchants and the Tatars. Yet you draw back before the insult of a stripling priest."

Khlit wheeled his horse toward the gate jerking the bridle of the Afghan's mount.

"Aye, I am old," he said, half to himself. "And I have seen before this the loom of a man-trap. Come."

Sullenly the other trotted after him. Back on the trail, the moon, breaking from the clouds by degrees, cast a network of shadows before them. The two rode in silence until Abdul Dost quickened his pace to take the lead.

"Perchance," he observed grimly, "that miscreant astrologer abides yet at the crossroads. The flat of my sword laid to his belly will teach him not to guide better men than he astray."

Khlit lifted his head.

"Aye, the astrologer," he meditated aloud. "Surely he must have known the way to Thaneswar, as well as the temple path. It would be well, Abdul Dost, to watch better our path. Why did he speak us false? That is a horse will need grooming."

"Aye, with a sword."

The *mansabdar* rode heedlessly forward until they had gained the main road. Khlit, looking shrewdly on all sides, thought that he saw a figure move in the thicket at the side of the path. He checked his horse with a low warning to his companion.

But Abdul Dost, lusting for reprisal, slipped down from his saddle and advanced weapon in hand to the edge of the brush, peering into the shadows under the trees, which were so dense that the rain could barely have penetrated beneath their branches. Standing so, he was clearly outlined in the moonlight.

"Come forth, O skulker of the shadows!" he called. "Hither, false reader of the stars. I have a word for your ears—*Bismillah!*"

A dozen armed figures leaped from the bush in front of him. Something struck the mail on his chest with a ringing *clang*, and a spear dropped at his feet. Another whizzed past his head.

Abdul Dost gave back a pace, warding off the sword-blades that searched for his throat. Excellent swordsman that he was, he was hard-pressed by the number of his assailants. A sweeping blow of his scimitar half-severed the head of the nearest man, but another weapon bit into his leg over the knee, and his startled horse reared back, making him half-lose his balance.

At this point Khlit spurred his horse at the foes of Abdul Dost, riding down one and forcing the others back.

"Mount!" he cried over his shoulder to the Afghan.

Abdul Dost's high-strung Arab, however, had been grazed by a spear and was temporarily unmanageable. Khlit covered his companion, avoiding the blows of the attackers cleverly. They pressed their onset savagely.

Abdul Dost, cursing his injured leg, tossed aside the reins of his useless mount and stepped forward to Khlit's side, his sword poised.

Then, while the two faced the ten during one of those involuntary pauses that occur in hand-to-hand fights, a new element entered into the conflict at the crossroads.

There was a sharp twang, a whistling hum in the air, and one of the assailants flung up his arms with a grunt. In the half-light Khlit saw that an arrow had transfixed the man's head, its feathered end sticking grotesquely from his cheek.

A second shaft and a third sped swiftly, each finding its mark on their foes. One man dropped silently to earth, clutching his chest; a second turned and spun dizzily backward into the bush.

One of the surviving few flung up his shield fearfully in time to have an arrow pierce it cleanly and plant itself in his shoulder.

There was something inexorable and deadly in the silent flight of arrows. Those who could stand, in the group of raiders, turned and leaped into the protecting shadows.

Khlit and Abdul Dost heard them running, breaking through the vines. They stared curiously at the five forms outstretched in the road. On the forehead of one who faced the moon, a shaft through his breast, they saw the white caste-mark of Jagannath.

Already the five had ceased moving.

"Come into the shadow, O heedless riders of the North," called a stalwart voice.

Khlit turned his horse, and was followed by Abdul Dost, who by this time had recovered his mount.

Under the trees on the farther side of the road they found Sawal Das, chuckling. The archer surveyed them, his small head on one side.

"Horses and sword-blades are an ill protection against the spears that fly in the dark," he remarked reprovingly.

"How came you here?" muttered Abdul Dost, who was in an ill humor, what with his hurt and the events of the night.

"*Ohé—Oho!*" Sawal Das laughed. "Am I not the right-hand man of my lord, the Rawul? Does he not ride hither with his bride tomorrow? Thus, I watch the road.

"A short space ago when the rain ceased I heard an ill-omened group talking at the crossroads. There was a half-caste *feringha* who said that the two riders would return to seek the Thaneswar path—"

"The astrologer!" muttered Abdul Dost, binding his girdle over his thigh.

"Even so, my lord. Who is he but a spy of the temple? Ah, my bold swordsman, there be jewels in your turban and sword-hilt.

"Likewise—so Bhimal whispered—the low-born followers of the temple have orders to keep armed men from Thaneswar gate. I know not. But I waited with bow strung, believing that there would be sport—"

"Bravely and well have you aided us," said Khlit shortly in his broken *Mogholi*. "I saw others moving in the bush—"

"Perchance the evil-faced Kurral and his friends," assented Sawal Das, who understood.

"I will not forget," grunted the Cossack "Nay."

The archer took his rein in hand.

"This is no spot for our talk. I will lead you to Thaneswar, where you may sleep in peace."

He led them forward, humming softly to himself.

"Men of Jagannath have been slain," he murmured over his shoulder. "That will rouse the anger of the priests. Already the hot blood is in their foreheads at thought of the honor and wealth of my lord the Rawul. We will not speak of this, lest a cloud sully the bride-bringing of my lord.

"Verily," he said more softly, "did Perwan Singh, the chanter of epics, say that before long this place will be as it was in the days of the Pandas and the higher gods. Aye, Perwan Singh sang that blood would cover the mountains and bones will fill the valleys. Death will walk in the shadows of the men of Thaneswar."

Now, after they had gone, a form scurried from the thicket down the muddy highway, a heavy pack on its back. It paused not, nor looked behind. Merghu, the astrologer, was leaving Kukushetra.

III

There is One who knows the place of the birds who fly through the sky; who perceives what has been and what will be; who knows the track of the wind
He is named by many names; yet he is but one.

Hymn to Vishnu

Khlit was disappointed in the sight of Thaneswar castle. On the day following the affray of the crossroads the Cossack was early afoot, and as the retainers were busied in preparing for the coming of their lord, he was able to make the rounds of the place undisturbed save by a few curious glances.

The abode of Rawul Matap Rao was not a castle in the true sense of the word. In the midst of the wheat fields of the province of Kukushetra a low wall of dried mud framed an enclosure of several buildings. The enclosure was beaten smooth by the feet of many animals, and against the wall were the stables, the elephant-stockade, the granaries, and the quarters of the stable-servants and the *mahouts*.

In the center of the site grew the garden of Thaneswar, a jumble of wild flowers, fern trees and miniature deodars cleverly culti-vated by gardeners whose hereditary task it was to tend the spot and keep clean the paths through the verdure, artfully designed to appear as if a haphazard growth of nature.

An open courtyard ornamented by a great pool of water shad-owed by cypresses fronted the garden. At the rear of the courtyard, it was true, a solid granite building stood—the hall of the Rawul.

Pillars of the same stone, however, supported a thatched roof, under which ran layers of cane. Numerous openings in the granite wall provided sleeping-terraces.

The inner partitions were mainly latticework, and only one ceiling—that of the main hall—was of stronger material than the thatch. This was of cedar, inlaid with ivory and mosaic, and brightly painted.

To Khlit, accustomed to the rugged stone structures of Central Asia, the small palace was but a poor fortress. He had no eye for the throng of diligent servants who were spreading clean cotton cloths over the floor mattresses or placing flowers in the latticework.

"The temple of the hill god, yonder," he muttered to Sawal Das, who had joined him, "was stronger."

The archer fingered his mustache.

"Aye," he admitted restlessly. "I would that the Rawul had kept the heavy taxes upon the peasants, so that the armed retainers of Thaneswar would be more numerous and better equipped. I have scarce two-score able men under me. And my lord has not many more men-at-arms to attend him. He would give the very gold of his treasury to the peasants, if need be.

"When I say that we should have more swords—when yonder eagle—" he pointed to the glittering dome of the temple—"cries out in greed—he laughs and swears that a word will rouse the peasantry and villagers of Kukushetra on our behalf. But I know not."

He shrugged his shoulders and dismissed his forebodings.

"Ah, well, warrior, who would dare to lift hand against Rawul Matap Rao, the last of the Thaneswar clan? Come, here is the choicest defender of Thaneswar, with his companions."

Sawal Das pointed to the stockade in one corner of the great enclosure. Here a half-dozen elephants were being groomed for the reception of the chieftain and his bride.

It was the first time that Khlit had seen the beasts nearby and he strode over to gaze at them. Seeing his absorption in the sight, the archer left to attend to his own affairs.

First the elephants were washed down well in a muddy pool outside the enclosure, reached by a wide gate through the wall. Then their heads, trunks and ears were painted a vivid orange, shaded off to green at the tips of the flapping ears and at the end of the trunk.

Then crimson silk cloths were hung over their barrels, and a triangular piece of green velvet was placed over their heads between the eyes. This done, silk cords with silver bells attached were thrown about their massive necks.

The largest of the huge animals, however, was attired in full war panoply. Bhimal, who had come with several of the household to gaze at the sight, touched Khlit's elbow.

"Behold Asil Rumi," he said in *Mogholi*.

Khlit and Abdul Dost had treated the lame peasant kindly—something rare in his experience—and he was grateful.

"The favorite elephant. He was a gift to the grandfather of the Rawul from a raja of Rinthambur. He has not his match for strength in this land. He is mightier than the storm-wind, which is the breath of the angry gods, for he can break down with his head a tree as big as my body."

The peasant sighed.

"Oftentimes, when the Rawul hunted tiger toward Rinthambur, Asil Rumi has trod down my wheat. But always the Rawul flung me silver to pay for the damage. A just man."

Khlit glanced at the old peasant.

"Have you left your farm?"

"Is it not Jagannath's? I would not dishonor the faith of my dead brother. See!" he cried.

Asil Rumi, with a thunderous internal rumbling, had planted his trunk against a post of the stockade a few yards from them. The elephant wore his battle armor—a bronze plate, heavily bossed, over his skull, stout leather sheets down either side, and twin sword-blades tied to his curving tusks.

Under the impact of the elephant's bulk the post creaked. Khlit saw it bend and heard it crack. The house servants ran back.

Asil Rumi leaned farther forward and the post—a good yard thick—gave as easily before him as an aspen. Then his *mahout* ran up. Khlit was surprised to hear the man talk to the beast urgently. The *mahout* held a silver prong, but this he did not use. Asil Rumi drew back.

At a second word from his master, the elephant coiled his trunk about the post and straightened it. Then he stood tranquil, his huge ears shaking, muttering to himself.

"How is it," asked Khlit, "that a small man such as that can command a beast like Asil Rumi? The beast could slay him with a touch of the tusk."

"Aye," assented Bhimal gravely, "the father of this *mahout* was slain by Asil Rumi when he was angry. But today he only plays. So long as this man speaks to him, Asil Rumi will obey because of his love for the man."

And Bhimal told how two generations ago the elephant had taken part in one of the battles of Rajasthan. The standard of the warlike Rinthambur clan had been placed on his back, and his *mahout* had led him well into the van of the Rájputs, ordering him to stand in a certain spot.

The battle had been closely fought about the beast, and the *mahout* slain. The elephant had been wounded in many places and the greater part of the Rinthambur Rájputs slain about him. Still Asil Rumi had remained standing where he was placed.

The Rájputs had won the battle, so Bhimal said. The soldiers had left the field during the pursuit, but Asil Rumi had stayed by the body of his *mahout*, refusing food or water for three days in his sorrow for the man who had been his master.

Then they had brought the boy who was the son of the *mahout*. Him the elephant had recognized and obeyed.

"Asil Rumi will go to meet the bride of Rinthambur," concluded Bhimal. "She will mount his *howdah*, with her lord. It will be a goodly sight."

Presently came Abdul Dost, resplendent in a fresh tunic and girdle, to announce that it was time they should groom their horses for the ride to meet the Rawul.

But Khlit remained in the elephant-stockade watching the beasts until the household cavalcade had actually mounted, when he left the animals that had so stirred his interest. He washed his face hastily in the garden pool, drew his belt tighter about his *khalat*, pulled at his mustache and was ready to ride with the others.

Bhimal excused himself to Sawul Das from accompanying the leaders of the peasants, saying that he was too lame to walk with the rest. Khlit, however, noticed that Bhimal kept pace with them as far as the crossroads.

The bodies had been cleared away, and the feet of men and beasts had obscured the imprint of blood here. Bhimal lingered.

"So," said the Cossack grimly, "you go to Jagannath, not to your lord."

"Aye," said the peasant simply. "In the temple above is he who is greater than any lord. *He* is master of death and life. My brother died in his worship. Wherefore should I not go?"

Khlit lingered behind the other horsemen, scanning Bhimal curiously. As the elephants had been strange beasts to him, so Bhimal and his kind were a new race of men.

It was Khlit's habit to ponder what was new to him. In this he differed from Abdul Dost.

"Have many of the Thaneswar peasants gone to the temple festival?" he inquired, noticing that the foot retainers with the cavalcade were few.

"Aye."

"What is the festival?"

"It is the great festival of Jagannath. *Janam*, the holy priests call it. They say it is to honor the birth of the god. It has always been."

"Will the Rawul and his woman go?"

Khlit did not care to revisit the temple after the episode of the night before.

"Nay. The Rawul has no love for the priests of the temple. He has said—so it is whispered through the fields—that they are not the true worshipers of Vishnu."

Down the breeze came the sound of the temple drums and cymbals. Khlit thought grimly that he also had no love for the servants of Vishnu.

"What is this Jagannath?" he asked indifferently.

To Khlit the worship of an idol by dance or song was a manifestation of Satan. He was a Christian of simple faith.

His tone, however, aroused the patient Hindu.

"Jagannath!" he cried, and his faded eyes gleamed. "Jagannath is the god of the poor. All men stand equal before him. The raja draws his car beside the pariah. His festival lasts as many days as I have fingers, and every day there is food for his worshipers. It is the holy time when a bride is offered to jagannath."

He pointed up to the temple.

"A woman is chosen, and she is blessed. She is called the bride of Jagannath. Food and flowers are given her. She rides in the front of the great car which we build with our hands when Jagannath himself comes from his temple and is borne in the car to the ruins of the holy edifice, which was once the home of the older gods themselves.

"The woman—so Kurral said—abides one night in the shrine of the god. Then Jagannath reveals himself to her. He tells the omens for the coming year, whether the crops will be good, the rains heavy and the cows healthy. Then this is told to us. It is verily the word of the god.

"Ah!" He glanced around. "I am late."

He hobbled off up the path, leaning on his stick, and Khlit spurred after the others, dismissing from his mind for a time what he had heard about the festival of *Janam*.

He soon forgot Bhimal in the confusion attending the arrival of the Rawul, and the banquet that night.

There was good cheer in Thaneswar. The young Rawul with his bride and his companions feasted on the gallery overlooking the main hall. The soldiery and retainers shared the feast at the foot of the hall, or without on the garden terrace.

Khlit and Abdul Dost had discovered that wine was to be had by those who so desired, and seated themselves in a corner of the hall with a generous portion of the repast and silver cups of sherbet between them.

"Eh," cried the *mansabdar*, "these Hindus lack not a free hand. Did you mark how the Rawul scattered gold, silver and gems among the throng? The beauty of his bride has intoxicated him."

Khlit ate in silence. The music of Hindustan—a shrill clatter of instruments—held no charm for him. Abdul Dost, however, was accustomed to the melodies and nodded his head in time, his appreciation heightened by the wine.

"Last night," he said bluntly, "I spoke in haste, for I was angry. You are my brother in arms. By Allah, I would cut the cheek-bones from him who dared to say what I did."

He emptied his cup and cast a pleased glance over the merry crowd.

"It was a good word you spoke when Sawal Das led you to the horse of the Rawul and spoke your name to Matap Rao. Eh, Matap Rao asked whether you had a rank as a chieftain."

He smiled.

"You responded that a chieftain's rank is like to the number of men who will follow his standard in battle. That was well said.

"I have heard tales that you once were leader of as many thousands as Matap Rao numbers tens among his men. Is that the truth? It was in Tatary, in the Horde."

"That time is past," said Khlit.

"Aye. Perchance, though, such things may arise again. Sawal Das says that there may be fighting. Yet I scent it not. What think you?"

Abdul Dost glanced at Khlit searchingly. Much he had heard of the Cossack's craft in war.

Yet since their meeting Khlit had shown no desire to take up arms. Rather, he had seemed well content to be unmolested. This did not accord with the spirit of the fiery Afghan, to whom the rumor of battle was as the scent of life itself.

"I think," said Khlit, "that Matap Rao had done better to leave guards at the gate."

The Afghan shrugged his shoulders. Then lifted his head at the sound of a ringing voice. It was aged Perwan Singh, and his song was the song of Arjun that begins:

As starlight in the Summer skies,
So is the brightness of a woman's eyes—
Unmatched is she!

Silence fell upon the hall and the outer corridors. All eyes were turned to the gallery where behind a curtain the young bride of Thaneswar sat beside the feast of Matap Rao and his companions, among them Perwan Singh.

The sunbeam of the morning shows
Within her path a withered lotus bud,
A dying rose.

Her footsteps wander in the sacred place
Where stand her brethren, the ethereal race
For ages dead!

A young noble of the household parted the curtain at the song's end. He was a slender man, dark-faced, twin strings of pearls wound in his turban and about his throat—Serwul Jain, of Thaneswar.

"Men of Thaneswar," he cried ringingly, "the Lotus Face is now our queen. Happy are we in the sight of the flower of Rinthambur. Look upon Retha, wife of your lord."

There was a murmur of delight as the woman stood beside him. She was of an even height with the boy, the olive face unveiled, the black eyes wide and tranquil, the dark hair empty of jewels except for pearls over the forehead. Her thin silk robe, bound about the waist and drawn up from feet to shoulder, showed the tight underbodice over her breast and the outline of the splendid form that had been termed "tiger-waisted."

"Verily," said Abdul Dost, "she is fair."

But Khlit had fallen asleep during the song. The minstrelsy of Hindustan held no charms for him, and he had eaten well.

A stir in the hall, followed by a sudden silence, aroused the Cossack. He was wide awake on the instant, scenting something unwonted. Abdul Dost was on his feet, as indeed were all in the hall. Within the doorway stood a group of Brahmans, surrounded by representatives of the higher castes of Kukushetra.

The castle retainer stood at gaze, curious and expectant. Through the open gate a breath of air stirred the flames of the candles. "What seek you?" asked Serwul Jain from the gallery.

"We have come from the temple of Kukushetra, from the holy shrine of the Lord of the World," responded the foremost priest. "Rawul Matap Rao we seek. We have a message for his ears."

By now the chieftain was beside Retha. The eyes of the throng went from him to the Brahman avidly. It was the first time the Brahmans had honored Thaneswar castle with their presence.

"I am here," said the Rawul briefly. "Speak."

The Brahman advanced a few paces, drawing his robe closer about him. The servants gave back respectfully.

"This, O Rawul," he began, "is the festival of *Janam*. Pilgrims have come from every corner of the Punjab; aye, from the Siwalik hills and the border of Rajasthan to the temple of Jagannath. Yet you remain behind your castle wall."

He spoke sharply, clearly. No anger was apparent in his voice, but a stern reproach. Behind him Khlit saw the gaunt figure of Kurral.

"The day of my wedding is just past," responded Matap Rao quietly, "and I abide here to hold the feast. My place is in my own hall, not at the temple."

"So be it," said the priest.

He flung his head back and his sonorous voice filled the chamber.

"I bear a message from the shrine. Though you have forgotten the reverence due to the Lord of the World, though you have said harsh words concerning his temple, though you have neglected the holy rites and slandered the divine mysteries—even though you have forsworn the worship of Jagannath—the Lord of the World forgives and honors you."

He paused as if to give his words weight with the attentive throng.

"For the space of years your path and that of the temple have divided. Aye, quarrels have been and blood shed. Last night five servants of the temple were slain on the high road without your gate."

A surprised murmur greeted this. News of the fight had been kept secret by the priests until now, and Sawal Das had held his tongue.

"Yet Jagannath forgives. Matap Rao, your path will now lead to the temple. For tonight the bride of Jagannath is chosen. And the woman chosen is—as is the custom—fairest in the land of Kukushetra. Retha of Rinthambur."

Complete silence enveloped the crowd. Men gaped and started. Youthful Serwul Jain started and clutched at his sword. The lean hand of Perwan Singh arrested midway as he stroked his beard. The girl flashed a startled glance at her lord and drew the silk veil across her face.

A slow flush rose into the face of Matap Rao and departed, leaving him pale. He drew a deep breath and the muscles of his figure tightened until he was at his full height.

To be selected as the bride of the god on the *Janam* festival was held a high honor. It had been shared in the past by some of the most noted women of the land. The choice of the temple had never been denied.

But in the mild face of the Rawul was the shadow of fierce anger, swiftly mastered. He looked long into the eyes of the waiting priest while the crowd hung upon his word.

"Whose is the choice?" he asked slowly.

"Nagir Jan himself uttered the decree. The holy priest was inspired by the thought that Retha, wife of the Rawul, should hear the prophecy of the god for the coming year. Who but she should tell the omens to Kukushetra?"

Matap Rao lifted his hand.

"Then let Nagir Jan come to Thaneswar," he responded. "Let him voice his request himself. I will not listen to those of lower caste."

IV

Upon the departure of the priests the curtain across the gallery was drawn. A tumult arose in the hall. Many peasants departed. The serving women fled back to their quarters, and the house retainers lingered, watching the gallery.

Abdul Dost leaned back against the wall, smiling at Khlit.

"By the beard of my grandsire! If I had such a bride as Retha of Rinthambur I would yield her not to any muttering Hindu priest."

He explained briefly to Khlit what had passed. The Cossack shook his head moodily.

"There will be ill sleeping in Thaneswar this night, Abdul Dost," he said grimly. "The quarrel between priest and chieftain cuts deeper than you think."

"It is fate. The Rawul may not refuse the honor."

Khlit stroked his gray mustache, making no response. The prime of his life he had spent in waging war with the reckless ardor of the Cossack against the enemies of the Cross. The wrong done to Bhimal had not escaped his attention. Nor had the one glimpse of the Kukushetra temple been agreeable to his narrow but heartfelt idea of a place of worship.

"When all is said," meditated the Afghan, "this is no bread of our eating."

"Nay, Abdul Dost. Yet we have eaten the salt of Matap Rao."

"Verily, that is so," grunted the Afghan. "Well, we shall soon see what is written. What is written, is written. Not otherwise."

Khlit seated himself beside his comrade and waited. Soon came Sawal Das through an opening in the wall behind them. Seeing them, he halted, breathing hard, for he had been running.

"*Aie!*" he cried. "It was an ill thought that led Matap Rao to thin the ranks of his armed men. Nagir Jan has watched Thaneswar ripen like a citron in the sun. He has yearned after the wheat fields and the tax paid by the peasants. Truly is he named the snake. See, how he strikes tonight.

"*Aie!* He is cunning. His power is like that of the furious *daeva*s. His armor is hidden, yet he is more to be feared than if a thousand swords waved about him."

Abdul Dost laughed.

"If that is the way the horse runs, archer, you could serve your master well by planting a feathered shaft under the ear of the priest."

Sawal Das shook his head.

"Fool!" he cried. "The Rawul would lose caste and life itself were he to shed the blood of a higher priest of Jagannath. He would be left for the burial dogs to gnaw. The person of Nagir Jan and those with him is inviolate."

"Then must Matap Rao yield up his bride."

The archer's white teeth glinted under his mustache.

"Never will a Rawul of Thaneswar do that."

Both men were surprised at the anger of the slender archer. They knew little of the true meaning of the festival of Jagannath.

"Perchance he will flee, Sawal Das. Khlit and I will mount willingly to ride with him. Your shafts would keep pursuers at a distance."

"I have been the rounds of the castle enclosure," observed Sawal Das. "The watchers of the temple are posted at every gateway and even along the wall itself. Their spies are in the stables. Without the enclosure the peasants gather together. They have been told to arm."

"On behalf of their lord?"

"Vishnu alone knows their hearts."

Abdul Dost reached down and gripped the arm of Sawal Das.

"Ho, little archer," he growled, "if it comes to sword-strokes— we have eaten the salt of your master, and we are in your debt. We will stand at your side."

"I thank you."

The Hindu's eyes lighted. Then his face fell.

"But what avail sword-strokes against Jagannath? How can steel cut the tendrils of his temple that coil about Thaneswar? Nay; unless my lord can overmaster him with fair words it will go ill with us."

He shook both fists over his head in impotent wrath.

"May the curse of Siva and Vishnu fall upon the master of lies! He has waited until the people of the countryside are aflame with zeal. He has stayed his hand until the Lotus Face came to Thaneswar as bride. Did not he ask to look upon her when she rode hither? *Aie*, he is like a barbed shaft in our flesh."

Came Bhimal, limping, to their corner.

"Nagir Jan is at the gate, Sawal Das," he muttered. "And behind him are the peasantry, soldiers and scholars of Kukushetra, many of them armed, to receive Retha as the chosen bride."

The archer departed. Bhimal squatted beside them, silent, his head hanging on his chest. Abdul Dost glanced at Khlit.

"Your pony is in the stable," he whispered. "Perchance if you ride not forth now the going will be ill."

"And so is yours, Abdul Dost," grunted Khlit. "Why do you not mount him?"

The Afghan smiled and they both settled back to await what was to come.

Nagir Jan entered the hall alone. Matap Rao advanced a few paces to meet him. Neither made a salaam. Their eyes met and the priest spoke first, while those in the hall listened.

"I have come for the bride of the *Janam*. Even as you asked it, I have come. Tonight she must bathe and be cleansed of all impurity. The women of the wardrobe and the strewers of flowers will attend her, to prepare her to mount the sacred car on the morrow. Then will she sit beside the god himself. And on that night will she kneel before him in the chamber in the ruins and the god will speak to her and manifest himself in the holy mystery. Where is the woman Retha?"

Matap Rao smiled, although his face was tense and his fingers quivered.

"Will you take the veil from your face? Will you withdraw the cloak from your words, Nagir Jan?"

The cold eyes of the priest flickered. His strong face showed no sign of the anger he must have felt.

"Nagir Jan, I will speak the truth. Will you answer me so?"

"Say on," assented the Brahman.

The young lord of Thaneswar raised his voice until it reached the far corners of the hall.

"Why do you hold me in despite, Nagir Jan? You have said that I am without faith. Yet do I say that my faith is as great as yours. Speak!"

A murmur went through the watchers. The youths standing behind Matap Rao glanced at each other, surprised by the bold course the Rawul had taken.

"Does a servant of Jagannath speak lies?" Nagir Jan smiled. "Is the wisdom of the temple a house of straw, to break before the first wind? Nay."

He paused, meditating. He spoke clearly, forcibly in the manner of one who knew how to sway the hearts of his hearers.

"Is not Jagannath Lord of the World, Matap Rao? In him is mighty Vishnu thrice incarnate; in him are the virtues of Siva, protector of the soul; and the virtues of Balabhadra and Subhadra. Since the birth of Ram, Jagannath has been. The power of Kali, All-Destroyer, is the lightning in his hand. Is not this the truth?"

Nagir Jan bowed his head. Matap Rao made no sign.

"Surely you do not question the holiness of Jagannath, protector of the poor, guardian of the pilgrim and master of our souls?" continued the priest. "Nay, who am I but a lowly sweeper of the floor before the mighty god?"

He stretched out a thin hand.

"Jagannath casts upon you the light of his mercy, Rawul. He ordains that your faithlessness be forgiven. Thus does Jagannath weld in one the twin rulers of Kukushetra.

"If you seek forgiveness, Kukushetra will prosper and the hearts of its men be uplifted. To this end has Jagannath claimed the beauty of Retha. Your wife will be the bond that will bind your soul to its forgotten faith."

He smiled and lowered his hand. Dignified and calm, he seemed as he said, the friend of the Rawul.

"Is not this the truth, Matap Rao? Aye, it is so."

The priest ceased speaking and waited for the other to reply.

In his speech Nagir Jan had avoided the issue of Matap Rao's faith. He had spoken only of the claim of Jagannath. And a swift glance at his hearers showed him that his words had gone home. Many heads nodded approvingly.

The Rawul would not dare, so thought Nagir Jan, to attack the invisible might of Jagannath. By invoking the divinity of the god, Nagir Jan had made Matap Rao powerless to debate. And personal debate, he guessed, was the hope of Matap Rao.

Something of triumph crept into his cold face. Matap Rao was thoughtful, his eyes troubled. The chieftain was an ardent Hindu. How could he renounce his faith?

Abruptly his head lifted and he met the eyes of the priest.

"What you have said of Jagannath, incarnation of Vishnu, is verily the truth, Nagir Jan," responded the Rawul. "Yet it is not all the truth. You have not said that the *priests* of Jagannath are false. They are false servants of Vishnu. They are not true followers of the One who is master of the gods."

He spoke brokenly, as a man torn by mingled feeling.

"Aye. Wherefore do the priests of Kukushetra perform the rites in costly robes? Or anoint themselves with oil? With perfume, with camphor and sandal? Instead of the sacred Vedas, they chant the *prem sagar*—the ocean of love. The pictures and images of the temple are those of lust."

His voice was firmer now, with the ring of conviction.

"Aye, you are faithless servants. The rich garments that are offered by pilgrims to the gods, you drape once upon the sacred images. Then you wear them on your unclean bodies.

"What becomes of the stores of food yielded by peasants for the meals of Jagannath? Four times a day do you present food to the wooden face of the god; afterward you feast well upon it."

Nagir Jan showed no change of expression, but he drew back as if from contamination.

"You have forgotten the wise teachings of Chaitanya, who declared that a priest is like to a warrior," continued the Rawul. "The *gosain* preached that sanctity is gained by inward warfare, by self-denial and privation.

"You of Kukushetra follow the doctrine of Vallabha Swami. He it was who said that gratified desire uplifts the soul. And so do you live. What are the handmaidens of Jagannath but the prostitutes of the temple and its people?"

An uneasy stir among the listeners greeted this. Many heads were shaken.

"It is the truth I speak," cried the Rawul, turning to them. "Nagir Jan claims to be the friend of the poverty-afflicted. Is it so? He seeks devotees among the merchants and masters of wealth.

"He takes the fields of the peasants by forfeiture, contrary to law. He has taken much of my land. He seeks all of Thaneswar." The young chieftain spread out his arms.

"My spirit has followed the way of Chaitanya. I believe that bloodshed is pollution. My household divinity is the image of the sun, which was the emblem of my oldest forebears, whose fields were made fertile by its light. Is it not truth that a man may uplift his spirit even to the footstool of the One among the gods by *bahkti*—faith?"

While the watchers gazed, some frowning, some admiring, Abdul Dost touched the arm of Khlit and nodded approvingly.

"An infidel," he whispered, "but—by the ninety-nine holy names—a man of faith."

Nagir Jan drew his robe closer about him, and spoke pityingly. "Blind!" he accused. "Does not the god dwell in the temple?"

"Then," responded Matap Rao, "whose dwelling is the world?" He pointed at the priest. "What avails it to wash your mouth, to mutter prayers on the pilgrimage if there is no faith in your heart, Nagir Jan? For my faith, you seek to destroy me, to gain the lands of Thaneswar. And so you have asked Retha as the bride of Jagannath."

The shaven head of the priest drew back with the swift motion of a snake about to strike. But Matap Rao spoke before him.

"Well you know, Nagir Jan, that I will not yield Retha. If it means my death, Retha will not go to the temple."

"Thus you defy the choice of Jagannath?"

"Aye," said Matap Rao, and his voice shook. "For I know what few know. Among the ruins will the bride of Jagannath remain to-morrow night—where you and those who believe with you have said the god will appear as a man and foretell the omens, in the mystery of *Janam*. But he who will come to the woman is no god but a man, chosen by lot among the priests—perhaps you, Nagir Jan."

His tense face flushed darkly. He lowered his voice, but in the silence it could be heard clearly.

"The rite of *Janam* will be performed. But a *man* violates the body of the bride. It is a priest. And he prophesies the omens. That is why, O Nagir Jan, I have called the priests false.

"Never will the Lotus Face become the bride of Jagannath," he added quietly.

"Impious! Idolator!"

The head of Nagir Jan shot forward with each word.

"It is a lie, spoken in madness. But the madness will not save you." His eyes shone cruelly, and his teeth drew back from the lips.

"You have blasphemed Jagannath, O Rawul. You have denied to Jagannath his bride." He turned swiftly. "Thaneswar is ac-cursed. Who among you will linger here? Who will come with me to serve Jagannath? The god will claim his bride. Woe to those who aid him not—"

He passed swiftly from the hall and a full half of the peasants as well as many of the house-servants slipped after him. The soldiers around the Rawul stood where they were.

Rawul Matap Rao gazed after the fugitives with a wry smile. Old Perwan Singh laid down his *vina* and girded a sword-belt about his bony frame. Serwul Jain drew his scimitar and flung the scabbard away.

"The battle-storm is at the gate of Thaneswar," he cried in his high voice. "Ho—who will shed his blood for the Lotus Face? You have heard the words of your lord."

A hearty shout from the companion nobles answered him, echoed by a gruffer acclaim from the soldiery, led by Sawal Das. Matap Rao's eyes lighted but his smile was sad.

"Aye, blood will be shed," he murmured. "It is pollution—yet we who die will not bear the stain of the sin."

He laid an arm across the bent shoulder of the minstrel.

"Even thus you foretold, old singer of epics. Will you sing also of the fate of Thaneswar?"

Abdul Dost spoke quickly to Khlit of what had passed. His face was alight with the excitement of conflict. But the shaggy face of Khlit showed no answering gleam.

"There will be good sword-blows, O wayfarer," cried the Muslim.

"Come, here is a goodly company. We will scatter the rout of temple-scum! Eh!—what say you?"

Khlit remained passive, wearing every indication of strong disgust.

"Why did not yonder stripling chieftain prepare the castle for siege?" he growled. "Dog of the devil—he did naught but speak words."

He remained seated where he was while Abdul Dost ran to join the forces mustering under Serwul Jain at the castle gate. He shook his head moodily.

But as the Rawul, armed and clad in mail, passed by, Khlit reached up and plucked his sleeve.

"Where, O chieftain," he asked bluntly, "is Asil Rumi, defender of Thaneswar? He is yet armored—aye—the elephants are your true citadel—"

Not understanding *Mogholi*, and impatient of the strange warrior's delay, the Rawul shook him off and passed on. Khlit looked after him aggrievedly.

Then he shook his wide shoulders, yawned, girded his belt tighter and departed on a quest for food among the remnants of the banquet.

It was Khlit's custom, whenever possible, to eat before embarking on any dangerous enterprise.

V

And they paused to harken to a voice which said, "Hasten."
It was the voice of the assembler of men, of him who spies
out a road for many, who goes alone to the mighty waters. It was
Yama, the Lord of Death, and he said:
"Hasten to thy home, and to thy fathers."

Nagir Jan was not seen again at Thaneswar that night. But his followers heard his tidings and a multitude gathered on the road. Those who accompanied the Brahman from the hall could give only an incoherent account of the words Matap Rao had spoken. The crowd, however, had been aroused by the priests in the temple.

It was enough for them that the Rawul had blasphemed against the name of Jagannath. They were stirred by religious zeal, at the festival of the god.

Moreover, as in all mobs, the lawless element coveted the chance to despoil the castle. Among the worshipers were many, well armed, who assembled merely for the prospect of plunder. They joined forces with the more numerous party.

The ranks of the pilgrims and worshipers who had been sent down from the temple by the Brahmans was swelled by an influx of villagers and peasants from the fields—ignorant men who followed blindly those of higher caste.

The higher priests absented themselves, but several of the lower orders such as Kurral directed the onset against the castle. Already the enclosure was surrounded. Torches blazed in

the fields without the mud wall. The wall itself was easily surmounted at several points before the garrison could muster to
defend it—even if they had been numerous enough to do so.

"Jagannath!" cried the pilgrims, running toward the central
garden, barehanded and aflame with zeal, believing that they
were about to avenge a mortal sin on the part of one who had
scorned the gods.

"Jagannath!" echoed the vagrants and mercenary soldiers, fingering their weapons, eyes burning with the lust of spoil.

"The bride of Jagannath!" shouted the priests among the
throng. "Harm her not, but slay all who defend her."

Torches flickered through the enclosure and in the garden.
Frightened stable servants fled to the castle, or huddled among
the beasts. The neighing of startled horses was drowned by the
trumpeting of the elephants. A *mahout* who drew his weapon
was cut down by the knives of the peasants.

But it was toward the palace that the assailants pressed
through the pleasure garden, and the palace was ill-designed for
defense. Wide doorways and latticed arbors guided the mob to
the entrances. The clash of steel sounded in the uproar, and the
shrill scream of a wounded woman pierced it like a knife-blade.

The bright moon outlined the scene clearly.

Khlit, standing passive within the main hall, could command
at once a balcony overlooking the gardens and the front gate. He
saw several of the rushing mob fall as the archers in the house
launched their shafts.

A powerful blacksmith, half-naked, appeared on the balcony,
whither he had climbed, dagger between his teeth. A loyal peasant rushed at him with a sickle, and paused at arm's reach.

"Jagannath!" shouted the giant, stepping forward.

The coolie shrank back and tossed away his makeshift weapon,
crying loudly for mercy. He stilled his cry at a melodious voice.
"Chaitanya! Child of the sun!"

It was old Perwan Singh, walking tranquilly along the tiles
of the gallery in the full moonlight. The smith hesitated, then

advanced to meet him, crouching. The minstrel struck down the dagger awkwardly with his sword. Meanwhile the recalcitrant peasant had crept behind him, and with a quick jerk wrested away the blade.

Perwan Singh lifted his arm, throwing back his head. He did not try to flee. The black giant surveyed him, teeth agrin, and, with a grunt, plunged his dagger into the old man's neck. Both he and the coolie grasped the minstrel's body before it could fall, stripping the rich gold bangles from arms and ankles of their victim and tearing the pearls from his turban-folds.

Before they could release the body an arrow whizzed through the air, followed swiftly by another. The giant coughed and flung up his arms, falling across the body of the coolie. The three forms lay on the tiles, their limbs moving weakly.

Sawal Das, fitting a fresh shaft to string, trotted by along the balcony, peering out into the garden.

The rush of the mob had by now resolved itself into a hand-to-hand struggle at every door to the castle. The blood-lust, once aroused, stilled all other feelings except that of fanatic zeal. Unarmed men grappled with each other, who had worked side by side in the fields the day before.

A woman slave caught up a javelin and thrust at the assailants, screaming the while. For the most part the house-servants had remained loyal to Matap Rao, whom they loved.

By now, however, all within the castle were struggling for their lives. A soldier slew the woman, first catching her ill-aimed weapon coolly on his shield. Khlit saw a second woman borne off by the peasants.

At the main gate the disciplined defenders under Matap Rao, aided well by that excellent swordsman, Abdul Dost, had beaten off the onset. Serwul Jain and several of the younger nobles had been ordered to safeguard Retha.

They stood in the rear of the main hall, the girl tranquil and proud, her face unveiled, her eyes following Matap Rao in the throng. The Rawul, by birth of the *Kayasth*, or student, caste, proved himself a brave man although unskilled.

It was when the first assault had been beaten off and the defenders were gaining courage that the crackle of flames was heard.

Agents of the priesthood among the mob had devoted their attention to firing the thatch roof at the corners. Matap Rao sent bevies of house-servants up to the terraces on the roof, but the flames gained. A shout proclaimed the triumph of the mob.

"Jagannath!" they cried. "The god claims his bride."

"Lo," screamed a pilgrim, "the fire spirits aid us. The *daevas* aid us."

Panic, that nemesis of ill-disciplined groups, seized on many slaves and peasants who were in the castle.

"Thaneswar burns!" cried a woman, wringing her hands.

"The gods have doomed us!" muttered a stout coolie, fleeing down the hall.

Serwul Jain sprang aside to cut him down.

"Back, dogs!" shouted the boy. "Death is without."

"*Aie*! We will yield our bodies to Jagannath," was the cry that greeted him.

"Jagannath!"

Those outside caught up the cry.

"Yield to the god."

The backbone of the defense was broken. Slaves threw down their arms. A frightened tide surged back and forth between the rooms. A Brahman appeared in the hall and ran toward Retha silently. A noble at her side stepped between, taking the rush of the priest on his shield.

But the Brahman's fall only dispirited the slaves the more.

Khlit saw groups of half-naked coolies climbing into the windows —the wide windows that served to cool Thaneswar in the Summer heat. He walked down the hall, looking for Abdul Dost.

He saw the thinned body of soldiers at the gate struggle and part before the press of attackers. Then Bhimal, who had remained crouched beside him during the earlier fight, started up and ran, limping, at Serwul Jain.

"Jagannath!" cried the peasant hoarsely. "My brother's god."

He grappled with the noble from behind and flung him to the stone floor. Coolies darted upon the two and sank their knives into the youth. Bhimal stood erect, his eyes staring in frenzy.

"Jagannath conquers!" he shouted.

Khlit caught a glimpse of Matap Rao in a press of men. He turned in time to see Retha's guards hemmed in by a rush of the mob, their swords wrested from their hands.

Retha was seized by many hands before she could lift a scimitar that she had caught up against herself. Seeing this and the agony in the girl's face, Khlit hesitated.

But those who held the wife of the Rawul were too many for one man to encounter. He turned aside, down a passage that led toward the main gate.

He had seen Abdul Dost and Matap Rao fight loose from the men who caught at them.

Then for a long space smoke descended upon the chambers of Thaneswar from the smoldering thatch. The cries of the hurt and the wailing of the women were drowned in a prolonged shout of triumph.

The Rawul and Abdul Dost, who kept at his side, sought fruitlessly through the passages for Retha. Those who met them stepped aside at sight of their bloodied swords and stern faces. They followed the cries of a woman out upon the garden terrace, only to find that she was a slave in the hands of the coolies.

Matap Rao, white-faced, would have gone back into the house, but the Muslim held him by sheer strength.

"It avails not, my lord," he said gruffly. "Let us to horse and then we may do something."

The chieftain, dazed by his misfortune, followed the tall Afghan toward the stables, which so far had escaped the notice of the mob, bent on the richer plunder of the castle. Here they met

Khlit walking composedly toward them, leading his own pony and the Arab of Abdul Dost, fully saddled.

"Tell the stripling," growled Khlit, "that his palace is lost. Retha I saw in the hands of the priests. They will guard her from the mob. Come."

He led them in the direction of the elephant-stockade. He had noted that morning that a gate offered access to the elephants' pool. Avoiding one or two of the great beasts who were trampling about the place, leaderless and uneasy, he came upon a man who ran along the stockade bearing a torch.

It was Sawal Das, bow in hand. The archer halted at sight of his lord.

"I had a thought to seek for Asil Rumi," he cried. "But the largest of the elephants is gone with his *mahout*. *Aie!*—heavy is my sorrow. My lord, my men are slain—"

"Come!" broke in Abdul Dost. "We can do naught in Thaneswar."

Even then, loath by hereditary custom to turn their backs on a foe, the chieftain and his archer would have lingered helplessly. But Abdul Dost took their arms and drew them forward.

"Would you add to the triumph of Nagir Jan?" he advised coolly. "There be none yonder but the dead and those who have gone over to the side of the infidel priests.

"This old warrior is in the right. He has seen many battles. We be four men, armed, with two horses. Better that than dead."

A shout from the garden announced that they had been seen. This decided the archer, who tossed his torch to the ground and ran outward through the stockade and the outer wall.

Avoiding their pursuers in the shadows, they passed by the pool into the wood beyond the fields. Here a freshly beaten path opened before them. Sawal Das trotted ahead until all sounds of pursuit had dwindled. Then they halted, eyeing each other in silence.

Matap Rao leaned against a horse, the sweat streaming from his face. His slender shoulders shook. Khlit glanced at him, then fell to studying the ground under their feet.

Sawal Das unstrung his bow and counted the arrows in his quiver.

"Enough," he remarked grimly, "to send as gifts into the gullets of the Snake and his Kurral. They will not live to see Retha placed upon the car of Jagannath. I swear it."

Abdul Dost grunted.

Matap Rao raised his head and they fell silent.

"In the fall of my house and the loss of my wife," he said bitterly, "lies my honor. Fool that I was to bring Retha to Thaneswar when Nagir Jan had set his toils about it. I cannot face the men of Rinthambur."

"Rinthambur!" cried Abdul Dost. "Ho—that is a good word. The hard-fighting clan will aid us, nothing loath—aye, and swiftly. Look you, on these two horses we may ride there—"

"Peace!" said the Rawul calmly. "Think you, soldier, I would ride to Rinthambur when they still hold the wedding feast, and say that Retha has been taken from me?"

"What else?" demanded the blunt Afghan. "By Allah—would you see the Lotus Face fall to Jagannath? In a day and a night we may ride thither and back. With the good clan of Rinthambur at our heels. Eh—they wield the swords to teach these priests a lesson—"

"Nay, it would be too late."

"When does the procession of the god—"

"Just before sunset the car of Jagannath is dragged to the ruins."

"Then," proposed the archer, "if Vishnu favors us we may attack—we four—and slay many. Twilight will cover our movement near the ruins. Aye, perchance we can muster some following among the nearby peasants.

"Then will we provide bodies in very truth for the car of Jagannath to roll upon. From this hour am I no longer a follower of the All-Destroyer—"

Matap Rao smiled wanly. "So have I not been for many years, Sawal Das. My faith is that of the Rinthambur clan, who are called children of the sun. I worship the One Highest. Yet what has it availed me?"

He turned as Khlit came up. The Cossack had lent an attentive ear to the speech of the archer. He had completed his study of the trail wherein they stood. He swaggered as he walked forward—a fresh alertness in his gaunt figure.

"It is time," he said, "that we took counsel together as wise men and as warriors. The time for folly is past."

Abdul Dost and Sawal Das, nothing loath, seated themselves on their cloaks upon the ground already damp with the night dew. Matap Rao remained as he was, leaning against the horse in full moonlight notwithstanding the chance of discovery by a stray pursuer.

The mesh of cypress and fern branches overhead cast mottled shadows on the group. The moon was well in the West and the moist air of the early morning hours chilled the perspiration with which the four were soaked. They drew their garments about them and waited, feeling the physical quietude that comes upon the heels of forcible exertion.

Khlit, deep in the shadows, called to Sawal Das softly.

"What see you here in the trail?" he questioned. "This is not a path made by men, nor is it a buffalo-track leading to water."

The archer bent forward. "True," he acknowledged. "It is the trail of elephants. One at least has passed."

He felt of the broad spoor. "Siva—none but Asil Rumi, largest of the Thaneswar herd, could have left these marks. They are fresh."

"Asil Rumi," continued Khlit from the darkness. "It is as I thought. Tell me, would the oldest elephant have fled without his rider?"

"Nay. Asil Rumi is schooled in war. He is not to be frightened. Only will he flee where his *mahout* leads. Without the man Asil Rumi would have stayed."

"This *mahout*—is he true man or traitor?"

"True man to the Rawul. It is his charge to safeguard the elephant. He must seek to lead Asil Rumi into hiding in the jungle."

"A good omen."

Satisfaction for the first time was in the voice of the Cossack.

"Now may we plan. Abdul Dost, have you a thought as to how we may act?"

The Muslim meditated.

"We will abide with the Rawul. We have taken his quarrel upon us. He may have a thought to lead us into the temple this night, while the slaves of Jagannath sleep and the plundering engages the multitude—"

"Vain," broke in the archer. "The priests hold continued festival. The temple wall is too high to climb and the guards are alert. Retha will be kept within the sanctuary of the idols, under the gold dome where no man may come but a priest.

"The only door to the shrine is through the court of offerings, across the place of dancing, and through the audience hall—"

"Even so," approved Khlit. "Now is it the turn of Sawal Das. He has already spoken well."

"My thought is this," explained the archer. "There will be great shouting and confusion when the sacred car is led from the temple gate. A mixed throng will seek to draw the car by the ropes and to push at the many wheels.

"We may cover our armor with common robes and hide our weapons, disguising our faces. Men from the outlying districts will aid us, for they are least tainted by the poisonous breath of the Snake—"

"Not so," objected the Afghan, ill pleased at the archer's refusal of his own plan. "Time lacks for the gathering of an adequate force. Those who were most faithful to the Rawul have suffered their heads and hands cut off and other defects.

"Besides, the mastery of Thaneswar has passed to the Snake. When would peasants risk their lives in a desperate venture? Eh— when fate has decreed against them?"

"Justly spoken," said Khlit bluntly. "Sawal Das, you and the Rawul might perchance conceal your likeness, but the heavy bones of Abdul Dost and myself—they would reveal us in the throng. It may not be."

"What then?" questioned the archer fiercely. "Shall we watch like frightened women while this deed of shame is done?"

"Has the chieftain a plan?" asked Khlit.

Matap Rao lifted his head wearily.

"Am I a warrior?" he said calmly. "The Rinthambur warriors have a saying that a sword has no honor until drawn in battle for a just cause. This night has brought me dishonor. There is no path for me except a death at the hands of the priests—"

"Not so," said Khlit.

The others peered into the shadows, trying to see his face.

"You have all spoken," continued the Cossack. "I have a plan that may gain us Retha. Will you hear it?"

"Speak," said Abdul Dost curiously.

"The temple may not be entered. The multitude of worshipers is too great for the assault of few men. Then must the chieftain and Abdul Dost ride to Rinthambur as speedily as may be."

"And Retha?" questioned the Rawul.

"Sawal Das and I will fetch the woman from the priests and go to meet you, so that your swords may cover our flight."

Matap Rao laughed shortly. To him the rescue of Retha seemed a thing impossible.

"Is my honor so debased that I would leave my bride to the chance of rescue at other hands?"

Whereupon Abdul Dost rose and went to his side respectfully. He laid a muscular hand on the shoulder of the youth.

"My lord," he said slowly, "your misfortune has befallen because of the evil craft of men baser and shrewder than you. Allah—you are but a new-weaned boy in experience of combat. You are a reader of books.

"Yet this man called the Curved Saber is a planner of battles. He has had a rank higher than yours. He has led a hundred thousand swords. His hair is gray, and it was said to me not once but many times that he is very shrewd.

"It is no dishonor to follow his leadership. I have not yet seen him in battle, but I have heard what I have heard."

The Rawul was silent for a space. Then, "Speak," he said to Khlit.

While they listened Khlit told them what was in his mind, in few words. He liked not to talk of his purpose. He spoke to ease the trouble of the boy.

When he had done Sawal Das and Abdul Dost looked at each other.

"*Bismillah!*" cried the Afghan. It is a bold plan. What! Think you I would ride to Rinthambur and leave you—Khlit—to act thus¿'

"Aye," said the Cossack dryly. "There is room for two men in my venture; no more. Likewise, two should ride to the rajas, for one man might fail or be slain—"

Matap Rao peered close into Khlit's bearded face.

"The greater danger lies here," he said. "You would take your life in your open hand. How can I ask this of you?"

Khlit grunted, for such words were ever to his distaste. "I would strike a blow for Retha," he responded, but he was thinking of Nagir Jan.

His words stirred the injured pride of the Hindu.

"By the gods!" he cried. "Then shall I stay with you."

"Nay, my lord. Will the chieftains of Rinthambur raise their standard and mount their riders for war on the word of a stranger —a Muslim? So that they will believe, you must go," adding in his beard, "and be out of my way."

So it happened before moonset that Abdul Dost and the Rawul mounted and rode swiftly to the West through paths known to the chieftain.

At once Khlit and Sawal Das set forth upon the spoor of Asil Rumi, which led north toward the farm of Bhimal. Now as he went the little archer fell to humming under his breath. It was the first time he had sung in many hours.

VI

When the shadows lengthened in the courtyard of the temple of Kukushetra the next day a long cry went up from the multitude. From the door under the wheel and flag of Vishnu came a line of priests.

First came the strewers of flowers, shedding lotus-blossoms, jasmine and roses in the path that led to the car of Jagannath. The bevy of dancing women thronged after them, chattering excitedly. But their shrill voices were drowned in the steady, passionate roar that went up from the throng.

The temple prostitutes no longer drew the eyes of the pilgrims. Their task in arousing the desires of the men was done. Now it was the day of Jagannath, the festival of the *Janam*.

Bands of priests emerged from the gate, motioning back the people. A solid wall of human beings, straining for sight of the god, packed the temple enclosure and stretched without the gates. A deeply religious, almost frenzied mass, waiting for the great event of the year, which was the passage of the god to his country seat—as the older ruined temple was termed.

A louder acclaim greeted the appearance of the grotesque wooden form of the god, borne upon the shoulders of the Brahmans. The figure of Jagannath was followed by that of the small Balabhadra, brother to the god, and Subhadra, his sister.

Jagannath was carried to his car. This was a complicated wooden edifice, put together by reverent hands—a car some fifteen yards long and ten yards wide, and lofty. Sixteen broad wooden wheels, seven feet high, supported the mass. A series of platforms, occupied by the women of the temple, hung with garlands of flowers and with offerings to the god, led up to a wide seat, wherein was placed Jagannath.

This done, those nearest the car laid hold of the wheels and the long ropes, ready to begin the famous journey. The smaller cars of Balabhadra and Subhadra received less attention and fewer adherents.

Was not Jagannath Lord of the World, chief among the gods, and divine bringer of prosperity during the coming year? So the

Brahmans had preached, and the people believed. Had not their fathers believed before them?

The decorators of the idols had robed Jagannath in costly silk and fitted false arms to the wooden body so that it might be sightly in the eyes of the multitude.

The cries of the crowd grew louder and the ropes attached to the car tautened with a jerk. A flutter of excitement ran through the gathering. Had they not journeyed for many days to be with Jagannath on the *Janam?*

As always in a throng, the nearness of so many of their kind wrought upon them. Religious zeal was at a white heat. But the Brahmans raised their hands, cautioning the worshipers.

"The bride of Jagannath comes!" they cried.

"Way for the bride of the god!" echoed the pilgrims.

The door of the temple opened again and Retha appeared, attended by some of the women of the wardrobe. The girl's slim form had been elaborately robed. Her cheeks were painted, her long hair allowed to fall upon her shoulders and back.

A brief silence paid tribute to the beauty of the woman. She glanced once anxiously about the enclosure; then her eyes fell, nor did she look up when she was led to a seat beside and slightly below the image of the god.

Once she was seated the guardians who had watched her throughout the night stepped aside. In the center of the crowd of worshipers Retha was cut off from her kind, as securely the property of the god as if she still stood in the shrine. For no one among the throng but was a follower of Jagannath, in the zenith of religious excitement.

The priests formed a cordon about the car. Hundreds of hands caught up the ropes. A blare of trumpets from the musicians on the car, and it lurched forward, the great wheels creaking.

"Honor to Jagannath!" screamed the voice of Bhimal. "The god is among us. Let me touch the wheels!"

The machine was moving forward more steadily now, the wheels churning deep into the sand. The pullers sweated and groaned, tasting keen delight in the toil; the throng crushed closer. A woman cried out, and fainted.

But those near her did not give back. Instead, they set their feet upon her body and pressed forward. Was it not true blessedness to die during the passage of Jagannath?

Contrary to many tales, they did not throw themselves under the wheels. Only one man did this, and he wracked with the pain of leprosy and sought a holy death, cleansed of his disease.

Perhaps in other days numbers had done this. But now many died in the throng, what with the heat and pressure and the strain of the excitement, which had continued now for several days.

Slowly the car moved from the temple enclosure, into the streets of the village, out upon the highway that led to its destination. The sun by now was descending to the horizon.

But the ardor of the pilgrims waxed higher as the god continued its steady progress. For the car to halt would be a bad omen. And the dancing women, stimulated by bhang, shouted and postured on the car, flinging their thin garments to those below and gesturing with nude bodies in a species of frenetic exaltation.

Those pushing the car from behind shouted in response. The eyes of Nagir Jan, walking among the pilgrims, gleamed. Kurral, crouched on the car, had ceased to watch the quiet form of Retha.

Rescue now, he thought, was impossible, as was any attempt on her part to escape. For the car was surrounded the space of a long bowshot on every side.

The wind which had fluttered the garlands on the car died down as the shadows lengthened. The leaders of the crowd were already within sight of the shrine whither they were bound.

Retha sat as one lifeless. Torn from the side of her husband and carried from the hall of Thaneswar, she had been helpless in the hands of the priests. A proud woman, accustomed to the deference shown to the clan of Rinthambur, the misfortune had numbed her at first.

Well knowing what Matap Rao knew of the evil rites of Jagannath, to be exhibited to the crowd of worshipers caused her to flush under the paint which stained her cheeks.

She would have cast herself down from the car if she had not known that the Brahmans would have forced her again into the seat. To be handled by such a mob was too great a shame.

She had heard that Matap had escaped alive the night before. One thought kept up her courage. Not without an effort to save her would the Rawul allow her to reach the shrine where the rites of that night were to take place.

This she knew, and she hugged the slight comfort of that hope to her heart. Rawul Matap Rao would not abandon her. But, seeing the number of the throng, even this hope dwindled.

How could the chieftain reach her side? But he would ride into the throng, she felt, and an arrow from his bow would free her from shame.

At a sudden silence which fell upon the worshipers she lifted her head for the first time.

Coming from the shrine of the elder gods she saw a massive elephant, appareled for war, an armored plate on his chest, sword blades fastened to his tusks, his ears and trunk painted a bright orange and leather sheets strapped to his sides. And, seeing, she gave a low cry.

"Asil Rumi!"

The elephant was advancing more swiftly than it seemed at first, his great ears stretched out, his small eyes shifting. On his back was the battle *howdah*. Behind his head perched the *mahout* wearing a shirt of mail. In the *howdah* were two figures that stared upon the crowd.

Asil Rumi advanced, interested, even excited, by the throng of men. Schooled to warfare, he followed obediently the instructions of his native master, scenting something unwonted before him. Those nearest gave back hastily.

For a space the throng believed that the elephant was running amuck. Never before had man or beast interfered with the progress of the god. But as Asil Rumi veered onward and the leading pullers at the ropes were forced to scramble aside an angry murmur went up.

Then the voice of Kurral rang out.

"Infidels!" he cried. "Those upon the elephant are men of Matap Rao."

The murmur increased to a shout, in which the shrill cries of the women mingled.

"Blasphemers! Profaners of Jagannath! Slay them!" Nagir Jan raised his arms in anger.

"Defend the god!" he shouted. "Turn the elephant aside."

Already some men had thrust at Asil Rumi with sticks and spears. The elephant rumbled deep within his bulk. His wrinkled head shook and tossed. His trunk lifted and his eyes became inflamed. He pushed on steadily.

A priest stepped into his path and slashed at his trunk with a dagger.

Asil Rumi switched his trunk aside, and smote the man with it. The priest fell back, his skull shattered. A soldier cast a javelin which clanged against the animal's breastplate.

Angered, the elephant rushed the man, caught him in his trunk and cast him underfoot. A huge foot descended on the soldier, and the man lay where he had fallen, a broken mass of bones from which oozed blood.

Now Asil Rumi trumpeted fiercely. He tasted battle and glanced around for a fresh foe.

The bulk of the towering car caught his eye. With a quick rush the elephant pressed between the ropes, moving swiftly for all his size and weight.

The clamor increased. Men dashed at the beast, seeking to penetrate his armor with their weapons; but more hung back. For from on the *howdah* a helmeted archer had begun to discharge arrows that smote down the leaders of the crowd. The *mahout* prodded Asil Rumi forward.

The elephant, nothing loath, placed his armored head full against the car. For a moment the pressure of the crowd behind the wooden edifice impelled it against the animal. Asil Rumi uttered a harsh, grating cry and bent his legs into the ground.

He leaned his weight against the car. The wooden wheels of Jagannath creaked, then turned loosely in the sand. The car of the god had stopped. A shout of dismay went up.

Then the *mahout* tugged with his hook at the head of Asil Rumi. Obedient, even in his growing anger inflamed by minor wounds, the elephant placed one forefoot on the shelving front of the car. The rudely constructed wood gave way and the mass of the car sank with a jar upon the ground, broken loose from the support of the front wheels.

By now the mob was fully aroused. Arrows and javelins flew against the leather protection of the animal and his leather-like skin, wrinkled and aged to the hardness of rhinoceros hide.

A shaft struck the leg of the native *mahout* and a spear caught in his groin under the armor. He shivered, but retained his seat. Seeing this, Khlit clambered over the front of the *howdah* to the man's side.

"Make the elephant kneel!" he cried.

Asil Rumi knelt, and the forepart of the car splintered under the weight of two massive knees. It fell lower. Now Asil Rumi was passive for a brief moment, and Sawal Das redoubled his efforts, seeking to prevent the priests with knives from hamstringing the beast.

"Come, Retha!" cried Khlit, kneeling and holding fast to the headband beside the failing native.

The woman was now on a level with him. She understood not his words, but his meaning was plain. The shock to the car had dislodged many of the men upon it.

The temple women clutched at her, but she avoided them. She poised her slender body for the leap.

"Slay the woman!" cried Kurral, scrambling toward her.

A powerful Bhil perched beside the head of the elephant and slashed once with his scimitar. The blow half-severed the *mahout's* head from the body. Before he could strike again Khlit had knocked him backward.

Retha sprang forward, and the Cossack caught her with his free arm, drawing back as Kurral leaped, knife in hand. The priest missed the woman. The next instant his body slipped back, a feathered shaft from the bow of Sawal Das projecting from his chest.

"Ho—Kurral—your death is worthy of you," chanted the archer. "Gully jackal, scavenger dog—"

His voice trailed off in a gurgle. And Khlit and the girl were flung back against the *howdah*. Asil Rumi, maddened by his wounds and no longer hearing the voice of his master, started erect.

He tossed his great head, reddened with blood. His trumpeting changed to a hoarse scream. The knives of his assailants had hurt him sorely.

The sword blades upon the tusks had been broken off against the car. The leather armor was cut and slashed. Spears, stuck in the flanks of the elephant, acted as irritants. His trunk—a most sensitive member—was injured, and his neck bleeding.

While Khlit and Retha clung beside the body of the *mahout*, Asil Rumi shrilled his anger at the throng of his enemies. He broke crashing from the ruins of the car wherein lay the unattended figure of Jagannath, and plunged into the crowd. Weaving his head—its paint besmirched by blood—Asil Rumi raced forward.

He rushed onward until no more of his tormentors stood in his path. Then the elephant hesitated, and headed toward the trail up the hill which led down to his quarters at Thaneswar.

"Harken," said a weak voice from the *howdah*.

Khlit peered up and saw the archer's face strangely pale.

"Asil Rumi will run," said Sawal Das, "until he sees the body of the native fall. Hold the *mahout* firmly."

A few foot soldiers had run after the elephant in a half-hearted fashion. There were no horsemen in the crowd, and few cared to follow the track of the great beast afoot. Asil Rumi had struck terror into the worshipers.

His appearance and the devastation he had wrought had been that of no ordinary elephant. Among the Hindus lingered the memory of the elder gods of the ruins from which Asil Rumi had so abruptly emerged. And some among them reflected that Vishnu, highest of the gods, bore an elephant head.

So had the deaths inflicted by Asil Rumi stirred their fears.

The sun had set, and the crimson of the western sky was fading to purple. The calm of twilight hung upon the forest through which Asil Rumi paced, following the trail. A flutter of night birds arose at his presence, and a prowling leopard slunk away at the angry mutter of the elephant, knowing that Asil Rumi was enraged and that an angry elephant was monarch of whatsoever path he chose to follow.

Again came the voice of Sawal Das, weaker now.

"My heart is warm that the Lotus Face is saved for my lord," it said—neither Khlit nor the girl dared to look up from their precarious perch where the branches of overhanging cypresses swept.

"An arrow—" the voice failed—"tell the Rawul how Sawal Das fought—for my spirit goes after the *mahout*—"

A moment later a branch caught the *howdah* and swept it to earth. Retha and Khlit clung tighter to the head-straps, pressing their bodies against the broad back of Asil Rumi. Khlit did not release his grasp on the dead native.

The wind of their passage swept past their ears; the labored breath of the old elephant smote their nostrils pungently. Ferns scraped their shoulders. They did not look up.

It was dark by now, and still Asil paced onward.

Dawn was breaking and a warm wind had sprung up when Matap Rao and Abdul Dost with the leaders of the Rinthambur clan passed the boundary tower of Thaneswar. A half-thousand armed men followed them, but few were abreast of them, for they had ridden steadily throughout the night, not sparing their horses.

Dawn showed the anxious chieftain the unbroken stretch of the Thaneswar forest through which he had passed on his bridal journey. He did not look at those with him, but pressed onward.

So it happened that Rawul Matap Rao and two of the best mounted of the Rinthambur riders were alone when they emerged into a glade where a path from Thaneswar crossed the main trail. And here they reined in their spent horses with a shout.

In the path lay the body of a native. Over the dead man stood the giant elephant, caked with mud and dried blood, his small eyes closed and his warlike finery stained and torn. And beside the elephant stood Khlit and Retha.

What followed was swift in coming to pass. After a brief embrace the Rawul left his bride to be escorted back to Rinthambur by Khlit and Abdul Dost at the head of a detail of horsemen while he and the Rinthambur men wrested Thaneswar from the priests.

It was a different matter this, from the assault upon the palace by Nagir Jan, and the followers of the temple were forced to give way before the onset of trained warriors.

The religious fervor of the Kukushetra men had suffered by the misfortune that befell their god before the ruins, and the fighting was soon at an end.

But it was not until Matap Rao was again in Thaneswar with Retha that Khlit and Abdul Dost turned their horses' heads from the palace. Peace had fallen upon the province again, for Matap Rao had sent a message to the shrine of Puri, and the high priests of Vishnu, among whom the ambitions of Nagir Jan had found no favor, had judged that Nagir Jan had made wrong use of his power and sent another to be head of the Kukushetra temple.

"Aye, and men whispered that there was a tale that the mad beast of the ruins was the incarnate spirit of an older god," laughed Abdul Dost, who wore new finery of armor and rode a fine horse—the Rawul had been generous. "Such are the fears of fools and infidels."

Khlit, who rode his old pony, tugged his beard, his eyes grave.

"It was not the false gods," he said decidedly, "that saved Matap Rao his wife. It was verily a warrior—an old warrior. But how can the Rawul reward him."

Abdul Dost glanced at Khlit curiously.

"Nay," he smiled; "you are the one. You are a leader of men, even of the Rawul and his kind—as I said to them. Belittle not the gratitude of the chieftain. He would have kept you at his right hand, in honor. But you will not."

"Because I am not the one."

"Sawal Das?"

"Somewhat perhaps."

Khlit's voice roughened and his eyes became moody.

"Asil Rumi is the one. Truly never have I seen a fighter such as he. Yet Asil Rumi is old. Soon he will die. Where is his reward?"

Whereupon Khlit shook his broad shoulders, tightened his rein and broke into a gallop. Abdul Dost frowned, pondering. He shook his handsome head. Then his brow cleared and he spurred after his friend.

The Masterpiece of Death

In the dust of the crossroads are marks of many feet. Some have come from the desert to the well; some have passed through the jungle—and they are weary. Some there are that have passed under the spur of fear and others follow after these.

He who is keen of eye will read the tale that is written in the dust of the crossroad. He who is dull and heavy with sleep—he sees the mark of a snake in the sand and thinks it a trailing rope.

But a snake has crossed the road.

Beside the road, in the jungle, a grave is dug for the one who is blind of eye, and dull.

This is the tale of the crossroad, and it is true.

Jhond, the money-carrier, walked slowly, aiding his tired feet with his staff. Behind him plodded a mule weighted with heavy saddlebags. The shadows were lengthening across the shimmering heat of the highway. And the mule lagged on its halter, sensing the approach of evening and a halt under the cypress trees that lined a nearby water course.

This was on the road that entered the Ghar Pass, at the headwaters of the Jumna River in Pawundur province. In the accounts of the great *vizier*, master of the treasury of Jahangir, Mogul of Hindustan, the Pawundur province was written down as the most northeastern of Hindustan proper, and was noted as lawless. All this being in the year of our Lord 1609.

Obedient perhaps to the mute urging of his mule, Jhond turned into the cypress *nullah*, followed by his dog, a nondescript of brown skin and visible bones, a byproduct of the Delhi bazaar and a beneficiary of the kindliness of aged Jhond, who was scarcely less beggarly or less sharp and furtive of eye.

Those who were walking beside the money-carrier guided him down the *nullah* away from the road to a cleared space. They were chance wayfarers, not guards, for the men of Jhond's profession traveled alone. Their pride of caste rendered large sums safe in their keeping and their poor garb made them safe from ordinary thieves.

Jhond was tired for he had made a long stage on an important mission. He was glad that the Muslim merchants—they were four—who had caught up with him at the entrance of the Ghar knew the way. One who had gone ahead awaited their coming in the glade beside a ditch, wherein two coolies sat.

Two of the merchants led him to a brook. He was thirsty. The fourth had lingered behind to see that no thieves had marked their passage from the main road. The dog whined.

"Drink," said one. "Here is the place."

"Aye," said Jhond and knelt.

A strip of cloth passed over his eyes and tightened around his neck. One of the men at his side gripped both his arms. While Jhond was held thus, the noose closed until he could no longer breathe. The dog ran about in little circles, whining and barking at the men.

When there was no longer any life in Jhond, his body was mutilated by kicks in the vital parts and cast into the ditch. The two filled in the ditch with fresh earth. This done, a fire was lighted on the grave so that the upturned earth should be concealed.

Not until then did the watch return from the high road with the word that they had not been seen. The six men went to the mule and ransacked the heavy leather sacks. They had, before this, searched the grimy clothing of the money-carrier and found nothing.

Nor was there gold or silver in the sacks; nothing but meal and a few pieces of cloth. Jhond, the money-carrier, had not had anything of value about him; nothing except the mule. This was strange.

But fate also was strange. And the men who had slain him were accustomed to the vagaries of fate. Besides, they had the mule. And they would have slain for less.

An owl hooted in the gathering darkness. Whereupon the men chattered anxiously together. Again came the cry of the owl. This time they took up their belongings, loaded them upon the animal and departed. They were heedful of omens.

But before they went they killed the dog by a blow on the skull with a stick. Otherwise the mourning beast might have dug into the grave or attracted other men to the spot.

So when they had gone there was nothing upon the spot where Jhond had planned to camp for the night: nothing, that is, except the dead dog and the embers of the fire, which soon went out.

Which was—all of it—as the six men dressed as merchants had planned.

"And after Jhond," explained the elegant Nazir u'din Mustafa Mirza, "was sent one named Chutter."

Mustafa Mirza—a tall man with narrow eyes and a thin beard, surnamed "the Moghuli"—leaned back upon the carpet which was spread on the balcony, halfway down into the well. The well was in the outer court of the Pawundur palace and it provided a grateful shade for those who wished to escape the heat that beat into the sun-dried clay of the courtyard.

"Chutter," he said, "was a trusted servant of my master. Alas! Few may be trusted in this land of dust and wind and thorns and tangled ferns. But my master, the *ameer*, trusted Chutter."

He inserted a portion of betel nut in his crimson-stained mouth and yawned, expelling thereafter the wind from his stomach after the manner of a beast. For Mustafa Mirza was sure of the interest of his two listeners. He had a rare tale to tell and it concerned them.

Idly he fingered the turquoise chain at his scrawny throat and gazed attentively into the tiny mirror upon a ring which ornamented a none-too-clean thumb. He was weaponless, yet his tunic was rich with spoil, taken after the manner of the conquering Muslims from the Hindu merchants and their women.

"It was perhaps two moons ago during the festival of Miriam that Chutter was sent to the pass of Ghar, to the tower of Ghar," he resumed. "And no trace—not so much as a sandal or the skin of his mule—had we found of the money-carrier Jhond. It was said that the half-eaten body of his dog was seen in a *nullah* where an owl feasted. Ho! Yet where the dog was Jhond was not. He may have camped there. Some ashes were seen. I know not."

"What of Chutter?" asked one of the listeners.

"Aye, Chutter. A slave. A dog of many fathers. He was mounted on a good horse. A pity, that; for the horse also was lost. He rode from here toward Ghar. An armed trooper followed him. That was at my bidding. Although my master, the *ameer*—may his shadow be long on the land of Pawundur—trusted Chutter, yet I trusted not the child of a *Gentu*, or Hindu."

He chewed at the betel and spat, after picking his teeth.

"Nevertheless it availed not. After sunset one day the trooper thought he heard a scream, choked off in the middle—thus." Mustafa Mirza snarled shrilly, then coughed gutturally. "The rider put spurs to his horse, for Chutter, the Gentu dog, was a bare double bowshot ahead. He saw lying upon the road a man clothed like a merchant of Samarkand. The man was writhing in a fit and foam was on his lips. So the trooper dismounted.

"The sick man, however, was not Chutter. And when the trooper reined forward again there was naught to be seen on the road save many footprints in the dirt. There was a deep pool near at hand. The man saw some shadows moving in the brush nearby and stayed not to look twice. He had a fear—a heavy fear."

The two listeners looked at each other and the Moghuli eyed them with satisfaction. His tale was worth hearing.

"The trooper swore," he went on, "that it was the voice of Chutter that cried out. He asked that the bottom of the pool be dragged and the body of Chutter found, to bear out his tale. But why should the *ameer* pay coolies to search for the body of a slave such as Chutter? Doubtless, he had died—after the manner described by the trooper. The man who lay in the road in a fit had been a trick. After the soul of Chutter had gone to join his fathers, whoever they be, it was hard to get a rider to seek Ghar on the mission. All said that death lay in wait under the cypress trees of the pass."

"Why did not you go, Mustafa Mirza?" asked one of his companions.

"I?" The Muslim stared and shrugged his shoulders. "Allah! This is a good land, full of jewels and slim women. I prefer them to the houris of paradise. Besides, my master, the liberal and gracious *ameer*, asked it not. Instead he purchased with gold mohars the services of one Jhat—a Sikh who was fresh come from Peshawar, a cousin by marriage of Chutter. The Sikh, who bore himself like a warrior, said that he had no fear. He swore that no evil demons or wayside thieves would keep him from gaining Ghar Tower on the mission.

"Jhat Singh traveled by night only. During the day he slept. He thus went far up the Ghar Pass, along the river Jumna. For a time we thought that he had reached the tower, and my master and I were glad. Yet his fate was otherwise. We learned it from a fisherman of the upper Jumna.

"This man was lying in his boat, having spread his nets. The sun was very hot and he was half-asleep when he saw Jhat Singh— he described the clothing and weapons of the Sikh and we knew it was the truth—he saw Jhat Singh pass along the trail by the river where the men walk who pull the ropes of the boats, going upstream. With the warrior were about a dozen other men who the fishermen said were boatmen. Yet they had no boat."

Mustafa Mirza nodded, pleased with his own acumen. "The Sikh was a fool, or overbold—perchance both. At this place, so said the man, the trail entered a thicket. He saw Jhat Singh and the others go into the thicket. One remained behind, looking at the fisherman who rowed over, hoping to sell some of his catch. The man on the bank bought some fish.

THE MASTERPIECE OF DEATH

" 'Perhaps,' said the fisher, 'if I go into the thicket after the others, they also will buy.'

"He was eager because a good price had been paid. The other man smiled. 'If they buy,' he said, 'another than you will spend the money.' Whereupon the fisherman rowed away after he had looked attentively upon the watcher. When he glanced back over his shoulder the man had gone."

"Why," asked one of the men who sat beside the *mirza*, "did this fellow row away?"

Mustafa Mirza smiled, baring his red tooth.

"*Ai*—he was wise. He recognized the watcher as one of a band of slayers. As he had thought, the party emerged from the farther side of the thicket, but Jhat Singh was not with them. The fisherman waited until near twilight. Then he crept into the thicket. He searched some time before he came upon the body of the Sikh. There was no mark or wound upon it. But it had been stripped of its weapons. Then the fisherman ran away hastily, for that was an evil place."

"He was a coward!" said the questioner gruffly.

"Nay," objected Mustafa Mirza, "he was wise. He had fished long in the waters of the Jumna and knew that there were those who slay men for spoil, so skilled that none ever see the manner of the slaying. He named them by some strange word, such as *tag*. I remember not. But the breath of Jhat Singh was no longer in his body, and a new man was needed for the mission of my master."

Yawning, the officer of the *ameer* lay back on the cushions and surveyed his two companions. There was curiosity in the glance of his quick, dark eyes—curiosity and cold appraisal.

"Thus, as I have said," he concluded, "the three who were sent on the mission to the tower of Ghar died. The generous *ameer* has offered you much gold to follow after them." Mustafa Mirza corrected himself hastily. "To go into Ghar Pass, I mean. For we desire not your death. Rather must the mission succeed. For it is time my master should have that which is in Ghar."

He offered his betel to the others, who refused.

"They died," nodded the *mirza*. "It was their fate—dogs of *Gentus*. But you, Abdul Dost, are a follower of the Prophet and a noted swordsman. And you, Khlit, surnamed the Curved Saber, are one who has grown gray in the path of battles."

Leaning forward, he placed a hand on the knee of each. Khlit, wise in the ways of men, had no doubt of his earnestness.

"I have a thought," said Mustafa Mirza. "You twain may win to Ghar. For Khlit is a *Ferang**★* and the slayers of the pass seldom lift hand against a *Ferang*."

Khlit looked up from under shaggy brows. He did not like others to touch him. "The *ameer* pays well," he grunted. "What manner of men are these slayers?"

"Who knows?" Mustafa Mirza stretched forth both hands, palms up. "My master and I have heard but a word here, a whisper there. Bands of the slayers go throughout Pawundur province; aye, and Hindustan. By no mark are they known. Often they have the appearance of merchants. It is not well to ask too closely. They are powerful."

"You have a fear of them in your heart," grumbled Khlit. "Does the governor of Pawundur, this *ameer*, allow murderers to walk the roads of his province?"

The other shook his head helplessly.

"By the beard of my grandsire! How can we do otherwise? The Mogul asks only that the tribute gleaned from Pawundur be given promptly to his *vizier*. And the slayers have harmed none of our household. Yet they have girded Ghar about like waiting snakes. Perhaps they have a smell of what is within the tower."

Abdul Dost swore impatiently.

"*Bismillah!* Give us spare horses and we will ride through the nest of scorpions like wind through the jungle!"

★ European.

"Horses!" The *mirza*, sighed, then assented eagerly. "Aye, you shall have two—the best. Think you, then, you will go to Ghar?"

Khlit made a warning sign to Abdul Dost who was ever impatient of precautions. Not so the Cossack. He had lived too long and seen too many men die at his side to be reckless of safeguards.

"Is there not another way to Ghar?" he asked thoughtfully.

"Nay—from here. The tower is at the summit of the pass. Hills, and below them blind forest mesh and swamps, make the Jumna trail the only road. It would be the ride of a month to gain the other side—the East. And there the paths are ill. You must go and return within the month. Has not my master promised as much gold as you can hold in two hands?"

"Aye," said Khlit dryly. "Have you seen these slayers?"

"Not I. It is said they live in the villages, like the usual *Gentu* farmers and drivers of bullock carts. Only when they wander in bands do they slay. Perhaps they are magicians, for they are never seen to slay nor is blood-guilt ever fastened upon them. It is said they have a strange god. I know not. I have spoken thus fully, for it is my wish that you return unharmed. Will you accept the mission?"

"We will talk together," said Khlit, "and in the morning we will come to the *ameer* with our answer."

"So be it," assented Mustafa Mirza. "Perchance, if your decision is as I expect, my master, who is the soul of generosity, will give the two good horses in addition to the gold."

With that Khlit and Abdul Dost rose and left the shadow of the well. They went to their tent, pitched in a corner of the village caravansary—an open space within a tumble-down wall by the high road, littered with dust and the droppings of beasts who had been there with former caravans. While Khlit boiled rice over his fire in silence and set out the melons and grapes they had purchased with their last silver in the bazaar, Abdul Dost talked.

"What are these slayers," he questioned idly, "but some bands of coolies? *Aie*—would they attack two riders such as you and I? We who have earned a name for our swords in Kukushetra?"

The two wanderers had aided the young Rawul of Thaneswar, nearby, and the fame of their exploit had preceded them—reaching, probably, the ears of the *ameer*, and arousing his interest in them as warriors useful for his own ends.

"The *ameer* promises reward to the value of a half dozen fine horses, and you and I have not a dinar in our girdles to buy a new saddle or a bracelet."

"Promises cost little to the speaker."

"Aye, but the need of the *ameer* is great."

This was true, as Khlit knew. Within a month the *vizier* would come from the court at Delhi for the annual payment of the tax of Rawundur—of the *jagir* sold to Ameer Taleb Khan.

It was customary in the empire for the Mogul to lease the various provinces to his officials, who would pay him a settled price for the privilege of squeezing all possible tribute from the people of the district—the Hindu farmers, priests and landholders.

The *ameer* had already begged off his first year's payment, on plea that Rawundur was rebellious. He had actually been engaged in putting down the gathering of certain hill clans. During his efforts he had deposited the accumulation of his treasury in a safe spot.

This had been the tower of Ghar, where a watchman had been posted. Khlit wondered why one man should be entrusted with so much wealth—pearls, diamonds, Venetian ducats, with various assortments of gold and silver trinkets.

The treasure, explained the *ameer*, was safe for two reasons. No one outside Mustafa Mirza and the watchman knew of its location in the tower. And the watchman was well able to protect his charge. Taleb Khan had smiled across the whole of his broad, good-natured face when he said this.

But now the disaffection was put down and the *vizier* was coming. Taleb Khan had no valid excuse to refuse payment of his two years' tax this time. He had gleaned much wealth by crushing the district. He must pay the tax or satisfy the *vizier*. So he dispatched three trusted men to Ghar Tower, bearing missives written by him and signed with his signet. All three had been slain.

This was unfortunate. Although he did not admit as much, Khlit gathered that the *ameer* was afraid to go himself, and the *mirza* likewise.

He dared not send a party of soldiers, so great was the wealth of the treasury. He had, he said, heard of Khlit and Abdul Dost. Sufficiently he trusted them to send them on the mission. They would be rewarded well.

The slayers, he thought, would not molest a *Ferang*. Nor did they ever rob where they did not first slay their victim.

Somewhat Khlit wondered at this. Who were these bands that went unarmed? How was it they had killed unmolested? How had Jhond, the carrier of money, been spirited off the face of the Earth? Or Jhat Singh slain without leaving a trace upon his body? Khlit had reason to know that the Sikhs were excellent fighters and well able to take care of themselves.

"Why," he observed to Abdul Dost, "will this *ameer* entrust us with the carrying of his treasure?"

The Muslim was partaking of the rice and bread cakes. He had a ready answer, although it came from a full mouth.

"Why does a dog trust a man with his bone when the dog is chained? Our worthy *ameer* has no other staff to lean upon. The chains that bind him are fear—of the slaying bands and the coming of the *vizier*. He has no other riders to send save you and I."

He swallowed the rice and muttered a brief phrase of thanksgiving to Allah. Abdul Dost was a devout man, of the finer type of Muslim.

"Likewise," he reasoned shrewdly, "the *ameer* knows to a grain the sum of his treasure. He will satisfy himself that we render it in full. If we chanced to flee—and I would not scorn to take his wealth from yonder stout official—his outposts in the district would catch up with us."

Khlit looked up curiously. The speech of Abdul Dost had struck deeper than the Afghan knew.

"Why barter further?" grumbled Abdul Dost. "The *ameer* needs his gold, and we also have need of the reward. Have you a fear of the thieves?"

Khlit grunted. The Muslim was well aware of the Cossack's bravery. But Khlit was in the habit of pondering a venture well. He, contrary to Abdul Dost, was in a strange country. His sagacity had kept him alive and had served his companion well.

"What think you, *mansabdar*?" he asked, wiping his hands on his sheepskin coat. Khlit would not abandon his heavy attire for the lighter garb of the country.

"With two good horses, and a remount each, you and I will ride to Ghar. Eh—if the low-born thieves come against us on the way, we will swing our scimitars and their blood will moisten the dust. But Taleb Khan must pay us the price of ten Kabul stallions for this deed."

Khlit did not answer at once. He was wondering what the tower of Ghar would be like. Why had the wealthy *ameer* selected it as a treasure house? He rose and went into the tent, stretching his tall bulk on the cotton cloths that the cleanly Abdul Dost provided for their sleeping.

"Tomorrow we will seek this *ameer*," he said.

The broad face of Taleb Khan lighted at sight of the two warriors. He was relieved that they had come. They were hardy men, he thought, and hardier riders. If any could win through to Ghar, these two could. Had they not withstood many times their number of foes, fighting without reward, when they had been guests at Thaneswar?

Ameer Taleb Khan reasoned that they would serve him as faithfully since he was paying a reward. He reckoned the value of men in mohars. He had calculated to a nicety the sum of gold that could be drained from the province. He knew to an ounce of silver the treasure now lying in Ghar. Aye, the two warriors would fetch back the gold and silver and jewels. And after they had left the dangerous pass of Ghar—

Smilingly Taleb Khan bent his head, although neither Khlit nor Abdul Dost had made the customary salaam. He wanted to show them he was in a gracious mood. He had dire need of their services. But this he did not care to reveal to them.

His small, womanish features puckered pleasantly. An olive hand stroked the gold chain at his throat. He lifted his face to feel the refreshing draft from the peacock fan that a woman slave moved over his head. She was a fair woman. Taleb Khan had an eye for such. He had sought out among the villages the comeliest maidens who were not yet given in marriage. In this Mustafa Mirza had been no mean agent.

For his good offices the *ameer* had allowed his favorite official to keep certain of the women for himself. True, the villagers murmured. But what were they save low-born? The Hindu nobles had become restive. Yet what availed their frowns and hard words when the power of the Mogul rested like a drawn scimitar behind the plump, silk-turbaned head of the *ameer*?

Still, unless the money was forthcoming to be given into the hand of the approaching *vizier*, displeasure of the Mogul would fall like a blight upon Taleb Khan.

The *ameer* sighed. He liked well the feel of gold coins and the luxury of Chinese silk, of perfume of attar, of the delight of opium and bhang, the light of great diamonds, the solace of boat festivals upon the lakes of Pawundur.

But greater than his lust for treasure was his fear of his imperial master. Somehow, the *vizier* must be appeased.

"You will undertake the mission?" he asked, not quite concealing his anxiety, as Abdul Dost noted.

An Afghan, whether warrior or merchant, is a born barterer. Not so Khlit.

"Three men have died upon the journey," parried Abdul Dost. "We ask a price of five fine horses each—of Kabul stallions, flawless, of straight breeding."

The plump lips of Taleb Khan drew down. He motioned to the slave to dry the perspiration on his cheeks with a cloth scented with musk.

"It is too high a price," he objected. "All that I have I must render to the Mogul. Would you rob the Lord of Lords?"

"Liar!" thought Abdul Dost. Aloud he said: "The slaying thieves beset the forests of Ghar. I am *mansabdar*, not a common soldier to be bought and sold. Ten horses or their price—"

"Agreed," said the *ameer* hastily. "But the treasure must be intact."

Abdul Dost frowned. "Am I a bazaar thief, O man of the Mogul? The treasure will be given to your hands."

"I meant but that none should be taken from you. Is the thing then agreed?"

"Aye," said Khlit impatiently. "Give to us the money and an extra pony apiece. We shall ride hard."

"Verily," assented the *ameer*, smiling again. "You are brave men." He drew a rolled sheet of parchment from the breast of his tunic and glanced at the seal which had been affixed with his ring.

Abdul Dost started. The letter, if it was such, was blank. Seeing his surprise Taleb Khan nodded reassuringly.

"My watchman is not a scholar. He cannot read. But the seal and the message—that Taleb Khan waits at Pawundur for the wealth that is his—will be sufficient. Eh, if a letter were stolen from you, and the thieves could read, would they not then proceed to Ghar and despoil the tower?"

He spoke idly and Khlit wondered how much of truth was in the words. Evidently the *ameer* had little fear that his treasure would be wrested by other hands from its abiding place.

"These thieves," he said gruffly, "the dogs know of the treasure. Or they would not have slain the other messengers."

"They suspect," admitted Taleb Khan. "But they know not. Likewise, they have a fear of the watchman of Ghar. But you will be safe." There was unmistakable earnestness now in his modulated voice. "Ride swiftly, as you plan," he added. "Mingle not with others, no matter who."

Abdul Dost nodded, taking the missive and securing it in his girdle.

"Take the trail by the Jumna, on the return journey. It is best, if you can, to hire a boat on the river. But make sure that no others are on the boat. Going up the valley you must ride, but when you turn your faces hither the current of the river will bear your boat."

When they had gone he leaned back upon the cushions, frowning in thought. Once he made as if to call them back; then he changed his mind, snuggling his plump shoulders among the cushions after the manner of a cat. But clearly Taleb Khan was not altogether at ease.

"All the others have died," he muttered. "Yet these two be tall men and masters of the scimitar."

He repeated that phrase as if to satisfy himself.

"If it is the will of Allah, they will come back in the boat."

Suddenly he threw back his head and laughed shrilly. He motioned to the slave.

"Bhang!" he commanded. "It is my wish to eat bhang. I would be eased of the heat of your demon-ridden land!"

Abdul Dost and Khlit had mounted after selecting with discernment two of the best ponies of the *ameer*'s stables. These they led by the halters. In their saddlebags they had placed rice, oatmeal cakes and, in Khlit's case, dried meat sufficient for a journey of eight or nine days.

As they had promised, they rode at a good pace, and on the evening of the second day reached the caravansary at the crossroads some miles from the entrance to the pass. All the other three had journeyed safely past this point.

Now at the crossroads was a group of tents. A seller of garments had taken up his station here, also a vendor of Ganges water and rotting fruit. Within the wall of the caravansary was located a more elaborate tent of reddish color before which was stretched a carpet.

As Khlit and the Afghan rode their tired horses into the enclosure and looked about for a clean space—no easy matter to find—where the Muslim could say his sunset prayer and the Cossack cook supper, an ancient beldame emerged from this tent and laid hand upon their reins.

"*Aie*—you are men from the North," she greeted them. "Your throats are dry and you are stiff from the irking of the saddle. This is verily a goodly spot for you to alight."

She pointed with a wizened arm, covered with cheap bangles, to the carpet.

"Therein is Daria Kurn," she explained, "one of the most beautiful of the nautch—women of Lahore. Verily she is a favorite of the wealthy nobles of Lahore. She will play upon the oina and your ears will be charmed with music as fine as the rustle of silk; perhaps, if she is minded, she will dance the dance of the ascent of the stars and your spirits will be comforted."

The aged woman rambled on. Abdul Dost, peering at the tent entrance, saw a girl seated on the carpet within. A pair of dark eyes sought his and he saw a *kohl*-stained face, shaped, as he thought, like the interior of a pink shell.

Abdul Dost shrugged his shoulders and would have dismounted but Khlit checked him with a gesture.

The nautch-girl was walking toward them, swaying on her slippered feet after the manner of slaves. Her silver anklets clinked gently. In the soft light of that hour the brocade of her bodice gleamed and the silk of her trousers, worn after the Persian fashion, glimmered.

Her dark hair was confined under a cloth-of-silver cap, the lower part of her round face concealed by the *yashmaq*. In one hand she bore a tambourine, which she jingled idly as she scrutinized the two men. Although her dress was that of a Persian Muslim, she resembled more a Hindu type.

"Come, my diamond-sheen," crooned the beldame, "my pretty dove, my precious pearl. Lower your veil and show the noble lords the light of your sun-adorning fairness. We will dance for the exalted *ameer*s and their souls will sink in an ocean of delight. Oh—" to the men—"Daria Kurn is verily a moon of resplendent beauty. Her henna toes spurn the silk carpet as lightly as wind kisses silk—"

"I will not dance!" said the girl abruptly.

She spoke carelessly but decisively. The faded eyes of the old woman gleamed harshly.

"Unutterable filth!" she cried. "Scum of the back alleys of the bazaar! Parrot-tongue—disobedient wanton! Eh—will you starve your friends with your whims? Will you—"

Abdul Dost had quietly dismounted and washed in the well at one corner. He had spread the prayer carpet that he always carried upon the ground by the well. Now his sonorous voice, as he faced toward the *Kaaba*, cut into the shrill harangue of the woman.

"*L'a illoha ill Allah*," he repeated devoutly. "There is no god but Allah. *Allah, ill karim Allah ill hakim*—"

He continued the course of his sunset devotions. Daria Kurn eyed him curiously, jingling her tambourine. Once an owl hooted and she turned her head on one side, much after the manner of the parrot that her protectress had just proclaimed her.

Khlit saw the two women speak together in low tones. Presently Abdul Dost rose, folded up his carpet and mounted with a leap. He urged his tired horse after the Cossack as Khlit left the caravansary.

As long as they were visible in the dull, golden afterglow of twilight, Daria Kurn watched them silently as they trotted down the highway, raising a cloud of dust that swirled upward in the breeze.

Abdul Dost had something to grumble about. "No thieves were there," he muttered. "It is customary for the singing and dancing girls to frequent places on the main roads. Have they bewitched you?"

"Better a dozen thieves," said Khlit dryly, "than two women. We will sleep in the forest."

In this manner did the two enter the pass of Ghar.

II

That same evening dusk brought out the lights of a nearby village. The bullocks had been stabled, the few sheep were penned, an array of smoke columns moved up from the thatched hamlets. Torches were visible, crossing from hut to hut. Somewhere a woman was singing softly, perhaps to a child. Boyish laughter shrilled from the vicinity of the water tank. It was followed by the deep cough of a beast close by in the bush.

Whereupon silence fell briefly on the village.

For the most part the men—farmers, hunters and merchants—squatted on their mats, chewing or drinking slowly and absorbing the cool of evening into their tired bodies. But one went quietly from house to house and talked with the owners.

He was Dhurum Khan, one of the chiefs of the village.

Those to whom he spoke girded their waist-cloths, yawned, stretched, and went out into the darkness, bearing bundles. One or two led forth a laden mule. Few spoke to their wives who watched intently.

Said one:

"The trading caravan goes to Lahore. It will be absent long, perhaps one month, perhaps two, perhaps three."

"I will bring back ten lengths of cloth—you will have a new garment. Peace be with you!" said another.

Yet all who assembled were not merchants. Several were weavers, some tillers of the soil, one a money-changer—he was a Muslim of the North—another a water-carrier of lower caste than the rest.

They formed into an irregular line, led by Dhurum who walked for some distance before he halted. Then he faced the dim figures, for the group carried no lights, and laid his hand on the shoulder of a youth.

"My son comes upon this journey, men of Pawundur," he announced slowly. "He will become a *bhurtote*."

A murmur of assent, even of mild admiration, went through the crowd, which numbered perhaps a score and a half.

"Aye, Dhurum Khan, *Jemadar*," they said.

Whereupon the leader ran his eye along the line of dim faces, calling softly a roster of names. Each man responded promptly. They spoke softly, understanding each other readily, yet their words were neither *Turki*, Hindustani, *Mogholi*, or Persian, nor any of the Punjab dialects. It was an argot of comparatively few phrases, but one with which they were very fluent.

"Come!" concluded Dhurum Khan. "It is the time ordained by the earth mother, the season sacred to Kali, to Bhawani, the All-Destroyer. A sixth of our goods have we already given to her priests, who are well content. Is this not so?"

"Aye, it is truth."

"Aforetimes did one of us see Kali in human form, feeding upon a body that the servant had slain. Since then has Kali grown great with our worship. Her shrine has its allotted gifts. Blood, sunk into the earth, is as pleasing to her divinity as water falling upon the roots of a dry plant. Come, we will perform the offices of Kali."

"It is time," assented a voice.

"It is time to trade," added another with satisfaction.

"Jaim Ali," responded Dhurum Khan, "my son, will share our trading venture. For the first time, he will buy goods—as one of us. But he will no longer bury them underground. He must be taught. Bhawani Bukta, the Hindu, will teach him. He will be the *guru* of my son."

Dhurum Khan turned in his tracks and resumed his progress. "The *Kassi* awaits," he said.

Now as they went a strange thing occurred. Bhawani Bukta, the bent carrier of water, still lugging his goatskin, stepped to the front like an assured leader. A weaver and a scavenger—the last of the lowest caste in the village—began to assume the guardianship of others who had been highly regarded merchants of illustrious ancestors in the village. Methodically the caste of all in the group underwent a silent change and those who had been ignoble straightened and expanded before the tacit reverence of their comrades.

They walked on silently, eyes and ears keen. Was it not the time for the omens to be observed?

They went silently, leaning slightly forward, their bare legs invisible in the dark, their turbaned heads turning alertly this way and that. The warm spell of evening faded into the clamorous night of the bush. Heavy dew moistened their arms and shoulders. Dhurum Khan halted beside a field where one of them had been wont to nurse growing grain.

As quietly as before they followed him into the field. A dark form, slender as a woman, stepped to the front of the group and pointed out a spot where a tuft of lush weeds showed in the grain.

"Herein is the *Kassi*," he whispered, and straightway the *jemadar* and the water-carrier began to dig with their hands.

When they uprose they held an object between them. It was a short pickax. Carefully Dhurum Khan wiped the dirt from it with the corner of his girdle. Again his soft voice came to their attentive ears. An undistinguishable murmur went through the gathering, an instinctive, almost feline voicing of satisfaction; it resembled the *purr* of a cat.

"The *Kassi*," said Dhurum Khan pleasantly, "has been tempered according to the ritual of our fathers at the forge of a high-caste smith. It has been washed first in water, then in water mixed with the sacred *gur*. Then in milk and in wine. It is marked with the seven spots."

"Aye, I have seen it." Young Jaim Ali tried hard to make his voice sound unexcited.

"It has been burned with cloves, sandalwood and *gur*," repeated the *jemadar*. "Yet the fire injured it not. Is it not verily the tool of Kali? On this journey we will carry it for the first time."

"May it be auspicious!"

"Heed then the omens!" Dhurum Khan's deep voice became stern. "We are not masters of our acts. We serve another. The omens are the talk of the other. Make sure that your ears are keen. Tell me what you observe. The voice of Kali speaks from the top of the temples. Yet our eyes cannot see all of her temples. Oftentimes does she call from a tree-top or the rock of a ravine."

"We will hear."

Along the road passed the silent group, some walking well in advance, others behind. Except for their characteristic watchfulness, they betrayed no unusual interest in their progress.

In this manner did the *thags*, sometimes called *thugs*, march from a village of Pawundur.

"A lizard chirped," called one eagerly.

"Good!" echoed Dhurum. "An auspicious omen, although not of the highest order. In the direction of the sound we will go. Is there a trail?"

"A bowshot beyond is a trail," growled Bhawani Bukta. "It leads to the Ghar Pass."

The night passed swiftly without further omen and the band went ahead with more assurance. The first streaks of dawn were gleaming in their faces when the foremost scouts sighted the glimmer of a fire. Three persons—Punjabi traders, they reported —were encamped by the fire and were already stirring to resume their journey.

Dhurum Khan gave orders with the skill of long experience. Several of the band, including those bearing the sacred pickaxes, plunged into the jungle, skirting the fire of the traders toward a point farther ahead on the road.

Two *thags*, dressed as coolies, plodded past the fire down the road without heeding the salutation of the traders. They were to form the advance lookout. If any strangers came toward them, the two were to delay them in talk, or, if need be, pretend sudden sickness—even a fit!

A similar outpost was sent back along the way they had come. The bulk of the gang who wore the garb of merchants then proceeded slowly forward, leading the mules.

They talked as they went, and laughed. The good omen was bearing swift fruit. Bhawani Bukta, hidden in the group beside the anxious Jaim Ali, untwisted the folds of his turban—a yellowish cloth. This he doused with water and tied one end in a firm knot.

"So your hand will not slip back along the cloth," he whispered in the *thaggi* jargon.

He bound the free end into a dexterous slip-noose, sliding it back and forth to make sure it was clear.

"Twist not the *rumal* into too small a cord," he advised sagely, "or it will leave a mark on the man's throat. Nor leave it too wide or it will catch on his chin."

Jaim Ali nodded, understanding. He had ridden with the band twice. The first time, two years ago, he had been a child of eleven and they had only permitted him to linger near the murders and to share the spoil. The second time he had witnessed first a burial, then a strangling. Now he was ready to become a full-fledged *bhurtote*—a slayer.

No knight, watching beside his arms in a church, was more intent on performing the ordeal in a fitting manner; no warrior-father more anxious than Dhurum Khan that the deed should go well and the auspices be good for his son's advancement.

So as they went they chanted softly the hymn to Kali that few outside the ranks of *thaggi* have heard. Breaking off sharply near the traders' fire, they fell to chattering and laughing. Dawn was outlining the treetops.

The Punjabis had adjusted the packs on their mules and were stamping the stiffness from their limbs after sleeping the night. Then Dhurum Khan gave a low exclamation of dismay. The Punjabis were in the road ahead of them, but one, revealed in the clearer light, proved to be a woman mounted on a mule.

"An ill fate!" he cried. "They are not our prey. We may not slay a woman."

It was not chivalry that restrained the *thag*s from the killing of women, only the belief that the female form was molded after that of Kali, their goddess. Even so, they often strangled women, especially when the victims were in the company of other men and the spoil was good.

For the laws of *thaggi*—rigid as the doctrines of the Buddhist faith—prescribed that no victims should be robbed without being first slain: also that none in a party should be permitted to escape. True, very young children were sometimes taken and adopted, but only if they showed no overmastering grief for the slain parents.

In northern Rájputana the *thag*s thus slew women often. And in the Punjab, where the *thag*s were powerful, it was done by the Mohammedans who were most numerous in these gangs. But even so it was considered an unfortunate thing, and penance was generally offered—gifts to the Brahmans or days of prayer—when a woman was strangled.

"Jaim Ali must not become a *bhurtote* if a woman's blood sinks into the earth," said Dhurum Khan, but hesitantly, for the omen had been good.

Bhawani Bukta slipped to his side.

"Nay, it is true," assented the *guru*, or teacher, of the boy. "Yet another may slay the woman."

"But the deed will be the same."

Bhawani Bukta shook his head slowly.

"The deed must come to pass. These are the victims we have sighted. It was ordained by fate. Already is their grave being dug."

"Then let my son not try his hand at this time."

Again the water-carrier, who was experienced in the lore of the cult, demurred. "We have said the prayer to Kali for the creation of a new strangler. It must be. Likewise, it would be unpardonable to ignore the omen of the lizard."

Dhurum Khan hesitated anxiously. A wave of uncertainty swept through the throng. A vital issue was at decision. They awaited the word of their elders in the cult, as they walked forward, apparently carelessly, toward the three who were awaiting their arrival, glad to have the company of merchants of their own class on the dangerous road.

Then from the right came the wailing cry of a single jackal. As one man the throng sighed in relief.

"It is *one* jackal," cried the water-carrier softly.

"An omen of the highest order," assented Dhurum Khan, not quite assuredly.

"Kali has spoken," put in another.

"Jaim Ali is marked as fortunate—if he slays swiftly and well."

The *thag*s pressed forward cheerily. The dark clouds of doubt had vanished, even as the sun flooded in on them through the trees. They waved happily at the waiting merchants and the woman—a slip of a girl perched on the mule, regarding them gravely from dark eyes under a hood.

Likewise, the Punjabis caught the contagion of their mood. Dhurum Khan's mild, benevolent face dispelled any doubt they might have felt that these were thieves. They had all the seeming of wealthy and reputable merchants.

Besides, the Punjabis were strangers in the district. They fell into step beside the *thag*s. Quietly the latter shifted their positions until two men were on either side the girl, one with the *rumal* hidden under his cloak being a Mohammedan who had been hastily allotted the venturous fate of slaying the woman.

Bhawani Bukta and Jaim Ali stepped near one of the men. Dhurum Khan fell to the rear. He had explained to the strangers that his group were merchants of the upper Jumna, bound for Simla with rare Portuguese cloths laden upon the mules. The Punjabis expressed a desire to see the cloths.

Willingly Dhurum Khan halted the animals when his keen eye told him he was abreast the spot where certain men were digging in the thicket.

The Punjabis bent over the unrolled lengths of cheap muslin. Bhawani Bukta cleared his throat.

"*Ae ho to ghiri chulo,*" he said to the girl. "If you come to join us, pray descend."

It was the signal. One of the Punjabis, recognizing the jargon or taking fright too late, cried out and sprang away.

"Death!" he shouted and began to run wildly down the road.

But his comrade groaned and staggered. Jaim Ali's cloth was about his throat. The knot was drawn tight.

The girl gave a startled gasp, and was pulled from her mule by strong hands. A *rumal* passed over her slender throat, and the Muslim strangler watched until her frail, twisted features had frozen into quietude. The *thag*s gave no heed to the escaped Punjabi.

But presently Dhurum Khan, who was watching, saw two of his comrades slip from the shadows at the side of the road and bury their knives in the body of the fugitive.

This done the slayers stepped aside and burial *thag*s took their places. The three bodies were carried quickly to the newly dug grave. There they were stabbed under the armpits to make certain of their death. Skillfully the earth was piled over them.

Some coolies, passing by the spot presently, saw a group of jovial merchants seated about a fire, some asleep, others sorting out the contents of the packs of the mules with them. The coolies went on, not suspecting that the bodies of the three Punjabis were under the ashes of the fire.

When they had gone the throng came to Jaim Ali and bent before him. He stood proudly beside Bhawani Bukta.

"He is a slayer!" they cried. "He has done well."

Unstinted admiration was in the words. Dhurum Khan smiled.

"We will eat *gur,*" he proclaimed, "in honor of my son."

They partook solemnly of the rich and heady sugar, which is doctored highly by the *thag*s. It was in one a food, a sweet and a stimulant. But the brow of the *jemadar* was not altogether clear. He was gratified by his son's success, no less than by the omens. But he still doubted because of the forbidden slaying of the woman. Perhaps he should have kept her to be the wife of his son.

"A shadow lies over us," he announced gravely.

"Perchance," admitted Bhawani Bukta, "for no other good omens have appeared since to indicate the approval of Kali."

"It is an evil thing," said Dhurum Khan.

A heavy silence fell upon the group who looked at their two leaders. The *jemadar* lifted his head in decision.

"My share of the spoil," he announced, "I will give to the Brahmans. But more we must do to avert the shadow. Else must we return to the village, and that is not wonted."

They waited expectantly. They had committed the murders with the dreadful skill of which they were masters. They considered that they had but done what was fated, that the gods were pleased.

"Six days will we pray," said Dhurum Khan, "and the place we will pray will be the presence of one who is high in our faith. We will go just beyond the mouth of the Ghar and rest there. Thus we will pray and lighten the shadow. For my doubt is heavy."

Thus it happened that Khlit and Abdul Dost, riding fast along Ghar Pass, found the way free of slayers, nor did they set eyes upon a thief, because the slaying of the woman had led the gang back toward Pawundur.

III

The shrine of Naga is covered with weeds. It is hidden in the forest. The passersby see it not. Other shrines have they built and worshipped.

Many have cried, "Naga is dead!"

Does a god die? Nay. For the passerby, parting the leaves of the forest, will see the stones of the shrine and one who watches thereon.

The wind of the foothills of the Siwaliks whistled up the Ghar Pass, stirring the ferns that clung to the giant oaks and sounding a strange tune as it pierced the tall, fragile bamboos.

Quivering, the delicate stems of the bamboos bent and nodded to the wind. The sound grew to a melodious, multitudinous whistle. For many hands had made holes in the bamboo stalks cunningly, leaving round apertures for the passage of the wind. Its coming was heralded up the pass as it bore the heavy scent of decaying lush grass and the odor of dying dahlias and jasmine.

Vividly the sun etched the shadows of the bamboo leaves and touched the moss on the piles of stone about the tower foot. A man, squatting against a stone, lifted his face to the sun and sighed.

His form was like that of a bamboo, lean so that the bones of his shoulders, ribs and arms showed through his gleaming brown skin. A turban of immaculate white muslin bound his head tightly. His beard grew low on his naked chest. His dark face was stamped with weariness.

"Little Kehru," he chanted gravely, "I hear you. You are coming through the sirki grass, walking like a panther upon your four limbs. You are holding your breath, and just now you gave the hiss of a contented cobra."

The man's eyes were closed but he pointed directly at a clump of grass, tall as an elephant's back, which was waving strangely in the wind.

"Little Kehru," he said mildly, "our friends, the sweet bamboo stalks which we cook and eat, you and I, they also are making a hiss. But the sound of a snake is not like to the rustle of the grass. And the sound of your coming is like the trot of a fat pig. I hear you."

The clump of grass was still a moment, then a child burst from it, laughing. He was naked except for a clean breech-clout. In a basket slung to his back he carried some mangoes.

"You were awaiting me, Ram Gholab," he accused. "Soon I will deceive you, O grandsire, and I will pounce upon you like a falcon that has marked a sparrow in the thicket. O, I am clever. I am wise. *Grrh-uugh*! I will pounce upon you someday and then you will laugh. Now you never laugh."

The lad reached his grandfather's knee and laid down the fruit. Ram Gholab reached forward and felt of it approvingly. Kehru might have been ten years of age. Probably he had no reckoning of the years. In his estimation he was already growing to the stature of a warrior. Was he not sole master, with of course Ram Gholab, of the upper Ghar?

"What saw you, O Kehru?"

"I saw that the kites have left the thicket far, far down where they flew to feast during the last moon—the thicket by the jumna bank. I saw no fishermen in the upper river. There were no feet marks in the upper trail, save those of sleek agni."

"No horses have passed upward?"

"Nay. Only, I saw the white crane of Saravasti and harkened to the talk of the *bandur.*"

"Were the *bandur* clamorous or slothful?"

"*Aye*—they called to me lazily, as if their bellies were full. All is well, they said, though not in words. They would have liked me to climb the trees, but I was running."

Kehru stretched himself proudly. "How well I run!" he said reflectively. "Soon I will keep pace with the antelope of the plain. But I would rather ride a horse. Why have not you a pony, Ram Gholab?"

"I have no silver. How could I have silver, O one-of-small-reason?"

"There is plenty in the inner cavern where—"

"That is forbidden." A stern note crept into the mild voice of the old man. "It is kept for our master."

"The fat *ameer*?"

Curiosity was mirrored in the boy's changing face. He was fathoming new depths. Ram Gholab talked little.

"Nay. Who is the Muslim but a slave of a slave? The master I named is Lord of Lords. He also is a Muslim by prayer, yet his mother was a Hindu and we of Pawundur serve him because of this."

"I have no mother. I am a free man." Thus Kehru soliloquized while Ram Gholab listened gravely. "The Lord of Lords is the Mogul. That is true. I know. He never goes forth except upon a picked elephant, and when he sets foot to ground the earth quakes. He has warriors as many as the ants in the sand-heaps. I have seen some riding through the villages when I climbed the trees of the lower forest. They had plumes on their turbans and the sun shone on their mail. Why have not you a bright scimitar, grandsire?"

"It is not lawful. My caste bears not weapons."

"But I do not want to play upon a pipe. I would like a horse between my legs and a good sword to cut off the heads of my enemies."

Ram Gholab's eyes puckered. He had not once opened them. The sadness deepened in his face.

"It is in the blood," he murmured. "Yet how may I who am blind teach the use of sword?" He took up a reed-like instrument and set it to his lips. "Eat, Kehru," he said. "I have brought grapes."

While the boy munched the fruit, Ram Gholab played upon his pipe. One at a time from various crevices in the stones issued cobras. They moved slowly toward the two, their beautiful brown and purple-green forms twisting lazily.

"Is the milk set for their eating?" questioned the master of the snakes.

"Aye," responded the child from a full mouth.

A hooded cobra had crept across his foot. Kehru lifted it partially between his toes with a slow, caressing motion and set it down farther away. The shrill, sweet notes of the pipe went on.

Suddenly Ram Gholab ceased, and at the same instant Kehru lifted his shaggy head. The ears of each were equally keen, but the hearing of the elder was more significant, from the experience of years. Some of the snakes moved away.

"Horses—several," mused Ram Gholab. "Two by their gait bear riders."

The boy had wriggled away, carefully stepping over the snakes, and darted to the clump of grass from which he had recently emerged. This point gave on the half-overgrown trail to Ghar Tower.

"Two strange warriors," he called softly, "and two led horses."

The snake charmer nodded.

"Perhaps, Kehru," he assented, "they have come—whom we awaited. Hide until I am certain of this thing. Are they armed?"

"Both. They have swords as big as my leg."

Kehru hid himself instantly in the grass. A crashing of bamboo stems, a quick *thud-thud* of tired horses spurring up a slope, and Khlit and Abdul Dost drew rein before the watchman of Ghar.

"Ho!" cried the Muslim, wiping the sweat from his eyes. "This is an evil place to find. We were not told that Ghar was a ruin and veiled in the forest."

He was about to swing down from his horse, but hesitated. "By the face of the Prophet! Never have I seen so many snakes!"

"Soon they will go," said Ram Gholab calmly. "But speak your names and your mission in Ghar."

Abdul Dost did so in broken Hindustani, eyeing the snakes alertly. Khlit glanced curiously over the tumble-down tower and the stone-heaps.

"The *ameer*," grumbled Abdul Dost, "warned of certain slayers in the forest. *Bismillah!* We have slept in our saddles and crossed the river thrice to escape pursuit, but not a thief has shown his evil face."

"It is well you did so. They are afoot. Throw me the letter."

Abdul Dost did so. Ram Gholab felt toward the sound of the paper striking the earth and picked it up. He felt of the seal.

"He is blind," observed Khlit.

"A strange watchman!"

Ram Gholab smiled under his beard.

"I have other eyes," he said. "Kehru! Come, light a fire before me."

The boy emerged from his nook, staring round-eyed at the tall warriors. He fetched dried sticks, leaves and a flint-stone. This he struck skillfully until the spark caught in the leaves.

When a small flame was flickering brightly, Ram Gholab extended the blank letter Abdul Dost had given him over the fire. He waited until it had become alight. It burned slowly in his fingers, and the two horsemen smelled a strong odor, strange to them, that resembled musk.

Then the Hindu withdrew careful from a knot in his own girdle a similar sheet of white parchment. He burned this also, sniffing at the odor. Apparently he was content.

"It is well," he said. "You have come from the fat slave of the Mogul."

Khlit mused upon the unusual method of identification and realized its advantages. As the *ameer* had said, no one seizing upon the missive would know for what it was intended. And certainly, despite his blindness, Ram Gholab was not easily to be deceived. He did not know, however, that a further precaution had been adopted.

"Dismount," instructed the snake charmer, "and tether your horses in the grove at the rear of the tower. There they will be less likely to step upon the snakes."

"The snakes!" cried Abdul Dost. "You mean the horses will be safer there."

"Nay. What I have said is the truth. Here the cobras are worshipers at the shrine within the tower. It is the shrine of Nagi. Molest them not. And likewise beware of them for your own sake."

He picked up a great, mottled cobra and showed its poison fangs intact.

"By allah!" muttered Abdul Dost to himself. "If one moves toward me Nagi will lack a worshiper."

He was beginning to understand why the tower of Ghar was safe from intruders.

"Come, O watchman of the snakes, our bellies yearn and we are weary of dried meal cakes. Give us food."

Ram Gholab rose and moved back to the tower in the manner of one who well knew his way. Khlit and his comrade followed, after seeing to the comfort of their horses.

The tower itself, although in ruinous condition, was of more recent building than the shrine it surmounted. Khlit scrambled over the stone-heaps—not without a wary eye for the cobras despite the stout, yak-hide boots he wore—into the rear postern gate. Here he found Kehru busied in preparation of porridge, milk, curried rice and mangoes.

Wide-eyed, the boy gazed on the tall warrior, noting Khlit's broad leather belt and smooth, leather boots, his black sheepskin hat, and the gold chasing on his scabbard. He marked the swagger of the Cossack—the walk of a man better accustomed to a saddle than the earth. And he drew in his breath with a hiss of admiration.

Khlit gazed at the framework of the tower. A broad aperture opened into the older shrine of Nagi. The shrine was of stained marble, without window or light of any kind. A rough flight of granite steps led up to the second story of the tower where Abdul Dost, doubtless mindful of the worshipers of Nagi, had persuaded Ram Gholab that the two warriors would prefer to spread their saddlecloths for sleep.

Having satisfied himself that the place contained no other inmates, the Cossack yawned, stretched and seated himself upon a wooden bench by the fire. He produced his black Cossack pipe and a small sack of what passed in China for tobacco. Kehru blinked and stared.

Khlit filled his pipe with tobacco, a rare delicacy that he husbanded with care in this land where the merits of the weed were as yet unknown. He picked a burning stick from the fire and lit the pipe, drawing into his lungs a mixture of smoking hemp, opium, and noxious weeds that would have instantly nauseated a man of less hardened constitution.

"*Aie!*" cried Kehru, sitting back on the stone floor abruptly.

"*Chota hazeri!*" grumbled Khlit, nodding at the food.

He knew but a word or two of Hindustani, picked up from Abdul Dost, but his gesture was significant. Kehru resumed the stirring of the pot and twining together of plantain leaves, which were his only plates. His eyes shone. Verily, here was a man of authority who took his ease right royally and indulged in a noteworthy solace, such as a man should!

He grinned and shook the trailing hair back from his eyes. He extended a mess of curry to Khlit who immediately fell-to with his fingers. Kehru was astonished as well as delighted. This tall warrior with the scarred face and swaggering feet had not only the bearing but the appetite of a warlike god.

Kehru hastily added more rice to the pot. He had measured the hunger of the two riders by the slender needs of himself and old Ram Gholab. A thought came to him. Khlit had appeared ill content with the frugal fare.

"Wait but the space that water boils," he chattered, "and the thrice-born chieftain may taste what is more fitting to his manlike gullet."

Assuring himself by a crafty glance that Ram Gholab was not within hearing, Kehru flitted from the tower. He ran to a thicket and dug with his hands into a hollow covered with cypress branches. He disclosed the body of a small antelope. An arrow had transfixed the beautiful beast behind the forelegs.

Kehru had gratified his ambition toward prowess by fashioning a slight bow with which he had become wonderfully skilled. An arrow was silent, and Ram Gholab, whose caste prohibited the taking of animal life, could not see its flight. But, alone, the boy had not dared to cook his prey. Also he would not eat meat. But the tall warrior quite evidently had stronger tastes.

Somewhat doubtfully he showed the dead antelope to the Cossack, who sniffed it appraisingly and took it readily.

"Ha!" he muttered, well pleased, and Kehru smiled joyfully.

In a trice Khlit had cut off a hind quarter, which he skinned with his dagger swiftly and tossed into the pot. Then impatiently he swept the whole of the boy's stock of wood upon the fire until it roared hotly and the water boiled.

This done, be nodded in friendly fashion to Kehru and stretched himself beyond the heat of the blaze, his sword near his right hand, and was asleep in a moment. Kehru harkened to his snores and crept nearer to gaze upon the splendidly engraved curved scabbard. He touched the weapon fleetingly in admiration.

At once Khlit was awake, his eyes hard, and the hilt of the sword close-gripped in a ready hand. Seeing only the startled boy, his tense figure relaxed and Kehru breathed again, well understanding that he had been close to death.

When Abdul Dost climbed down to the fire, attracted by the smell of meat, he found Khlit heartily engaged upon the antelope quarter, half-cooked.

"Ho!" remarked the Muslim. "The smell is good. How was the beast slain?"

Khlit was well acquainted with the Mohammedan scruples as to food.

"In fitting fashion," he remarked dryly. "Eat."

Abdul Dost sniffed and sat down. He tried some of the fruit and curry, eyeing the rapidly vanishing meat enviously.

"Ram Gholab says that peril awaits us on our return," he observed.

"Then will you need more strength, Abdul Dost. Eat, therefore."

The Muslim needed no further urging. When the food had vanished and the fire was cooling into ashes, he lay back on his cloak contentedly.

"You and I are marked by the slayers, Khlit," he said, "as a hare is marked by a goshawk. So says Ram Gholab. The slayers have doubtless seen us as we came hither. They have knowledge of the treasure—eh," he broke off, "then why have they not attacked the tower, O watcher of the snakes?"

The Hindu pointed into the dark shrine.

"Nag guards what is there. The *thag* fears the cobras. Likewise, it is their custom to slay only upon a journey. If they marched against a dwelling they would fear the anger of Kali."

"A strange folk," meditated the Muslim, "low-born Hindus, doubtless."

"Nay," Ram Gholab spoke sharply, "they are followers of the Prophet for the most part. Their ancestors were laborers behind bullocks and such dishonorable pursuits."

"That is surely a lie." Abdul Dost's religious pride was aroused. "For it is forbidden in the law to slay murderously."

"The *thag*s believe that they keep the law. They say that their victims are marked for death by fate. Thus the *thag*s do naught but carry out what is already ordained. If they did not slay—and it is a sin in their evil minds if they do not—the victims would die otherwise."

"Still the guilt of blood is on their souls."

"Are not you also a slayer?"

"In battle. Arm to arm and eye to eye, in a just quarrel. Never have I slain save in open fight."

"Death is death." Ram Gholab closed his blind eyes. "Thus I heard the father of this boy say—for he was once a scout-*thag*, but repented swiftly."

He ceased abruptly, fearing that Kehru had heard. Abdul Dost looked at him sharply.

"So—the *thag*—slayers believe that I and the Curved Saber are fated to die?"

"Assuredly."

"Hm. They will watch for our coming with the gold."

"But," pointed out Ram Gholab, "Taleb Khan has devised a means of leaving the tower. A *panshway*—a river boat—lies nearby on the Jumna bank below the tower. This will bear you back to the *ameer*."

"A boat!" grumbled Khlit when this was told to him. "Nay, rather will we ride where we may choose our going."

A shadow crossed the thin face of the Hindu. He had had his instructions. Ram Gholab was a faithful man and worthy of trust. Moreover, he had the single-mindedness of the aged, whose sole task had been the care of a trust.

The treasure of Ghar Tower had been the somber delight of his lonely life. His pride was at stake—for the safety of the gold. His hand trembled slightly as he answered:

"Ameer Taleb Khan spoke with me and said that thus should the gold be taken from the tower—and in no other manner. There is a roof over the deck of the *panshway* and under it you may lie hid, with horses. The current will bear you downstream. The long end of the rudder can be handled, so said the *ameer*, from within."

"It is well said," mused Abdul Dost who liked to take the other side of an argument from the taciturn Khlit. "But if the *thag*s see us enter the boat—"

"Tomorrow night you must embark. They will not see for they have not eyes of an owl. Aye, the boat is best. For the *thag*s have spies, so I have heard, along the Ghar Pass. They will see you ride down the trail."

"We bear swords," grunted Khlit who had no love of a ship of any sort. "Our horses are swift—"

"But not so swift as an arrow," pointed out Abdul Dost, yawning. "Nor can we ride for three days and nights without watering the horses. The slayers will be watching the trail. They will not look for us within the boat."

Khlit was silent.

"Where lies this gold?" he asked presently.

When Abdul Dost had translated his request, Ram Gholab rose. Kehru lighted a torch from the embers of the fire. But the master of the snakes needed no light to find his way into the shrine.

It was a bare chamber of stone, perhaps ten feet square, great fissures showing between the slabs. Khlit, peering keenly at the walls and floor, saw no sign of an opening which might serve as a hiding place. The only object in the shrine was a square block of jade, placed against the wall, wherein was carved the image of Vishnu with the hood of the seven snakes above the figure of the god.

Ram Gholab squatted on the floor.

"Be silent," he whispered, "and move not. The servants of Nag are quick to strike, and their touch is death."

Abdul Dost, guessing vaguely what was to come, glanced back at the doorway uncertainly; but as Khlit stood his ground so did the Muslim. Ram Gholab's pipe began its soft note. His turbaned head moved slightly, almost in the fashion of the hood of one of his snakes. Kehru was like a brown figure turned to stone.

The voice of the pipe rose shriller. The flickering light from the torch faded then grew greater. Ram Gholab nodded his head and Kehru stepped toward the jade slab. Abdul Dost glanced from side to side uneasily. He was not at all comfortable. His religious scruples did not favor his presence in a Hindu shrine, especially that of Nag—even though deserted. Besides he felt a distinct sense of danger.

Kehru thrust the unburned end of his torch into the crack of the stone directly over the jade. He pried vigorously and the slab turned as if revolving on a hidden axis. When an opening about a foot in width had been made the boy stepped back alertly.

The hooded head and tiny eyes of a giant cobra were visible in the black hole. Khlit heard a sound like that of steam passing through a narrow hole. The snake darted its head forward and the glistening coils followed.

It was a magnificent specimen, the spectacle mark clear and shining, the long, beautiful body nearly the length of a man. A second cobra followed the first.

"Come, beloved of the god, guardian of Door-ga—master of Ghar. Come. We are calling thus. Do not harm us. We also are servants of Nag."

So chanted Ram Gholab, removing the pipe from his lips. The cobras which had turned aside, running their heads along the wall, moved toward him, their hoods lifted.

Abdul Dost felt his brow strangely warm. He had heard no sound, but Khlit had drawn his sword and held it poised in his hand. Meanwhile the boy slipped to the opening in the wall. He drew out an ebony box of some size.

The snakes seemed to pay no heed to him. Kehru gently walked from the shrine, bearing the box and his torch. For a moment the place was in half darkness. The pipe of Ram Gholab continued its soothing note.

Then Kehru returned, and light flooded the chamber.

"*B'illah!*"

It was a full-voiced oath, torn from the throat of Abdul Dost. One of the snakes of the shrine had moved its coils toward him with dreadful grace and silence, and the torch showed that its coils were passing over his foot. Its head waved not a yard from his hand.

And at his voice the coils of the snake on the floor contracted instantly. A cobra does not draw back its head to strike, such is the strength of its lean body. But this one struck simultaneously as it moved.

Khlit's action was involuntary. He had seen vicious tensity leap into the snake. He had not waited for the head to strike.

Even so, his blade moved with deadly swiftness. The snake had darted its fangs at Abdul Dost, but midway the sword met it and the splendid hood fell to the stone floor, cleanly severed from the writhing trunk.

Kehru gave a cry of dismay and dropped the torch. The chamber dwindled into gloom. Abdul Dost and the Cossack both ran from the shrine into the tower at the same second.

They paused by the fire with drawn weapons. The Muslim's teeth were chattering as if from a chill. But he mastered his emotion quickly.

"Well did you serve me!" he cried. "I was near to death."

Kehru stood beside them, staring affrightedly at the shrine. Khlit took a step forward and hesitated. Ram Gholab must be in peril. But it would be vain to return to the stone chamber without a light. Then an angry voice came from the darkness.

"Death! It is near to you now. O fool! O blunderer! O accursed of the gods! An evil deed."

The old Hindu advanced into the light, his blind eyes rolling fruitlessly. And Khlit swore. The second cobra was held on the arm of the snake-charmer, its coils about his waist and leg.

Although the giant snake was plainly agitated, its hood erect and venomously swelled, it made no effort to strike its friend. Both warriors recoiled hastily.

"Well for you," said Ram Gholab bitterly, "that I seized upon the second servant of Nag. O well for you that I am blind and my senses are keen in the dark. If I had not seized him, he would have struck once—twice—as you fled. Fools, to think that your clumsy feet could outstrip the dart of the cobra. Half am I minded to release him upon you."

His teeth glimmered through his beard. The blue veins stood out in his forehead. His voice was like the angry breath of the serpent he held. Then his head drooped.

"Nay," he murmured. "You are but the dull slaves of a master who is also my master. You shall go free. But the shrine of Nag is profaned. Take the gold of the Mogul. I shall abide in the shrine. Kehru, build up the fire. The servant of Nag must be burned upon the pyre or evil will descend upon your head and you—aye, though a child—will be accursed."

Throwing back his head he laughed. The giant snake twisted in his arm. "Verily," he cried, "have you said that the slayers have marked you. Now will you not escape uncaught from Ghar. Now it is assured. The shadow of death will close upon you. No sword will guard you this time. Ohé—my work is done, but your fate you may not escape."

Abdul Dost felt a cold pulse stir in his back. Khlit stared curiously at the Hindu, wondering why the life of a snake should be so valued.

To Abdul Dost, however, the words rang with an ominous portent. The Muslim, as well as Ram Gholab, was a believer in fate.

The form of Ram Gholab slipped back into the darkness of the shrine, bearing the snake, and the glimmer of his white turban was lost in the shadow. Whereupon the boy raised the lid of the ebony box.

Within gleamed the soft luster of gray pearls, the rainbow glitter of diamonds, the wine-hued sparkle of rubies. Beneath the gems were sacks of gold.

Abdul Dost fingered a diamond curiously, turning it in his lean hand so as best to catch the light.

"A rich nest," he grunted, "with rare eggs therein. I have a thought, Khlit, that our path back to Pawundur will be set with the thorns of trouble."

"Close the casket," advised the Cossack, "and bear it with you to your couch above. We must sleep, but first I will see to the horses."

At a sign from him Kehru produced a fresh torch and lighted it, following Khlit's tall figure to the thicket behind the tower where the four horses were picketed. It was a mild night and the trees sheltered the beasts from the heavy dews.

Having satisfied himself that the horses were fed and secured, Khlit undid the saddle-girths and laid the furniture on the ground. Then he paused to watch the boy.

Kehru had stuck his torch in the earth and approached one of the Cossack's shaggy Turkoman ponies. Caressingly his hand went behind the horse's ears, and he crooned softly. He fetched dried ferns and spread them for a bed under the animal.

Whereupon the pony nuzzled Kehru, lipping his hand and sniffing, well content. The boy of Ghar was at home with animals. They were, indeed, the only friends of his life, except for the blind guardian.

Wistfully his dark eyes dwelt on the pony. Khlit grunted.

"*Oho*, little warrior! Did not Abdul Dost say when he was well fed that you desired a horse and had none? Aye, the pony will not be too large for your small legs."

Kehru looked at him inquiringly. On an impulse Khlit placed the halter of the beast in the boy's hand, resting the other hand on the pony's neck.

"Scarce will there be space for four horses in the boat," he mused. He nodded. "Yours," he explained in broken Hindustani.

Kehru started with surprise and excitement. His white teeth shone from his brown face in a wide grin. He had understood, but hardly credited his good fortune. Khlit nodded again and walked away carelessly.

Straightway his hand was seized in a warm clasp. Kehru knelt before him and pressed the scarred hand of the warrior to his brow. Then he bent his dark head to the ground and touched Khlit's boots reverently.

Impatiently the Cossack drew away and swaggered off to his sleep. He knew it not, but his generosity had stirred a tumult in the boy's mind. Long after Khlit was asleep the boy lingered proudly by his new possession. In his soul was arising a great doubt.

While he felt the back of the horse for saddle sores and examined teeth and legs in the dark, he was debating a most important matter. For the first time in his life he must decide upon the conduct of a warrior.

He glanced at the dark shrine where muffled sounds indicated that Ram Gholab still labored. Then he undid the halter from the tree trunk and sprang upon the pony's back. Swiftly he guided his mount from the tower, using only the halter cord and his bare heels.

Beyond the tower he struck into the Ghar trail and quickened to a gallop.

All was silent now about Ghar Tower, save for the grieving prayers of Ram Gholab, who squatted above a fresh mound in the earth between the stones, and the nightly tumult of insects—the strident hum where the dwellings of men are few and the forest is moist.

IV

On the broad plain by the Jumna, just below the Ghar Pass, the camp of the Pawundur *thags* spread, like a brown anthill resting upon green sward. The six days of prayer had passed without further ill omen, and Dhurum Khan, the *jemadar*, was easier in spirit, although he still felt vague misgivings at the death of the woman.

He was walking restlessly along the high road near the encampment, accompanied by the *guru*, Bhawani Bukta, whose bent figure was alert with new eagerness now that the time was drawing near for the band to march again.

"According to the custom of *thaggi*," he told Dhurum Khan, "we have waited at the crossroads, lifting hand against none, while the six days have dawned and ceased. Rather, we have aided and given comfort to passing traders, as well as entertainment in the tents, owing to the advice of the one to whom we came in our trouble."

"Well did the one counsel," admitted the leader, "for by our quietude none suspect that we be slayers. Nay, not the riders of the *ameer* himself, who have stopped in our tents."

"Blind slaves!" The water-carrier grimaced. "Our time is come and we will act. Look!"

Where the roads crossed were strange marks in the sand, as if men had turned to the right, toward the river, dragging their feet and leaving small piles of dirt at intervals. This was a well-known signal.

"The scouts bid us hasten," interpreted Dhurum Khan, "to the Jumna."

They quickened their pace, plying their staffs vigorously, looking to those who might chance to watch like wandering tradesmen. Presently they emerged upon the sand flat through which the tranquil Jumna threaded, its sacred waters a deepest blue in color. For the Jumna, although taking its source from the snow ravines, retains its clear color, unlike the Ganges.

At the *ghat*, the river landing place, a small skiff was tied to a pole in the sand. In the skiff were two men.

"O *Jemadar*," reported one, "as you commanded we have rowed until our backs are blistered with the sun and sore with a great soreness. We have made our eyes like to the eyes of vultures and we have seen them enter a *panshway*—even as our spies among the fisher folk foretold. Behold, protector of the poor, our poverty is like to a ragged garment."

"Two lengths of cloth you shall have."

"Our hands are raw."

"An ounce of silver each."

"O generous master!" The scout-*thag* bent his head. "Another word have I. When we rowed hither a raven called twice. Is not the omen good?"

Both Dhurum Khan and the *guru* gave an exclamation of pleasure. Bhawani Bukta stroked the outlines of his noosed cord under his dirty tunic.

"Are you assured it is they?" demanded the *jemadar*. "We have waited long for news of their coming to the river."

"Their faces were hid," responded the man in the skiff. "And they loosened the boat at night. But we followed, where we were not seen, and harkened to their talk. We are not mistaken. Within a day, or perhaps two, they plan to land near this spot."

Dhurum Khan nodded, reflecting. He glanced along the *ghat* and saw one or two river craft tied up nearby, their crews asleep under the awnings that kept off the hot sun. He lowered his voice earnestly.

"Harken," he whispered. "This day the band will move. We will leave the one who counseled us wisely. The omens are good. But the skiff is too little for a crew. Do you, Bhawani Bukta, and these two, assume the manner of weavers who are seeking cloth to buy. In one of the vessels in the bight there are sellers of cloth— so they told us when they rested in our tents and refreshed their spirits with the magic of a song. O, the one is wise!"

"Aye," responded the three, "it is the truth."

"Then," continued Dhurum Khan, "will I retrace my steps and give the order for one-half the band to break camp. Some boys under my son, Jaim Ali, will I send hither in advance of the rest. The boys will drive mules without burdens and pretend that the mules have broken loose."

"Aye," they nodded expectantly.

"When the boys and the mules come, you will be upon yonder *panshway*, bartering with the owners. Ask permission to cook your rice at their fire under the roof of the boat."

"We will slay those who sit about the fire," hazarded Bhawani Bukta.

"Aye, thus you will do. Bhawani Bukta will give the *jhirni*—the signal for murder—which is three raps upon the deck, on a boat. He will watch and see that no men on the other craft take alarm."

"But what of the men sleeping on the upper deck?" asked the *guru*. "Shall I stab them quietly as they sleep?"

"Unworthy!" Dhurum Khan frowned, for he had grown careful since the murder of the woman. "Kick them awake and say that one of their comrades by the fire has been taken with a fit of vomiting."

"Nay," broke in the quick-witted water-carrier, "I will say that he writhes with torment of worms in his body and barks like a dog. Thus they will have a fear lest he become mad and go hastily."

"So that these two clever *thag*s may strangle them. Then, when all of the five men on the *panshway* have become offerings to Kali, make a hole in the side of the boat away from the other craft and let the bodies fall into the water."

Bhawani Bukta bent his gray head in assent smilingly.

"You spoke of boys and mules, *Jemadar*. What is their mission?"

"To make a loud noise and outcry upon shore, to drown a cry if one of the men on the boat struggles against the noose. Thus will the crews of the other vessels have eyes and ears only for the mules and the running boys."

The dark eyes of the three glistened.

"O wise leader," they whispered. "It is verily a plan of plans."

The dark eyes of Dhurum Khan were alight with purpose. For six days he had pondered this scheme. His spies had brought news of a treasure being carried on a *panshway*. And he—with the counselor at the crossroads whom they all held in reverence—had planned a great theft, a masterpiece of death.

"Take heed," he cautioned. "If the men in the other craft should ask what has become of the dead men—for they will not suspect they are dead—say that your victims have gone to the camp at the crossroads to hear another song. Should strangers come along, say that the crew have sold the *panshway* to you."

"Verily," assented the *thag*s.

To one not understanding the great skill of these men in their profession, the murder of five boatmen on a public landing place, and the disposal of their bodies in broad daylight, would appear a difficult, if not disastrous, feat. Yet by following these instructions of Dhurum Khan the thing was done. And the *thag*s who had come to the *ghat* were in possession of a serviceable river craft as well as the few goods of the dead boatmen.

The boys and the mules returned to the roadside camp with Dhurum Khan, while Bhawani Bukta was appointed *manji*, or captain, of the boat.

He ordered the fastenings loosened as soon as the stains and disorder of the murder upon the lower deck had been cleared away, and the patched calico sail was raised to the breeze. The squat little vessel veered away from the land while bystanders on shore waved at it.

Invisible under the river surface rested the five bodies, well weighted with stones taken from the ballast of the boat. The hole in the side was filled up hastily and the vessel stemmed the current of the river on its mission of death, its blunt bow headed upstream toward Ghar.

Until that afternoon Khlit and his companion had had the upper reaches of the Jumna to themselves, except for some flocks of fishing skiffs. They remained carefully under the overhang of the half-cabin beside the horses, guiding their *panshway* by the long oar which passed through the stem.

It was hot under the dome-shaped wooden shelter; the lower deck of the vessel was musty and the timbers waterlogged. There was no place to stand on the upper portion except at the bow—for the mast penetrated the curving wooden screen—or on the steerage platform. These points they shunned and concealed themselves furthermore by placing the horses in the open pit between the overhang and the stem.

By situating the three beasts here, they made certain that no casual eye would wonder whether their craft was masterless. They did not try to raise the sail, knowing nothing of how it should be done. They were content to drift down the rapid current and steer clear of the shore by clumsy use of the oar.

"It is like to a pot floating in a trough," muttered Abdul Dost, "and it is well that we are near to the end of the trough, for a sickness comes upon me."

Khlit did not remind the Muslim that the boat was his choice. The Cossack leaned back against the bare beams of the side, where he could watch the river through a crack in the opposite timbers. His silence irritated Abdul Dost, who was thoroughly weary of the *panshway*.

"We are like sheep in a pen," he grumbled. "Better had we risked the arrows in the forest than this thing of evil."

"Now that we are here," pointed out Khlit, "it would be the folly of a woman to depart from the boat. For we would easily be seen and our place of landing would be marked by many eyes."

He squinted thoughtfully ahead, where a sail was visible.

"Did you see aught of Kehru during the second day at Ghar?" he asked.

"Nay, the boy had vanished with one of your ponies. Only Ram Gholab was there, at the grave of his snake. He said in parting that our graves, also, were being dug beside the Jumna."

"Likewise," mused Khlit, piecing together certain thoughts in his mind, "did Ram Gholab say, unthinking, that the father of Kehru was a *thag* for a space. But this, I think, the boy knew not."

"He has a desire to be a warrior of the Mogul."

"Yet is he gone from Ghar. And hereabouts the *thags* seem the only warriors."

Abdul Dost glanced at his companion and shrugged his shoulders. He pointed to a pile of skins under which the corner of the ebony box protruded.

"Eh," he grumbled, "you have claimed the care of the Mogul's treasure. But that is an ill place. If the boat should gallop the box might overturn and the diamonds would strew the deck."

"The chest," said Khlit complacently, "is my care—as the boat is yours."

"Aye," muttered Abdul Dost, "you have spent more time in counting over the bags of gold than in watching what is before the muzzle of the boat."

"Nevertheless, I am watching a sail that is trotting up the highway of the river toward us."

Abdul Dost swore and peered through the ramshackle deck. The approaching *panshway* was nearing them rapidly, its sail bellying in the wind. He could see a brown figure on the steering platform. But no others.

"I wonder," Khlit stroked his beard, "why Kehru left the tower."

"He did but steal the pony."

"The pony was given him." The Cossack pointed aft grimly. "The thought came to me that he might have ridden from the tower bearing a message—because another sail is behind us. It crosses from one side to the other like a shying horse."

"By the face of the Prophet!" Abdul Dost stood up and knocked his head soundly against the overhang of the deck. "*B'illah!* This is an evil place. It was ill done to give the boy a horse. He may have betrayed—"

"He had honest eyes." Khlit thought briefly that Kehru had appeared uneasy when he had last seen him. "Besides, if he had wished evil he could have lifted the horse."

Abdul Dost marked the course of the first *panshway* with care.

"It will pass us by, far to the flank," he decided, and so it proved.

"But the other gains," observed Khlit. "And our pot wallows like a full-fed turtle. Abdul Dost, you lifted your voice in favor of the boat. Tell me then how to put spurs to it."

The Muslim gazed at the bare deck, the pile of the sail and the rotting timbers, and shook his head. He had never been afloat before, having crossed rivers after the manner of his kind by swimming his horse.

"I see no spurs," he responded moodily. "I think the boat that follows in our tracks gains on us because it wears a sail. But how can we place a sail upon this turtle? Nay, perhaps it were best to swim our horses ashore."

Khlit measured the distance to the bank and shook his head. Before they could gain land the following vessel would cut them off. He had noticed that it moved more quickly when tacking.

"If it is our fate to be taken in this pot," ruminated Abdul Dost, "it will come to pass. What is written is written."

"Look," said Khlit.

The *panshway* that had passed them by had come out in the wake of the second boat and now both were heading downstream. Their brown sails fluttered as they were hauled by the crews. Behind them the green slopes of the Ghar rose to the blue sky. The broad bosom of the Jumna was spreading wider as the gorge opened out. They were nearly at their destination. But the pursuing vessel was within arrowshot.

Khlit drew his Turkish pistols from his belt and saw to the priming carefully. He rose and adjusted the saddlebags on his horse, despite the danger of being seen. Then he called to Abdul Dost.

"The riders of the nearest boat are running about the deck in confusion. They are crying out as if in fear."

What Khlit said was true. To a man accustomed to sailing craft, it would have been evident before now that the crew were endeavoring to make all possible haste, nursing the boat along against the wind, under the loud orders of the steersman. The crew were glancing back at the third vessel, which was following steadily some distance in the rear.

"They have a fear!" cried Abdul Dost.

The fleeing vessel was now abreast of them. Two men, dressed in the manner of merchants, gestured at them wildly from the after deck.

"*Thags*!" they cried. "Fools! Lift your sail and flee. Do you not see that the boat behind is a craft of the slayers. They follow, waiting for their prey."

Khlit and Abdul Dost glanced at the swelling brown sail in their wake. The Muslim smiled ruefully.

"Verily, that is wisdom!" he cried. "But we know not how to bridle this boat for speed."

"Fools!" said the merchant again. "It is death to linger."

They cried shrilly at the crew who were fumbling with the sail. The two vessels had drifted almost together, for the other *panshway* had lost the wind.

"A handful of gold," offered Abdul Dost, "to one of your men who will come to our boat and rein it for flight."

Even in the danger of capture by the pursuing craft, he was not willing to venture on the merchant's ship with the telltale chest. Inwardly he cursed Khlit's obstinacy in leaving the treasure in the chest.

The coolies stared at him and glanced at each other. The two boats were now rail to rail. One of the crew leaped to Abdul Dost's side.

He was a half-naked Mussulman coolie, his eyes rolling in excitement. He glanced sharply down into the lower deck, noting the tangled sail, the pile of skins, and the watching Khlit.

"I will aid you!" he cried. "It is time!"

Silently a half-dozen turbans appeared over the rail of the larger boat. Brown forms sprang down upon Abdul Dost, their naked feet bearing him to the deck, with the breath knocked from his broad chest. No chance had the Afghan to draw weapon or even shout a warning to Khlit.

But the Cossack had seen. Instinctively—for he was never startled by sudden danger—he had grasped the halter of his pony, the beast being already weighted with his saddlebags, and freed it. He stepped back, drawing the horse with him to the boat rail opposite the point of attack.

The thought flashed upon him that Ram Gholab had said the *thag*s never attacked without slaying. Abdul Dost was already under their feet and seemed doomed, for he lay passive, struggling with his breath. By a leap over the rail Khlit and his pony might perhaps have escaped into the water and reached the shore before the sailing craft could be brought about after them.

But the Cossack would not leave his friend. With an angry shout he drew his weapon and leaped forward. He had seen the treachery in a flash, too late. The panic on the other *panshway* was assumed. They had been cleverly surprised.

As he sprang, swinging his blade overhead, there was a hiss in the air. Something settled about his shoulders and drew taut. Striving vainly to strike at it with his sword, he was jerked to one side and thrown heavily.

A fleeting glimpse he had of the merchant—a slim, bearded fellow whose face was vaguely familiar. The man was pulling at the cord, the noose of which had closed over Khlit.

Savage hands struck at the Cossack. Others gripped his sword-arm. Several naked bodies pressed upon him. Struggling, he was cast face down and held firmly. The horses reared in fright.

Khlit expected momentarily the bite of a knife against his ribs or the tension of a cord about his throat. He struggled in grim silence, only to feel other ropes wound about his legs and around his body.

Then he was picked up bodily and thrown heavily into the other *panshway*. A *thud*, and Abdul Dost lay beside him, likewise bound and breathing in great gasps.

"The horses!" cried the merchant's voice. "They are valuable."

"Master, we cannot fetch them," a coolie's voice made answer. "Their fear is too great."

"Dogs! Then do two of you man the boat that has them. Sail it to shore. Your death if the horses are not landed safely."

With that the merchant scrambled down beside Khlit. In his arms was the ebony chest. He shouted an order and the square sail was hastily dressed. The boat swayed and lunged forward as it caught the wind. Several of the coolies had leaped back after the merchant. Khlit had a glimpse of the sail running up on the *panshway* he and Abdul Dost had occupied.

Khlit wondered why they had not been slain. Surely they were helpless. He had strained fruitlessly at his cords and now lay passive. Abdul Dost was glaring at their captors.

The merchant had set down the box and was regarding them complacently.

"Well done!" said a smooth, familiar voice.

Khlit rolled over upon his other side to peer at the speaker. Under the overhang of the cabin sat a stout man, wearing the cloak and long, gray tunic of a Mussulman trader. A broad face beamed upon the surprised Cossack and a pair of pig eyes puckered in a smile.

In spite of the tradesman garb, Khlit recognized Ameer Taleb Khan.

His first impression was relief that they had not fallen into the hands of a *thag* band. His second was a swift foreboding that all was not well. But he lay silent, thinking. Why was the *ameer* so costumed? Why had he and Abdul Dost been attacked? The Muslim, who had also seen their captor, found his voice readily.

"Is this the manner that you greet your riders, Taleb Khan?" he snarled. "By Allah and the ninety-nine holy names! It was ill done. My ribs are cracked. Unloose us!"

Taleb Khan's smile broadened. He sat on his heels upon a comfortable rug, a water jar and dish of sweets at his side. Now he lifted a sugared date carefully and placed it in his mouth. He seemed well pleased with the situation. The merchant sat down beside him, and Khlit knew him to be Mustafa Mirza, also disguised after a clumsy fashion.

"Peace!" ejaculated the servant of the *ameer*. "Make your tongue gentle in addressing your master."

Abdul Dost worked to a sitting position, stifling a grunt of pain. He had been roughly used.

"Is this a jest? Do not those dirty garments offend your nicety, Mustafa?"

The *mirza* scowled.

"Nay, it is no jest. We have taken two thieves in the act."

"Thieves!" Abdul Dost grappled with this new thought. "The thieves are behind you in the pursuing boat. You named them *thags*."

"It is the truth—most like. They had evil faces and they stared at us as they passed. But then my men were below deck. Now the *thags* have seen our number and weapons and they have headed about, up the river, being wise—as you are not."

A glance showed Abdul Dost that this was so. The third boat was but a diminishing square of sail, already rounding a bend of the Jumna near the shore. His own boat followed close behind that of the *ameer*.

"Wherefore have you done this thing, Taleb Khan?" The Afghan was still bewildered. "There was no need to set upon us. Here is the gold and the jewels in the chest."

"Aye, the chest." Taleb Khan stroked its black surface fondly and eyed the bronze clasp. "Well do I know my treasure chest." He shook his head moodily. "Aye, a pity. I deemed you worthy of trust. Yet is the treasure of my box gone."

"Gone?" Abdul Dost gaped, but Khlit's eyes grew hard under the shaggy brows.

"Aye—vanished. Stolen!"

"Nay!" cried the Afghan roundly. "Look within and you shall see the jewels and gold mohars. Even so. Did I not see them with my eyes?"

"I doubt it not. You coveted the wealth with your eyes. And you took it. It is written that the fate of a stealer of the goods of another man shall be like to the reward of a jackal."

"But look within the chest and see the truth."

The *ameer* glanced tentatively at the watching coolies and shook his head.

"No need," he observed, "to verify your guilt. You have stolen the treasure entrusted to your care. I—watchful in the affairs of the Mogul—have caught the thieves. But the treasure is gone. A pity. The *vizier* will grow great with wrath. Already he rides hither, not an hour from Pawundur. He will deal with you as you deserve, being a faithless servant."

Khlit sat up, biting his mustache.

"Harken, O *ameer*," he said bitterly. "In all things we have done as you bade us. We are not thieves. We journeyed in the path back to Pawundur by the boat as you ordered."

"I?" The official's brows went up. "Did I mention a boat? I think not—Mustafa!"

"Nay," amended that person promptly, "you bade these low-born ride back by the trail. I heard it."

"A lie!" cried Abdul Dost.

Taleb Khan and Mustafa laughed; they rocked on their heels with mirth; they looked at Khlit and Abdul Dost and the skin of their smooth faces grew wrinkled with mirth.

"Nay, O harken to the low-born snatchers of goods—the faithless messengers!" they said in concert. "Did not you steal the *panshway* from the landing place of the shrine? Did you not slay the thrice-blessed snake of the shrine? Nay, for you stole down the river, thinking to outwit us and escape from Pawundur. Verily, but we were watchful."

While Abdul Dost stared, the truth began to glimmer into the shrewd brain of the Cossack. He spat vigorously.

"So—we have been tricked, *mansabdar*," he growled, shaking his head like an angry dog. "Doubtless Ram Gholab helped in the trick. And Kehru—"

"The boy rode to us," explained the *mirza*, taking pleasure in the discomfiture of his prisoners and wishing to while away the hour before they should land. "Thus he had been ordered. He rode swiftly by the byways that he treads like an antelope. A good half-day he came before your slow boat. *Ai*, we knew that you were no sailors."

At this Abdul Dost subsided into silence, for he understood now the trap that had been set. Taleb Khan had sent them to Ghar meaning to give them over to the agent of the Mogul as stealers of the gold. The *ameer* had sent others on the mission but they had been slain by the unexpected activity of the *thag* bands that were rife in the valley.

He saw now why Taleb Khan had not wished to go himself or to send a body of soldiery for the gold. The covetous official had desired to keep the wealth that should be paid to his master. He had devised this stratagem to provide men to accuse of the theft. Khlit and Abdul Dost had no friends in Pawundur. Their case would be decided long before they could get word to the Rawul of Thaneswar. The Mogul's justice was swift, and the Afghan had no proof here among the lesser agents of the throne that he had once served Jahangir, Lord of Lords.

Khlit was reasoning along similar lines, but unlike his friend he did not sulk in silence. He was curious concerning the manner of their betrayal; also he fancied he saw certain weak spots in the scheme of Taleb Khan which might be useful.

"Thus," he said slowly, gaining time to think, "Ram Gholab was ordered to send us into your hands?"

He spoke almost admiringly, as if he could relish the superior cunning that had trapped him. Taleb Khan stared, then leaned back upon the ebony chest with a smile. Verily this aged wanderer was providing excellent sport for his enjoyment.

"Not so, O wise owl. Ram Gholab is a fool of fools—a dotard who is bemired in his own magic of the snake. He believes that he truly serves the Mogul!" The *ameer* broke off cautiously. "That is, he is no agent of mine. He was ordered to send the message of your departure, believing that I would safeguard your journey. *Aie*, it was well thought upon. Also he was ordered to send you by the ship."

Taleb Khan, relishing his words, had lowered his voice to a whisper so that the coolies might not hear. A faithless man himself, he did not trust others.

"And Kehru likewise. He came to my tent like a fledgling warrior upon a mission of state. Naught he knows of your theft."

"Then," mused Khlit, "this tale of the slayers is but a tale. We saw them not."

"Oh, there is some truth in it, most wise old owl. Aye, there be bands of *thags* hereabouts. But two swift riders, strangers like yourself, could have passed through them unmolested. They seek lesser prey. Yet Ram Gholab has heard much of their doings and his solitary musing has made them great, like huge shadows cast by a small fire at night."

Whereupon Taleb Khan wearied of his sport and rose to give heed to the landing of the boat at the *ghat*. Khlit also had food for thought. He was silent while the vessel was worked to the shore and the sail dropped.

It was mid-afternoon and the heat was great when he and Abdul Dost were led over the sands to the Pawundur road. Behind them the coolies brought their horses. Taleb Khan mounted one, for he was bulky and the heat irked him. Mustafa led the way.

At the crossroads were the tents of some merchants, likewise a stained crimson canopy at one comer of the caravansary. The *ameer*'s round tent had been pitched in the enclosure, and under the open fly slaves had set meat and drink for the refreshment of their master.

When Taleb Khan was partaking of the food, seated upon his carpet, Khlit nudged Abdul Dost. They were seated, still bound, near their captors, but at one side of the tent opening in the full glare of the sun.

"Take heed," he whispered, "and watch. There is something that the *ameer* does not yet know."

"What matter?" asked the Afghan moodily. "Ram Gholab spoke truly concerning our fate. We know the treachery of the *ameer*. Will he let us live? Nay. Already he has planned the manner of our death and but awaits the coming of the *vizier* who is nearby, so the coolies said."

But Khlit caught the wandering eye of Taleb Khan. The *ameer* was refreshed by food—while Khlit and Abdul Dost were suffering the first pains of a long fast—and he was restless because of the excitement of his attempt to defraud the Mogul. He was restless, looking for diversion, and his eye strayed to the rug under which the box had been placed for concealment. Perhaps he meant to open it, but the Cossack's words arrested him.

"If a bridge is built with a hole in the middle, is it safe to walk upon, Taleb Khan?"

The *ameer* was surprised. He did not quite know what to make of the graybeard who sat bound by his tent, but who faced him as one chieftain to another.

"Not so," he responded, motioning the slave behind him to stir the air with his fan of peacock plumes.

"Then is your plan like to a bridge, Taleb Khan. You will fall through the hole and perhaps die. The Mogul deals swiftly with a faithless servant."

"Aye. You and your comrade will be slain on this spot by the *vizier* and your heads will be put in a cage. The cage will be hung outside the walls of Delhi by the caravan gate."

"And what of you, Taleb Khan?" Khlit's voice was stern. "Think you the *vizier* will not see the hole in your scheme? He will ask why you sent two riders for the revenue at Ghar instead of going yourself. What will you answer?"

The *ameer* lay back luxuriously upon the rug. His eyes twinkled. He hesitated, then spoke, for the pleasure of his stratagem was still strong upon him.

"With words I will not answer, O unfortunate one. You know not the officials of the Mogul."

"*One* we know," observed Abdul Dost grimly. "It is sufficient."

Taleb Khan waved his hand airily. The Afghan's dark face flushed and the veins stood out in his forehead.

"By the tomb of Mohammed!" he cried softly, for he was a proud man. "There be chieftains at court who count the name of Abdul Dost, *mansabdar*, warrior of Akbar—may he rest in peace—among their friends."

"Akbar rests in peace. Likewise, who will know the blackened skin of a severed head for that of Abdul Dost? We will permit the ravens to pick at your eyes and the carrion birds to tear your lips—a little. Thus your friends will not know you. Have you a name?" He looked around for Mustafa and saw him not. "Nay, we know not your name."

Khlit pressed his arm warningly upon the Afghan's knee. Threats were useless against the *ameer*. "You have not said," he remarked, "how you will cross the hole in the bridge."

The ragged turban—for the *ameer* had not desired to exert himself sufficiently to change his garb—of Taleb Khan nodded affably.

"I like your wit, graybeard. It is delightful as the pretty trick of a wanton woman. I shall cross the hole with a gold plank. Ten ounces of gold will I put into the hand of the *vizier*. He has his price. Who has not? A jewel—a blood ruby—for the head treasurer over the *vizier*, and my tale will not be doubted. As for the Mogul: if he asks, there will be the two heads—yours—of the thieves to show."

"Will that content him?"

"Why not? He knows Pawundur is restless."

Taleb Khan smiled, pleased with his own shrewdness.

"Many will tell," he added, "if need be, of the theft of the *panshway* and how you sought to escape. Death of the Prophet! Shall I not keep the gold I labored to wring from this heathen land?

The villagers are like barren curs, so wretched are they. Only by seizing the wives and virgins of the dead men did I obtain the full quota of wheat and grain."

Khlit looked at him inquiringly.

"Aye, it was cleverly done. Mustafa saw to it. And when we had the quota, the women were returned, although, of course, some were no longer virgins. My men must have some sport, for they are weary with this cursed land."

"And the tax of the merchants?"

"I sold them the grain at double price. Those that bought not were hung for traitors. Few were hung."

It was a pleasant day for the *ameer*. He felt the full tide of success reward his efforts. And to crown his delight came Mustafa to the tent, pulling after him the slim form of Daria Kurn, veiled.

"A nautch-woman have I found, Lord," explained the *mirza*, "within the soiled tent. Oh, a fair woman with soft eyes."

"Bare her face!"

Mustafa jerked the veil from the cheeks of the dancing girl. The cheeks were *kohl*-stained. The beautiful eyes glanced swiftly, sidewise, at Taleb Khan. The *ameer* crowed joyously and straightway forgot Khlit and Abdul Dost.

"A prize, Mustafa, a prize! Come, my precious jade, my splendid dove! Dance and let your feet be light. I am weary."

Daria Kurn looked slowly about the tent at the watchers who had crowded into the shade at the coming of Mustafa.

"I will not dance," she said sullenly.

"Sing then, my bracelet of delight, my pretty trinket of love. Sing!"

"Lick your palm!"

Taleb Khan scowled at this abrupt refusal of his request. He was accustomed to having his commands obeyed. Mustafa struck the nautch-woman on the cheek. Straightaway she fastened her slender fingers in his beard, screaming with anger, one side of her sharp face crimson.

The *mirza* bellowed with rage and felt for his sword. Daria Kurn scratched his hand. Many coolies and followers of the merchants came running from their sleep at the outcry and formed a staring ring about the two struggling figures. Taleb Khan lay back on his rug, the better to laugh, for he was stout.

"Master," came a stifled voice from behind Khlit, "I have your curved sword and the scimitar of the Muslim warrior."

Schooled by bitter experience, the Cossack did not turn his head. He recognized the voice of Kehru. Abdul Dost sat up abruptly.

"I took the weapons from the low-born slaves who tended the horses. They know it not." The whisper of the boy trembled with eagerness. "I hid them in an antelope skin and I crawled hither. For I heard them talk of how you were to be slain. I know not why you are bound. But you gave to me a round-bellied pony without flaw, and I am your man. Aye—your warrior."

Mustafa had freed himself from the angry woman and drawn his dagger. In his rage he would have slashed the painted face of Daria Kurn, but Taleb Khan cried him halt.

"Would you spoil me this gem, Mustafa—this oasis in the sands of Hindustan? Nay, touch her not. I have not laughed so much in a fortnight!"

Khlit glanced sidewise at the throng. Intent on the spectacle of the woman, the bystanders had no eyes for him. He sat with Abdul Dost slightly back from the group, near to the side of the tent. Legs bandaged and naked rose about him. Slowly he rose to a kneeling position until his feet and bound limbs were behind him and concealed from view of those within the tent.

"Bid the boy look to see if any watch from the caravansary," he whispered to Abdul Dost, who had quickly assumed a similar position.

"No one watches," informed Kehru. "Those who have not come hither sleep."

Hope was arising like the rush of fresh water in the parched body of Abdul Dost. He lifted his dark head for the first time in many hours and felt the burning of the sun across the back of his neck.

"Allah is good," he said.

Khlit glanced at him warningly. They were in a throng of full thirty men. Others rested in the nearby tents. Around all ran the stone wall of the caravansary. Guards were at the entrance. Their position, despite the unexpected aid of the boy, was little short of deadly. Both he and Abdul Dost seized upon the thought at the same instant.

"Sever our accursed cords silently, from beneath," whispered the Afghan from still lips. "But let them rest as they are, once they are loosened. Then leave our swords in the skin. Seek the horses—"

"Pick out our mounts," added Khlit, "and the pony. Bring them to the rear of the tent swiftly."

He thought of the *vizier*, riding toward the caravansary with his followers, and leaned forward slightly to glance into the tent. Daria Kurn was tossing fragments of beard disdainfully into Mustafa's purple face. She swayed mockingly before him, poising bird-like on her toes.

Taleb Khan sat up and stroked his mustache.

"Sing!" he cried. "By the footstool of God! So fair a form must have a voice like to that of the nightingale."

"Am I a bazaar scavenger," stormed the woman, "to lift my voice before coolies?"

"But—"

"The sun is hot."

"I will pay a gold mohar."

"I will sit by your knee, in the shade of the tent, my lord."

With a smirk Taleb Khan piled high the cushions at his side. Daria Kurn tripped forward swaying and seated herself daintily. He clapped his hands.

"Wine!" he ordered. "Snow cooled—the best of Shiraz!"

"Aye, wine!" cried the girl. "Wine for the pleasure of my lord."

She stroked his cheek and he lay back against the cushions, well-content. The discomfiture of Mustafa had only made Daria

Kurn more desirable in his eyes. Was not a woman of spirit more fitting to attend him than a whimpering maiden of the people?

Khlit felt a light tug at his hands and the cords loosened. His feet likewise were free. A glance assured him that Abdul Dost also had only the severed thongs upon his wrists and that the antelope skin was upon the sand behind them within arm's reach, and something bulky under it.

Kehru had vanished silently, leaving only the prints of his naked feet.

Then Mustafa, smarting under his ordeal, saw fit to wreak his ill humor upon the captives.

"Aye, bring wine," he growled, "and let it be poured upon the beards of these thieves. Thirst shall teach them the first lesson of their crime."

He knew that neither of the warriors had tasted drink for the space of many hours during which they had lain in the sun.

Catching a goblet from a slave, he strode over to the two, his eyes gleaming wickedly. Khlit measured him silently, cursing the ill luck that had drawn Mustafa's attention upon them. The men in the crowd laughed carelessly.

"Guard well that wine, Mustafa," cried the Cossack quickly. "For I will truly drink of it and my thirst shall be eased—by your hand."

"Wherefore?" grunted the *mirza*, hesitating.

Khlit had spoken as if by authority.

Taleb Khan paid no heed. He was staring greedily at Daria Kurn, who knelt above him, her dark eyes straying about the throng, her lips humming softly the words of a song. The subdued light in the tent glimmered on her bare arms and waist. The fat hand of the *ameer* wandered among the strands of her brown hair. It pleased his vanity to play with this woman before his followers.

Khlit threw back his head and laughed, laughed with a ring of real merriment.

"Wherefore? Why, Taleb Khan has been robbed!"

The *ameer* ceased his gallant efforts and glared at the Cossack. Khlit sat back upon the loose cords of his feet. The woman glanced at him once with the cold anger of a startled snake.

"Robbed!" Taleb Khan was uneasy; those who covet gold are ever quick to fear theft. "How? When? The man is mad!"

"Not long since. I have watched the woman," growled Khlit. "Ho! It is a good jest. The thief has had his gains lifted from him."

"Verily," said Daria Kurn musically, "the sun has made him mad."

She smiled upon the bewildered *ameer* and loosened the girdle about her waist. It was a thin, silk girdle, redolent of musk. Her hand strayed artlessly to the *ameer*'s stout fist, and Taleb Khan's frown lightened. Not so Mustafa.

"No madness is it," he grumbled, "to beware of the craft of such a she-jackal. Speak, graybeard—what have you seen?"

Khlit, listening for sound of horses' hoofs moving behind the tent, made answer boldly.

"I have seen what the *ameer* will pay well to hear. I have seen the gold taken from the ebony chest. I have seen Taleb Khan robbed of his treasure. If he would know where the gold has gone, he must bargain with me."

Mustafa uttered a round oath. The faded eyes of Taleb Khan widened slowly and his mouth opened. He glanced uneasily at the outline of the chest on the farther side of Daria Kurn. He grunted and extended a tentative hand to the rug, across the knees of the nautch-girl. Then he hesitated.

He glanced at those who watched. It would not be well to bare the treasure to the sight of these merchants and their servants, if it were actually in the chest, for some would go to the *vizier* with the tale.

Then Taleb Khan would be obliged to pay a heavier bribe for the *vizier*'s silence—heavier, that is, than if the official really thought that the *ameer* had been robbed of the revenue. For the *vizier* would be forced to pay the merchant for the information.

But, he thought hastily, what if Khlit's words were true? He flushed and stared narrowly at the woman. She took his hand in hers and kissed it.

"You have lied!" he muttered to the Cossack.

But his tone was far from assured. Suppose the gold was actually gone? The woman was artful.

"I have not lied," Khlit's mustache twitched in a smile. "The bags of gold are gone. What I have seen, I have seen."

With a cry Taleb Khan snatched the rug from the ebony box. His avarice had overcome his caution. He fumbled with the bronze lock. The men pressed nearer.

Khlit saw a noose descend over the head of Taleb Khan and close about his throat.

Daria Kurn had sprung erect. In both hands she held the girdle that she had slipped around the *ameer*'s neck. It had been knotted cleverly. She tugged with all the strength of her slender frame, placing a slippered foot against the back of the man. Taleb Khan's round face changed from red to purple. The cry that had started in his throat choked to a gurgle.

At the same instant, Khlit's hand darted behind him. He had felt the touch of muslin against his cheek. He flung himself backward.

"Your sword, Abdul Dost!" he shouted, and his words were tense with peril.

For simultaneously with the strangling of the *ameer* he had seen nooses appear magically from nowhere and drape about the throats of Mustafa and the followers of the *ameer*. He had acted without waiting for more.

The man who had sought to strangle Khlit had been, perhaps, a trifle slower than his companion *thags*, believing that his victim was bound. He held an empty noose. He had not long to dwell upon his mistake.

Khlit's sword flashed up as the Cossack lay on the ground and the man's legs were cut from under him. He sank down groaning, but Khlit was no longer under him. A second stroke cut through the *thag*'s waist to his backbone.

The strangler who had stood beside Abdul Dost had thrown his noose over the Muslim's head and drawn it tight. Yet the Afghan was hardly slower to act than Khlit. He caught the cord firmly in one hand and grasped his sword from under the antelope skin with the other.

The *thag* yelled in alarm and plucked his knife from his girdle. He lifted it to spring on Abdul Dost. He struck at the Afghan, but only the bloodied stump of an arm reached the chest of the *mansabdar*. The hand and the knife fell to earth.

Abdul Dost was one of the most expert swordsmen in Hindustan. Although slow to think, he, like many men of great physical activity, was alert to move. Having rendered their assailants harmless, he and Khlit glanced hastily about the tent.

They saw a strange sight. Mustafa's lean form was writhing helplessly on the sand. Taleb Khan leered at them like a hideous toad, his fat arms waving weakly and more weakly to catch the perfumed girdle of Daria Kurn which was draining his breath. The dozen followers were suffering a like fate.

"*Gurkha men dina!*" screamed an angry voice. "Strangle!"

Dhurum Khan pointed at Khlit and Abdul Dost in a frenzy. Except for the unexpected resistance of the two supposedly bound men, all had gone well with the *thag*s.

In their guise of merchants, they had assembled unsuspected at the caravansary during the absence of Taleb Khan and his followers upon the river.

They had waited by the *mirza*'s empty tents, knowing that the men must return to their camp. Quietly they had joined the throng about Daria Kurn when all eyes were upon the woman. They had awaited their opportunity, each strangler standing beside his victim with their habitual calmness.

Only two men had survived the massacre. These faced the *thag*s, sword in hand.

"Attack!" cried Daria Kurn. "Fools! Bunglers! They are but two."

Several half-naked *thags* leaped forward with drawn knives at Khlit and Abdul Dost. The *mansabdar* stepped to meet them. He was smiling and his eyes were alight.

The first slayer dropped to the sand with his skull split under the folds of his turban. The second had his throat nearly cut through by a swift half stroke. The rest hung back, fearing the tall Muslim who seemed to joy in a conflict.

Khlit gazed about the scene of battle curiously. He wondered at the swift action of the *thags*. A moment since Taleb Khan and his men had been alive. Now they were in the last death throes, kicking and gasping on the sand.

The thought came to him that Taleb Khan had paid dearly for his disguise. Probably the slayers had thought him an ordinary merchant.

"Back to back!" he growled to Abdul Dost.

The two placed themselves in readiness. They knew better than to flee. By now figures were running from the nearby tents. Dhurum Khan had planned his masterpiece of death. All the unfortunates who slumbered in the tents had awakened from their dreams only to slip struggling into a deeper sleep.

His guards posted at the gate in the wall would have cut down any who escaped the stranglers. But no one ran from the tents except the *thags*.

"Oh, cowards!" The shrill voice of Daria Kurn reviled her companions. "Will you let two stand unhurt? Give me a sword!"

Khlit swept the crowd with an appraising glance. He was glad that no bows were to be seen—not knowing that the *thags* always worked with noose and steel, which were silent and left no traces. But momentarily the number around them grew, as the stranglers left their other victims to hasten to complete the killing.

In the unwritten law of *thaggi*, the ritual of Kali, it was unheard of to permit any of the destined victims to escape. If one died all must die.

Jaim Ali caught the arm of Daria Kurn as she was rushing upon the two warriors with streaming hair.

"Let me strike!" she wailed. "Mine—and Dhurum Khan's—was the plan. They are marked for my sword."

"True it is," the boy cried, "that you are the one whose counsel we sought. We are your servants, O Daria Kurn, beloved of Kali."

He swung a long noose in the air, stepping toward the waiting two. But the woman would not be denied. She darted forward, and seeing this the *thags* under Dhurum surged after her.

"We must complete the work," they whispered to each other. "If not, we are doomed. The evil omen of the slain woman is bearing fruit."

"Aye, the evil omen," chanted Dhurum Khan, hearing.

"Ho!" laughed Abdul Dost. "The slayers come—faithless followers of the Prophet. The low-born cooks taste of the feast they have prepared!"

Knives and short swords were ill weapons against the two finest sword-arms in Hindustan. At each sentence the Afghan, now thoroughly warmed to his work, struck aside a leaping *thag*. When he struck, men crumpled to earth.

Jaim Ali's noose closed over Khlit's blade and arm, but Abdul Dost cut the cord and sent the youth reeling with the same blow. Daria Kurn sprang at him, and her knife caught in his cloak, biting into his chest.

Khlit had never slain a woman. He turned his blade as he cut at the mistress of the *thags* and she was knocked senseless. But Dhurum Khan, thinking to take advantage of the opening, was slain swiftly.

The *thags* hesitated at sight of the bodies on the earth. They gave a wailing cry of grief. It was drowned in the quick tumult of rushing horses.

"Mount, master!" cried the voice of Kehru. "The horses come behind you!"

The trained ears of the two warriors located the horses without obliging them to turn their heads. The slayers looked up, startled at sight of the three mounts trotting from behind the tent. Kehru, unnoticed by the *thag*s because he had been hidden among the animals during the massacre, had acted swiftly and well.

Khlit and Abdul Dost leaped back as one man and grasped the manes of the passing horses. Neither warrior needed aid of the stirrups to mount. The Cossack, in fact, landed standing on the saddle, a favorite trick, and gave a yell of triumph. It was good to be mounted again.

His wide coat-skirts flapped out and his gray hair swayed behind him as he headed straight for the caravansary gate, his horse at a round gallop.

Kehru chortled joyously and dug his bare heels into the flanks of his pony. The guards at the gate were without bows. One ran forward uncertainly, but dodged back at the sweep of the Afghan's blade.

They were through the gate and the broad road to Pawundur stretched before them. Within a few moments—so swiftly they went—they met the cavalcade of the *vizier* with his servants and soldiers.

Straightaway, at the tidings they brought, the cavalcade broke into a gallop and gained the crossroads just as the sun reached the level horizon of Pawundur plain. At the gate they halted— Khlit and Abdul Dost and the *vizier*, who rode a mule and was attended by two slaves who had held a sunshade over him during the heat of the day.

"Allah!" said the *vizier*.

It was a strange sight. Tents, animals, ropes, bales of goods, and men were gone as if swept away in the brief interlude by a magic hand. The level gleam of the setting sun shone redly on the stretch of sand.

Upon the sand in grotesque and grim attitudes lay Taleb Khan, Mustafa and their men, coolies and officials alike. No wounds were to be seen on their bodies—save for a certain redness about the throat and bulge of the staring eyes. Their weapons were taken from them, but their common garments, assumed as a disguise, remained. The *vizier* went from one to the other and paused at the round body of Taleb Khan.

"By the thrice-blessed name of God!" he said, and was silent. "It is written that those who don the garb of trickery shall drink the cup of deceit. Where is the revenue of Pawundur?"

Khlit dismounted and showed him the ebony box in the sand by the dead *ameer*.

"Herein was the revenue of Pawundur," he said.

Abdul Dost had already related the tale of the *thag* attack, saying nothing however of the treachery of Taleb Khan. A righteous man, the *mansabdar* was loath to speak ill of the slain.

In the chest were numerous rocks, and nothing more. Again the *vizier* looked about the caravansary and stretched out his arms in resignation. The tale of the crossroads—and he read it with his own eyes—was complete. He ordered his followers to make camp and bury the bodies. But Khlit would not linger in the caravansary. He sought out Kehru and led him to the *vizier*.

"Here is a stripling, O man of the Mogul," he said, "who will make a brave warrior. Take him into the service of the Mogul and it shall one day profit you."

Whereupon he mounted and lifted a hand in farewell. At the gate he turned in his saddle.

"Perhaps," he called, "you may find the revenue of Pawundur —in the villages from here to the border. But seek it not after the manner of Taleb Khan."

The *vizier* had a tender skin. He knew of the *thags*. He did not care to seek the revenues of Pawundur. Nevertheless, in time strange tales came to him, and he wondered.

After this fashion the tales came to be told in the bazaars and the highways of Pawundur. Abdul Dost had been thinking as he rode beside Khlit away from the caravansary and turned his horse's head into the road that led to the North.

"Eh," he pondered, "it was a clever thought—your thought to cry 'robbery' to Taleb Khan. Did Daria Kurn verily take from the chest that which was within?"

Khlit shook his head.

"Then it was a lie. It was a good lie, full-tongued. It was fated to save our lives."

"It was not a lie."

For a dozen paces the Afghan considered this. He was puzzled. Either the *thags* had taken the gold and gems from the chest, or they had not. This was as clear to him as his horse's ears before his eyes. He told this to Khlit.

The Cossack leaned forward and silently drew a handful of gold from one of his saddlebags—the bags that had rested at his saddle peak since their departure from the boat. From the other sack he pulled out a jewel or two mixed with grain and oaten cakes.

"The treasure of Taleb Khan!" said Abdul Dost, staring.

"Aye," responded Khlit. "Taleb Khan. On the boat I had a thought that the wealth would be safer in these bags. So I took it—when you looked the other way—from the chest. I would have rendered it truly to Taleb Khan, but he seized upon us."

Abdul Dost drew rein for his sunset prayer.

"Verily," he mused, "the fate of the *ameer* was a strange fate. What is written, is written. Not otherwise."

Thereafter, at each village they passed, the inhabitants gathered around them while a tall *Ferang*, dressed much like a wild wolf, scattered handfuls of gold among them, laughing the while, and spurred away before they could prostrate themselves in gratitude or rob the two warriors.

And at the final village of Pawundur province, the dark-faced Afghan who rode with the *Ferang* showed a double handful of fine gems, red rubies of Badakshan and blue diamonds of Persia. He replaced the jewels in his girdle.

"Say to the *vizier*," he cried, "that this is the price of the guilt of one who was named Taleb Khan."

The Curved Sword

I

In the mountains the light of the sun is strongest; there the shadows are deepest. The herds find there the richest grass, and the water that rushes from the snows overhead.

In the mountains the herder sleeps under the open eyes of God. And he hears the voice of the winds, betokening sunrise and storm.

In the mountains the eagle beholds the world beneath his wings.

Is an eagle to be found in the lowlands? Nay—naught is there but the sparrow-hawk and kite.

Afghan proverb

Chan, the minstrel, rose and girded tight his shawl-belt. It was the hour of sunset and the *namaz gar*—the evening prayer. From the village below his tent Chan could hear the *mullah*'s cry; but although scarcely a village in the southern foothills of the Himalayas did not join in the prayer to the Prophet in the year 1609, Chan heeded neither *mullah*'s cry nor his own spiritual welfare.

Sunset to Chan the minstrel meant sometimes supper of mutton or rice and sometimes a yearning stomach. This evening, however, he had left the stock of rice and dried apricots in his felt tent untasted. He had been engaged in the more important work of composing a love lyric.

The song was finished—and the Afghan youth boasted a critical ear, schooled in the musical modes of the wandering bards of Samarkand, likewise a skilled finger to stir the one string of his guitar—and Chan sprang into the saddle of his pony, which had been grazing behind the tent. He adjusted the shagreen quiver of arrows behind his left shoulder, slinging his guitar over his right arm.

Chan was a dark-faced, merry-eyed youth—although a wisdom beyond his years, born of many privations and no little fighting, lurked behind the smile in those same brown eyes. The *zirih*— sleeveless coat of mail—gripped his lithe body tightly under the ragged and travel-stained red-velvet cloak. Blue turquoise glimmered on the dagger-hilt that peered from his girdle, and a brown cap of sable fur topped his black locks.

His pony began to trot mechanically down toward the village as the minstrel hummed the refrain of his new lyric triumphantly. An unstrung bow bobbed at his saddle-peak. Chan, who was as skilled at making play with bowstring as guitar string, had long ago passed the test of Afghan archery—to shoot, at full gallop, an arrow at a mark, loosen the bow and use it as a whip, then restring to let fly another arrow at the same mark.

"My bow for an enemy, my song for my mistress," he hummed, "and both, my faith, reach to the heart—aye, both to the heart."

Thus sang Chan as he trotted onward, fully prepared to take either weapon in hand—so uncertain were these times in the hills of Hindustan.

"Nay," he murmured to the ears of his pony that twitched back responsively; "shall we sew the pearls of wit upon the cord of love or ply the arrow-stitches of vengeance! *Hai—ohai*, the day is fair and soon we shall see the gray stone walls that enclose the fairest jewel of paradise!"

Meditating in this manner, he passed through the village—not without a tentative sniff at the odors that rose with the smoke of the cooking-fires before the huts. He called cheerily at the flocks of black-faced sheep that pressed home from the pasture trails. Snatching at a cluster of dying, yellow roses, he arrayed the blossoms bravely in his cap.

The pony, knowing well the way, passed rapidly under twisted junipers, over grassy downs, and by glens already shadowy with evening. A wind, stirring in lazy gusts from the mountain passes overhead, tossed the dried balls of gray thistles before the rider, who struck at them readily with his bow.

Chan's hut had been on the mountain slope just within the upper timber line where he could watch what was going on in the valleys, fully prepared to flee to the rocky passes if need be. Overhead, the giant shoulders of the Koh-i-Baba thrust up from the pine forest; still farther rose the barren wastes of the heights to the snow peaks, encrimsoned by the setting sun.

He was now riding through the fertile uplands of the province known to his race as Badakshan, which was on the marches of the empire of Hindustan, the border above Kabul Valley, and the passes through the Hindu Kush—the Shyr and Khyber Passes, already scenes of age-old battles—and a thorn in the side of the emperor of Hindustan, *Padishah* Jahangir, the Mogul, Lord of the World and Master of Ind.

Without guidance the pony turned aside from the valley trail through the dried broom that led to a gorge under one of the cliffs. Here an apple orchard almost concealed a tiny sandstone house. Chan tethered his mount to one of the trees and advanced, peering about him in the uncertain light.

Overhead the sky was still blue and the sun was blood-colored behind the summits, but in the gorge darkness fell swiftly, and already a star or two was winking into being in the East. A dog slunk off at his approach. Chan glanced at it in some surprise, humming still as he took his guitar in hand.

Under a rose-bush near the house wall he sat cross-legged, and smiled. Within the stone wall, he thought, a lovely girl would be expecting his song. Chan, of course, had never seen her face, but he had talked with her and knew that she must be lovely.

Then his figure stiffened and he looked attentively at the ground.

Many horses had passed here since his last visit. The bushes were broken through in places and the earth trampled. The minstrel ran an exploring finger over one of the imprints and drew in his breath sharply, feeling the mark of leather shoes.

For a space the man was silent, his senses keenly alert. The quietude of the stone house weighed upon him, and he remem-

bered the furtive manner of the dog. He even fancied that he heard
a moan issue from within.

Abruptly the howl of the dog disturbed him. Chan sprang up
and ran into the door, stooping under the low portal. At his feet he
could make out a human body that moved and sighed. A glance
around the bare stone chamber, and a second, more hesitant, into
the screened woman's quarters, showed him that no one else was
to be seen.

He bent over the form at his feet and saw that it was the mother
of the house.

"*Aie!*" she cried, seeing Chan. "*Aie!*"

"What has come to pass? Whither your daughter—"

The mother rose to her knees, tresses disheveled about her
shoulders and her hands bloodied. She who had often driven him
from the orchard with abuse grasped his knees, leaving thereon
the stains of torn fingers.

"Evil has come upon this house. Riders passed along the road,
and one saw the child of my heart and liver watching from under
the trees. They took her, and beat me when I cried out—taking
the rings from my fingers—"

The woman held up her hands and Chan saw that two fingers
had been cut off. He freed himself from her grasp, drawing a long
breath, and stepped toward the door.

"Who were the riders, and whither did they turn their horses'
heads?"

For a space the mother was silent, looking fearfully out of the
door. Then a fresh outburst of grief overcame her.

"Alacha, the Slayer, it was, with his men. May Ali the just
pursue him with retribution! May he taste the evil he has stored
up for others! *Barkallah!* O Chan, brave Chan, men say you are
quick and shrewd. Mount, good Chan, speed your shaft—"

Mechanically the young minstrel slung the guitar over his
back and strung his bow.

"Went they south or north?"

"South, toward the camp of that black Turkoman, Alacha."
Her weak voice rose in sudden terror. "Strike not at Alacha, foolish one! Anger not those who hold the valley within their grasp.
Nay—send the shaft into the breast of my pearl of beauty, my
innocent daughter—"

But the minstrel strode from door and house, mounting with
a single leap. Behind him the peasant woman rocked in her misery, heedless of her own hurt. Chan wore no spurs, yet the pony
wheeled away at full gallop at the urge of its rider.

Alacha, sometimes called the *Kara*, or Black Turkoman, was
the landholder of the valley of Badakshan—that wide, fertile valley which was more like a plain, high in the foothills of the
Himalayas, wherein were the villages of the Afghans and the
Mongol Hazaras and great Balkh, the mother of cities. Alacha
was *jagirdar*, or fief-holder of the Mogul, and his authority over
the land was absolute so long as the yearly tax of grain, animals,
cloths, and silver was paid by him to the Mogul and judicious
presents were sent to the court at the festivals.

Surrounded by his Turkoman, Persian and Uzbek followers,
living in his stately, moving camp, the Slayer had well earned
the name bestowed on him by the Afghan tribes of the countryside. Perhaps for this reason he had been selected by Jahangir,
the Mogul, as a fitting ruler of Badakshan, which was far from
peaceful. Once the warriors of Badakshan had aided the Mogul
during the stress of battle, but the memory of an emperor is short,
and independence is the breath of life to an Afghan.

To resist the authority of Alacha was to strike against the
might of the Mogul. To lift weapon against the rulers of the valley
was to risk the terrors of fire and pillage. So the mother in her
grief had known, and so Chan knew. But the minstrel was great
of soul.

Riding swiftly beyond the confines of the village, he passed
the last of the tilled land and so came at full gallop to a rise in
the trail where, silhouetted against the afterglow of the sky, two
riders sat their horses.

They were tall men, fully armed. One by the drape of his turban and his long cloak appeared an Afghan. But Chan made out at his shoulder a small, round shield of a kind worn by followers of the Mogul. The other rider, bearded and wide of shoulder, wore a peculiar sheepskin hat tilted on one side of his shaggy head.

Both sat their horses easily, watching him. Both were powerful men, travel-stained. Neither spoke as he neared them, but he of the turban dressed his shield swiftly, seeing Chan pluck forth an arrow from over his shoulder.

Never doubting that the two were an afterguard of the armed party that had carried off the girl, Chan loosed the arrow. It rang against metal on the chest of the turbaned rider. The next moment Chan was on his foe, discarding his bow for the long Persian dagger in his girdle.

The minstrel struck swiftly, wheeling his pony as the rider maneuvered his own mount readily. Steel clashed against steel as Chan sought to close with his adversary, who faced him silently without giving ground. Momentarily Chan thought to feel the weapon of the other warrior strike his unprotected back. But the tall wearer of the sheepskin hat watched passively, even laughing once deep in his throat.

"Ho, stealer of women!" grunted the minstrel hotly, for it was his fashion to speak aloud while fighting and ever to voice the thought that was in his mind. "Despoiler of a home! Tearer of the veil of a maiden's chastity! Dog—"

Thus addressed, he of the turban caught Chan's wrist with his free hand and with a grip of remorseless fingers loosened the minstrel's hold on the dagger until the weapon clanged to earth.

Unarmed, Chan fronted his foe resolutely, stunned by the swift skill that had overcome him as if he were a child in arms.

"Aye, dog," he muttered, "for you bear the insignia of shame, being yet an Afghan—" he pointed at the round shield—"for, like a dog you stray about seeking the scraps that fall from the Mogul's table and lick the hand that crushes the life from your race!"

Instead of striking the youth, the warrior of the turban drew a long, hissing breath and peered intently at Chan's face as if to mark his adversary. His own features were veiled by a loosened fold of the turban. And, bending head upon chest, he seemed to draw back into the screening shadows of evening. It was the silent watcher who spoke.

"Stripling, do your arrows burn in their quiver that you loose them thus? We are no takers of women. Some riders passed, at speed, two bow-shots before you, and in the dust of their going I saw a woman across the saddle-peak of one. Likewise another woman ran after them screaming. If you seek them, go—but look before you loose a second shaft."

Chan peered from one to the other, bewildered.

"Be you not men of the Mogul?"

"Aye, and—nay. Go!"

Glancing at the fierce eyes that bored into his from under shaggy brows, Chan stooped to snatch up his dagger without quitting saddle. He gathered up his reins, muttering to himself, "This is no man of human mold—" measuring the long waist, high shoulders and massive thews of the taller warrior—"and verily his mate is a swordsman of the brood of hell—"

"Of the Mogul's bodyguard," grunted he of the sheepskin hat. "O one of small wit, you have crossed steel with him who is master of the scimitar in all Hindustan. There is another riddle for your addle-pate. Now, go!"

And Chan galloped away, not before his late adversary had checked him long enough to learn his name.

He urged his horse along the grassy trail, peering into the gathering shadows as he went. It was not long before he reined in suddenly, throwing his pony back on its haunches.

Leaping from the saddle, Chan ran to a white huddle that lay across the road. It was the form of a young woman, unveiled. Where throat met breast the hilt of a dagger projected, and under the still head and scattered tresses the earth was damp.

Chan shaded his eyes to search the trail ahead, but saw only a haze of dust at a distant turn.

"Alacha has passed," he sighed.

Barely could be make out the face of the dead woman—rounded, innocent features, stained with dust, dark eyes that strained wildly up at the empty vault of the skies, a full, young mouth twisted with strange, sudden pain.

He touched the dagger-hilt gently without moving it and found it to be heavily jeweled, of Persian workmanship. Once or twice the minstrel had seen the weapon in the girdle of the Slayer.

"Aye," he sighed again, "my precious flower of beauty was fair, even as I foreknew. Her cheeks are like the rounded rose-petals, her throat is fair as the soft throat of a pigeon.

"*Aie*—my fair one, my pearl of love, my bird that fell from the nest! Allah in His wisdom has taken you to His mercy—so Muhammad Asad, the holy man would tell me. I mocked at him, yet can I doubt the meaning of death?"

As if the story were written in the dust of the road, its message was clear for Chan to read. Held upon the saddle-peak of Alacha, the girl had managed to draw his dagger from his girdle unseen in the dim light and had struck, not at her foe but at herself, choosing the surest release from her bondage.

It was like Alacha, the minstrel pondered bitterly, to toss the body aside into the road when he saw that the woman would die. By tomorrow he would have forgotten the incident. Alacha, by nature and political position, was scarcely afraid of consequences.

So Chan, grieving at the death of the woman he had wooed without seeing her face, took up the body in his arms. With some difficulty he mounted, bearing his burden, and set off back along the way he had come, toward the village.

Far overhead on his right the snow peaks were turning from dark crimson to purple. Darkness was in the valley, and a cold wind stirred the dust under the pony's hoofs, wafting a strong, chill scent of willows and aspen from the nearby thickets.

Man and horse moved slowly as if tired. Chan's thoughts were numbed.

"The mountains are red," he said to himself, "and red is the road. It is the color of blood."

The muscles of his face moved spasmodically and stiffened. His teeth drew back from set lips.

"In the law of the Prophet is it written; there is the price of blood to be paid. Aye—to be paid."

II

The Sign at the Crossroads

The light had not failed when the two riders who had recently encountered Chan passed by the village without attracting attention and followed the path as it wound upward along the edge of the forest.

They rode in silence, yet keeping abreast and looking occasionally at each other or at the trail ahead or behind in the fashion of men who have been much together and are accustomed to notice their surroundings with a wariness that is the mark of troubled times.

Here the forest gave back and numerous fields of lush grass appeared cut by ravines, down which unseen streams murmured over worn stones. An owl hooted somewhere in the direction of a bare pine that towered against the darkening sky. And ahead of them a flight of wide-winged birds rose lazily. At the same time a stringent odor came to them on the wind.

The Afghan motioned his companion to halt and pointed out another path running athwart their own. Midway where the two met, a stout stake projected from the ground. A last, lingering vulture flapped away from the stake, rising from the body of a man transfixed by the wooden point.

"This is my homeland," observed he of the turban slowly, "and I have not slept within its borders since some months before I joined company with you. Behold the sign for the traveler."

He laughed once shortly, and passed on, his horse shying at the dead body.

"Even so," remarked the elder rider calmly, "we must sleep and our horses have come far this day from the pass you call the Khyber."

The Afghan glanced back at the stake and the form over which the carrion birds were assembling, now that the two riders had passed the crossroads.

"Not here, old warrior. Nearby in a ravine should be a holy man, Muhammad Asad, whom I seek. Come!"

Up one of the watercourses which descended from the slopes of the overhanging hills there was a granite cliff bearing certain writings in the *Turki* tongue, chiseled into the face of the rock. These writings, maxims of the Koran, were laboriously traced by the hermit *mullah*, Muhammad Asad, whose blindness precluded his writing upon parchment.

Unlike the Hindu *fakirs*, Muhammad Asad lived not upon mendicant charity, but was supplied with food by the villagers. A thin native boy who had kindled a fire in the mouth of the cliff's base—the abode of the *mullah*—stared at the two newcomers who walked their horses into the circle of light.

The hermit, a lean man with white beard and skin darkened almost to black by the sun, stood up in his neat cloak and spotless turban and greeted the two, seemingly without surprise.

"It is written," he cried in a melodious voice, "that guests are a blessing from Allah. Doubly fortunate am I, in this ill-omened year, that I should share my evening meal. Dismount!"

"A true Afghan greeting," observed the turbaned warrior to his companion, turning his horse loose to graze.

At this the blind *mullah* lifted his head sharply, as one who hears a familiar note of music.

"A true believer speaks," he murmured. "Aye, in the hills of Badakshan it is the law that even an enemy may sleep unafraid beneath the roof of an Afghan. Are you friend or enemy?"

His sightless eyes peered in the direction of the two visitors as if seeking out the secrets that were hidden from him. The Afghan strode to the fire.

"A friend, Muhammad Asad," he responded almost roughly. "Aye, one who rides pursued by sorrow. My companion is a warrior known to many lands and courts, although a *caphar*— unbeliever. Come, give him food."

Muhammad Asad still stood as if listening for something he did not hear.

"It is written," he said again gently, "that he who is pursued by sorrow knows not what the road may bring to him."

He motioned his guests to the fire, but refused to share their repast, saying that hunger lacked. Then he dismissed the boy and bade them spread blankets by the fire within the shallow cave, which was little except a depression in the face of the cliff.

"Enough to an Afghan," he observed quietly, "his rug and blanket. Let the hired mercenaries of the World-Gripper* have their silks and cushions."

The Afghan warrior looked up sharply, his glance straying to the round shield that rested against his quiver, within arm's reach. In the firelight his hawk-like features stood out clearly, the skin tight upon the bone, his keen eyes quick and clear, his thin-lipped mouth straight as a knife-cut in the dark face.

A man in the prime of life, his bearing and actions suggested a soldier, and a scar running from cheek to eye indicated a severe wound sustained years ago. He ate little, and watched the *mullah* thoughtfully.

His big-boned, bearded companion, however, made away with enough for two men and looked regretfully at the last remains of the *pilau*—a dish of rice and mutton, highly seasoned. Then he lay back upon his sheepskin coat, paying little attention to the talk of the other two, for he knew only a smattering of *Turki*.

"Warrior," observed the *mullah*, folding thin arms in his wide

---

* Jahangir, the Mogul.

sleeves. "You have come far this day. Aye, from the Khyber neck where the guards of Alacha watch the land. You are a soldier of the Mogul, and you have come hither to hear what Muhammad Asad can tell you about the valley."

The Afghan started and glared at the priest.

"This is sorcery!" he grunted. "You are blind—"

"Sight, Muslim," smiled Muhammand Asad, "lies inward as well as outward. A lame sense is aided by the crutch of wisdom. Nay—you walk and sit like one who is sore and wearied, as I can hear. Were you not a follower of the World—Gripper—may Allah heap upon him the fruits of his tyranny—Alacha's guards would not lightly let you pass. And since my poor home is hidden from the high road, you have sought me out."

The other fingered his sword irresolutely.

"On the farther side of the village, O *kwajah*, we beheld a youth who calls himself Chan, and he rode in pursuit of men who had taken a woman from the village. Know you aught of this?"

"A woman!" Muhammad Asad's thin face darkened. "That is an evil thing. So Alacha has dared openly to pierce the veil of the harem?

"Yet it is like to other deeds of the Slayer. He struck down with his sword the child who brought out to him the keys of Balkh—because it was thought he would not strike a child—and laughed, saying that the bandits of the Hindu Kush should taste the power of their emperor."

He paused, shaking his head.

"My years are many, O honored guest—" the blind man dwelled forcibly on the last two words—"and much have I heard of the warfare of the tribes, sometimes between themselves, for that has been the fate of the Afghan, and more often to defend them from the Uzbek of the West or the Persian of the South. But never before have I heard the name of emperor cried out in the valley of the Hindu Kush that is Badakshan. So I have proclaimed from the minaret of Balkh that this is a year of danger and peril, wherein the evil omens cluster about Badakshan as the vultures sink to the body of the slain messenger on the high road. For that Alacha had the soles of my feet beaten with wands, and I gave thanks to Allah, for I suffered in a just cause."

"I have been in Hindustan," said the soldier, "and there also have wars been. I have not heard of these things."

"Doubtless the emperor of Hindustan has paid you in good gold," responded the priest. "Watching from our hills, we have seen the armies of the Mogul overrun the province of Kabul, and once our fighting men under our leader Abdul Dost saved the World-Gripper his life. Has Jahangir forgotten that?"

"The court is far from Badakshan, and the revenues from the hills have been scanty, O *kwajah*. Money is the thews by which the Mogul holds his empire together."

"Yet Jahangir sent Alacha. Once we dispatched a messenger to complain to the Mogul. When the Slayer learned of this the messenger did not return to us, nor did his word reach farther than one of the lesser *ameer*s."

And Muhammad Asad, kneeling by the embers of the fire, told of villages stripped of their stores of grain so that hunger walked ominously through the valley, of droves of horses requisitioned for the imperial army, of *bakhshi*s, treasurers, who made a list of the goods of each man and took one-third for Alacha.

He described hunts, ordered for the pleasure of Alacha, in which farmers' crops were trampled by the riders, and of cattle driven off in nightly raids which the *jagirdar* countenanced.

"It is our fate that this should be laid upon us. What could we do? The imperial standard is set before the tent of Alacha. Through him the Mogul speaks. There is no one to call him to account. Once when our councilors of Balkh were trying to keep the young men and the wandering Hazaras from revolt, I sent a second messenger, this time to our former leader-in-arms, Abdul Dost. But Alacha is shrewd and the messenger lies on the high road near my abode."

The Afghan stared into the fire, plucking at his beard.

"Yet, O *kwajah*, you should be a man of peace and I and our older men fought for Akbar, the father of Jahangir. It was he gave me rank of *mansabdar* on the battlefield—"

"And now the pay for which you have sold your sword is gleaned from the empty bellies of our tribe. The Mogul is no longer a hill man, and he has forgotten that his grandsire was of Mongol blood. He has turned Hindu, and it is said he eats the drugs of the Persians. The shadow of his hand lies over the land."

"Only in a united India, O *kwajah*, is there hope of peace. The Mogul's hand binds together the empire."

"Evil, Muslim, is to be spurned. And Alacha is evil. Doubtless you fear him—"

"*Bismillah!* I, who have turned my horse from no man, fear the Black Turkoman?"

The *mullah* smiled a little. "There speaks Abdul Dost." He nodded as if in confirmation of what he had previously suspected. "Once, Abdul Dost, I heard your voice on the high road, in the year of the Ox. And I do not easily forget."

At this the Afghan soldier who had taken service with the Mogul fell to stroking his short black beard, as was his habit when disturbed. Since the death of his master, the last Afghan ruler of Badakshan, Abdul Dost had followed the path of war behind the standard of the Mogul, though more often engaged in independent forays with his old companion who now slept profoundly by the fireside, secure in the presence of friends.

Mingled emotions showed in the dark face of the Muslim warrior. He had heard something—for little news drifted south through the mountains save what Alacha chose to send—of the tyranny that had oppressed his people. Yet he had honored the service of Akbar, the Great, father of Jahangir, from childhood, and like the best type of Mohammedan soldier, he was faithful to his leader.

Muhammad Asad with uncanny perspicacity seemed to follow the trend of his visitor's thoughts.

"The time I heard your voice, Abdul Dost," he meditated aloud, "you helped to save a child from the path of charging buffalo. Behold, the child is grown to half-boyhood and he honors your name. He it is who tends my fire and who is now gone to the village. Have the drugs and wine and the flung gold of the Mogul changed your spirit? Are you no longer a true Afghan?"

Abdul Dost looked up with smoldering intensity but said nothing.

"Dreams, Abdul Dost," continued the blind priest, "are the visions of the soul in flight without the body. In the first of this moon I dreamed that one who was skilled in war, whose name is a talisman in Badakshan, who had the noble stamp of the ancient race of Sulieman in his features, came to the oppressed people of Badakshan and placed upon his strong shoulders the cloak of faith, and took within his hand the staff of leadership."

Again he nodded with the assurance of the aged.

"And, behold, Abdul Dost, you came to my fireside and the first portion of my dream was true. Yet because you cherished the rank of *mansab*, in the pay of the money-gleaner Jahangir, I would not share bread and salt with you until I knew whether you were true Afghan or—" and his mild voice strengthened in righteous wrath—"a dog that feeds at the table of the Mongol who has forgotten his birth, his faith, and the two laws—the law of the Koran and the law of Genghis Khan, who was the first and greatest Mongol."

The subtle oratory of the ardent-spirited *mullah* worked profoundly on the simpler emotions of the soldier. But to Abdul Dost truth was self-evident: his mind was shaped for action, yet before acting it was not his nature to ponder at length.

"*Bismillah!*" He flung out an eloquent hand. "O *kwajah*, hither I came to drink at the refreshing well of your wisdom. What avails it to reproach me for that I have been a warrior of the Mogul. It is no shame. Were more of our heedless and quarrelsome men obedient to authority, the balm of peace would heal the sores of past wars that afflict Badakshan. In a just ruler lies the solution of our unrest."

"Not so, Abdul Dost. Can a tiger be prisoned within bars? Is an eagle fashioned by God to fly with clipped wings? Jahangir has proclaimed himself lord of Badakshan. It is the heritage of the Afghans to have no rulers except themselves!"

His low voice rang with conviction. Abdul Dost stretched an appealing hand toward the *mullah* as if beseeching relief from his own trouble.

"Then would you have Badakshan rebel against the Mogul?"

As he said this, footsteps sounded outside the cave. The *mansabdar* moved on his knees and his hand went to his sword-hilt, but the *kwajah* smiled, saying, "It is the boy."

The stripling, panting from a hard run, salaamed respectfully to Abdul Dost and burst into pent-up speech.

He had been to the village and had come with news warm on his lips. Chan, the minstrel, the master of artful song, had entered the village with the body of a young woman across his saddle. Chan had shown the knife of Alacha fast in the throat of the woman. He had shown the body to the headmen of the village.

"The Slayer has crossed the barrier of the harem," cried the boy. "So said the elders. And Chan asks that the price of blood be paid."

Muhammad Asad turned to Abdul Dost, his fragile countenance dark with religious zeal.

"Allah has ordained it thus, Abdul Dost. Here is the answer to your question. A woman has been slain, and Alacha must pay the price. When a freshet from the snow-line rises and rushes downward, who can stay its course?"

The *mansabdar*, concealing his deep anxiety before the boy, stared into the fire. He knew that this murder of a woman, unlike the previous slaughter of tribesmen and peasants under the thin guise of justice, meant war in Afghan territory.

"No man can stay the working of fate," cried Muhammad Asad. "The will of God will come to pass, even thus. And I prophesy! *Ai*—the spirit that has come into my soul calls for speech."

He rose, extending emaciated arms to the roof of the cave, against which the smoke rose, blackening the rock. His sightless eyes turned skyward.

"*Ai*—hear these, my words. I, Muhammad Asad, humblest of the servants of God, foretell what will come to pass. In my soul it is clear. I know—I have long known. Blood will cover the mountains; bones will whiten in the valleys. The hand of Death will strike upon Badakshan!"

Abdul Dost and the boy watched the aged man with mingled feelings in which awe predominated. Often had the blind *mullah* foretold events of importance, perhaps purely from keen judgment arising from his close knowledge of affairs in the hills, perhaps from premonition sharpened by deep meditation, the fruit of long fasting and inward thought.

"There will be a battle in the valley," he cried. "The cannon and the elephants of the World-Gripper array themselves against the horsemen of the hills—and others.

"I see clouds of riders coming, dense as the flight of arrows from the passes where no riders are. I see bright swords drawn from scabbards that are now rusted. I see these horsemen, who once rode through Afghanistan, Kwaresan, Iran and Khorassan, but are not now in the land—"

He resumed his seat on the ground by Abdul Dost, his eyes closed. For a space there was silence, save for the deep breathing of the boy.

"What riders mean you?" asked Abdul Dost at length, for the words had puzzled him.

"How should I know, Afghan? But this thing you will see, for it is written."

His delicate, strained features became all at once very gentle.

"Aye, Abdul Dost, there will be war, and the terrors of war. But out of the fighting peace may come. Will you take up the reins of leadership?"

Hereupon the boy gazed avidly at the veteran warrior, the light of hero-worship strong in his brown eyes.

"I have a bow, O great Abdul Dost," he ventured, "and I can shoot crows very skillfully. Will you grant me the honor of riding behind your left side?"

The mind of the warrior was upon other things.

"Too much strife and taking of life have I seen, O *kwajah*, lightly to draw the sword of conflict. War? I know not. I must think. A leader?"

He turned at this to look at his sleeping companion, who had wakened alertly at the priest's outburst but now reposed again, his harsh face lined with fatigue.

"*Hai*—a leader, say you! Here is one who is a father of battles. At his side I have learned much of the art of war."

The boy looked his disbelief that Abdul Dost had aught to learn, and the *mullah*, hearing, became immersed in meditation.

"Verily is this man a master of battles," went on Abdul Dost. "He has led the *caphar* Kazaks who wield curved swords, like that at his side. And his voice has commanded the hordes of Tartary. The wiles of the Turk he knows, likewise the Rájput charge, and the battle-plan of the Mogul generals."

"Then his infidel sword is for sale?" Muhammad Asad spoke bitterly. "The Afghans lack gold, while the Mogul scatters diamonds from the back of his gold-quilted elephant—"

Abdul Dost shook his head with a laugh.

"You cannot see, O *kwajah*, that this old warrior wears a torn sheepskin coat and his belt is worn leather, while his horsehide boots are stained with usage. His weapon is a curved sword, very heavy, but without jewels.

"Much wealth, perhaps, has he been given, but I have seen him fling it among hungry villagers. I have seen him go hungry to pay for fodder for his horse—"

"So he will aid—"

"*Kwajah*, my companion does not seek war. He rides where he wills. I know not what is in his mind. His aid to us is worth three

times a thousand fine horsemen. Yet he will not draw sword for
pay or for what we Afghans cherish—renown in our history."

At this Abdul Dost lay back on his blanket, resting his head
on his arm.

"This man is Khlit, who is called the Curved Saber," he said
finally. "He—and I also—seek not war. Tomorrow we will ride to
Alacha and hold council, seeking to adjust the wrongs of Badakshan."

Almost immediately Abdul Dost slept. The priest sat passively, drawing nearer to the embers as the heat of the fire dwindled. The boy fidgeted with tiny bow and arrows until the healthy
drowsiness of childhood claimed him. The light of the fire had
vanished and the cave was in darkness.

But in the village a fire had been kindled that grew and spread
to other villages as Chan the minstrel rode through the valley,
calling upon the tribes to see the body of the fair woman, his
dead mistress, carried upon the saddle of his pony.

III
The Slayer Speaks

In the satin tent of Alacha, *jagirdar* of Badakshan, slaves set forth
the morning meal. A scarlet canopy embroidered with images
of birds and beasts worked in sewn pearls shaded the entrance,
inside which a white cloth had been laid. Scent had been thrown
into the air by the experienced servitors.

Alacha himself reclined on cushions by the cloth. A slender
man with olive face and dark, neatly dressed hair, wearing the
undress silk tunic and white cotton trousers of the Mogul court.
His black eyes were restless and insolent. One jeweled hand cherished a falcon on an adjacent perch.

Barely did he taste the dishes of rice, minced fowl, jellies,
sugar candies and rose-water. His full-lipped mouth smiled as
he stroked the bird, but he was engrossed in meditation. Waving
away the dishes, he clapped his hands for the guard that stood
without the tent.

"The horsemen who were on post at the Shyr," he commanded briefly.

Alacha was ever sparing of words and was a master of cutting irony. It was characteristic of the *jagirdar* that, unlike the ordinary *ameer* of the court, he disliked to have courtiers and lieutenants attend him.

Attentively he surveyed the two warriors, who bowed nine times—the imperial salaam—before the tent entrance. He spoke in a very clear, high-pitched voice.

"So you passed into Badakshan him whom I ordered to be brought to me?"

"May your forgiveness anoint us, unworthy! Abdul Dost gave rank and showed signet ring of *mansabdar*. So we passed him, not knowing his name. And his companion we passed, for he is the warrior that you in your wisdom sought—Khlit, of Tatar blood."

Not a flicker of the full eyes nor a movement of the jeweled hands showed that Alacha was surprised. He studied the two men inscrutably and dismissed them with a nod. They salaamed and departed, thankful to escape punishment.

Alacha reached into a silver casket by his side and drew out a rolled paper. Attentively he scanned this, noting the seal of the imperial *vizier*. Then he lay back with closed eyes while a stolid slave slowly waved a plumed fan of peacock feathers back and forth over his head.

But the Slayer was not asleep. When a sentinel appeared to announce that two riders sought speech with him, he scarcely stirred.

"Admit them."

Only once as Abdul Dost and Khlit rode their horses into the enclosure before the satin tent did the *jagirdar* glance at them, marking faces, bearing, and clothing. When the two visitors stood before him, Alacha was stroking the feathers of his pet, seemingly indifferent to their presence.

This irked Abdul Dost, who was ever straightforward.

"I have a message for your ear alone, Alacha, landholder of the Mogul," he said directly. "Dismiss your men." For some Turkoman guards had lingered near at hand.

Alacha turned his head enough to make certain that the untouched dishes of the morning meal remained on the cloth for the entertainment of guests.

"Sit, distinguished *mansabdar*," he murmured, "and partake of my humble bounty. Alas, these savage hills offer little that is dainty in food."

Abdul Dost remained grimly erect.

"Until I have spoken my message and received an answer I will not break my fast, Alacha, and then not at your cloth."

"Know you not the courtesy of the court, worthy warrior?" responded Alacha. "Why have you come, bearing arms, to the tent of your superior?"

With a short laugh Abdul Dost tapped the hilt of his scimitar.

"This weapon, Alacha, has served the Mogul more than once; and as for my companion, because of aid he once rendered to Nur-Jahan, who is to be Jahangir's queen-bride, his right to wear sword is unquestioned."

Alacha did not press his point, yet signed to his men to remain where they were. So the three faced one another, Khlit watching quietly, only half-catching what was said, Abdul Dost impatient and more than a little surprised at the almost effeminate aspect of the man who had brought terror into the hills of his people. The Slayer noted every move of his visitors and every change of expression without seeming to do so, but for the most part his attention was devoted to Khlit.

He heard immovably Abdul Dost's recital of the oppression that had come upon Badakshan, of the hunger of the villages, the anger at the hunting and the spoil taken by the agents of the *jagirdar*.

"There is no merchant but seeks to leave Badakshan because when by hard labor and thrift he increases his property, the *bakhshi* who is your treasurer levies upon him the sum of his profits. No peasant can keep his herds, for the animals are driven off by your soldiers. Weapons are seized wherever found—and how is an Afghan to live, weaponless?"

Carefully Alacha adjusted the silk hood over his pet.

"Those who had gold or silver—and they are few in this land," went on the *mansabdar* bitterly, "have buried it, so now none is to be had, save what you seize. One-third of the young men of the tribes are called upon for military service, and their sisters have been carried off by your men in raids, which you have not sought to punish. Badakshan bleeds, and your hand holds the knife. That is my message."

The hood tied to his satisfaction, Alacha turned his attention to a dish of sweetmeats and selected a sugared pomegranate with care.

"When sickness afflicts a human body, worthy *mansabdar*, does not a skilled physician bleed the patient?"

"Nay—if death is the result of the bloodletting. Allah alone decides the life and death of men."

"Of men, verily. Yet these scum of the hills be but low-born beggars, and their fathers before them were thieves. Who shall treat a jackal like a hunting-dog, or a miscreant like a man of honor?"

Alacha's black eyes snapped as he glanced swiftly up at Abdul Dost.

"Soldier, who sent you?"

Under his mustache the *mansabdar* smiled.

"Am I one to carry another's words? Alacha, it is the truth I speak. What will you answer?"

"You have been in the villages?"

The Turkoman's keen eyes seemed to probe out the information he sought.

"Bah—the bazaars will have their tale, and dogs will growl. Perchance the threadbare *mullah*s have poured the poison of their anger into your ears. Muhammad Asad, perchance?"

Abdul Dost's scarred face gave him the secret he angled for.

"By the beard of the Prophet! It was Muhammad Asad."

"Alacha, you have the blood of a woman on your hands. You know the law. Men will gather in pursuit of blood—"

"So they talk thus? Nay. The wanton of the village who was enamoured of a wandering minstrel slew herself."

Abdul Dost shook his head grimly. Always a man of meager speech, anxiety weighed upon him. Much depended upon the reply of Alacha.

"Your answer?" he asked again.

"To the men of Badakshan—nothing. To you, Abdul Dost, who are in the service of the Mogul, this."

The Turkoman spoke softly, almost idly.

"You complain of money exacted. It is to pay the price of my *jagir* to the treasurer of the Mogul, who bestowed it upon me. You speak of men slain and other hardships. Consider the maxim of the Koran that ill-doers shall taste the fruits of their evil. The Afghans are lawless; the hand that governs them must be stern."

At this Abdul Dost stroked his beard gravely.

"Then you will not hear the council of the headmen, nor make amends for the misdeeds of your men?"

"Nay."

"Then, Alacha, give heed to what also is written in the book of our faith. An eye shall be given for an eye, a tooth for a tooth, a life for a life—"

Swiftly the noble rose, drawing back the flap of the tent. Standing almost breast to breast against Abdul Dost, he pointed to the embroidered banner that hung at the enclosure entrance.

"Behold the standard of the Mogul, soldier," he said calmly. "It is the standard you have followed in battle. By this sign may you know I am master of Badakshan."

Before Abdul Dost could reply Alacha turned quickly to Khlit and spoke in the steppe dialect of *Turki*.

"Warrior, my heart is opened like a flower at sight of your face. The Master of the World has sent for you. Too long your sword has been absent from his court."

Khlit, hands thrust into his belt, booted feet wide apart, and sheepskin hat thrust carelessly askew on his gray hair, looked at the Slayer curiously. Alacha stooped to draw the parchment *firman* from his silver chest. Before exhibiting it to Khlit he asked quickly:

"You have skill to read? You also, Abdul Dost?"

"Not I," responded the old warrior indifferently. "Such scrawls are for priests and dogs of councilors who live by words."

Abdul Dost shook his head, moody at the reception accorded his message.

"This is from the hand of Jahangir, the Sun of Benevolence, Monarch of Hindustan."

Alacha exhibited the imperial seal.

"It is a summons to the court which now holds festival at Lahore, not six days' ride from the southern passes of Badakshan. There welcome awaits you, gifts that Jahangir alone can bestow, a robe of honor, a horse from the pick of the imperial stable, and rank in the army of India."

Khlit took the missive in his gaunt hand curiously and passed it back to the *jagirdar* silently.

"Do not fail to obey the request of the emperor," pressed Alacha. "The imperial favor shines upon few. Nur-Jahan, it is said, is your friend, and the Light of the World sways our prince with a single word. High honor is yours for the taking; rest and wealth for your old age."

"I would like a good horse," observed Khlit.

"It is yours. It is my exalted privilege to be bearer of the *firman* of my lord the Mogul." Alacha bowed his dark head. "Jahangir desires your presence. I would that I were in your place!"

Smilingly he watched his two visitors depart. When they had mounted and vanished through the enclosure gate the smile passed from his olive face as if by magic and he scowled, spitting upon the ground where Abdul Dost had stood. Then he called for a mounted messenger.

Kneeling upon the white cloth, he seized parchment and a feathered pen and laboriously wrote something. These he read over carefully before sealing. They were addressed to a high official of the court—to the *vizier*, in fact, who had sent the missive Alacha had shown to Khlit, and who was in favor with Jahangir and his queen-to-be.

As the letter of the *vizier* had been in Persian—a language unknown to Abdul Dost, who clung to his native tongue, and hence undecipherable by the *mansabdar* as the Slayer well knew—Alacha had written his reply in the flowery phrases of the Persian courtiers:

> *Perfection of nobility, star of grandeur, glorious son of Jamshyd, pillar of empire and monument of magnanimity: I, unworthy as the dust beneath thy horse's hoofs, presume to address thee in the matter of the unrest amid the scorpion-nest of Badakshan.*
>
> *The exalted message of thy wisdom, that "all who lift high their heads among the Afghans should have their heads stricken from their shoulders," has delighted my eyes. Yet to accomplish thy lofty aim, it has been necessary for me to pretend that thy words were otherwise—to the warrior known as the Curved Saber who now rides to Lahore with my assurance that the sun of imperial favor is inclined to shine upon him.*
>
> *Since this warrior is notable in craft and feats of arms, thy wisdom will perceive that it is best to retain him at court away from these ill-omened ones of Badakshan. Gain then the ear of Jahangir, to the end that Khlit be granted some trifling favor such as a robe of honor or a horse. Nur-Jahan, the favorite, has regard for the ancient warrior.*
>
> *If gifts will not nourish his restless spirit in peace, then, O vizier, chains and perchance the cells of eye-blinding Gwalior must play their part.*

The missive closed with elaborate compliments and promises of extensive payment of presents of camels, cloth, weapons and women and boy servitors from Alacha to the Mogul at the coming festival.

This accomplished and the messenger dismissed, Alacha instructed certain spies among the Hazara peasants who had been won to his cause by rich bribes to keep close track of the movements of Abdul Dost. No Afghans, as Alacha well knew, would play the part of a spy or betray their leader.

From the peasants he turned with a grimace to his own officers.

"Hold a muster of my soldiery," he commanded. "Send a party of horsemen to hunt down that mad priest, Muhammad Asad, and another to fetch me the witless minstrel Chan. Strip him of weapons and clothing and sew him into the fresh hide of a bullock where he may have his fill of blood and sing odes to his dead mistress to his heart's content."

Abdul Dost and Khlit reined in their horses by mutual consent where the path to the Shyr neck intersected the trail along which they were riding. Here they were on a slight hillock that afforded a view over the fertile, rolling plain of Badakshan.

But the fields beside the trail, illumined by the warm sun of early Autumn, showed only trampled grain, in which a broken wooden plow lay like some forlorn gravestone in a desecrated cemetery.

On the other side of the highway a shepherd watched them listlessly, lying with his dog at the edge of a willow thicket. No sheep were visible, as Abdul Dost noticed. Below them the huts of a village clustered about a dark pool of water, and around this squatted a ring of cloaked figures.

Along a wooded ridge beyond the village trotted a body of horse, their spear-tips glittering within the thin foliage of aspens and cypress, and the glint of armor showing under rich vestments—Turkoman riders in the service of Alacha.

Abdul Dost surveyed them moodily, gazing from the almost inanimate villagers to the dark stretches of pines that reached up over his head to the edge of the timberline. He raised his eyes to serried peaks, towering high against the blue vault of the sky. The rarefied air of that altitude revealed valleys and peaks alike with startling distinctness.

Emerging from an ice-coated moraine, two eagles circled over the pine-tops on tranquil wings. Abdul Dost pointed to them.

"They are of the hills," he muttered, "and freedom is their life. Allah the all-wise has decreed that they shall be spared the yoke of servitude."

Long and searchingly he gazed at Khlit's rugged features.

"You and I have slept under the stars together these many nights, and we have partaken of the same salt. You have drawn your reins along the path I have followed—until now. Do you abide in Badakshan, or ride through the Khyber to the court at Lahore?"

Carefully he concealed his own deep interest in Khlit's answer. The presence of the veteran warrior in Abdul Dost's land meant much to him. He had come to rely upon the wisdom of the former Cossack. With unrest and strife in the air of the hills, he was loath to have Khlit depart.

On the other hand, with honor and ease awaiting him at the court of India, Abdul Dost would not ask Khlit to share his own unsettled fortunes further.

Torn between soldierly loyalty to the Mogul and love for his own people now suffering at the hand of Alacha, Abdul Dost had his problem to thresh out, his decision to make. And so he yearned for the companionship of the man who had been a true friend, sharer of his tent and food through many adventures, in which the skilled sword of Abdul Dost had aided Khlit as often as the old warrior's craft had served them both.

"What think you?"

Khlit leaned thoughtfully upon his saddle-peak, questioning his friend with shrewd gray eyes set in a network of wrinkles but still keen.

"The good-will of Jahangir is a jewel beyond price."

Khlit nodded slowly, meditating aloud.

"Never have I seen this Mogul, Abdul Dost, who calls himself Lord of the World. There should be great warriors at his table, and much feasting and wise words."

"Aye," said Abdul Dost.

"Also gold. I have no gold. Nor a good horse, other than this steppe pony."

"Aye."

In spite of himself Abdul Dost's frank face clouded under Khlit's gaze. "These things, assuredly, you would have. Did you not fetch Nur-Jahan safely from the mountains of Tartary—" he waved a lean hand to the North and East where the giant peaks of the Himalayas were dimly to be discerned—"when you rode hither from the horde of the Tatar Khans?"

"She, also, will remember."

"Aye," replied Abdul Dhost, somewhat dryly.

"As for the Mogul, is he not of the blood of the ancient Mongol khans whose forebear was Genghis, the Great? In my veins runs the blood of Genghis. This thing I would tell him, Abdul Dost. As for a woman, her will is the wind's will."

"And so you go to the court?" Abdul Dost checked what he would have said, and lifted hand and head. "That is well. May your shadow grow, and your years be ripe with honor."

"My years come to an end. And honor—" Khlit smiled grimly —"is there any honor other than the friendship of true men?"

He took up his reins, squaring his shoulders, and felt of saddlebags and girdle wherein were whetstone and a brace of Turkish pistols.

"Abdul Dost, give me your hand. I ride far, but with the first snowfall in the mountains I shall come back to Badakshan and seek you."

Just a little, the Afghan shook his head, his eyes straying to the valley.

"What is written is written. This is farewell."

Long and earnestly the two looked into each other's eyes as they clasped hands after the custom of Khlit. And thus each spoke briefly, concealing the anxiety that weighed on them.

In Khlit's mind rang the words of the blind priest, foretelling battle in the land of his friend, and in his soul was a great curiosity as to the friendship of princes, and whether indeed the Mogul was a man of his word.

In Abdul Dost's thoughts was the certainty that he would not see Khlit again, in his heart the crying need of companionship in difficulty. But of this he would not speak, fearing to obstruct the path of Khlit's good fortune.

He watched his friend ride away along the path to the South, between rising shoulders of barren, sandstone summits. Until Khlit's sheepskin hat had vanished around a turn in the trail he remained motionless.

Then he picked up his reins and moved onward along the highway at a walk, tugging the head of his horse aside as the beast, from long habit, sought to follow Khlit's mount.

IV

To the builder of empire, the opener of roads, the healer of sickness, the planner of cities—respect.

For the bearer of water, the tiller of fields, the wielder of a protecting sword—gratitude.

To the wearer of another's sword, the crown of another's greatness, and to him who sits in another's throne—terror.

From father to son, the thrones of Agra, Delhi, Chitore, Kabul had passed, from Babur, the first great figure in history among the Moguls, who carved the empire of India out of chaos with his sword, to Humayon, the chivalrous, to Akbar, Jallal' u'din Akbar, who knit together the warring provinces of the empire by supreme diplomacy and humane law making, to Jahangir.

And during the reign of Jahangir the empire of the Moguls reached its zenith.

The World-Gripper inherited much of the hardiness of his forebears, and added thereto many vices of his own. Born in the shadow of a mighty throne, already acclaimed by a multitude of servants, he was not forced to undergo the healthful discipline of privation. Clever, unquestionably, supremely courteous at occasion, he was narrow of mind, hasty of temper, cruel when aroused, and always suspicious.

Of Turki-Mongol father and Hindu mother, schooled by Persian wiseacres, he revealed the traits of mixed breeding. A lover
of women of many races, pampered of body and gross of appetite,
the traces of degeneracy that were to mark the downfall of the
Moguls already appeared in him.

Yet at that time, as it is written in the annals of his reign,
when the favorable constellation of Aries was rising into the sky,
the supremacy of Delhi and Agra over the world from the Indian
Sea to the territory of the once-powerful Mongol khans, from
Ethiopia to China, was at its height.

The brilliancy of the Mogul court was the talk of the outer
world. Ambassadors came from Tibet, Khorassan, and Africa to
receive magnificent presents. Portuguese priests, envoys and soldiers had established themselves at court; Hawkins was sailing
thither from England, to be the forerunner of the East India Company; France, under Louis XIII, was rising to greatness in Europe;
the Ming dynasty in China was at its brightest.

But the empire of the Mogul was supreme. Envoys from Ferangistan—Europe—were regarded as visitors from inferior states.
The fiery Rájputs were held in temporary check; the Maharattas,
Persians and Turks acknowledged the overlordship of Agra; only
the Afghans maintained pretense of liberty.

At this time the revenues of the Mogul are estimated at two
hundred million rupees, and the men under arms at four hundred
thousand. And these were composed largely of the pick of the
warlike Rájputs, the Punjabis, Turks, and Persians with a smattering of Portuguese mercenaries—musket-men, or matchlock-
men.

And in the rising tide of his power Jahangir held festival at
Lahore, capital of the province of the Five Rivers, in that year. The
rainy season had passed and the river had sunk to its bed, leaving
a vast stretch of mud between water and the lofty buildings of
the palaces.

On the high-water mark of the river bank Jahangir in his whim
had ordered a gold chain to be placed. This chain ran into the main

hall of his palace, where it was connected with a series of sixty golden bells.

"So that any man of the land may have justice," Jahangir had said. "No matter who he may be, let him touch the gold chain and the bells will sound in my ear. Thus will I dispense the imperial mercy."

Courtiers had acclaimed the words, yet guards had been placed at the river bank to protect the gold of the chain, and it came to pass in time that these guards had considered it part of their duty to keep away any who sought to meddle with the Chain of Justice, as it was called. Their officers had hinted that the peace of the mighty monarch was not lightly to be disturbed.

Thus the bells had been silent, and as Jahangir feasted on a certain night in his banquet hall their presence was all but forgotten by himself and the *ameer*s in attendance.

Jahangir sat upon a slight dais facing the rows of nobles, Hindu and Muslim, who shared with him the dainties of northern fruits; wine—for the monarch chose to ignore the Muslim laws at nights—and meats cut skillfully from the choicer portions of game slain that day in the nearby jungle, whither the court had come to escape the heat of late Summer in the dry plain of Hindustan.

He was a stout, broad-faced man, with sharp black eyes, clean-shaven except for a dark mustache. Garbed in a comfortable silk tunic and small, pearl-sewn turban, his hands, neck and head were brilliant with jewels. Behind him, unnoticed, glimmered the gold bells in torch and candle light. Often he laughed at a compliment or jest from his *ameer*s, for the banquet had endured many hours and heating cups of spirits had touched bearded lips as musicians made merry behind screens of latticework.

So, being in high good humor, the World-Gripper listened to a favorite *vizier* who whispered respectfully in his ear.

"My *Padishah*, light of my eyes and guider of my fortunes, a common soldier waits to attend you, sent from your zealous servant Alacha. Khlit is his name, and he is the Ferang (European) who once had the all-desirous privilege of serving Nur-Jahan, Light of the World—"

"I will receive his presents."

The monarch's geniality was heightened by mention of the favorite whom he desired above all others to make his wife.

At this the *vizier* hesitated, for Khlit had brought no gifts, as was customary—in fact, had none to bring. Mentally the courtier summed up the old warrior's meager possessions and announced smilingly that Khlit's most valued treasures—a fine, curved sword, declared the courtier, and his horse—were at the disposal of the Mogul.

"My *Padishah*," he purred, bowing, for Alacha had remembered him with no little gold, "your *jagirdar* who holds the turbulent Afghans trembling before the sound of the voice of your authority, has sent a string of fifty long-haired Bactrian camels laden with gold and silk cloth as a gift to lay before your feet. He humbly asks that some robe of honor be accorded the warrior, who is a power among the wild Mongol khans of the North. One of Alacha's spies—a priest, among the Mongols of the steppe— spoke to him before this of the power of the khan."

Jahangir's benignity waxed amain. The camels were a welcome addition to his animals of the military train. He nodded, and the sentries at the farther end of the hall ushered in Khlit.

Courtiers and monarch alike stared at the gaunt figure of the Cossack, and many whispers went the rounds exclaiming upon the uncouthness of the newcomer's dress and the rude insolence of his bearing.

For, instead of performing the salaam as he had been instructed or even touching his hand to the floor and then to his forehead, Khlit advanced among the banquet cloths with his accustomed swaggering gait and raised his hand, bending his head slightly.

The spectators looked from him to the emperor and at the *vizier* curiously.

Khlit stood before the sitting monarch quite calmly, meeting his frowning stare fairly. *"Padishal salamet!"* he exclaimed in broken *Turki*, and the plump, bejeweled councilor frowned and grimaced behind Jahangir, at the unequaled effrontery of utterance before the emperor should be pleased to speak.

But chance worked in Khlit's favor. Jahangir had frowned, whereat the courtiers murmured and half-rose, sensing the displeasure of their lord. Yet the World-Gripper was meditating, rather pleasantly than otherwise.

"I am told," his cultured voice observed clearly, "that you have been a leader of the Mongol khans who enjoy the honor of being our neighbors. Doubtless you have come to pay your respects to the Presence. It rejoices us greatly that the barbarians of the North have bent their eyes before the sun of India."

The idea of a representative from the descendants of Genghis Khan attending upon his pleasure rather interested the man to whom power was the breath of life. Uncouth as Khlit might be, and uncertain as his mission to the court certainly was—save for the hinted message of Alacha that the *vizier* had not seen fit to reveal in full—it was characteristic of Jahangir that he chose instantly to assume that Khlit could be placed on par with the other outlandish envoys of Ethiopia, Abyssinia and Tibet who at present added to his pomp, eating their heads off the while.

Khlit, not understanding, looked calmly and inquiringly at the *vizier*, who quickly paraphrased the monarch's remarks, altering their meaning.

"Warrior, the Master of the Universe asks if you be related by blood to the Mongol khans. Alacha informs me you once held rank among them."

"Aye," assented Khlit readily.

The *vizier* salaamed.

"My *Padishah*," he cried, "the warrior places himself at the call of your pleasure."

In this fashion did a skillful diplomat cover over the perils that threatened from Khlit's introduction. Jahangir was pleased. The reminder of his own importance went to his head like wine.

"Let the graybeard keep his horse and sword," he responded, which was well, as Khlit would never have suffered parting from his weapon. "We will add the word-defying grace of womanly beauty to the value of the slight gifts from our hand. Let Nur-Jahan herself be summoned from the imperial quarters to place at his waist a better sword. Meanwhile robe him in a cloth-of-gold *khilat*, as is meet for the eyes of the Splendor of the World."

Khlit looked curiously at the resplendent garment that was drawn over his rough sheepskin coat and at the girdle of many-colored silk placed around his leather belt. He listened silently to the announcement that a satin tent had been placed at his disposal near the cantonment of the personal cavalry of the emperor, a tent with a native servant—in the pay of the *vizier* who was Alacha's friend. Only at mention of a blooded Arabian horse did he nod, well pleased.

Jahangir turned to his wine, relishing his whim, and looked on with all the artless pleasure of a pleased child when the stately figure of veiled Nur-Jahan came into the room. The nobles rose and bowed profoundly.

Khlit scanned the woman who had come in his care from the plains of Tartary to the arms of the Mogul, admiring the brilliance of her Indian dress, the pearls in her black hair. But—as etiquette demanded—she did not speak before she took a gold-inlaid scimitar from one of the *bakhshi*s in attendance.

This she passed through the silk girdle about the warrior, saying:

"It is a weapon of proved, Damascus steel, precious as the metal with which it is wrought. Wear it on behalf of the one who gives it."

At this Jahangir smiled, and the courtiers murmured politely. Only one—a northern noble related to Alacha, Paluwan Khan, of the Mavr-un-nahr Turks—whispering that to gird on two swords was an omen of war to the death.

But Khlit reflected that Nur-Jahan had changed. Once she had been talkative, had laughed readily and artlessly. Now her fine

eyes—all that he could see—were melancholy. Bending closer as
she gave the weapon a last pat, she said softly—

"You have won the favor of Jahangir, yet watch for treachery
among the *ameers*."

She bent her veiled head profoundly before the monarch who
had sent for her from the ends of his kingdom and who loved her
deeply, acknowledged the salutation of the courtiers and vanished between the draperies through which she had come.

Had Nur-Jahan enjoyed at that time the mastery over the
narrow-minded emperor which she assumed—to the everlasting
good of India—at a later period, she might have spoken more
boldly. Perhaps, for she was a woman of keen insight and rare
statesmanship, she might have averted the tragedy that was to
come to pass among the Afghan hills.

"Bid the Mongol take his place among the lesser *ameers*," ordered Jahangir, "and see that he never lacks for food or comfort.
Request him to be often before our eyes, and especially when we
debate, as we will soon do, upon certain matters of warfare."

Thus Khlit took his place at one of the farther settees, at
the banquet, and ate and drank heartily, meditating the while
upon the reception he had been accorded, upon the man who
was monarch of many million souls, and upon the warning of
Nur-Jahan.

The *ameers* accepted him for the most part with polite curiosity, some with friendliness and some few—from the northern
provinces—with veiled jealousy.

Silently, for he understood little that was said, he watched the
pomp and panoply of the richest court in the world. He appeared
at the levees, came mounted on his new Arab to the ceremonious guard-mount, wherein Rájput and Muslim alternated in
attendance before the quarters of the emperor.

He studied the immense throngs of camp followers, merchants, soldiery, and envoys that filled the narrow streets of
Lahore, crowding the tall, wooden buildings. He even asked the
meaning of the gold chain at the river bank.

Thus for several days Khlit dwelt in the camp of the Mogul, awaiting the time when he had been told he would be called upon to speak in council, received generally with respect, thanks to the favor Nur-Jahan had shown him. Unlike the *ameers* and the officers who went everywhere mounted on elephants and accompanied by gorgeously clad followers, Khlit kept to himself for the most part, spending long intervals in meditation in his tent.

"The woman remembered," he said to himself. "Will the man forget?"

Always he watched the faces of the *ameers*, studying their customs and looking on at the machinery of empire, especially the routine of the army. Long hours were spent in investigating the elephant artillery, the corps of camel guns, the Portuguese company of musketeers and the numerous native cavalry. What he saw he kept to himself, awaiting the time to speak.

V

The Bells of Justice

It was one evening when the coolness of early night brought the nobles to the palace and the usual feasting that Khlit made his memorable response to a question of Jahangir.

The emperor had been closeted with some of his more intimate councilors, and had instructed certain officers of the army—Abdullah Khan, newly arrived from victories in the Dekkan; Raja Man Singh, leader of the Rájputs; Paluwan Khan and the aged I'timad-doulat, father of Nur-Jahan—to attend him. Khlit was among the number.

The screens had been drawn from the arched embrasures overlooking the river. The last glow of sunset cast a half-light over the lighted bazaars of the city, wherein throngs still bartered, quarreled and sang. Jahangir had drawn his officers slightly apart from the rest of the courtiers. Bowls of wine had been filled and emptied.

As a mark of high favor Jahangir had tasted some delicacy and ordered his servants to place the dish before Abdullah Khan, who rose and bowed. The monarch did likewise with Khlit, who, not liking the dainty set before him, left it untasted.

"What!" smiled the Mogul, who was disposed to be gracious. "Does our choice offend the taste of the great Mongol?"

"*Padishah*," bowed the *vizier* who was the friend of Alacha, "he is voiceless, overwhelmed by the ocean of your magnanimity."

"He is a boor," whispered one *ameer*.

"A witless barbarian," scoffed Paluwan Khan. "With but one horse."

Khlit understood much of what was said.

"A horse," he responded slowly, "carried Genghis Khan where an elephant could not go—to mastery in battle."

A heavy silence fell upon those of the assemblage—and they were many—who heard this remark. Experienced courtiers, smooth-faced Turks, intriguers from the court of the Sultan of Constantinople, bearded Armenian money-lenders, elaborately robed emissaries from the declining Caliphate of Baghdad, alert Persians—all glanced discreetly at the Mogul to see how he would take the words. For only Jahangir and his *ameer*s rode upon elephants. But the Mogul, still disposed to treat Khlit agreeably for certain reasons known to himself, laughed, taking the response to apply only to Paluwan Khan.

"*Kaber dar*—have care—warrior," he cried. "Did not we ourself mount this day upon the back of a favorite royal male elephant and shoot blunted arrows of gold among the multitude in honor of the victories of worthy Abdullah Khan over the low-born malcontents of the Dekkan? Aye, we scattered jewels from the balcony of the palace—"

He broke off, struck by a fresh thought. Khlit was silent, waiting for what was to come. The *vizier* had whispered, when the wine cups first circulated, that Jahangir would make a request of him.

"The constellation of Aries arises," murmured the Mogul. "The year is rife with omen for our reign. Come, our wisest mas-

ters of warfare are gathered here. Who can decide my question—
what is the best weapon?"

Inquiringly he glanced at the half-nude Ethiopians, who
grinned stupidly, their round heads rolling on sweaty shoulders,
what with the influence of strong distilled arrack that they guz-
zled greedily.

"Bah," murmured Jahangir to the *vizier* petulantly, "their
skulls avail not save for drinking-cups for their foes. No presents
did they bring save some worthless slaves, the hide of an ass and
an ox-horn filled with civet."

"*Padishah*," smiled the councilor, "doubtless the slaves were
some of the three hundred children of the barbarous Negro chief."

"And the skin," put in Paluwan Khan, who possessed a sharp
tongue, "was taken from a dead ass by the roadside—"

"The civet," added a Persian, not to be outdone, "is what they
covet to drown the stench of their bodies—"

The good-natured but uncomprehending Negroes grinned on.
Jahangir passed by the leopard-skin-clad Abyssinians with the
remark that only an animal would take the hide of a beast to
cover its buttocks.

But Paluwan Khan gave answer that the mace, favorite weapon
of the Turkomans, was best. A slim Kashmiri noble raised a voice
for the arrow, which struck down at a distance. Soft-spoken Hindus argued for the spear, and the talkative Persian avowed that
the javelin was most useful, since it combined the functions of
spear and arrow.

The discussion was witty, ceremonious. Khlit tried to understand it, his head bent as if listening for something he did not
hear. Then Raja Man Singh, descendant of kings who traced their
lineage to the gods, leader of the clans of Marwar and Oudh—
warriors born and bred—called out in a clear voice:

"The sword, O prince. The sword is the arm of chivalry, the
weapon of the Rájput. With these others a man may strike but
once; with a sword is he master of many blows."

At this Khlit, to whom the speech was translated, nodded sagely. Closely he looked at the Rájput noble, marking his open, intelligent face as if he wished to remember it well.

"Yet these weapons suffice but for the individual," began Jahangir again. "I speak of battles. You have all said that never was there an army in the world such as mine. What is the best weapon by which we may strike those who are our foes?"

Those who knew him best were well aware that a purpose underlay the idle words of the monarch. Eyes met eyes inquiringly, and jeweled hands fingered well-trimmed mustaches.

"How may we smite those of ill-fortune who on our marches have sinned against Allah and our empire by arraying themselves in battle-ranks?"

A massive, black-faced Turk salaamed, bellowing in a hearty voice:

"Great Sultan, give me leave to set my cannon-mouths against the miscreants. Verily I will erect a barricade of withes, carts and iron chains between my roarers and blow this accursed scum to ____."

So spoke the chief of the artillery, one Ra'dandaz Khan, the Lord Thunder-Thrower.

"And by the thundering cannon," added the captain of the Portuguese mercenaries, "I will place my matchlock-men to pick off the leaders of the traitors and stay their charge. Thus will I serve the Lord of India!"

Jahangir glanced at Abdullah Khan, fresh from conquest.

"Mirror of the Glory of Allah, Index of the Book of Creation, Refuge of the World," uttered that successful leader smoothly, "under your gracious words my heart expands. Yet before your wisdom my knowledge is like a grain of sand, lying below a lofty mountain. As you know, wise intrigue and offers of wealth undermine the strength of our foes."

Raja Man Singh frowned at the stilted phrases. "Lord," he cried, "the best of battle is the charge at pace that scatters the ranks of an enemy fairly."

Jahangir smiled at the Rájput whose reckless bravery was a saying in the land, and turned to Khlit.

"Warrior," he observed, "men say that you are a Rustum of the Age, a master of battles, leader of the Mongols. I await your answer."

Thoughtfully Khlit looked from the raja to the Mogul. "Lord," he said gravely, "have you forgotten the *tulughma*?"

Frowning, the Mogul shook his broad head as if trying to recall a familiar phrase. *Ameer* glanced at *ameer*. The *vizier* hastily prompted Khlit to explain the word.

"It is the weapon of Genghis Khan, your ancestor," continued the old warrior. "It is the 'Mongol swoop.' By it he defeated—" Khlit looked in turn from Paluwan Khan to the man from Baghdad, and to Raja Man Singh—"Turkoman, Caliph, and Hindu."

"I have heard the phrase," Jahangir nodded, leaning back upon his cushions almost under the golden bells. "What is the maneuver?"

"A charge," responded Khlit through his interpreter, "yet not the charge of the Rájput. A flight of arrows, yet not the arrowflights of your archers. A strategem that is not the deceit of Abdullah Khan."

"The *tulughma*? I know it not."

"Lord, if your army faced the Mongols in battle you would see the swoop of Genghis Khan. Are the deeds of the first of your race no longer sung by your bards?"

Impatiently Jahangir toyed with his necklace. Petulantly he spoke:

"Graybeard, these are parables. Come, I have a thought for what you must do. You will reveal this maneuver in actual warfare. Warrior, I have shown you favor, and I have decided that you will accompany my army which is about to set out."

He sat erect, glancing at his *ameer*s.

"My servants, the dark head of rebellion has arisen in the empire. The message came to my ear this nightfall. You must mount for war on my behalf—"

The Mogul fell silent, but no spoken word had arrested his speech. The golden Bells of Justice had given tongue.

Close by his head they echoed in chiming melody, faint tinkling mingled with sonorous deep-toned note. For the first time in Lahore, the bells had sounded.

Dust-stained, haggard of face, and feverish of eye, his clothing streaked with mud, his velvet cloak bespattered and torn, Chan the minstrel kneeled before the Mogul.

"Justice!" he cried. "My lord, justice for the wronged!"

Rather pleased than otherwise was Jahangir the Mogul at sight of the suppliant form. Not a little surprised was he, however, for since the day of the guards no commoner had lightly approached the gold bell-rope. Still more aroused was he when a slave whispered that the newcomer had cast the guard at the rope into the mud of the riverbed when the sentinel had sought to restrain him.

"Speak!" he commanded. "The gate of the court of mercy is open to you."

Chan raised his bare head, his features tense with youthful anxiety.

"Lord of the World," he muttered, his voice rising as he half-chanted his message, "holy men have been slain. *Mullah*s, brothers of Muhammed Asad, who is beloved of God, have been done to death by lawless men. I saw women taken into the bondage of lust, and villages burned. I have come from the tribes over which you are lord in pursuit of justice."

"Who is this slayer?"

"Lord, your lips have framed his name—Alacha, the Slayer. And the tribes are the Afghans."

At this the sparkle died from the black eyes of the monarch. The interest that had given life to his pale face faded, and he frowned.

"The Afghans sent you?" He spoke sharply, evidently irritated.

"Nay, my lord."

Chan dwelled on the face of the monarch anxiously.

"Unbidden I came to beg of you the royal justice. The Afghans ask no mercy."

Almost indifferently Jahangir turned aside, speaking softly to his nearest attendants, among them the *vizier*. The *ameer*s stared curiously at the minstrel as if at a man condemned.

"My servants," the Mogul addressed them again, ignoring Chan, "this ill-fortuned one has voiced the tidings I was about to relate. In the hills of the Afghans within rebellious Badakshan men are arming for revolt, as is their custom. The tribes have mounted for war, impiously spurning my authority and acclaiming a leader of their own—"

"Lord," the minstrel, unused to court etiquette, interrupted, "they seek but to defend themselves against oppression. Wrong has been done by Alacha. Wherefore I, a suppliant, came to the gold bell of which I had heard. Would you close the gates of justice against my plea—"

His high voice trailed off hopelessly as two armed servitors approached him at a sign from the *vizier*. Jahangir's frown deepened. He did not altogether relish having the tale of how a claimant for justice had been received repeated throughout his kingdom.

"Personal wrong-doing," he salved his conscience, "ever merits our attention. Yet this Alacha is a faithful servant of our standard, and his acts are in the interest of our rule. We cannot pardon rebellion."

A wave of his hand dismissed the minstrel, who had risen moodily to his feet.

"Throw him from the summit of the palace. Yet—" he fingered his tiny gold scimitar irresolutely—"hold! Even to such a villainous conspirator does our mercy extend. Bear him to the quarters of our outer guards and there have the sinews of his knees severed, that he will bear no more messages."

A complimentary murmur greeted this manifestation of the royal clemency. Only Chan, drawing his slim figure erect, smiled bitterly.

"For his mercy," he said slowly, "I thank my lord, the Mogul."

Unseen, Khlit rose in his corner and moved toward Chan. This act, however, caught the eye of the watchful *vizier*, who whispered to Jahangir. "*Padishah*, River of Unending Forgiveness, before this dark one came you were speaking to the Mongol—"

"True. Your reminder reveals the zeal of a faithful servant."

New animation flooded the smooth countenance of the monarch, who motioned to Khlit as Chan was led out—the minstrel casting the while a scornful glance at the warrior whom he had last seen in company with Abdul Dost.

"Dog, who feeds from the Mogul's table," whispered the boy with the hot scorn of youth, passing Khlit as he went by between the guards.

Khlit, heedful of Jahangir, paid no attention beyond a quick glance.

VI

The Song of Chan

"Old warrior, now is the moment when you may show gratitude for the costly scimitar given to you, and the robe of honor. When my army mounts for the Afghan campaign, you will ride with the *ameer*s—Raja Man Singh, the Brave (the Rájput bent his head at this); Paluwan Khan; the Lord Thunder-Thrower; and my faithful *Ferang*s, the musket-men. Your words of the Mongol battles have struck my fancy. Teach Raja Man Singh this *tulughma* of yours and gifts you have received will be as nought beside the treasure I will bestow."

So spoke the Mogul, and the warrior heard the words interpreted, standing in silence, his lined face thoughtful.

"Can the Rájputs ride as the Mongols did?" he asked bluntly.

"By the many-armed gods!" The raja sprang from his seat, but Jahangir waved him aside.

"We shall see. That will be your task—to cooperate with the Prince of Marwar in crushing this snake which has turned against me. Abdul Dost has assumed the leadership of the Afghans and raised the unholy standard of revolt. He—son of Suleiman—was once in my pay. Now is he branded an outlaw, and rebel."

Moodily Khlit raised his eyes.

"Lord," his deep voice addressed the interpreter, "is not Abdul Dost the son of Mongol fathers? His ancestors were yours— Genghis and Timurlane, the Conquerors. His land is the homeland of the Moguls."

Sheer surprise kept Jahangir silent.

"Abdul Dost served you well," went on the warrior gruffly, for he chose his words with difficulty. "Have you forgotten? Nay, it was to ask you this and to require your aid for him and his people that I rode hither."

Ameer glanced at *ameer* mockingly. Paluwan Khan lay back on his cushions well-pleased. The *vizier* sighed in sheer relief. His task of spying upon Khlit was done.

With a single sentence the warrior had cast into the balance the favor he had earned from Jahangir.

"The quarrel of Abdul Dost is just," explained Khlit earnestly. "Consider it in wise council among your captains. His quarrel is with Alacha, who is both evildoer and tyrant. Behead Alacha and place Abdul Dost in his stead."

A courtier laughed impulsively at this, and the sound broke the gathering wrath of Jahangir, who reflected that Khlit was after all a common soldier and an uncouth man, knowing nought of affairs of state.

"Set an Afghan to rule Afghans?" he cried. "A wolf to lead wolves? Nay, Alacha at my bidding has had the heads of the leading men in Badakshan carried around on poles. As fast as he does so these dark ones set up another leader. So long as there is any trace of the people of Badakshan they will keep up this disturbance."

His brow darkened again at this, and a flush rose in his cheeks. That morning during the hunt two beaters had unluckily come upon the scene when Jahangir had been about to shoot down a

fine nilgau and the incident still rankled, although the monarch
had had the feet cut from under the two.

"Ho, warrior, by Allah and all his saints!"

Jahangir bethought him of the Hindus present.

"And by Vishnu and Siva! You presume upon our goodwill
mightily. Yet you may atone for your mistake—"

Twice within the hour had the voice of Chan interrupted his
imperial master. The notes of a song in a strong youthful voice
wafted through the open embrasures that gave on the river, where
the guardhouse stood.

> *False as Hell is the Mogul's word,*
> *Tarnished and broken the Mogul sword!*

Several of the courtiers moved toward the windows to draw
the screens.

> *Evil fruit from the Mogul's seed,*
> *And the faith of the Mogul is lost indeed—*

Came the echo of a distant struggle, a single short cry of pain.
And then silence.

"Unlike that unfortunate," resumed Jahangir impassively,
"you may yet win honor at our behest. Ride with the *ameer*s
against Abdul Dost. You have knowledge of the country and
the Afghan wiles. Defeat him, and claim greater favors at our
all-forgiving hand."

"And if the ungrateful warrior refuses?" put in the *vizier*
swiftly.

"Death of the gods!" The Mogul's slender patience gave way.
"Has he not our robe of honor on his poverty-stricken back? Will
he choose the cistern of ——, rather than my service?"

Uncomprehending and no little troubled, Khlit stood his
ground, trying to grasp what was passing. He had hoped to speak
a word to Jahangir for his friend. To aid Abdul Dost he had come
to Lahore, and had been gratified by his reception. Now he saw
his plans scattered as dust before the wind. He turned to the

vizier, whom he thought to be his friend. That shrewd councilor straightaway looked at the floor.

"Take the boor hence," cried Jahangir, "and learn his answer. Raja Man Singh, Paluwan Khan, attend me!"

Khlit looked up as the *vizier* and others approached him.

"I must think," he responded to their inquiries. "Come to my tent, and you will learn what I have decided."

With that he turned and stalked from the chamber. Those who clustered about him hung back, unwilling to leave the important council that was under way, and appreciating the fact that Khlit could not quit the Mogul's camp without being observed by the guards.

So it happened that because of their anxiety to learn what was passing in the hall where the Afghan campaign was being discussed, it was some moments before the *vizier* and others went to the warrior's tent by the posts of the outer guard, never doubting that his decision would be favorable. They judged him by their own standard, and thus were startled as well as genuinely surprised at what they found.

Khlit's tent was empty, his couch and scimitar—the gift of Jahangir—lying on the carpet. Both horses were gone, likewise the robe of honor. As to this last, they had an inkling from the palace sentinels.

"A warrior in an imperial *khilat* we passed out, verily, for we could not gainsay one of such a rank. A servant followed him, riding unsteadily upon a horse of the royal stable. They drew their reins to the North."

Puzzled, the men of the court searched the vicinity with torches and found the servant, who had been in the pay of the *vizier*, bound and gagged behind the satin tent.

It was not long before they came to understand the truth—that Khlit had substituted the maimed Chan for his servant, carrying him from the guard tent, saying that he would care for the minstrel's hurt.

"Said the Mongol aught when he bound you?" they demanded
of the trembling native.

"Aye, my lords. He said, 'Beware the *tulughma.*'"

VII
Word to Abdul Dost

Far above the Shyr Pass stood a round hut of woven cypress and
pine branches, its entrance overlooking a grassy glade, around
which the pine forest pressed on three sides. Up the mountain,
open tracts of grass were revealed, rising to the region of barren
shale rock.

By climbing a giant fir a view could be gained of the whole
Shyr Pass, through which the Amu Daria threaded its ribbon-like
length.

Beside the river almost directly under the fir—so steep were
the sides of the gorge—appeared the trail through the pass, looking for all the world from that height like a yellow ant road.
And like ants were the moving black specks, coming and going
busily along the trail. Sometimes singly, sometimes in groups,
they passed under the hut—sometimes the long cavalcade of a
caravan was visible.

For many days a girl—she who had put together the hut with
her own hands—had climbed the sticky branches of the fir to
spend hours in scanning the trail with keen eyes, oblivious of
the movements of her cattle, which grazed at will on the upper
pastures.

Now she was standing in the hut entrance, nibbling at a round
bread-cake and frowning at the mist that drove down from the
summits overhead. She was slender and very erect of figure, this
Afghan girl, with a ragged woolen coat, plainly designed for a
man, about her boyish shoulders.

She braced herself against the *bad-i-purwan*, the Wind of
Purwan—the northern wind—that moaned daily through the
pass, harbinger of the Autumn season. Behind the hut, like some
gigantic field of ripened grain, the pine trees bent and rocked.

Branch rubbed against branch; massive treetops lifted, to bend low with a crackling protest the next moment.

Feeling the chill of the blast—for the upper slopes of the Afghan hills, the Koh-i-Baba, were many degrees colder than the valley below, where the yellow grain of late Summer was still visible—the solitary maiden rubbed one bare foot tentatively against her leg, drawing the hood of the cloak over her streaming black hair. Her attitude was wary, even defiant. And suddenly she ceased munching the bread, to draw a startled breath.

Within, or rather against, the rush of the wind the note of a high voice reached her ears.

> No more I watch at the noble's gate.
> For I gaze at the world from the mountain peak—

The roving glance of the hill girl, keen as it was, failed to discern any human being nearby.

"Now the sweet Ghilani saint aid me!" she murmured, dreading the approach of the invisible singer.

Had not tales been told in the hill villages of Ghils and other terrifying spirits of the heights that rode on the breast of the wind and carried off the souls of men to eternal damnation?

> No vulture I, to hover over carrion.
> An eagle I, to strike down my prey!

At this, a horse burst through the underbrush in front of the hut, and the song halted abruptly as the rider sighted watching girl and hut.

He sat a wearied Arab in curious fashion, and he was weaponless. A very tarnished red velvet cloak was wrapped about his slender shoulders, a fur cap pulled over his ears. His face was dark with cold, and his cheeks hollowed by privation. Chan, despite his lusty singing, had lost somewhat of his debonair manner during a hard journey.

But he swept off his cap with a flourish.

"Allah the generous be thanked," he murmured to himself. "Food, shelter, woman—a fair maid of my own people and one that I have seen before, methinks. Peace be with you!" he greeted her, his eyes dwelling upon her face, which seemed strangely familiar.

"And upon you also be peace," she replied gravely, scanning him with the determined interest of those who must distinguish between friend and foe.

Chan walked the horse to her side, and she noted seriously that the beast was of excellent breed, its saddle costly with silver mountings and cloth-of-gold trappings.

The horse was plainly of better quality than the rider—stolen without doubt, she guessed at once. This somewhat lulled her suspicions, for Chan was undoubtedly an Afghan.

"Who are you?" she demanded, returning to her bread. "What are you doing here? Whither do you ride?"

"One thing at a time, magpie," smiled Chan. "At present I hunger, and for the present I ride no farther than yonder hut. As for my name, have you never heard of Chan of the Hills, the minstrel of the chieftains? Verily it is my ill-fortune to lack my guitar, which was reft from me by certain ill-omened slaves of the World-Gripper. Allah grant that—

> Every fool who made me bow my head,
> His head will be bowed by my sword.

"Of course," he meditated, "I lack a sword; yet I have a horse, see you—a notable horse, given me by a thrice-exalted warrior. Help me down from my horse."

Chan's smile vanished as he felt of a limp leg that hung useless.

"A mark of the benevolence of the River of Mercy and Fountain of Forgiveness, in other words, the Mogul. By the mercy of God was it ordained that my warrior friend should grasp the executioner by the scruff of his dirty neck when he swung scimitar to hamstring my other leg. So I can yet stand on one foot, but I cannot climb down from this noble steed."

With an exclamation the girl helped the youth to a bench in the hut and busied herself with lighting from flint and tinder a fire of brushwood on the flat stones that served for a hearth. Then she offered him milk and began to heat a bowl of rice—after she had unsaddled the Arab and left it to graze.

Food and warmth brightened the eyes of the minstrel.

"*Aie, kichik gul*—Oh, little flower—scarce did I think to find a woman of my people so close to the Shyr. What is your name? Why are you alone?"

"I am called Tala-i-Nur. My brother was sent as *jighit*, or mounted messenger, to look for our leader some time since and was slain by Alacha—and also was my sister slain. Because of this my father with all of our family joined the Afghan standard."

Curiously Chan looked from the girl to the ill-made hut.

"Then must you love the smell of danger, Tala, for Alacha and his men hold the Shyr beneath us—wherefore came I climbing over the mountain."

"Aye—I have seen."

Chin on hands, the Afghan maid smiled somberly, gazing into the crackling fire. At this Chan was silent, thinking that the girl had chosen her lofty pasturage in order to watch what went on in the pass.

"Verily," he mused, "it is cold and windy here for the *yailak*— the Summer pasture. Perchance you watch other things than cows."

"Who can know what Allah has ordained?"

Suspicion smoldered half-hidden in Tala's dark eyes. An Afghan does not like to be questioned. And the spies of Alacha were thick on the countryside.

"That horse of yours bears the Mogul's brand on its flank."

Chan nodded.

"Aye, little sharp-eyes. Well for me he was the pick of the imperial stables. Never were men so pressed as I and my warrior lord. We rode like the fiends of the wind up the Jhilam bank to the North, where we parted—he for the mountains of the Roof of the World, and I for Kabul and the Shyr. I rode at night along goat-path and sheep-track and ate what I could pluck by the way—for dismount I could not."

He grimaced ruefully and glanced up as a patter of rain struck against the felt roof of the hut. Through the many gaps in the woven walls, wind whistled and swept the swirling smoke into Tala's intent face.

"Tell me what goes on in the land," asked the minstrel eagerly. "Where lies Abdul Dost? Has he many followers? Has he seized Balkh and Khanjut?"

The girl seemed not to heed him. She was fingering a bow, stringing it and fitting an arrow to the cord. Presently she glanced at her guest from under the tangle of black hair—dark as a raven's wing, he thought admiringly.

"Would you know what is in my mind?" she questioned.

"Aye."

"You are a spy!"

Springing erect, Tala drew taut the bowstring, leveling the arrow-point at Chan's chest with a steady hand. She breathed deeply, her strong young body rigid with defiance.

"You are the one who tried to slay Abdul Dost. You ride a horse of the World-Gripper. Claiming to be a minstrel, you lack tambour or guitar—and lie about it clumsily. Now you seek to make me talk of the Afghan army."

Chan's mouth opened wide. Then he laughed, a flash of admiration in his brown eyes.

"Clever little magpie! Yet you know the Afghan code. Even a foe is safe under Afghan roof."

"But you are—a spy of the World-Gripper."

The arrow-point drew back to the haft of the bow as the girl deftly pulled bowstring to ear. The boy's eyes did not waver, nor did the smile fade from his lips.

"Tala," he said slowly, "your brother was sent as a messenger—and slain."

"Aye, and my sister also, at the hand of Alacha."

"Yet am I sent as a messenger from my warrior friend to Abdul Dost, your leader. The word I bear means much to the Afghans. Would you slay me?"

"I do not believe you."

"But you must believe."

Chan's smile had vanished. Earnestness shone from his tired face. Stretching forth his crippled leg, he began to unwind the bandages. Stiff with dust and blood, they came off slowly, finally revealing the purple line of a fresh wound behind the knee.

Turning, with an involuntary twitch of agony the boy pulled up his torn cotton trouser, and Tala saw the raw ends of the severed ligaments. Her arms dropped a little and the bowstring slacked.

Chan stared at his crippled limb dumbly. Gone was all the merriment that the boy assumed so bravely, nourishing his own courage thereby.

"I shall never walk as a man again. Ever I must crawl with a crutch. *Ai*—at a word from the Mogul did they this thing. And he called it mercy."

Now a flush overspread the girl's cheeks—a flush that changed swiftly to a nerveless pallor. Arrow and bow fell to her feet. Chan raised his clenched hands toward the roof of the hut.

"I cannot walk, Tala. But I can ride—and loose arrow from bow. Aye, I shall sew the arrow-stitch of vengeance. It will heal my wound."

He turned on the girl savagely.

"Think you this is a disguise? Would the wise Alacha, the shrewd, fox-like Alacha, choose a cripple for a spy? Ha—think you so?"

Tala's hands flew to her face and covered her eyes. Tears dripped from between her fingers to the earth that was the only floor of the hut. Then she ran to Chan and fell on her knees.

"Forgive me!" she cried. "I doubted, but now your words ring true. Oh, it was the poison of Alacha that made me doubt. I deemed you the one that had caused my sister's death."

Uncertainly, for she still wept, Tala cleansed the bandages in fresh water and bound them about Chan's knee, because she had no other linen. As she did so, she released long pent-up emotion in swift speech.

"I never doubted you were Chan. Often have I heard you sing under the trees of our orchard in the village before I came here. But Alacha spoke of you, and I believed, because I could not know it was but a trick of the Slayer."

"Alacha—you?" The Afghan youth stared, bewildered.

"Aye. You remember the woman to whom you sang love songs in the evening, and who listened behind the lattice of her window. The window looking out upon the orchard."

"But she is dead."

"My sister, older than I. Chan, I listened too, for I was envious of your singing, knowing that you had seen the form of my sister who was more fair than I. Aye, Chan, I sat by her knee in the evening after sunset prayers and saw her splendid face grow lovelier at your song. At such times the poison of jealousy was in my heart.

"Then came Alacha, riding by from a hunt. He saw the face of my sister unveiled and seized her, beating me to earth when I struggled to aid her."

Tala, the labor of her dressing finished, sat up, the tears still bright on her cheeks.

"I heard Alacha whisper to his men that here was a means to make the low-born Afghans draw the sword of open revolt. Chan, Alacha had been ordered by the Mogul to stir up the Afghans to rebel—so Badakshan could be despoiled, and the strength of the Afghan tribes scattered to the winds. Seeing that I had heard what was said, the man to whom he spoke would have seized me also, but Alacha stayed him, smiling slowly after his fashion.

" 'Chan, our spy,' he said so that I could hear, 'has shown us a fair flower to be our victim.' "

"But," observed the minstrel, "I did not see you when I rode to the hut that night."

"Nay, I tried to follow the Slayer and his men. I was soon tired and fell by the road. Then I heard that you had carried the body of my sister through Badakshan to arouse the tribes, and so I believed all the more what the Slayer had said. When my father, mourning for my sister, said that you had gone to the Mogul camp I felt in my heart that you were a traitor. But now I see the truth. Forgive me!"

The boy laid his hand on her shoulder, sighing.

"We are but children, Tala, before the craft of the Mogul and his agents. See how he turns Afghan against Afghan. What have I to forgive? So you came here to watch the movements of the Slayer?"

"Aye—and more."

Tala related how when the Afghans took up arms, Alacha—who was well-prepared—had given up Balkh, but had fallen back on the Shyr Pass, the main road to Kabul and the Mogul's cities. He held Khanjut, the "Iron Gate" of the pass, on the Afghan side, while Abdul Dost assembled his forces in the plains.

"The Mogul musters his army at Lahore, not far from Kabul," mused the boy. "And by the Shyr he will pass his men through the Koh-i-Baba hills, which are the walls of Badakshan. Oh, they are shrewd. How can we oppose such men?"

"By the sword of the tribes." Tala's brown eyes flashed. "And even the women will do their part—even I. Here I can see little, for the mists and the rain veil the movements in the pass below. So I have decided on what I must do. Alacha has an eye—so it is said—for the Afghan women. I will drive my cows by the trails I know to the bed of the pass. The Slayer's men will seize the animals for their food, but I—"

"You will be taken!" cried the boy.

"That is what I plan."

The girl's serious brow was stern with purpose. Her eyes fell, but she nodded bravely.

"I have heard that Alacha keeps the fairest women for himself. Thus shall I see what goes on in his camp and hear something of his plans—for I am quick of ear."

The boy's face fell; then he laughed—checking himself swiftly, as he put his hand on the tangle of her hair. "O little flower, I am very wise. I have journeyed among the camps of the world—and seen Alacha and the Mogul. Such men as they, Tala, have eyes solely for the elegant women of Persia and Hindustan. The Slayer scarce would notice you in your rags—"

"Am I not fair?" She gazed at him wide-eyed, questioning. "Alas, Alacha had eyes for my sister! And, somewhat, I resemble her."

At this Chan gazed at the girl keenly.

"True, Tala. You are very like her. Yet we Afghans are not spies and, therefore, are blind to the tricks of our foes."

Tala rose with a nod, bravely determined. "I shall go to the camp of Alacha and watch, and if any one tries to harm me I shall shoot him with my bow."

Chan shook his head moodily. Then his eyes brightened.

"So be it, Tala. If you could learn aught to aid Abdul Dost . . ." He smiled, merry again. "And I will join you, after I have delivered my message. I will come to seek you at the Shyr bank, behind the Iron Gate, wearing some old garments of the holy man, Muhammad Asad."

"Alacha would slay you."

"Nay, for I will be a begging *kwajah*, lame, for all to see."

He caught the girl's slim wrist fiercely. "O Tala, you and I will contrive a mighty thing. We will be a thorn in the side of the World-Gripper! For we will sow the seeds of fear."

While the Afghan maid listened, wondering, Chan told her the message that he bore to Abdul Dost—that the old warrior who had befriended him was bringing aid to Abdul Dost. That a horde of wild riders would come to Badakshan from the North, through the mountain passes.

"Such men as you and I have never seen, O Tala. They live for fighting alone, and they ride like the demons of the air. They wear the hides of beasts for armor, and their bodies are like iron."

"Who are they?" Tala was amazed.

"The Tatar Horde. They, like the Afghans, are the children of Genghis Khan. Eh, little flower, we will spread fear in the camp of our enemy. We will foretell the coming of the spirits of the dead warriors, of whom the Mogul's bards sing."

His eyes were smoldering as if with fever.

"Thus will I knit the arrow-stitch of vengeance. Once before, the Tatar Horde swept through the Caliphate and Samarkand crumbled like a house of dust before them, and Balkh and La-hore. *Ameers* and sultans were cut down like ripe grain. So, we will sing, you and I—"

Chan laughed, clutching her slender shoulders. "We will sing a chant of doom—of doom from the mountains. We will say that the Ghils are a-horse, and the dead walk again. The Mogul's men live by omens. Eh—we will give them an omen, a mighty omen. They will hear the trumpets of the Conqueror, Genghis Kahn."

He leaned back against the wall, his small body exhausted. "Now I will sleep."

So Tala cast wood upon the fire and dragged her blankets close to the stone hearth, and made Chan comfortable thereon. She sat close to him, watching until he slept.

But she did not sleep. From time to time she replenished the fire, gazing into its glow and turning over in her mind the strange things the minstrel had said.

And in this manner did a boy and girl plan to match their wits against the intrigue of a master plotter.

In the early morning they parted, Tala assembling her herd and driving it down to the valley, while Chan turned his horse's head toward Badakshan and the Afghan camp.

Before sunset the tidings he brought were repeated to Abdul Dost, where the chief of the Afghans had planted his standard in the plain.

"Do not give battle with your full strength until I join you. With my men, I will reach Badakshan from the northern passes before snow closes the valleys."

That was the message from Khlit. On hearing it Abdul Dost flushed with pleasure and uttered a broad oath, saying to the blind Muhammad Asad, who sat near him, that they would have the aid of the old warrior whose wisdom was worth more than two thousand swords.

The *mullah* nodded gravely.

"Verily does it seem that the aid of this warrior could not be bought with gold. It is in my mind that he has felt the tie of friendship, and that he keeps faith with you. Yet what tribes are these of the North and how may they come hither?"

Neither Muhammad Asad nor Abdul Dost had seen the Mongol clans. Between the Afghan valleys and Mongolia rose the mountain barrier of the Himalayas. No merchants went to the steppe. Only some legends and tales of travelers had reached their ears.

What manner of men were these from the steppe? They did not know.

"And how," asked a warrior, "are they to surmount the barrier of the hills? Can an army pass over the Roof of the World? Nay, it may not be."

Abdul Dost realized the force of this.

"We are in the hand of God," he repeated gravely. "We will wait."

His men—villagers, shepherds, hunters, clansmen—were impatient for action. Afghans, Hazaras, Kirghiz—all had assembled to fight for their liberty. From the distant tribes of Ferghana and from the desert itself they had come. Old men and former soldiers, boys and priests, had cheerfully taken up the burden of war.

The boy who had been the ward of blind Muhammad Asad rode proudly at the left hand of the *mansabdar*. Hope was rife in Badakshan—the reckless exuberance of the Afghan who never reckons the strength of a foe.

Meanwhile in the Shyr Pass Alacha sat in his red tent, hearing the messages of his spies, drilling his men, plundering cattle and grain. And in Kabul the high *ameer*s of the World-Gripper mobilized the imperial army. Raja Man Singh and Paluwan Khan planned the coming campaign. The Lord Thunder-Thrower cast more shot for his camel artillery. The matchlock-men furbished their weapons under the eye of a Portuguese captain of mercenaries.

The imperial army, the *corps d'armée* of the Mogul, formed itself slowly into a gigantic, machine-like whole. Levies of horsemen from the northern provinces trotted in daily, the warriors resplendent in silver armlets, silk and cloth-of-silver and precious jewels sewn into turban and tunic—bearing upon their backs more often than not the whole of a year's pay while their families in the villages hungered.

Camp followers, bazaar-merchants, armorers, courtesans, flocked to Kabul until a veritable city of tents arose in the valley by the winding river.

Then came the day when Jahangir placed robes of honor on Raja Man Singh, Paluman Khan and the *ameer*s of his host; the *alam*, the imperial standard, was raised, the kettledrums sounded, and the long camel-trains began to move forward to the northern pass, attended by the advance guard of Rájput cavalry. From the balcony of his palace the World-Gripper watched the dust that rose over the moving host.

"See that an accounting is made to me," he observed idly to the *vizier* who stood by him. "An accounting of the spoil taken from the Afghans. It will add in my memoirs to the glory of my reign."

VIII

By the waters of Kerulon, by the hills of Khantai Khan, in the heart of the ocean of grass, a palace is.

Above the waters of the sacred river, under the breasts of the mountain, there is the court of a monarch.

The eyes of a warrior host turn toward the lord of souls. Yet he moves not and the standard over his head stirs not. For the palace is a tomb, and the standard is dust. And no man may see the warrior host that lies at the feet of Genghis Khan.

Yet in the hearts of men still lives the fear that was fear of Genghis Khan.

In the annals of the Mongol khans it is written that the Horde journeyed south and west from their homeland by the Kerulon and the basin of Jungaria in the Autumn of a year early in the seventeenth century, and this was to escape the Winter cold that was creeping down from Lake Baikal, as well as the inroads of the Chinese.

For the khans and their people lived not in cities. Their *yurts*, great felt tents, moved over the mid-Asian steppe drawn by bullocks, and with the *yurts* moved the herds that were the remaining wealth of the Mongols.

They roved restlessly, seldom dismounting from their shaggy ponies, passing aimlessly over the vast spaces, ringed by distant snow ranges that lay just to the north of the Himalayas.

The clans of Mongolia were thinned in numbers; their glory was a thing of the past, recited in song by the minstrels, brooded over beside the fires at night. They wore the sheepskin and leather taken from the animals slain for food. Their weapons were antiquated, being fashioned for the hunt—bows, and short swords.

Powerful, slow-thinking men, warriors and herders, the khans ate what they might, drank deep of mare's milk and slept much, listening at times to the songs of the minstrels.

So Khlit found them by the lakes north of the Thian Shan.

"It is well," they said. "He who was our Kha Khan has come to us to sleep in our tents and eat of our food."

Word passed swiftly along the invisible channels of the steppe that the Cossack in whose veins ran Tatar blood, and who—

himself a descendant of their royal chiefs—had once been their leader, had returned to them out of the mysterious splendor of Ind beyond the mountains to the South.

"He has come in the twilight of old age," they said. "It is well. For the steppe which is our home is his also."

And then swiftly the messages changed. The gray-haired chiefs of the *kurultai*, the council, assembled and spoke together.

"The warrior who was Kha Khan has followed the path of battle in the land of Ind," they repeated gravely. "He has come with a word for our hearing."

Hunters who were following the gazelles and wild horses of the plains began to drift back to the *yurts*, hearing the rumor. Khans, seeking Winter quarters for their clans, rode to the *kibitka* where Khlit sat.

"There is war beyond the mountains to the South and West," they said next. "A people of our race live in a valley there—the valley of Badakshan."

Then also riders passed from the lakes to the outlying hordes, as the Tatars still called their tribes, although now but a shadow of the numbers that had overrun China, the Himalayas, Iran, Persia, and the Caucasus.

"The Kirghiz and the Afghans, who are like to us, ask aid," they remarked to each other. "They are the children of Timurlane, the Lame Conqueror, who is of the line of Genghis Khan."

"The army of Ind rides to the hills," replied shrewder ones, "and there is the wealth of a kingdom in the camp of the Mogul's men. Aye there is gold and weapons—horses, jewels and cattle."

Under the magic stimulus of war the men of the hordes gathered about the lakes. Once assembled, they sought Khlit out. The elder men of the Jun-gar brooded silently. And Khlit addressed his old friends of the *kurultai*.

"To the South," he said. "lies a road that the khans have not followed for the space of eight times the life of a man. In the time of Genghis Khan the road led to the Caliphate; now it leads to Ind."

Bearded heads bent attentively to catch his words; slant eyes peered at him immobily from under tufted brows. Massive, scarred hands clutched spear-shafts as the Tatar chieftains leaned on their spears to listen.

"At the end of the road danger awaits the rider," went on Khlit's deep voice. "I have been your leader. Brothers, khans, you know I speak not idle words—" his glance roved from face to face—"nor make promises that may not be kept. I have made a pledge that I will bring aid to a warrior, my brother-in-arms, Khan of Badakshan."

"Aye." The fur-capped head of youthful Berang, khan of the Torgot clan, nodded. "O Khlit, we know."

"Then hear my message. Before this I have said that I would lead those who dare follow against Jahangir, the World-Gripper, the Mogul. Now I say, brothers, khans, that of those who follow me few will return."

Silence greeted this, and the hard eyes did not falter.

"Well said, by the blood of the horse of Natagai!" bellowed a lion-like voice—Chagan, the sword-bearer, a man thick-set as a gnarled oak, powerful enough to break the neck of a yak by a twist of his hands. "That is no lie. Good!"

Khlit lifted his hand. "Spoil there may be—spoil from the tents of the Chatagais.* Yet those who are slain may bear away no gold. I want no riders to follow me who think of naught but plunder."

"Aye," said the khans. "In flashing sword-strokes does a warrior find honor."

"If there be a battle—and a battle I seek—those who follow me must face the tramp of elephants and the thunder of cannon. I want no cowards."

The khans growled at this, clutching their weapons the tighter. One grumbled that Genghis had overmastered the "moving castles," the elephants, when he vanquished the emperor of Han.

"And among those who come with me there will be no leaders. I will lead, and he who disobeys will die. At my side will be the

* The Mogul race of India.

yak-tail standard, as when we drove the Chinese banners before us at the Kerulon."

"Ho!" cried one. "That was a battle. The minstrels will sing of that."

"But not of this," broke in Khlit harshly. "For we will be in a strange, southern land, and the bards of Ind will not remember the bravery of the Tatar khans. Nay, we will have naught but hard blows and hard words, for we go to the aid of an oppressed people. Nor—" he faced them gravely—"do I seek the leadership save that one man must be chief and not many. And I know how we may strike the Mogul."

His aged countenance lighted up at this, and his keen eyes gleamed. "Ha, lords! We be old, many of us, and our race is passing into the shadows. Come, shall we strike one good blow with the sword—" his curved sword flashed in his hand at this—"of Genghis, the Conqueror! Shall we ride into battle once more? Has our blood grown too thin to shed?"

The somber faces shone, and the intent eyes held his fiercely.

"Tomorrow at daybreak—" Khlit sheathed his weapon and folded his arms across his broad chest—"I ride to the South. Those who will go with me must be mounted and assembled at the council place by then."

Such was his last address to the Tatar khans.

That night beside the campfires that sprinkled the plain and flickered into the lakes the men of the Horde sat in unwonted talk. Here and there the one-stringed fiddle of a minstrel strummed and a deep voice recited an endless chant of former glory. And with this rose the plaint of the women—the sound of mourning that has since the world was new attended the departure of the warriors.

And with the dawn, when the fires had sunk to embers, there was a stirring of figures, the soft tread of horses, and the clink of weapons.

The first glow of scarlet sunrise over the steppe showed a multitude of riders gathered around the tent of Khlit.

Truly it was a strange army. For there was no baggage save the saddlebags on the spare horses—each Tatar brought an extra mount. Nor was any ammunition train to be seen. Each warrior carried his own weapons.

There was no muster, no fretting of waiting ranks. The riders of the clans grouped about their respective banners, and the whole hive-like mass centered around the yak-tail standard.

This was outlined clearly against the yellow of the flooding sky. It moved forward, and helmeted heads and spear-points followed swiftly. Once a woman burst from a tent to run, weeping, beside the horse of a young warrior, who thrust her aside with his foot.

Again rose the song of the minstrels, harsh and discordant in the semi-darkness. Groups of old women, straining aged eyes, clutched the young ones to them in silence.

"*Hai*—the Horde is onward bound . . . the khans of Tatary ride . . . they follow the standard of Genghis . . . Woe to those who stand in their way . . ."

It was the chant of the riders, remembered from ancient times. And, in the half-light of dawn, the black mass of riders under the banners seemed not otherwise than the mass of the ancient Horde.

IX

Alacha Hunts

Tala sat watchfully upon the broad rump of a buffalo, the last of her herd. While the beast drank from a pool in one of the icy mountain streams, the girl eyed the surrounding thicket thoughtfully. She had drawn a fold of her heavy cloak across the lower portion of her face, and only her alert eyes were visible, under a dark tangle of hair.

The echo of a distant shout pierced the quiet of the glade. Overhead the echo reverberated from lofty sandstone cliffs, winding in and out among narrow rock ravines, and returning unexpectedly from the face of some distant mountain. The buffalo raised its

dripping muzzle inquiringly, but Tala made no move to pull its
nose-cord away from the stream.

She listened keenly as the voices of men approached through a
willow thicket along the bank of the stream. Then horses' hoofs
were heard, trampling on stones. Tala sat upright, her small figure
tense. She had been waiting for the coming of the riders.

And presently, as she had anticipated, a brilliant cortège trotted through the willows, led by two noblemen. She recognized
the silks and velvets of Alacha and the russet-and-green overtunic
of Paluwan Khan—the Northern Lord. On the gloved wrist of the
Slayer rested his favorite gyrfalcon, hooded.

In contrast to the light hunting-garb of the handsome, olive-
skinned Turkoman, the khan rode fully armed in *khud*—steel
headdress—and *zirih* beneath his tunic, with mace and sword at
his girdle. Paluwan Khan was a dark-browed, stoop-shouldered
man, and more than a little bow-legged.

Tala faced them defiantly, only drawing the cloak closer under
her eyes.

"An Afghan, by the soul of Ali!" cried Paluwan Khan, scowling.

"And not ill-shaped," added Alacha, fingering his mustache.

"No place this, for a brat of the ill-omened brood," grunted the
khan.

"After all," murmured Alacha, his slant eyes straying idly back
to his falcon, from the girl, "she is dirty, and rags distort even the
finest limbs. Ho, little thief, what do you here? What seek you in
the hunting-ground of the Mogul?"

Tala's eyes blazed.

"This land was my father's field," she cried. "And you, O
Alacha, are a greater thief than I, for your men have taken my
cattle, leaving only this buffalo that is sick and like to die."

"Then is your father a traitor, wench," said Alacha in a color-
less voice. Unlike the khan, he seemed to enjoy the hot words of
the girl. "For he is with the black standard of rebellious Abdul
Dost."

Under his gaze, curiously thoughtful, as if the aspect of the woman called up a familiar thought, Tala turned her head aside.

"Am I not to be paid for the cattle?" she asked passively.

Paluwan Khan laughed in his beard and would have spurred on, but Alacha turned cold eyes from Tala to the foremost of his retinue, a gigantic Turk, Hossein by name.

"Hossein, offspring of sin," he observed, twisting the end of his light mustache delicately, "your race is covetous of the women of other lands. Let me see, I have given you Georgian, Circassian, Khorassani and Kirghiz, but never—before this—an Afghan. Would yonder sharp-tongued baggage please you?"

"Aye, my lord," bellowed the stout warrior. "There is no bounty like my lord's."

He was clad in the barbaric splendor that was then the fashion in Constantinople. A blue *kaftan*, fur-tipped, enveloped his massive shoulders, over a white robe embroidered with cloth-of-gold, somewhat soiled. Hossein had wrestled in the courts of the Osmanli, and his garb mimicked the splendor of the sultans, just as the jewels on his black paws imitated the Greek fashion, and also the chain of turquoise about his bull neck.

"Aye, fountain of imperial mercy," he salaamed, small eyes glittering. "If her tongue be too sharp for my taste, a knife will blunt it—"

Tala thrust out a contemptuous lower lip. "Is this the justice of Alacha?"

Neither of the nobles deigned to reply. Hossein advanced on Tala, seizing the nose-cord of the buffalo. Alacha looked on, much amused.

The Slayer was something of a philosopher, having passed his boyhood as disciple in a *meddresse* of Samarkand, and wandering from there to Bokhara and its mosques, to idolatrous Antioch and cosmopolitan Constantinople. Nominally a Mohammedan, he was familiar with the doctrines of Shiite and Sunnite, Zoroastrian and Hebrew, and the *shaman*s, or conjurer-priests, of Mongolia.

Thus he had the intelligence and capacity for evil of the mosque-raised boy and the ready wits of a wanderer.

He could quote readily from the Persian poets, the astronomy of Uleg Beg, or the hero epic of the *Ramayana*. Supremely intelligent, he allowed others to do his fighting for him, and his quarreling. In great favor with the petulant Jahangir, he was skilled in anticipating the moods of his monarch.

Some said that the cruelty of the slender Turkoman was not natural to him, being assumed to satisfy Jahangir; others that by cruelty he hoped to make his name feared, being loath to hazard his person in battle to that end.

Now he glanced up, his smooth face revealing as much surprise as it was capable of showing. A broad, bent figure clad in heavy sheepskins had approached Hossein silently and laid a massive hand on the Turk's shoulder.

"By the gods!" murmured Alacha.

He stared at the companion of the newcomer, a veiled woman mounted on a white Arab.

"Stand aside," said, or rather growled, the man of the sheepskins.

Hossein gaped and stepped back to shake off the hand that gripped him. Failing in this, he reached for a knife in his girdle.

"Unmannered dog!" he shouted. "Child of a dog—"

His heavy voice waxed shrill with anger. He had noticed the brown, curling hair and the blue eyes of the man who faced him—a Circassian.

Between Turk and Circassian there was a world-old feud. The stranger folded his arms, his eyes hard. Upon shoulder and swelling forearm the leather garments clung tightly, molded over iron-like muscles. He did not move to touch the short, bare sword thrust through his belt.

Alacha, who was a keen observer, noted that the sheepskins of the powerful stranger seemed ill in keeping with the splendid workmanship of the sword. And he fancied that the woman, although wearing the heavy wool of a commoner, bore herself too well on the blooded horse to be a person of the countryside. Her veil and the pearl chaplet bound over her dark hair were of Persian design.

Paluwan Khan, impatient at the second interruption, commanded Hossein to knock the stranger down, seize the girl and continue on with the hunt, in the name of Allah's mercy.

"Nay," cried the woman on the horse, "he is my man—" nodding at the broad figure in sheepskins—"and he will take the Afghan woman for me."

Alacha toyed with the silver chain of his hawk and frowned, puzzled by the imperious voice of the woman and the boldness of her servant.

"Hossein," he purred, "are you minded to give place to a boor, a shepherd clown?"

His glance still dwelt on the veiled stranger, noting the stately figure and the wealth of dark hair. Why did such a one ride alone, except for a single slave? Who was she? What did she want of the Afghan child?

Paluwan Khan spurred to his side.

"In the name of Satan and all his brood, why barter words with a woman? They profit a man nothing, and they sting like serpents."

Alacha waved him aside. Surely the newcomer was beautiful. Probably, since she was alone, she was masterless. If he could know for certain that she was not wife or mistress of some noble more powerful than himself—

"O *khanum*—" he bent his handsome head slightly—"have you a claim to this wretched girl, that you countermand the word of Alacha?"

"I desire her." The woman seemed to be smiling behind her veil. "And I have been listening, my lord, behind yonder thicket to—the words of Alacha."

"Ah."

The Turkoman bit his carefully tended mustache reflectively. The woman had wit. Likewise—so he assured himself—there must be a purpose behind her speech. If he only knew—

"*Khanum*, it is never my wish to forgo the desire of beauty. You have a sturdy scoundrel to attend you—eh, he is not lacking in boldness. Then let him try his strength with the wrestler, Hossein. Let the Afghan maiden be the prize."

He expected a protest, perhaps the disclosure of her name and rank. And by soft words he hoped to win her favor.

"So be it," she said after a pause. "Geron is no weakling."

At this the Circassian silently discarded coat and belt and stood forth in leather jerkin and woolen trousers. Hossein, after a glance at his master, did likewise, baring hairy shoulders and arms, massive and full-fleshed.

"Ho, Circassian dog," he bellowed, "I will make *kohl* for your blue eyes out of the dust. Nay, I will redden your pale cheeks with blood."

Geron glanced at him impassively. He stood not as tall as the Turk, but he was broader across the shoulders and chest. Moreover his arms were of gorilla-like length, and his legs—unlike Hossein's—were heavily thewed.

"Is your man skilled as a wrestler, *khanum*?" growled Paluwan Khan, becoming interested. He had pressed forward, to form a ring about the two champions, with others of the hunting-party.

"If not, his bones will crack like twigs, and I shall take that bright sword of his, for it likes me well."

"He is no wrestler," observed the woman. "*Ai—*"

Hossein with professional shrewdness had suddenly gripped Geron about the shoulders, his plump arms twining for a headlock. The Circassian, taken by surprise, twisted about and broke free with some trouble. He stood erect, breathing deeply, and then gasped wholeheartedly. The Turk, angered by the failure of his first hold, butted him full in the stomach.

"Is your man a wrestler?" asked the woman quickly. "I think he is a ram."

She broke off as Geron was heavily thrown by a more successful trick of the Turk. The breath seemed to have been knocked from his stout body by this second impact, yet when Hossein would have fallen upon him with a cry of triumph, he wriggled aside and stood erect, glaring at his tormentor.

Squealing with self-inspired rage, Hossein rushed at him head down. Again they grappled, and the two powerful bodies swayed and staggered over the turf. Alacha barely glanced at them. He was sure of the outcome, and he was more interested in the woman who took delight in a man's sport.

The Turk, feinting craftily, jerked Geron's knees from under him and pounced upon his sweating shoulders, driving home the head-hold he sought—his forearm locked under the chin of his adversary, his weight full on Geron's neck.

"Now the twig will snap, *crack*—like that!" Paluwan Khan grinned, and snapped his fingers

The woman clapped her hands.

"Geron!" she cried. "Make an end."

But the Circassian's broad face was purple, and he gasped. Be a man ever so strong, he cannot put forth his strength without wind in his lungs. Hossein was silent now, striving wickedly to break the neck of his foe. The wrestling match had become a deadly struggle.

Tala sat her buffalo, scrutinizing combatants and spectators with sharp interest. Such sport was in her mind the play of slaves. Men of her race fought with sharp sword-edges. Although she might well have done so, she made no effort to run off.

She had noted every detail of the appearance of the woman on the horse. But chiefly she watched the Slayer.

The two wrestlers had sunk to the ground, Geron underneath. The friends of Hossein had raised a triumphant shout. This seemed to act as the spur the great Circassian needed, for a brown arm shot out from the writhing mass and closed about the throat of the Turk.

The watchers saw Hossein thrust back and his grip broken as easily as a severed vine is pulled from a tree trunk. The muscles of Geron's arm swelled and cracked as he rose slowly to his knees, gulping deep breaths of air into a laboring chest.

Out of red eyes, under sweat-dripping brows, he stared at the struggling Hossein. The Turk, by a crafty twist, jerked free, blood spurting from his throat and mouth as be did so. Then Geron, still kneeling, caught him sidewise by the waist and rose with his burden to his feet.

Gripping the Turk fast on his shoulder, Geron stared about him and stepped to the edge of the pool. His hands shifted from waist to the neck of Hossein and his broad shoulders heaved.

Hossein, the skilled wrestler, flew through the air and fell, a good four paces away, into the pool near the watching Tala. The water was shallow, yet Hossein lay passive beneath it, stunned.

"Let him lie," said Alacha softly. "I have no service for a weakling."

But Geron paced forward a trifle unsteadily, stooped, and drew the unconscious body from the water. Without looking at it he walked to his sheepskin coat and belt, girded on his sword and seized the nose-cord of Tala's buffalo. Then he spoke to Paluwan Khan.

"This blade—" he smote the haft of his short weapon—"was fashioned for my hand, not for yours, my lord."

The noble shrugged his shoulders and would have urged Alacha forward on the hunt, but the Slayer had been whispering to the woman.

"In the name of all the gods, who is your champion? He handled Hossein like a sack of grain."

"My lord," she laughed, "he is no miller but a maker of swords. He is Geron, the armorer of the Mogul."

Alacha stared at the man who for half a generation had tempered and shaped the Damascus and Persian blades for Jahangir.

"The imperial favor would shine upon us coldly," swore Paluwan Khan in his ear, "if your stupid wrestler had broken the neck of the great smith. Said I not a woman was a breeder of trouble—"

"But such a woman," whispered Alacha. "Half the spoils of Afghanistan for a sight of her face."

To the stranger he added:

"The Afghan girl is yours; verily your wrestler is a worthy servant indeed. Yet for you a champion of nobler blood should be supplied. Will you lighten my eyes with gladness by allowing me to escort you to the camp? Perhaps if you have no tent, or await some one from the court—"

"I wait for no one, Alacha," she responded. "But I will ride with you to your tent."

Whereupon, preceded by Geron and Tala on her buffalo, the woman and Alacha turned back along the stream toward the camp of the Mogul's army.

Within the inner recess of Alacha's tent the woman of the pearls seated herself upon the cushions of the Slayer, yet when he would have knelt upon the rug in front of her, she checked him with an imperious gesture.

"It is not fitting you should sit," she explained, adding softly, "You know not my rank. "

This indeed was causing Alacha no little worry. He frowned, for he fancied that his visitor was making game of him. If he could but know her name, and her purpose in seeking him—

Smilingly he offered his visitor dainty refreshment of sherbet, ice-cooled, and figs in syrup. These, however, the woman commanded to be taken to Tala in the entrance compartment of the tent, with more substantial fare for Geron.

Alacha's smooth brow flushed darkly at this affront to his hospitality. He fumbled with the jewels at his throat, trying to meet the glance of the dark-eyed beauty who was tranquilly scrutinizing the splendid coloring of a peacock—one of the Slayer's pets.

"Now, my lord." she observed at length, "I wish you to tell me how the campaign goes—how you and the pillars of empire have fared against the Afghan."

Politely, slightly ironically, he bowed. "To do that, my lady, I must first know your name."

"Then—" the brown eyes flashed at him mockingly over the veil—"I must needs tell you. The whole of the Mogul's army has

passed through the Shyr into Badakshan; you have burned to the
ground a score of villages, and planted as many headmen upon
stakes. Balkh you have seized, and levied tribute of half their
wealth upon its merchants. Slaves you have taken—"

"From the thieving Pathans."

"Who must become the servants of Jahangir. Was it wise?
My lord Alacha, you have advanced the imperial army over half
Badakshan, destroying the crops, fruits and vineyards that you
have not stripped for yourself—"

"*Khanum*, we have driven the Afghans before us."

"Verily? You have not engaged them in battle."

"Nay, they fly before the imperial standard. True, they harass
our foraging parties and our supply caravans. They be born brig-
ands."

"Who love their freedom."

Alacha's full lip curled. Was the woman seeking to play upon
him? She wore the headdress and veil of a married woman, yet
she rose alone near the army. She had befriended an Afghan girl.
Wherefore?

"Your words are a well of wisdom, *khanum*," he parried. "Perchance also your wisdom has found a part for the hill maiden to
play."

His visitor nodded gravely.

"Aye, my lord. I shall send her to Abdul Dost with a message."

The Turkoman laughed. If this were intrigue it was poorly concealed. He became more bold, for he fancied the woman sought
to win his favor. That she should be a friend of the Afghans he
doubted. The men of the hills had no wits in their empty skulls.

"It is written that the fairest of women unite the pearls of
wisdom to the diamond of beauty," he smiled, approaching her.
"Happy is the hour when such a companion comes to my tent—"

"Have you not bound the girdle of fidelity to your master, the
Mogul, about the cloak of war?" she asked calmly. "Alacha, I have
seen the manner in which you serve your lord. No eyes have you

for aught save the women you may take, or the spoil you may pile beside your tent."

The Turkoman shrugged his shoulders, staring curiously at the woman who treated him as a servant.

"Alacha," she continued thoughtfully, "I also serve the Mogul, and he trusts me above his generals. Wherefore I say to offer Abdul Dost fair terms. Let the Afghan make peace in honor. Offer amends for the pillaging done by your men. Send the girl Tala with the message."

"Amends—to the Afghan? When we have the imperial army mustered for battle? What would Jahangir say?"

He laughed tolerantly. It pleased him to match words with his fair visitor.

The brown eyes fell serious at once, and she spoke with masculine directness.

"Alacha, you and the other *ameer*s think much of the glory that may be won in a battle. Yet are we all servants of India, and the Mogul of India." Her voice quickened and she sat erect. "Where have your spies been? Have you no tidings of aid coming to Adbul Dost from the northern tribes?"

"Aye—some talk there has been among the mountain men of Mongol clans gathering beyond the hills. But naught have I heard from the priest who is my spy among the Mongols."

"Talk! If you meet these same clans in battle the imperial army will feel the weight of a skilled sword. Grant them peace and you may win strong allies—Afghans and Mongols. Then will the empire of India wax greater thereby."

Alacha smiled, adjusting the folds of his elaborate cloak.

"The clans will never win through the passes of the Roof of the World, my lady. Verily, this is a matter for the wisdom of men, not for a woman's tongue. Will you not rest—"

"Nay. Alacha, once I came through the passes of the northern hills from the desert and the city of the black priests—Khoten. For guide I had a warrior of the Mongol clans. Now he has gone back to his people."

"Can horsemen ride over the rock passes? Can horses find feed in the snow? Nay, have no fear—"

He sought to touch her hand.

"Fool!"

The woman rose swiftly. From under her veil she drew a long string of pearls, unwound from about her throat.

"You have an eye for spoil. Know you these royal jewels? Know you their owner?"

Alacha's olive face paled and his lips quivered. He stepped back, raising both hands to his forehead. For he had looked into the gateway of death, and his usually placid nerves failed him momentarily.

"Nur-Jahan!" he cried "Light of the World, queen-to-be of Jahangir! Pardon. How was I to know? *Kulluh*—I am your slave."

With a quick thought he drew his dagger and held its hilt toward her. "Slay me if I have displeased—"

She waved him back impatiently, smiling under her veil at the transparent attempt at heroics. Adjusting the splendid pearls once more about her throat, she made a sign for quiet.

"Jahangir knows not I have left the court. When I heard the news from Mongolia I hastened hither, for those at the court had no thought for the coming of the clans. Only Geron knows, and he is my faithful slave, for he came from my home in Persia."

Her voice softened at this, and Alacha breathed a sigh of relief. Nur-Jahan was unlike the women of India. Once a wanderer, daughter of a poor caravan-follower, her beauty and splendid intellect had made a name for her at the court of Akbar, father of Jahangir.

Her former husband, Sher Afghan, the Tiger Lord, had been slain by Jahangir's order—almost the first act of the young Mogul's reign. Nur-Jahan, formerly called Mir-un-nissa, alone of those at the court of Delhi was unafraid of Jahangir—had even received his wooing coldly.

Sorrow and the vicissitudes of life had left their stamp on the woman's soul, although her fairness seemed to have grown the

greater for suffering. Her courage in holding up the mirror of truth
to the eyes of the narrow-minded and short-tempered monarch
had increased her influence over him. Fearless, prone to follow
her own path, her wisdom overmatched the wits of the statesmen
of the court.

Nur-Jahan was destined to be the greatest empress of India.
And the love of the Mogul for her was the brightest spot in a
dissolute life. Although the Taj Mahal was built as the tomb of
another woman, Nur-Jahan, the Persian, was the fairest figure of
the Mogul era.

And it was this love, headstrong and jealous, of Jahangir for
the Persian that Alacha had feared.

"Tomorrow," said Nur-Jahan, "we will send the girl with the
message to Adbul Dost. Oh, Alacha, much have I risked in coming hither. The Mogul has greater foes near his side than the
Afghans. He must not suffer a defeat on this border of his kingdom. Nay, now is the time for peace."

With that she withdrew to a small tent on the outskirts of the
camp that Geron had set up, and with her went Tala.

And the great Persian out of kindness to the maid gave her fresh
garments of the Afghan fashion to replace her rags and ordered
her to sleep at the foot of her own couch.

Now when the cry of the *namaz gar* went up and the manifold
activity of the camp was stilled while ten thousand Muslims
knelt in worship, Nur-Jahan crouched by the carpet that was her
bed and prayed.

And when she ceased she heard without the tent the curious
song of a minstrel to his love, low-toned and musical. Yet when
she and Geron looked from the tent canopy they saw a slender
beggar, wearing holy garments, sitting beneath the wide limbs of
a plane tree, and looking up tranquilly into the evening

Alacha did not pray. He sat on the cushions where the fragrance
of the attar of rose—Nur-Jahan's favorite perfume—still clung

faintly, and in his soul was the poison of a temptation that twined into his thoughts and would not be dismissed.

"Jahangir knows not she has come hither," he repeated under his breath.

He rested his handsome head on clenched hands, feeling again the fear that had gripped him when he thought of the Mogul.

"By the gods—whoever they be—she is fair. For a glimpse of her face I would hazard—much."

And his new longing drove out the fear. His mind had ever dwelt on women. And Nur-Jahan, whose beauty pierced the veil that concealed it, had been in his tent, at his side.

"Aye, the Persian has risked much," he communed with his thoughts. "Verily she has hazarded the favor of Jahangir to ride hither. Why? She came to me. Perchance she does not dislike me—"

Isolated from the court, monarch of a kingdom, Alacha had fed upon his own vanity. He had fashioned a shallow heaven out of his own desires.

"She seeks mercy for the Afghans—unknown to the Mogul. Is she the empress of the age, or—fool?"

While the shadows deepened in the tent, he sat in meditation. Impatiently he ordered away attendants who would have brought candles and the evening meal. He glanced from time to time across the space between the tents to where the silk curtains of Nur-Jahan's shelter glowed, shaking slightly in the cool, evening breeze.

"Geron knows."

He rose to pace the carpets of his pavilion restlessly. Once be glanced up at the distant peaks of the Himalayas, where the snow summits loomed chilly and roseate with the afterglow of the sun, and thought amusedly that Nur-Jahan had come to the camp to make peace with Abdul Dost because she feared an army of horsemen might cross a half-thousand miles of those ravines.

This reflection encouraged him in a subtle fashion. No one would credit the warning of the Persian. That was well. If the campaign were ended at this stage there would be scant triumph for Alacha.

So it must not be ended.

He nodded to himself slowly, then started with a hissing breath of alarm as a dark figure crawled to his feet. It was a great, silent form, like an animal's.

"Mercy, lord. Do not turn the warmth of your favor from Hossein!"

The wrestler, stripped of his finery, with tattered tunic and baggy trousers water-soaked, rose to his knees. Light from a torch at the gate of the *khanate*—the strip of heavy calico, upon bamboo poles that encircled the tent—shone upon his white eyeballs rolling in a blood-stained face.

"Lord of the Northern World, Monarch of the Stars," he chattered, his teeth unruly with the cold, "your slaves say that you cursed me because the Circassian dog tricked me. But I—"

"You would like revenge upon Ger—upon the blue-eyed Circassian?" observed Alacha thoughtfully.

"My lord, it is my prayer—"

"Come then."

The Turkoman moved toward the gate of the *khanate*. Hossein followed, happy that Alacha had not struck him or sent him away. A defeated wrestler, cast off by his master, Hossein's fortunes would have sunk to the dust, and the prospect of further largesse and slaves been as naught.

At the gate Alacha dismissed the spearman who stood guard, and commanded the torch to be borne away. Leaning against the post of the barrier, he gazed silently over the encampment. An arrow's shot away glimmered the tent of Nur-Jahan in the shadows under the grove of plane trees.

The smoke of a thousand cooking fires was dwindling into the cold air of evening, and the sky overhead, shot with the brilliance of myriad stars, was curiously transparent. Somewhere behind the hills an invisible gateway was opening through which the light of a full moon—the harvest moon—was flooding.

But as yet the only illumination in the camp came from the moving torches, where men threaded their way between the tents, or a noble passed hither and yon with his retinue.

Flares reflected ruddily upon the standard of Paluwan Khan, among the dark lines of horses of the Punjabi cavalry. Voices echoed from the water tank, about which groups of footmen, armor and weapons put aside, gambled and sang.

As an undertone to this came the ceaseless mutter of camels, coughing and grunting over their fodder, and—at intervals—the bellowing call of an elephant.

"Soon, Hossein," whispered the Slayer, "the moon will be up."

"Aye, lord."

"Before then—"

Alacha's low voice dwindled into silence. His forehead was very hot, although the chill of evening had settled upon the earth. Restlessly his hands twitched at his throat. Every nerve seemed to be on fire.

What monumental folly had sent Nur-Jahan incognito to the camp and to him? Was she truly without a protector other than stout Geron? Was it all not the invisible working of fate?

Fate had been kind to Alacha. He was fast rising to greatness. A moment's boldness—

"My lord?" came the servile voice of Hossein, fawning.

Tomorrow—Alacha's racing thoughts resumed their trend—Nur-Jahan might reveal her identity to the other *ameers*. She might influence them to peace. Aye, she might well strip Alacha of his prestige by a single word whispered in her soft voice into the ear of Jahangir. Already she had hinted she thought Alacha unfaithful to his master.

In this she had wronged Alacha, who served Jahangir well, serving himself the while, as a clever man should. So the Turkoman reasoned with his thoughts. And there came into his mind unbidden the vision of the clear, brown eyes of the famous Persian, the alertness and vital energy of her figure, full-fledged in beauty.

"A jewel of paradise," he breathed. "Aye, more splendid than the throne of the Mogul—"

"My lord?"

"Before the moon rises," said Alacha slowly, harkening curiously to the sound of his own words, "go unseen to yonder tent."

He pointed, and as he did so the glimmer faded from the silk.

"The Circassian lies there asleep, doubtless across the threshold. Note his position and keep watch. Remain there until I come."

"Aye, lord."

In the darkness Hossein smiled, seeing how his fortunes might be replenished. He bowed and slipped away along the dark stretch of the *khanate*, moving softly for all his bulk.

Alacha clapped his hands, and a servant ran from his pavilion to his side.

"Horses," be commanded. "Two of the best. Have them brought to the outskirts of the grove—" again he pointed—"and tethered there. Do not abide by the horses, but return hither. Haste!"

Scarcely had the footsteps of the man, running barefoot, ceased, when Alacha turned aside and stalked rapidly through the tents toward the pavilion of Paluwan Khan.

By now Alacha knew that the northern Lord would be abed, on his cloak spread on the bare ground, half-unconscious from the effects of a drinking bout. And not otherwise did he find the khan.

Without returning the hurried salute of the guard at the pavilion door, the Turkoman leaned over the squat figure snoring on disordered garments and shook him by the shoulder.

A man awakened from sleep is bemused, and, if tired, angry. Having emptied many cups of rare wine of Kabul and Ferghana, Paluwan Khan first reached for his sword, then swore roundly.

"Hide of a dog—"

Alacha squatted close to him, speaking swiftly. A spy, he said, had come to the camp. A wandering Persian courtesan in the pay of their enemies had sought to beguile him—Alacha.

"Carcass of Satan!" observed Paluwan Khan drowsily. "Well she knew in what quarter to ply her arts! You have a dagger. Make an end of her and let me sleep."

"She it was who rode up to us when the sun had crossed the midway,* the mistress of the Circassian—"

"Geron? He is no traitor."

Alacha's bright eyes narrowed. For a moment he had forgotten that Paluwan Khan knew the identity of the armorer. He smiled at the drowsy chieftain ironically.

"Ha, my lord! Think you the armorer of Jahangir would wander afield in rags like a stray beggar? Nay. I believe the two to be friends of the Mongol warrior who invaded the court of the King of Kings—"

"Say you so?"

Paluwan Khan had a blunt brain. Jahangir had once observed that while Alacha held too much pride in his brain-cup, Paluwan Khan held too many cups in his brain. Now he thought dully of the act of Nur-Jahan in befriending the Afghan girl, and swore drowsily.

"Send her then," he growled, "to —— or the Mogul. What affair is it of mine?"

"She is quartered near to you," responded Alacha quickly. "Grant me a following of four Punjabis—your men—and I will seek her out—"

"Aye," muttered the khan. "Make an end, by Allah. It is written that the tongue of a woman is evil as the bite of a serpent . . ."

He was already asleep. Alacha summoned the two spearmen who had heard the speech of the nobles, and called up two from the outer guard. With these Punjabis he hastened back to his tent, giving them whispered instructions on the way. From the tent

---

* The afternoon.

they sought the grove of trees, under which shadows were just forming as moonlight swept the sky over the mountain peaks.

Came Hossein to his side with a sibilant word.

Laying aside their spears—clumsy weapons for hand-to-hand work—the four sturdy men of Paluwan Khan slipped to the door of the tent and disappeared within.

Alacha, who had been at some pains to have others than his own men attack Geron in case his plan should miscarry, moved nearer. He heard a low exclamation, the sound of a blow.

Dimly he made out struggling figures within the pavilion. Hossein with a grin of hate drew his dagger and stepped warily nearer. Then, running forward, he struck viciously at a man who grappled with two others.

Alacha saw the two draw back, saw the mottled moonlight glimmer on the light curls of Geron, who took an unsteady step forward, staring at the Slayer with wide eyes that saw naught but a red mist of pain.

Geron gave a grunting cry and sank to the earth, clutching his throat. Pausing only long enough to make sure that Hossein had dealt the giant armorer a deadly blow, Alacha stepped over the prone form of a Punjabi and peered at the woman, who had risen from the couch.

Within the tent the moonlight took on a strange, silvery semblance, shot through with the black arms that were shadows from the branches of trees. It sparkled faintly on the jewels upon the hands of stately Nur-Jahan, and glowed with a flame-like radiance along the string of pearls at her smooth throat.

Swiftly she drew veil across her mouth.

"What means this? Where is Geron?"

"Slain by some Punjabi revelers. Oh *khanum*, there is peril for you here. Come!"

Alacha stepped toward her and grasped her wrist, his own hand far from steady. The woman's quick intuition warned her, and she drew away.

The man's arm closed about her throat; fingers pressed against her lips. Nur-Jahan thrust at him, her body tense with anger and fright. A quick word and Hossein came, gathering her in huge arms, lifting her to his stout shoulder. To the horses he carried her, being skilled in the handling of women, and laid her across the saddle-peak of one.

Alacha, breathing deeply, stared into the shadows in the tent-corners, moving silently about. His pulse was unruly, and he shivered more than once.

The Afghan girl, he knew, must be within the tent, and her mouth as well as Geron's must be sealed, for there was no way to know what Nur-Jahan had said to Tala in the earlier hours of the night.

Then did Alacha pause in his tracks, his dark head thrust forward between his slender shoulders, the fingers of a groping hand outstretched rigidly.

"Death of the gods!" he swore.

So near to him that his fingers almost touched her cheek he saw, not a tousled-haired, tattered Afghan girl, but a shapely maiden whose black ringlets hung down over her breast, whose garments were of fine silk and velvet, who wore across her throat a slim chain of bead-like black pearls.

The silver-like radiance from above touched her high forehead strongly. Her motionless eyes stared stolidly into his. It seemed to Alacha—such illusions being sometimes wrought by overstrained nerves—that the figure of the woman had stepped forward through the fabric of the tent.

In reality Tala, who had remained motionless, hoping to escape unseen, was half-paralyzed by the nearness of the Slayer and by the menace of his silent search.

Yet Alacha saw only the likeness of a young girl, who had worn those same pearls and garments like to these—an Afghan girl who had slain herself while he held her upon his saddle.

"How came you here?" he muttered, feeling a chill course through his nerves. "What—"

Not until now had he seen Tala's face unveiled, nor did he

know that she was sister to the woman he had caused to die. Instinctively, mastered by mounting fright, Tala raised her hand to her throat.

To Alacha the gesture was significant, menacing. He drew back a step; then, overcome by an impulse of fear, he turned and fled from the tent.

When the Punjabis, ordered by Alacha to search the tent, came to look for the woman he had seen, they saw naught but the empty recess of the pavilion and the deserted couch of Nur-Jahan. Tala had slipped under the tent wall and fled into the grove.

Presently Hossein moved away through the trees, with his prisoner in his arms. From the grove he struck into a winding path that led through the scattered bazaars of the camp followers, to the outer lines of the imperial forces and thence to a sheep-track up the hillside.

And after him, slipping from shadow to shadow, came two ponies, stolen from the mounts of the cavalry, and upon these rode Tala and Chan, the minstrel, wearing the garb of a begging *kwajah*.

"For," Chan had whispered to Tala, "the Slayer said to Hossein that before long he would come to seek the woman, and it is my thought that he will come alone."

"It is the will of God," responded Tala.

At the council of the *ameer*s the following morning Paluwan Khan smote impatiently with his scabbard upon the carpet before his feet, crying in a mighty voice:

"An end, say I. By the beard of Ali, we will bring these ill-omened ones to a battle. My horsemen have pushed them back and up the broad valley of Badakshan, and now they are at the last of their villages—the whole scum of the devil brood. Now they must fight or give up their lands—"

"A scant battle will it be," remarked the chivalrous raja, who had all the Rájput distaste of facing an inferior foe. "Yet some tidings have come to me of horsemen riding hither from Mongolia. What say you, Alacha?"

The Turkoman smiled ironically.

"One horseman might come, but not an army. Even the raja's men would not face the Autumn cold of the upper passes, where snow will soon cover the ground."

"Nor," nodded Raja Man Singh, "can even the fiends of the air find sufficient food to feed a clan on yonder rock ravines and desolate forests."

"Aye," growled Paluwan Khan impatiently, "it is said that demons and the likeness of foul creatures infest the spaces of the Roof of the World, who prey upon travelers. What manner of men would follow a leader through such-like? *Khosh.* It may not be."

He turned to Alacha with reawakened curiosity.

"Ho, lord, what did you with the Persian wench—send her to —— or the Mogul?"

Boisterously he laughed, but Alacha, whose face was somewhat strained, did not smile.

"Not to the Mogul," he said.

Now, following upon this council of the chiefs, the bulk of the imperial army pressed onward toward the upper limits of Badakshan, moving in an orderly mass—artillery and musketmen with the baggage in the center and the cavalry upon the outskirts.

And the chiefs of many villages of the North came to Abdul Dost, crying, "We have seen the flames of our homes and the slaughter of our cattle. Will ye not give battle before all Badakshan is lost?"

To each of these the Afghan leader made the same response.

"It is not yet time."

And the Afghans saw that he looked much to the dark lines in the distant hills that were the passes to the North, and steadfastly watched the sky for signs of storm.

"It is not yet time," he said again.

X

Through the gate in the mountain comes the buran, the wind that destroys. Shepherds and the flocks of shepherds die at the cold touch of the buran.

From the iron gate of the winds in the sky comes the buran, and where it breathes is desolation.

Before the time of our fathers and their fathers and the memory of the oldest men there came through the gate of the mountain the Destroyer.

Genghis Khan, the Destroyer, rode through the gateway of Mongolia and in his path there was desolation.

"Aye, before the memory of man there came the sea of ice, and the mountains of ice, and no life was in Sungaria.

"Aye, khans of the Horde, the ice moved down from the North, sweeping across the plains of the Mongols as the waves of sand now move across the plains; but when the ice came to the mountains of the Roof of the World it went no farther. Yet here, lords of Mongolia, are the traces of the ice to be seen, graven upon broad, flat stones.

"And before the ice fled the great elephants with tusks as long as a bent tree, and hide heavy-coated—like yonder yak, lords of the Horde."

A minstrel who rode with the Mongols pointed to a herd of the shaggy, clumsy yaks grazing by the shore of the lake. Already hunters had circled from the Horde to slay the beasts and bring their meat to the next camp.

"That was the age of the hero-spirits, lords," he recited. "The *tengri-bogdo* dwelt upon the heights, and many were the battles they waged. Aye, many the palaces they built of mountain rock that reached to the heavens.

"Upon the winds they rode, leaping from hilltop to plain at a single bound, *pouf*—like the blast of the wind. The arrows they shot were fashioned of the shafts of pine trees, and still you may see the marks where the arrows pierced the mountain slopes."

Whereupon he pointed to gullies and giant crevices in the range of hills they were approaching to the South.

"After the spirit heroes came the yellow-haired men from the West, my lords. With long swords they drove the servants of Berkhan before them, driving the Mongols east. They died, and then through the gate came Genghis the Mighty. Aye, his banners moved before the winds to the West, and many were the lands he conquered."*

With a shout of approval the khans greeted the song of the minstrel, pressing their horses forward eagerly. They did not know that Khlit, who rode at their head, had asked the minstrel to repeat his song as they rode, thus driving fatigue from the minds of his followers.

The Horde had passed through the lake region of Sungaria, splashing along the flooded shores, finding game abundant. They had slept little, covering some seventy miles a day.

Khlit had not wished to urge his horsemen to their speed until the Sungarian Gate should be passed, knowing that it is not well to start too hastily upon a forced march.

He knew well the great task that had confronted them—the journey from the southern limit of the Mongolian plain to the northern tip of Afghanistan. And he calculated that this was to be done in three weeks if he was to aid Abdul Dost as he had promised. By that time, even allowing for a late season, the passes of the Hindu Kush would be ice-coated and impenetrable.

They had followed the horse track that led to the South beside the lake of Ebi Nor—the Wind Lake—and Sairam Nor, instead of the broader, more passable caravan route that made a detour to the West.

Some of the Tatars had brought *yurts*—heavy, felt tents, erected upon poles—on the backs of pack horses. Seeing this, Khlit had said nothing to the warriors in question. Yet at their first camp and their second, he made these men fetch the water and collect dried camel-dung for fires.

---

* Legends of the Sungarian Gate, leading from Mongolia into Europe.

When he repeated this performance at the third camp, within the entrance of the Sungarian Gate, and it became clear that his selection of the men was no longer a matter of mere chance, the offending Tatars left their *yurts* standing and rode on, baggageless like the rest.

"In the Gate," they grumbled, being aggrieved, "we will meet the spirits of the *buran*, and the icy wind will bar our passage. Aye, the spirits of the heights will be angry. By what right does this warrior make himself our lord?"

Khlit heard, and remembered, and said nothing.

He mounted before daylight, nor did he call a halt that day or night. The Tatars shifted from time to time to their spare horses, and ate strips of smoke-cured meat in the saddle. Many slept as they rode.

To the West appeared a wide level of steppe, dotted with lakes, stretching to the horizon—a vast expanse of blue. Far before them the snow peaks of the *Ala tau* loomed in the veils of mist.

"This is the limit of our land," said some within hearing of Khlit. "And this is the last of the steppe. Before us are the spirit mountains where we have never gone. Upon their summits the Ghils call to men, unseen, plaintively, and the men follow and die—"

"Once through the Sungarian Gate, how may we win back to our Sungarian land?" assented others, feeling perhaps the first irking of fatigue, or being desirous of their homes.

These were the younger warriors, with some of the *shamans*.

At noon that day, midway through the pass, Khlit rode back into the gatherings of the grumblers.

"Aye," he said to the younger men, "this is the end of your land. If you would return to the *karaul* of your people, do so now. Because from this point you must go forward with me."

He had halted the long ranks of riders that stretched the length of the pass like an endless caravan, the sunlight glittering on lines of spear points.

"The Horde will wait," he said grimly, "while you ride past."

The Tatars who had been talking of the Gate looked at each other, and no one moved. It was their fashion to grumble, and they knew that never before in the annals of their armies had men forsaken the standard during a campaign.

"Ha!" Chagan, the sword-bearer, pulled at his long mustache that hung down on the sides of his massive chin, blackened to the eyes by exposure to the sun. "That is well. The first warrior to move would have died at my hand,"

He surveyed the cloaked forms of the *shaman*s, the priests who had scented spoil in the expedition.

"It is fitting," he added, "that the masters of magic should abide in this accursed place of spirits, so that the *tengri* of the air will send no evil magic upon the heels of our passage."

In speaking thus he followed carefully the words of Khlit, who had reason to know the treacherous greed of the conjurers. The Tatar warriors, those who had spoken too freely, seized this occasion to wax mirthful at the expense of the *shaman*s, who were forced—perhaps not unwillingly—to remain in the Gate.

All but one did so, and returned to the *karaul* by the lakes. This one, Gutchluk by name, brooded much over the words of Chagan, and suspected Khlit to be the author thereof.

This Gutchluk, having traveled to the holy city of Lhasa, and learned many secrets of religion and priesthood from the disciples of the arch-priest, the Dalai Lama, bethought him of the Turkomans, whom he had once visited, and the wealth that was reputed to be in the coffers of the *ameer*s of the Mogul—especially of Alacha, who was known to him.

And so that night he rode south and west, circling the moving lines of horsemen, carrying with him a small pack upon the back of his pony.

And in this manner in the course of a few days word began to drift through the passes to the adherents of Alacha, the Slayer, that the Horde was riding south.

That night there was a moon and the Tatars gazed down upon the troubled waters of the lakes below the pass, seeing their ruffled, wind-tossed surface and the white lines of breakers on the shore—although at the altitude of the pass no air was stirring.

"Lo," muttered a broad-faced warrior, "the pent winds have escaped; they have come to the Gate."

"Yet," responded Chagan readily, "the spirits of the air be friendly to us, for they smite not at us. They ride with us, against our foes."

This remark was passed from mouth to mouth, and worked the leaven of courage.

The next day, when dawn struck into the gray sky overhead, Khlit, glancing back, saw the loom of heavy clouds above the pass and the darkness of hail. He shook his head and glanced before the moving ranks of the Horde, to the gray mists and the hidden ravines of the mountains.

Now within the hour the riders in the van came upon the skull of a wolf resting in the branches of a tree and below it the weather-smoothed skull of a man.

"An evil omen," cried some.

Others, noting the fresh track of a pony leading south, were puzzled, not knowing of the flight of Gutchluk.

After watching the last of his men file from the Alau ravines, Khlit halted Berang, khan of the Torgot clan and commander of the rear guard.

The youthful chieftain, keen-eyed and quiet, had been a close companion of Khlit in the days when the Cossack had been Kha Khan of the Horde.

"Yield your banner to another," ordered Khlit, "and prepare to ride ahead, seizing what guides you may—but in no case a Turkoman."

Riding bridle to bridle with the gaily dressed Tatar—for Berang, unlike his companions, rejoiced in green and red leathers, in silver accouterments, chased mail and a purple Chinese cap with peacock feather—Khlit explained that the khan was to seek out Abdul Dost in the northern limits of Badakshan, "striking equally south and west, by the course of the sun, past the eastern end of Issyuk Kul, the Lake of the Clouds, and so up into the passes of the Hindu Kush—"

"Say to the leader of the Afghans that the Horde will join him within ten days. Before then he must not give battle. Return then up the course of the upper Oxus until you meet with us."

The brown eyes of the young leader flashed. "It shall be done. A swift journey to the Horde!"

"*Ahatou khan, temou chou!*"—Brother khan, dwell in peace!

Khlit watched the erect form of the warrior speed past the marching groups. Berang, he knew, could be relied on. And by now the followers of Abdul Dost must be in sore need.

Swiftly the black mass of the Horde, like the swarm of so many giant bees, spread over the green levels of the Ili Valley, where the sun was yet warm, and flowers were in the grass. Nor did they pause in crossing the river, for each warrior swam his horse into the bosom of the slow stream, tugging behind him the spare mount. And here were found herds of gazelle, to be shot down by youthful archers; likewise sheep, to be taken at will—the fat-tailed sheep of the Kirghiz.

By the Ili, Khlit halted for a day and a night to rest the horses, and the impatient Tatars grumbled thereat. Many khans who had not before this experienced the weight of Khlit's hand talked among themselves of seizing the leadership—for it was the Tatar nature to be restless under a strange leader, or under any leader at all.

Being restless, they drank overmuch—the fare being rich for the day—of *kumiss*, and so lay drunk in their coats about the camp.

Khlit had slept long that day, and on awaking at sunset mounted and made the rounds of the camp. Groups of warriors followed him idly to where the drunken men lay, to see how he would deal with this happening.

If the Cossack should ignore the conduct of the revelers it would countenance feasting and drunkenness on the march. And this would have pleased the warriors—all but the wiser heads.

So, many hard eyes followed the Kha Khan as he reined in his horse by the empty *kumiss* casks and the prone figures. No one was with him.

Noting this, the old Cossack signed for the watchers to approach, as they did, afoot and unarmed.

"These be thirsty dogs."

He pointed at the befuddled forms clustered about the casks.

"Give them to drink. Strip them and cast them into the river."

For a space warrior looked at warrior appraisingly. They were in an idle mood, not altogether harmless—an idleness bred of the sun's warmth and the long sleep on the grass. Some swore, others scowled. Khlit watched them silently.

"Blood of Natagai!" bellowed a reeling khan. "I and my brothers will die, for we cannot swim—thus."

"Die then," said Khlit coldly. "Those who have their wits will live."

He swung savagely on the watchers.

"Ye heard me?"

They moved uncertainly. Then a broad-faced, flat-backed youngster laughed aloud.

"Ho—we will see if they can swim!"

Whereupon the mood of the crowd changed. They grinned and sought out the offenders. A struggle began, and as it waxed the good humor of the crowd increased. Clothing and armor were torn from the drunkards. Naked forms were carried to the river-bank and cast into the stream.

It became a game—a game such as the blunt natures of these men could understand. Many more ran up, and of the newcomers the *kumiss*-drinkers were singled out and plunged into the cold current.

Some sank to their death, but the majority were revived sufficiently to swim and made their way ashore, more or less sobered.

Word of the jest spread through the camp, and the *kumiss* casks were shunned perforce.

And another word was passed from clan to clan.

"Khlit, the Kha Khan, has spoken an order. The Horde is on the march, and while it is so, and he is our leader, death will be the lot of the man who drinks fermented spirits. Our leader was once *ataman* of the Kazak horde, and this was the law he learned."

From this time forth the iron authority of the old Cossack was felt. Not for nothing had Khlit lived the greater number of years of his life in the war encampment of the Cossacks, where harsh discipline was visited upon the few for the welfare of the many.

Other things than this he had learned. When the Horde swarmed across the divide north of Issyuk Kul and the leather shoes of many ponies gave out on the rocks and the grit of sandstone, Khlit ordered rough shoes fashioned of the hides of slain yaks. And on leaving the shores of the lake he had the men cut grass, chop it fine with their swords and put it into the capacious saddlebags with the rations of barley for the horses—rations gleaned from the Kirghiz and Turkoman villages by the lake.

"For when the ponies suffer from thirst in the mountain ravines, they will not eat of the barley without the grass," he said.

And when in the passes of the upper Hindu Kush the Autumn hailstorms swept down upon their backs, and snow swirled about the giant peaks overhead, he cried to the minstrels to sing and would not halt.

"Sleep here is evil," he warned.

The Tatars dozed as they rode. This time there were no complaints. When Chagan carried the choice hind quarter of a slain sheep to Khlit, he had it divided among the nearest followers, saying that the barley which sufficed his horse would do for him.

He was silent at these times, and thoughtful. While the Horde was making speed over almost continuous obstacles—torrents that must be bridged, slippery slopes that must be climbed, in the growing cold that numbed men and horses inexorably—Khlit knew that as yet the warriors were not a whole, were not knit together.

But the Tatars themselves were now content. Endurance was bred in their natures, and they laughed from cracked lips at their sufferings.

"The Kha Khan is worthy," they said. "We will follow him."

"He is a wise leader," they said. "He has lost none of his old cunning."

Their confidence soared, for they believed they were invincible as the host of Genghis Khan, of which the minstrels sang.

But Khlit knew that he was leading a mass of undisciplined horsemen, splendid fighters individually, yet armed only with bows and their heavy, curved swords against the coordinated whole of the Mogul's array—elephants, cannon, foot and horse.

He looked back down the dark defiles where the ranks of horsemen trotted, heedless of suffering, intent only on winning forward under his guidance.

"O my brothers," he muttered in his beard, "God grant I keep faith with you."

Now as the Horde moved through the Hindu Kush, through the rock gates of the place that is called the Roof of the World, certain wandering Kirghiz huntsmen saw them from a distance and fled away, bearing a message of fear.

"In the mists of the passes spirits ride," they said in the hill villages. "Their faces are black and they move with the speed of demons of the higher world. Crows and kites follow their course."

"If birds follow," observed villagers who had not seen the Horde, "they must be men."

"But we have not seen the like of such men."

And in the grass valleys of the upper *pamirs*—stretches of moss-like meadows above the timberline—shepherds ran in, crying.

"Surely there is fear and doom afoot. For we heard trumpets at sunrise, and the *nacar*s, the cymbals of the Mongols, even as our fathers heard the trumpets of Genghis Khan. And the tramp of a multitude sounded, where we could see no riders."

Word of this passed from mouth to mouth, as such things do, and came at last to the ranks of the Mogul's army.

XI
The Eye of the Mountain

Until daybreak, the night of the slaying of Geron, Hossein rode steadily along the trails that led to the heights of the Hindu Kush above the timberline.

Nur-Jahan, held across his stout knees, cried that she was the bride-to-be of the Mogul, and Hossein laughed.

"A pretty song, my Persian nightingale! So have other captives of my master Alacha twittered and wept. You do not weep."

"I am Nur-Jahan."

The Turk threw back his massive head and roared with mirth.

"Aye, the Light of the World. Well, then the world will soon be dark. By Allah, would I had that necklace that lies about your beautiful throat, my *khanum*."

His hairy hand felt appraisingly of the pearls under her veil, but he knew too well the moods of his master to deprive Alacha of such jewels. So Nur-Jahan sank into disturbed silence as they rode under pines and ever upward beside waterfalls.

With daybreak Hossein dismounted and bound his captive skillfully by the hands and feet, using his own girdle. Then he drank heavily of the water from the freshet they were following, called Ali to witness that his belly yearned, and straightaway fell asleep, sprawled near the prone woman, his mouth open and snores vibrating from his nose.

Then for the first time Nur-Jahan wept at the disgrace, struggling vainly to undo her bonds. Strangely enough she once fancied that a small, turbaned man drew near the sound of her lament and peered through a tangle of dying junipers. Blinded by her tears, she was not sure, and when she cried out, Hossein wakened with a curse.

In time came a servant of Alacha, who gave Hossein whispered instructions, with food; and when the sun was high the Turk ate the best of the provender—tossing her an oatmeal cake that she would not touch—and climbed upon his horse, forcing her to walk.

Slowly they passed onward along the trails, seeing at times fleeing Afghan shepherds and children driving cattle headlong into secret places. The scent of smoke drifted to them, and when at length they came out into a clearing on the mountainside, the Persian could make out on the great plain to their left scattered bodies of Afghan horse wheeling in flight, and dense masses of Rájput cavalry moving through burning villages.

"What means this?" she cried.

Hossein pointed to clouds of dust in the distance.

"The army advances and drives the ill-omened ones, like animals, into the wilds, my Persian lady," he observed indifferently. "Come, Alacha has a nest just above here where he often spied out what passed on the plain. He bade us wait for him there at the eye of the mountain."

Nur-Jahan looked longingly at the steep slope, almost a precipice, stretching down from her feet. She was very tired and Hossein had kept her hands bound and the end of the girdle in his own hand.

The place he spoke of was around a bend in the trail they had been following—a nest of rocks overlooking the narrow ribbon of the upper Oxus. A cave of sorts afforded some protection. Here Hossein turned the horse loose to graze as best it might among ferns and thorns and thrust her into the cave, squatting in front of it sleepily.

Under the lofty sandstone roof of the cave there was no sun, and the chill of the place, where water dripped unseen down the walls, struck through the thin garments of the Persian. She sat passive upon the cold rock floor, mind and body alike numbed by hunger. As time passed she became conscious of a tumult on the plain below, of distant cries and the occasional clash of steel.

Anxiously she went to the cave entrance and inquired of Hossein what was happening.

The Turk, irritated by the lack of food and wine in the plentiful measure to which he was accustomed, muttered at her savagely.

"Back into your darkness, Light of the World! What cares a light-of-love such as you what passes on the field of battle?"

"A battle!" Nur-Jahan sighed. "Are the armies engaged?"

"Aye, yonder fools on both sides cut each other up as a Gulf Arab slices fish for a stinking bazaar. They sprinkle foul carcasses hither and yon, food for the kites. 'Tis but a skirmish in which the accursed Pathans seem to have the upper hand—yet I scent a wile of my master, Alacha. Heaven grant he come soon, with eatables and drinkables."

Whereupon he thrust her back and watched suspiciously until the evening, when the tumult below died out as the shadows lengthened from the mountains across the broad valley of Badakshan, and Alacha came jauntily riding a nimble Kabuli mare and clad in all his elegance.

He glanced sharply at the prostrate Hossein and ordered him to leave the cave entrance.

"A bite of food for your slave," mumbled the Turk, and Alacha impatiently waved him away.

"There be berries among the thorns, dog, and roots for such as thou."

Whereupon Hossein departed, scowling, and Alacha stood at the entrance to the cavern. Nur-Jahan faced him at once.

"A dog you called yonder cutthroat, yet what word will suffice for you, my lord?" she said softly. "When Jahangir learns that you have laid hand upon his bride?"

The Turkoman rested a slim hand against the rock and peered at her, smiling, in the gloom.

"Nur-Jahan? Verily she is at the court for all I know. You name yourself falsely, my beautiful Persian, christening—as do the Christian infidels—yourself with lofty lineage. *Ohai*, do you think to make me believe that you are the Light of the World?"

"When you slew Geron basely, you believed."

"The slave was a Christian *caphar*—unbeliever. His death has earned Hossein a niche in the Prophet's paradise, or purgatory—I care not which. Only fools pay obeisance to a god, and death is often the reward of folly. Yet you are wise, my lady. You have learned somewhat of my power—"

"Have you done this?"

The woman pointed down at the mist-covered expanse of the valley where campfires, numerous as the stars, sparkled from the hillside under their feet to the distant Hindu Kush.

"Against my warning and advice have you entered upon battle with the Afghans at this limit of their land?"

Alacha surveyed her in silence, noting how the shadows dwelt in her dark hair, and how fair her forehead was over the veil. Her voice, he thought, was chill as the sandstone cliff that towered overhead.

"Evil will come of this, my lord," she said softly. "Death will walk among your ranks in the valley, for cornered men fight like beasts—"

"And like beasts will we slay them," he nodded. "The Afghan blight will be cleansed from the border of the empire; we will wipe clean the blotch of treachery with the blood of punishment—"

"So that honor and gold will be paid to you and Paluwan Khan," she hissed.

"To me, yes; to the Northern Lord, perhaps. Verily, it was my doing, my lady. A spy of mine, a wretched *shaman* of the Turkoman race, Gutchluk, who once had the immeasurable distinction of explaining his beggarly faith to me—Gutchluk, I say, rode to my tent full of some tale of a Mongol Horde, hither bound. He mouthed big words, yet I know the northern passes and fear no Tatars.

"This Gutchluk I used. I sent him, pretending he was envoy from the Mongol chief, Khlit, to Abdul Dost—"

"And this false priest advised the Afghan to give battle?"

"Ah, you are clever, my beautiful courtesan."

Nur-Jahan stiffened in the insult.

"Aye, that was his tale. Who may pen the waters when the dam is burst? Abdul Dost's soul—does a man of slow wit possess a soul?—was harassed by continued retreat. His followers were nagging him to let them cast their bodies against the chained cannon and the musket balls of the Mogul's men. So did he draw up his wild clans for battle, and some few horsemen of his—"

"Were permitted to score a false victory?"

"To smite off a few heads of opium-besotted Rájputs. This, like strong wine, will go to the heads of the Afghans, and on the morrow or the next day—Gutchluk will contrive to steal back to me here this night and report the hour chosen by Abdul Dost for the final assault—these same Afghans will go heedless to their bell, like masterless sheep before the storm."

"Most wise Alacha! Have you thought of your fate?"

"To be beloved by the fairest flower of the Persian garden—a fair fate, and to my liking."

His soft voice became musical, and he bent nearer to the woman, who stood like a slender lily, outlined against the face of the rock. Over their heads a moon was rising, and its glow pierced the cavern mouth. The dark eyes of Nur-Jahan were raised to its light.

Alacha reached forth and tore the veil from her head, drawing a quick breath as he gazed upon the dim features of the Persian girl whose beauty had made a slave of a monarch.

"Fair, most fair." he mused. "Soon the moon will be higher, and then will I drink of your loveliness closer, my lady. Ah, the Master Potter to whom men pray under one name or another, never fashioned with greater artistry the clay of a human form. Aye, the Master Weaver who knits the threads of human fate has given you to me. Will you not sit and drink of the rare wine I have carried hither, and the sweetmeats?"

"Aye," said the woman suddenly, "I will."

So, watched closely by the Turkoman, Nur-Jahan fetched a clean linen cloth and twin gold cups, with a small wine jar and

dishes of rice, fruit and sugared dates, from his saddlebags. These
she spread before the mouth of the cavern and seated herself upon
a stone, partaking a little of the rice and dates and pretending to
drink.

No opportunity offered for her to escape. Down the path up
which Alacha had come she perceived the bulk of Hossein, and in
the thicket beside the face of the rock she fancied that the form
of another watcher was visible. Overhead the cliff rose almost
sheer; below there was a gradual slope covered by an impenetrable
tangle of thorns.

True, the upper trail was clear. But Nur-Jahan's dainty feet
and slippers were not fashioned for running, nor could she hope
to outdistance the Turkoman.

Alacha poured a slight oblation upon the turf.

"To *kismet*, by whatever name suits best."

His voice had become gentle. He reminded the woman that no
one except Hossein knew of her coming to the camp, and Hossein
was his man. Paluwan Khan knew a little, but the Northern Lord
might well be slain in the coming battle.

Victory, thanks to the good offices of Gutchluk, was certain.
What tribes could stand against the Mogul's ranks?

The victory would make Alacha an *ameer*, a mighty noble.
India from the Indus to the Oxus would be under his rule. He
would be wealthy as a caliph.

Nur-Jahan would find her lot as mistress in one of his castles
a pleasant one. Willingly or not, this would be her fate. Better
willingly. Was it not pleasanter than her lot as a wanderer in
Persia?

"So this," she replied quietly, "is the way you serve your lord?"

Alacha found her calmness a trifle disconcerting; nevertheless,
her pride satisfied his vanity. He tasted of the sugared fruit and
smiled, thin-lipped.

"Jahangir—he who was to be your potent husband, my *khanum*—Jahangir has said, 'Kingship knows no kinship.' Thus do
I say, 'Service knows no mastery.' Myself alone I serve. I cannot

win to greatness save through the Mogul, so—I cannot risk that he should know what has passed here."

"And I?"

"You are a precious pearl, beyond price. You are the fairest woman of two lands. Like the essence of the poppy is your beauty—intoxicating, poisonous, deadly."

Nur-Jahan had lifted the cup to her full lips, dissembling to drink there from. Some drops escaping the cup as her hand trembled, fell dark upon the linen.

As Alacha leaned nearer, seeking words to express the passion that swelled at his heart, she slipped a small hand forward along the cloth. Her fingers rose toward his belt.

Smiling, Alacha caught her hand away from his dagger-hilt.

"A dangerous plaything—steel—my fair flower. Was it for this you drank with me?"

He gripped her other wrist, drawing her toward him, his eyes seeking hers, which flew desperately to cliff and thorn-patch—then riveted to stillness.

"I would drink the charm of your eyes," he whispered, breathing quickly through parted lips.

It was Alacha's moment of triumph, when success and mastery over a matchless woman were his.

It was but a brief moment. With a sharp exclamation he released her wrists, staring at the thing that Nur-Jahan had been watching over his shoulder. A rider in armor sat a horse at the bend of the trail by the cavern, and neither horse nor rider moved.

By now the moon had come up into the sky and shed a clear light upon the grassy terrace before the cave. In its dancing glow—for moonlight has the quality of a transparent veil cast over the objects of earth—Alacha saw that the horseman was strange in seeming.

A squat, erect body appeared to melt into the outlines of a shaggy pony. Where a fur cloak parted over broad shoulders the moonlight glinted on mail. Above a square, dark face as expressionless as an obelisk, a thin feather projected fantastically. To the rider's knee clung a curving sword that was fashioned by no smith of Persia, India, or Khorassan.

"Who comes?" cried Alacha, stumbling to his feet. "By the heart of Satan—what man are you?"

Startled, his quick nerves never of the steadiest, Alacha fancied that the uncouth form was truly one of the Ghils of the heights that descended upon humankind. The silence of the rider stirred his fear the more.

"Hossein!" he cried shrilly. "Hossein! Fat whelp—aid me!"

To this cry also there came no answer. But the rider paced his horse forward, and stood, with a single movement, upon the earth within reach of Alacha. No move he made to draw weapon, but stared curiously from the woman to the Turkoman.

Then Nur-Jahan laughed, although unsteadily. "My lord Alacha," she cried, "a Mongol has come to Badakshan."

"A spirit of evil," he muttered, drawing back. "Hossein, good Hossein, a hundred gold mohars if you slay me this evil one."

The Mongol warrior had caught but one word of Nur-Jahan's speaking.

"I am Berang Khan," his deep voice growled.

The words rolled gutturally from his chest.

"In the mists along the river I lost my way. To this height I came, to see the better. Who is this prince?"

He nodded his broad head at Alacha, and Nur-Jahan, who had picked up some fragments of the Tatar tongue in her early wandering through the northern lands, made quick, albeit broken reply.

"A noble of Ind."

Berang took a step forward to peer with childlike interest at the first foeman who had crossed his path.

Alacha waited for no more, sensing the menace in the fearless approach of the Khan. Berang in fact would have slain him the next moment had not the Turkoman drawn his knife and struck like a flash, reaching for his scimitar simultaneously.

The Slayer had moved with feline quickness, but had made no allowance for Berang's mode of fighting. A born swordsman, the khan did not grasp his weapon hurriedly, but stepped back a short pace that brought Alacha's dagger-point down upon his broad chest instead of his throat.

The slim blade snapped against the heavy mail, and when Alacha's scimitar slashed at his foeman's neck, Berang's short, heavy sword, curved like a crescent moon but square at the end, knocked the stroke aside as a bear sweeps down a deer's horn with a blow of the paw.

Berang swung his weapon in a glittering circle of steel that knocked Alacha to earth, with crushed ribs and chest cut half in two under the severed Damascus mail. Under impact of such a blow the Slayer rolled over twice on the grass and lay while air whistled through the cut in his side from the pierced lung.

Then the khan wheeled alertly, seeing two figures glide into the moonlight. He checked the sweep of his sword as he saw them to be a turbaned cripple bearing a bow without arrows, and at his side a young girl.

"Hossein," observed Chan to Nur-Jahan, "will not come. For once the stomach of the Turk is filled—with arrows."

He stared at Berang eagerly. "You are from the Horde?" he cried. "What do you seek?"

"A khan of the Afghans. Abdul Dost."

Chan turned to Tala, with whom he had waited for a day and a night, until the coming of Alacha. The Afghan girl was bending over the dying Turkoman, holding his head close to hers by the hair.

"Now, O Slayer," cried Chan, "look upon Death!"

And in very truth it must have seemed to the dying Turkoman that he looked upon one who was dead, for the aspect of Tala's face and dress was like that of the woman who had died under his hand.

"I swore an oath," nodded the minstrel, "that Alacha should die, yet it has come to pass at another hand than mine."

Abruptly he ceased as Berang caught his shoulder, asking gruffly where he might find Abdul Dost. To the Tatar the death of a foe was a slight thing. But to the three others a tyrant had crumbled into dust, and Tala and Chan stared wide-eyed, even in their triumph.

The minstrel pointed to the dark blotches of groves beyond the river, and to the distant summits of rolling hillocks half-veiled in the shimmering moonlight.

"Yonder lie the Afghan lines," he said. "Stay—I will guide you; two horses have I seized, that I might ride—"

He had the gift of tongue, and Berang understood readily. He asked the position of the Mogul's lines, but Chan knew little of this. As they talked, Nur-Jahan stepped to the side of the dead noble, wondering slightly at the swift course of fate that had driven the ambitious, the ready-witted Alacha down into the shadows. His handsome face was turned up to the sky, the full mouth twisted in pain.

"*Tamam shud*," she murmured—"that is finished."

The thought came to her to escape while the others talked, yet on the instant the Mongol gripped her shoulder.

"I will take the woman of the prince," he growled, "to tell us what secrets she may. If she will not, torture will loose her tongue."

Whereupon without glancing at the cold beauty of Nur-Jahan he swung her upon one of the horses brought thither by Tala. The girl and the minstrel mounted the other and led the way along the path, Berang bringing up impatiently in the rear.

When they had passed beyond the turn in the trail, the terrace before the cavern was very quiet for a space. An owl hooted in the scrub trees nearby, and suddenly there was a rush of wings, a dart of powerful talons, and the feathered assassin of the night descended upon the face of the dead man.

The talons struck and tore, yet the great bird sprang away, its pallid eyes gleaming. It had felt the rending of flesh under its claws, yet it flew away, knowing that the dead thing had been a man.

And straightaway there was a rustle on the lower path; the bushes parted, and Gutchluk peered about the glade. Seeing Alacha, the *shaman* ran forward, looking cautiously over his shoulder. He knelt, muttering:

"Exalted lord, harken to the message of thine humble servitor. I have run but now from the camp of thy foes. At dawn, the dawn after tomorrow, will Abdul Dost attack with all his force—My lord, harken—"

Gutchluk bent closer, thinking that Alacha slept, and so gained full sight of the cold face, streaked with dark talon marks, of the sightless eyes staring up at him.

With a gasp that ended in a muttering cry, the spy of Alacha scrambled to his feet, looked down wildly, and fled away along the trail, his dark robe clinging to outstretched arms.

Very much like a huge bat he seemed, winging its way upon the earth.

So the Slayer lay dead on the turf of the place where he had come, as to the eye of the mountain. Yet the plot that he had begun, the deceit he had formulated, the treachery he had fostered—all these lived.

Because of Alacha the mission of Nur-Jahan to make peace between the hereditary foes was fruitless. Abdul Dost had been tricked.

In the books of wisdom of the Muslims it is written that the dark *ferrash* strikes and a sultan dies, passing like as a drop of water from the surface of the desert. But the fruits of the tree of evil do not pass away.

Because of Alacha the prophecy of the blind Muhammad Asad was to come to pass, and the valley of Badakshan was to be filled with the bones of men.

All Berang's haste could not undo the harm that had been done. He found the Afghan camp astir with preparation. Sentries challenged sharply at every goat-path of the upper plain, bodies of horse moved slowly into position beside the river or occupied villages.

Foot soldiers—the mass of the Afghan force—furbished shields and scimitars and watched for dawn. Wounded men bandaged their hurts. Women and children, thronging in from the nearby hills, brought milk and mealcakes.

The Afghans had tasted battle. They were entering battle at the side of their families and remaining flocks, camped in a large village, almost under the Hindu Kush.

Abdul Dost was silent, hearing the tale of the deceit that had been practiced upon him—for Berang quickly identified himself as the true messenger sent by Khlit. His forehead flushed hotly.

"Draw back your men, Afghan," advised Berang brusquely. "The wisdom of the Kha Khan must be obeyed. He may not reach here before a night and a day and another night and day."

The *mansabdar* looked around at the circle of his leaders' faces, glowing in the firelight before his tent, and shook his head. Every face was exultant, for the news of Berang's coming had been passed through the ranks swiftly.

"The Mongols near the end of the passes," the tidings had gone forth. "The Horde has come from the steppe."

"I cannot hold back my men—now," said Abdul Dost harshly to Berang.

"Did ye not believe the word of the Kha Khan that he would come?"

"I believed. Yet for the space of thrice ten days have my men seen the smoke of their houses, and their flocks slain, to fester in the fields, their children coursed down and their women taken to the lust of the Mogul's soldiery."

Berang swore roundly under his shaggy mustache. Implicitly he trusted Khlit, and to have the Kha Khan's advice set aside on whatever grounds was blasting.

Abdul Dost thrust his lean, scarred face close to the Mongol.

"Eh, Tatar," he growled. "I and my Afghans will hold the ranks of the Mogul in battle so long as may be. Get you hence, to Khlit.

Tell him what you have learned and say that by the ninety and nine holy names of Allah I thank him—I and my men, for his coming. Bid him make what speed he may to the battle—"

He broke off, resuming his seat by the fire. Abdul Dost was too experienced a warrior to share the unthinking exultation of his men, and he knew well the true strength of the imperial army.

He knew likewise that it was hopeless for him to try to postpone the conflict further. Not only would it dishearten his men and perhaps scatter them to abandon the last position they had taken, but an attempt to do so would be useless. The Afghans had made their last ablutions before battle.

So Berang spat upon the earth and sprang to horse. An Afghan caught at his bridle rein.

"Warrior of the Horde," he cried, "in which quarter will the Kha Khan strike when he comes? What is his plan, of which you speak?"

"The *tulughma*—the Mongol swoop," Berang made answer. "And no one save the Kha Khan knows in what quarter it will come."

So he galloped away, muttering to keep his rendezvous with Khlit, and with him went Chan as guide, and Tala with Chan. The minstrel still kept Nur-Jahan at his side watchfully. Tala, yielding to the plea of the Persian, who shrank from having her face exposed to the gaze of the soldiery, had procured for her fellow Muslim a veil. Thus the presence of Nur-Jahan was unnoticed and unsuspected in the excitement.

She rode through the darkness, the bridle of her horse in Tala's hand, and slept as she rode.

XII
The Lord Thunder-Thrower Laughs

Shortly after morning prayers on the next day a mounted messenger from the Mogul bearing a jeweled sword to Paluwan Khan and another to Raja Man Singh—as presents on the eve of battle— passed swiftly through the village of Anderab, which served as the base of supplies for the army of the *ameers*.

Here mobs of porters, *dak*-runners, wrestlers and palanquin bearers gathered to gaze on the imperial messenger. Painted women, followers of the army, peered out from behind the screens of upper balconies; drivers of beasts looked up from the pens by the road indifferently.

Caravaneers, striding in the dust behind lines of long-haired camels, cursed him under their breath, bending their heads abjectly the while, or springing aside to escape his horse's hoofs. Hangers-on, conjurers, astrologers, blacksmiths—all came to the opening of their booths or huts to gaze.

"The battle is on," they said. "Soon the Afghan army will be no more."

The emissary made haste during the forenoon along the road to Talikan, the headquarters of the *ameer*s. Soon he began to pass powder-trains, idle camels of the falcon-gun artillery, and guard posts. Camps of irregular horse, waiting until the crisis of the battle be past before venturing on the field, lined the road.

The streets of Talikan were filled with bands of captives, roped, laboring at carrying supplies and water-sacks, with troops of sick men clustered under awnings, with slaves and the idle horses of the Rájput cavalry which formed the third line of battle.

The messenger passed the Rájput warriors, galloping into their clans, streaking their faces with turmeric, drinking, singing and laughing.

Here the ground was tilled fields, trampled by thousands of hoofs, and a mass of mud by the riverbank. The tents had been struck and sent to the rear. Squadrons of horse, mailed and fully armed, waited in the fields.

An arrow's flight ahead of them stretched the long line of footmen, pikemen, and household troops: Uzbeks, Turks, and Punjabis facing north: also the Portuguese mercenaries, matchlockmen, in solid ranks.

They faced the foremost line—the cannon. Here the Lord Thunder-Thrower had stationed carts and piles of baggage in squares, between which were stakes driven into the ground and from the stakes to the carts long leather bands, with iron chains, at the height of a man's waist above ground.

At intervals along the chains were the *feringha*, the heavy brass artillery that was the joy of the Lord Thunder-Thrower. In the carts and grouped on the flanks were the lighter pieces.

One flank—the left—rested upon a mass of hillocks, rocky, broken ground, and the other—the right—upon the river.

So in two days had the *ameers* of Jahangir arrayed themselves for battle. They received the messenger at the foremost tent just behind the infantry, where the elephants were placed— huge beasts, armored on head and fore quarters, their *howdah*s bristling with archers. Paluwan Khan girded on the new sword with his old one, and smiled.

"Tarry, honored sir," he bellowed at the messenger, "and you will see the Afghan host go to —— by way of the flashing scimitar. Alacha, who has vanished like a dream of the night, was to tell us the time of the rebels' onset, but we are ready mustered, and await but the hour."

Raja Man Singh pointed to the clouds of Afghan riders clustered not more than a gunshot away and urged an attack by his cavalry. The Lord Thunder-Thrower threw back his head and laughed long.

"Stay, my gentle scion of Marwar! Let these agile riders taste of my *feringha* balls and iron chains, cleverly hidden by sheaves of wheat, and of the rockets and blast of the falcon pieces—then may you cut them up as a sharp sword cuts a trussed sheep."

This was roughly the plan of the *ameers*. Their numbers were somewhat more than those of the Afghans—about twelve thousand as opposed to nine thousand. More potent by far than numbers was the advantage in weapons, in cannon and in discipline.

Throughout that day the *ameers* feasted the envoy and listened to reports of skirmishes between the lines. Raja Man Singh fretted when the Afghans rode before the Mogul position, crying challenges. Paluwan Khan smiled.

"Would you loose the prisoned wolf from the pen, Raja? Alacha has tricked the ill-omened ones into a decision to attack and then . . ." He broke off with a scowl. "In the name of Allah the All-wise, where is the Slayer? After some woman, it is likely—"

He shrugged his shoulders and arranged to assume command of the Turkoman's followers himself. This caused some necessary confusion and had its effect later.

During that day and night the length and breadth of the camp was searched for Alacha without result. At dawn Paluwan Khan and Raja Man Singh were in sole command of the Mogul's forces.

And at dawn the first ranks of Afghans threw themselves against the foe.

Almost Ra'dandaz Khan, the Lord Thunder-Thrower, master cannoneer, was taken by surprise. There was barely light enough to make out the dark groups of hillmen advancing over the fields.

Paluwan Khan's outposts were driven in swiftly, and at first silently—for the Afghans crept up on the sentries and slew them. Shouts resounded, kettledrums were beaten, and steel weapons dashed.

Running swiftly, the Afghans surrounded and cut down mounted pickets of the *ameer*s and rushed upon the staked line of the Thunder-Thrower. Here and there a falcon gun bellowed and flashed in the half-light of early morning.

The Afghan van, picked from the tribes by Abdul Dost for this desperate venture, never reached the line of stakes. The leather ropes and steel chains were lowered at certain points and squadrons of irregular horse under the lieutenants of Paluwan Khan issued forth, checking the clamorous Afghans and cutting them up.

Whereupon the Lord Thunder-Thrower swore a pleased oath and hastened to his guns, flaming match in hand. The imperial standard was raised in front of the tents of the *ameer*s, and Raja Man Singh ran from his pavilion in time to see the solid mass of

Afghan cavalry led by Abdul Dost follow forward upon the heels of the broken infantry screen.

The Mogul's irregulars, their task half-performed, scattered—some to the wings and some back through the breaks in the staked line, which were fast being closed. Scimitars flashing and cloaks flying, the Afghans charged, crying shrilly:

"*Allah akbar! Ho—Allah-ho!*"

The roaring of the *feringha* answered them as the Lord Thunder-Thrower and his cannoneers touched matches to the bronze breeches of the heavy artillery. Fiery rockets charged with powder were flung high into the air by the Mogul's men, to fall among the horses of the attacking ranks. Pikemen dressed their weapons behind the chains.

Wide gaps were opened among the Afghans by the blast of the *feringha*, and the rockets set horses to plunging. Yet the Afghans cared not whether their lines be ordered; they swept onward, slaying the few irregulars who had tarried too long to plunder the fallen.

Horses screamed in pain as they were thrown against the pikes that stretched behind the chains; cloaked figures sprang from saddle and across the chains, weapon in hand. Here and there the impact of mounted riders snapped the cords of bulls' hide, and horsemen rode through shouting and smiting.

And as they did so there came the steady reports of the weapons of the Portuguese matchlock-men stationed behind the guns, their pieces resting upon wooden supports. Matchlock balls pierced through mail shirt and quilted corselet, sending riders here and there plunging to earth.

"Now will the Rájput clans mount for attack," cried Raja Man Singh, fingering his drawn weapon.

Ra'dandaz Khan, striding through the confusion, gripped his arm. The Turk's broad face was smoke-blackened, but his smile was as wide as ever.

"My men will deal with these dogs," he shouted. "Save your sword for a second brood. Abdul Dost has more in store."

And as he had guessed the Afghans withdrew from the staked line slowly, their strength sadly broken by the cannon and the pikes. For a space quiet held the bank of the Oxus—a quiet broken by the moans of the wounded. At noon Abdul Dost knelt on his prayer carpet, his men doing likewise. It was the hour of midday prayer.

"God is great," they chanted, lifting burning eyes to the dear sky. "There is no God but God—"

Straightaway they launched their main attack—first mounted archers that wheeled and sent arrow flights speeding among the men behind the staked line, then a solid mass of five thousand Afghans, mad with the lust of conflict.

"Alacha has contrived well," muttered Paluwan Khan, picking up his shield and signing to Raja Man Singh.

The sweep of the Afghans carried them through and over the cannon, casting the *feringha* to earth after one bellow—for these giant pieces could be loaded and discharged but once during the attack. They slew the defenders of the bullock carts and surrounded the Lord Thunder-Thrower's men—that official having prudently retired behind the cavalry, his task performed.

And now the watchers on the housetops of Talikan saw the dark forms of the armored elephants move forward, sun glinting upon the arrows that sped from the *howdah*s. These beasts, veritable moving castles, advanced among the Afghans, who engaged them desperately, the warriors dismounting and attacking the bellies of the elephants with knives and hacking at the flailing trunks with their scimitars.

Paluwan Khan, sitting within a swaying *howdah*, gazed forth upon a struggling mass of men and horses, stretched from the river to the distant hillocks, and caused his standard to be lifted as a signal for Raja Man Singh to attack with the Rájputs.

A shout resounded above the tumult, and the fluttering garments of the Rájput clans appeared charging upon the flanks and center of the embattled ranks.

Whereupon there was a glad clamor of trumpet and cymbals from the onlookers at Talikan, and the camp followers began to run forward to seek the spoil for which they had been waiting.

Slowly, inexorably, the elephants plowed forward as the Afghan riders gave back. The fresh troops of Raja Man Singh cleared the flanks of foemen, and the Lord Thunder-Thrower turned to the imperial envoy who watched at his side—a safe distance from the fighting.

"Speed with word to Jahangir, my lord," cried Ra'dandaz Khan. "Say that by Allah's aid the servants of the World-Gripper are driving the evil ones of dark fortunes to death and captivity, and by nightfall a mound of skulls will be erected to the glory of the Monarch of the Earth. Speed!"

And the envoy, nothing loath, mounted, knowing that a truly regal gift would be his for the bringing of such tidings.

In this manner is the message inscribed in the annals of Jahangir. Yet of what followed in the battle of Badakshan naught is said. Perhaps this is because of those who saw the battle some said one thing, some another, and still others, being dead, had naught to say. Yet chiefly is it because the Mogul wrote down only those things which added to the glory of his reign, and, being outwardly a follower of the Prophet, would not give belief to the tale that powers other than human fought against his *ameer*s that day.

For into the ranks of the Afghans spurred a huge figure, clad in rough sheepskins, smiting aside those of the imperial riders who opposed him with a sword as great as a man's thigh.

Seeking out Abdul Dost, sitting grim-eyed upon his horse in the center of his men, this stranger cried:

"Word to the Afghan leader from his ally. Give back! Seek

safety. Draw back to the mountains, Afghan, and give place to
the Mongol."

Quickened hope caused Abdul Dost to turn and gaze back at
the fields and woods in his rear, at the scattered villages through
which bodies of horsemen fought, Rájput and Afghan alike, to
the valleys that led down from the mountains to the North. Yet
he saw no others than his own men, and the slain that sprinkled
the fields.

"Come you from Khlit?" he asked harshly.

"Aye, the Kha Khan."

"He has passed the mountain barrier? He comes to the battle?"

"Aye. He grants the Horde a space to breathe deep and eat. He
has seen the course of the battle from the mountainside, and he
bids you draw back if you have faith in him, for he cannot leave
his men to come to you."

The Tatar rider glanced around at the tumult.

"Ho, Afghan, give place to the Mongol!"

Crying his war shout, the warrior spurred his horse into the
struggling groups before him, hewing mightily with his sword,
and was lost to view among the enemy.

And Abdul Dost, fighting doggedly, drew back to his own camp
in the Afghan village. Here his men gathered together the whole
of their remaining strength, and, with women and boys in the
ranks, resisted the advance of the Rájputs, refusing to retreat farther and determined to die if need be upon the field.

The *mansabdar* remained with his men, who were soon surrounded in the village by the forces under Raja Man Singh.

Thus the intrigue of Alacha and the strategy of Paluwan Khan
had overcome the Afghans. To drive home the victory, Raja Man
Singh prepared to administer the last blow, sure of himself and
the strength at his command.

"What care I for new foes?" he laughed when warned of the
appearance of a Mongol among the Afghans. "The field is in our
hands, and the spirit heroes, nay, the gods themselves, could not
drive our army back from its conquest."

XIII

*Greater love hath no man than this, that a man lay down his life
for his friends.*

As Khlit brought the last of his men through the lower passes
of the Hindu Kush, after sunrise of the day of the battle, above
the plain of Badakshan and overlooking the winding course of
the Oxus, they rode through a flurry of snow and hail and passed
from under storm clouds.

For the last day and night the Horde had not halted to rest or
to sleep. Those who still had extra horses rode these until they
dropped, saving the better ones as best they might. Under Khlit's
driving the Tatars had made the journey of a hundred miles over
the ravines in twenty-four hours. Now at the place where Berang
waited, Khlit commanded that they dismount and kill such spare
horses as remained in order that they might eat.

From the broad valley underfoot came the rumble of cannon
and the dull murmur that told the veteran warriors a battle was
on, although they could see nothing of the field itself, being deep
in the pine forest at the headwaters of the Oxus.

Berang, however, had climbed a tree farther down the valley
and had made out much of the conflict, especially what had taken
place by the river which ran directly down from the pass, being
but a slender stream at that point.

"We must hasten," he growled to Khlit, "for good sword
strokes are dealt yonder, and it is my thought that the Afghans
ride to defeat, for their ranks are broken."

"The men must eat," Khlit answered, and the Tatars stretched
themselves on the ground under the pines, while some kindled
fires.

The faces of all were blackened by exposure and lined with
fatigue. The bleared eyes were dull, and the thick-set, powerful
bodies swayed as they moved afoot, for they had lived in the
saddle during the greater part of a week, and the cessation of
continued motion bewildered them.

Yet they chuckled, staring at each other and their leader. They had come over the passes where Genghis Khan had been before them, and they were looking down upon India.

Some scooped up handfuls of the snow for themselves, but carefully led their shaggy beasts—the steppe ponies, possessed of the iron-like endurance of their masters—to the streams that ran into the Oxus to drink.

Khlit leaned upon his saddle-peak, his brown face the color of the saddle itself, his sheepskin coat bound close to his body. While Berang talked, he listened intently.

Savagely he shook his head, hearing of the first assault of the Afghans and their repulse. He knew the strength of the Mogul's army, and its manner of fighting.

"We are late, late," he murmured. "Would I could see Abdul Dost. Ha, Berang, tell me the lie of the land."

The khan sought out Chan, and the minstrel, who knew the plain of Badakshan like a book, described it to the Cossack, who memorized every detail with painstaking care, glancing the while at his men, who ate wolfishly by the fires, and, having eaten, fell instantly into sleep.

"Talikan!" broke in Khlit. "The rearmost village—there be captives therein? The spare horse-herds of the Rájputs?"

"I have heard talk of Afghan prisoners laboring there, my lord," responded the boy, then looked up brightly. "We also have a captive my lord—a noblewoman—and she may be made to tell you what you would know."

At the Cossack's impatient nod he hurried back among the trees and presently appeared with Tala, leading the horse whereon sat the veiled Nur-Jahan.

The Persian held herself proudly erect, gazing mutely at the masses of uncouth warriors moving hither and thither among their horses. She was very pale, and her dark eyes were bright. Khlit barely glanced at her, not recognizing the empress-to-be in the lone woman dressed in the woolen robes of a commoner.

"How many Afghan prisoners are in Talikan?" he barked. "How many guards?"

"I know not."

Something in her voice caused the old warrior to look at her sharply.

"Ha, woman, fail not to speak!"

"I know not."

"You have seen the numbers of the Mogul's army—what numbers?"

"As many as the head leaves underfoot, or the stones in the riverbed."

At this Berang muttered an oath and drew sword. He stepped to Nur-Jahan's side and grasped her hair in a mighty hand.

"Speak or die."

The form of the woman stiffened and her eyelids fluttered. She lowered her eyes, keeping silence.

"What name bears she?" Khlit turned to Chan.

"Lord, we know not. Because of her, Berang, your man, slew Alacha. I heard her say that she was called the Light of the World; but that surely was madness."

"Lord," Tala put in, bending her dark head, "I know not if it be madness, for this princess is of Isphahan, and she said to me in the Mogul camp that she would contrive peace between Afghan and Mogul. Then Alacha had her carried away. Not once but many times she spoke as Nur-Jahan, and great is her pride."

The keen eye of the Afghan girl had read much truth in the unveiled features of Nur-Jahan. Khlit reined his horse forward until his shaggy head was close to the eyes of the captive woman.

"Speak, witless one," he growled. "Tell the numbers that Raja Man Singh holds as reserve. Where lie they? In Talikan? With the prisoners?"

When the Persian remained silent he snatched the veil from her head, and muttered in his beard.

"Aye, you are Nur-Jahan. Once I carried you safely from Khoten to Kashmir, to your lord, the Mogul. And now, forgetting that, he has put a price upon my head. Speak, for here it matters not whether you be Nur-Jahan or slave."

The woman shook her head mutely. But now Tala and Chan pressed forward, eyes agleam.

"O Kha Khan, know you the prize that you hold? Threaten her with the torture; send word to Raja Man Singh that Nur-Jahan will suffer for the wrongs of Badakshan—"

"Little Afghan—" Khlit spoke impatiently—"said you not that the Light of the World sought to bring about peace between your people and the Mogul—and failed? How may she succeed now, when the battle is on? The *ameers* will have no thought for a woman. They follow their own path—" he nodded toward the plain below—"and twice ten thousand warriors are deaf to words."

"Then," cried Berang and others of the khans, "let her suffer until she voices the tidings you would know."

He bent back the fair head of the captive with a twist of his wrist, and the others muttered hoarse approval. Khlit glanced once searchingly into the strained face of the Persian and caught Berang's arm, thrusting it aside.

"She is Nur-Jahan, and she will not speak. Brothers, khans, are ye dotards and fools to wage war upon the body of one woman?"

He looked from man to man, his gray eyes hard under the shaggy brows.

They scowled at each other and fingered their weapons.

"Content you, Kha Khan," they barked. "We follow where you lead. Take us therefore to this horde of India—minions of the false prince sired by the great Genghis."

Khlit glanced briefly a last time at Nur-Jahan.

"Ha, woman of the Mogul, you shall bear the tidings to your lord. Say that the Tatars yield you back to him—unharmed. Tell him of the Mongol swoop, and the events that come to pass this day."

So speaking, he gave Nur-Jahan into the care of Chagan, the mighty sword-bearer, bidding Chan also ride with her until she should be given over safely into the care of some Mogul noble. This done, he looked hastily at the sun, noting likewise that the

tumult on the plain below seemed to have died out somewhat—
for Abdul Dost had drawn back from his first charge, and ordered
the kettledrums sounded for assembly.

Throughout the forest in the gorge, swarthy Tatars sprang up,
cursing stiffened limbs, and mounted. The khans lifted their standards and rode forward, striking aside those in their way, until
they reached Khlit's side.

The Cossack signed for them to follow and led the way forward
for some distance until the gorge fell away and a wide stream
appeared at their feet. Berang pointed out the hillock whence he
had observed the opening of the battle, and on this spot Khlit
faced his khans.

He indicated the course of the stream, widening to a small,
shallow river down by the battlefield to the South, and pointed to
the distance on the right, where some five miles away miniature
groups of men moved slowly about the plain and the smoke of
burning huts rose into the air. Faintly they could make out the
dark line that was the Mogul's front, against the river bank.

"There we must be with utmost speed, brothers, khans," he
said quietly. "How?"

"Let us ride to the Afghan horde," muttered Berang. "They be
sore-pressed. Aye, what else?"

Khlit looked at him impassively.

"We be but one against five of the Mogul's men. Our Horde is
thinned by death in the passes. Already you have said the Afghans
are beaten back, having men to three times our number. By joining the Afghans we would swell their number—true—but avail
nothing more."

"Let us then ride forward alone against the Mogul," bellowed
an old Tatar, his thin, white mustache hanging to his naked chest,
blackened by the sun. "Aye, to slay mightily, as is fitting—"

"Then would we be but one against five, and five that are facing
us, ready for an onset—"

"The flank, then," cried another, pointing to the right.

"There the ground is too rough for horses."

Khlit lifted his hand.

"Hear me, brothers, khans. A way there is to double our numbers and to charge over fair ground and to strike where we are not looked for. We will ride in the *tulughma*, the Mongol swoop."

"Ho, that is good hearing," nodded the khans, their fierce eyes gleaming. "Aye, that is good."

"By inspiring fear, brothers, khans, we will make greater our numbers. And we will be feared when we strike where no foe is looked for."

Khlit still held them with his eyes.

"Yet by so doing we will cut ourselves off from escape—verily, there will be no hope if we fail. Mightily will we slay, yet death will follow us fast. Will you come with me?"

As one man the Tatars made answer.

"Lead, by Natagai's blood—lead. By the hide of the gods, lead us on, Kha Khan. We be wearied of talk."

Just a little Khlit smiled under his mustache, glancing calmly at the ring of faces. It was a moment of pride for the old warrior. Three thousand men and more had followed him over half a thousand miles of mountain land, enduring the while hardships that no army of India, Russia, Persia or China would have faced. He had done what the *ameer*s of the Mogul, as Chan had related, had said that no man could do—and what the Afghans had feared could not be done. And now, without sight of friend or foe, the survivors of these men would follow him blindly into what seemed to him to be certain death for the most part, if not for all.

Then it was that Khlit sent the warrior—him of the bare shoulders and white hair—headlong to Abdul Dost, bearing the command to draw back from the battle to where the Afghan forces would be safe and leave the field to the Tatars.

Thus Khlit hoped to make good his promise to Abdul Dost. He was under no illusions as to what his own fate might be.

"Yet," he muttered to himself as he led the van of his riders across the stream to the farther bank, opposite the plain of battle, and turned swiftly to the South down a shallow valley pointed out by Chan, "when my sword is broken and my men are wearied or slain, the army of Jahangir will be an army no more."

In the scattered hamlets along the left bank of the river, the villagers, old men, and the women and children who had been staring across the shallow bosom of the Oxus—the watchers turned in amazement, perceiving that dark masses of horsemen rode down the valley behind them to the South. They heard a steady thunder of hoofs, and saw harsh faces and the glint of steel through clouds of dust.

"*Ai!*" they cried. "The tales of the hillmen were true. Verily there are spirits of the heights afoot."

Being frightened and superstitious, they thought this—having seen no men like the Tatars.

The Horde passed steadily athwart the battle lines on the farther side of the Oxus, and children in the fields, bending in the midday prayer wherein they besought aid for the Afghans, stared round-eyed as the riders trampled through wheat fields burned by Alacha's men, and behind thickets of willows, cypress and tamarisk that screened them from observation by the Mogul's forces.

Chan, called forward by Khlit, served as guide. Here and there they encountered the skirmishing parties flung out across the river by Paluwan Khan, and engulfed them. It was ever the way of the Horde to strike so swiftly that no news of their coming reached ahead.

They heard the distant roar of conflict as Abdul Dost flung his men forward in the noon charge, before Khlit's messenger could find him in the affray.

Khlit looked up somewhat anxiously at this. But his lean face was tranquil. He smelled once more the smoke of battle, heard the impact of charging ranks. A great peace held his mind, and he smiled.

His thoughts went back to the steppes, to the Ukraine and Tartary, where he had gone forward like this, but at the head of shouting Cossacks against the Turk and the Pole. Like this he had passed down the bank of the Volga, the Dneiper—aye, and the Kerulon, in the homeland of the Tatars.

He wondered how the old chiefs of Cossackdom had fared during the years after he had left the war encampments. He would have liked to see their faces again, hear their oaths and see the glitter of their swords. Yet he knew his old companions were dead.

So likewise had the elder khans of Tartary passed from his life, Chepé Buga and the others—their souls loosed from their bodies in the swift tide of battle.

Only Abdul Dost remained.

Khlit's life had been long and full. He had chosen the open plains and the hard fortunes of war instead of the peace of cities and the honors of the courts. No comfort had he won out of life, nor had he gained anything to serve him except his sword. He had seen the coming of a new era, of wide-flung empires and far-venturing ships, and his friends had been the last of a warrior race—in Cossackdom and Tartary . . .

"Kha Khan—" Chan broke into his thoughts—"we come to the ford that leads to Talikan."

"Lift high the yak-tail standard," shouted Khlit, rising in his stirrups. "Sound the *nacars*—Berang, take the Torgots across the river; Chagan, abide with me; brothers, khans, assemble your men into the clans and let each one look to me for orders. Draw your swords, brothers, khans."

In silence, until they gained midway across the stream, the Torgot clan rode. Debouching from twin clumps of willows, they were not noticed at first by the Mogul's forces holding the village, who had heard that the Afghans were driven back. And even when espied the Tatars were at first taken for some fresh body of imperial cavalry.

Not until the strange aspect of Berang's men was noted did the scattered troops in Talikan take alarm. By then the Tatars were riding through the streets.

Without difficulty they drove the ill-armed and unprepared detachments in Talikan before them, striking down all who bore arms. The tide of the Horde swept across the river, trampled down the riverbank bazaars, sending the wondering inhabitants scurrying indoors.

So suddenly had they appeared that rumors began to fly toward the rearmost lines of the *ameer*s.

"Demons out of purgatory have sprung from the ground . . . Men came out of the river and laid waste Talikan . . . They are like to wild beasts and no man may face them."

Thus the message came to Paluwan Khan, sitting his elephant in the midst of his scattered foot soldiery, and to Raja Man Singh, who pressed the attack on all sides against the Afghan camp where Abdul Dost had rallied his men.

At Talikan Khlit remounted half his followers from the spare horses of the Rájputs. Seeking out the Afghan prisoners and scattering their guards, he ordered them to mount the horses discarded by the Tatars and to arm themselves from weapons cast upon the ground by fugitives and from the stores of the *ameer*s. The village itself he fired, and a giant column of smoke soon rose against the sky, causing the imperial forces on the field of battle to glance back and wonder.

Reforming his clans at the remount camp of the Rájputs, now emptied of guards, Khlit gave his men only scant breathing space before leading them forward.

This time he altered his column into a fan-shaped formation, the standard in the center. Before advancing he summoned a Rájput noble, wounded, who had been spared by Berang. Pointing out the still figure of Nur-Jahan, he bade the man escort her out of the conflict.

"Take her to Jahangir, Raja," he said grimly. "Say to the World-Gripper that his empress has a braver heart than he—and is more faithful to a friend."

He did not even watch the noble take the bridle of Nur-Jahan's horse and lead it back through the village, stumbling onward in mute amazement. Yet his words were afterward to prove true. Nur-Jahan was the heart and the brains Jahangir's reign.

And now came youths and old men running from houses here and there, crying:

"Allah be praised! Aid is come for the Afghans. We will go with the Tatar Horde."

These Khlit ordered curtly back, but took the freed prisoners with him, some running at the stirrups of his men. Broken by torture and fatigue, the Afghans ran on, silently, nursing their longing for revenge.

Within the space of a few moments the Horde had reached the main camp of the Mogul's forces and cleared it of defenders. The fugitives ran to Paluwan Khan, crying that the Mongols were upon them, and their coming added to the general confusion that had ensued upon the heels of the temporary victory of the *ameers*.

But Paluwan Khan, cursing mightily, formed his battalions to face the rear and sent a rider speeding to Raja Man Singh with urgent summons to draw back to aid him. The movements of the Tatars had been so swift and their change of mounts so quickly accomplished that the tale of their numbers had grown.

"Fetch back your cannon!" roared Paluwan Khan at the Thunder-Thrower. "Where are your pikemen? Send me the leader of the Portuguese infidels! In the name of Allah, form your ranks!"

Before this could be done the Horde was among the main array of the *ameers*. The Tatars hitherto had met but the scourings of the camp, the bazaar hangers-on, servants, slaves and camp followers. Now they gave a great shout at sight of the line of footmen drawn up behind pikes.

Chagan carried the yak-tail standard into the front of the attack, followed closely by Khlit, and a thousand horsemen—hewing, slashing, and mad with the intoxication of battle—had broken into the ranks of Paluwan Khan.

Short, broad swords smote the steel heads from pikes; flights of arrows sped over the foremost riders to fall thick among the men of Paluwan Khan. The imperial lines, disconcerted, broken, began to give back.

A second line of Tatars came forward, driving into the melee just as the elephants, or those that could be brought up from the engagement at the Afghan camp, came plodding forward, their *howdah*s a-bristle with archers.

Until now Khlit had made full use of the advantage gained by the *tulughma*—the encircling movement that was the favorite stratagem of Genghis Khan, who sent his cavalry from the rear of his own lines clear into the rear of the enemy.

He had reasoned that he would find the forces of the *ameer*s scattered and in part disorganized after the affray with the Afghans. In advancing as he did into the heart of the Mogul's army, he foresaw that he would meet with different detachments separately. Yet now he realized that the strength of the enemy had been barely touched by the reckless assaults of Abdul Dost upon a prepared defense.

And the huge elephants were veritable citadels of strength.

"Bid the clans," he shouted to the nearest warriors, "fight clear of the elephants—all but the beast bearing the standard of Paluwan Khan."

He pointed to the *howdah* of the Northern Lord, glittering with its costly trimmings.

"Chagan, take a score of followers and slay me that chief."

By now the arrows from the *howdah*s were flying among the Tatar riders, and their own arrows were deflected off the armored coverings of the beasts. Khlit rose to a standing position in his saddle and surveyed the masses of fighting men. He rode swiftly from clan to clan, bidding them draw away from the riverbank. In so doing they passed near the elephant of Paluwan Khan.

Chagan had driven his horse at the head of the giant beast, clearing a path for himself with his sword. He swung at the black trunk that swayed above him, missed his stroke, and went down as his horse fell with an arrow in its throat.

"Bid your elephant kneel, cowardly lord," he bellowed, springing to his feet and avoiding the impact of the great tusks, "and fight as a man should!"

His companions being for the most part slain, Chagan seized a fresh mount that went by riderless and rode against the elephant's side. Gripping the canopy that overhung the elephant's back, with teeth and clutching fingers he drew himself up, heedless of blows delivered upon his steel headpiece and mailed chest.

"Ho!" he cried from between set teeth. "I will come to you, Northern Lord!"

An arrow seared his cheek and a knife in the hand of an archer bit into the muscles of a massive arm. Chagan's free hand seized the *mahout* and jerked him from behind the ears of the elephant as ripe fruit is plucked from a tree. At this the beast swayed and shivered, and for an instant the occupants of the *howdah* were flung back upon themselves and Chagan was nearly cast to earth.

Kneeling, holding on the *howdah*-edge with a bleeding hand, he smote twice with his heavy sword, smashing the skull of an archer and knocking another to the ground. The remaining native thrust his shield before Paluwan Khan.

But the Northern Lord, no coward, pushed his servant aside and sprang at Chagan, scimitar in hand.

The Tatar sword-bearer, kneeling, wounded, was at a disadvantage. Swiftly he let fall his own weapon and closed with Paluwan Khan, taking the latter's stroke upon his shoulder. A clutching hand gripped the throat of the Northern Lord above the mail and Chagan roared in triumph.

Pulling his foe free of the *howdah*, the Tatar lifted Paluwan Khan to his shoulder and leaped from the back of the elephant.

The two mailed bodies struck the earth heavily, Paluwan Khan underneath, and it was a long moment before Chagan rose, reeling. In his bleeding hand he clasped the head of the Northern Lord. And, reeling, he made his way to Khlit, through the watchers who had halted to view the struggle upon the elephant.

"Kha Khan, look upon your foe!"

And Chagan tossed the head aside, to run, staggering, at Khlit's stirrup as the Tatars swept athwart the Mogul's line, away from the river.

Under cover of arrow flights discharged from horseback, the Tatar clans fell in behind their leaders, riding slowly, being reluctant to leave their foe.

"We have not quelled them, lord," panted a one-eyed warrior at young Berang Khan. "Aye, more ride up. Why do we not stay them?"

"Peace!" roared Berang. "Still your clamorous tongues, dogs, and await your time."

Grumbling and glancing often back, the Tatars drew clear of the Mogul's main array, drawing ever to the hillocks, away from the riverbank. Khlit, watching shrewdly the movements of the fighting men, had seen that detachments of Rájputs were coming up from the beleaguered Afghans.

Moreover, the elephants were causing his Tatars sore hurt, and his men were wearied. So he led the Horde, once again assembled in its hive-like entirety, to what had been the left flank of Paluwan Khan, behind the broken, rocky ground, out into the plain. And here he bade his men dress their wounds and wait, under cover of the rising ground.

As they did so, from the grove and field of grain, from *nullah* and waterbed came groups of Afghan men and women who had concealed themselves during the battle, and these bore milk and goatskins of water to allay the thirst of the Tatars.

And more—groups of armed riders galloped up, leaderless, having been separated from the Afghans in the camp of Abdul Dost. Frightened herds of cattle were rushing about the fields behind the Tatars.

Khlit, standing on the uppermost rocks, the sun behind his back, was now facing the river. After passing through Talikan, the Mogul camp, and charging the rear of the main line of Paluwan Khan, he had turned aside and brought his men to the extreme flank of the enemy.

"Gather your men into their clans," he said briefly to the khans. "See that each one has arrows and a sword. Send riders to head those herds—" he pointed at the trampling cattle on the plain—"this way. Make haste."

Carefully he studied the forces of the Mogul a pistol-shot away. He saw that they were moving about, forming a new line to face him. Cannon were being brought up on camel back. Some men tried to cut down the stout leather ropes bound to the stakes that now divided their own position—as Khlit was on their flank.

He saw mounted Rájputs riding through the multitude, and companies of mercenaries marching first here, then there.

"It is well," he smiled. "They have no leaders."

What had happened was this. Paluwan Khan until his death had commanded Alacha's men as well as his own. With both *ameer*s lost, only the *mansabdar*s and company leaders remained, with the exception of the Thunder-Thrower, who was swearing in his endeavor to make his pieces bear on the new position of the Tatars.

Khlit saw that some six thousand fighting men faced his own horsemen, who did not now number two thousand. And the elephants remained.

Though he longed to do so, he could not ride on to where the Afghans still fought Raja Man Singh, on his left, to the North behind several gullies and groves. For the ground there was broken, and he could not leave six thousand men, and elephants, close in his rear, to ride farther to the North.

But he smiled, seeing the masses of cattle driven up, and turned to Berang. "If the Mogul's men had advanced upon us here among the rocks the battle would be theirs," he growled. "Yet, having no leader, they held back. Now will we charge."

He cast a last glance to the North, wondering how Abdul Dost fared. Then he seized the standard from Chagan's weakened hand, shouting for the riders to head the cattle forward, toward the enemy and the river.

"Nay, lord," groaned the sword—bearer. "That is my task—to hold the standard—"

"Give back, Chagan," Khlit urged, "for you are half-slain."

But the sword-bearer spurred after him, reeling in the saddle. The Horde followed after the standard, their eyes fastened on the flying yak-tails, a mighty shout rumbling from their throats.

And before them went the frightened cattle.

Crash, and again *crash* came the blast of the *zam zan*, the cannon of the Lord Thunder-Thrower, and many cattle and some Tatars were blown to earth. Urging on their spent horses, rising high in their stirrups, sending arrows swiftly from their short bows—so that the sun glinted upon them as upon drops of rain—the Tatars charged home, riding in among the cattle, sweeping first to one side, then the other with their strange swords, hacking, wheeling, shouting.

The Portuguese mercenaries discharged their pieces and caught up their short swords fearfully; the men of the Lord Thunder-Thrower had time for but one blast of their light pieces, for the *feringha* could not be moved to face the Tatars; the imperial archers found their shafts fruitless against the swift, short bows of the Mongols.

"Allah turned his face from us," said a cannoneer of the Thunder-Thrower that night, speaking of the charge, "and the spirits of the air fought against us; since we had slain our foe and they had passed from our sight, yet they came again to be slain, and the cannon balls did not check them. Aye, they were like to the spirits of the dead, like to the Horde of Genghis, the Terrible."

He had seen Chagan cut half in two by a sweep of a pike, yet strike down the man who held the pike, and grapple with a matchlock-man who had turned to flee.

"We cannot slay them!" cried an archer of the household troops, flinging down his bow. "Our shafts pass through them, but they do not fall. Woe—woe!"

"They be spirits of the air!" shrieked a wounded Punjabi, his turban falling over his bloody face. "The gods fight against us—the many-armed gods!"

Whereupon a cursing Rájput struck him down and rode forward at the Tatar standard until Berang spurred against him and he too went headlong to death, but valorously.

"Flee, flee!" cried a small, cloaked figure, running about among the horses' legs.

It was a shriveled man in a dirty purple cloak, fear blazoned on his black face. Gutchluk had sought safety in the Mogul's ranks, yet found it not.

"Flee!" bellowed a brawny Turk, flinging down his scimitar and rushing toward the river.

Now after the Tatar charge came a curious array. Horseless Afghans, wearied and bloody, stumbled on; old men caught up weapons from the trampled fields; stripling youths shrilled their war shout, plying bows and dashing nimbly among the embattled host—Chan the minstrel riding at their head and singing as he rode.

Khlit and the bodyguard of the Tatars were fighting grimly about the standard when these new, strange friends slipped among the horses to their aid. The Cossack had chosen the moment well. He had not given the enemy time to form into orderly ranks; he had charged with the sun at his back and the river at the rear of the foe. He pressed on, his curved sword red, his eyes alert. And with the standard came the swarm of the Horde.

That stout Turk, the Thunder-Thrower, had forsaken his cannon in judicious foretaste of what was coming. Halting two slaves with him at his scimitar point, he beat a ponderous retreat and arrived panting at the muddy bank of the river.

Rushing into the water, he scrambled up, upon the shoulders of his slaves, grasping their hair.

"Now bear me across the water, jackals, or you die!" he muttered.

One man slipped and the Lord Thunder-Thrower subsided into the brown current of the Oxus gasping, impregnating the water with a smell of musk. Seeing this the other native, eyes agleam, caught at him, wrenching the pearls from throat and turban.

"Aid me to swim, in the name of God!" roared the Turk.

But his follower had gone, swimming away among the other fugitives.

Then did the stout Thunder-Thrower espy a goatskin filled with air, floating upon the current—such a skin as the common natives used to ferry them from bank to bank—and upon this was a water-soaked, brown man, shriveled of face, his purple robe clinging to shrunken shoulders.

Gutchluk had fled before the Turk. In a moment the bulky master cannoneer had struck the *shaman* heavily on the side of the head, and Gutchluk sank back into the brown water, his fingers still clutching at the life-giving skin. The Thunder-Thrower wrenched away the groping hands and spurned Gutchluk with his foot, as the *shaman* disappeared under the surface.

The Mogul ranks had been broken. Panic had seized the men of the Mogul. They cast away their arms and ran back to the riverbank. Here some tried to flee north and south in the mud, to be cut down by the Tatar horsemen. Others swam across the river—mainly horsemen.

Mailed Turks gathered into groups and rode desperately south into Talikan. Only the elephants and scattered Rájputs held the field, for the footmen had been the first to flee.

Against the elephants Khlit ordered huge fagots, torn from the defenses of the Thunder-Thrower, to be carried, flaming. The Tatar archers shot arrows into the necks of the huge beasts, and soon the elephants were retreating trumpeting, into the river, or running amuck south to Talikan.

The sun was now setting, and the fight had become a shambles.

Talikan and the Mogul camp were burning. Khlit sounded the *nacar*s and assembled a remnant of his men, others joining him as he advanced forward again, north along the river toward the Afghan camp. His men reeled in their saddles from weariness; some slept as they rode; no one shouted or sang, save the Afghan boys and men who had aided them.

"On to Abdul Dost!" they cried.

In the smoky twilight the array of the Horde drew near the Afghan village, where Raja Man Singh saw them and gathered his Rájputs about him. Some three thousand good men he had, of the Marwar clan, of Oudipur and Sindh. The Rájput code of honor would not permit him to withdraw from the field.

And then the sun sank, plunging the plain of Badakshan with its hideous carpet of dead, the dark flood of the river Oxus, and the overhanging hills into gloom—save for where flames soared into the sky from the bazaars of Talikan and the tents of the Mogul; and in the light of the fires Afghan children and wounded Tatars plundered the riches of the *ameer*s.

In the deepening twilight the Afghans issued from their lines— the lines they still held at the village—and joined the Tatars. United, they sought the Rájputs in the dark.

Here was no orderly charge of mounted ranks, but a hand-to-hand struggle, fierce and silent, except for the clash of steel and the cry of the stricken. Men moved numbly over the plain, and oftentimes foemen stared at each other in the gloom, too wearied to strike. But always the Rájputs were pressed away from the river and the Afghan village, into the plain, fighting until they could fight no more.

By moonrise the battlefield was cleared, and dark bodies of riders passed far afield into the plain, some fleeing, some pursuing. Raja Man Singh was carried away bodily by two servants, his sword lost and he himself wounded. It was many days before the Rájput clans reformed their ranks, broken by the Tatars.

"Lord of the World, Monarch of the Universe," the Lord Thunder-Thrower made plaint subsequently to the Mogul, "I did assemble some forces beyond the river, but demons pursued us through the night, and Ghils shrieked at us in the moonlight. They followed, nor could we lose them."

"The gods walked the earth again that night," chattered a native soldier.

"Nay," said another, "I heard the trumpets of Genghis Khan, and the tramp of his host in the air."

Thus was the battle won and lost in Badakshan. And the broken army of the Mogul withdrew from Badakshan, leaving the Afghans free. Some said that forces more than human had fought against the Mogul; others, that intrigue and treachery had planted the fear of the coming of the Horde in the breast of the Mogul's men, and that they heard and saw naught but the image of their own fears in the moonlight. The *mullah*s of the North declared that the sins of the *ameer*s had worked their undoing.

For how otherwise, asked the *mullah*s, could the imperial army be routed by a small band of Tatars who came from nowhere and who went—nowhere?

Yet no one knew that a master of cavalry tactics had outgeneraled the *ameer*s of the Mogul by a maneuver as old as the campaigns of Genghis, and had outfought six times his numbers with men who had not their match upon horses.

Khlit had drawn back from the pursuit at moonrise to seek for Abdul Dost in the Afghan camp. He walked a spent horse alone into the rows of fallen tents from fire to fire, holding a broken sword clasped in his hand.

He did not go far alone. Men and women who had thronged to the camp fell in behind his horse. Chan rode up, singing, followed by a group of Afghan youths chanting their victory.

"Where is Abdul Dost?" asked Khlit.

At this the singing was silenced. Torches came, and the gathering throng passed with him to the center of the Afghan lines, where the torches grouped themselves about a figure in armor prone on the ground—the armor slashed and bloodied, and the lean, dark face very harsh in the moonlight. The Afghan khans and their women and children looked on as Khlit dismounted stiffly, for he also was wounded.

By the side of Abdul Dost squatted a white-robed figure in a clean turban, bearing a staff in his hand, and by his knee was a slim boy. Muhammad Asad stared up into the sky from his blind eyes, his lips murmuring gentle prayers, but the boy whispered something into the ear of Abdul Dost.

The *mansabdar* glanced up and smiled.

"It was a good fight. I shall not see another like it."

He tried to lift one arm, and Khlit saw that his hand was mangled, and heard men whisper behind his back that the ribs of Abdul Dost were broken about his heart and that he would be a cripple henceforth. Khlit barely heard. He let the hilt of his broken sword fall to the earth, and took the other hand of his friend in his for a moment.

"Leave us," he said harshly to the onlookers.

He sat down by Abdul Dost, his dust-stained, weary face alight with gratitude and relief. Abdul Dost would live.

In the silence came the faint mutter of prayer from the bearded lips of Muhammad Asad—"*Allah akbar—Allah il allah!*"—and presently the blind man turned his face toward Khlit.

"O Kha Khan," he whispered, "you have saved my people. How may we do you fitting honor?"

He reached out a questioning hand, but the boy at his side spoke softly, saying that Khlit was asleep.

On the morrow, as swiftly as it came, the remnant of the Horde drifted away to the northern passes before snow should close the way. And because of the speed of their departure many tales arose in the Afghan land and the hill country—tales of spirits that had fought in Badakshan. To these stories Muhammad Asad, who became *kwajah* of the Afghans and leader of his people, made reply—

"Not by spirits, nor by the strength of warriors, was the Mogul defeated—but by the fellowship of two men."

Appendix

Adventure magazine, where all of the tales in this volume first appeared, maintained a letter column titled "The Camp-Fire." As a descriptor, "letter column" does not quite do this regular feature justice. *Adventure* was published two and sometimes three times a month, and as a result of this frequency and the interchange of ideas it fostered, "The Camp-Fire" was really more like an Internet bulletin board of today than a letter column found in today's quarterly or even monthly magazines. It featured letters from readers, editorial notes, and essays from writers. If a reader had a question or even a quibble with a story, he could write in, and the odds were that the letter would not only be printed but that the story's author would draft a response.

Harold Lamb and other contributors frequently wrote lengthy letters that further explained some of the historical details that appeared in their stories. The letters about the stories included in this volume, with introductory comments by *Adventure* editor Arthur Sullivan Hoffman, follow, and appear in order of publication. The date of the issue of *Adventure* is indicated, along with the title of the Lamb story that appeared in the issue. Lamb did not write a letter about every story.

November 1, 1919: "The Skull of Shirzad Mir"

The old Cossack, Khlit, has been a friend of ours for some time and now H. A. Lamb is introducing us to some new people whom

I think you will also come to like. There are more of these tales to come and it may be that after a while Khlit may wander down and meet these new people himself. But not for quite a while.

Incidentally, how do you pronounce his name? I always sounded it as if it were spelled "Kleet" but Mr. Lamb tells me it should be pronounced with the "i" short—"Klitt." However, I've known him too long by the former sound and can't make the change comfortably.

A word from Mr. Lamb about these Moguls of the early seventeenth century:

Tales of Abdul Dost deal with the Moguls of India, in the early seventeenth century. Scene of "The Skull of Shirzad Mir" laid in northern hill country of Afghanistan.

As for the skull in question. They were frequently made into drinking cups. A fashion of the time—to have an enemy chieftain's skull on exhibit, ornamented with gold or silver according to the wealth of the possessor.

There's a good deal of history in back of Abdul Dost's tales. Badakshan, home of Shirzad Mir, was the backbone of the Mogul kingdom before the great conquerors descended from the hills into Hindustan and central India. Once in India, the Moguls never returned to their homeland; but they had a great fondness for Kabul and Kashmir, showing it was from politic rather than personal reasons that they favored Delhi and Agra over the hills.

In the time of Abdul Dost Jahangir was on the throne of India, and Jahangir did not match up to his two great forebears, Babur and Akbar. It was the old story of the fighting conqueror whose descendants became palace figureheads and ruled through women and eunuchs.

Babur was a man's man, and his memoirs are an unbroken tale of fighting, mostly against odds. He won the respect even of his Rájput enemy, Rajah Sanga, who must have been an experienced judge of fighters as he was blinded in one eye, without one arm, lame and with eighty other battle scars. Babur enjoyed picking up two men and carrying them, leaping across the battlements of a rampart. In his own words, the year before he died:

"I swam across the Ganges for amusement. I counted my strokes and found that I swam over in thirty-three; then I took my breath and swam back. I had crossed by swimming every river I met except (until then) the Ganges."

Akbar also was a fine strain of man, and Jahangir displayed flashes of his heritage of courage, will and humor. The Mogul was absolute owner of most of the land within the empire, and when Jahangir took the throne there was a general rush on the part of the amirs and begs to register their claims. It was a case of first heard, best rewarded. Likewise, the powers at court were of mixed nationality—Rájputs, Persians, Afghans, Uzbeks and Turki-Mohammedans. The Mogul couldn't afford to play favorites. Shirzad Mir was late.

Sir Ralph Weyand I have drawn from the historical John Mildenhall, or Midnall. Mildenhall sailed from London for Syria in 1599, bearing a letter from Queen Elizabeth to the Mogul. Left Aleppo 1600 for Kandahar. Received at court at Agra about three years later. Portuguese intrigue defeated his efforts to gain trade *firman*. The Portuguese were then firmly dug in at Goa and Surat. They had valuable trade rights, and their priests were in favor at court (owing to the Moguls' policy to countenance every creed).

Mildenhall suspected his interpreter—probably with reason— of a fondness for Portuguese gold, and determined that he must be able to speak Persian in person. Learned Persian in six months, escaped poisoning by his enemies, put some of said enemies out of action, returned to court and argued his own case. Said the Moguls had received little hard cash—although the satellites of the throne had got much—and won his trade concession. The first, I think, granted to an Englishman.

Mildenhall's second chapter doesn't make such good reading. He was, as the chronicle has it, in "an exceeding great rage" at his enemies; bartered his concession somehow for money; got together a fortune of 120,000* after returning to Persia; later, changed his religion, turned rogue and disappeared.

In order to keep the Englishman of the Abdul Dost tales clear of this second chapter, I've re-christened him Sir Weyand and set him on his own, but his adventures follow closely the first part of Mildenhall's career.

December 12, 1919: "Said Afzel's Elephant"

A few points about "Said Afzel's Elephant." It may seem improbable that three men could do what Abdul Dost and his friends tackled. In India at that time, however, a noble from the court traveled with a large following of slaves, personal attendants, eunuchs, wives, buffoons, *hafiz*, or poem readers, bearers, et cetera.

Few of such gentry were fighting men by inclination or training. And even today the hillmen of Afghanistan, such as the Afridis, are excellent combatants when so inclined. At that time tribal warfare was the rule and the hillmen were skilled in weapons. They had to be.

As to Said Afzel. The character of the opium-using poet is not overdrawn. Drugs of varied sort were in general use, and it was the fashion to remain stupefied for certain lengths of time. The Rájputs were addicted to opium in very large quantities. One passage in the memoirs of Babur relates that he kept sober at a drinking party of his friends in order to see what the bout would be like. He watched them drink wine, then change to bhang and distilled spirits, ending up with opium and more wine until "they became senseless or began to commit all manner of follies, whereupon I had myself carried out."

A good deal has been written of the treasure of the Moguls. This was hardly so very great in money, but consisted of enormous quantities of jewels, especially diamonds and rubies, horses, cloth-of-gold, et cetera. The amount of an amir's treasure measured the number of fighting-men he could buy; hence the

*Denomination unspecified by Lamb.

possession of a store of riches as in this story was more valuable to an ambitious noble than a small kingdom.

April 15, 1920: *"Ameer* of the Sea"

A word on the "bracelet-brother" custom of the Rájputs, from Colonel Tod, annalist of Rajasthan. The custom is quite ancient, and has more than once played an important part in the wars of central India.

"The Rájput lady sends a bracelet either by her handmaid, or the family priest, to the knight of her choice. With the *rakhi* she confers the title of adopted brother; and, while its acceptance secures to her all the protection of a cavalier servant, scandal itself never suggests any other tie to his devotion. He may hazard his life in her service, and yet never receive a smile in reward.

"No honor is more highly esteemed than that of being the *rakhi band bhai* or 'bracelet-bound-brother,' of a princess."

The bracelet was generally sent when the woman in question was in distress, in warfare. Naturally, the *rakhi* usually passed between Rájput and Rájput, but at least on one occasion—that of Humayon, mentioned in the story—the bracelet was bestowed upon a man of another race. There is no reason why an Englishman of this period could not have been selected as a brother-in-arms, inasmuch as the choice was determined more by the courage and known fighting ability of the man than by rank or caste.

July 15, 1920: "Law of Fire"

Most of us are familiar with the Hindu custom of suttee. It prevailed until stamped out by the British—and they had a hard time doing it—in the middle of the last century. Not all of us, perhaps, are aware of the religious significance of the act—the burning of a widow on the funeral fire.

It seems that the widows—often several in number—believed that their voluntary death insured themselves a higher life, according to the doctrine of the transmigration of souls. Thus, if they died in this manner seven times, they became perfect. Most of the women went to the funeral pyre voluntarily, and displayed extraordinary courage. But the Brahmans always had along an orchestra of horns and cymbals to drown the cries of the victim, in case the woman's strength gave way under the ordeal. Also, the priests had long poles ready, to prevent any attempt to escape from the pyre.

As to those who did escape the suttee, Francois Bernier, the French physician who wandered over India during the seventeenth century, says:

> *I have been often in the company of a fair idolator who contrived to save her life by throwing herself upon the protection of the scavengers (*halakhors*) who assemble on these occasions, when they learn that the intended victim is young and handsome, that her relations are of little note, and that she is to be accompanied by only a few of her acquaintance.*
>
> *Yet the woman whose courage fails at the sight of the horrible apparatus of death, and who avails herself of the presence of these men to avoid the impending sacrifice, cannot hope to pass her days in happiness, or to be treated with respect.*
>
> *Never again can she live with the Hindus; no individual of that nation (religion) will at any time or under any circumstances, associate with a creature so degraded, who is accounted utterly infamous and execrated because of the dishonour which her conduct has brought upon the religion of the country. Consequently she is ever afterward exposed to the ill-treatment of her low and vulgar protectors.*
>
> *There is no Mogul [meaning, probably, Mussulman—H. A. Lamb] who does not dread the consequences of contributing to the preservation of a woman devoted to the burning pile, or who will venture to offer asylum to one who escapes from the fangs of the Brahmans. But many widows have been rescued by the Portuguese.*

I'm not sure that Mohammedan women were burned, but often slaves were sacrificed with their mistress. The girl of the tale, being a Mohammedan, was not bound to the Hindu ritual.

As for Abdul Dost, he was hardly a man to be influenced by the power of the Brahmans. And Khlit conducted himself upon the favorite phrase found in U.S. Army instruction—"as circumstances may direct."

September 18, 1920: "Masterpiece of Death"

Concerning those interesting professional murderers of whom we've all heard, and in connection with his novelette in this issue, Harold Lamb gives us some facts that are doubtless new to most of us:

Most of us have had experience with thugs of various kinds. And we are still alive and kicking. Not many of us know about the *thag*s of India.

They were not *dacoits*—as the British government supposed until Seringapatam and 1799—nor were they organized gangs of robbers and murderers. Rather, they were murderers and robbers, the one thing coming before the other. They were professional men, law-abiding and harmless except in this one respect, and they took immense pride in their profession.

This pride was not religious pride, and the *thag*s were not essentially Kali-worshipers, I think. In fact nearly half were Mohammedans. Kali was a kind of tutelary deity and a certain percentage of spoil gained from the murders by *thaggi* was set aside as a propitiatory offering to the goddess. Regarding these Mohammedans Captain Sleeman—who devoted a lifetime to stamping out *thaggi* in India in the nineteenth century and failed of complete success—says a curious thing. He asked some condemned *thag*s whether the taking of life was not proscribed by the law of the Prophet. The answer was that the victims of the *thag*s were without doubt predestined to die. In slaying them the Mohammedan *thag*s only aided destiny and hence were guiltless of bloodshed.

Another general misbelief among us is that the *thag*s murdered Europeans. They vary rarely did so, unless necessary. When one member of a band of travelers had been killed by these hereditary students of death, it was a law of their cult that all members of the party must meet a like fate. Nor did they kill women, not from any reverence for woman as a sex but because it was generally considered unlucky. They went entirely by omens. Many a traveler on the highway was saved when in company with *thag*s by a snake crossing the road from the wrong side.

It was a curious profession, this, and very skillfully conducted. Estimates of the known deaths by *thag*s run as high as fifteen hundred per year in Central India alone. And the actual deaths were many more, for the simple reason that the *phansigars*—stranglers—rarely left any evidence of their work. Those who were condemned to death attended to the matter themselves, knotting the halter rope under their right ear, and jumping off into oblivion—perhaps actuated by the rigid caste of the professional and also by firm conviction that to be hanged by the hand of a *chumar* was unendurable.

And it is one of the curiosities of human life that these devotees of human death never held themselves to be criminals. The son followed the trade of the father. Wives sometimes never knew their husbands were *phansigars*. The young lads who were—as they termed it—"hard-breasted" enough to be given a *rumal*, or strangling noose, were as proud as an English youth of the same age upon whom knighthood had been conferred.

During Khlit's time the *thag*s were powerful and usually unmolested. They were rich, and an established part of the community. In "The Masterpiece of Death," Khlit, who was a warrior by profession and a believer in the merits of a fair fight with bare weapons when a fight was necessary, meets some members of this cult.

Sleeman archives. What I meant was this: "the peculiar customs of *thaggi* appearing in the tale have the confessions of the stranglers themselves and testimony before Catpain Sleeman for authority."

November 3, 1920: "The Curved Sword"

When I first read Harold lamb's story "The Masterpiece of Death" in the mid-Sept. issue my brain was shipwrecked on the mixture of "thag," "thug," "thuggi," and "thaggi." So I wrote Mr. Lamb for help and here's his reply. I admit I passed the buck to Mr. Noyes as to whether we'd use an "a" or a "u." I refused to look at those words again and don't even know which he chose.

You see, any magazine has to adopt one system of spelling and stick to it, despite awkward exceptions that will arise under any system. We happen to use the Standard Dictionary in the office and now and then the spellings grieve Mr. Lamb (and others).

How come? Highbinders and gunmen are called "thugs" in this country. We derived the word from England, via India, where a curious assassin-robber fraternity called itself *thags* (singular, *thag*). The cult or science of the murderers is known as *thaggi*, just as the cult of masons is known as masonry. (The word "thuggi" was a slip on my part.)

If you must give the Standard its pound of flesh, spell 'em "thug," "thugs," and "thuggi." The "a" is, I think, correct, if you look on the word as a quotation from the native language. That's just what it is—in the story.

But if we spell "thag" "thug," we should write "Jagannath" as "Juggernaut." As to this last, I've seen it spelled at least twelve ways by the authorities. Why not write down all the variations, put 'em in a hat on separate slips of paper, and let the foreman of the composing-room draw one?

About the Author

Harold Lamb (1892–1962) was born in Alpine, New Jersey, the son of Eliza Rollison and Frederick Lamb, an artist and writer. Lamb later described himself as having been born with damaged eyes, ears, and speech, adding that by adulthood these problems had mostly righted themselves. He was never very comfortable in crowds or cities, and found school "a torment." He had two main refuges when growing up—his grandfather's library and the outdoors. Lamb loved tennis and played the game well into his later years.

Lamb attended Columbia, where he first dug into the histories of Eastern civilizations, ever after his lifelong fascination. He served briefly in World War I as an infantryman, but saw no action. In 1917 he married Ruth Barbour, and by all accounts their marriage was a long and happy one. They had two children, Frederick and Cary. Arthur Sullivan Hoffman, the chief editor of *Adventure* magazine, recognized Lamb's storytelling skills and encouraged him to write about the subjects he most loved. For the next twenty years or so, historical fiction set in the remote East flowed from Lamb's pen and he quickly became one of *Adventure*'s most popular writers. Lamb did not stop with fiction, however, and soon began to draft biographies and screenplays. By the time the pulp magazine market dried up, Lamb was an established and recognized historian, and for the rest of his life he produced respected biographies and histories, earning numerous awards, including one from the Persian government for his two-volume history of the Crusades.

Lamb knew many languages: by his own account, French, Latin, ancient Persian, some Arabic, a smattering of Turkish, and a bit of Manchu-Tartar and medieval Ukranian. He traveled throughout Asia, visiting most of the places he wrote about, and during World War II he was on covert assignment overseas for the U.S. government. He is remembered today both for his scholarly histories and for his swashbuckling tales of daring Cossacks and Crusaders. "Life is good, after all," Lamb once wrote, "when a man can go where he wants to, and write about what he likes best."

Source Acknowledgments

The stories within this volume were originally published in *Adventure* magazine: "The Lion Cub," June 1, 1920; "The Skull of Shirzad Mir," November 1, 1919; "Said Afzel's Elephant," December 1, 1919; "Prophecy of the Blind," February 1, 1920; "Rose Face," March 1, 1920; "*Ameer* of the Sea," April 15, 1920; "Law of Fire," July 15, 1920; "The Bride of Jagannath," August 1, 1920; "The Masterpiece of Death," September 15, 1920; "The Curved Sword," November 3, 1920.

DATE			